THE COMPLETE TARGET CRIME FICTION SERIES

RICKY BLACK

MAILING LIST

If you want more information regarding upcoming releases, or updates about new content on my site, sign up to my mailing list at the end of this book - You'll even receive a novella, absolutely free.

ORIGINS

BEGINNING

CHAPTER ONE

Monday 10 March 1997

HE JUST NEEDED *a few more seconds*

He was close, his arm stretching out. The stacks of twenty and fifty-pound notes were in front of him. He grinned as he grabbed the money.

'Lamont!'

Lamont Jones jerked awake, vaulting from the bed. Stretching and wiping his eyes, he quickly trundled downstairs. Carmen Jones sat at the table, a middle-aged black woman with long black hair and great bone structure, just barely hanging onto the looks that had once enticed many men.

'Good morning, Auntie.'

Carmen ignored her nephew, looking over him with a critical eye. Lamont was gangly, with similar cheekbones to his Aunt, and messily curly hair. A jagged scar at the bottom of his chin slightly marred his features. He was long-limbed with a quizzical nature and dark, rose-wood eyes that showed a vulnerability that intrigued those around him. Auntie was immune to it.

'Get back upstairs and wash your face. You look disgusting,' she said coolly.

Lamont hurried to obey, heading back downstairs afterward. Auntie had lit a cigarette, the disgusting smoke wafting around the kitchen. Lamont was just getting over a chest infection and the smoke tickled his lungs. If Auntie noticed, it didn't show.

'Get started on breakfast. Your sister will be up soon and I don't want her to be late.'

Lamont busied himself turning on the hob, then went to the fridge for eggs and bacon. Auntie watched, still talking.

'Comb your hair too. You're a mess. What is wrong with you? Are you slow?'

The usual anger simmering within, Lamont ignored Auntie. She did this daily and rising to it would only make things worse. Instead, he skilfully prepared and served breakfast, made her a cup of tea, and then went to wake his sister. Marika Jones was snoring softly, the quilt pulled over her head.

'Rika . . .' Lamont gently rocked her. 'Rika, you need to wake up.'

'Mhmm,' Marika stirred, looked at Lamont and then closed her eyes again. Mumbling, Lamont yanked away the quilt.

'Oi, what are you doing?'

'You've got school today.'

'I'm tired. I wanna go back to sleep.'

'Don't make me get Auntie.' Lamont would never utilise this threat, but it sometimes paid dividends.

'I don't care. Get her. I'll tell her I'm ill.' Marika pulled the quilt back over herself.

'Fine.' Lamont left to take a shower. Auntie normally timed him, so he made sure he was out within minutes to avoid her complaints about him using all the hot water. Like everything else in the house, the shower was top of the line but Auntie still found fault. Dressing for school in a worn pair of jeans and a baggy shirt, Lamont threw on a pair of cheap trainers with damaged soles. Marika was drinking a glass of milk in the kitchen, beaming when he re-entered the room.

'Hurry, Rika. Are you going to school by yourself, or with Danielle?' Danielle was a friend of Marika's. Her mum had a car and she would often drive Marika to school. Lamont had wanted Marika at his high school so he could keep an eye on her, but Auntie hadn't cared, choosing to send Marika somewhere else.

'Marika isn't going to school today. She doesn't feel well,' said Auntie.

'She's lying though, Auntie.' Lamont glared at his sister, whose smile widened.

'You don't dictate to me. My niece said she is ill, so she isn't going to school. It's as simple as that.' Auntie lit another cigarette. This time though, she unlocked the back door and stood outside.

'How often do you think you're gonna get away with this?' Lamont hissed at his sister. Giggling, she continued sipping her milk and completely dismissed him. Marika seemed to take several days off school a week. Whereas Lamont attended school every day even when he was ill, Marika took liberties.

There was nothing Lamont could do about it though. He had no say in the household. Lamont saw school as his way out and because of that, he soaked up everything taught to him.

Putting a jacket on and grabbing his school bag, Lamont left the house without saying goodbye. Once outside, he embraced the air of Chapeltown, or the *Hood* as it was affectionately known. A diverse, multicultural suburb in Leeds, Chapeltown had a reputation for violence. Lamont saw beyond that though. There was beauty in the Hood, a certain energy that sometimes made the hairs on Lamont's arms stand on end. He couldn't explain it, but he felt it.

Lamont headed towards the main road, his steps halting slightly when he saw the group of boys skulking on the corner. They smirked when they saw him.

'Look who it is; *Trampy Lamont*,' one of them called out. He was a lanky kid named Tower. Tower came from a big family and had a lot of brothers. He was always throwing his weight about and targeting Lamont. They'd fought before, but Tower's friends always jumped in when it looked like he would lose.

Lamont sighed. There was no way to avoid them. If he tried to run, they would either chase him or spread the word that he was a coward. He froze as the group approached.

'Where'd you get them trainers from? Africa?' Tower stood in front of Lamont. His friends guffawed as if Tower had told the funniest joke in the world.

'Nah, even the Africans wouldn't wear them,' Another boy piped up.

'Look how his toes are nearly poking through! And look at them trousers,' Tower continued. Lamont stood, hands in his pockets, taking the insults. Tower was trying to bait him and Lamont would not rise to it. Seeing that his strategy wasn't working, Tower tried another tactic.

'Gimme all the money you've got. Now.'

Lamont had nothing to spare. He had change for the bus but he had left early with the express purpose of walking to school.

'I don't have anything, Tower.'

'Why do you talk like that?'

'I don't talk like anything.'

'Yeah, you do. You talk like a white man, all prim and proper. You're from the Hood. Act like it,' Tower snarled. 'Gimme your money. If I don't get a pound in sixty seconds, we're gonna rush you.'

Sighing, Lamont removed his school bag and jacket. Putting them on the floor, he faced Tower and the others.

'Have you seen this guy? Why are you taking your coat off like you're looking to rumble? You wanna go?' Tower taunted. Lamont tensed, waiting for them to make the first move. Before Tower could do anything, another voice spoke up.

'I'll go with you.'

Tower and his cronies froze, recognising the harsh voice. Tower swore quietly as Marcus strolled towards them. Marcus Daniels was sixteen years old, but he was over six feet tall, with the build and the attitude to prove it. Unlike Lamont, Marcus wore a plain black t-shirt, jeans and black trainers without a speck of dust or dirt on them. He glared at Tower and his gang, eyeing each of them. None could meet his gaze.

'Yo, safe, Marcus.' Tower's tone softened.

'Don't *safe* me. Why are you lot surrounding my brother like you're gonna take him on?' Marcus asked in his slow voice. Marcus was soft-spoken. It was his eyes that constantly gave away his true intent. They were full of malice and rage against the world. Anyone who knew him, knew Marcus was the real deal.

'Nah, we were just playing with him. Lamont's cool,' Tower back-pedalled. His boys slowly backed away.

'L, are they troubling you?' Marcus addressed Lamont now. Lamont needed only a second to reply.

'Nah. Like Tower said, we were just messing.'

Tower shot Lamont a look but didn't refute his statement.

'Are you sure?'

'Yeah, man. I'm sure.'

'You lot, go away. Trouble my bro, you'll have me to deal with,' Marcus promised. The boys hurried up the road.

'You should have let me stomp them out,' Marcus said.

'There's no point. It'll just make it worse next time.'

'Doesn't matter. Sometimes you need to take the licks. People will never respect you if you don't stand up for yourself.'

Lamont knew Marcus meant well, but he resented being spoken down to by anyone. It was easy for Marcus to preach about standing up for himself. He was built like a monster. Lamont was on his own most of the time and he had no one to back him up.

'Whatever, man. Have you been out all night?' Lamont changed the subject.

Marcus grinned. 'Had some business, then I stayed with Mia.'

Lamont laughed. Mia was Marcus's girlfriend, for lack of a better term. Having moved out of her house as quickly as humanly possible, Mia now lived with her older sister. Marcus was always around and if the rumours were true, had also slept with Mia's sister.

'What kind of business?'

'Don't worry your head about it, *schoolboy*,' Marcus reached into his jeans pocket and peeled off five, ten-pound notes. 'Keep hold of that. Don't let the witch see it.'

'I won't.' The first time Marcus had given him money, Lamont fool-ishly left it on his bedside table. The next day he awoke to the lash of the belt striking his legs and Auntie screaming that he was a thief. Ever since, he had become more practised.

'I'm gonna head home. Why don't you skip school and come with me?'

Lamont shook his head. 'I'm not missing school. I'll get with you later if you're about.'

'Let me know if Tower and his people trouble you again.'

'I will,' Lamont lied. Tower was an annoyance but the last thing Lamont needed was people thinking he needed Marcus to fight his battles for him.

For the past few years, Marcus had lived with Lamont, his Auntie, and Marika. The son of a pair of hardcore drug abusers, his father was murdered trying to rob a drug crew, and his mother died of an overdose when he was six. Marcus had been in his fair share of foster homes. Moving in with Lamont had calmed him down, but the demon still lived below the surface.

Once Marcus turned to walk home, Lamont quickened his pace. If he didn't hurry, he would have to get the bus. Folding the money that Marcus had given him, Lamont put it in his sock and was on his way.

* * *

Lamont was hurrying out of the school gates that afternoon when he heard someone call his name. Tower strode toward him with his gang following.

'Oi, don't think you're rough because you've got *Psycho Marcus* backing you. My brother will end him if he steps out of line, understood?' Tower pushed out his chest.

'I do,' Lamont said listlessly.

'You better. I want some money tomorrow. Don't try avoiding me either, because I'll come to your yard and smack up you and your sister, you get me?'

'Don't talk about my sister,' Lamont's tone had changed. He sounded colder. Tower and his people picked up on it.

'Or what? What are you gonna do?' Tower challenged him. Lamont glared, his eyes burning with anger. The sight of Lamont's stare made Tower feel uneasy.

'Don't forget what I said. Come, you guys. Let's go.' Tower's team hurried away. Lamont watched them go, taking a deep breath.

'Are you walking home, L?'

Lamont hid the smile that appeared on his face as Erica Anderson sashayed into view, two of her friends flanking her. Erica was tall, with skin the colour of dark honey. Lamont had liked her for the longest time, but painfully knew that he was in the friend zone. Erica had an older boyfriend, but she often talked with Lamont and sometimes they would walk home together.

'Hey, Erica. Yeah, I am. Are you?' he said eagerly.

'Yeah. These two are getting the bus, but I'm meeting Leon at the park. Do you mind if I walk with you?'

'No, course not.' Lamont again tried hiding his smile, wondering how desperate he had sounded. Erica's friends giggled, shaking their heads.

'Let's go then. See you two later,' Erica said to her friends. Walking with Lamont, the two of them crossed the road, walking down the long path that led to the park.

'Did you do Mr Silver's homework?' Erica asked as they walked.

'Did it on Sunday. It was hard though. Did you?'

'Yeah, did it at Leon's house. When he let me anyway. I swear, all he does is try to feel me up!'

'Bet that's annoying,' Lamont said, jealous of Leon being able to put his hands on Erica.

'It's sweet. He's not a talker, so I guess it's his way of telling me what I mean to him.' Erica giggled, running a hand through her hair.

'Yeah, there's always that.'

'What were Tower and his boys talking to you about? You looked mad.'

'Nothing. Just Tower being Tower.' Lamont didn't want to think about him.

'Okay. Just be careful. You know what he's like.'

'I'm always careful,' said Lamont, smiling. Erica grinned back.

'What are you doing this evening?'

Lamont shrugged. 'Should be good. I'll either get the chance to do all the washing, or if I'm lucky, Auntie will let me do the ironing or cooking.'

'She treats you worse than a slave.'

Lamont had confided in Erica occasionally about Auntie's treatment. Once he had even shown her the welts on his back from the belt. He didn't know why; all Lamont knew was that he trusted Erica and enjoyed talking to her. Marcus was his best friend, but he wasn't the easiest guy to converse with. Erica showed Lamont the affection and sympathy that he needed. That was enough.

'I'll be out of there soon,' Lamont said with conviction.

'What would you do though? How would you live?' Erica looked thoughtful.

'I'll get a part-time job and start college. I can't stay under that roof forever.'

Erica nodded. Lamont had mentioned his desire to leave home before. They walked along after that, talking about school life and playground dramas.

'Lavinia likes you. Do you like her?' Erica was referring to a girl in their year at school.

'She's all right. Not my type though.'

'Really? So what's your type then?' Erica pressed.

You, Lamont wanted to say. He didn't.

'I don't have a proper type. I just know that Lavinia's not for me. She's cool to talk to, but I don't have feelings for her.'

Erica smiled. 'Give her a chance. I bet she'd let you sleep with her.'

'I'm not interested in that,' Lamont lied. He was sixteen. It was all he thought about.

'Really? You're not? Have you done it before?' Erica asked him.

'Yeah. Loads of times,' Lamont's voice took on a boastful tone. He was lying though. He had virtually no experience with the opposite sex. He had kissed a few girls, but absolutely nothing had materialised from it. Between his mismatched clothing and being prey for every bully going, Lamont wasn't top of the social spectrum. Life had dealt him nothing. He was smart, but it was getting him nowhere. Lamont hoped college would change things for him, but struggled to see how it could.

'Really? Who with?' Erica sounded interested now.

'No one you know,' Lamont furtively replied.

'You're no fun. Did you enjoy it? I always do.'

Lamont's stomach lurched at Erica's words. He knew Erica had slept with Leon, but he didn't want to hear about it.

'It was okay. Nothing special.' Lamont hated himself for lying, wishing he could tell Erica the truth; that she was the only girl he wanted to sleep with, mainly because of the kindness she had shown him. He couldn't though. Lamont had committed himself to the lie, and now he would have to see it through to the end.

'You must not be doing it right. Talk to Leon. He's great at it. I suppose it's because he's older.'

'Yeah, must be,' Lamont grumbled. The park was coming into sight now.

'Gosh, you're so moody sometimes, L.' Erica linked arms with him and kissed him on the cheek. Lamont felt his face burn, his jeans tightening. Erica smelled amazing. Like apricots.

'Shut up,' He said good-naturedly, enjoying the contact. They crossed the road and trudged up the steps to the park. Lamont spotted Leon and his friends sitting on the swings. They were all hard-faced, towering over Lamont. Leon, a bullet-headed eighteen-year-old with facial hair and a sneer, looked Lamont up and down. Lamont disentangled himself from Erica.

'I guess I'll see you tomorrow at school then,' he said, not liking the way Leon and his friends were staring.

'Why don't you stay and hang out? Leon won't mind. His friends are cool,' Erica said. Lamont shook his head.

'Nah. Auntie will flip. I'll see you later.'

Lamont hurried away. Washing his hands and face as soon as he got in, he headed to the kitchen. Raucous laughter greeted him. Auntie and two of her friends sat around the table, smoking, drinking and laughing almost manically at some joke. They all looked up as Lamont entered.

'Good afternoon, Auntie,' The practised words rolled from Lamont's tongue with passable conviction. Auntie stopped laughing.

'Don't stand around talking. Grab the dustpan and brush and sweep the stairs. Come back when you're done. I've got more for you to do.'

Lamont did as instructed. Getting the dustpan and brush from the cupboard under the stairs, he began to sweep. It was tedious work, bending over to sweep the stairs causing him a backache. He didn't know why he couldn't use the big brush but the last time he had asked, Auntie had hit him in the head with it.

When Lamont finished, he looked into Marika's room, where she draped on her bed reading a magazine. She looked at Lamont haughtily when she saw him.

'What do you want?'

'Where did you get that magazine from?'

'Auntie bought me it. For being so good today.' Marika grinned. Lamont clenched his fists.

'You little faker. You could've at least swept the stairs for me.'

'Nah. That's your job.'

'Whatever. Is Marcus in?'

'He's in his room. Think he's sleeping,' Marika replied, turning back to her magazine.

Lamont left, picking up the dustpan and brush. Emptying the dirt into the bin downstairs, he washed his hands again, put the dustpan away and went back to Auntie for further instructions.

When all his chores were finished, Lamont flopped onto his bed, spent. He was sure that Auntie made up jobs for him to do. She seemed to get a kick out of watching him sweat. Lamont had homework, but before he started, he needed to relax. Yawning, he stared up at the ceiling, gathering his thoughts.

Lamont dreamed of a time when he would be on his own. He would be a working man, free to live his life any way he wanted. The thought was daunting, yet something he did for himself now. Other than the roof over his head, Auntie provided nothing for Lamont. He did everything. Lamont had tried making money getting part-time jobs in the past, but Auntie always seemed to scupper his hustle.

Not for much longer though. School was nearly finished. If all went well, he would not have to suffer much longer.

'L?' There was a heavy knocking at the door.

'Come in, Marcus,' Lamont called out. Marcus sauntered into the room, smirking when he saw Lamont lying down.

'The fuck are you doing, thinking and strategising and shit!' he laughed.

'Just trying to get my mind right,' replied Lamont.

'Get money, you get your mind right. Money opens doors,' Marcus said matter-of-factly. To him it was that simple.

'When I finish school, I'll get money,' Lamont assured his friend. Marcus made a face.

'When? Any job you get, it's gonna take time to make real cash,' Marcus pointed out. Lamont didn't respond. Marcus had touched upon the flaw in his life plan. Whatever job Lamont ended up in, it would take time to build up. He would need to be patient.

'Forget that anyway,' Marcus scratched his head. 'Me and you are going out.'

'Nah, I'm tired,' Lamont replied, stifling another yawn.

'I'm not asking. I'm tired of seeing you sitting up here, night in, night out. Throw on some aftershave too; we're gonna be around women.'

CHAPTER TWO

Monday 10 March 1997

MIA GREETED Marcus with a long kiss at the door. Lamont averted his eyes when Marcus started feeling her up. Eventually, they broke apart.

'L, this is Mia. Mia, this is my brother, L,' Marcus introduced them. Mia was curvy and caramel skinned, with a round baby face and slightly slanted hazel eyes. She kept her hair in neat crotchet braids and wore light pink lipstick.

'Nice to finally meet you, L. Marcus's mentioned you before,' Mia's tone was friendly, but Lamont saw the way she looked at his clothing. He forced himself to stay respectful.

'Same, Mia. He talks about you all the time.'

Marcus chuckled, disguising it as a cough when Mia shot him a glance. They all headed into the main room. Lamont expected a mess, but the room gleamed. The TV alone was bigger than Auntie's, and the sofa looked to be top of the range. An older girl who Lamont guessed was Mia's sister glanced at them, wearing a jumper and a pair of cut-off shorts. Her gaze lingered on Lamont for a second, then she went back to reading.

'This is my older sister, Rochelle. Shelle, this is Lamont. He's Marcus's friend.'

'Nice to meet you, Rochelle,' Lamont said politely. Rochelle gave him another glance, dismissing him without a word.

'Ignore her; Rochelle's always on her period,' Marcus put his arm around Lamont. 'C'mon, what do you want to drink?'

'Just some juice or some water please,' Lamont replied. Marcus and Mia shared a look and sniggered. Even Rochelle seemed to hide a smile.

'A real drink. You think we came here to sip Kia Ora?' Marcus was still laughing. Lamont wet his dry lips. He'd never tried alcohol before. Marcus strode into the kitchen, returning with a bottle of Courvoisier and four large glasses.

'Come, Shelly. Have a drink with us.' Marcus poured a liberal amount into one glass.

'I don't want a drink.'

'Have one or I will take your little magazine and rip it up,' said Marcus. Tutting, Rochelle held out her hand and took the glass. She downed it and handed it back.

'Happy?'

'Over the moon,' Marcus shook his head at Rochelle, then turned to Lamont and Mia. 'Come on.'

Mia took her glass. Lamont picked up his, trying to not make a face. He sniffed the glass, his nose curling from the strength alone.

'Just down it in one, L,' said Marcus. They toasted, and both poured it back. Lamont swallowed the alcohol, then launched into a huge coughing fit. His chest and throat felt like they were on fire. Marcus laughed at him.

'Lightweight. Here, the second one will go down nicely.'

* * *

By the time Lamont finished the second drink, he was leaning big time. The room swayed around him, and he was struggling to focus. He heard Marcus and Mia giggling; the sound distorted. His head pounded, and he could feel the liquor in his belly. He felt free of the usual woes he seemed to carry around. Lamont wished Erica was nearby so he could tell her the truth about his feelings. Somewhere amid his thinking, Mia and Marcus had disappeared. Only Rochelle remained, now watching the television.

'Do you mind me watching with you?' Lamont cringed at how foreign and magnified his voice sounded. Rochelle shrugged.

'Tell me about yourself,' Lamont said, wanting to make conversation with Rochelle. She glared, turning back to the TV.

'There's no need to be rude,' The liquor made Lamont confident. 'I'm trying to get to know you, that's all.'

Rochelle gave Lamont another look, this one seemed devoid of aggression or attitude. It was deeply speculative.

'You're much more attractive when you're quiet,' she said flatly. Her words punctured Lamont's vibe. He closed his eyes and rubbed his head, suddenly wishing he'd declined the liquor.

'Do you mind if I have some water?'

* * *

They didn't stay long. Marcus and Mia came downstairs a while later with rumpled clothing. Marcus counted out some money and threw it on the coffee table, then he and Lamont left.

The chilly night air removed whatever vestiges of alcoholic influence remained for Lamont. He swayed slightly for a few steps, then became steadier on his feet. Marcus prowled alongside him, tense, eyes flitting in every direction. The Hood was his jungle, and he always had to be on point.

'Where did you disappear to?' Lamont asked. Marcus laughed.

'Where do you think? I went to see my girl, not to sit around watching *London's Burning*.'

'So what did you bring me for?' Lamont was curious.

'Because, you sit in that house all day reading books and cleaning up after your Auntie like *Cinderella*. I just wanted you to loosen up.'

'Fair enough.'

'What did you think of Rochelle?' Marcus surprised Lamont with this question.

'She seemed nice.' Lamont picked his words carefully.

'I'd love to hit that,' admitted Marcus, rubbing his hands together.

Lamont paused. 'Wait, I thought—'

'I know what you thought. I let people believe it. Truth is, Mia's always watching me. I would though. Rochelle's sexier than Mia,' Marcus went on. 'Still, Mia knows her role. She lets me store shit in the yard, and she gives a blowjob that'll curl your toes.'

Lamont was quiet. He was happy to walk along and let Marcus ramble about blowjobs.

'You should bang Rochelle. Get her to take your cherry,' Marcus said offhandedly. Lamont stopped in the middle of the street.

'What are you talking about?'

Marcus laughed, 'I know you're a virgin. Doesn't matter. Just lose it ASAP. You do that and you might develop some game.'

Lamont stuck a finger up at his friend, and they began walking again. He didn't know how Marcus had worked it out. He had never confided in his friend about anything to do with girls, but Marcus was more perceptive than Lamont gave him credit for.

They had almost reached home when Lamont's stomach churned worse than ever.

'Oh shit!' he groaned, doubling over and throwing up. Marcus laughed in the background as Lamont retched two more times, holding his stomach, groaning like someone had hit him.

'C'mon, lightweight. Let's get you inside and get you some water.' Marcus was still laughing like a madman. He held out his hand. Lamont grabbed it and Marcus helped him. They walked the rest of the way in silence.

* * *

The next day, Lamont was still messed up from the alcohol. Shaking it off, he traipsed to play football as he did several times a week. A man named Nigel Worthington held the sessions. Nigel was a broad-shouldered man who had always been around the Hood. He'd had a promising football career until a bad tackle had put an end to that. Undeterred, Nigel refused to sit around. He started his own business and began coaching some local kids for free on the side. Most disliked him and his methods, but respected his desire to get the best out of them.

Lamont changed into the provided uniform and dutifully completed the rigorous callisthenics that Nigel had everyone perform at the beginning of the session. They were forced to complete press-ups, sit-ups, sprints and a whole other medley of exercises. Lamont loved it. He loved the discipline, and he loved pushing himself. It also remained the only time Auntie allowed him to have any fun. By the time they finished, everyone was sucking in air.

Nigel allowed them to drink some water, then laid out a succession of football drills for them to complete. The rules were simple. He expected everyone to take part and if one person didn't, then all the kids were banned from playing the end-of-session match. As the kids came down hard on anyone who didn't take part, this rarely happened.

Once the drills were over, Nigel selected two captains and they picked the teams. Once done, Nigel blew his whistle, and the match was up and running.

Lamont received the ball and went past two players like they weren't even there. He wanted to go all the way, but forced himself to pass to another player, who scored. It was a one-sided match after that. Lamont got two goals and set up three more. Playing football was the only time he felt accepted. Everyone knew his background but on the football pitch it didn't matter that he wore cheap clothing. All that mattered was his performance.

Once they had tidied up and the other kids had gone, Lamont was alone with Nigel. He was about to leave when Nigel called him back.

'I'll give you a lift, Lamont. You don't need to walk.'

'It's not far,' Lamont quickly said.

'I don't mind. Give me two minutes to put these cones away and we'll set off.'

Lamont was quiet as he sat in Nigel's Volvo listening to *Phil Collins*. He only recognised the particular song because he'd heard it on the radio countless times. It surprised him that Nigel was a fan.

'How are you doing, Lamont?'

'I'm doing fine,' Lamont replied. Nigel had never offered him a lift before, nor had he ever asked how Lamont was doing. He wasn't rude, but his focus was teaching them to play football, not trying to pry into their lives.

'You played well today. You've taken on board everything I've taught you. You were really implementing some good one-touch football and your movement off the ball is amazing.'

'Thanks.' Lamont didn't know what to say. He had joined the football sessions with an inflated ego, believing he was the best. When he began playing for Nigel, he was determined to show everyone. Nigel refused to start him for any matches, but Lamont never complained. When given the opportunity, Lamont scored hatfuls of goals, before being dropped again. Lamont almost quit, but finally realised the point Nigel was trying to make.

During the next match, Lamont waited to start and when he came on, set up two goals and kept the ball moving with some tight passing. After that his relationship with Nigel improved.

'Have you ever thought about taking it further?' Nigel asked.

'Taking what further?'

'Football. You could go far. Seriously,' Nigel continued. 'You have the traits teams look for when selecting young talent. You could get to the top.'

Lamont's eyebrow rose. He was good, but didn't think he had anywhere near the talent needed to play professionally.

'What do you think? I know it's daunting. I'd be there to help you out though. I have good contacts and I'm certain I could get you a trial. What do you say?'

Lamont sensed Nigel meant well, but he didn't like the fact he was pressuring him into a decision. Auntie would never agree to it anyway, and she was still his legal guardian.

'I'd need to have a think about it.'

Nigel frowned, slowly nodding.

'No problem. That's no problem at all. Let me know when you've decided. I'll set everything up. You won't need to worry.'

Lamont wondered about Nigel's angle. *Was he offering to be his agent? Was Lamont his ticket to the big time?*

'How are things with your Auntie?' Nigel glanced at Lamont as they stopped at a red light.

'Fine,' Lamont mechanically replied. He had shut down now. Occasionally he had given the same answer to teachers when they had enquired about Auntie.

'Good. That's excellent,' Nigel said. 'I'll shut up and get you home now.'

* * *

The next night, Lamont was reading a book when there was a loud knock at the front door. Auntie and Marika were out. Lamont smiled when he saw his friend standing there.

'Yes, L!' Levi Parker greeted Lamont. Auntie didn't allow his friends in the house, so Lamont shut the door and they sat outside.

'Easy, Levi. What's up?'

Levi beamed. He was the same age and size as Lamont, but more confident, living well thanks to the drugs his older brother sold. He wore his hair in neat, thin cornrows and rocked a sports jacket and tracksuit bottoms with Nike's and a thin gold chain.

'I've got some real good news, L. We're gonna make some money!'

'Doing what?'

Levi glanced around.

'Can you leave here?'

'Auntie said to stay until she got back.'

Levi frowned. 'Stop by my Nana's yard when you can. I've got summat to show you.'

* * *

Once Auntie returned, Lamont headed out to see Levi. He lived two streets down so Lamont didn't have far to walk.

A few of the elders in the Hood were milled around, talking in loud voices and laughing. They greeted Lamont warmly, and he was polite in return. Some had been friends of his parents and occasionally told him stories about them; stories Auntie was too lazy to share.

Knocking on Levi's door, Lamont waited for an answer.

'Lamont! How have you been?' said Nana Parker, warmly greeting

Lamont. She was in her sixties and seemed to be perpetually cold. Every time Lamont saw her, she wore a thick cardigan and warm clothing, even in the summer.

'Hello, Nana P. Are you okay?' Lamont made conversation for a few minutes, then walked up the stairs to Levi's room, knocking on the door.

'Come in, L!' Levi called out. It startled Lamont to see Levi sitting on his bed smoking. Next to him was the biggest bag of weed Lamont had ever seen.

'What's that for? Are you gonna smoke it?' Lamont asked.

'Course not. We're gonna sell it. Craig's gonna hook us up. Are you in?'

Lamont wasn't stupid. He knew how things worked in the Hood. More people were selling drugs these days, and there was a lot of potential profit. Craig Parker had started out selling weed and was now moving heroin and crack for one of the local shot callers. He made enough money to show off and also pay his Nana's bills. Their father had run out on them, their mother was too strung out on drugs to be a good parent. Craig had stepped up at an early age to feed his family, and Lamont admired that.

'No, I'm not in.' Lamont was struggling, but he didn't want to become just another black kid selling drugs. He had worked too hard and taken too much crap at school to give in now.

'Why? You need the money more than I do. Your Auntie's got you living on some real slave shit, man. What else are you gonna do? I wanna go fifty/fifty with you, L.'

'I just can't do it.'

Levi sighed, shrugging.

'I just wanted to help you. Here, try this.' He held out the spliff. Lamont shook his head.

'No thanks.'

'C'mon L, you don't go to prison for having a couple' burns.' Levi sucked his teeth and took a deep toke. He tried holding it, but ended up coughing.

'Nicely done,' said Lamont, laughing.

'Whatever. Where's Marcus at these days?'

'Marcus is doing his thing. He's not at home much. He's out, or he's at Mia's.'

'Mia . . . I'd have her,' Levi said almost reverently.

'Yeah, she's nice.'

'Her sister's sexy too. I was chilling with Dennis, and he said Marcus is doing them both, and that he's got them on Spencer Place making money. That true?' Levi asked. Spencer Place was a road in Chapeltown, synonymous with prostitution. Lamont and Levi knew people their age who had slept with the women who roamed there.

'No, it's not true. They're cool. I was chilling with them last week.'

'For real? Yo, you need to rush her sister. If it was me, I'd have made a move by now,' Levi bragged. Lamont just let him go on. He liked to listen, Levi liked to talk. Their personalities were in sync.

'Whatever, man. I need to go anyway, before Auntie complains.'

Levi finished his spliff and emptied the ashtray into the bin.

'Look, if you change your mind about selling, you know where I am. Got it?'

'Got it.'

* * *

Levi's offer remained on Lamont's mind for days, the temptation growing. He could work towards building his future. He could get out from under Auntie's tyrannical reign, get somewhere nice for him and Marika to live. They would be happy.

If he didn't get caught.

Weed was minor compared to some other drugs on the streets, but it was still illegal and people still went to prison for selling it. If Lamont was locked up, even if it was only in a young offender's institute, Marika would be at the mercy of their Auntie. He knew Auntie favoured Marika and wouldn't mistreat her. She would dote on her more. That was what Lamont feared most of all; his sister becoming like their poisonous Aunt.

When school finished, Lamont and Erica walked to the park together. Erica talked non-stop but Lamont stared at the ground, wondering how much he could make.

Would Craig let them step up or would he leave them selling only ounces? Would Levi stick to a fifty/fifty split? Was it all worth it?

As he looked down, Lamont noticed his well-worn Gola trainers. He fixated on them, imagining them as a fresh pair of Nike's, the sort Marcus wore. He'd said Lamont could borrow them, but he couldn't bring himself to share his friend's trainers.

'Lamont?'

Startled, Lamont looked up. Erica wasn't next to him. He turned, noting that she had stopped walking now, looking at him strangely.

'Yeah?'

'Are you okay? You looked like you were in a trance.'

'I'm fine. Just thinking.'

'About what? You looked proper serious.'

'Nothing much. Just school stuff,' he lied. Judging by the raised eyebrow, Erica didn't believe him.

Leon and his friends were in the same place when Lamont and Erica reached the park. Leon again glared at Lamont, but he wasn't intimidated this time. He smiled to Erica, said goodbye and turned to walk away.

'Oi!' Leon's booming voice called out. Lamont faced him.

'Yeah?'

'Come here. I wanna chat to you,' Leon ordered. Lamont held his ground for a moment, then ambled into the park. He could feel the eyes of Leon's friends on him, but ignored them and concentrated on Leon. He swayed on the swing in a baby blue tracksuit with white trainers. Despite the hot sun, he wore his hood, trying to ignore the bead of sweat dripping down his forehead.

'What's up?' Lamont asked. Leon eyeballed him for another moment before he spoke. Erica draped over him, trying and failing to look relaxed.

'What's your deal?'

Lamont frowned. 'My deal with what?'

'Are you a puff?'

Leon's friends fell about laughing at the wit of their leader. Thankfully, Erica looked as embarrassed as Lamont did.

'Leon, leave him alone. He's my friend.'

'I know. You told me. I just wanna know if he's your gay friend or if he's after a piece. He's always around you.'

'Like I said, he's my friend. That's why he walked me up here. I came to see you but if you're going to act like this, then I'll leave.'

'What you gonna do? Get this tramp to comb your hair?' Leon cracked. His friends laughed harder. Enraged, Lamont moved towards Leon with his fists clenched.

'What? Are you stepping?' Leon rose, ready to fight, before Erica got in the middle.

'No! L, just leave it. He's being a prick,' she said, pushing him gently away. Leon's friends were on their feet, still glaring at Lamont. He didn't care. He'd had enough. Enough of people treating him like crap because of circumstances that weren't his to control. Lamont hadn't asked for any of it.

'Fuck this,' he spat. Turning on his heel, he left, ignoring Erica's pleas for him to come back, the abusive taunts of Leon and his cronies.

Lamont's rage hadn't diminished by the time he arrived home. He slammed the front door as he stormed into the house.

'That you, Lamont? Who do you think you are, slamming my door!' Auntie shouted. Ignoring her, Lamont stomped upstairs and dropped his school bag on the floor.

'Oi, I'm talking to you? Did you hear what I said?' Auntie barged into his room. She glared at Lamont and he returned the look without flinching.

'I heard you.'

'Take that look off your face, before I knock it off,' Auntie warned. Ignoring her again, Lamont continued to glare. Her eyes flashing, Auntie slapped Lamont across the face, the sound ricocheting around the room. Lamont stayed where he was, willing himself to ignore the stinging feeling.

'Did you hear me!' she screamed. Still Lamont didn't say a word. His eyes desperately wanted to water, but Lamont wouldn't allow it. He wouldn't give Auntie that satisfaction. Not this time. He was done being the victim. Lamont's hands balled into fists, but remained by his side. Auntie noticed.

'You wanna fight do you? You ungrateful piece of shit. Get your chores done before I call someone round to teach you a lesson. Is that what you want?'

The front door opened before Lamont could answer and they heard Marika's voice from the bottom of the stairs.

'Auntie, I'm home! Are you here?'

'Coming, sweetness,' Auntie called out with false enthusiasm. She gave Lamont an ugly scowl. 'We're not done, boy. Chores. Now.'

With that she left.

CHAPTER THREE

Tuesday 11 March 1997

LATER THAT NIGHT, Lamont left the house without telling Auntie. The night air was mellow and people were out in force, chilling and shooting the shit. It was one thing Lamont had always liked about Chapeltown. There was a sense of community that you didn't get in other areas. Heading briskly along the roads, Lamont stopped at Levi's place.

'Yes, L. You good?' Levi greeted him. He wore a vest and a pair of long shorts with no socks.

'Can we talk?'

Levi nodded. 'Come. We'll go upstairs.'

The two boys traipsed to Levi's bedroom. Lamont had always liked it. It had everything; a colour TV, a PlayStation, and a CD player with two tape slots. The walls were adorned with posters of everything from *Wu-Tang Clan* to *Tupac*.

'What's up, man? You look stressed,' said Levi.

'I've changed my mind.'

'About what?'

Lamont stared at Levi until finally, his friend caught on.

'I forgot all about that. What changed your mind?'

'Look at me,' Lamont said, tone still solemn.

'What are you on about?'

'I'm broke, living with a woman that hates me, and everyone thinks I'm some tramp. Like it's my fault my parents died.' All Lamont's frustration seemed to explode from him. Levi watched in stunned silence as Lamont vented about the altercation with Leon.

'You shoulda smacked them up, L. Never let anyone take you for an idiot,' he said when Lamont finished.

'That's the thing. Everyone takes the piss; all because of how I look. I'm sick of it. You want us to sell weed, we'll sell it. Tell me what you want me to do.'

Levi grinned, not even bothering to hide it. He wanted to sell for his brother but he didn't want to do it alone.

'Gimme a couple' days to talk to Craig and set summat up.'

'Why so long?' Lamont wanted to get started as soon as possible. The quicker they started selling, the quicker he would make money.

'Craig's never here. He pays Nana's bills and gives her money for food and stuff, but he's always out and about, staying at different yards and shit.'

'Okay. Get at me as soon as you can.'

'I like this fire! Keep it up and we'll get rich!'

* * *

By the time Lamont slipped back inside, Auntie was already in bed. Quietly locking the door, Lamont took his trainers off and padded carefully up the stairs. He was about to go into his room when Marcus's door opened.

'C'mere.'

Surprised, Lamont entered Marcus's room. Like Levi's it was kitted out with the latest electronics. Marcus also had a set of large dumbbells and some barbells. There were several Flex magazines tossed all over the place and a foldaway weightlifting bench in the corner.

Lamont stood awkwardly by the door. As cool as he and Marcus were, he didn't spend much time in Marcus's room. It was amazing how different it was to his own though.

'I need a favour,' Marcus didn't waste any time, rummaging in his drawers. For whatever reason he was shirtless, wearing only a pair of black tracksuit bottoms and all black trainers.

'What's up?'

'I'm doing a move, but one of my guys can't make it. I need you to step in. I'll pay you two hundred quid. Cash in hand.'

The money immediately swayed Lamont, but he held back.

'What kinda move?'

'You know what I do, L, so don't try playing dumb. You don't need to do anything. Stand there and let me and my dude handle it. Jump in if it goes wrong. Easy money.'

Lamont hesitated, thinking about what he could buy. Since his argument with Leon, he thought only about bettering his circumstances. He would not wallow anymore.

'L, we're family, so I'm gonna kick it up to two fifty. We need to go though. My boy's got us a car, and he's gonna be outside any minute. Are you in?'

Lamont took another second to think, but his mind was made up.

'I'm in.'

* * *

Marcus told Lamont to dress to blend in, so Lamont picked out a pair of frayed black trousers and a black hooded top. He kicked on his black trainers and was good to go. He and Marcus headed down the stairs and left the house. A Vauxhall Cavalier waited, a youngish boy with a rough-looking face behind the wheel. He nodded stoically at Marcus and stared Lamont down.

'Yo, this is, L. L, this is Victor, or *Big V*,' Marcus introduced them both. They climbed into the car, and Victor drove away. The radio wasn't playing. Victor was focused on the road and Marcus stared out of the window.

Lamont sat in the back, his heart hammering. He was going on his first ever move. He'd heard of them before. People went on moves for all kinds of reasons, mostly for money or fun. Lamont wanted to ask what they were doing, who they were doing it to. Most of all, he wanted to go home. He felt like Tre from *Boyz N' Tha Hood*, in the back of the ride and wanting to have the guts to tell Big V to pull over. He didn't though. He was a third wheel. Lamont was doing this for the money.

After a long drive, the car pulled to a stop on a random street. Marcus and Victor climbed out. Lamont followed suit, not recognising the area.

'Keep a lookout, L,' Marcus instructed as he and Victor opened the car boot. Lamont watched in horror as he saw Marcus slip what looked like a gun into his trouser waistband. Victor gripped two worn-looking baseball bats. He handed one to Lamont.

'Here, put this on too.' Marcus threw a balled-up black item to Lamont, and he unravelled the balaclava. It clearly belonged to the guy Lamont was standing in for and reeked of sweat. Lamont put it on though, tugging it down to ensure it concealed his face.

'Right then. L, take the back. Me and Vic will take the front. Anyone comes at you, smack 'em with the bat. Understand?'

Lamont nodded, trying to ignore the jitters in his stomach. He felt like if he opened his mouth he would throw up. Evidently his fear showed on his face because Victor finally spoke.

'He looks shook. Are you sure he's up for it?'

'He'll be fine. Come on, let's get in place.'

The trio hurried along. Slipping down two streets, they stopped in front of a dilapidated looking terraced house. It seemed to loom in front of Lamont like some haunted house from an old vampire movie. Imposing and eerily majestic.

Remembering his instructions, Lamont went around to the back of the house. He listened out for noises and he didn't have to wait long. There was a loud crash, the sound of a woman's screams, then a scuffle. Trying the backdoor, Lamont was startled to find it open. He hurried into the house toward the noise. Lamont entered the room just in time to see Marcus hit a mousy-haired man in the face with the butt of his gun.

'Where's it at?' he bellowed.

'Mate, you've got the wrong house. There's nowt here,' The man moaned, blood staining his greying white vest. In the room's corner, Victor restrained a chubby, screaming blonde woman.

'Shut your mouth!' he shouted, slapping her. The man was about to rush at Victor when Marcus hit him again.

'I said, where is it? Don't play with me!' Marcus hit the man a third time, then instructed Victor to hit the woman again. Victor did so, throwing her on the floor and jabbing the bat into her ribs as she retched and coughed.

'That's enough!' Lamont shouted. Victor and Marcus both looked at him.

'Shut up! You know why we're here, so don't go acting like a punk,' Marcus shouted, turning back to his victim. 'I'm gonna ask you one more time, then my man there's gonna open up your missus! Where is it at?'

'It's u-upstairs,' The man finally stammered.

'Upstairs where?'

'Main bedroom. Under the mattress.'

'Yo!' Marcus got Lamont's attention, 'go get it. Don't come back down without it.'

Lamont's legs felt like lead as he willed himself to walk up the stairs. The hallway was a complete mess. The front door was still wide open, probably from Marcus's entry. When he reached the top, Lamont walked into one room. It was a cluttered, boxy mess. He quickly checked it anyway and found nothing. He didn't know what they had come for, but he assumed it was money or jewellery.

The next room Lamont was in was larger, though equally messy, with clothes and shoes strewn all over the place. Lamont put his bat down and lifted the mattress. He found a carrier bag there, which he grabbed. Leaving the mattress where it was, he headed back downstairs and handed the wares to Marcus. Marcus peered into the bag.

'Did you look?' he asked.

'No, I didn't,' Lamont's voice was calmer than he expected it to be.

'Okay,' Marcus turned back to the blooded man, still moaning in pain. 'Listen, I'm gonna take this and that's the end. You wanna make an issue of it, I'm gonna come back and pop one in your woman. When the police come, don't fucking tell them anything or we'll be back.' Kicking the man again, Marcus signalled for them to leave.

They were running now, heading down the roads back to the car.

Lamont felt like he was in a dream. It all felt too surreal. He couldn't believe what he had just taken part in. Feeling his stomach bubbling again, he took deep breaths, trying to avoid being sick.

'L! Come on!' Marcus yelled. Lamont got his bearings and began running again. They climbed into the car and Victor sped off down the road.

'Right, slow down, Vic,' Marcus said when they were away. 'We don't wanna get a pull with this strap on us.'

Victor did as ordered. Lamont was shaking in the back, still shocked at what had transpired.

'Oi, L?' Marcus called from the passenger seat. Lamont looked at him.

'Take the mask off, you plum.'

Victor laughed as Lamont removed the smelly balaclava and threw it to the side as if it were contagious.

'Where did you find this guy? He's a pussy!'

Marcus's face darkened.

'Pull over. Now.'

Victor pulled the car to the side of the road. Without warning, Marcus's arm shot out and he began choking Victor.

'Yo! What are you doing?' Victor spluttered, trying in vain to break Marcus's grip.

'Lamont is my brother. Talk to him with respect or I'll end you. Understand! Well, do you?' Marcus looked demented.

'Yeah! Y-Yeah I understand! Let me go,' Victor yelled. Marcus released the hold.

'Good. Start the car. Pegz is waiting for us.'

Subdued now, Victor drove to a park in Harehills. The three of them walked to the swings. It was pitch black now, the park deserted, save for two figures in tracksuits sitting on the swings. They stood up when they saw Marcus and company approaching.

'Yes, Pegz,' Marcus greeted him.

'Safe, Marcus. You get it?' Pegz asked. He was a peanut coloured man, very skinny, with shifty looking eyes. He appeared older than Marcus, spoke with an obvious familiarity. His companion was overseeing the proceedings with his heavily muscled arms folded. He was so big he even made Marcus look small. And that was saying something.

'Yeah. It's here.' Marcus held out the carrier bag. Pegz peered inside, taking the package out of the bag and smiling. Lamont looked at it. It was drugs, a white block that Lamont assumed meant it was cocaine. He didn't know what size it was, but Pegz seemed pleased.

'You're a legend, Marcus. Did Daryl give you any trouble?'

'Nah. We smacked him and his missus around.'

'That's my Don! What did we agree on? Two grand?'

'That sounds right.'

Pegz handed Marcus a stack of money. Marcus counted it, slapped hands with Pegz and they were on their way back to the car. When they were in the car, Marcus handed them both their shares.

'Good work, L. For real.'

'How did he know the man's name?' Lamont immediately said what was on his mind.

'Who?'

'Pegz. How did he know who you robbed?'

'Oh. That's his brother-in-law.'

'Are you serious?'

'Pegz has a baby to his sister. Some horrible little thing from Seacroft. Pegz is the one who told us where to go.'

'That's wrong though.' Lamont couldn't get his head around it. Marcus glanced at him.

'This is the life. Everyone is looking for a come up. You just got two-fifty for standing in the corner looking like you were gonna shit yourself. Sit back and enjoy. Don't worry about the hows and whys.'

Victor laughed, but turned it into a cough when Marcus glared at him. When they reached Auntie's, Marcus turned to Victor and slapped his hand.

'Good work, man. Ditch the car. Store the tools for next time. I'll get at you tomorrow. Stay quiet too, okay?'

'I know the drill,' Victor assured him. He gave Lamont a nod and drove away.

'That was easy,' Marcus yawned. 'I'm gonna grab some food and maybe go to Mia's. You coming?'

Lamont wanted to be by himself, needing to process what had transpired.

'I have school tomorrow.'

'So what? You had school last time. Come and have another drink.'

Lamont shook his head. 'Not tonight.'

'Check you later then.' Marcus touched fists with Lamont and disappeared down the road.

When Lamont was inside, he brushed his teeth, stripped down and climbed into bed. His heart was still pounding. He lay there, thinking about everything that could have gone wrong. They could have been arrested, or badly hurt if more people had been at the house.

Lamont hadn't found the robbery itself difficult, but the casual violence unnerved him. Watching Victor hit the woman in the stomach had appalled him. Lamont didn't want to be associated with that. He hid the cash he'd received, feeling ashamed for taking part. He hadn't harmed Darryl or his woman, but he felt shame just the same.

So much had happened today. All the events seemed to hit Lamont at once. He grew angry as he recalled the way Leon had treated him. The way Auntie attacked him. Lamont had made some money, but he was still in the same position as he was before the robbery. He was still a piece of shit, looked down on by everyone around him.

* * *

Lamont's mood continued into the next day. He kept his head down, but found he was answering the teachers back with more force than normal. He was hurrying toward the gates after school, when he found Tower and two of his friends waiting.

'Look who it is,' Tower laughed to his cronies when he saw Lamont. 'It's our favourite tramp.'

Lamont ignored them, keeping his eyes on Tower. Tower liked to bait him, but he wasn't vicious. He was just a bully who liked an audience. Lamont found himself strangely calm, weighing up the situation.

'You good though, L? You doing well? Because those trainers are leaning to the side!'

Tower and his friends laughed. He reminded Lamont of Erica's boyfriend, needing to poke fun at Lamont to make himself feel better. Had he looked at Lamont — truly looked at him — he would have known that today wasn't the day to provoke him.

A small crowd gathered around now. It was the end of the day and everyone wanted to see the drama. No one really liked Tower, but they laughed anyway.

'Seriously though, L. It must be hard in your household. You're pathetic If I was you, man, I'd just kill myself.'

Lamont was reaching boiling point. Some noticed in the crowd, whispering to one another, pointing at him like he was in a zoo. Lamont trembled, a lone tear rolling down his face. Tower noticed.

'Are you serious? Yo, he's crying!' he bellowed with laughter. Lamont was on the verge. Tower was in his face now, clowning around. He patted Lamont on the head like a dog, and that was all it took. With a guttural roar from deep within the recesses of his soul, Lamont struck.

Tower was completely off-guard. The blow caught him flush on the cheek, distorting his features for a second, his face almost clay-like. He staggered back, eyes narrowing as he threw a sloppy return punch. Lamont stepped to the left and caught Tower with a hook, sending him to the ground. The bully tried scrambling to his feet, only to see stars as Lamont kicked him in the face. One of Tower's friends tried to intervene but tripped over his own feet. Lamont began kicking him, keeping him down. Tower was struggling to his feet so Lamont whaled on him with lefts and rights.

The other two bullies threw Lamont to the floor and began kicking him. Lamont curled up, then lunged and tackled one of them. They rolled around now, trying to pin Lamont down, but he was unhinged, his hands free, lashing out in all directions, hitting anyone he could.

Finally, several teachers waded into the midst to break up the fight. It took two of them alone to contain Lamont, who struggled to get free so he could rip Tower's head off. Physically dragging him away, they led him up the path and back into school.

* * *

That evening, Lamont sulked in his room. For his antics at school they had suspended him for a week. The head teacher had threatened expulsion, but several kids came forward saying that Lamont had been provoked. This combined with his stellar attendance record and schoolwork led her to change her mind.

Lamont was calmer, but he didn't feel better. He thought he would after finally getting the better of Tower but he felt hollow. Tower wouldn't take the beating lightly. He would probably make Lamont's life even more hellish than it already was.

Lamont shrugged, his head bowed low. He needed someone. Someone he could talk to and unload on, but he had no one like that in his life. He hadn't spoken to Erica since leaving her in the park with Leon. She had tried speaking to him during the day but he had rebuffed her. Lamont knew it wasn't Erica's fault that Leon had started with him, but she went out with him, which made her partly responsible.

There was a knock at Lamont's bedroom door. He ignored it. Auntie had ripped into him earlier, threatening to kick him out onto the streets. After striking him several times, she ordered him upstairs. Lamont had been there ever since, stomach rumbling with hunger. He could have gone downstairs and made something, but his body wouldn't cooperate.

The person knocked again, louder.

'L, I'm coming in,' Marcus said. He walked into the room and shut the door behind him. 'Why are you sitting in the dark?'

'I like the dark. It's peaceful.'

Marcus shook his head and turned the light on, the glare making Lamont squint for a second. Marcus looked down at him, concern evident in his obsidian eyes.

'I heard about what happened today. Are you good?'

Lamont nodded. 'Yeah. I'm fine.'

'I heard you spazzed on Tower and his boy's, bro. Word is you were brawling with like five of them, and then teachers came and you were fighting with them too!' Marcus sounded impressed.

'He pushed me too far,' Lamont replied.

'Tower's a prick, thinking he's connected. I'm gonna talk to his brother, and I promise he ain't gonna trouble you again. What did the witch say?'

'Usual line. *I'm a disgrace, blah blah*. She's threatening to throw me out.'

'How many times has she used that one though? This place would turn to shit without you and she knows that. Let her say what she's saying,' Marcus paused then. 'Are you sure you're okay?'

Again, Lamont nodded.

'I'm just saying . . . I know how I can be, but you're my brother. If there's anything you really need to talk about, I'm always gonna be here for you.'

Lamont smiled at Marcus, 'I know, man. I appreciate it. I don't know what's wrong with me . . . I guess I'm just tired of it all. Is this the best it gets for me? Someone troubles me constantly, I finally stand up for myself, and I end up getting suspended from school? When's it supposed to change? When are things gonna get right for me?'

'Make it better, blood. Don't sit around waiting for it because I'll tell you something; people are so screwed up that you can't rely on things being right. Make them right by doing your own thing,' Marcus paused again. 'I've got another move if you're interested.'

Lamont shook his head. 'No thanks. It's not for me.'

'You sure? There's three hundred quid in it for you.'

'I'm sure. Thanks though. What you said; I think you're right.'

Marcus grinned. 'Read one of your books or something. Just kick back.'

'Yeah, I think I'll do that.'

CHAPTER FOUR

Saturday 15 March 1997

LAMONT WOKE early and tiptoed down the stairs. Marika had stayed at a friend's house the night before, and Auntie was sleeping in, so neither were in his way.

Making himself some juice, Lamont did some press-ups on the kitchen floor, then ate some breakfast. When he finished, he tidied up, then rushed through the usual chores before taking a shower. He swiftly dressed and rooted around his room, collecting his hidden money.

Including what he had made working with Marcus, Lamont had saved over four hundred pounds. What he had been saving it for, he wasn't sure. The goal of independence for he and Marika was still a while away. For now, Lamont was tired of looking how he did. It was time to change that.

Since going to live with Auntie, Lamont couldn't recall ever having new clothes. Auntie would buy a lot of his clothes from various jumble sales and charity shops. Her clothing was all designer, and even Marika had some nice pieces. With Lamont, she told him he grew too quickly for her to be buying him new stuff. He heard it so often that he almost started to believe it.

Gathering his money and making sure the notes were neat, Lamont shoved them into his pocket and left the house, locking the door behind him. He hurried down the street and crossed the road, debating whether to wait at the bus stop or to just walk all the way to town. By the time he got to the stop it was empty. Assuming he had just missed a bus, Lamont walked.

It was a beautiful morning. It wasn't warm, but the breeze was pleasant on Lamont's face. By the time he reached the city centre, Lamont was hungry again. Buying a sandwich and a drink, he ate quickly, standing against a wall opposite the St John's centre. When he finished, he went into a shoe store.

As soon as Lamont entered, he smelled the suede and the leather of the different trainers and shoes. When Auntie would take him shopping when he was younger, Lamont wasn't allowed to even look in the shop's direction. As he had grown older he would go in with Marcus or one of his other friends, usually just to look. Now, he would buy.

Lamont navigated his way through some other shoppers and gazed at the Nike section of trainers. He noticed the shop staff watching him out of the corner of his eye. One stood near the exit in what she thought was a discreet manner. It galled Lamont that they would just assume he was some scruffy thief. Nostrils flaring, he reached for the best pair of trainers he could see; a pair of white, grey and royal blue Nike Tailwinds. Signalling to one of the staff, he beckoned him over. The man came, but dragged his feet. He was bald and wiry, his black and white polo shirt and black trousers hanging loosely on his frame.

'How can I help?' he sounded bored.

'I want these in a size nine,' said Lamont. The man hesitated, sharing a look with another member of staff. The nerves Lamont felt walking in dissipated. This person didn't know him; he would not let them look down their noses at him.

'Is that a problem? Do you not have any in stock?' Lamont raised his voice slightly, causing people to look over. Abashed, it galvanised the man into action.

'Sorry, I'll go look now.'

Lamont watched the man hurry away. He glared at the woman standing by the door, and she turned away. After trying on the trainers, Lamont paid at the till, hiding a smile at the look of shock that appeared on the retailer's face. He tried getting Lamont to buy a host of other accessories, but Lamont turned him down and left the shop with his head held high. He went to a few other shops buying various t-shirts and a few tracksuits.

His hands heaving with bags, Lamont went to Waterstones, his favourite bookshop. The second he walked in, he was as always enthralled by the books. He glanced around, mooching around the different sections and selecting two paperbacks along with a copy of *Prince* by *Machiavelli*. After paying, he treated himself to a taxi home.

As Lamont sat in the back of the car, lost in his own thoughts, he felt like a different person. He had new clothes, new books to read, and he was travelling home in style. It all seemed surreal, and he wondered if it was a sign, if fate was trying to tell him that crime paid. Lamont had toed the line for years, receiving nothing but scorn from those around him. He had turned to crime for the first time and now he seemed to be on an entirely different path. It was strange.

Lamont paid the driver around the corner from his house, climbing out with his bags. He unlocked the front door, then locked it behind him.

'Lamont!'

Ignoring Auntie, Lamont went straight upstairs, hesitating outside his room.

'Lamont, come here right now!'

'Thinking fast, Lamont opened Marcus's door and put the bags in there. Hurrying to the bathroom, he flushed the toilet and pretended to wash his hands.

'Didn't you hear me calling you?' Auntie was on him the second he entered the living room. She was smoking with a vengeance, taking full advantage of Marika being out of the house.

'Sorry, I needed the toilet,' lied Lamont.

'Where were you?'

'I went for a walk.'

Technically, he'd walked into town, Lamont rationalised.

'Who said you could do that? There's work for you to do.'

'I needed some fresh air, and I didn't want to disturb your sleep.'

Auntie glared. Finishing her cigarette, she beckoned Lamont to come with her. They traipsed upstairs and Auntie barged into Lamont's room, looking around. Her eyes narrowing, she turned back to Lamont, eyes flashing with anger.

'Next time you wanna leave the house, tell me first. You're not a damn grown up yet.'

'Yes, Auntie. I will.' Lamont did his best to hide the glee he was feeling inside. If Auntie had found the clothing, all hell would have broken loose. Once the clothes went into his battered wardrobe, she would be none the wiser. It wasn't as if she ever did his washing, anyway.

'Get downstairs and do your chores.'

'I did them this morning,' said Lamont. Walking past Auntie, he didn't even wait for her to say anything else as he headed to make a drink. Shopping was thirsty work.

* * *

Lamont resisted the urge to wear his new clothing when he ventured out later on that night. Marika wasn't back from her sleepover and Auntie had gone out. Not wanting to remain in the house, Lamont roamed the streets.

Levi had contacted him earlier, ringing Auntie's landline to let him know he was still waiting for Craig. Lamont's intent to sell drugs hadn't abated. He would do whatever was necessary to leave Auntie and all her mess behind. Working with Levi would help him put something together.

Stopping at a paper shop, Lamont bought a bottle of Ribena, sipping it as he slouched against a nearby wall. He was so lost in his thoughts that it took him a moment to realise someone was trying to talk to him.

The baby-faced teenager was Lamont's age, with skin the same shade as a peanut shell, closely cropped hair and harsh, dark eyes. He was stockily built, the outlines of muscle visible through the grey hooded top he wore.

'What's up, Shorty?' Lamont greeted his friend.

'Nothing, saw you chilling over here so I thought I'd come see how

you were doing. Heard you got kicked out of school for stabbing someone?' Shorty raised an eyebrow.

'I got into a fight and ended up suspended. It involved no knives.'
Lamont couldn't even think where that rumour would have come
from.

'Thought it sounded a little dodgy. How come you were fighting?
You're usually trying to walk away when people trouble you.'

'They provoked me.'

'Always with the big words,' Shorty scoffed. 'Go on then; who
provoked you?'

'Tower.'

Shorty looked disgusted, 'Ninja's little brother? He's a geek. I hope
you smacked him up.'

'I did all right.' Lamont wouldn't boost his ego and tell Shorty the
whole story. He sighed, realising he would have to face everyone at
school when he went back. He thought about the altercation with
Leon. Even after fighting to be left alone, Lamont would still have to
deal with Leon's nonsense. He could walk another way home, but the
road leading to the park was the quickest route. He could even take
the bus, but pride wouldn't let him do that.

'L?'

Lamont jerked out of his reverie.

'Are you high? Why are you acting all spaced out?'

'I've just got some things on my mind. Do you know a dude called
Leon?'

'Leon who? What's his surname?'

'I'm not sure. He's about eighteen, nineteen. Hangs around that
park near Chapel Allerton. He's kinda light skinned, and he's got a
bullethead.'

Shorty thought about it. 'The name ain't ringing a bell. Why
though? Is he troubling you?'

Lamont didn't reply. He hadn't asked Shorty because he wanted
Leon hurt. He'd hoped he knew Leon and could talk to him.

'Is he?'

Lamont sighed again. 'He hasn't put his hands on me or anything.

He doesn't like me being around his girl, and he's threatened me before.'

Shorty's eyes darkened as they analysed Lamont. They had stuck together since the age of five, where they were two of only a handful of ethnic children at their Primary school. By the look Shorty gave him, Lamont knew how this would turn out. It never took much to set off Shorty.

'Where do you see this guy again?' Shorty's voice was even, but Lamont wasn't convinced.

'Chapel Allerton Park, near my school. He's always there with his crew.'

'How many of them?'

'Four or five usually.'

Shorty scratched his chin, his nostrils flaring. He nodded his head as if internally agreeing to something.

'When do you go back to school again?'

'Next week Wednesday,' Lamont replied. Shorty nodded again.

'Cool.'

* * *

Lamont left school next Wednesday, not surprised to see Shorty and another local goon. His name was Kieron, but everyone called him *K-Bar*. K-Bar was dark-skinned and bony, with thin shoulder length dreadlocks and dead eyes. He was Shorty's crime partner and though more doleful than Shorty; he didn't need any excuse to cause trouble.

'L, c'mere,' Shorty called out. Looking left and right, Lamont hurried across the road.

'What are you lot doing up here?'

Shorty laughed. 'We're gonna handle your problem. Come.'

Falling in step, Lamont followed Shorty and K-Bar towards the park.

Leon and his cronies sat in their usual spot, laughing and telling jokes. There were a few girls lingering around. Scanning their faces, Lamont saw none were Erica. Recognising Lamont, Leon scowled.

'What are you looking at?'

Shorty cut his eyes to Lamont, 'Is he the one?'

Lamont nodded.

'Oi! I'm talking to you! Erica's not here to look after you now!'

Shorty rubbed his nose. 'I'll deal with this.'

Without missing a beat, he entered the park and walked right up to Leon. Sensing trouble, Leon's boys closed ranks, causing Lamont and K-Bar to stand at either side of Shorty, ready to back him up.

'Who are you?' Leon didn't like Shorty eyeballing him.

'You need to back off my boy. If I hear that you or any of these dickheads have been troubling him, I'll deal with you myself.'

Leon stood. He towered over Shorty, but the younger man didn't flinch.

'I don't think you know who you're dealing with.'

'No. I don't think you know who *you're* dealing with. L is off limits to you and your crew,' Shorty's voice was calm but he was definitely ready for war. Lamont knew the signs. He had seen Shorty in action before. He took a step back to give him space.

'Listen, little man, dig up before I get mad. Take that tramp there with you. If I catch him around Erica again, I'll fuck him up,' said Leon.

That was enough.

Before Leon could react, Shorty levelled him with two swift hits, knocking him into the swing. The girls screamed and ran. Leon's friends waded in, but K-Bar pulled a knife, causing them to freeze.

'Back up. It's one-on-one, or I'm cutting everyone,' K-Bar's voice had enough conviction to cause the group to step back.

Leon was up now. He looked dazed, but the hits had hurt his pride more than anything. He charged Shorty, who saw the move coming and planted his feet into the ground. Grabbing Leon in a front headlock, he brought his knee up, catching Leon in the face. Bringing his elbow down on Leon's spine, Shorty let go, allowing the older boy to crumple to the ground.

'That all you've got?' Shorty taunted, panting slightly. When Leon tried to rise, Shorty brought his foot back and kicked him in the head. Leon fell back and didn't move. Standing over him, Shorty looked to

Leon's friends, frozen with fear at the sight of Shorty's calculated assault on their leader. Without him they were powerless.

'Yo, when *Mr Untouchable* here wakes up, tell him to stay away from L. I'm warning you all once. Find someone else to touch, or we're coming back with more weapons.'

Shorty walked away. K-Bar followed him without a word. Lamont snuck a glance at Leon's friends, then he trailed Shorty and K-Bar.

* * *

'I don't think he'll be troubling you anymore, L.'

It had been less than an hour since the fight. The three of them were standing in the Hood drinking bottles of Lilt and enjoying the sun.

Shorty was all smiles after beating Leon. Lamont had seen this reaction from his friend before. Violence didn't make Lamont happy. He wasn't ungrateful though. Shorty had beaten up Leon for bullying him. Shorty and Marcus were alike in that way; they cared for little, but protected anyone in their circle. Lamont was lucky to have friends like them.

'Yeah. I think you put a stop to that.'

Shorty drained his bottle and threw it into the street. 'Dudes like him run their mouths because they've got people around them. Hit them a couple times, they crumble like he did.'

Lamont wasn't listening. His eyes were on the bottle that Shorty had thrown.

'Pick that up, man.'

Shorty was talking to K-Bar now. He evidently hadn't heard what Lamont had said.

'Shorty.'

Shorty turned.

'What?'

'That bottle. Pick it up and put it in the bin, man. It's right next to it.'

'What?' Shorty frowned.

'We have to look after our streets. It doesn't hurt to put it in the bin.'

'Is he serious?' Shorty cut his eyes to K-Bar, who shrugged For a second, Shorty grilled Lamont, then burst into laughter and went to get the bottle.

'You're a funny guy, L. People are becoming millionaires selling poison, and you're quibbling over a Lilt bottle.'

'Doesn't matter. It begins with us. We need to look out for our community,' Lamont replied.

'Whatever you say, *Malcolm-X*. Come on, let's go get a ball and play footy.'

* * *

Lamont had maths with Erica the next day, but she looked like she had been crying, and did her best to avoid him. It stung, but Lamont expected it. Leon was everything to Erica, and the word was already out about the beating Shorty had given him.

Lamont had PE as the last lesson of the day. When he exited the changing rooms afterward, swinging his tattered sports bag, Erica waited.

'Afternoon.' Lamont knew she wouldn't speak first.

'That's all you have to say to me?'

'About what?'

'You and your psycho friends beat up Leon! You should see his face!'

'I won't talk to you if you're going to act like this,' Lamont said calmly, seeing his crush in a whole new light. The fact she had stuck by Leon after he verbally abused Lamont had been a turning point. Their friendship would never be the same.

'How am I supposed to react? Was that really the best way to handle it?' Erica lowered her voice, but people walking by were still looking at the pair.

'We just wanted to talk. He wanted to act the big man in front of his boys and those girls, so my friend called him out.'

'One of your friends had a knife!' Erica hissed. Her expression changed. 'What girls?'

'That's for you two to discuss. He was a prick to me for no reason, so if you want to analyse anything, analyse that.'

'He's my boyfriend!'

'So what!' Lamont bellowed. 'So what if he's your boyfriend? Are you gonna be with him forever? No! It's a silly, schoolgirl relationship and you know it, so grow up.'

Erica gaped at Lamont as if she had never seen him before. He seemed to radiate an aura. A power resonated, and it was unnerving to see the meek, quirky boy who walked her home, evolve before her eyes.

'He was asking for what he got. I don't feel sorry about it. Hopefully, he'll watch his mouth now.'

'L, what happened to you? When did you stop being nice?' Erica asked softly.

'The second I realised that nice guys get crushed by pretty girls like you. I'll see you around.' With that, Lamont strolled past Erica, leaving her openmouthed.

* * *

When Lamont arrived home, Marika was watching TV. She had changed out of her uniform and was devouring cereal like she hadn't eaten in days. Lamont kissed her on the cheek, put his bags down and took his coat off.

'Where's Auntie?'

'Out. She said you'd make me dinner,' Marika said, with her mouth full of Coco Pops.

'Okay. I'll make it in about ten minutes.'

'No! I'm hungry now! Why do you think I'm eating cereal?' Marika shouted.

Lamont stood in front of the TV and looked at her. Marika opened her mouth to say something clever, but stopped herself. The fiery look in her brother's eyes scared her. His jaw was clenched tight, his gaze unflinching. Something was different about Lamont, and Marika didn't want to make the wrong move.

CHAPTER FIVE

Friday 21 March 1997

LAMONT FOLLOWED Marcus as he knocked on Mia's door. She answered, giving Lamont a double take when she noticed him. His hair was trimmed, and he wore a new sports jacket with a pair of jeans and some trainers.

'Wow, you look different, L,' she said, her mouth open. Marcus nudged her.

'Let us in then. I've got liquor.' Marcus held up the bottle of brandy. Mia led them into the living room. Rochelle again sat on the sofa, this time reading a book. She acknowledged Marcus and Lamont with a nod.

'Get some cups,' Marcus ordered Mia, who hurried to obey. 'Shelly, what's happening, darling?'

'Nothing, Marcus. Just chilling.'

'Cool. What you reading?'

Rochelle held up the book. It was *To Kill a Mockingbird* by Harper Lee; one of Lamont's favourites.

'Never read it. Any good? You know who else is a big reader?' Marcus didn't even wait for Rochelle to answer his first question.

'Who?'

Lamont's stomach lurched.

'My boy L here. He loves reading, I swear. His room at home is just full of books. Isn't it?' Marcus elbowed him.

Lamont wanted to strangle Marcus. He knew that action wouldn't end well though, so instead, he nodded.

'Yeah. I like to read. I've got a copy of that at home. I love it,' he mumbled.

'Really?' Rochelle sounded sceptical.

'Yeah. When I was younger, I . . .' Lamont broke off. He had been about to launch into a story about his parents.

'Spit it out then,' Marcus said, not realising.

'Leave him, Marcus,' Rochelle said. She met Lamont's eyes for a moment, then Mia entered with three glasses.

'What are you doing?' Marcus said, his voice rising.

'What do you mean?'

'There's four of us. Go get another fucking glass,' he barked.

'Marcus, you need to watch the way you talk to my sister,' Rochelle said.

Marcus scowled. 'What are you on about?'

'You know what I'm on about. If she's your girl, talk to her properly, not like she's any chick off the streets.'

'Why don't you chill out and go back to your fucking book? This is nothing to do with you.'

'You're in our house, so I think you'll find it has a lot to do with me. Talk to her properly, or leave.'

Mia's timely arrival stopped Marcus from retorting again.

'Come on baby, let's go upstairs. We'll take the drinks with us.'

Marcus fumed, but allowed himself to be led upstairs, taking the bottle of brandy.

'You need some better friends,' Rochelle remarked when the door closed. She picked up her book.

'Marcus is family.'

'Marcus is a fool. He has good qualities, but he's got no manners. He talks to my sister like shit, and I won't accept that.'

'That's fair enough. Marcus is family though, like I said, and I don't want you badmouthing him around me.'

Rochelle raised an eyebrow.

'Well, look who grew a backbone while they were away. Guess you got over that whole stuttering thing from last time.'

'Guess I did,' said Lamont, smirking.

'That's good. I like the confidence. Just remember one thing, Lamont.'

'I'm listening, *Shelly*.'

'Good. First, it takes more than some new clothes and a haircut to get me. Remember that. Don't call me Shelly either.'

'You let Marcus call you Shelly . . .'

'If I told Marcus to stop, he'd probably call me it more. That's his mentality. What I'm trying to work out is if it's yours too.' Rochelle looked at Lamont again. There was none of the hostility she had shown last time, and this spurred him on. He stared back, entranced by the way her long dark hair fell over her face; the pronounced curves of her body in the sweatpants and tank-top. Rochelle was extraordinary. It was more than looks though. There was something about her assertive attitude that he liked.

'Marcus is Marcus. I'm me.'

'Yeah and who are you?' challenged Rochelle.

'I told you; I'm me.'

'I need more than that. You and Marcus live together, right?' Rochelle began.

'Yeah.'

'Mia said you both live with some relative of yours. Is that true?'

'Yeah.'

'And you go to the same school?'

'Marcus dropped out last year.'

'I see.'

'I might join him.' It was the first time Lamont had admitted that to anyone.

'Why?' Rochelle shot him a sharp look.

'Why what?'

'Why would you want to drop out?'

'I need to make money,' Lamont said, as if it were the most obvious answer in the world.

'And you don't think that staying in school a few more months and completing your education will lead to a better job?'

'There's no guarantee of that.'

'Oh, so you want easy, street money then?'

'I didn't say that. I'll take whatever money I can,' Lamont corrected.

Rochelle shook her head. 'There was me thinking you had more principles.'

'You know nothing about my life, so don't you dare pass judgement on me for wanting something right now.' Lamont was breathing hard now, incensed at Rochelle's comment.

'Slow your roll. I'm not passing judgement on you. I'm entitled to my opinion, which is that you're an idiot if you even think about leaving school.'

'Okay, what are you doing that's so special?'

'I work in an office in town.'

'What are you working towards?'

'What do you mean?'

'Look at you; there's no way you're going to be just working in an office forever. So what is it? What are you working towards?' asked Lamont.

Rochelle blinked, surprised by Lamont's perceptiveness.

'I want to be a teacher.'

'Makes sense, what with that little speech you just gave me about education. Primary or high school?'

'Primary. I don't think I could handle teenagers.'

'If you can handle Marcus, you can handle some cheeky teenagers,' Lamont joked. They both laughed. Hers was a melodic throaty sound that made Lamont think of serene nights, laid on the grass, staring at the stars in the sky. It was so easy talking to Rochelle; no more nerve-wracking than talking to Erica.

Rochelle was older and more assured, but she was still a girl. Lamont no longer felt daunted.

'Thanks. I guess. Can I ask you something?' Rochelle started.

'Yeah, go for it.'

'You were going to say something earlier about this book.' She pointed at *To Kill a Mockingbird*. Lamont's stomach lurched again.

'Yeah. I was.'

'What were you going to say?'

'I used to read it with my mum and dad,' Lamont admitted.

'What happened to them?'

'They died. In a car crash.' Lamont's words were hollow. He remembered the screech of tyres, then the darkness. Lamont had woken to a pain that never dissipated. He rubbed his chin, feeling the familiar scar.

'Oh my God. I'm so sorry to hear that.' Rochelle's hand went to her mouth.

'When I was younger, my parents were always trying to get me to read, but I couldn't concentrate. One day, my mum put that same book in front of me and offered me a pound if I read the first three chapters.'

'Did you?'

'By the time I got to chapter three, I'd forgotten to ask for the money. That story made me love reading. I've never looked back.'

Rochelle beamed. 'That's sweet. I feel sorry for people that don't read. Music and books are two of God's greatest inventions.'

'You're not wrong.'

'Lamont?'

'Yeah?'

'Don't leave school. Okay?'

Lamont said nothing. He was woefully inexperienced with girls, but even he was sharp enough to realise that with the story he had just told Rochelle, the dynamics of their conversation had changed.

'I know it's hard. But just promise me you won't. You're so close to the end. I hear what you're saying about the money, but education is important.'

'Okay, I promise,' Lamont said. They looked at each other for another long moment before he changed the subject.

'What part of the book are you up to?'

Rochelle smiled then and began describing to Lamont exactly what Scout Finch was doing. They both began discussing the merits of the book. The conversation was fast-paced and passionate. By the time Mia and Marcus drunkenly lurched downstairs, Lamont and Rochelle were like old friends.

'Aww, this is what I like to see. Don't they look sweet, babe?' said Marcus.

'Yeah, look at them giggling like some school kids,' Mia teased.

'Leave it alone, Mia,' Rochelle's voice changed. She had grown cold and distant again. Lamont internally sighed, knowing that the night was over.

'Okay, okay, just saying, Shelle.'

'Yo, L, we need to jet. Ladies, it's been fun.' Marcus kissed Mia and waved at Rochelle. They were nearly at the door when Rochelle spoke.

'Lamont?'

'Yeah?'

'You can call me Shelly if you like,' Rochelle said quietly. Then she picked her book back up as if nothing had happened.

* * *

'*You can call me Shelly . . .*'

Lamont rubbed his eyes. Ever since they had left Mia's place, Marcus hadn't shut up.

'What was that about? While I was grinding, what were you two yapping about?'

'We weren't talking about anything in particular. We were just talking,' Lamont tried downplaying it.

'Whatever. I've never seen Rochelle smile like that before. I know when a man is talking smooth. You were running some serious game on her.'

'Just leave it.'

'Yo, I'm proud of you, man. That's a good place to start. Tell you what, if she's anything like her sis, then the grind will be amazing!' Marcus exclaimed. 'We need to go there again tomorrow, then you can vibe her and see what happens.'

'She's just a friend.'

'Don't gimme that nonsense, L. I know more about this stuff than you do. Rochelle is feeling you. You need to handle that.'

'Whatever you say.'

Marcus was laughing now. Loudly. A front door opened as they walked past, and a man glared out at them. Marcus glared back, and the man hurriedly closed the door.

'This is a new start for you. Your balls are dropping. You punched up one kid at school, you're going on moves with me and making money! All you need now is to shag Shelly, and you're straight.'

'Focus on shagging Mia right and leave me to my business,' Lamont said jokingly.

'Oh, I see what this is . . . you get a pair of Nikes, and suddenly you're Superman? Let me see how quick you can run in them!' Marcus lunged at Lamont, who dodged him and scarpered up the road. Marcus followed, the pair of them laughing.

* * *

The next day, Lamont was at Levi's. His Nana was at some function, so they were at the kitchen table, studying a Morrison's carrier bag filled with weed.

'It stinks,' Lamont remarked, making a face and peering into the bag.

'That's good. Means it'll sell quicker.'

'What do we need to start then?'

'I don't know.' Levi scratched his head.

'Didn't Craig tell you?'

'Nah,' Levi laughed, rubbing the back of his neck, 'I made out like you knew what you were doing.'

'Why?'

'Because. He's my brother, man. You know how much shit he gives me. I wanted to show him I could be an asset.'

'We need to find someone who knows what they're doing with this.' Lamont motioned to the bag.

'I know a couple' dudes, but they're like Craig's age. They'll never entertain us.'

Lamont racked his brains, trying to think of someone they could go to. He thought of Marcus, but that was a last resort. Just then, he thought of the right person.

'I know who we can go to.'

* * *

'L, what's cracking?' Shorty said, slapping hands with him and Levi.

'You busy? Kinda need to talk to you.'

'Nah, y'all come in. Kick those shoes off though. The carpet's new.'

Shorty's place was laced. It was a small flat on Harehills Avenue that appeared unkempt on the outside. Lamont didn't know who Shorty made decorate, but they knew their colours. It had all the latest entertainment devices, similar to Marcus's and Levi's rooms.

Shorty directed the pair to sit on the leather sofa. Reaching onto the coffee table, he picked up his spliff from the ashtray and lit it. Taking two burns, he offered it to Lamont, who declined. Levi eagerly took it, coughing loudly as the weed hit his lungs.

'Don't hit it so hard. Take time,' said Shorty, laughing. 'What's up, anyway?'

Lamont glanced at Levi for a second.

'We've got some weed. We want your help to sell it.'

Shorty's reaction was immediate. He doubled over laughing, almost burning himself with the joint. Levi and Lamont watched as Shorty's laughter grew louder and more animated. After several minutes, he calmed down.

'Seriously. What's up?' he repeated.

'We've got an ounce of weed, but we don't really know where to start with it. We hoped you could give us some pointers.'

Shorty wiped his eyes, 'L . . . you know what I do, don't you?'

Lamont did. Shorty had been selling weed for a few years. He and K-Bar had started off small, but were growing in reputation.

'Yeah. You can help us.'

'L, y'all are competition. That's gonna mess with my money. What if you pinch my customers? I can't allow that.'

'I feel what you're saying,' Lamont started. 'We're boys though. I'm just asking for some help.'

'This is business. I can't fuck with you,' Shorty said firmly.

'Are you serious?' Levi's tone was hostile. 'We're supposed to be boys. Why are you going on dodgy?'

Shorty's expression hardened. '*Going on dodgy?* You lot turn up on my doorstep like the *Chuckle Brothers*, talking about you've got weed to sell, but you don't know what to do with it? This is my life. I'm on this shit, twenty-four-seven, get me? I'm not fucking about going to school like you lot. Your brother hustles. Dig up and go talk to him.'

'Shorty,' Lamont interjected before Levi could open his mouth again. 'We can all help each other here. You know my situation, and you know what I'm like. How desperate must I be to turn up here, talking to you like this?'

'That's true,' Shorty admitted.

'Nothing goes on for free. You said yourself, Craig's doing big things. Come on board with us. Help us get started, and Craig will give us a better price. That means more money for you.'

'What?' Levi spluttered. Lamont impaled him with a look. Shorty leant forward, looking more interested now.

'You sure you can speak for Craig?'

'Course. Work with us and you'll make more money,' said Lamont. Shorty thought it over.

'Deal.'

* * *

'Lamont, what are you playing at?'

They were headed back to Levi's. He had kept quiet while Lamont and Shorty were talking, but now he was furious.

'We needed Shorty's help,' Lamont said.

'What about that crap about a better price?'

'You need to talk to your brother. Make him see sense.'

'Are you serious? Craig will kill me.' Levi's eyes widened.

'No, he won't. This is about money. Tell him you've found someone with a solid client base, meaning he gets a better return. He'll be happy with the extra business,' Lamont assured him. Levi took a deep breath and nodded.

'I hope you're right, bro. I'm gonna get the weed bags and the scales. I'll get back at you when I've spoken to Craig again.'

* * *

The next few days passed without incident. Levi bought the equipment. He spoke to his brother who agreed to Lamont's proposal, just as Lamont suspected he would. Craig wanted to speak to them directly though, summoning them to meet him.

Craig Parker could usually be found on Chapeltown Road, around Landport Street. He was surrounded by an entourage which comprised two large goons, and a smattering of female admirers. Craig had the dark good looks Levi was getting. He dressed the part, usually sporting fresh designer clothes that no one else on the street had. He burned a hole through Lamont as they approached. Lamont met Craig's gaze, knowing instinctively that movements were critical at this point.

'So, you're slanging now?'

It seemed an innocent question, but Lamont sensed Craig wanted more. The street life was cold. Everyone suspected the others' motives. Craig was wilful, always willing to get what he wanted rather than sitting around. He was the Ghetto Prince at the moment, gaining momentum as he surged through the drugs game. He was doing well for himself. Better than most people expected.

'Yeah,' Lamont kept his response simple, wanting to lure Craig in. It worked.

'Why?'

'Because I'm broke.'

'So? Get a paper round.'

Craig's entourage burst into peals of laughter as if he had said the funniest thing in the world.

'Like you did?'

Lamont's comeback silenced everyone in the vicinity. Even Levi gaped, wondering how he had the gall to make such a fresh remark.

Craig surveyed Lamont, trying to compare the hustler confidently staring him down, to the scared kid his little brother used to bring to their house. Lamont seemed prepared, and another bonus for Craig was that he was working with Levi. Craig didn't have the patience to teach his little brother about the hustle. If they flopped, it wouldn't backfire on him.

'I went out and got it. That's the difference. You kids want it all handed to you nowadays.'

'I'm ready to work for mine. We all are.'

'And you're speaking for Shorty?'

Lamont nodded.

'He's a little maniac. Can you control him?'

'It's not about control. It's about working with him. Shorty's my friend.'

'And Marcus? Is he your *friend* too?'

'Marcus is my brother,' Lamont corrected.

Craig nodded slowly, sharing a look with one of his guys, a large black boy in a Reebok hooded top. Whatever passed between them, Lamont didn't understand.

'Your brother robbed some of my people, did you know that?' Craig sounded pleasant enough, but Lamont sensed the viper within. He needed to be careful. Craig might have been referring to the robbery Lamont had taken part in. Playing dumb was his best defence.

'No, I didn't.'

'What if I told you that to work for me, you had to give up your brother? Would you do it?'

Lamont's reply was immediate.

'No, I wouldn't.'

Craig smiled.

'As long as you keep them away from my people, I will give you a shot.'

Lamont smiled. 'You won't regret this.'

The smile slipped from Craig's face. 'If I regret it, you and your whole team will too. Understand?'

'I understand, Craig.'

'I'm gonna hook you up on trust. I want my money every Friday. I don't care if you sell out or not. Understand?'

Lamont nodded.

'The money goes through Levi. If you run out, let him know and he'll let me know. Don't send any of your other people to meet me. Understand?'

Lamont nodded again.

'If you get into a beef, handle it. If it gets out of hand, I'll step in, but don't be ringing me because a sale slapped you and stole your draws. Understand?'

'Yes, Craig. I understand.'

'Good. Now, get out of here.'

CHAPTER SIX

Wednesday 26 March 1997

'L, man? Where did that come from?' Levi exclaimed when they were halfway down Chapeltown road. He'd expected Craig to bully Lamont and make him look stupid, but Lamont dominated him. Levi wondered what Lamont was truly capable of. He seemed so harmless most of the time, but then sometimes . . .

'I had to show him it was beneficial to work together. Can you speak to him about supply? We need to know the weed will be available when we need it.'

Levi scratched his head. 'I'll speak to him later. He'll diss me in front of his boys if I press him now.'

'He seemed very interested in Shorty and Marcus,' mused Lamont.

'They're crazy. People know you roll with them. Marcus, man . . . he's dark. He scares the crap out of me. Dunno how you can just chat to him normally. When I speak to him, I feel like I need my guard up.'

'They're family. With family, sometimes you only see the good parts,' Lamont replied. He quickened his pace, forcing Levi to hurry to keep up.

* * *

With their supply secure, Lamont and Levi arranged a meeting at Levi's place. They camped in the kitchen around a chipped wooden table while his Nana watched her programmes in the living room, the TV volume at a deafening level.

Levi closed the door and faced the gang. Lamont was at the far side, with K-Bar and Shorty at either end.

'It's all sorted, Shorty. We spoke to my bro. He'll hook us up with a cheaper rate,' said Levi

Shorty grinned. 'Deal's a deal then. Let's talk business.'

The crew ironed out the details, deciding they would start from tomorrow, with the work being kept at Shorty's. He and K-Bar had their own spot so no-one would find out what they were doing. As they spoke, Lamont felt Levi giving him funny looks. He waited until the others left before speaking to him about it.

'What's wrong?'

Levi shrugged, scraping his index finger along the table, 'I'm not sure I like how this is going.'

'What do you mean?'

Levi stewed a moment.

'I brought you in, and now it just feels like you're taking over. You're talking with Craig even though he's my brother. You brought your own people into the plan without even speaking to me about it. Seems you're trying to push me out.'

Lamont saw the anger on his friend's face. He needed to handle this. Lamont was committed now, and he would do what he needed to make money. If that meant making Levi happy, he'd do it.

'This is on you, Levi. It's your thing. If you think I'm making too many decisions, just tell me to step off. I wanted to bring Shorty and K-Bar in because they have the links to sell quick, and people won't trouble them. If you wanna do something different though, tell me. Craig's your brother. This whole thing falls apart without you.'

Lamont sounded sincere, but it was necessary. Levi and Shorty had a thing about respect. If Lamont placated them both, the operation would run smoothly.

Levi tried hiding his delight at Lamont's words.

'Okay. You're right. We'll get started tomorrow like we agreed.

Meet me at Shorty's. We'll bag up the drugs there, and sort out who deals where.'

Lamont nodded.

'Sounds good, Levi. Great plan, bro.'

* * *

Things quickly escalated. The crew bagged the weed and using Shorty's network of buyers, sold out in no time. After repeating this a few times, Craig began to take them seriously. He gave them two kilos of weed on credit to see if the crew could handle it. They could.

Word of their good product was landing in the right ears. The school crowd was a goldmine too. Lamont often found himself besieged by classmates wanting to buy, but only dealt with them off the school grounds.

In no time, they had the chain of command down to a T. Levi was in charge of making sure Craig received his return, and would pick up the drugs and drop them on Shorty. Shorty and K-Bar would weigh and bag all the weed, then they would all slang it.

Being the strongest with numbers, Lamont oversaw the money side, making sure everyone was paid equally and promptly. Everything ran like clockwork, and that was down to Lamont. He tailored the strategy he used with Levi and was using it on Shorty too. He allowed both to think they were dictating things and because of that, there was no strife in the ranks.

* * *

Lamont strolled down Chapeltown Road with Levi one night. They had just gone to meet some clients near Reginald Terrace, and Lamont wanted to see if anyone was at the park to play football. They were almost there when a car pulled up alongside them.

'Lamont, can I have a word?' Nigel Worthington rolled the window down. Lamont sighed. He had avoided Nigel since the man's admission about wanting to become his agent. The last thing he needed was another adult trying to manipulate him.

'Yeah. What's up?'

Nigel cut his eyes to Levi, 'I'd prefer to talk alone.'

'I'll be at the park, L.' Levi glanced at Nigel and strolled away.

'Are you getting in?' Nigel asked. Lamont hesitated. Not wanting to press it, Nigel parked and climbed out. He wore the navy tracksuit and worn Reebok trainers he normally wore for coaching, giving Lamont a once-over.

'New clothes?'

Lamont shrugged.

'Did your Auntie give you some money?'

Lamont just stared. Nigel knew where the money had come from.

'Is this what you want to do, Lamont? I'm giving you an opportunity to be a superstar. I have people in place and you can ascend. I can help you. Why would you throw it all away?'

'That's your thing. Not mine,' Lamont finally spoke.

'And this is your thing, is it? You want to hustle, like all the other idiots on the street? You wanna go prison? Do you want to die?'

'I'm tired of the way I'm living. I wouldn't expect you to understand,' Lamont snapped, forgetting he was talking to a grown man.

'Do you really think you're the only person who has had it hard? There are many people out there who have struggled! I know you've been through a lot of crap with your Auntie. I sympathise, but you have a chip on your shoulder. Is this what your parents would have wanted?'

'Don't talk about my parents,' Lamont's voice had an innate chill. Nigel was aware he was going too far. Wisely, he backed down.

'I'm sorry, Lamont. I just don't want to see you waste your talent. You are capable of so much more. When you're on that field, you're composed, you're in the moment. I'd even venture to say you're happy. Don't throw that all away over a street dream.'

Lamont measured Nigel with a hard stare. 'You want the truth? Football's the street dream. It's all a game, and If I'm gonna play, I might as well get paid for it. Right now. Not years down the line.'

Nigel took a deep breath, picking his words carefully. Deep down, he knew it was futile. He had lost Lamont. It was written in the boy's eyes. He tried again anyway.

'Okay, come and play anyway. Just for fun. We can take it from there.'

'There's nothing to take. I'm sick and tired of being treated like shit and manipulated.'

'I've never treated you like shit. I've treated you the same as the other boys, but I knew that you could go further. I still do. You're closer than you know to hitting the next level with football,' Nigel retorted.

'How many other kids are you giving that speech to? Let me guess, I follow you all the way and then I become just another player? Lost in the shuffle, probably end up dropped after a few games? No, I'll take my chances with what I'm doing,' Lamont's words had an adult's finality, which Nigel recognised and respected.

'I'm sorry to hear you talking like this. If you come to your senses, you know where to find me.'

Nigel drove away. Lamont watched after him for a second, wondering briefly if he had made the right decision. He turned on his heel and walked towards the park.

* * *

One night, the gang drove to a meeting. Their exploits had reached the ears of a shark named Blair. Blair had a distribution network of his own and was always looking for new links. He had reached out to Levi, and they agreed a price for an entire kilo of weed.

'Blair is the business,' Levi was saying from the passenger seat. 'I've asked around about him. He's definitely paid. If we deal with him, we're gonna make loads.'

'I've seen him about in town. He likes rocking chains and shit. He's a flashy guy,' added Shorty.

'Nothing wrong with being flashy,' said Levi, grinning. To emphasise his point, he wore a large gold chain which rested easily on his chest. Lamont hated it, thinking it made Levi look like a target. He couldn't tell him what to do though. Levi was fragile and Lamont had to go to great pains not to undermine him.

He disagreed with this meeting. Blair was established. There was no reason for him to be buying such a large amount of weed from some up and comers. Lamont had been outvoted though. If they shifted the entire kilo, they could reload quicker and restart the process. The team was hungry for more success. More accolades. More profit.

'We're nearly there anyway,' Shorty said, steering the car masterfully through the streets. He had borrowed the car from an associate, and wouldn't hear the end of it if he damaged the ride.

They parked down the road from the house where Blair waited. K-Bar and Shorty were at the back as Lamont and Levi led the way towards the house. Lamont scanned in all directions, looking for anything suspicious. Something wasn't right. His instincts screamed it, but he couldn't gauge the cause.

'Glad you could all make it,' a man Lamont assumed was Blair said, opening the door. 'Come right through.'

Blair closed the door behind them. Lamont looked around the room. It was basic. There was an old TV, peeling walls and wooden floorboards. He thought he heard a creak in the adjacent room, but then there was nothing. Blair clapped his hands together loudly, getting their attention. He was older — Lamont assumed late twenties. His hair was neatly tapered, and the chain around his neck made Levi's look invisible. He wore a fresh tracksuit and a gold watch on his right wrist. His hands were adorned with large rings and he rubbed his hands together, odiously smiling.

'You got the stuff then?'

'Yeah. We've got it. Where's the money?' Shorty replied.

'It's upstairs. I'll go get it.' Blair left the room and headed upstairs.

'Why didn't he have the money down here?' Lamont quickly spoke.

'What are you on about?' Shorty asked.

'We arranged this. Why wouldn't he have the money?'

'Lamont, just chill. I've got this,' said Levi. Before he could say another word, the doors on either side of the room burst open and two masked guys rushed at them. Lamont froze.

'Get on the floor!' one of them growled, wielding what looked like a pipe. The second the doors opened, Shorty was in motion. Whipping a gun from his waistband, he pointed it at the two would-be robbers.

'No. You lot get on the floor.'

'Wait . . . Shorty?' the man with the pipe said, surprised. Recognising his voice and build, Lamont stepped forward.

'Marcus?'

'L? What are you doing here?' Marcus pulled the mask off his face. Victor did the same thing.

'Doing a buy. What are you doing?'

'A buy? You're dealing now?'

Lamont nodded.

'We got a call earlier. Blair promised us half the take if we rushed some kids. We didn't know it was you lot though. Oi,' Marcus turned to Victor, 'go grab that snake. We're gonna deal with this.'

Victor hurried to do Marcus's bidding.

'I can't believe this.' Marcus rubbed his face, breathing heavily. Lamont knew the signs. When Marcus got worked up, it never ended well for the perpetrator.

The sounds of a scuffle attracted everyone's attention. Victor was dragging Blair into the room, the man digging his feet into the floor. Shorty smacked Blair in the mouth with the gun. There was a crunch and Blair sagged, allowing Victor to throw him to the floor.

'You little weasel. You thought you could send me after family?' Marcus spat at Blair, who cowered away.

'It's not like that! I didn't know he was your family! I swear,' he moaned through bloodied lips.

'Well, you've had it now. Vic, go back upstairs and search for the stash. I know it's here somewhere. In the meantime, you can take off those jewels. I'm taxing them for my pain and suffering.'

'Marcus, man, please—' Blair started, silenced by a kick to the ribs.

'If I have to strip you down myself, I swear I'm gonna break every finger on your hands. Take them off. Now.'

Shaking with fear, Blair took off his watch, his rings and his chain. Marcus pocketed them. Victor came back downstairs with a brick-sized wad of money, which he handed to Marcus. Marcus thumbed through the notes, nodding his approval.

'This'll do. You ever try anything like this again, and I'll kill you.' Marcus gave the beaten man one more kick, then they all left.

'Well, that was a result. Simple bit of work. I almost got shot, but still. Here,' Marcus split the brick of money and handed half to Lamont. 'For you and your little team.'

Lamont held the money, his heart beating. Selling weed had been easy, but tonight had been a stark lesson that anything could happen. He nodded at Marcus, willing himself to calm down.

'Anyway, we're gonna bounce. We're gonna lick another move. We were relying on robbing you lot, but luckily we had it as a backup.'

'What's the job?' Shorty asked, ever the opportunist.

'Like this one, only with better planning. Half a kilo. Maybe more. You in? We could use that gun.'

'I'm in. K is too. What about y'all?' he looked at Lamont and Levi.

'I'm going home. I'm tired,' Lamont said.

'Me too. Just drop us off on the way,' Levi added. Marcus nodded. He and Victor climbed in their ride. When Lamont and the others were in their own car, they all drove off.

CHAPTER SEVEN

Wednesday 16 April 1997

LAMONT WAS CHILLING at Shorty's after school, watching television. Shorty had cut Lamont a key, so most of the time he would hang out. Shorty didn't care. He was usually out scheming or having sex. Lamont was about to make a drink, when the door opened and Levi bounded in.

'Yo, L!' he called out.

'I'm here, man. No need to shout.' Lamont appeared in the doorway.

'Well c'mon. We need to go.'

'Where to?'

'Craig wants to see us.'

Lamont put his shoes on and followed Levi. A taxi waited. Levi gave the driver directions, and the driver drove off. It seemed pointless to Lamont. Craig was within walking distance. It was as if Levi was spending money for the sake of it.

As predicted, they were out of the car less than a minute later. Levi paid the fare, and they headed towards Craig. He was slouched on a wall, kissing a girl Lamont had never seen before. She had large, dark eyes, skin the shade of cooking chocolate, and a body that poked out in all the right places. Lamont avoided staring, but Levi looked the girl up and down, almost licking his lips. Eventually Craig stopped kissing the girl and faced them.

'Everything good?'

Both boys nodded.

'I'm asking because I heard about last night.'

'Just a misunderstanding, bro,' Levi started. 'We were dealing with someone and he tried snaking us. We handled it though.'

'You handled it, or Marcus did?' Craig smiled at the look of surprise that appeared on Levi's face. 'C'mon, baby bro. I know everything that happens on these streets. Why do you think I called you here? Blair is a punk. If you'd told me you were dealing with him, I would have told y'all not to.'

'He wanted to buy a keg,' Levi said. 'It was easy money.'

'Easy money had you getting stuck up. Don't be stupid chasing quick money. Grind for it. Stop smoking and shagging little girls and keep track of what's happening. If you'd bothered to check, you would have realised that me and Blair had beef.'

'Beef? Over what?'

'Over this fine girl I've got my arms around,' Craig palmed the girl for emphasis. 'See, Kierra here, she had a spell with Blair. When she realised what a bitch he was, she wanted me. He didn't like it, but he can't do anything. Me and that idiot used to run together.'

'What happened?' Lamont spoke for the first time.

'He was skimming. We were partners, splitting all the money down the middle. He was doing deals on the side and didn't want to cut me in, so I kicked his ass out of the squad.'

'Do we need to worry about him?' Lamont was trying to establish what they were dealing with. This was why he hadn't wanted to do the deal. You just never knew what another person was bringing to the table, drama-wise.

'Blair's already shouting his mouth off about getting set up. He's not putting it on you lot directly, because you're nobodies. What he's doing is telling people I did it. He's harmless, but since I kicked him out, he's running with some crazy Yardies. Those are the ones you need to watch out for.'

'Understood,' Lamont said. Annoyed at being cut out of the conversation, Levi spoke up.

'We're not worried about that bitch. If he comes for me, I'll cut him and anyone he wants to bring along,' he exclaimed. Craig and Lamont stared at him, unmoved by his posturing.

'Shut up. I don't wanna hear about you running your mouth, trying to start shit to impress me. Sort your head out, think about the money. Understand?'

Levi stared his brother down. Craig's eyes narrowed.

'I said, do you understand?'

'Yeah, bro. I understand.'

'Get out of here. I've got stuff to handle.'

* * *

'Who does he think he is?'

They were almost back at Shorty's place. Since leaving Craig, Levi had ranted non stop.

'He's just worried. We can't make money if we're watching our backs waiting for Blair.'

'Are you scared? I'm not scared. That motherfucker set us up.'

'It worked out for us though. Marcus robbed him. We made money from an impossible situation,' Lamont replied.

'Why are you talking like you're in charge? Craig is my brother, so stop sucking up to him and support me. I brought you in!' Levi shouted. Anger flared within Lamont. It wasn't the time for an outburst though. Levi had shown his petulance. Lamont wouldn't lower himself to that level. It was about the money, nothing more.

'Okay, bro. Whatever you say. Like you said, you brought me in,' he replied.

Levi took a deep breath.

'L, I'm sorry, man. You're my bro. It's just Craig. He thought we would flop, and now that we're making money, he wants to play boss. He should have told us about Blair beforehand, then we would have known not to deal with him. He was probably in on it from the beginning.'

Lamont let Levi vent as they walked up the stairs to Shorty's flat. K-Bar was back from his excursions. He watched the pair enter as he smoked a cigarette.

'What's up?' he asked.

'More drama,' Lamont said, summarising what Craig said about Blair.

'That's a bad situation. Blair got humiliated, so we need to be careful,' K-Bar said when Lamont finished.

'Forget Blair. We put him in his place,' Levi snapped, heading to the kitchen, returning with a bottle of Courvoisier and a clean glass.

'Shorty's not gonna like you touching his liquor,' K-Bar pointed out.

'Fuck Shorty. He's not gonna say anything if I buy him a bottle back, is he?'

K-Bar's eyes narrowed, but he said nothing. Levi poured himself a glass, drank it and poured another, which he downed. He began coughing loudly, then poured himself another glass.

'Take it easy,' Lamont said.

'Fuck taking it easy,' Levi slurred, the brandy already touching him. 'Remember whose team you're on. I'm out.' Slamming the glass on the table, Levi tottered from the house.

'He's out of control,' K-Bar said as soon as the front door closed.

'Don't worry about it. He knows not to go too far.'

'Shorty might see it differently if he keeps running his mouth. He'll knock him out.'

'Levi's just angry. He wants Craig to think he's an asset. He doesn't realise that this isn't about Craig. We're just workers. We need to keep profiting and stay above water.'

'Did Craig say anything about who these Yardies were?'

Lamont shook his head. 'He just said they were crazy.'

K-Bar stroked his chin. 'I'll find out, so we know what we're up against. I'll let you speak to Shorty. You need to calm Levi down too, because he's moving too fast, too quickly.'

* * *

The gang took it easy after that. They did their business, but didn't arrange any deals with anyone they didn't know.

Lamont passed on Craig's warning to everyone. Only Levi remained belligerent. Lately, he was drinking more, smoking weed, and bringing random girls to Shorty's place, nearly causing he and Shorty to fight. Levi thought Craig would protect him if things escalated, but Lamont didn't believe he was taking Shorty seriously.

There were rumours about the things Shorty had done, some even involving murder. Lamont believed the tales. He recalled how easily Shorty had pulled the gun when he thought they were in danger. Shorty was ruthless and there was nothing to gain by Levi provoking him.

Still, he kept out of it. Lamont's prime focus was getting paid, and he did that. He had money hidden all over his room and there was no danger of Auntie finding it. Lately, she was spending more time out of the house, which Lamont took to mean that she was hunting for a new sponsor. Lamont passed through and made sure Marika was okay, did his chores, then left again. The less he was in the house, the less chance there was he would argue with Auntie.

Lamont also hung around Marcus more, which mostly meant standing around outside different houses.

Marcus had heard the rumours about Blair, but wasn't taking them seriously. He was cool with the Yardies backing Blair, stating that as long as Craig kept himself to himself, there would be no problem.

* * *

Lamont hurried towards the front gate after school one day. He wore a black tracksuit and matching trainers with a new backpack, walking with his shoulders set and his head held high. Tower and his crew shot him dirty looks, but he strolled past them without a word.

Erica was outside the gate with her friends. She looked away when Lamont walked by, but her friends stared, their faces no longer holding looks of disgust. He heard them whisper, but Lamont ignored the pair, heading to the park. People were waiting for him.

By the time he arrived, the two boys were standing there. Spotting several parents in the small park, Lamont motioned for the boys to come to him, which they did. The trio walked to a secluded corner.

'What are you after?'

'Two tens,' one boy replied. He was a chubby black boy named Tyrone. Tyrone was another kid Lamont had known for years. He had realised early on that rather than letting the fact he was overweight get him down, it was better to embrace it. Because of this he was well-liked.

The other kid was a pale, bespectacled boy named Robert. Robert had started smoking to get over nerves for an exam. He started buying more, and in no time, Lamont had a reliable customer.

Reaching into his bag, Lamont opened his pencil case and quickly took two ten-pound draws from where he had strategically placed them. He gave them to Tyrone, taking the two ten-pound notes from his sweaty hands.

'Safe. Get at me when you want more.' Lamont touched fists with them both and walked off.

* * *

By the time Lamont arrived home, Auntie was in the living room with Marika. She looked up when Lamont entered.

'Where have you been?'

'Out.'

'Don't get cheeky, boy. I know you were out. Where were you?'

'I was chilling in the park,' Lamont lied. Auntie glared at him.

'You don't have time to chill in the park. You have work to do.'

'I know that. I'll do it now.'

'What did I just say about getting cheeky?' Auntie shouted. Marika immediately looked at her, lip trembling. Noticing her niece's reaction, Auntie visibly calmed down.

'Get a dustpan and brush and sweep these floors. They're filthy.'

Lamont flashed a smile.

'No problem, Auntie. I'll do it now.' Without another word, he practically skipped from the room.

* * *

Life went on for Lamont and the team. For a while, they were paranoid over a potential beef with the Yardies Craig and Marcus had mentioned. It felt like Lamont was seeing crews and gangs everywhere, and he believed he would be the target of a retaliatory attack.

'I keep telling you,' Marcus said one day, as they lifted weights at a gym in Harehills. 'There's no problem. It's been ages, so leave it alone. You still getting money?'

Lamont nodded.

'Focus on that then,' Marcus laughed to himself. 'Still can't believe you're slanging though. If you wanted to make money so bad, you should have just kept working with me.'

Lamont didn't reply until he'd completed his set on the bench. They'd been in the gym over forty minutes, and his body ached.

'You saw how I was that one time. I'm not cut out for it,' he said finally, recalling the disastrous robbery he'd been part of.

'It was your first go, L. No one's a master criminal their first time. You did as you were told and kept your nerve mostly,' Marcus shrugged. 'You're doing well, so it doesn't matter I guess. I'm hearing you're about it. Proper natural leader.'

'Who said that?' Lamont was curious. No one had said anything to him. Marcus refused to continue the conversation until the session was complete.

They were home eating tinned tuna and pasta in the kitchen before Marcus revisited the subject.

'So, yeah, I'm hearing you've got skills. You're on point with the money, and you're good at keeping things flowing. Keep it up, and you're gonna see real money, bro.'

'Who told you this though?'

'I work with your people, L. I know Shorty and them lot too, you know. We talk business and your name comes up. Him and K can't say enough good things about you.'

'I'm glad they think so highly of me,' Lamont noticed Levi's name hadn't come up. 'It's funny though, because they didn't even want to work with me at first.'

'Course not. They thought you'd fuck up their hustle. You proved them wrong, and now you're all benefitting.'

Lamont finished his food, taking Marcus at his word. He'd never thought of himself as a leader. Levi had a more forceful personality, which was why he clashed with Shorty so much. Lamont just steered the ship. He focused on the bottom line, which was money.

'What's happening with Shelly?'

Lamont rolled his eyes.

'C'mon, Marcus, not this again.'

'Not what? Do you like her?'

'You know I do.'

'So, what's stopping you?'

'We're just friends,' Lamont's reply sounded weak, even to him.

'Well, I was there the other night, and she was asking about you.'

'Nothing wrong with asking about a friend,' said Lamont, though his chest tightened at those words.

'Whatever you say, L. Step up and get it done.'

* * *

A few days later, Lamont fought to control his nerves as he approached Rochelle's place. He looked down at his outfit, having settled for a white t-shirt, denim jeans and a high-top trainers. He could feel the warmth of the sun on his arms, glad he'd left his coat at home. Forcing himself to stand with confidence, Lamont knocked at the door, holding a carrier bag.

'Easy, L, you okay?' Mia looked surprised to see Lamont. She had a smile on her face though, which startled him.

'I'm fine. Is Rochelle in?'

'Nah, she's out.'

Lamont's stomach dropped.

'Oh, okay. Could you give her this?' Lamont held out the bag.

'What's in it?' Mia didn't move.

'A book and a CD I thought she might like.'

Mia studied him a moment.

'Come in.'

'What?'

'Come and wait for her. She went food shopping, so she won't be long. You can stay for dinner.'

'I . . . Is that alright?'

'Course it is. Come on.'

Not arguing, Lamont entered the house, heading straight for the living room. He felt Mia's eyes on him, hoping it wouldn't become uncomfortable with Marcus's girl.

'Have you been going gym?' she suddenly asked.

'Me and Marcus go a few times a week.'

'You can see it. Your back looks proper broad.'

'Erm, thanks,' Lamont said, keeping his voice light. Mia's eyes surveyed him again, looking him up and down.

'You're scrawny compared to my man though.'

Just like that, they laughed, and it lifted the tension.

'So, you like my sister then?'

'We're friends.'

Mia raised an eyebrow. 'Do you buy books for all your friends?'

'If they like to read,' Lamont shot back.

'Fine. If that's the story you wanna go with, I won't argue. Do you want something to drink?'

Later, Lamont was sitting with a glass of apple juice, when the front door opened.

'Mia, I'm back. I swear, I need to get my licence. The taxi driver was a right pervert. Listen, they didn't have any Red Leicester, so I—' Rochelle stopped when she saw Lamont in the living room. 'L?'

'Hey, Shelly.'

'What are you doing here?' Rochelle stood in the doorway, holding the shopping bags. She wore a black jacket over some jeans and riding boots. Lamont rose to his feet more gracefully than he felt, taking the shopping bags from her.

'Let me help you with those.'

'Okay, but then you can answer my question,' Rochelle said, leading him to the kitchen. When they'd put the shopping away, Rochelle shot him a glance.

'So . . .'

Lamont raised his hands. 'So what?'

'Why are you here?'

'I was hungry. Heard you scrubbed up a good dinner.'

'L . . .'

Lamont grinned, jamming his hands in his pockets out of nervousness.

'Fine. I bought something for you today. Tried leaving it with your sister, but she made me stay.'

Rochelle processed this. 'Do you want to stay for dinner then?'

'Yeah.'

'When we finish, I want to see what you brought.'

* * *

Lamont helped Rochelle cook, using his vast experience from feeding Auntie. When the three of them finished, Mia left the room, giving the pair privacy. Lamont had relaxed from earlier, but some awkwardness lingered. It often seemed he was one step away from messing up whatever he had with Rochelle, and it was confusing.

Lamont wanted to be comfortable in her presence, but not too comfortable, in case he did something stupid. He'd never gone to her house without Marcus before, and was half expecting to hear his friends booming laugh and see him bounding into the living room, but he didn't. There was no one to take the attention from Lamont.

'Can I see this mysterious gift now?'

Lamont steadied himself and handed the bag to Rochelle.

'*Anita Baker.*' Rochelle's eyes were a question as she looked up at Lamont, holding the CD. He resisted the urge to put his hands in his pockets.

'You said once that music and books were two of the greatest inventions. I wanted to add to your collection. Anita Baker has a strong, distinctive voice. Reminds me of yours.'

'And the book? Why *The Colour Purple?*'

Lamont wasn't sure if Rochelle liked his gifts or not, but she was putting him on the spot.

'I just thought you you'd enjoy it.'

Rochelle beamed, surprising Lamont.

'I'm sure I will. And thank you. It's sweet of you.'

Relieved that she liked the gift, Lamont grinned.

'It's fine.'

They spoke for a while longer, and Lamont watched TV with Rochelle. He became distracted when Rochelle started to lean on him. His heart hammered against his chest, but he tried to look cool. She smelt like cherries and some jasmine aroma. Lamont liked it a lot. He liked everything about just sitting with Rochelle, almost like they were a couple. He wouldn't overthink it though.

'You're finishing school soon, aren't you?'

'Couple of weeks left and then I'm done. My exams are in June.'

Rochelle shifted against him. 'Are you revising?'

'A bit.' Lamont wouldn't lie. He had gone through old notes and school books, but he needed to make money too, He spent more time with Shorty and Marcus than he did revising.

'L, exams are important. Promise me you'll take them seriously.'

Lamont nodded. 'I promise that I will. When they're done though, let me take you out for dinner, okay?'

Rochelle glanced at him, her smile so sweet it threatened to over-whelm him.

'Okay.'

Lamont's chest felt warm. The evening had been one of the best he could remember. All of his drama, all the pressures of the street had evaporated in Rochelle's presence, and he loved it. He needed to leave though and with great regret, extricated himself from Rochelle's touch.

'I've gotta go.'

If Rochelle was disappointed, she hid it well as she walked Lamont to the front door.

'Thanks again for the presents, L. I'm going to put the album on now and start reading.'

'Good. Let me know what you think.'

'I will.'

They glanced at one another, not knowing what to do next.

Lamont took her in his arms, hugging her against him. Rochelle stiffened for a second, then hugged him back. Acting on instinct, Lamont kissed her on the forehead as he let her go.

'Night, Shelly.'

'Night, L.'

CHAPTER EIGHT

Tuesday 20 May 1997

LAMONT HAD books spread across his desk. He'd listened to Rochelle, and was revising for his exams, which started next week.

Lamont had officially left school, turned in all coursework, and he was ready. There was no fear over completing his exams. He had always been a dutiful student and his personal circumstances hadn't impacted his desire to learn. Scribbling notes as he pored through his year eleven maths textbook, Auntie's shrill voice cut through the quiet.

'Lamont! Door!'

Mumbling under his breath, Lamont hurried down the stairs. Levi waited in the garden, his movements jittery.

'L, I need you,' he started, nervously looking up and down the street.

'For what? What's going on?'

'I got into a situation and I need you, man. We need to go find Marcus, or—'

'Levi, are you gonna tell me what's happened?' Lamont cut across his friend. Levi made a noise of dissent, his eyes wide with fear.

'Look, people are coming for me. Are you gonna help me find Marcus or what?'

Lamont wanted to leave Levi to it. They were friends though, and he couldn't abandon him. Hurrying upstairs, he put on a hooded top, squeezed his feet into some black trainers, and made his way back to the front door. He heard Auntie call out, but Lamont had already closed the door.

'What's this situation then?'

'I was dealing on the side,' Levi hung his head. 'I gave some weed to someone I thought was harmless. It had loads of seeds and shit, practically unsellable. He's connected to a bigger guy. Now, they're after me. They nearly caught me near my house, but I ran and escaped them. They're probably still there.'

Lamont put out a hand to stop his friend.

'Why were you dealing on the side?' he asked, trying not to let his anger show.

'Why do you think? I needed money.'

'We all need money,' Lamont snapped. 'I look after that side of our thing though, so how did you do it?'

'. . . When I reloaded with Craig, I got some extra for myself.'

Lamont couldn't believe it. Levi needed money less than any of them. Craig made sure he wanted for nothing. Lamont regretted getting caught up in Levi's drama, but it was too late now.

'It wasn't the first time, was it?' Lamont already knew the answer. Levi couldn't look him in the eye, focusing instead on the ground. Lamont sighed, shaking his head. He couldn't bring himself to shout at his friend. Like it or not, Levi was the link to their supply.

'Let's just deal with this mess.' Lamont stalked towards Levi's place without even waiting for him.

* * *

Lamont stewed later, his mind alight. The guys Levi ripped off had been out for his blood, and it took Lamont offering them Levi's chain as collateral to call them off.

More often, Lamont wondered about the drugs game. It was easy to get caught up in the hustle. He was selling weed to people who wanted to smoke, and on the surface that seemed fine, but it was still an offence, and he couldn't afford to get caught.

Lamont absentmindedly played with the pieces of a battered chessboard. It had belonged to his father. Lamont remembered the nights spent listening to his dad explaining the significance of each piece, taking him the intricacies of taking his time with each move.

They would play and his dad would always win at first, but before his death, Lamont could beat him. He wondered to himself now if his dad had let him win.

Lamont had a few friends he could play with, but he hadn't seen them much since he had started dealing drugs. It was time-consuming. He enjoyed the money he made but there was a lot of running around involved. It was a distraction though, and a distraction was what he needed right now.

Lamont thought about Rochelle. He'd been to the house once or twice since the dinner. The awkwardness lingered, but there was none of the initial ice and scorn. Now they talked easily about TV shows, literature, but never about anything too deep. Maybe that was the problem.

Lamont was sure that Rochelle liked him the way he liked her. Marcus teased him, saying that they acted more like a couple than he and Mia did, and Lamont would play along, *but how the hell was he supposed to know?*

His experience with the opposite sex was minimal. He could talk to them because they didn't take him seriously. He was a friend to them, just like he had been to Erica, but it was different with Rochelle. It felt like there was something more there, but he had nothing to compare it to. And that was the problem.

If he and Rochelle were just friends, then he wouldn't feel how he did. He wouldn't be moping around, confused, not knowing if he was imagining anything between them. Blinking, Lamont looked down, realising, he was fingering the black queen piece. He glanced down at it, his eyes blurring for a moment, then he decided.

* * *

'L? What are you doing here?'

Lamont could have kicked himself for his impulsiveness. Rochelle looked out at him. She wore a tight sleeveless top with big gold buttons. Two of the buttons were undone, leaving a tantalising trail to her cleavage, her thick thighs encased in a skirt. She was barefooted, some minstrel brown polish on her toenails. He stared, thinking how dumb it had been to turn up on her doorstep.

'L?' She spoke again, louder this time. Lamont met her eyes. He wondered if she knew the sexual vibe she put out. He didn't think she did. There was no way she could know the full effect she had on him.

'I wanted to see you,' Lamont mumbled. The way the scenario had played out in his head and the reality couldn't have been more different. For a fleeting second he was tempted to run away. Instead, he met her eyes again.

'Why?' she asked.

'Because I like you.'

'I like you too, L. I think you're a great guy.'

'Good. If we both like each other, that's all it should take, right?'

Rochelle shook her head. 'It's not that simple. I have baggage. There are complications in my life I can't explain. Trust me when I say I'm the last person you want to get involved with.'

'You're wrong. When I'm around you . . . I feel like I can be myself. I don't have to put on an act or blend in. You make me feel secure. Surely if I have someone like that, I should keep them close, right?' Lamont fought to keep his words even, to stop his voice from shaking, heart madly pounding. He had never put himself out there like this before. The words were out now. He was being a man, telling Rochelle how he really felt, hoping to hell that she wouldn't shoot him down.

The insecurities whipped at him like an abusive partner. *How could she want him? What the hell did he have to offer her?*

Lamont's eyes watered now, unblinking. He wanted to break his gaze. He couldn't though; he had to show her. This was more important than he knew.

'L, please listen to me . . . you can't get involved with me. Please, just go home and let's forget about this.' Rochelle's voice had lost its usual assertiveness. Her eyes glistened with tears. Lamont didn't know why they were there. Only that she was weakening. She liked him.

That was all Lamont had needed to hear. If she liked him, then he was in control.

'No,' he replied, her fledging resistance strengthening his resolve.

'You don't have a choice. I can't do this with you. I *won't* do this with you.' Rochelle tried to close the door but Lamont jammed it with his trainer. Pain shot through his foot but he didn't care.

'I'm not going anywhere. I'm tired of shying away from things, too scared to stick a toe in the pool and risk getting wet. I like you. I'm not missing this opportunity to make you understand how much.'

'Lamo—' Rochelle didn't get his name out. Lamont moved forward, capturing her lips, hands grazing Rochelle's hips. She resisted only for a moment before she was kissing Lamont back.

Her mouth was like the sweetest honey, glorious nectar that Lamont savoured. He hungrily massaged her lips with his own, trying to avoid worrying if he was kissing her right. He seemed to be doing okay. She moaned in his mouth, grinding her hot body against his. Lamont's erection tented in his tracksuit bottoms now, so engorged that it hurt. It pressed into Rochelle. There was no way she couldn't know it was there. Lamont's embarrassment immediately evaporated when she rubbed against it.

They were in the house now, stumbling upstairs, lips glued to one another. Rochelle threw him on the bed, slowly undoing the buttons on her shirt. Raising her eyebrows, she paused. Lamont took the hint, quickly stripping. He lay on the bed fully naked, feeling foolish, yet more turned on than ever before. She watched him wordlessly, clad in a black bra and thong. Then, they were gone.

Lamont's breath seemed to catch in his chest. He had never seen a naked woman in the flesh before, so he had nothing to compare it to, but Rochelle was a vision. Her opulent breasts hung freely, complimenting proportioned hips and thighs. Her caramel skin seemed to glow in the streetlight's ambience outside the window.

'Do you have a condom?' Rochelle whispered.

Lamont nodded, rummaging through his trouser pockets for his wallet. He had two condoms in there that he'd started carrying around. He opened one with trembling hands, hoping he was putting it on the right way.

When it was secure, Rochelle started kissing his body, knowing precisely where to strike. Everywhere she touched left a warm tingling feeling that Lamont relished. His breathing was shallow. He was trying to stay calm, to avoid finishing before he had even started. Rochelle reached down and stroked him slowly. Her grip was loose, slowly grazing, sending bolts of pleasure down his shaft. He groaned out loud, unable to hold back, then reached out and probed her with one finger. Rochelle gave a shudder and threw her head back. Lamont stopped.

'Sorry! Did I hurt you?' he spluttered. Rochelle gripped his jaw.

'Don't stop. Do that again,' she ordered. Lamont obliged, amazed at how wet Rochelle was. She moaned his name softly, and he revelled in the power of giving her pleasure.

'That's enough.' Rochelle moved his hand and climbed on top, lowering herself onto him. Lamont closed his eyes and braced himself. This was it. He was finally losing his virginity. And it was like nothing else he had ever experienced. As enjoyable as everything else had been until this point, the feel of Rochelle cancelled everything out. The heat from her was powerful, so intense Lamont felt it constricting through the protective sheath of the condom.

Putting her hands on Lamont's chest, Rochelle's hips bucked, slowly rotating in circles. Lamont closed his eyes, trying to stave off how good it felt. He couldn't finish now. He had to go the distance. Rochelle was moaning, rocking faster, her eyes closed, mouth parted. Lamont grabbed her breasts. Raising his body off the bed, he began sucking as if they were the most succulent fruit he had ever tasted.

Rochelle's moans spurred him on more. He pushed his hips into her, wanting to increase Rochelle's pleasure as much as his own. They were both moving at a clumsy pace but it was an enjoyable clumsiness. Rochelle was trying to dictate the pace, but in his inexperience, Lamont didn't realise. He greedily grabbed at her body, unable to keep his hands to himself.

'Let me do it,' Rochelle whispered, the softness of her voice sounding like the song of angels. She began bucking her hips crazily, Lamont unable to keep up. His teeth gritted together, his toes wiggling, a twinge in his midsection. What Rochelle was doing felt too good and before he could stop himself, Lamont exploded. His body jerked a few times as he filled the condom, and then he was still.

Lamont breathed heavily, Rochelle too. She placed both her hands on his chest, digging her nails in. It hurt, but he wasn't going to tell her to stop. He was semi erect, and it didn't feel comfortable. Sensing this, Rochelle climbed from him, hurrying to the bathroom. Using both hands, Lamont removed the condom, wrapped it in tissue and threw it in the bin. He felt awkward being naked, so he put his boxer shorts back on.

A few minutes later, Rochelle came out of the bathroom. She smiled, but it flickered, never showing in her eyes.

'What's wrong?' He asked, praying she wasn't disappointed with his performance.

'I'm just mad.'

'Mad at me?'

Rochelle's expression was rueful.

'Madder at myself. I told you nothing could happen, and then I slept with you . . . I can't believe I was so stupid!'

'Rochelle, I wanted this. I've never wanted anything more in my life. I mean that.' Lamont, openly staring at her magnificent body, wanting to file away every inch for future reference, scared he was dreaming. Reaching out to touch her, it surprised Lamont when she recoiled.

'I think you should go. Please, just leave.'

Lamont watched in dejected bewilderment as Rochelle burst into tears. Respecting her wishes, he dressed himself. As he was putting on his t-shirt, he couldn't help it. He tried to hug Rochelle, but she pushed him away.

'Don't touch me! Don't ever touch me again!'

Startled, Lamont backed away. He opened his mouth, then closed it. He tugged his hooded top over his head, mumbled an apology and hurried down the stairs. He left at the same time Mia was walking in. They stared at one another awkwardly. Mia gaped at him like he was a ghost.

'L? What are you doing here?' she asked, noting his rumpled hoody and tracksuit bottoms. His hair was tousled, and he had what looked like teeth marks embedded in his jawline and neck.

'Gotta go.' Lamont darted past Mia, out of the front door and was halfway up the street before her mouth could close. He needed the safety of his bedroom. One thing was for sure though, Lamont thought sadly as he turned the corner. He would never have another shot with Rochelle again.

CHAPTER NINE

Tuesday 20 May 1997

MARCUS CAME into Lamont's room later that night. Lamont stared into space as Marcus closed the bedroom door behind him. Lamont didn't even look up.

'You cool, L?' Marcus started, looming near the wall. It was funny how different Lamont's room was to his own. In Marcus's room, you could tell it was his. Lamont's room could have belonged to anyone. Apart from the books and writing notepads, it was practically empty. There was a battered wardrobe for Lamont's clothes, some shoeboxes and an old cassette player. Apart from that, there was nothing. Nothing to show Lamont belonged.

Marcus wondered to himself if that was the reason Lamont acted as he did sometimes; because he didn't believe he had a home.

'I'm fine,' Lamont's voice was hoarse. Awkwardly, Marcus wondered if he'd been crying.

'I spoke to Mia,' Marcus was trying his hardest to be subtle. 'She said she saw you at the house.'

Lamont didn't speak. Marcus continued.

'Said you left in a hurry, and that Shelly was quiet. Didn't even come down from her room. What's up with that?'

'What do you want me to say, Marcus?' Lamont said, finally looking at him. Marcus's face broke into a wide grin.

'You know what I want you to say. Tell me you handled your business,' he said gleefully. Lamont looked at Marcus but didn't reply. He hesitated a moment too long, and that was all the inclination his friend needed.

'Yes! That's my fucking boy! I knew you had it in you!' Marcus clapped Lamont on the back.

'Chill. It's not a big deal.'

'Course it's a big deal! You finally lost your v, and more importantly, you lost it with a thoroughbred. Rochelle is all that man. I bet it was good. Be honest, was it good?'

Lamont smiled at Marcus's enthusiasm. 'How would I know? I have nothing to compare it to. I enjoyed it though.'

'Did she?'

'She looked like it . . . during, anyway.'

Lamont confided in Marcus what had happened after they had finished. Marcus made a face.

'That is strange. Shelly's quiet though. You never know what she's thinking. She's like you. Why do you think I said you needed to grind her? You're a lucky dude, man. Wait till I tell people. You're gonna be the man around here.'

'Don't tell anyone,' Lamont's voice was firm.

'Why? L, this is a good thing. This is what you need. Finally, people are gonna see what I see. You're stone cold, but within you, I dunno. Hard to say, but there's like . . . I don't know, an aura,' Marcus said. Lamont stared at him.

'An aura?'

'Yeah, man. Listen, you know I'm not good with words. But you're a quiet motherfucker. Lot of people, they see that and it makes them think you're weak. But I know different. Always have. You're a force. You just need to let people see it.'

It was Lamont's turn to gape at Marcus now. They had joked over the years, but he had never heard Marcus speak with as much conviction as he was now. Lamont didn't know if he was drunk or high, but he immediately dismissed Marcus's words.

'Don't tell anyone. I want you to give me your word that you'll keep it to yourself.'

'L, man, c'mon,' Marcus kissed his teeth.

'Please. This is important to me.'

'Fine. You wanna keep quiet on the best piece of news you've ever had, then fine. I'll do one better and tell Mia to keep her big mouth shut too.'

Lamont smiled again. 'Thanks, bro.'

* * *

One Thursday, Lamont had finished his History exam and headed home. Later, he was walking down to the shop when he heard a voice calling him. Turning, he saw Shorty. They touched fists.

'How's it going, Shorty?'

'It's all good. Just went to go meet someone,' Shorty replied, his eyes flashing excitedly. 'Did you hear about Craig?'

Lamont hadn't, but lately, Craig seemed more stressed than normal. The last time Lamont saw him, he had been wearing the same hooded top and trousers he had worn the time before that.

As Lamont and Levi weren't seeing eye to eye, he didn't know what was happening, but he suspected it concerned Blair and the Yardies. Lamont couldn't help but think about the incident where Marcus had beaten up Blair. He wondered if that was the right way to handle the situation.

'What happened?'

Shorty laughed. 'Him and two of his boys stomped out Leader on Francis Street. It was wicked!'

'Which *Leader*? Who's that?' Lamont asked. Shorty kissed his teeth.

'You need to stop reading them books and hit the streets. Leader runs one of them little Yardie groups. He's the one Blair ran to for protection. He's a psycho.'

'So why would Craig attack him?'

'Because he's an idiot. Everyone knows about Leader. This ain't gonna be the end, I guarantee that.'

Lamont didn't understand why there needed to be a war. There was enough money for everyone to get rich. There was no profit from the violence.

'What's the point?' He finally said.

'What?' Shorty looked at him.

'In fighting. Craig is supposed to be about making money. Why would he allow himself to get caught up?'

'Hype, nothing more. Craig's snorting, running with pure fools who just wanna see him in trouble while they steal his money. I'm telling you, when he flops, they'll move on to the next guy.'

'Craig's on drugs?' Lamont was surprised.

'Yeah. Has been for a while. Why do you think he's entertaining this stupidness? He's taking coke, trying to keep hold of that slut he stole from Blair. That's what all this shit is over. He's fronting like he's got a real piece, when really she's always been available to dudes. Even I shagged Kierra.'

Lamont's mouth hung open. 'When?'

'Ages ago. Met her at a party. Linked her afterwards and banged her in an alleyway.' Shorty laughed at the expression on Lamont's face.

'Why would you do that? What about Craig?'

'What about him? He's got a couple guys he chills with that slap people around, but he's got no heart. He was just in the right place when Delroy was looking for people and he got put on. He's nothing.'

Lamont said nothing. Delroy Williams was known for importing and supplying drugs all over Yorkshire. Lamont hadn't known he was Craig's supplier, but it made perfect sense. Craig had access to weed whenever he wanted it. There weren't many suppliers who could accommodate this. Shorty sighed, his expression changing.

'Listen, you need to learn the streets if you wanna survive. Craig's running around on that powder thinking he's invincible. If he thinks Delroy will back him in this war, he's a dickhead. Delroy likes it quiet.'

'So what's gonna happen?'

Before Shorty could reply, they heard gunshots.

'L! Down!' Shorty hit the deck. Lamont mirrored his actions, his heart pounding with fear. There was no way to tell where the gunshots were coming from, but Shorty seemed to think they were close.

'C'mon, we're alright. The gunshots were round the corner. C'mon, let's go see who it was.' Shorty hurried down the street. Lamont followed, not knowing what he was getting into. They were running now. Lamont could feel his nose dripping. He wiped it hastily, noting that it was snot rather than blood. He had hit the pavement hard, but he was okay.

A crowd gathered a few streets down, loudly whispering about what transpired. A woman in tears ran past Lamont and Shorty. He wondered if she would call an ambulance. They moved in closer now, pushing their way through the crowds.

Two guys were stretched out on the pavement. They were so still it looked like they were sleeping, but the blood seeping from their bodies was a sign that they wouldn't be waking up from this nap. They were face-down, so it was impossible to tell who they were, but Lamont was sure he recognised the hooded top one of them was wearing. He hoped he was wrong, but the nauseous feeling in his stomach told him otherwise.

Finally, an ambulance turned up, two flashing police cars behind it. The police began pushing people back and trying to establish order. The local youths didn't take kindly to the pushing, and there was a stand-off, resolved when the police threatened to call for backup.

When Lamont finally got a good look at the clothing, his heart leapt in his throat.

'C'mon, L, we need to leave. Now.' Shorty was already stomping up the road.

'Shorty, that was Craig!' Lamont hissed, hurrying after him.

'I know it was Craig. He's dead and standing around won't do anything. We need to find Levi.'

'We need to go back; find out who did it.'

'We know who did it. It was Leader's guys. Craig thought he could beat him up and get away with it,' Shorty was half talking to himself.

'So, now what? Do we get him?'

Shorty stopped in his tracks. 'You wanna go after Leader? I'm telling you; you do that, you're dead. Simple as that.'

'Yeah, but—'

'But nothing. Craig did something stupid. I'm not letting you do the same thing. Now, cut that suicide talk and let's find Levi. He needs to hear from us, not someone else.'

* * *

Hours later, they gathered in Levi's kitchen. His Nana was upstairs, but every once in a while they would hear a wail. Lamont didn't know why Levi wasn't up there comforting her, but kept it to himself. Shorty had bought brandy. They'd each had a glass out of respect, but Levi had drunk three more. With each glass he became more animated, before finally standing, tears streaming down his face.

'They're all dead. I'm gonna wipe the lot of them out,' he shouted. Draining the last dregs of the glass, he threw it against the wall.

'Levi, calm down,' Lamont said. Shorty stared at the floor. K-Bar dolefully watched Levi's tirade.

'How am I supposed to calm down? They killed my fucking brother, L. Murdered him on the streets and you want me to just let it go?'

'I'm just saying; think rationally. There's no use getting mad. It won't solve anything. We need to plan our next move.'

'I know exactly what my next move is. Shorty, get me a strap and I'll dead every one of them!'

Shorty finally looked up. He met Lamont's eye before he replied to Levi.

'I'm not getting you a strap. You wanna go prison over your brother's beef?'

'Fuck you, Shorty. You got away with murder; why shouldn't I?'

'Shut it. Don't talk about things you don't understand,' Shorty snapped.

'I'll talk about anything I want.'

'Lay off that brandy, because you can't handle it. Your bro knew what he was getting into. He rolled with a crew. Fall back and let them handle it.'

'If you don't gimme a strap, then Marcus will,' Levi said matter-of-factly.

'No, he won't. We're not gonna let you go shooting up the streets over this. Calm down, sleep off the liquor and comfort your Nana. Listen to her, man. She needs you to be there for her.'

'Shut the fuck up! I run this team. I brought you all in. If it wasn't for me, then—'

'Are you still harping on about that?' Shorty kissed his teeth. 'Levi, get real. I was doing this long before you. You ain't the boss of nothing. L kept this in line. Don't go thinking you're Nicky Barnes because your brother supplied us. Chill out and stay in your lane.'

Levi stormed over to Shorty. 'Get up.'

'Why?' Shorty said, sniggering.

'We're gonna fight.'

Shorty grinned at Levi. 'Are we?'

'Yeah, we are.' Levi's voice shook.

'This won't get us anywhere,' Lamont interjected. They ignored him.

'C'mon. Get up,' Levi urged.

Shorty shook with laughter. 'What did I just say about staying in your lane?'

'What did I just say about getting up?'

'You wanna hear the truth? If I get up, they might end up burying you next to your brother.'

That was the last straw. Levi caught Shorty in the side of the head with a good shot. The blow stunned Shorty enough for Levi to pull him to the ground, but that was where the advantage ended. Levi was drunk. Even if he was sober, he wouldn't have been a match for Shorty, who quickly overpowered him, punching him twice in the mouth before K-Bar and Lamont could pull him off.

'Get off me,' Shorty roared, trying to break free. Levi crawled into a sitting position, his mouth bleeding. He glared at Shorty, but didn't make another move.

'Shorty, chill! His brother just died,' Lamont tried reasoning with Shorty.

'Fuck him and his brother.'

'No, fuck you, Shorty,' Levi screamed. 'I'll deal with it myself.' stumbling to his feet, he hurried upstairs, leaving the three of them in his kitchen.

* * *

They didn't see much of Levi after that. Every time Lamont called for him, Levi's Nana would say that he was out. Lamont hoped this meant he had calmed down, but knowing Levi he doubted it.

In the meantime, the streets were buzzing with different stories about Craig's murder. Even his crew were swapping tales rather than doing anything. Just as Shorty predicted, the second Craig died, they moved on. Their lack of loyalty disgusted Lamont, but he couldn't do anything about it.

Supply-wise, they were stuck. Craig had been the only connection to Clint, and now he was dead, they were in the cold. Shorty was forced to link up with his old supplier. He hadn't forgiven Shorty for ditching him, and hiked up the price, knowing they were powerless to do anything about it. People were put off by the decline in quality and it showed in their profits.

Lamont had to continue though. He dealt with more people outside of Chapeltown, sweet-talking them into taking the substandard drugs. He didn't convince everyone, but he was making the most of a bad situation.

Marcus and Shorty, who always had their ears to the streets, reported back on what was going down in the Hood. Leader and a few of his guys had been questioned about the murder of Craig and his worker, but without evidence other than rumours of a street beef, they were forced to let the killers go on bail.

After finishing his exams one day, Lamont slumped on Shorty's sofa, half asleep, when the door burst open and Shorty charged into the living room, scaring Lamont.

'Get up!' he yelled, his face panicked.

'What the hell, Shorty? Why are you shouting?'

'Levi got arrested.'

Lamont was up now. 'What for?'

'He went after Leader. Stabbed him on the street in front of witnesses and then ran off. Police snatched him from his Nana's. He's in custody now.'

'What about Leader? Is he alive?' Lamont's head was buzzing.

'One of his boys shouted a warning when Levi ran up. Sliced his chest a little, and there was loads of blood. He's all right though. He's already out of hospital.'

Lamont shook his head, his mind alight with the nonsense of it all. He should have tried harder to get in contact with Levi. He had known exactly what his friend was capable of, and he had just dismissed it. Now Levi was facing prison time.

'I can't believe it . . .'

'Well, you need to. He's got no sense. Craig shoulda schooled him better on the game. He's done summat dumb and now he's going away for it.'

'Levi's our boy. Don't talk about him like that.'

'He's a dickhead. Him and his brother, they never used their heads and now look at them. Dead and in jail,' Shorty kissed his teeth. 'I'm not getting into an argument, anyway. I'm off to get some food. You want summat?'

Lamont shook his head again. Shorty left. Deep down, Lamont knew he was right to be annoyed. Levi had acted rashly and now he would pay the penalty for it.

The situation was causing Lamont to think about his own future. *Was this really what he wanted? Pitching on the streets, dodging overzealous drug squads and rival dealers?* He needed to think about his next move.

* * *

They'd had a good run.

That was all Lamont thought to himself in the following days. With all the drama surrounding Craig's murder and Levi being locked up, things were turbulent. Shorty and K-Bar were out in town getting drunk, doing drugs and waiting for things to fix themselves. Lamont didn't see how they could without a decent supplier.

He had visited Levi's devastated Nana, and told her he would look out for her, but she insisted she didn't need it. Craig had always been generous, and she had money saved. Still, she loved her grandchildren and the fact that everything was so fractured had wounded her.

Lamont tried finding Levi's mum in the streets, but she was in the wind. The streets had a way of hiding people who didn't want to be found, and Lamont didn't have the resources to track her down.

Life at the moment was a lot of reading and soul-searching. Exams were finished, so Lamont was giving more thought to the future. He was confident he had done well on the exams, and he would use that to secure something more worthwhile.

The jig seemed to be up. It felt like Lamont was waking up from the dream of spending drug money on new trainers and clothes. Even as he sat on the bed, he saw the Nike shoe boxes piled against the battered chest of drawers Auntie had found for him when he went to live with her. He had his Walkman at full blast, listening to *Life After Death* by *The Notorious B.I.G.*, absorbing every word.

As he tried reading a *Stephen King* novel, he thought about the promise he had made to himself. After shuffling from Rochelle's house, he had vowed that he wouldn't contact her until he knew where they stood. Rochelle had Auntie's number. She could call at anytime to explain what had happened, what he had done wrong.

In the heat of the act, it seemed he was doing okay. She was making all the right noises, and she seemed as connected as he was. She had seemed just as into it, but the aftermath made him wonder. Every time Lamont thought back to the night they had shared, he remembered the aftermath more than anything. He hated replaying the way she had recoiled afterwards when he tried to touch her. He wanted her to feel what he had felt. He wanted to tell her she had made him feel whole for the first time since he was ten years old.

And that was when Lamont decided to break his promise. He would go to Rochelle. Tell her he would get a job; that he wanted them to be normal together. He was smart. He knew how to get the best out of people. *Surely there was something out there for him on the job front?*

Talking to her and baring his soul had worked well for him last time, and Lamont was willing to bet it would work again. Hitting the stop button on his Walkman, he hurried to get ready.

* * *

Lamont hurried along the streets, Rochelle's house soon looming in front of him. The bedroom light was on but the downstairs lights were off. Lamont knocked loudly, laying out the game plan. When the door opened, Lamont's rehearsed words vanished.

'Yeah?' A man looked out at him. He looked older and more unnervingly, he was half dressed, his defined upper body on show. His shaggy afro was unkempt, and he had a five o'clock shadow across the underside of his face. There were marks all over his body, along with a scar that went through the middle of his right eyebrow down to his eyelid.

Lamont stared, not knowing what to say. He felt like he had seen the man somewhere, but couldn't think where.

'Oi? What do you want?' the man said, louder this time. Lamont heard footsteps and Rochelle appeared next to the man. Her mouth fell open at the sight of Lamont.

'L?'

'This is that little kid you were grinding?' The man looked Lamont up and down.

'Ricky, let me handle this,' Rochelle said. He didn't even acknowledge her words.

'Yo, piss off. You got a little shag, and that's the end. This is mine,' Ricky taunted, putting his arm around Rochelle. Instinctively, Lamont's hands balled into fists. Ricky noticed.

'Oh? You wanna go? C'mon then!'

'Ricky. Go back upstairs. Please, let me handle this,' Rochelle repeated. Ricky gave Lamont a scathing look.

'Guess I'll warm the bed back up.'

An awkward silence lingered in Ricky's departure. Lamont's heart hammered as he gazed at Rochelle. He hadn't noticed she wore nothing but a bed sheet. Once he saw it, something in him seemed to shift, his insides turning to lead. He wanted to fall to the ground. He realised then, at that horrid moment, that he was in love.

Lamont wanted to cry. He wanted to hit Rochelle. He wanted to hit Ricky. He wanted to keep attacking them both. Most of all, he wanted to hold Rochelle, and he wanted her to hold him back. To be there for him. Lamont wanted to call her names. He couldn't though. He couldn't speak.

'I'm sorry.'

Rochelle's simple words cut through Lamont like a knife. He forced himself to maintain her gaze, his eyes filling with tears that he quickly blinked away.

'Is he the baggage?' Lamont's words came out as a croaking sound. Rochelle hesitated, then slowly nodded.

'So, what happens now?' he asked, trying his hardest to control his words. Rochelle didn't hesitate.

'Now, you go home and forget all about me.'

With that, Rochelle closed the door on both Lamont and his broken heart.

TEFLON

CHAPTER TEN

Thursday 23 April 1998

'WE NEED A PLAN.'

Lamont didn't immediately reply to Shorty's words. They stood outside a local shop in the Hood, enjoying the warm evening, well-received after two weeks of wet weather. He knew his friend was right though. They needed something solid.

Lamont had finished his education the previous year, scoring highly in all of his exams. Upon picking up his results, Lamont's teachers tried talking to him about his future goals, only to be coldly rebuffed.

Lamont, Shorty and K-Bar had continued to sell weed, but the profits they enjoyed with Craig were long gone, and Lamont had to dip into his savings more often.

Auntie knew he had money and turned up the pressure on him, first by demanding he pay board, to which Lamont agreed, then by badgering Lamont about what he was doing. He was storing more things in Marcus's room. Marcus didn't mind. He had all but moved out, spending his time in the streets.

Lamont hung with Shorty most of the time, and with Shorty anything could happen. A trip to the shop to buy milk one day, escalated into Shorty shaking down a sale for twenty pounds and repeatedly stomping on him. Why Shorty had done it, Lamont couldn't say.

'I know,' he finally replied.

'We can't keep going like this. I still think robberies are where it's at. Marcus is making grands.'

Lamont shook his head. 'You can, but I'm not getting into that.'

'What then? What's the big plan? Trevor is going on funny ever since I ducked him and started working with you lot. He doesn't give a damn how much money we're bringing. He's never gonna give us a break.' Shorty was referring to their weed supplier.

Lamont was half-listening, his attention on a black Mercedes Benz ghosting down the road. Loud rap music blared from the speakers. When the driver looked out of his window, Lamont's stomach lurched when he realised who it was. He was now fully clothed, but it was the man Rochelle had been with that night.

Ricky slowed the car down, staring at Lamont over the top of expensive sunglasses. The exchange only lasted a second before he was down the road and out of sight.

'Yo, how do you know Ricky?' Shorty frowned at Lamont.

'What?' Lamont stared after the car.

'Ricky. Ricky Reagan. He works for Delroy, man.'

'I've seen him around,' Lamont lied. He didn't need Shorty to tell him about Delroy. Delroy Williams was the biggest criminal in Leeds, and had been so for decades, heavily involved in drugs and other forms of crime.

'Ricky's the guy Craig wanted to be. Delroy has him running most of his street teams. I heard he bought that Benz brand new. Cash.'

'That's impressive,' Lamont replied through gritted teeth. He couldn't help but remember Ricky's arrogance that night as he'd stared down Lamont. It occurred almost a year ago, yet Lamont was as affected now. Shorty babbled, oblivious to Lamont's change of mood.

'There's pure money in those hard drugs. I know a couple guys selling coke small-time. They make loads off them white people in town,' said Shorty, laughing. Lamont's brow furrowed.

'Let's do that,' he said.

'Do what?'

'Sell coke.'

Shorty sniggered. 'You wanna sell coke? *You?*'

Shorty's laughter grew. His shoulders shook, tears of mirth streaming from his eyes. Lamont didn't say a word. He didn't need to. He stared down his friend in a way he never had before, and when Shorty noticed the look, he immediately sobered up.

Lamont's face was placid, but his nostrils flared, and his eyes were like ice. Shorty didn't know what had caused the change, and he stood there, stumped.

'Do you want money?' Lamont said, when he was sure he had Shorty's full attention.

'What kinda question is that? Course I want money. We're dying out here, L, for basically nothing. We make enough to do what we're doing, but where's the profit?'

'This is the chance to get ahead. I've been considering something similar for a while, and we can do it. We only need one thing.'

'Yeah. Cash. Packages cost money, bro. Drugs aren't cheap. I doubt that even between you, me and K, we could come up with enough. Unless you wanna rip off Trevor and not give him his end?'

Lamont gazed into the distance again, his mind on Mercedes Benzes' and women he couldn't have.

'If we were to sell, do you think you could find us a customer base?'

Shorty needed only a second to think about that.

'Yeah, I know people. They'd buy from us.'

Lamont smiled now, the icy look in his eyes fading.

'We'll need to get someone to give us credit then.'

'Don't talk shit. No-one's gonna front us for some coke. Everyone is out for themselves. No one's trying to bring anyone else in. It's not that kinda game.'

'We'll make it that kinda game. Get us a meeting and I will do the rest,' Lamont said.

Shorty stared at his friend in wonder. Lamont quietly went about his business, ruffled no feathers and kept it moving. At times though, he was a different person, driven, seeming to radiate some inner power that demanded you take him seriously.

Shorty first noticed when they were selling drugs with Levi. Levi would act like he was the boss but when it was crunch time, Lamont made the crucial decisions. It confused Shorty, but also filled him with a sense of reassurance. He didn't quite know what was going on with Lamont, but he was calculated and intelligent. Shorty was in.

'Cool, L. I'll see what I can do.'

* * *

'Lamont? Why haven't you swept the kitchen floor yet?'

Lamont slumped over the table, eating cereal and listening to *Mobb Deep* on his Walkman. He could hear Auntie shouting, but she didn't need to know that. The Walkman and cassette tapes he'd purchased were proving a worthwhile investment. Realising Lamont wasn't listening, Auntie snatched the earphones from his ears.

'Do you hear me?' she screamed. Lamont looked at her blankly.

'Yes, I hear you. I'll sweep when I'm finished.'

'No, you'll do it now.'

Lamont swallowed another mouthful of cornflakes and looked at his Auntie.

'No, I won't.'

Auntie eyes bulged at Lamont's defiance. 'Yes, you will. I'm not sure where you think you are, but this is my house and you'll do as I say.'

'I don't think you heard me the first time,' Lamont put the spoon in the bowl without taking his eyes from his Aunt. 'No. I. Won't.'

Auntie shook her head. 'You think you can take me on?'

Lamont smiled, viewing Auntie as if for the first time. She was attractive, but it was a faded, marred beauty, the hair still long and dark, but without the shine. The clothes were still expensive, but tight on a body that had put on a lot of weight and couldn't face it.

'*Take you on?* What is it you think is going on here? I'm a grown man and my days of being bossed around by you are over.'

'Oh really?' Auntie's sunken cheekbones quivered, her mouth opening and closing as she tried to gather her words. Lamont didn't give her a chance.

'Yes, really. I pay you rent. Why should I even do chores?'

'I'll tell you why, because—'

'The question was rhetorical,' Lamont interjected. 'I'm not doing chores anymore. So either you do them, or get Rika to.'

Auntie gasped at Lamont's words. Before she could retort, there was a knock at the door. Lamont smiled sweetly and stood. 'I'll get that shall I?' Leaving Auntie in stunned silence, he left the kitchen.

'We need to talk,' Shorty said when Lamont opened the door. It had been a week since Lamont had given Shorty his task. They'd chilled since, but Shorty hadn't mentioned it, and Lamont hadn't pushed the issue. Lamont stepped outside, closing the door behind him.

'I've been all over the place, L. No one wants to deal with us.'

'What?'

'People turned me down left right and centre. A couple' people said they'd sell to us for a price, but no-one's trying to give anything for free. Not to me anyway,' Shorty kissed his teeth. Lamont read between the lines; Shorty had done robberies in the past, making it hard for people to trust him.

'No one would deal with you?'

Shorty nodded. 'One guy said he would. He's a loser though.'

'What do you mean?'

'This dude called Louie. Lives near Bankside. He said he'll meet us.'

'So, let's deal with him.' Lamont didn't understand.

'He's a drunk, L. A proper loser. He's got a few kids running for him and even they rip him off. He's no good for us.'

'We have to start somewhere, Shorty. Set the meeting up.'

Shorty shrugged. 'Fine. If this fucks up though, it's on you.'

* * *

Days later, Shorty and Lamont stood outside Louie's place. The house itself was unforgettable. It was a ramshackle terraced spot with shutters over the windows and a brown front door with the paint peeling from it. Leading the way, Shorty knocked. After a few moments, they heard movement and what sounded like cursing. Soon both doors had been unlocked and an old man glared out at them.

'Shorty? What do you want now?' Louie growled. He was a stunted man with a round belly, fleshy face and a copious amount of grizzled facial hair. He wore a pair of greying tracksuit bottoms and a rumpled sweater.

'You know what I want. I'm here to do business, unless you want to do it out here?'

'Who's he?' the man looked at Lamont now. Lamont met his gaze.

'He's my boy. I told you about him. He's with me in this thing.'

'What's his name?'

'Lamont.'

'Surname?' Louie all but shouted.

'Jones. His surname is Jones,' Shorty muttered.

'Jones . . . *Carmen Jones?*' Louie's eyes were wistful. Lamont didn't have to ask how he knew the name.

'She's my Auntie.'

'Come in. Quickly.'

The living room looked even worse than the outside of the house. Cleaning evidently wasn't one of Louie's talents. There were plates of food on the coffee table, everything covered in a fine layer of dust.

'Take a seat,' said Louie, sitting in a dilapidated armchair. The pair remained standing. 'Fine. Suit yourselves. What do you want?'

Lamont started to speak, but Shorty beat him to it.

'You know what we want. An ounce of coke. You'll get your fee back plus interest when we move it.'

Louie took a second to reply, loudly sucking his teeth. The sound was disgusting, but both boys ignored it.

'I give you that, I'm shorting myself. It's bad enough I've got little kids out there making me look dumb trying to rip me off. People think I don't know, but I do.' Louie met Lamont's eyes, then Shorty's.

'That's between you and your people. We're looking to get our feet in the door. Furthermore, we already talked about this, so why are you messing around?' Shorty's voice rose.

'Because I've already got one set of people ripping me off. You lot might make it two sets, and then I'm losing out even more. I dunno if it's worth it. Not without summat up front.' Louie picked his words carefully. Shorty's hands balled into fists, a prominent vein throbbing from his neck.

'You're taking the piss.'

'I'm not trying to—'

'Don't interrupt me,' Shorty thundered. 'I don't care what little pricks you've got juggling for you on the streets. Never think you can treat me and my people like shit, understand?'

Louie nodded, swallowing hard. 'I'm not trying to mess you around, but I have to do what I think is right.'

'What are you talking about? You're a slanger. Take that *save the streets shit* elsewhere, because this is business. You said we were getting an ounce, so we're not leaving without one.'

'What, so now you're threatening me?' Louie shouted. Lamont saw Louie's hand slip into his pocket. In his rage Shorty seemed to have missed the movement. The whole thing was getting out of hand.

'Does anyone want a drink?'

Lamont's words were even, but had the desired effect. Louie and Shorty stopped shouting.

'You what?' Louie had taken little notice of the quiet Jones boy. He wore a black crewneck sweater and jeans, and had an air of healthy confidence about him.

'I'm thirsty. I'd like a drink. Does anyone else want one?' Lamont replied.

'I wouldn't mind a beer,' Louie said slowly, unsure of what was going on.

'Shorty, can you get Louie a beer please while I speak to him?'

Shorty glared at Lamont but rather than argue, he stomped to the kitchen. There was another moment of silence when he left, both men trying to feel the other out.

'So, you know my Auntie,' Lamont finally spoke. Louie assessed the words before he replied.

'I know a few members of your family. I knew your mother too,' he looked Lamont in the eyes. 'You look a lot like her.'

Lamont felt a jolt in his stomach at the mention of his mother. Louie wasn't the first to say this. People had been saying it to him all his life, and every time they did, he had the same feeling.

'So I've heard. You and my Auntie . . . was it serious?'

'Why?' Louie's tone was suspicious. Lamont maintained the eye contact. He stood by the window, the light from outside the dirty windows illuminating his profile, making him appear more dominant, bathed in the brightness.

'She raised me after my parents died. I guess I just don't understand what men saw in her.'

'You don't?' Louie raised his bushy eyebrows. Lamont laughed, conceding the point. He was old enough to understand the sexual effect women had on men.

'Okay, maybe I don't want to see it from that angle.'

'Your Auntie, she was something special. Even now, people still talk about her in her heyday,' Louie paused, checking if Lamont seemed offended before he went on. 'She had this wild energy. Pure passion. She could go in a room and get any guy she wanted. Any guy!' Louie's voice rose. Lamont gave him a moment before he spoke.

'And she wanted you.' It wasn't a question. The answer was already clear.

'You probably see me as some grubby old man, but back then, I had the wardrobe, the jewellery, a big car. People waited around for me. I guess your Auntie liked that because we started spending time together,' Louie's eyes darkened then. 'She used me. Got what she wanted . . . money, powder, everything, and then she just switched. Didn't avoid me or anything; she just changed. When a woman as passionate as your Auntie turns cold on you, you feel horrible. That was how I felt. Ill.' Louie's words were tinged with a sadness that Lamont himself understood.

What Rochelle had taken from him was far worse than any money, or clothes or jewellery. She had taken his heart.

Lamont had spoken to no-one about it, not even Marcus. At times, he felt he was over his feelings, and then they would intensify, returning more powerful than ever. Lamont needed to convince Louie, because he had no intention of ending up like him.

'I understand, Louie. Really, I do.'

Louie seemed surprised at Lamont's sincerity for a moment, and then his eyes narrowed.

'I wanna ask you summat now.'

Lamont nodded.

'Why do you wanna sell drugs?'

'Why not?' Lamont quickly replied, before he'd even considered the question. Louie shook his head.

'Seriously. Be straight up.'

'I need to. You weren't the only one who got bled by my Auntie. Any money my parents might have left, I never saw. I remember the wild parties she held that I had to clean up after though. As a kid,' Lamont shook away the memories, focusing, determined to make the older man understand. 'I need to build something and this is the best way to do it.'

'You're different though. I can see that. You can fit in out there, in that normal world. You don't need to stay in the darkness.'

'The other reason I need to do this,' Lamont went on as if he hadn't heard Louie, 'is because I had someone I cared about too, and she screwed me over. The *normal* life is what I might have had with her, but that's done. I always listen to my instincts, and when my instincts tell me to do something, I do it. More importantly, I make sure I do it better than anyone else.'

Neither spoke now, knowing a level of understanding connected them. Shorty re-entered the room. He gave Lamont a funny look and handed the beer to Louie.

'What's the deal then?' he said, his voice still thick with anger. Louie rose with a grunt and went upstairs. He returned and handed a carrier bag to Lamont.

'There's two ounces in there. Shorty knows the price. Come back when you have my end, plus ten percent.'

CHAPTER ELEVEN

Monday 4 May 1998

NEITHER LAMONT nor Shorty spoke after leaving Louie. Lamont glanced around as they walked, his earlier confidence buried. Chapeltown was full of predators, and the police were always around in some form. The last thing they needed was to get caught with drugs.

The fear propelled Lamont forward, his step quickening. Shorty moved more assuredly next to him. He didn't look daunted about walking with drugs. Instead, Shorty looked thoughtful.

'I heard what you said to Louie,' he finally broke the silence. Lamont didn't respond, though by the look in his eyes, it was obvious he had heard his friend speaking. 'Who did you catch feelings over?'

Lamont stopped, turning toward Shorty. Shorty was taken aback by the seriousness etched into every line of Lamont's face.

'I don't want to talk about it. Not now. Not ever. Okay?' Lamont's tone was chilling, and Shorty nodded.

'Fine,' Shorty changed the subject. 'I'm gonna link up with K-Bar. We'll cut and bag these ounces. He's getting hold of the equipment for us, so I'll get at you when it's done. There's this crackhead named Chalky. He'll let us use his place.'

'Sounds like a plan.'

When Lamont entered his home, the noise from the TV was deafening. Auntie sat in the living room, watching her evening soaps with a cup of coffee. She glanced at Lamont standing in the doorway. A frown appeared on her face but she didn't say a word. Instead, she turned her attention back to the TV.

Lamont headed upstairs, smiling at the reaction. Auntie had grown comfortable with Lamont giving her money. It was why she hadn't pushed back after their argument. As much as she disliked him, Lamont knew Auntie would do anything to make sure the cash continued coming in.

Upstairs, Lamont tried to read a book, but found himself restless. He made some food in the kitchen, washing the tasteless microwave meal down with a glass of water, thinking about the venture they were undertaking.

Convincing Louie to give him a package was only the first step. Selling weed was relatively safe. They dealt mostly with people he knew and there was no real danger. Cocaine, crack and heroin were different ball-games. The stakes were larger and people were willing to maim to keep what was theirs. Lamont needed to be tough, but more importantly, he would have to use his brain like he never had before. It was vital that he succeed.

Lamont thought again to the Mercedes Benz; the cool assuredness of the man driving it. The way Shorty had spoken about him. Ricky had it all. A flash car, money, a reputation . . . Rochelle.

Putting his plate in the sink, Lamont quickly washed and dried it then left the house, needing some air.

Lamont moved along the streets with his head down, fighting the urge to yawn. He was tired after the day but he knew if he laid down, he wouldn't sleep. He was wired, his brain refusing to shut down, to stop thinking about Rochelle. Lamont hated himself for the weakness. He wanted to be more like Marcus and Shorty. They could effortlessly detach from whatever girls they were seeing. They were ruthless, and that was what Lamont wanted to be. He wanted to be callous. Cold.

He couldn't help but yearn for her though. He only had to close his eyes to remember the feel of Rochelle's body against his, the parting of her mouth as she moaned, the sexual dynamite in her eyes just waiting to explode. So many months had gone by, but Lamont could still see it all, and it was killing him. He had messed around with other girls since, but Rochelle was burrowed under his skin.

Lamont's feet took him to Chapeltown Road. He stood outside Warsaw Stores, one shop amongst a row, staring straight ahead. Street lights threw the row into prominence. Lamont wasn't the only one hanging around, but the older men gave him his space, talking in loud tones.

Lamont thought of Rochelle, and of prison. Most of all, the thoughts of failing were overwhelming to the point of crippling him. He closed his eyes. He needed this. He needed to succeed.

'Lamont?'

He almost didn't hear the soft voice calling him, but looked up instinctively as a girl walked confidently towards him. It took a second before he realised they'd gone to the same school. She wore a black jacket, fitted denim jeans and flat shoes, carrying a leather portfolio and a handbag. Her skin was a butterscotch shade that seemed to gleam under the streetlights. Lamont found his depressive thoughts dissipating slightly under an obvious beauty he didn't recall her having a year ago.

'Layla, how are you doing?' he said after finding his tongue.

'Good. Just coming back from college. How are you though? I haven't seen you since school ended. Didn't you go to the end-of-year party?'

Lamont shook his head. He'd heard that Erica and some of her friends were organising a party, but he had given it a miss.

'I couldn't make it. So, how's college? Are you still wanting to be a solicitor?' Lamont remembered Layla's passion from school. Her eyes widened slightly, and he could tell she was surprised at him remembering.

'Yeah, that's right. I'm loving college. It's good to be around new people and the classes I'm taking are enjoyable. What are you doing with your days?'

Lamont shrugged. 'Would you believe me if I said I was still trying to find myself?'

Layla grinned, looking at Lamont's tracksuit and expensive trainers. It didn't take a genius to work out what he was into, and it was made obvious by his vague answer. Layla had spotted him when she was sitting on the bus, and the sorrow in his eyes intrigued her enough to get off the bus a few stops early to speak to him. They had only spoken a few times in school, but this somehow felt different.

'What's wrong with you? You don't have to tell me if you don't want, but talking about whatever it is might help.'

'I've just got things on my mind. It's not even worth putting into words.'

'That means women.'

Lamont grinned, but didn't deny it. Traffic whizzed along behind them. A kid and his friend dribbled a football down the road, passing it between them and keeping it from the edge of the pavement. For a moment, Lamont remembered doing the same thing as a kid. He watched them harder than he should have. Layla entered Warsaw Stores whilst he was distracted and bought herself a bottle of water.

'Well . . . It was nice running into you, L, but I'm gonna go. I got off the bus to speak to you, but I have an early start tomorrow.'

'Where are you walking to?'

'St Martin's.'

'Can I walk with you?'

Layla nodded, and they began walking up Chapeltown Road. Lamont felt himself warming to Layla as the conversation flowed. She told funny stories about college and they shared memories from school. He ambled along, feeling freer than he had in a long while.

Layla was surprised at Lamont. She remembered him chasing after Erica in school and stuttering around women. Now, Lamont was more confident and direct. He smiled easily, but Layla couldn't help but notice that his eyes, a beautiful rosewood shade, were hard, none of the supposed joy reaching them. It was thought provoking. By the time they reached Layla's house, the pace of their walking had slowed, trying to make the talk last.

'Well, here we are,' Layla said, motioning to her house. 'It was nice running into you, L.'

'You too. I'm glad you're doing well. I'd like to stay in touch if it's cool with you? Feels weird to reconnect and then forget about each other again.'

Layla smiled, reaching into her portfolio and writing her number on some paper. She handed it to Lamont.

'You're right. Ring me and we'll hang out sometime.'

Lamont grinned and hugged Layla, enjoying the feel of her slim curves against his body. He inhaled a vanilla scent and pulled away slightly.

'I'll speak to you soon.'

* * *

The next morning, Auntie stormed into Lamont's room at the crack of dawn. He snored gently, his head burrowed into a simple white pillow.

'Lamont! Wake up!'

'What do you want?' Lamont yawned, not even opening his eyes.

Auntie's eyes narrowed. 'I want some money. Do you know how much things cost around here?'

Kissing his teeth, Lamont clambered from the bed.

'Get out of my room. I'll bring it down to you.'

Auntie gaped at him, fury resonating in her eyes.

'Who the hell are you talking to?'

Lamont looked at her, not at all bothered by the outburst.

'If you want your money, leave.'

Glaring at her nephew for a long moment, Auntie turned on her heel and flounced from the room. When he heard her stomping back down the stairs, Lamont smiled, happy to have won another verbal spar. He washed and dressed, sauntering downstairs with four ten-pound notes. Laying them on the kitchen table, he was about to walk back out when Auntie called after him.

'What's this?' Her lip curled.

'You wanted money. There's your money,'

'This isn't enough. I need more.'

'Tough. You'll get the rest on Friday. Until then, make it last.' Without even waiting for Auntie to reply, Lamont walked out of the house, realising with a jolt that he was thinking of Layla, and not Rochelle.

* * *

Lamont was in his room reading when the call came through. K-Bar met him outside Auntie's, and they drove to Chalky's place. He lived near Bankside, close to Lamont's home. He took a deep breath, trying to calm his nerves. When they entered, Shorty was in the kitchen, the drugs haphazardly wrapped. There was cocaine residue on numerous surfaces, but Chalky was nowhere to be seen.

'We're good to go, L. We've got everything cooked and bagged. Chalky's putting the word out that we've got some strong shit, and I've let my people know, so it's time to get cracking.'

Despite the fear gnawing at Lamont, he felt uplifted to hear Shorty state they were ready. Ever since he'd spoken to Louie, Lamont had flip-flopped so many times between wanting to sell drugs and wanting to get out and get a real job before it was too late. When he sat down and gave the subject some thought though, he realised there was nothing else he wanted to do.

* * *

Lamont stood near Spencer Place in the Hood, doing his best to remain inconspicuous. He rubbed his hands on his trousers, glancing around, his heart racing. Every time he saw someone he recognised, he would keep his head down, praying they wouldn't guess what he was doing. Every person who looked at him from a passing car was an undercover officer, determined to lock him up.

Lamont kept his hands in his pockets, the wraps stored there burning a hole in his palm. He had refused to store the drugs in his mouth the way the others did. He couldn't believe people did this every day. Selling weed had been easy by comparison. Lamont dealt with people he knew, and everything was lovely. Crack was a whole different game. It presented much more risk. Lamont's stomach twisted nervously the longer he stood there.

After a while, a dusty-looking man shuffled towards him, dirty faced and limping. As he drew closer, Lamont scanned his face, trying to gauge if he the man was legit, or an undercover officer.

'Have you got owt?' the man mumbled. His heart pounding, Lamont remembered Shorty's teachings, and signalled for the man to walk down a nearby alley. With a quick glance around, Lamont followed him.

'What are you after?' his voice shook slightly. Clearing his throat, Lamont tried getting it under control. 'What do you want?'

The sale watched Lamont intently. Lamont met the look, the beating of his heart more frenzied. He was sweating, but willed himself not to look away first. Finally, the sale began coughing profusely, 'Gimme three please.' He scratched his neck.

'Got you.' Lamont scrambled in his pockets for the wraps. The sale took them with sweaty fingers, gave Lamont the money, then hurried away as fast as his limp would allow. Letting out a deep breath, Lamont stuck the money in his sock, glanced around again, then slowly walked back out to Spencer Place.

* * *

After the initial selling of his first wraps, it took almost a week for Lamont, Shorty and K-Bar to move both ounces. For a few days, they clipped sales — addicts — where they could, before deciding to try working shifts. Lamont worked the day, K-Bar the evening, and Shorty overnight. After they sold out, Shorty brought Louie his profit, and took another two ounces.

Some days were slower, but they slowly built up a rhythm. Shorty helped when he went to town one day and purchased some pay-as-you-go mobile phones. These phones were cumbersome, but would help the trio build up their drug line, and become more known.

* * *

A few weeks later, Lamont was at Shorty's eating when the mobile phone rang. Hastily swallowing his food, Lamont answered.

'Yeah?'

'You got owt? I need eight.' A scratchy voice asked. Lamont was pleased. The morning had been dry so far. If this sale was serious, Lamont would be closer to selling out for the day.

'Meet me at Spencer's. Two minutes.' Lamont waited for the sale to confirm, then hung up. Wolfing down the rest of the sandwich, Lamont guzzled a glass of water and hit the roads.

The sale was waiting in the alleyway by Spencer Place. He looked shifty, but that was becoming more normal to Lamont. What struck him as strange was that he didn't recognise the sale. Assuming he had got the number from another customer, Lamont approached him.

'You got that?' he asked, referring to the money. The sale didn't move though. Lamont was about to repeat himself when he heard scuffling from behind. Lamont had no time to react before he was barrelled to the floor, a flurry of feet repeatedly kicking him.

There were three men, stinking and tattered. Surging to his feet, Lamont hit one man, sending him reeling. The other attackers dragged him back to the floor, desperation lending them strength as they rained hits on him. When Lamont stopped moving, one of them rummaged through Lamont's jacket pocket, relieving him of his wraps.

'Check his pockets! Get his money!'

Luckily, Lamont had left the rest of his money at Shorty's. Hitting him twice more, the trio scampered away, leaving Lamont moaning on the ground in pain.

* * *

'L! What the fuck happened?' Shorty leapt to his feet when Lamont staggered inside. His jacket was torn, his mouth bleeding.

'Got jumped by some fiends.' Lamont collapsed into a chair and massaged his ribs.

'Did they get anything?'

'Eight shots.' Lamont moaned.

'Motherfuckers!' Shorty growled. 'What did they look like?'

Lamont gave the best description he could, but everything had been a blur, and he'd struggled to see his attackers. Shouting for K-Bar, who was resting upstairs, Shorty hit the roads to look for the thieves,

K-Bar following. Once the door had slammed, Lamont closed his eyes, shaking slightly.

* * *

Shorty and K-Bar searched all over for the thieves, but they had gone to ground. Eventually, they had to take the loss, and let it go.

Lamont spent the next few days in deep thought. Being attacked by people he believed to be the lowest of the low was degrading. It made him wonder if he had the heart to be a drug dealer. Everyone in the game was out to win. Lamont played out in his mind all the different ways the situation could have gone. If the fiends had knives, he might be dead. The thought of Marika being alone scared Lamont as much as being shot or stabbed.

Lamont was nearly eighteen. He was smart enough to get a legitimate job if he put his mind to it. When it came down to it though, he refused to fail. He had goals, and a group of decaying smack-heads would not determine his destiny.

* * *

Lamont's robbery was glossed over fairly quickly, and he decided he would not be a victim. He stepped up his training, sparring with Marcus and Shorty, ensuring he was in peak physical condition and ready for any conflict.

The goal for the team was to make as much money as possible, and Lamont made sure they did that. He, K-Bar and Shorty would pitch around the Hood, serving as many fiends as possible and making sure Louie got his return.

In no time, they were his best customers, and though Shorty and K-Bar would drop off the money and collect the drugs, Lamont made sure they treated Louie right, forever grateful to the man for giving him his start.

They hit the streets with a vengeance, working hard, letting the crack heads know who they were and where to find them. When they disagreed with other teams, Shorty and K-Bar would handle it, and their reputations were enough to keep people at bay.

The money was improving, but not quickly enough for Lamont's liking. One day, he sat down with Shorty. They were at his spot, Lamont pacing the boxy living room while Shorty relaxed with a beer.

'Why are you so worried, L? We're smashing it.'

Lamont paused, scratching his chin, weighing up his words and debating what to say.

'I want more.'

'We all want more, but we need to keep moving carefully. Isn't that what you're always saying?'

'I am, and we are, but we also need to step our game up, or we'll be like everyone else, hustling every day to stay ahead. We need people working for us.'

Shorty nodded. 'I feel you on that. I've got a couple dudes that would work for us if the money was right. We need to keep making links though, plus we need to move on from Louie, bro. The man is dead weight. His own people rip him off, for fuck's sake.'

'That's them. We do our own thing, and for now, Louie's supply will do. When we've grown, we'll look to other suppliers. I want you to reach out to any who you think can work with us. Speak to K-Bar, make sure we're all in agreement.'

'K-Bar will be down with whatever makes us more money, L. I'll speak to him, but he's cool.'

Lamont agreed. K-Bar didn't like to weigh in on many of the big decisions. He was an asset though, and like Shorty, had a vibe that warned against messing with him.

'We need to trim the fat too.'

'What the hell does that mean?' Shorty frowned.

'It means there are a lot of dealers in similar positions to us. We need to be above them, and we need them working for us, so that we grow. We're seen as the bottom of the barrel, and I don't like that.'

Shorty yawned. 'I get what you're saying, but like you said, we're at the bottom, so there's no reason for any of them to come and work with us.'

Lamont grinned, but there was no joy in it. It was bloodless, full of menace, and made Shorty feel uneasy.

'This is where we get creative. We need to meet Marcus, and I'll fill you both in on the plan.'

* * *

Days later, Lamont was on the streets, wanting to get inside so he could eat and chill. He had a few wraps left to sell, but he wasn't seeing as many fiends around, and no one was calling the phone boxes he hung around, nor were they calling the mobile phone he carried.

Lamont was exhausted after a long night and day, but he also had a rule about finishing his shift with product on his person, so he would stay outside until he'd sold out. The longer he stayed, the more risk of running into police or stick-up dudes who preyed on dealers.

Dipping down a side-street with his hands jammed into his pockets, Lamont noticed a prostitute he'd sold drugs to in the past. She was tottering along, trying to light a cigarette.

'Daisy, how are you doing?' He asked, startling the woman. She was shorter than he was, with bedraggled blonde hair, pale blue eyes and truckloads of makeup. Once upon a time she'd been a looker, but life and drugs had worn her down. She was good-natured though, and Lamont didn't avoid her.

'I'm knackered, L,' she said, finally lighting her cigarette. She offered Lamont one from the battered pack, but he declined.

'I know how you feel. I'm looking to get inside and get some food.' He reached into his pockets for the wraps, showing them to her. 'I'll sell you these three for forty quid.'

Daisy sighed, shaking her head.

'I've barely made anything, L. My man will kill me if I go home with no money.'

L would have walked away, but he could tell by the gleam in Daisy's eyes that she was interested.

'Daisy, baby. We both know it's only a matter of time until you get scooped up and paid. When the punters come cruising, you'll be the first port of call. I'd have a go myself, if I thought I could keep up,' he said, smiling widely at Daisy, watching her grin.

'I'm sure you'd do fine, L. You can have a go for half-price,' she offered, leering at Lamont. He resisted the urge to shudder, forcing the grin to remain on his face.

'Maybe next time. Gimme thirty five and they're yours. You know no one else will do you a better deal, and you can go home and get merry.'

Daisy considered it for all of two seconds before she fumbled in her pockets and gave Lamont his money. He gave her the wraps, then watched her totter back down the alley. Deep down, Lamont knew she'd likely not make anymore money, which would infuriate her pimp, but he couldn't find it within him to care. Turning on his heel, he hurried away, keeping his eyes open for any activity.

CHAPTER TWELVE

Monday 15 June 1998

LAMONT LEFT THE PARK, beaming. He'd gone to hang with some old football friends. Since he stopped training with Nigel, he had seen little of them. They'd had an impromptu football game. Lamont had held his own, scoring multiple times against his skilled friends. It was a boost to his confidence and even as he walked home covered in sweat, he just couldn't stop smiling. For nearly a year he had allowed the darkness to overwhelm his thoughts. Now, he was thinking clearly. He hoped.

As Lamont approached Auntie's place, thinking about where to watch the Germany vs USA World Cup match that night, he noticed Marcus waiting, leaning against a car smoking a joint. He eyed Lamont carefully, touching his fist.

'Where are you coming from all sweaty like that? I hope it's a woman.'

'I was kicking ball with some friends. What you doing round here?'

'Come to see you obviously.'

'How's independent life?' Lamont asked. He hadn't seen much of Marcus since he moved out. The times they had spoken were mainly in passing, so he was surprised that he was waiting for him.

'You know me, I've always been independent. Forget that for now though,' Marcus motioned to the ride. 'Let's go for a drive.'

'Have I got time to get a shower first?'

Marcus raised an eyebrow. 'We're not going on a date, blood. You don't need to freshen up.'

'I've been playing football for hours, bro. Gimme twenty minutes to get a shower and then we can go wherever.'

Lamont hurried inside, quickly showering and dressing in a sweater and jeans. He shrugged his feet into some black Nike trainers and headed out the door, grabbing his wallet and keys. Marcus was already sitting in the car. When Lamont climbed in, he drove away.

'How's things?' Marcus asked after they'd been driving for a while.

'Can't complain. Just trying to make things happen.'

'Drugs?'

Lamont turned to Marcus, wondering who he had been talking to. He immediately ruled out Louie, as he couldn't imagine Marcus making time with the small-fry.

'Shorty?'

Marcus nodded. 'He told me you secured a connect so you can start slanging Class A.'

'What else did Shorty tell you?'

'He said you spoke to Louie, and that you were sharing stories. Said you caught feelings.'

'Did he also say that I told him I never wanted to discuss it?' Lamont's voice was cold. If Marcus noticed, he didn't comment.

'Maybe you didn't wanna discuss it with him, but I know who you were talking about. Guess it explains a few things too.'

Lamont tried to control his breathing, but he could feel himself growing angry. He had tried for so long to put his feelings behind him where Rochelle was concerned. What she had done to him had shattered his core, and the hardest thing at the time had been to go on as if nothing was wrong.

The pressure had nearly broken Lamont, and he never wanted to go through anything like it again. Marcus wouldn't listen though, Lamont knew that. He had sought him out for a reason, and nothing would prevent them from having the conversation, as painful as it would be for Lamont.

'Are you hungry?' Marcus asked after a while. Lamont shook his head, but was betrayed by his rumbling stomach. Marcus laughed but didn't say anything.

They stopped at a West Indian spot near Roundhay Road. Marcus practically ordered the whole menu, whereas Lamont settled for oxtail with rice and stewed peas. They sat inside the crowded restaurant to eat. Marcus nodded and greeted a few people, some of whom Lamont was familiar with. They ate in silence for a while and then Marcus began talking again.

'She was fucked up, you know.'

Lamont wanted to pretend he didn't know who Marcus was talking about, but it wasn't worth it.

'I tried asking about it. Mia did too. She wouldn't speak though. It was obvious she was hurting. Just like you.'

'How do you know something happened if she didn't speak on it?'

Marcus paused. 'I saw Ricky.'

Lamont's fingers tightened around the fork he was holding. Everything about Ricky Reagan made him want to kill the man, and that was a dangerous mindset to have. If Lamont wanted to survive the drugs game, he needed to keep his emotions in check.

'What did he say?'

'He wanted to know about you. Said you came by the place, and that he'd heard about you sexing Rochelle. He wanted it to stop.'

'Did you know about him?' Lamont looked his friend in the eye. Some of his anger must have slipped out, because Marcus looked startled for a minute.

'Yeah.'

Lamont grit his teeth, his breathing intensifying for a moment.

'Why didn't you tell me?'

'Because . . .' Marcus blew out a breath.

'Because what?'

'Because I didn't know, okay?'

'Didn't know what? Stop skating around it and just answer me.'

Lamont's voice rose, and people glanced over at them. He took a deep breath, calming down.

'I didn't know how you felt for her.'

'What are you talking about? Course you kn—'

'I just thought you wanted to have sex with her. I didn't know you were caught up. Whatever happened though, it fucked her up. She hasn't been the same since.'

Lamont didn't speak. He wasn't sure how he even felt about that. He didn't want Rochelle to be hurt but, he couldn't deny feeling a certain relish that her decision had affected her that day. They ate again without speaking, but Lamont enjoyed the comfort. He knew that Marcus had his best interests at heart, as annoying as it was that he'd held information from him.

'So, you're stepping your game up then?'

Lamont looked up, wiping his mouth with a napkin as he finished his food.

'Do you think I should?'

Marcus shrugged. 'You'll have thought it all through. The streets are rough, but I know what you're like, and I definitely know what Shorty is like. You'll be stacking in no time, no doubt.'

Lamont scratched his chin, secretly pleased at Marcus's words.

'Did he say anything about the other thing?'

Marcus frowned. 'What other thing?'

'I need your help with something. I'll pay well.'

* * *

Marcus stopped his car down the road from an unkempt terraced house. Pulling on a pair of leather gloves, he tugged his hood tighter over his head, and climbed from the car, keeping his head down.

In front of the dirty house, a group of guys were laughing and cracking jokes, one talking on a mobile phone almost the size of his head. Marcus didn't hesitate. Assessing the biggest man first, he caught him flush with a blow, sending the man sailing through the air. Two of the others turned and ran, the last man frozen on the spot. Marcus grabbed him around the throat, lifting him off the ground like he weighed nothing.

'You need to get off this strip, you little punk. You're not man enough to be out here. Look how quickly your people dusted and left you?'

Marcus flung the man to the floor and kicked him in the ribs. Looking around, he took his money and drugs, then walked away.

* * *

Marcus and Victor repeated the same tactic on half a dozen different independent dealers over the next few weeks, beating them senseless, robbing their product, and leaving them for dead. After a while, Shorty or K-Bar would pass through, feigning concern and promising safety if they started buying from Lamont directly.

The plan was a success, and every affected person began indirectly working for Lamont. Marcus received five thousand pounds and was impressed with Lamont's cunning in manipulating a situation to get paid. With Lamont's help, he devised a similar strategy, and waded into the protection market, quickly swelling his profits.

'You're a crafty guy, L,' Shorty later remarked, as the pair sipped drinks in a club in town. 'How did you know that would work?'

'I took a shot,' said Lamont shrugging and lifting the drink to his lips.

* * *

In August, Lamont and Layla left the cinema, both grinning as they navigated through the city centre. They had been to see *The Negotiator*, and both enjoyed the film immensely.

'Do you want to go for food, or do you fancy something to drink?' Lamont asked, looking around him as they walked. It was early evening, and still warm enough for Lamont to be in a white t-shirt, and Layla to be wearing a blouse and skirt. They were an attractive couple, and men and women alike were checking out the pair as they strolled.

'Let's go for food. I don't need to be getting drunk around you,' said Layla, grinning.

'What do you mean by that?' Lamont replied, laughing, but Layla refused to answer until they'd settled down for food at a Chinese restaurant near the market. After they placed their orders, she spoke.

'You knew exactly what I meant; I don't even know why you asked.'

She was right. As always. Ever since running into Layla on Chapeltown Road, Lamont had spent a lot of time with her. She was fun, and he found talking to her simple. Rochelle had damaged him though, and Lamont was fully aware of that fact. As much as he enjoyed spending time with Layla, he knew that he often backed away at crucial moments. If Layla realised, she'd never commented on it.

'You think I need you to be drunk to take advantage of you?'

Layla shrugged, tucking into her food when it arrived.

'Maybe you would. I don't know; as long as I've been spending time with you, you've been nothing but a perfect gentleman.'

'I thought that would be seen as a good thing.'

'It's strange. I mean, you're a good-looking guy. You're smart and you dress nice; the dirty looks I was receiving from other women are proof of that. I guess I just don't know what your game is.'

Lamont mulled that one over, deciding exactly how he would answer.

'When we were in high school, I started juggling weed, as you know.'

Layla nodded, eating her food as he spoke. Lamont took a bite of his chow mein before he continued.

'I met a girl. You saw me in school; I was a complete loser, spending all my time chasing after a girl who wasn't worthy. I met one who seemed to understand me, who had similar interests, who seemed to want the best for me.'

'I'm guessing it didn't turn out that way.' Layla met Lamont's eyes.

'We grew closer, I let her know how I felt, and we had sex,' Lamont's stomach churned, remembering seeing Reagan in the doorway, Rochelle's face as she closed the door on him. He willed the images away, taking a deep breath. 'She destroyed me.'

That was it. Lamont didn't need to say anymore. Layla reached over and squeezed his hand, then went back to her food. They spoke after that about regular topics, speaking about the movie, their plans for the rest of the year. They left town and Lamont ordered a taxi. Outside Layla's house, he asked the driver to wait as he climbed out. They stood in the street for an awkward moment.

'I'm sorry if I ruined the mood. I don't want you to think I don't like you, because I do. The way I am though; the life I'm in. I don't want to ruin you.'

Layla smiled, pulling Lamont in for a hug and feeling him stiffen. She kissed him on the cheek and let him go.

'Thank you for being honest, L. I can tell it wasn't easy. When you want to spend more time together, call me.'

With that, she grinned and headed inside, Lamont watching her every step of the way.

* * *

Lamont, Shorty and K-Bar continued to plod along. They were becoming more known to the fiends and were making good money.

As months passed, Louie was finding it difficult to keep up with them. He was making more money than before but still he wasn't happy. When Shorty took Lamont with him to reload one day in September, he made his feelings clear.

'I'm glad you're here, Lamont,' he said, jerking his thumb at Shorty. 'He never wants to listen to me.'

'Because you talk shit, that's why. I swear, the more money we make, the more you complain.'

'Oi, don't forget who got you started. You'd still be scratching your ass if it wasn't for me.'

'Guys, we don't need this,' Lamont interjected, when Shorty opened his mouth to reply. 'What's the problem, Louie?'

'The bloody problem is I'm too old to be running all over the place. I need to keep you lot happy, but now my other youngsters are complaining. They need product too.'

'Fuck them little pricks. We're getting through ten times as much as them. Cut them loose,' Shorty said.

Louie bristled, 'Hang on a—'

'—Guys,' there was more bite in Lamont's tone now. Both men heeded this. 'We're all working together, and we're all getting paid. There's a way around this.'

'What ways that then?'

'You sit back and let us make the money for you.'

'I thought that was what I was doing now?'

'What I mean is, introduce us to your guy. We supply you, and you supply your regulars with no fuss.'

'So you wanna cut me out?'

'No, not cut you out. Make it easier for you.' Lamont said.

'Sounds like you're trying to cut me out.'

Shorty narrowed his eyes at Louie's petulant tone. Lamont smiled though, like he'd expected this response.

'Cutting you out makes little sense, and it's not productive. We want to continue making money but our demand is higher, Lou. If you have a better suggestion, let's hear it.'

Shorty and Louie both stared at Lamont, mouths agape. Lamont could be so quiet and unassuming that it was easy to overlook the dominance he showed. Shorty coughed inaudibly, Louie shifting slightly in his seat.

'Look, take a quarter for now. Gimme time to have a think.'

* * *

'That motherfucker is getting too cheeky for his own good,' Shorty grumbled as they left.

'Louie's grouchy, but he's just used to being ripped off.'

'Why you always taking his side?' Shorty stopped and glared at Lamont.

'It's not about taking sides. If we keep Louie comfortable, he'll be easy to control. He's on the way out; he just doesn't wanna admit it.'

'You think?'

'Louie's lazy. The game has left him behind and he doesn't want to chase after it. We need his supplier so we can keep growing.'

'Okay. I get you.' Shorty was starting to understand now. Lamont jokingly nudged him.

'Let's turn up the pressure and get rich, Shortstuff.'

Grinning, Shorty slapped hands with Lamont. He didn't know who Lamont had caught feelings over, but he'd never seen his friend looking so focused. He liked it.

* * *

Lamont slouched over the kitchen table at Auntie's. Nowadays, he spent most of his time chilling at Shorty's or out and about, meeting links and selling.

The life had hold of him, and Lamont was obsessed with making money. His team was growing, and Lamont's portion at the end of each week was increasing. It wasn't enough. The streets were wide open, and Lamont wanted to be one of the established cliques making big money. It was possible, but he needed to keep pushing and continue watching the angles.

Raising his tea to his lips, Lamont's eyes narrowed as Auntie hovered next to him. He forced himself to meet her eyes, lowering his cup.

'Yes?'

'I need more money.'

'I gave you your money yesterday.'

'I used it. I need more. You definitely have it.'

Lamont gave his Auntie another look. He'd done his best to keep the peace. They argued, but he never crossed the line, comfortable having a place to stay near Marika.

'Where does your money go?'

The reaction was immediate. Auntie stepped back, her mouth wide open, but no words coming out. Calmly, Lamont waited.

'What do you mean? I've never had any money because I spent half my life looking after you and your little sister. Don't you remember any of that?'

'Are you serious?' Lamont's eyebrows rose. He shouldn't have been shocked at Auntie's complete white-washing of the facts, but he was.

'You lot never wanted for anything. I fed and clothed you, made sure you were both looked after, and you've never been grateful for any of it. Marika always was. You never were.'

Lamont laughed in her face, the sound chillingly devoid of mirth.

'You profited from my parent's death. You received a live-in slave, and never once did you show me anything that resembled love. You treated Marika well, but you taught her nothing but your disgusting bad habits. For you to stand there and talk about us being looked after is nothing but a joke.'

'You're nothing but a little lia—'

'What happened to my parent's money?'

Auntie visibly paled at Lamont's question, running a hand through her hair.

'What do you mean?'

Lamont rose to his feet, noting that he towered over his Auntie. After her years of bullying, it was indescribable to see her on the back foot, unable to hit him or think of a decent comeback. The years of fear were over.

'My parents worked all their lives. They paid off the house we lived in when they were still alive, which everyone in our family knows. Where did the money from the sale of that same house go?'

'Are you crazy! Do you know how expensive it was to take care of everything? That money was eaten up by legal costs, inheritance fees, all of that stuff. I took care of you lot out of my pocket, with no help from family, and no gratitude. You'd have gone to a home if it wasn't for me.'

'I'd have preferred that to growing up around you,' retorted Lamont, his words calm despite the utter rage he felt toward this woman. 'Do you think I'm stupid? I was ten years old when I came to live with you. I remember the drink and drugs, and your little parties, the expensive clothing. I know about you falsifying details to become a foster mother, even though you were claiming benefits and living off my dead parents blood and sweat. You have no idea of what it means to struggle. You're nothing but a bitter, out-of-touch lush who never wanted to earn any money for herself. No wonder everyone hates you.'

'That's it!' Auntie screamed. 'Get out of my house. I've put up with you and your ways long enough. I want you out!'

Lamont smiled, shocked at how free he felt.

'I'm leaving, don't worry. I won't spend another night in this house.'

'Good! You drug dealing piece of shit. I should call the police and let them know what you're doing.'

'I'd rather be a dealer than a user,' Lamont tilted his head, staring at the vile woman. 'A question; how did you keep paying for all of those drugs after your money ran out?' Not even waiting for her to answer, he made a face. 'On second thoughts, I don't want to know.'

'You piece of shi—' Auntie went to strike Lamont, but he grabbed her wrist, overpowering her with ease.

'You'll never lay a hand on me again,' he said, enunciating each word as Auntie struggled against his grip. 'You have no power anymore. I'm leaving, and you get nothing from me. Not a single penny. Any money I give Rika from now on is hers. If I hear you've taken any of it, or you've mistreated her, you'll regret it. That I can promise you. If you know I'm dealing, you know what I can do to you. Do not push me.'

Shoving Auntie to the side, Lamont finished his drink and left the room, Auntie cowed into silence behind him. He went to his room and packed his belongings, then left without another word.

CHAPTER THIRTEEN

Wednesday 10 February 1999

FINANCIALLY, Lamont was doing well. After abruptly leaving Auntie's, he'd stayed with Shorty and K-Bar for a few weeks, before getting his own place nearby on Cowper Street. It was enough. For now.

The streets remained steady, and their crew continued to hold its own against others. Everything hummed. The cash came in fast and everyone did as instructed. Lamont ran a tight ship and Shorty was on hand to ensure discipline was maintained. That was the smart thing Lamont did. He managed Shorty correctly, allowing him to do what he needed, keeping him sharp, knowing that Shorty would then do the same for the guys below. Lamont had hit a snag now though: He had too much money.

At first, Lamont saved his money in shoe boxes like a lot of guys he knew. He gave money to his sister, put some in the bank, and had even started hiding money outside, wrapping it well.

It wasn't sustainable. Lamont was wary of the police. He needed to set himself up. Just because things were going well, didn't mean they would continue. Lamont made a black coffee, staring into space and holding the piping porcelain mug in his hands. He thought about investing the money and buying more drugs, but that would just lead to more cash lying around.

As Lamont thought about what he could do, an idea came to him. With a grin he reached for his phone and dialled a number.

'It's L. Where are you? We need to talk.'

* * *

Lamont took a taxi into town, heading for a pub near the university. Outside, scores of drunk, boisterous students ran around making noise. Lamont made his way through the masses. Inside, the pub was stuffy and full almost to capacity. Pushing his way to the bar, Lamont ordered a pint and scanned the room, finally spotting him in the corner, whispering in the ear of a giggling girl. Making his way over, Lamont plopped on the seat opposite them.

'How's it going, Xiyu?'

'L! What the hell man, where have you been?' Xiyu Manderson's eyes twinkled. The pair were old friends and had spent a lot of time together before Lamont started selling weed.

Xiyu was fair skinned, with straight jet black hair and piercing almond eyes that he'd received from his Chinese mother.

'Busy working. Same as you.' Lamont smiled at the girl Xiyu was entertaining. She smiled back.

'Uni man . . . It's crazy. You should start going. You'd love it.'

'Maybe I will. I need to talk to you. It's urgent.'

Xiyu nodded, rubbing his hands through his hair.

'Babe, go sit with the others. I'll come and get you after.'

The girl didn't like it, but she forced a smile on her face and moved.

'What's the drill then? How can I help?' Xiyu asked.

'You're studying business at Uni aren't you?'

'You already know I am.' Xiyu rolled his eyes.

'I want to invest some money.'

'Into what?' Xiyu sipped his drink. Lamont didn't know what it was, but it smelt fruity.

'Something legitimate. I was hoping you could help.'

Xiyu scratched his chest. He was dressed like the other guys in the pub; white t-shirt, jeans and canvas shoes. His clothes seemed to be in better condition though which didn't surprise Lamont. Xiyu had always been finicky about his outfits. Lamont assumed it came from growing up poor; trying to look your best when you didn't have the resources to do it.

As they sat, people kept approaching Xiyu, slapping him on the back, offering to get him another drink. It surprised Lamont just how popular he was.

'I work in an office to pay for Uni, mate. Barely earning above minimum wage. I dunno what I could tell you,' Xiyu said a few minutes later, after his fan club dispersed.

'You know business though. I want to know it too. Money isn't an issue. I'll pay you for the information.'

Xiyu shook his head. 'I don't need you to pay me. You're my friend and I want to help you. I'm just . . .' Xiyu trailed off, staring intently at the table. Lamont didn't interrupt. He had seen Xiyu's thinking face before, distracting himself by scanning the bar.

A couple of girls were scantily clad, several glancing in Lamont's direction. He smiled, but didn't make a move. He was on the clock tonight. Pleasure would have to wait. He wondered how many of the students in the pub had lectures first thing, and if they would even show up. Lamont's phone rang, but he ignored it. He needed to get this sorted.

'There's a guy I know. He's older and works in the same building as me. He's called Martin. Trust fund kid who got cut off by his parents. He's doing well for himself, and he's always looking for investors. I could speak to him.'

Lamont beamed. 'That would be great. While you're ringing him, I'll go to the bar. What are you drinking?'

Lamont returned with Xiyu's drink, annoyed to see that his lady-friend from before draped all over him again. Xiyu had a seedy smile on his face now as she whispered something into his ear that made him glance around to see if anyone overheard. Approaching, Lamont gave Xiyu his drink and sat down with a glass of water. If he had another pint, he'd end staying all night.

'I spoke with Martin. He's busy this week, but said to give you his number. You can have a meeting on Tuesday. Ring him for the details.'

'Thanks, Xiyu. Means a lot.' Lamont took out his phone, ignoring the missed calls and texts. Xiyu relayed Martin's number and Lamont stored it in his phone.

'I'm gonna be off then.'

'Stay and finish your drink at least, pal,' Xiyu insisted, pointing at the water that Lamont hadn't touched. Lamont did as bidden. 'Can I ask you a question, L?'

'Go for it.'

'How much are we talking about here?'

'In terms of?'

'How much are you wanting to invest? I mean, Martin's small-time, but he's not gonna want an investment of like five hundred quid or summat. He's a serious guy.'

'So am I.'

'How much then?'

Lamont drained his water and stood.

'Don't worry about that,' he reached into his pocket and handed Xiyu a fifty pound note. 'Buy yourself a few drinks on me. Thanks for the introduction.' Nodding at his girl and shaking Xiyu's hand, Lamont made his way out of the pub, phone already to his ear to call a taxi.

* * *

Lamont sat in the reception of an office building in town, reading a magazine and trying his best to relax. True to his word, Xiyu had set up everything for Lamont. He'd spoken to Martin over the phone and they arranged a sit down to get a feel for one another.

Lamont felt out of his element. Everyone around him seemed immaculate in their neat business attire. They carried briefcases, fancy bags and containers of coffee. They seemed busy, sure-footed, never hanging around to chat, always moving from point A to B. Even the receptionists were demure and professional. For Lamont it was a brand new environment, but he was determined to navigate it.

The reception was spacious, with marble flooring and mahogany desks, neutral walls covered with various paintings and certificates announcing the authenticity of the company. Lamont was definitely sold. He wasn't sure if that was a good or a bad thing yet.

As Lamont waited for Martin, he realised he didn't even know what the man looked like. He was about to ring Xiyu and ask for a description when he heard a small voice call his name. He turned, watching as a red-faced, lumpy man hurried towards him. The man held out his hand and as he did so, the folder he carried fell to the floor, papers going everywhere. If possible, the man's face turned an even brighter shade of red. Several workers passed, openly sniggering.

'You must be Martin.' Lamont bent down to help Martin pick up the paperwork.

'Yes, I'm Martin Fisher. It's good to meet you. And thank you.' Martin gestured to the papers. He forced them together in a haphazard pile, then shook Lamont's hand with his clammier one. They went into the lift and took it to the second floor. Lamont was led into the work area, dozens of others dressed like Martin talking loudly on phones. The smell of sweat, sickly sweet aftershave and coffee were prominent.

Lamont took everything in on his way to Martin's shabby cubicle. It was boxy, the wooden desk too small for the assortment of paperwork covering it. There were two dirty coffee mugs that needed cleaning and a copy of a broadsheet newspaper that Lamont saw that was three days old. He sat opposite Martin and waited for him to begin.

'I'm sorry about the mess. I haven't had much time to do a clean.'

'Don't worry about it.'

'Can I get you something to drink?'

'No thank you.'

'Did Martha downstairs offer you something?'

'She did.'

'And you're sure you don't want anything?'

Lamont nodded. Martin copied the movement, nodding his head frenziedly like an idiot. He quickly stopped, taking a deep breath. With shaking hands, he reached for the prospectus folder he had dropped in reception and opened it. His eyes scanned the first page quickly. Cursing under his breath, he moved it to the side.

'Really sorry about this. I had them all in order, and now . . .' He ruffled his floppy black hair, breathing hard. 'I'm just going to get a drink. You sure I can't bring you one back?'

'I'm fine.' Lamont's words had a slight edge now, that Martin recognised. Shuffling from his chair, he tottered to the kitchen at the far end of the office. He came back a minute later, drinking from what looked like a canister of water. Wiping his mouth with his hand, he reached for the papers again.

'So . . . Xiyu says that you were interested in investing some money? Depending on the figures, I think I can help.'

'In what way?' Lamont asked. Xiyu had given little insight into what Martin actually did.

'I mainly deal in property. Buying into houses, doing them up, renting or selling them. In terms of business, I know of quite a few companies looking for investments. One of these companies is a letting agency. I think it could be a good fit for you in terms of what you're wanting to invest.'

Lamont mulled that over, not wanting to speak before he understood what Martin was saying.

'If I'm interested, what happens then?'

'I put you in play, introduce you to the others, and you can decide, sign the contracts, whatever.' Martin seemed more relaxed now, more confident talking figures.

'Can I take the prospectus away with me?'

'Of course. You're in control here. This doesn't move forward without you being fully committed,' said Martin.

'If you don't mind me asking, what do you get out of this?'

'A simple middleman fee. A percentage from you and a percentage from whoever you work with.'

'So, you don't invest in any of these companies yourself?'

'I have a share in the letting agency.'

'Do you make money from it?'

Martin took another sip from his water.

'Yes. The aim of the game here is steady, consistent profit. Xiyu said you'd probably deal in mainly cash. What I will help you do is invest that cash into a portfolio so you're much more flexible in terms of capital. Cash is good, but also not good if you understand my meaning.'

'It's why I'm here.'

'That's good. I promise you that any of these companies you consider will do wonders for you in the long run. Take the prospectus away, consider your options and then get in touch with me. I'll have a meeting set up in no time.'

* * *

MONDAY 22 FEBRUARY 1999

'This is big for us, L.'

After several months, Louie had finally stopped dithering, allowing Lamont and Shorty to run his drugs line for him. He had made the initial introduction to his supplier, and Lamont and Shorty were on the way to meet him whilst K-Bar handled business.

'I know, Shorty.'

'If we can go away with a kilo, then we're up and running.' Shorty continued, driving to the Hyde Park meet. They had rented a vehicle using Louie's name and credit card.

'Shorty, I know,' Lamont repeated. Shorty glanced over but said nothing. Louie had said little about the supplier, other than saying they went way back.

They climbed out after reaching the spot, knocking at the door. A woman opened it. She looked to be in her forties, busty with bleached-blonde hair. She smiled at the pair, and they smiled back.

'You lads here to see Bill?' she asked. They nodded.

'Follow me. I'll take you to him.' She led them to the kitchen. Two men sat there, eating large meals and talking to one another in quick tones. They paused when they saw Lamont and Shorty.

'You lot must be Louie's lads,' one of them said. He was bald with a thick moustache and the makings of a beard. He stared at the pair through pale blue eyes as he shovelled food in his mouth.

'That's right,' said Lamont.

'Sit down then. We'll talk when I've munched this,' he gestured to the food. Shorty and Lamont took seats. The woman waited by the wall.

'Do you want a drink or owt?'

They shook their heads.

'Sweet,' Bill turned to the woman. 'Go kick your feet up and watch TV, love. I'll be along soon.'

The other man continued to stare at Lamont and Shorty. His expression wasn't friendly.

'This is my bro, Jonny,' said Bill. Both men nodded at Jonny, who didn't respond. Lamont wondered if they should have brought Marcus.

'Right, let's talk,' Bill pushed his plate to the side and stifled a burp. 'Louie speaks bloody highly of you two. Says you're reliable and you've never tried fucking him over,' he nodded in approval to his own statement. 'Lou's a good guy. Used to help our old man a lot before he died.'

'He's been good to us too. We want to make him richer,' said Lamont. Bill laughed.

'And yourselves.'

'Definitely. No point doing this otherwise.'

'I normally give Lou half a kilo. He's gone over prices hasn't he?'

Lamont nodded. 'If possible, we want to step up. Order wise.'

Bill and Jonny shared a look.

'Step up to what?'

Lamont paused for a second, keeping his eyes on the brothers.

'A whole box of each.'

'Can you afford that?' Bill let out a low whistle.

'We can afford half up front. The rest plus five percent when we've shifted them.'

'Can you move it though?'

'Everything is in place,' said Lamont. 'We can move it with relatively little effort.'

Bill stared Lamont down again. Lamont matched his expression.

'I'm gonna give you lads a play. Mess about with my money though . . .' Bill didn't need to finish. Shorty's eyes narrowed, but Lamont held out his hand. Bill shook.

'I'd expect nothing less, Bill.'

'I'm gonna shoot off now that's sorted. Jonny will sort the particulars. I want my end in two weeks. Toodle-oo gents.'

As Jonny turned to address them, Lamont felt a happy glow in his stomach.

* * *

After meeting with Bill and Jonny, Shorty and K-Bar broke the drugs down, ensuring Louie got a portion for his runners. They hit the streets with a vengeance, selling out quicker than any of them expected. Bill and Jonny were stunned when Shorty returned with their profit after less than a week, asking for more.

They spread far, establishing new links. Bit by bit, the gulf between Lamont's faction and others grew. Lamont wanted more though, and intended to get it.

CHAPTER FOURTEEN

Friday 30 April 1999

LAMONT AND MARIKA sat in a high-class restaurant in the city centre. Lamont wore a grey shirt, black trousers and shoes, with Marika wearing a ruffled shirt and tight denim jeans.

For Lamont, it was difficult to see his little sister was growing up. She looked older than her years, with a fresh-faced beauty, intense eyes and dark hair tumbling over slender shoulders. Several patrons in the venue were openly eyeing her. Lamont shot each a vicious look, making them look away.

'Can I get some wine?' Marika asked.

'No. You're sixteen.'

'Why bother bringing me to this expensive restaurant then? May as well have bought me a takeaway.'

'Whatever. How's school?' Lamont ignored Marika's pouting.

'Boring.'

'Are you revising for your exams?'

'Yes. Every day.'

Lamont knew she was lying. Despite being bright, Marika spent more time trying to get out of school than applying herself.

'Take it seriously. Please. You can do whatever you want, with the right qualifications.'

'Is that why I barely see you anymore? Are you doing whatever you want?'

'I'm doing what I need to. You need to be better than me though,' Lamont sipped his sparkling water. 'How are things at home?'

'L, don't go there.' Marika shook her head. The waiter approached them to take their orders. They both settled for a pasta, fish and salad combo.

'I'm just saying. If you wanted to move out, I'd help you rent somewhere. You wouldn't even have to pay rent until you found a job.'

'Look, you're my big bro and I love you, so I'm not gonna mention the blatant disrespect you've shown Auntie.'

'You don't know what you're talking about.'

'Auntie told me about you threatening her before you moved out. Tell me your side.'

'You've already decided, so what's the point?' Lamont folded his arms, nostrils flaring.

'Cool.' Marika shrugged, and they sat in silence. When their food arrived, they kept their eyes down. Once they were finished, Lamont paid the bill, and they left the restaurant, walking through the city centre, particularly beautiful tonight, the moon shimmering amid the dark backdrop of the sky. People glanced at the striking pair as they ambled by.

'I don't want to argue,' Lamont finally said, breaking the tension.

'Me neither. Let's agree not to talk about home life.'

'I like that.' Lamont had a wide grin on his face now. He saw a movement out of the corner of his eye as a couple walked towards him. He was on edge until he recognised the man.

'Hello, Lamont,' said Nigel Worthington, his old coach. His eyes fell on Marika. 'You've grown up since I last saw you, girl.'

Marika beamed.

'How are you doing?' Lamont asked Nigel. He smiled at the woman by Nigel's side and she returned the gesture.

'I'm fantastic. This is my wife, Paulina. Paulina, this is a young man I used to train, Lamont, and his pretty little sister Marika.'

Marika's face lit up when Nigel introduced her. She made small-talk with Nigel's wife while the men moved a short distance away.

'How's it all going then?' Nigel asked.

'I'm living.'

'Looks like it. That's a very expensive looking outfit you're wearing.' Nigel gave Lamont a once-over.

'Look the part, be the part, right?'

Nigel nodded. 'That makes sense,' he glanced over at the women. 'I'm glad I ran into you. I always hated how we fell out. I was never trying to preach to you. I just wanted you to know.'

'I appreciate that.'

Nigel coughed, taking a deep breath.

'I walked your path. Long time ago, I was in those same streets, shotting poison because I thought it was all I could do. I saw the light after a while,' Nigel paused again, his dark eyes boring into Lamont's. 'I'm not trying to lecture you, L. Just think about what you really want,' he finished, heading back to the women. Lamont stared into space for a moment, shocked at Nigel's confession. It explained a lot. With another glance at the deep night sky, he followed Nigel.

* * *

When Auntie's home loomed into view later, Lamont tensed, but maintained his composure.

'You're not coming in are you?' said Marika, her voice quiet. Lamont reached into his pocket and gave his sister some money.

'Buy yourself something nice, sis.' He held her tightly.

'Can I see you again soon?' Marika said into his chest.

'Anytime you need me, I'll be there. I promise you that.' Letting his younger sister go, Lamont watched as she went inside, then turned to walk home, buoyed. It was important that he and Marika remained in a good place.

Lamont was almost at the corner of Hamilton Avenue when a black car pulled up next to him. The passenger window wound down.

'Are you Lamont?' A bald man said in a deep voice.

'Who's asking?'

'Get in the back. Someone wants to talk to you.'

'Who?' Lamont's eyes narrowed.

'If we wanted to hurt you, you'd be hurt. Don't be awkward.'

Weighing this up, Lamont climbed in the car.

* * *

The journey to the unknown destination proceeded in silence. Lamont had no idea who had summoned him. The driver and passenger looked solid. Lamont wondered if it was Marcus or Shorty's idea of a joke but when the car stopped at the iron gates of a mansion, he knew this was bigger.

After the driver spoke into a mouthpiece on the side of the gate, the gates opened and the car cruised in, pulling to a stop at the top of a long driveway.

'Get out.'

Lamont complied. The driver stayed in the car as Lamont and the lackey walked towards the front door and entered the house. The hallway was adorned with paintings. Knocking on a mahogany door, the lackey instructed Lamont to sit down, closing the door behind him.

A few minutes later the door opened again, another man ambling in, his large frame filling the doorway. He stared Lamont down, then took a seat opposite him in a regal leather armchair.

'You know who I am.' It was a statement, not a question. Lamont nodded. He'd recognised the man straight away.

'Who am I then?' The man barely spoke above a whisper. Lamont caught every word though.

'Delroy Williams.'

'Do you know what I do?'

'Whatever you need to.'

Delroy Williams controlled much of the local drug trade. He was a powerful man who had ordered people killed, even occasionally pulling the trigger himself. He'd moved to Britain from the West Indies, cutting a bloody swath through the streets as soon as he stepped off the boat. He was large and dreadlocked, with beady, piercing eyes, a bulbous nose and huge hands. He wore a polo shirt that stretched over a massive gut.

'*Whatever I need to*. I like that.' Delroy rose, heading to a drinks cabinet in the corner. He poured two glasses of brandy, handing one to Lamont.

'You wondering why you're here yet?' Delroy asked. Again Lamont nodded. 'You don't talk much do you?'

'Only when necessary.'

'Why?'

'You learn more when you listen,' replied Lamont. Delroy's eyebrows rose.

'I like that. I like that a lot,' he said, swirling his brandy around in the glass before taking a liberal gulp. 'I hear good things about you, kid. I knew your people.'

Lamont's stomach jolted as it always did at the mention of his parents.

'You look like your mother,' Delroy continued. Lamont nodded dumbly.

'I don't make it a habit to bring strangers to my home. I've checked you out though. You run that little team of yours to perfection.'

'I do my best.'

'Your best is brilliant. With the right coaching, you could be a big deal. What are you after?'

'What do you mean?'

'You went from selling ten pound draws to moving kilo's in what? A year? Two years?'

'Something like that.'

'I'm asking how far you want to go. You're a smart kid, I can tell that right off. You can make money doing anything, so why play the game?'

'Because what I do is the easiest way to win.'

Delroy studied Lamont carefully.

'I agree, and I wanna help you get there.'

Lamont was supposed to ask how. He didn't take the bait. Delroy chuckled.

'Work for me and I'll make you rich. I'll show you the view from the top and by the end, you'll be richer and bigger than me.'

Lamont saw the satisfaction on Delroy's face. He wondered how many greedy youngsters had swallowed what he told them hook, line and sinker. He sensed the malice in the older man's eyes, easily making up his mind.

'I appreciate the offer. Meaning no disrespect, I'm happy with how things are going for me right now.'

The smug look hadn't left Delroy's face, but his eyes hardened. Lamont knew of how dangerous the answer was, but had his principles. He wouldn't work for anyone else. *Even Reagan worked for someone else*, Lamont thought to himself with a certain satisfaction.

'Maybe you need a little incentive,' Delroy stood in front of a painting. Moving it aside, he revealed a wall-safe and typed a combination on the keypad with his fat fingers. Removing a stack of money, he locked the safe again. 'Ten grand. Call it a signing-on fee.'

'It's generous,' Lamont admitted. 'I can't accept it though.'

Delroy's eyes narrowed. 'Don't you like money?'

'I love money. I just love control more,' said Lamont. Delroy eyed him.

'Man to man, I have to respect your decision,' Delroy scratched the underside of his beard. 'Tell you what though . . . I have something that I know you'll take. Wait here.' Delroy left the room again. He sauntered back into the room with a box and handed it to Lamont. 'Open it.'

Lamont took the box. When he saw what rested there, he couldn't speak. Delroy watched him closely.

'Take it you recognise that?'

In the box was an old gold watch. It was more weathered than the last time Lamont had seen it. He nodded, feeling a lump in his throat.

'Me and your pops respected each other. I know he always wanted to give that to you.'

Lamont wanted to ask how Delroy had procured the watch but it didn't matter. When Lamont was younger, his father had promised he would give him the watch one day, but Auntie gave it to one of her boyfriends after his death.

'Thank you,' Lamont said, his voice more of a croak, eyes wet.

'Take it. Take the money too,' Delroy urged. Picking up the box containing the watch, Lamont stood, facing Delroy and holding out his hand.

'Thank you.'

Delroy nodded, mirroring the seriousness.

'You're a good kid . . .' he hesitated. 'My man will drop you where you need to go.'

* * *

That night Lamont lay in bed fingering the watch. He didn't think the gesture had been made out of kindness but right now he didn't care. Slipping the watch onto his wrist, Lamont smiled to himself. He couldn't explain it, but it felt good. The watch was loose, but he would get it resized. He felt a deep euphoria within, as if he had crossed some mythical line. Drifting into an easy sleep, Lamont felt truly happy for the first time in years.

The next morning, Delroy's people knocked and delivered the ten thousand pounds he'd turned down. He hadn't shown them where he lived.

CHAPTER FIFTEEN

Thursday 17 June 1999

LAMONT PAID for a brandy and coke, navigating his way across the room to Xiyu.

'What's up then?' Lamont asked. Xiyu had called, asking Lamont to meet him at the pub again. Like last time, it was packed, and Lamont was already wondering if it was worth investing in a pub in the city centre. He resolved to speak with Martin.

Xiyu was by himself, no women in sight. He was slightly hunched, and seemed to be avoiding the crowds. It was a direct contrast to their last meeting.

'Is business going well?'

'Business?' Lamont frowned. Xiyu scooted closer.

'I know what you do, L.'

Without warning, Lamont gripped Chink's shirt.

'What's your game? Are you grassing?'

'Course not,' Xiyu jerked away. 'Look, people talk. You're the man, and Martin's been dressing better. Obviously, he's making good money.'

Lamont nodded.

'Sorry for gripping you. Go on.'

'I want to borrow some money.'

'Are you in trouble?'

Xiyu shook his head.

'I'm not, L. Honestly.'

Lamont sipped his drink.

'How much?'

'Five thousand pounds.'

Lamont didn't immediately respond, watching Xiyu's fingers tighten around his pint. He admired his friends composure. If he knew what Lamont did, it was likely he knew about Shorty, K-Bar and the others too.

'That's a lot of textbooks.'

'I'm sure it is, but that's not what I want the money for.'

'Are you going to tell me what you do want the money for, or would you like me to guess?'

'I want to invest in some nightlife.' Xiyu didn't go into detail, but it intrigued Lamont.

'You'll have to be more specific.'

'I've been doing some experimentation in the clubs, and I believe I've found an easy resource that can be tapped to make us both money.'

'What kind of explanation is that?' said Lamont with a laugh. Xiyu grinned.

'I wouldn't ever mess with your money, L, but I can do this. There's money to be made on the club scene and I'm the man to make it.'

'When did you start hustling?'

Xiyu shook his head. 'I'm just someone who knows what he wants in life and is willing to take multiple pathways to get there. If you lend me the money, you'll get it back plus an extra ten percent.'

'When would I get it back?'

'Within a month.'

'And if you can't do what you think you can do?'

Xiyu met Lamont's eyes. 'I can do it.'

Lamont weighed it over. Five thousand pounds wouldn't leave him in any debt, and something in Xiyu's manner made Lamont confident. If there was another easy outlet for profit, Lamont needed to risk it.

'When do you need the money?'

'Whenever you can get it to me.'

'Take my address. Come tomorrow after seven. I'll have the money. I hope that this hunch of yours pays off,' Lamont said, studying Xiyu. The meaning was clear.

'I wouldn't ask if I wasn't positive,' said Xiyu, smiling widely again. 'Let's get another drink, and I can tell you more about it.'

* * *

SUNDAY 4 JULY 1999

Lamont stifled a yawn as the black cab pulled up outside his home. When he'd paid the driver and retrieved his luggage, he headed inside. Deciding to take care of unpacking later, he went to the kitchen and made a cup of tea. He drank it standing at the counter, reaching for his mobile to call Shorty.

'I'm back,' he said as his friend answered.

'Good to hear from you, blood. Pass through to my place anytime. I'm not going nowhere.'

Finishing his drink, Lamont made a quick meal, and had a shower. He dressed in a tracksuit, then drove over to Shorty's spot. The smell of weed stung his nostrils as he walked into the living room.

Shorty was slouched in front of the TV, staring at the screen as he puffed on a spliff. He had his feet on the coffee table next to a selection of mobile phones. He slapped Lamont's hand in greeting.

'Yes, L! What was it saying over there? How did you get back from the Airport?'

'Greece is all right, actually. I met some good people over there. You should head out for a trip sometime. I just got a taxi home from the airport. Forgot to arrange some travel.'

Shorty shook his head. 'I would have got one of the youths to pick you up if you'd let me know. Those black cabs are expensive.'

'Don't worry about it. I'm here now, so it's cool. How are things?' Lamont had left Shorty in charge for the week while he went to Greece. It was his first time leaving the country, and he'd enjoyed the experience. Shorty shrugged.

'Dead really. There was drama, but none of our people were involved.'

'What sort of drama are we talking about here?'

'Reagan killed someone. Out in public too. Blew this guys head off because he owed a chunk of money and apparently made it clear he wasn't paying. Police picked up Reagan and everything, but he had an alibi.'

Lamont's mouth tightened. His hatred for Ricky Reagan had never abated, and Lamont doubted it ever would. Even the thought of him brought back memories of his half-naked body pressed against Rochelle's in the doorway, and his parting words of disrespect to Lamont. It had been over two years, but those feelings lingered.

'Weren't there any witnesses?'

'Course. None of them were gonna testify though. Delroy would kill their whole families.'

'Business still strong?' Lamont changed the subject.

Shorty grinned. 'We're selling out everywhere. People can't take our product quick enough. K-Bar's got some new links out near Halton Moor, and they're begging him to get more product!'

Lamont was pleased, but concerned by Shorty's words. Their explosion had come out of nowhere. At one point they were growing in stature and gaining more clientele, then suddenly they had exploded into one of the largest teams on the streets.

They'd ramped up, with Shorty building up an army of runners and lieutenants, meaning less moving around for he and Lamont. He oversaw the streets and Lamont oversaw him and K-Bar. The pressure rose at the same time, and their growth was putting a spotlight on the team; a spotlight that led to increased police activity, among other potential threats.

'Make sure he's taking it easy. Make sure everyone is actually. Things are going well. We don't want to mess that up.'

'L, don't worry, bro. Things are cool. Now, take a fucking seat, stop being a baby and tell me about Greece. I know you got laid over there!'

* * *

Days after Lamont's return from Greece. He, Shorty and K-Bar went for food. They spoke as they ate, discussing the streets. People were still buzzed from Reagan's arrest, and the summer had everyone out to prove a point.

'Next reload is coming in on Thursday. Make sure you give more to Shane's lot. They moved loads last week. Think they've got some crews buying wholesale, so we'll take advantage of that.'

'Cool.'

Shorty wiped his mouth after finishing his food.

'What about Blanka? He's making a lot of noise.'

Blanka was named after the *Street Fighter* character. He was erratic, but had solid connections and a good supply. Lamont had heard his name before, hearing he treated his team badly and kept most of the profits for himself. Because of his reputation however, people gave him a wide berth.

'Blanka is a machine,' said K-Bar. 'Remember when Bali tried to take him out last year? He's been on the run ever since.'

'Bali was a dickhead, K. He had sloppy people trying to do the job. That whole situation made Blanka look better than he was. It helped his rep. His whole team hates him, and he's been slapping the wrong people around.'

'You want to take him out?' Lamont asked, scratching the under-side of his jaw. He could see the merit, as removing Blanka would increase their reputation and their market share. With Blanka's antics however, he was almost definitely a police target, and if they linked their team to his murder, it would mean more negative attention.

'Yeah, I'm ready to bump with him. Me and K could get the job done.'

'You could, but it's a big risk. Police are watching, waiting for us to mess up.'

'Get Marcus to do it then. He's built up a team of wolves. They'd do this easy.'

Lamont considered this. It wasn't a bad plan. Marcus was still involved in robberies, but he had diversified into other areas, and his team had adapted with him. He had several young killers who would do whatever he ordered without fail, and wasn't afraid to use them when necessary. Lamont mulled it over, feeling Shorty and K-Bar's eyes burning into him. He would not rush his decision though, and it was after a few minutes of silence that he finally decided.

'Speak to Marcus. Set it up and sort out a price. Treat it like a proper job, give him the right instructions and get it done. Reach out quietly to Blanka's number two guy and offer him money to sell out Blanka. If he says no . . .' Lamont let the words hang, but the meaning was clear to both Shorty and K-Bar, and they wore matching grins.

'Blood, it's already done. We'll sort all of this, don't worry.'

After the meal, Lamont headed home. The life was hotting up, and he needed to make sure he was ready to move. Shorty and K-Bar were out to make waves, and Lamont would need to keep them in line.

* * *

THURSDAY 7 JULY 1999

Lamont was slouched in front of the TV when his phone buzzed on the coffee table. Lazily picking it up without even checking who it was, he answered.

'L, are you at home?' Xiyu sounded breathless.

'Yeah. Is something wrong?' Lamont sat up now.

'I need to come and see you. Is that cool?'

'Course it is. I'll leave the door open.'

Less than ten minutes later, Xiyu bounded into the house, carrying his rucksack and two containers of coffee. He offered one to Lamont and greedily sipped at the other one. Lamont watched, disgusted.

'You could at least let it cool down.'

'I don't want it to cool down. Strike while the iron's hot. Drink while the coffee's hot. The two together.'

'Whatever, *Sun Tzu*. What was so urgent? You sounded like you were getting a blow job on the phone.'

'You might want to give me one when you find out what I've got for you.' Xiyu bounced on the soles of his feet. He wore a lightweight black jacket, jeans and shoes. Lamont wondered if he was going out tonight. Or, if he had been out already.

'I strongly doubt that anything you say could push me to those levels,' Lamont shook his head. 'What's up?'

Xiyu opened his bag and handed a brown envelope to Lamont. Lamont sifted through, surprised to see a bundle of neat twenty and fifty-pound notes. He fingered a few, tickled to see that all the queens heads were facing the same way.

'How much is here?'

'Six grand. I paid extra on top of the agreed amount.'

'I only gave you the money the other week. What the hell did you do?'

'I invested it like I said I would. Put some product out in the clubs. The money helped pay off a few of the little bouncer firms; the rest took care of itself.'

Lamont gazed from the money, to Xiyu. The club scene wasn't easy. Lamont had made a few feelers after he started dealing with Bill, but no one seemed able to handle it.

'How solid is your team?'

'Watertight. Everyone knows their role. I've been cultivating people for a while now. All that was missing was the money. Even after paying everybody off, I've cleared nearly ten thousand pounds. I'm going to flip that now.'

'What are you moving?' Lamont was wary talking drugs in his house, but enthusiasm won over.

'Everything I can. I have reliable clientele in the clubs. Not like the lagging crackheads on the streets. These are working guys; they're dependable, with good jobs. They don't want the aggro. They just wanna do business. Isn't that what it's about?'

Lamont nodded, looking down at the money again, doing calculations in his head.

'Xiyu, I think we need to have a talk . . .'

CHAPTER SIXTEEN

Saturday 10 July 1999

'I DON'T LIKE IT.'

'What's not to like?'

Shorty and Lamont were driving from a meeting, waiting in traffic. Lamont had mentioned Xiyu, and the money he'd made for them. The discussion had continued ever since. The car they were driving, a tidy grey Alfa Romeo, had been rented specifically for the trip. Neither wanted the police getting too familiar with their cars.

'Chink is legit. He's not dirty like us.' Shorty turned up the *Jay-Z* track pumping through the speaker. Lamont turned it back down.

'Why do you call him *Chink*?'

'Because. He's Chinese.'

'So if he called you *nigger*, you'd be okay with that?'

The lights changed to green. Shorty beeped at the Vauxhall in front of them to hurry.

'If he dropped the n-bomb, I'd smack his fucking face off. Fact is, I don't like it.'

'He made us six grand. In a few weeks. Think of the return if we gave him more money.'

'Why are you talking about *we* like you haven't already decided?' Shorty scowled.

'I haven't decided anything. I'm talking it over with you.'

'You don't need to. Do what you wanna do.'

'I want to know why you have a problem with it.'

'I have a problem with Chink. Like I said, he's not dirty like us,' Shorty repeated.

'What the hell does that mean? Is that a race thing again?'

Shorty shook his head as he swerved into the next lane, cutting off the driver behind him. It was a tactic he undertook now and then to ensure he wasn't being followed.

'We're grinders. We came up hard and that's why we're doing this. Chink is a little Uni punk. He's not built for this life.'

'Yet, he made six grand for us. Six grand in a few weeks, with no extra help. Why can't you see the potential in that?'

Shorty made a face, 'It's only six bags. Big deal. We make more than that daily. Much more.'

'Yes, but now we have another source of income, one that we don't have to do any groundwork for, because Xiyu did it for us. The club scene isn't easy. He's navigating it and that means a whole different type of customer. A more reliable, clean cut type.'

Shorty sucked his teeth but didn't reply.

'Shorty, this is a good move. At least consider it. If it doesn't work out, we don't lose much.'

'We lose money if he flops. When he flops.'

'Like you said though, we make more than that already,' Lamont reminded him, laughing. Shorty didn't reciprocate.

'I don't trust him.'

'Trust me. I've never steered you wrong yet, and I have a good feeling about this. It could take us to the next level.'

Shorty shrugged. They were approaching the city centre now. The music volume had increased again, but Lamont didn't mind. If it helped placate Shorty, he was fine with it.

Lamont wondered what he'd missed with Xiyu and Shorty. He'd hung out with both, but time spent with Shorty normally involved running around the streets, playing football. Lamont's time with Xiyu consisted of playing chess and practising maths for fun. It had been a weird balance but seemed to have worked out.

Lamont wondered if it was simple jealousy that was affecting Shorty's decision.

'Do you want me to arrange a meeting with Xiyu so he can explain the plan to you?'

'Nah, if you wanna deal with him, then do it. I'm down with you but I ain't gotta like that Chinky motherfucker and I don't. First time he messes up, he can fuck off back to those little puffs he goes Uni with.'

Lamont laughed again. Shorty was hilarious when he was grumpy.

'Let's get you some food and put a smile on your face. I'm buying.'

* * *

Lamont parked his car on Chapeltown Road, smoothing the folds of his jacket and walking towards the barber shop. The sign gleamed, but there was a sense of foreboding as he approached the shop. Lamont ignored the feeling and stepped inside. He hadn't been in a while, but it still reeked of sheen, hair grease, and a lingering fast food smell.

There were three ripped barber seats, unkempt and barely held together. The wooden seating area looked uncomfortable, and there wasn't a customer in sight.

'Lamont Jones, is that you?' Trinidad Tommy came from the back, limping toward Lamont. The pair shook hands. Trinidad didn't look like he'd aged in the few years it had been since Lamont had seen him. He was balding, but his skin shone and he looked healthier than some younger people Lamont knew. His grip was like rock. The strength never left some people.

'Nice to see you, Trinidad.'

'You too, you too. I haven't seen you in a long time, but you've grown up good. You favour your mother.'

Lamont swallowed a lump in his throat at the mention of his mother.

'Thank you.'

'Are you wanting a trim?' Trinidad half-heartedly gestured to one of the barber chairs. Lamont slid into the seat, instructing Trinidad to shape him up.

'How are you doing then?' Trinidad asked, combing out Lamont's hair before he shaved it.

'I'm doing well. In fact, when you're finished, I want to talk with you. Cool?'

Trinidad frowned, but nodded. When he'd finished Lamont's hair and cleaned him up, they went into the kitchen area. Trinidad sat down, Lamont remained standing.

'What's the problem?'

'I've heard about your money troubles,' Lamont said. Trinidad scowled.

'People shouldn't be telling tales. My problems are my own, and I'll sort them myself.'

'What do you need?'

'I don't need anything, Lamont. I've never needed anything. I've worked hard, looked after myself my whole life. I'll make it through this.'

'Trinidad,' Lamont looked at the wizened barber, holding his stare until the man looked away. Trinidad had known Lamont Jones since he was a child, and he'd never known him to exhibit such a quiet intensity.

Trinidad had heard rumours about what Lamont was into, and that he was doing very well. Looking at him now, it wasn't a surprise. 'I want to help you. I understand you're proud, but I'm asking you what you need, and I want an answer.'

Trinidad swallowed, sighing. 'I need ten thousand pounds to get the creditors off my back.'

Lamont scratched the scar on his chin, silently staring into space. Trinidad watched, not knowing what to do. Finally, Lamont smiled.

'I want to be partners with you.'

'Excuse me?'

'I want us to go into business. I'll give you twenty thousand pounds. Ten, you can use to pay what you owe. The other ten will be an investment. We'll breathe some life into your business and work together to grow.'

'Is this a joke?' Trinidad's eyes narrowed.

'I don't joke about money, Trinidad. We can draw up an official contract, but I'm deadly serious about this.'

Shaking his head, Trinidad smiled and shook hands with Lamont.

'I agree.'

* * *

'What's the plan here, L?'

Lamont and Shorty were at the barbers, sitting in Lamont's new office. In the background, they could hear the hammering and drilling as the contractors worked on renovating the premises. The office had been completed first at Lamont's request, and he was looking forward to filling the space with his own belongings.

'You'll need to be more specific,' replied Lamont, staring around the room, envisioning what he would put where.

'Why did you invest twenty bags in this piece-of-shit barbers?'

'Because, Trinidad needed help for starters, and I think some businesses are important in Chapeltown. A barber shop is one of them. Another reason is the money factor.'

'What do you mean by that?'

'We're growing. Our crew is already one of the biggest in the streets. It's only a matter of time before people look at us, and we have to be able to justify the money. Investing in a cash-rich business like this place is smart. I've been working with that white dude Xiyu put me onto, and he's helping me move my money around. There's more to life than buying new chains and clothes and cars.'

'Fam, look how we grew up,' Shorty replied. 'We were broker than broke. Now that I've got money in my pocket, you better believe that I'm gonna buy up everything that I always wanted. That's the Hood dream, L.'

Lamont shrugged. 'My dream is a little bigger, Shorty. And I don't want any police officer or person of authority to take my dream away from me whenever they wished.'

With that, the old friends sat in silence, listening to the work of the builders.

* * *

'We're here.'

Lamont and K-Bar climbed from the ride, approaching the meeting spot. K-Bar was armed, and his confident demeanour emboldened Lamont. The door opened as they cleared the garden. A man shook both their hands, leading them into the living room.

A few others milled around, glaring at the pair. Lamont held the eyes of everyone, K-Bar doing the same, until the men looked away.

'Clear the room,' Lamont said. They didn't work for him, yet didn't hesitate to listen, heading upstairs. The man they'd come to meet looked put-out, but said nothing.

'Is everything in place then?' Lamont asked Terry Worthy. Terry ran a hand through his slicked-back hair, making a sucking sound with his teeth.

'Blanka's proper paranoid. Doesn't know who he can trust. Spends most of his time snorting his own coke and snapping at people. His guys are looking to be led by someone else. A few are saying it should be me.' Terry puffed out his chest, smirking.

Lamont resisted the urge to laugh. Terry was a clown, but he was entertaining, and something often overlooked in this business of theirs. Terry was an independent dealer, but had links amongst Blanka's people and in wider circles. He'd been pushing to do business with Lamont for a while, and they'd fed him little crumbs, slowing introducing him to the plan to take out Blanka. He'd proved instrumental, and Lamont was good at keeping his ego in check.

'Do you want to lead?'

Terry shrugged. 'Sometimes guys step up, don't they? I mean, look at you. You came out of nowhere, and now you're top guy. Why can't I do it too?'

Lamont could have easily named fifty reasons Terry couldn't do it, but smiled. Terry was easy to control, and they only needed him a while longer. In the meantime, Terry had other links that Lamont had already started to plunder. His bank balance was increasing at an alarming pace, and a lot of it was down to the extracurricular moves he was making. Terry had unwittingly been a massive help in that regard.

'I'm on board with you stepping up. Spencer's in place and ready to work with us for now?'

Terry nodded. 'Spencer is a good lad. He's loyal when you give him reason to be, and Blanka has been taking him for granted for a while now. By the end of this week, everything will be in place, and he'll be gone.'

* * *

When the pair left Terry's and climbed into K-Bar's car, Lamont turned to him before he started the engine.

'Put a man on Terry, follow him wherever he goes. Until Blanka is dead, I don't trust him.'

'You've got it, L,' said K-Bar, before driving away.

* * *

WEDNESDAY 21 JULY 1999

Blanka was ready.

Nothing would stop his takeover. He'd seen the gaps for a while; weaknesses in the Hood infrastructure. There were a few established kingpins at the top. To topple them would take a lot of firepower and resources, which he didn't have at present.

Blanka had shown great patience in biding his time, building links, bullying those he could, and amassing money. He planned on waging war on a few factions that were getting too big for their boots, namely an organisation led by Lamont Jones.

Blanka knew a little about Lamont; he was supposed to be some kind of genius who everyone raved about like he was *Lucky Luciano*. He too had built his crew from the ground up and had solid people under him. Blanka knew about Shorty and K-Bar. The pair had earned their deadly reputations, but so had Blanka. He'd killed before too, and he'd do it again.

Blanka had told none of his people about the plan to take out Lamont Jones, unsure of whom to trust. He'd reveal it to them in time and put one of them in place to run the remains of Lamont's crew after he decimated them.

Snorting another line of coke and turning up the volume on the *Scarface* video cassette, Blanka wiped his eyes and reached for a bottle of water, chugging it before stumbling to his feet. He lurched upstairs to use the toilet. As he was washing and drying his hands, Blanka heard a banging noise from downstairs.

'Oi, what's going on down there!' He roared. He'd ordered two kids to cook crack in the kitchen, but he hadn't told them to have a party while they did it. When he didn't receive an answer, Blanka's nostrils flared. He hurried to one of the bedrooms, rooting under the bed for his equaliser; a Mac-10 machine gun with an extended clip. Making sure it was loaded, he hurried downstairs, noting the front door had been left wide open.

Eyes darting around, Blanka heard another noise and decided enough was enough. He began firing, hands jerking to keep the gun steady as he sprayed rounds, hearing the cracking sounds of bullets hitting walls, the churning of metal on metal. He paused, taking cover next to the door, then fired again.

There was return fire this time, bullets thudding around him. Blanka didn't know who was coming for him, but they would regret it.

'You ain't taking me!' Blanka continued to yell as he pumped out rounds. 'Come and take me head-on, you pussies! You think I'm scared?'

It was hard to see through the gun smoke and debris, but Blanka was sure he had more weaponry dotted around than whoever was out there. They were near the garden, but he had them pinned down. Blanka was so focused on the men in front, that watching his back hadn't occurred to him.

Marcus strolled through the back entrance Blanka's workers had unlocked, smirking at the sight of Blanka posturing like Pacino. He had all the time in the world to raise the gun clutched in his hand and fire.

Blanka screamed as the back of his leg seemed to explode. He lost his balance, and the gun tumbled from his grip. Blanka didn't have time to see who was shooting as two more bullets thudded into his back, dropping him. The last thing he saw was a smiling Marcus aiming the gun at his face. There was a bang and a flash before everything went dark.

Standing over Blanka's prone frame, Marcus shot him twice more in the head, then disappeared through the back again. He climbed into the waiting car, and Victor drove away. In the destroyed living room, blood seeped from Blanka, as *Scarface* continued to play out in the background.

CHAPTER SEVENTEEN

Tuesday 16 May 2000

LAMONT LEFT HIS HOUSE. A grey Suzuki jeep idled by the curb, and he climbed in the back.

'Moneybags, how you doing?' Marcus pulled away, the engine purring.

'I'm fine. Wish I knew where I was going though,' replied Lamont. All Marcus had said was that they were going to see someone. With Marcus that could mean anything. He stayed quiet as Marcus turned up the track. Marcus was heavily into his old school music, not that Lamont minded too much. It was easy to settle in and listen to *Rakim* blessing the tracks.

After a while, they arrived at a semi-detached home in Shadwell. Lamont glanced at the surrounding houses, wondering who Marcus knew in this area. He noted that Marcus had turned the music down and was tapping his hands on the steering wheel, almost as if he was nervous. Lamont knew they weren't going to see women. Marcus had dragged him to see them in the past, and there was never so much fuss.

'Right, c'mon then.' Marcus killed the engine and climbed from the ride. Lamont followed, eyeing his friend strangely. Marcus had his hands jammed in his pockets, and his face seemed tense. Lamont wondered if he was having problems with another crew. They knocked on the door which was answered a moment later.

'Marcus, good to see you.' A man smiled warmly at them. He was average height and build, with a lined face and salt and pepper hair. He led them to the sitting room. It was elaborately furnished, with thick carpeting and dark brown furniture.

'Drinks?'

Both men shook their heads. The older man fixed himself a glass of whiskey and sat in an armchair, his eyes on Lamont.

'Marcus has told me a lot about you. He wanted us to meet.'

'If you don't mind me asking, sir, who exactly are you? Marcus never said.' Lamont noticed Marcus tense up next to him, but the giant stayed silent. The old man seemed unaffected by Lamont's directness, smiling mildly.

'My name is Junior. I'm an old acquaintance of Marcus's.'

Lamont nodded. 'If you don't mind me asking, how did you make his acquaintance?'

'I import things. Marcus was introduced to me and we hit it off. He's mentioned you often. We figured it was time for us to meet.'

'What has Marcus told you?'

'He's told me you're the smartest person he knows. I have other sources too, and they tell me you're the future of our business.'

Lamont didn't respond straight away. He'd stepped up in the past few years, but he'd never met Junior, and was shocked Marcus knew someone he wasn't aware of.

'I see.'

Junior continued to smile. 'You're nervous. I understand. Your reputation precedes you, and I know you like things quiet. You have to realise that everything you do makes ripples. Blanka for example.'

Lamont was now paying attention. Marcus had murdered Blanka for him nearly a year ago, and the streets had been hotter than ever. The police investigated and kept up the pressure on the streets. Blanka had a reputation for violence, so there were many rumours of how he'd met his demise, and every crew in the area was linked to the murder.

The fact they found nearly a dozen weapons dotted around the safe house proved Blanka knew his days were numbered.

Lamont had spun a story through the streets that Blanka owed some Dutch gangsters money and was murdered because of this. The story gained traction, but eventually, people just stopped talking about Blanka and moved on.

Lamont took over his territory, absorbed his customers, and put one of Blanka's old workers, Spencer, in charge. Spencer paid Lamont sixty percent of his profits for the privilege and protection.

'Do you think it was handled badly?' Lamont was interested in Junior's opinion.

'Blanka's death was always going to cause waves. He was a force, larger than life to some. There is no way to quietly murder such men. He was a mad dog and needed putting down. Have you made the most of the situation?'

Lamont nodded, cutting his eyes to Marcus. The giant remained slouched against the wall, his muscled arms folded.

'Be careful. You're known now; people will seek to take advantage, and the authorities will be watching. I won't ask about your financial situation, but I imagine you're doing well, so let me give you the following piece of advice; diversify and don't let them come after your money.'

Lamont considered that information, sitting back and allowing Marcus and Junior to hold a conversation. He was making more money than he could manage. Some of it was lent to people at extortionate rates that they had to pay back. Most was invested into buying more drugs. He'd bought a stake of the barbers, and funded a few smaller businesses, but he lived in fear that he would lose it all, a fact Junior had cottoned onto immediately.

Lamont resolved to speak with Martin and his solicitor, and ensure everything was watertight.

* * *

'What did you think then?'

Lamont and Marcus were in town drinking beers. They'd gone to get some food after leaving Junior's, then Marcus suggested hitting the city centre.

'He's shrewd.'

Marcus nodded. 'He came up alongside Karma, Delroy and Mitch. You needed to be ruthless back then to survive, but Junior played them all and stayed out of the crossfire.'

Lamont lifted his beer. 'How did you meet him?'

'Did a job. Took something from the wrong person. Junior reached out, and I sent his guy packing. Gave him a few slaps and told him I was keeping what I took.'

'What did Junior do?'

Marcus grinned. 'He reached out again through some guys I respected, and they set up a meeting. This was in like 97/98. We spoke, and I guess I realised he would benefit me. I never gave him the work back, but I did other jobs he put me onto, and paid him back ten times over. He's given me money in the past, and even saved money and invested it. He's a good guy to know, that's why I wanted you to meet him.'

Lamont scratched his chin, glancing around the bar. It was fairly quiet, unsurprising as it was a Monday night. A few people having after work drinks were milled around, but nothing major.

'Has he ever advised you to invest?'

'All the time.'

'And?'

'And nothing. I like my money where I can see it. I don't know nothing about stocks and investments and all that shit. If I don't have money, I just go out and make more.'

'Is that enough for you?'

Marcus surveyed Lamont with a long look.

'Blood, I'm not you. I don't hoard money, because we're in the jungle, and I can always make more. Junior's been telling me about investments for the longest. He has loads of money but that's his thing. My thing is just to keep doing what I'm doing. When people step out of line, I show them. I enjoy spending money more than I enjoy saving it.'

The friends didn't speak much after that. Lamont understood Marcus's mindset in a way. It was similar to the mindset of other crimi-nals Lamont knew; they lived for today and barely considered tomorrow. Lamont had never been able to live that way, and he would not start now.

* * *

FRIDAY 18 AUGUST 2000

Lamont stared out of the taxi window as it pulled to a stop outside a house on Francis Street in the Hood. As Shorty paid the driver, Lamont surveyed the house, noticing the loud music shaking the ground. He didn't know whose party it was. Shorty had called, told him to throw on some clothes, and they were off.

'Shorty, good to see you.' A svelte woman in a t-shirt and equally tight jeans opened the front door. She kissed Shorty on the cheek before turning her eyes on Lamont.

'You too, Tash. This is Teflon.'

Lamont noted Tash's eyes widening. *Teflon* was a nickname Shorty and K-Bar had given him, mockingly proclaiming that nothing ever stuck to him, and that he was some wannabe Mob boss. Lamont had stopped protesting, mostly because he knew the pair wouldn't listen. It was a surprise that Tash seemed to know him though.

'Nice to meet you, Teflon. C'mon in, babe, have a drink.'

They did the rounds. Shorty knew everyone, and couldn't move without people stopping him to speak. He introduced Lamont and everyone that heard his nickname had the same awed reaction, following up with attempts to hold a conversation. Shorty left him in a corner saying he'd be back soon.

Lamont sipped the brandy and coke Tash had fetched, listening to the music in silence, tuning out the buzzing noise of the party. He didn't know how to interact with the party-goers. They were from the same area with similar experiences, but life was different for Lamont. He was different. Appearance wise, he dressed the same as many of the guys in attendance; navy crew-necked t-shirt, jeans and Air Max train-ers. His mindset set him apart though, and his cold eyes. Not that he knew that.

A movement caught his eye and Lamont noticed a girl dancing at the other side of the living room. His eyes were drawn to long legs that the tight jeans and boots only helped accentuate. Feeling his eyes on her, the girl danced a while longer, watching Lamont the whole time. He held the stare, a mirthless smirk flitting over his features.

She beckoned him over, but Lamont didn't move, killing the instinctive part of him that wanted to go to her. She took the hint, moving to him, ignoring the three guys who tried speaking to her on the way. She stood in front of Lamont, taking in his frame.

'What you drinking?'

In response, Lamont held out the plastic cup. The girl took a sip, wiping her mouth and giving it back. She'd missed some residue, the liquid hanging on her plump bottom lip. Lamont's eyes flickered to it.

'What's your name?'

'My friends call me L.' Lamont didn't ask her name. Part of him wanted to, but the past had him tethered, and he was different now.

'Okay, L. I'm Kim.'

Lamont smiled, but it didn't reach his eyes.

'Do you know Tash then?'

'We went to school together. Carr Manor. Where did you go?'

Lamont told her. He learned they had people in common and before long, an hour had passed. Lamont had finished three drinks and still couldn't see Shorty. Kim stayed by his side the whole night and even now she pressed against him, swaying to the music. Lamont blearily scanned the room, noting at least half a dozen guys glaring in his direction and grumbling to one another.

'Wanna come and have a drink at my place?'

Lamont needed less than a second to decide.

'Lead the way.'

* * *

Kim's place was a small, one-bedroomed spot near Roundhay Road. It appeared clean, with cream walls and bright furniture. Kim signalled for Lamont to sit down. She'd had more drink than Lamont, and this was evident in her movements. Without asking what he wanted, Kim came with half a bottle of brandy. She drank from the bottle, then handed it to Lamont. Kim clutched him tightly on the sofa, gazing through lidded eyes.

Lamont put the bottle on the coffee table, tracing Kim's jaw, drawing her even closer. His mouth covered hers, the kiss deepening. Kim moaned in his mouth, practically sitting on Lamont's lap as he clutched her body. His brain was surprisingly coherent, recalling the moves that worked for him.

Kim's moans increased, and soon Lamont peeled her out of her clothing, kissing her as Kim grinded on him, enamoured and wanting more. She tugged at Lamont's jeans and boxer shorts, devouring him with her warm mouth, causing Lamont to let out a hiss of pleasure. Her motions increased, the suction her mouth provided causing Lamont's body to jerk. Lamont collapsed onto the sofa, panting as Kim looked into his eyes, her mouth moist. Composing herself, she took his hand and led him upstairs.

* * *

Morning came, and Lamont's eyes slowly opened. He didn't recognise the room, but the previous night's actions quickly came back. Kim was fast asleep, her arm draped across his bare chest, her hair cascading over her face.

Lamont disentangled himself and quickly dressed, uninterested in a repeat performance. Without even looking back at the bed, Lamont made his way downstairs, located Kim's key and left.

It wasn't far to his flat, so Lamont walked rather than call a taxi. He was glad he hadn't been steaming drunk. His mouth was dry but other than that, he seemed to have avoided a hangover. He couldn't help but wonder about people's reactions to him.

As soon as Shorty had dropped the name *Teflon* last night, people had treated him with a certain reverence. He planned on speaking to Shorty and clarifying exactly what his friend had said. Putting all thoughts out of his head, Lamont quickened his step, looking forward to having a shower and going back to sleep.

CHAPTER EIGHTEEN

Saturday 2 September 2000

SHORTY AND LAMONT WERE INDOORS. A heatwave had recently hit
Leeds with a vengeance, and Shorty lay on the sofa with his eyes
closed. Lamont sat upright in his chair, apparently lost in thought.

'What time's the meet?' said Lamont.

'K'll be there now. It better go as planned too, or I'm gonna smack
up Terry.' Shorty didn't even open his eyes.

'Terry knows what he's doing. No reason it shouldn't go to plan,'
said Lamont. Privately, he was concerned. Terry had been cool for a
while after they murdered Blanka, but now he was overly cocky,
walking around the streets like he owned them.

'He's a flake. Always has been. Raider and them lot nearly killed
him after he flirted with Keisha that time.'

'Terry tried it on with Raider's sister?' Lamont asked. Raider was a
loud maniac, with a reputation similar to Marcus's.

'He's a clown. Watch he doesn't try that with Marika.'

'Rika would chew him up. You know what my sister's like,' said
Lamont. Shorty laughed.

'Raider's sis isn't all that, anyway. I tapped it last year.'

'Jesus, you need testing.' Lamont shook his head.

'How do you know I didn't use a rubber?'

Lamont glanced at Shorty. He had a small smirk on his face, eyes still closed.

'Did you?'

'She didn't gimme a chance. Got myself checked after though. Clean as a whistle.'

'For now.'

Shorty sat up. 'Fuck off. You need to get out there and start sampling these chicks.'

'Don't worry about me.'

'Are you sleeping with someone on the sly?' Shorty sounded interested now. Lamont just smirked, not bothering to reply. 'Tell me, man. I tell you about all of mine. Who are you fucking?'

Lamont was about to speak, when they heard a rush of quick footsteps. The door opened and K-Bar bounded into the room, panting.

'What happened?' Lamont asked, letting K-Bar catch his breath.

'Got rushed at the meet. Police licked us,' K-Bar pulled off his damp hoody and slid into a weathered armchair. Several of his dreads stuck to his forehead. Impatiently, he brushed them away.

'Did you lose them before you came here?' Shorty demanded. K-Bar cut his eyes to him.

'I was careful. Had to drop the pack though,'

'Where's Terry?' Shorty stood now, tense.

'He ran. All of us did. Everyone went in different directions trying to throw them off.'

'We need to go find him. He planned this deal. He needs to make it right.'

* * *

'Boss, I didn't know it was gonna happen either.'

They were at Terry's place, a spot he was renting in Chapel Allerton. It was a three-bedroom place, the living room hosting a gigantic flat-screen TV, along with a DVD player and the usual medley of action DVDs. Lamont glanced at a copy of the film *Commando*. Terry reclined on his cheap sofa, sipping a beer.

'We lost half a box, Terry. You organised the meet, and you were supposed to protect our interests,' said Lamont. K-Bar and Shorty brooded behind him, glaring at Terry.

'Half is nowt.' Terry waved his hand.

'We feel differently.' Lamont kept his eyes glued to Terry, who sat up, rubbing his palms on his trousers.

'It's your damn fault, so you're taking the hit,' Shorty cut in, tired of the slow dance.

'You what?' Terry frowned.

'Don't pretend you didn't hear me. K said you rolled to the spot in a Porsche. How hot is that?'

'It was a *TVR*. What's the big deal? It's a rental.'

'It draws attention, Terry. What we do isn't supposed to draw attention,' Lamont added.

'I've been doing this longer than you lot. I know the game.'

'That means you should know what you can and can't do. What we need to decide is where to go from here.'

'If you've got a couple more boxes knocking around, we can do the deal now,' said Terry. Lamont shook his head.

'We don't walk around with stuff—'

'—Yo, you need to pay back what we lost before you talk about more business,' Shorty snapped.

'It wasn't my bloody fault. Why should I have to pay for that?'

'Are you retarded, you forgetful prick? Didn't we just explain why?'

Terry turned to Lamont. 'Mate, call off your dog.'

Grabbing Terry by the throat, Shorty dragged him from the chair and punched him in the stomach. Terry folded from the blow, collapsing to his knees and dry-heaving.

'Shorty, that's enough,' Lamont pulled him back. Shakily, Terry staggered to his feet, pale and wincing. 'You want to do further business, Terry, you take the hit. Not us. You need to pay the difference, plus an extra two thousand, as a reminder not to mess up again,' said Lamont. Behind him, Shorty breathed hard, furiously eyeing Terry. Terry swallowed, his upper lip trembling.

'Fine . . . only because I wanna do more business with you lot though,' he glanced towards the door. 'Wait here and I'll go get it.'

Lamont made a decision right then. He would finish the deal, then he would distance himself from Terry Worthy. His help with Blanka aside, the man was a magnet for trouble.

* * *

THURSDAY 21 SEPTEMBER 2000

Lamont fiddled with the zip on his black jacket, looking both ways as he crossed the road and entered the Italian restaurant. He was shown to a table.

'Would you like a drink, sir?'

'A gin and tonic, please,' Lamont replied to the waiter. He settled back, waiting for the man he'd come to meet, to speak.

'Thanks for coming, L,' the man finally said. He wrung his hands together and took furtive sips from a glass of water. He was sallow-skinned, with lank black hair and a wispy moustache. His eyes were a washed shade of blue, beset with reddish, crisscrossed veins.

'You didn't leave much choice,' Lamont's tone was mild. Colin Leary was a former heavyweight. Once upon a time he'd yielded power within the Leeds night scene, using money earned from cashing in on selling ecstasy to set up a nightclub. People flocked and money flowed. Colin made friends with up and coming young gangs, allowing them to sell discreetly for a fee within his club. Everything ran smoothly until recently, where it all exploded.

Colin looked around the room, nearly jumping from his seat when the staff returned with Lamont's drink.

'Calm down,' Lamont told him. Colin rubbed the back of his neck, wetting his dry lips.

'They're after me, L. They threatened to chop my kid's head off if I didn't give them eighty grand.'

'So, why don't you?'

'No! I-I haven't done anything wrong,' Colin's voice shook, several tears tumbling down his pale cheeks. Lamont signalled for the staff to bring more water and handed Colin a tissue.

Colin had a point. All he had done was make friends with two rising hotheads, Parker and Blotto. The pair started out doing robberies, branching out to drugs, loans and whatever else they could get away with. Despite being reckless and temperamental, they made a cunning pair, skilled at staying out of trouble.

When a West Indian gang hailing from Tivoli gardens in Kingston demanded Parker and Blotto start paying a percentage of their drug money, the pair laughed it off.

A few weeks later, Blotto was leaving a restaurant with his girl-friend, when the pair were set upon by two men wielding knives. Blotto fought them off, but was stabbed twice. He lost a lot of blood and was taken to hospital. Parker refused to back down and shot up the house of one of the suspected gangsters. Unfortunately, he and his crew picked the wrong house, narrowly missing the six-year-old son of another Yardie, this man a known shooter.

Since then, the war had escalated, and Colin was forced into the conflict when his bouncers were shot at and jumped. He was also robbed and had his Porsche convertible set on fire. Parker assured Colin he would handle it, but he and Blotto were on the move, hiding underground and trying to plan a counter.

In the meantime, Colin was left in the open, easy prey for the Yardie gangsters. Colin reached out to Lamont in his panic, and here they were.

'That's the life we're in. Whether or not you've done anything wrong, you're involved. Guilty by association.'

Colin wiped his eyes. The waiters were hovering, but looked reluctant to approach. Lamont shook his head, and they dispersed.

'Can you help me?'

'How?' Lamont leaned toward Colin, his eyes never leaving the man.

'Talk to them, get them to leave me alone. You've got friends in that camp. I heard you do.'

'You know what rumours are like.'

'So, you're saying you don't?' Colin demanded.

'I'm saying, you're asking me to get involved in a volatile situation that doesn't concern me. Why would I do that? Would you?'

Colin didn't reply. Lamont steepled his fingers, letting the silence manifest until Colin couldn't stand it.

'What if I pay you? All you need to do is talk to the other side on my behalf. You don't have to raise guns or anything like that. Just, let them know we're friendly and that you're watching my back. I'll pay you ten grand.'

Lamont hid the smile that threatened his face, steeling his features.

'I want a piece of your business, and I want the names of the main people you do business with, along with an introduction.'

Colin's face paled further, if possible.

'Are you daft? That's worth loads more.'

'Depends on how you look at it. You approached me. I'm not forcing you to be here.'

Colin audibly swallowed, dabbing at his shimmering face with the same tissue from earlier.

'If I do all that, are you promising they'll leave me alone?'

Lamont met Colin's eyes again. 'I can't promise that, but I will intercede on your behalf, and I'll talk with the right people to get this sorted. In the meantime, we're gonna meet my associate, and I will leave you two to talk.'

Lamont signalled for the bill, still holding the smile back. Colin's misfortune would do wonders for Lamont's bank balance. As he paid, he was already ringing Xiyu.

CHAPTER NINETEEN

Friday 30 June 2001

LAMONT HUNG around across the road from an office building, checking his watch to make sure he had the right time. He jammed his hands in his jacket pockets, hoping he didn't look as nervous as he felt. When he saw a familiar face walking from the building, he headed over to them.

'Hey, Layla.'

'L?' Layla Kane looked shocked to see him. She was dressed in work gear; a simple blouse and trousers with a black coat. Her butterscotch skin seemed to emit an aura, and Lamont felt her presence. There was something special about her. It had taken him the longest time to realise it, but he was glad he'd reached out. Even if it had taken three years.

'How are you doing?'

'I'm . . . how did you know where I worked?'

Lamont winked, making Layla smile.

'I have my ways. I wanted to see you. Do you want to go for a drink?'

'I've been working for twelve hours straight, L.'

'Let's get you a coffee then.'

* * *

They sat across from one another in a cramped coffee shop. Lamont watched Layla sip her drink like she was dying of thirst.

'What the hell do they have you doing in that firm?' He asked.

'Too much. It's a nightmare. I work every hour of the day for very little money, on top of studying and prepping for exams. Doesn't leave much time for anything else.'

'I can imagine,' Lamont reached out and brushed his fingertips against Layla's palm. 'It's great to see you.'

'I have a boyfriend, L.'

Lamont didn't immediately pull his hand away, but he felt a jolt of something similar to something he felt in 1997. It stunned him. Lamont thought he had buried that part of himself, but here he was, getting in too deep with another woman who was too good for him.

'Do you love him?'

Layla laughed. 'Who asks a question like that?'

Lamont shrugged. She was right. It was a stupid question and the whole thing was none of his business. He was reminded of the last conversation he'd had with Layla, where she'd essentially told him to come and find her when he was ready. He'd taken too long though, and he was now painfully aware of that fact.

'Tell me about him.'

'Why?' Layla's brow furrowed, and Lamont couldn't blame her.

'Because I like you, and because you like him.'

Layla surveyed Lamont, but after a minute, she began talking about her boyfriend; how they'd met while studying, and how it was early days, but she thought he'd be good for her.

Lamont saw it for what it was. A sign that Lamont could never be that guy while he lived the life he did. He paid for her coffee, but knew he'd never seek her out again.

* * *

THURSDAY 5 JULY 2001

'So, we're gonna go out and have a big party in town.'

Lamont was sat on the sofa at Shorty's place with his arms folded, listening to his friend talk. He'd been rambling for ages, so Lamont was thinking about other things, namely the state of the streets.

Gunplay and gang warfare had broken out on a whole new scale. Several West Indian gangs were warring with several English ones.

Lamont had interceded for Colin Leary last year. Using Marcus and Shorty, he'd spoken with the aggressors, and they'd eventually agreed to leave Colin alone. Unfortunately, other conflicts had sprung up, and the people involved, didn't have Lamont's diplomacy.

'L, are you listening?'

'Yes, you're having a birthday party in town and you want me to be there. I heard you loud and clear.'

'What's the problem? Why do you look so emotional?'

'I'm worried.'

'What's new there then? All you do is worry, Teflon.'

Lamont resisted the urge to roll his eyes. He still hadn't grown used to the nickname Shorty and K-Bar had given him, but it didn't bother him as much anymore.

'The streets are nuts. There's the beef Marcus had with Mori, and now the Yardies are going crazy, shooting at people in broad daylight. There's tension. Don't tell me you can't feel it out there on those streets.'

'I don't care. Anyone comes for me, I'll drop them myself. You know I don't play.'

'There's no profit in it. We're here to make money, remember? Warring with Yardies who have nothing to lose is ridiculous,' replied Lamont.

'Yeah well, Ronnie and them other boys aren't gonna back down, so unless you're gonna weigh in and organise sit-downs, stay out of it and keep it moving.'

Lamont wished it were that easy. He had a bad feeling about the Yardies, and he was preparing for them to make a move against him. He was rising in stature and an obvious target. Lamont was careful about who he was around and had moved house to avoid anyone becoming familiar with his patterns.

'Just make sure you're prepared, Shorty. If things kick off, we need to move quickly.'

'Whatever. Can we go back to speaking about my birthday, please? How many people do you think I should invite? You know a couple' people will act proper emotional if they don't get an invitation. I want plenty of women there. Stace will come, but that doesn't mean I can't look. Are there any chicks you want there?'

Lamont shook his head, still thinking.

'Stop thinking about that war nonsense. No one is trying to mess with us. We're deep in the game, and we have the firepower to take out neighbourhoods if we need to. Make sure you're planning on fucking someone at my party, because you know women will be pointed in your direction.'

* * *

'You're worried then.'

Lamont and Marcus sat in Marcus's ride in the Hood. It was early evening, but the weather remained ridiculously warm. Marcus was shirtless, his muscled build on display, whilst Lamont wore a white vest and shorts. He was still sweating, and the heat was making him irritable.

'I don't understand why no one else is. The Yardies are coming after crews. People are getting robbed and chopped up. They don't care about the rules. All they care about is anarchy.'

'Do you wanna take them out?'

Lamont laughed. 'That's a great idea. Kill a few of them, then spend the rest of my life watching out for Yardie triggermen. It's nothing for them to sneak into the country and come after me.'

'If they try, I'll kill them. All of them. You never need to worry while I'm here.'

Lamont grinned. He and Marcus had an up and down friendship, but Marcus's loyalty had never wavered. He still went on robberies, but also had a few people selling drugs for him, so there was always money coming in. He wasn't in the same bracket as Lamont, but had enough for what he needed.

Lamont was constantly trying to get Marcus and Shorty to consider investing their money. They weren't interested though, so he left it alone.

'Yes Marcus!' A voice called out. Lamont looked to see who had spoken and his blood ran cold. He recognised the posture immediately, the wild hair and the scar on the face. The man slowed his Mercedes to a crawl and hopped out with the engine still running, music pumping from the speaker. Like Lamont, he wore a vest, his corded, wiry muscles on display. He looked at Lamont with cold brown eyes, then slapped hands with Marcus, who had climbed from the car.

'Yes, Ricky. What's happening?'

'Nothing much. Looking to chill for the evening. Just driving around trying to get into trouble.' Reagan's eyes flickered toward Lamont again. The two men stared one another down, neither budging. Marcus noticed.

'Ricky, this is my brother Lamont. People call him *Teflon*. L, this is Ricky Reagan. I'm sure you've heard the name.'

Lamont resisted the urge to cut his eyes to Marcus. He knew full-well Lamont knew who Reagan was. Lamont was sixteen again, waiting outside the door as Rochelle closed it on him to spend time with Reagan. His jaw tensed, but he controlled his thoughts. He wasn't going back. Lamont would never be that person again.

'Have we met?' Reagan awkwardly shook hands with Lamont.

'Years ago,' said Lamont. Reagan kept his eyes on Lamont a moment longer, then turned back to Marcus.

'Have you spoken to Lennox lately? I've been trying to reach him.'

'He's out of town. Should be back in a few weeks.'

'If you hear from him, tell him to bell me. Might have a job for him. In fact, you can take it if you want. Someone needs to go missing. Ten bags.'

Marcus grinned. 'I'll check you tomorrow and we can talk.'

Reagan cut his eyes back to Lamont, who hadn't stopped staring. The man who had been responsible for everything Lamont was now.

'Delroy's mentioned you a few times. He thinks you're the second coming,' Reagan's tone was hostile. Lamont wondered if he was jealous. Delroy hadn't slowed down his recruiting campaign over the years. Recently, he'd sent his son to talk with Lamont. Lamont had chilled around Winston Williams over the years, but it was so transparent that he was recruiting for his father. Lamont still wanted to work for himself, but Winston was cool, so he didn't make an issue.

'He's never mentioned *you*,' said Lamont. Reagan's eyes flashed, but he didn't move. His eyes flicked to Marcus then back to Lamont.

'I'll see you around, Teflon.'

Climbing back in the Mercedes, Reagan took off down the street. There was a short silence after he left.

'Fucking hell, L . . . I thought you were over that Rochelle mess?' Marcus, laughed. Lamont didn't reply, his attention on the spot where Reagan had stood, his thoughts filled with rage and a little anguish he tried pretending wasn't there.

* * *

TUESDAY 10 JULY 2001

'Would you though?'

Lamont closed his eyes. He was in another borrowed car with Shorty and they were waiting at some traffic lights for the light to turn green. Shorty was at the wheel, animated, bopping his head to *Mobb Deep* as he tapped on the steering wheel with both hands.

'It's not important if I would or not,' replied Lamont.

'For fuck's sake, L. I'm just asking a question. Why you gotta kill shit all the time?'

'Because you'll end up getting yourself in trouble.'

'I'm just asking a question,' Shorty repeated. 'Would you bang Bill's missus? Yes or no?'

'Fine. Yes I would,' said Lamont after thinking about it for a moment. Shorty laughed. Despite Bill supplying them with drugs, Shorty couldn't help mentioning his wife at every opportunity.

'I thought so! I've seen her looking at me like she wants a piece. I don't think Billy is hitting it right.'

'That's between Bill and his missus. Focus on business.'

'You need to have some fun once in a while. You're too damn seri-ous, man,' said Shorty, kissing his teeth. He turned up the volume on the music and rocketed ahead when the light changed.

It didn't take long for them to arrive at Bill's place. A few random faces milled around outside, staring at the pair when they pulled up. Lamont had seen a couple of them around before, but there were a few faces he didn't know. True to form, Shorty seemed oblivious, wading through the crowd like it wasn't even there. Lamont followed suit. No one made any move to stop them.

Bill's woman answered the door again, smiling widely. Her cleavage was prominent in her tight tank top, and Shorty openly leered.

'Nice to see you lot again. Bill and his brother are downstairs in the basement. I'll take you down to them.'

'You're looking sexy today,' Shorty piped up. She giggled, reddening slightly.

'Thank you. C'mon, before Bill comes up.'

They followed her down to the basement. Lamont shot Shorty a look, but he ignored him. Lamont planned to tell him to curb this one. Bill's woman was flirty. Lamont didn't want any lines crossed though, especially with the man who was giving them their supply.

The basement was already cramped. Bill's woman didn't hang around after showing them down. In the room stood Bill, Jonny, and two others that Lamont hadn't seen before. He didn't know what they had been talking about before he and Shorty showed up, but the second Bill saw them, everything stopped.

Lamont's instincts were going haywire now. He didn't know why Bill had requested the meeting but the whole setup was unnerving. He searched the faces of the men surrounding Bill and Jonny. They looked unfriendly, but they weren't giving anything away. Lamont forced himself not to look at Shorty, hoping his partner would be ready if things went bad.

'Nice to see you, boys,' Bill shook hands with them both. 'I wanted you to meet someone. This is Daz,' he motioned to one of the men behind him. Daz was taller than Lamont, with golden blonde hair, blue eyes and an easy demeanour. He wore a jacket over a t-shirt with some jeans and was beaming. 'Daz does a lot of business for me. He's one of my best.'

Daz nodded, almost preening at all the praise. Bill watched him for a moment.

'He *was* one of my best anyway, until he started shitting in the pot.'

Daz's face paled but before he could move, Jonny grabbed him by the throat and drove his knee into Daz's stomach. Daz slid to the floor, coughing and retching. Jonny kicked him repeatedly, spewing curses at him as Daz tried to cover up.

'Daz thought he could steal from me, and I can't have that. Do you understand?'

'Not entirely,' said Lamont. 'Are you trying to accuse us of something?'

The beating stopped. The whole room was silent, save for the whimpering and snivelling of Daz, crumpled on the dusty floor of the basement.

'Should I be?' Bill's voice was deadly.

'No, you shouldn't.'

'Good. I'm not trying to accuse you of owt. I'm showing that this isn't how to do business. Don't bite the hand feeding you. I've got a good feeling about you lot, but I'm getting old and sometimes I'm wrong. Had a good feeling about that one too.' Bill kicked Daz in the back.

'There's no mercy in this shit,' said Shorty, nodding at the beating in front of him.

'Definitely not. There can't be. I'm not a bloody soft touch and if I take a shot on some guy like Daz here,' Bill kicked him again, 'then I expect him to make the most of it. Not to cheat me.'

'That's understandable,' said Lamont. He understood the message that Bill was trying to share with him. Stepping forward, Shorty kicked Daz in the head and began whaling on him with hits. Jonny and the others did the same as Bill smiled with approval, looking at the scene like a proud father. He glanced at Lamont, who fought to keep his expression neutral. He wouldn't let Bill see that he had affected him.

CHAPTER TWENTY

Saturday 21 July 2001

LAMONT CLIMBED out of the shower, tripping over his own feet. He'd stupidly had a nap when he was supposed to be getting ready and now he was pushed for time.

Shorty had messaged him twice saying he was in the taxi. For a person who was always late, he was a stickler for the punctuality of others. Hurrying to the wardrobe, Lamont hastily ironed a white t-shirt and jeans. He wasn't sure which clubs they would end up at, so he opted for shoes. Popping his watch on, Lamont heard the taxi beeping from outside.

'Yes, L!' Shorty grinned, his eyes red and slightly drooping. K-Bar sat up front with the taxi driver. He nodded in Lamont's direction as the taxi drove towards town.

'How much have you drank?' Lamont asked Shorty.

'Half a bottle of Henny. Hit the fucking spot too,' Shorty replied. The driver frowned but didn't turn around.

'Make sure you get some water in you. If you start falling all over the place, I'm leaving you.'

'Forget that. I'm lean but I'll still out-drink you.'

The taxi let them out on Briggate. K-Bar tried paying the driver but Lamont cut across him, handing the driver a twenty.

As they approached the club, they heard the thumping sounds of Garage tracks along with the excited shrieks of the crowds. They headed inside; the atmosphere overwhelming. There were flashing lights, scantily clad women and enough goons to start a riot. Shorty was a thug, but he had charisma and people enjoyed being in his company.

K-Bar and Blakey had organised the party, and Lamont had paid. While Shorty began slapping hands and flirting with every girl in sight, Lamont hovered around the edges of the party, talking with the few who approached him. He was happy for Shorty to get all the attention.

'Why are you so quiet?'

Lamont smiled when he saw Xiyu walking towards him. He was dressed to impress in a plum-coloured shirt, blue trousers and expensive shoes.

'Finally, a friendly face,' laughed Lamont. 'How long have you been here?'

'Couple of hours. I had business here earlier.'

'Everything go as planned?' asked Lamont. Since bringing Xiyu into the fold, he had never failed to fill Lamont's pockets come payday. Lamont didn't know the specifics of what Xiyu did, but whatever it was, he did it well. Shorty and his clique still had issues with Xiyu, openly calling him *Chink* and trying to undermine him. Xiyu seemed to take it in his stride though.

'You're going to have another good week,' Xiyu winked.

'I'll need it after paying for this party.'

Lamont and Xiyu watched Shorty pouring champagne down his throat as the crowd cheered him on.

'He's living it up,' said Xiyu.

'He's earned it. It's his birthday party after all.'

'I hope he remembers he's representing you out there.'

'I'm not his boss.' Lamont looked at Xiyu.

'Whether you want to admit it, L, everyone knows this is your team.'

'I don't,' said Lamont. Xiyu smirked.

'Ask yourself this; does Shorty make any important decisions?'

'We make them together.'

'And, if it was just Shorty making them, would things run just as smoothly?'

'It's hard to say.'

'You're right, L . . . it's hard saying that I'm correct.' Xiyu took a smug sip of his Martini and Lemonade.

'I don't need to deal in hypotheticals. This is Shorty's night and short of getting locked up, he can do whatever he likes.'

'I thought Marcus would be here.'

'He's handling some business,' said Lamont. He said no more and Xiyu knew not to ask.

'How long are you staying out?'

Lamont checked his watch. 'Not too late,' he motioned towards Shorty. 'He'll probably be out until the crack of down. I'll be in long before that.'

'I'll probably finish this and go.' Xiyu motioned to his drink.

'Why? It's still early.'

'I haven't slept in nearly twenty-four hours, L. I just wanted to show my love to the *birthday boy*. I bought him the expensive champagne that he's currently spilling on the floor.'

'Just let him have his shine.' Lamont as always, played mediator.

'He's welcome to his shine,' Xiyu locked eyes with a girl walking by. She smiled at him and he smiled back. 'I'll get my own. Catch you later, L.' Xiyu moved towards the girl. Lamont chuckled to himself.

'Mate, don't you think it's getting crowded?'

Lamont turned to the sweaty man in the generic black t-shirt and trousers. His name tag announced he was the Bar Manager.

'Pardon?'

'The VIP. There's too many people squeezing in. Who is this guy? They're acting like he's a bloody pop star or summat,' said the manager. Lamont smirked at Shorty being referred to as *Pop*. He doubted Shorty was even aware how many people were trying to gain access. His tongue was firmly down the throat of a random girl. Lamont couldn't see Stacey, Shorty's girl. He wondered if she'd shown up tonight.

'I don't wanna jeopardise the licence if something kicks off,' the manager went on. Lamont tuned him out, thinking now might be a good time to leave. Xiyu and his companion had vanished.

At that point, Lamont spotted an older figure watching him from across the bar. He couldn't place the man, but there was something strangely familiar. The look on the man's face was speculative. He was tall and thin, with hard-faced features and cool eyes. A minute later he was gone, swallowed up by the crowd.

Lamont frowned, looking for K-Bar to let him know he was going when he heard a commotion.

'Get off me!'

A man was pushing his way through the crowds. Lamont didn't recognise him at first, but when he saw the jagged scar and the wild hair, he realised who it was. Ricky Reagan forced his way to the middle of the VIP section, eyes narrowed. Lamont wondered if angry was his default mindset or if it appeared that way because of his scarred face. Looking around, Reagan spotted Lamont and bounded toward him.

'What's happening?'

'Just having a few drinks. We're celebrating,' said Lamont. Three young goons appeared behind Reagan, each giving Lamont a hard stare.

'Can anyone join, or is it a private thing?'

'By all means, stay and celebrate.' Lamont said with a small smile. The previous meeting around Marcus had irritated Lamont, and he'd vowed to control his emotions around Reagan in the future. Reagan's face darkened for a moment, but he nodded and bullied his way to the bar.

'What is he doing here?' K-Bar appeared at Lamont's side.

'Looks like he wanted to party with his good friend Shorty,' said Lamont dryly. K-Bar chuckled. Everyone else seemed to have gotten over Reagan's brusque interruption, going back instead to having a good time.

Lamont's desire to go home abated. He ordered a bottle of water from the bar and chugged it, waiting.

It didn't take long. Twenty minutes later, Reagan stood near a booth telling loud stories to his cronies and a few stragglers. He was waving his arms wildly and gesticulating for effect. He knocked into a man walking from the bar, causing him to spill his drink.

'Oi, watch it,' the man said. Without hesitation, Reagan hit the man in the face. Lamont had a first hand-view and even he winced. Reagan was slim and slightly shorter than Lamont, but his power was evident. The man crumpled to the floor in a heap. Reagan grabbed a nearby bottle, ready to strike the man while he was down.

'Ricky, don't do it.' Lamont vaulted forward and got in Reagan's way.

'Get the fuck out the way, let me teach that bitch a lesson!'

'It's not worth the aggro. He's down, just leave it.'

'Is he your fucking man or summat?' Reagan shoved Lamont, causing an audible gasp from the gathering crowd. His eyes were red, almost popping out of their sockets.

'I'm just trying to look out for you. It's not worth the trouble,' Lamont tried again.

'Fuck you. I don't need your help. I ain't ask you to play *Mother Teresa*, did I?'

The crowd watched the exchange. Lamont stared Reagan down, the intensity from his gaze almost palpable. Reagan wiped his nose, more cautious now. His crew of hyenas grouped closer to him.

'Move,' said Reagan. Lamont ignored him. He saw the bouncers approaching behind Reagan, but then someone else pushed through the crowd.

'I know that's not my brother you're pushing.'

Shorty stood next to Lamont, his voice radiating complete and utter danger. He met Reagan's eyes, not backing down an inch.

'Stay out of it, Shorty. This don't concern you.' There was noticeably less bass in Reagan's voice now. K-Bar and Blakey stood with Shorty, eyeing Reagan's goons with disdain.

'If it concerns L, it concerns me. I don't even know why you're trying to beg it and be at my party, anyway. Fuck off.'

'You fuck off. Don't get lairy because you've had a few shots and a little dick rub, you little punk,' snapped Reagan.

Shorty moved forward. One of Reagan's hyenas blocked his path. Shorty caught him flush with a right hook so clinical it was heard over the music. He stepped over the crumpled thug, ready to rush Reagan, K-Bar and Blakey moving as well.

'Enough.'

Lamont didn't raise his voice, but it had the desired effect, and everyone froze. 'Back down. We don't need the situation getting any worse.'

Noticeably bristling, Shorty kissed his teeth but stayed where he was as the bouncers ushered Reagan and his cronies out of the section. Everyone stared at Lamont with awe. Most hadn't even noticed him at the party, and none had ever seen anyone impose their will on either Ricky Reagan or Shorty.

Walking towards the bar, Lamont got the attention of the shell-shocked staff.

'Champagne for everyone. Get that music back up,' he ordered, handing his black card to one of them.

* * *

'He's dead.'

It was the day after Shorty's birthday, and Lamont was lazing on the sofa watching him pace the room.

'Shorty, calm down.'

'Nah, he's dead. He violated. The guy was ready to fight you, and then he wants to step to me? I don't care about his rep. I'll handle him and his team. Me and K will do it. Or Marcus even.'

Lamont understood Shorty's frustration. He took his reputation seriously, and the fact Reagan had tried speaking down to him was a blow. Lamont was thinking about the bigger picture though.

'Reagan works for Delroy, Shorty. We can't go up against that power.'

'Course we can! Delroy's an old man. Reagan and his other son Eddie are the best he's got. We topple them, the other's will drop too. Delroy can get it too if he steps in, the fat prick.'

'You're not thinking clearly.'

'My head is always clear when there's killing to be done. You know that. Let me off the leash on this one. He tried to punk you too, remember?'

'He made himself look pathetic. He crashed your party, nearly got beaten up, then got dragged from the club. Think about it that way.'

Shorty didn't speak, his muscled arms folded as he breathed hard, nostrils flaring.

'Anymore drama from him and he's gone. You better speak to Delroy and tell him to get Reagan under manners, because it's open season right now, and people are being shot at for less.'

* * *

For days, Lamont considered Shorty's words, and hoped Reagan didn't do anything to make things worse.

So far, 2001 had been Lamont's most profitable year yet. Bill and Jonny were giving him more and more drugs and responsibility. Crack and heroin remained his biggest earners, but he made good money from other drugs too.

Lamont's investments were tiding over nicely, and he was in an excellent position. There was so much scope on Chapeltown at the moment though, and Lamont needed the gang wars to end. And quickly.

Lamont kept it close to home, working through his people, making sure everything was in place. Lamont had considered taking another trip abroad. He'd travelled a little over the years, but never for long, needing to be close to the Hood just in case something happened. Lately, it seemed that would happen more than ever.

Lamont's phone rang.

'Hello?'

'Ring me back from a phone box.' Shorty hung up. Lamont sighed and grabbed his keys. Driving to the nearest phone box, he put a pound in the machine and dialled Shorty's number.

'What's up?'

'Madness, blood. I was at Jukie's having a drink. Do you know Neville?'

Lamont did. Neville was a Jamaican who ran with a vicious gang. Lamont had met him a few times, but they'd never clicked.

'What about him?'

'He got stabbed. Some youths ran up and tussled with him, ended up poking him like three times. There was blood everywhere.'

Lamont's jaw tensed, and he clutched the receiver tightly. This wasn't a good situation.

'Is he dead?'

'I dunno. The kids ran off. The old man called an ambulance and people just dipped. I was the first guy out of there. I was strapped, and I wasn't waiting around for Police.'

'Wait, you had a weapon?'

'There's war, Tef. You need to get a weapon too and stop messing around. I'll check you tomorrow. I'm laying low tonight.'

There was a click and Shorty was gone.

* * *

After hanging up, Lamont made a few more phone calls to get an idea of what had transpired. It was early days though, and no one knew much.

Neville was alive, but was in intensive care, and no one knew if he would pull through. After mooching around for a while and stewing on the situation, Lamont called Marcus.

'I heard Neville's already dead,' were the first words out of Marcus's mouth when he stepped into Lamont's house later. He went to the kitchen and made himself a drink. Lamont trailed after him.

'He's still alive. At least I hope he is. Who did it?'

'I heard it was Brandon. You know the name?'

Lamont did. Brandon was a tearaway a year younger than Lamont, who was making a name for himself as a knucklehead. Lamont had heard his name in connection with the current conflicts, but hadn't paid him much attention. Everyone wanted to get ahead. It was hard to keep up with every new face.

'Why?'

'Dunno. Brandon's not as deep as you, but he's making good money selling crack. Maybe Neville thought he could set him up.'

'What's Shorty's relationship with Brandon?'

'They're cool. You know what Shorty's like. He gets on with everyone until he doesn't. Him and Brandon are basically the same guy.'

Lamont mulled this over. He was putting the pieces together in the way he believed an outsider would look at the situation. Neville and Shorty weren't enemies, but they weren't friends either and that would be enough to get people looking in his direction.

'I might need to reach out to some of Neville's people.'

'What for? Why are you taking this so seriously?' said Marcus, frowning.

'They're gonna blame Shorty and say he set up Neville.'

'How the hell do you know that?'

'Because it's too convenient. No one really knows how this crap started, but Shorty is definitely cool with the English lot. Neville's people are going to know this and they're gonna move against him. I guarantee it.'

'You don't think you might be looking too much into it, L?'

'Possibly. But, I'm willing to take the risk. I'll tell you right now that if a hair on Shorty's head is harmed, I'm in it. Whoever touches him, I'll wipe them off the face of the earth.'

Marcus grinned. 'I like the fire, L! When you get like this, you're like a different guy. Like when you boxed Tower that time. I heard he's still locked up.'

'Forget Tower. He's old news. I need you to come with me to speak with Neville's people.'

'Who we looking for then? Courtney?' asked Marcus. Courtney was Neville's boss, and was a cool guy to deal with most of the time. Lamont didn't know if that would be the case now though.

'Yeah. We'll take your car. Give me a strap too, just in case.'

CHAPTER TWENTY ONE

Monday 20 August 2001

IT TOOK a few hours and several phone calls to find Courtney, but they met him in the back of a house in Chapeltown. The spot was teeming with West-Indian men, talking in loud voices and eyeballing Lamont. He would have felt more nervous if it wasn't for Marcus's presence. Marcus strolled through the spot like he owned the place, daring anyone to say something. No one did.

Courtney was in the kitchen, talking on a phone, pausing every two seconds to shout at an older woman who stood over a stewpot. He signalled for Lamont and Marcus to wait, telling the person on the phone to ring back. Washing and wiping his hands, he greeted them both.

'How's Neville doing?' Lamont got to the point. Courtney's jaw tensed. He was a squat man, wearing a loose shirt and jeans.

'Bad. Doesn't look like he'll make it.'

Lamont glanced at Marcus, but his friend focused on Courtney.

'What does that mean for Shorty?'

Courtney rubbed his eyes. 'Was he involved?'

'Course he wasn't. He's had no dealings with Neville.'

'This boy Brandon though. He knows him?'

'I don't know the extent of their relationship,' said Lamont. Courtney smirked, but it was strained.

'You talk nice. Smooth. Women probably chase you down the street.'

Lamont didn't reply. Courtney took a sip of a foul-smelling drink Lamont hadn't noticed before. The old woman was still cooking, pretending she wasn't listening.

'My people think Shorty was involved. I can't keep them back on this.'

'Can't, or won't?' Lamont asked. Marcus straightened, his eyes hard.

'It's war. My people are getting killed out there. Brandon ain't the only one doing it. What am I supposed to think?'

'You're supposed to think that Shorty has nothing to gain from setting up Neville. There's a lot of money on our side. We don't need the drama.'

'No one needs drama. Sometimes we find it anyway.'

Marcus moved forward, scowling. Lamont waved him off, his eyes remaining on Courtney.

'Do your investigation. You'll find that Shorty had nothing to do with it. You have enough on your plate with Brandon and the others. You don't need more aggravation.'

'You threatening me now, boy?'

'My name is Lamont, not *boy*. I don't need to threaten to make a point. Enjoy your day.'

* * *

'You handled that well.'

They were back in the car now. Marcus was driving, his weapon within reach. Lamont had a pistol too. He was still getting used to it, but in the current climate it was likely necessary. Lamont didn't like how the meeting had gone. The Yardies seemed determined to blame Shorty, and he wondered if they'd orchestrated the attack themselves.

'You think?'

'No weakness. Those Yardies smell that shit. You handled it the right way. They know Shorty didn't have nothing to do with it.'

'So, they're looking for the excuse.'

'Course. Shorty's cool with the kids they're shooting at. It would send a message if they could clip him.'

'Shorty needs to stay hidden then. If he comes out, it might give them a reason to touch him. I need your people all over this. I know you've got connections amongst the Yardies, but I'll pay you well.'

Marcus shook his head.

'You're my brother. Fuck the Yardies. My people will be ready; don't doubt that.'

Lamont was relieved. Shorty and K-Bar had teams of shooters to call on, but Marcus's men were ruthless. If things escalated, they would need them.

* * *

THURSDAY 23 AUGUST 2001

Days passed. Brandon's house was shot at, as was his mother's house, and the house where his baby mother lived. Luckily, they were abandoned. The word was that Brandon had fled Leeds, avoiding the Yardies and the police.

Shorty was chafing under his forced stay, wanting to get back out onto the streets. Lamont had heard nothing from Courtney, but Marcus and his team remained on standby.

Lamont was at home flicking through the channels when his phone rang. It was Marcus.

'Someone sprayed one of Shorty's spots.'

Lamont sat up. 'Did they get anyone?'

'There was no one there. It'll be Courtney's people definitely. I'm gonna do some digging. Stay indoors and I'll have someone outside watching.'

Marcus was gone. Lamont sighed, feeling the beginnings of a headache. The Yardies needed to be dealt with. It meant wading into the war between them and the English youths, but Lamont didn't have a choice. He needed information. Taking out a spare phone, he dialled Shorty's number.

'Yo, L. I'm not waiting around like some little bitch doing nothing. The big man told me what happened. It's on.'

'Shorty, relax. This whole beef, what did it start over?'

Shorty kissed his teeth down the phone, making Lamont's head hurt more.

'Money. A few Yardie's were working with Keller and Mali. Summat went wrong with the deal, and Keller and Mali got ripped off. They tried getting their money back, but it didn't work, so they did a drive-by. It went wrong, and they hit the wrong guys. Suddenly there's a war, and no one's backing down.'

Lamont mulled that over. He'd heard about that shooting in passing, but hadn't known the specifics.

'And Brandon?'

'He's the hitter dudes were using. He disliked them Yardies, summat to do with how his dad treated his mum, so he was running around like *Rambo* doing stupid shit. Now, he's stabbed the wrong person, and he's on the run.'

'Didn't you consider telling him to stop?'

'For what? He's not a kid. He knew what he was doing. It was just a dumb plan.'

Lamont couldn't argue with that.

'Okay, Shorty. Let the big man handle this. Stay out of sight. please.'

Shorty grumbled before hanging up. Lamont drank some water, massaging his forehead. He knew why it had all started, and it was even more of a mess than previously.

The police were already making encroachments into Chapeltown. Lamont didn't want or need them poking around his activity. He needed to end the war, and he needed to do it quickly.

* * *

Marcus checked his gun, looking to Charlie in the driver's seat. He had his eyes on the road, totally in the zone. In the back, Sharma was ready to go. Marcus wished Victor could have rode with them, but he was still in recovery after a previous job had gone awry.

Marcus had spoken with Shorty, who all-but begged to go on the mission with them. Shorty was an excellent soldier, and they'd worked together in the past, but Marcus would handle this problem himself.

'I'm going straight for Courtney. Keep everyone else at bay and secure them in the room. If we're not gone in ten minutes, I've got a crew on standby, who will come in and spray the house. Cool?'

Both men nodded. They pulled up down the street from Courtney's spot. It was early evening and still warm, but there was no one outside to make an issue.

They headed for the garden, Marcus behind Sharma, Charlie covering their backs. At a nod from Marcus, Sharma kicked in the door. They heard immediate noise. Marcus surged through with his shotgun, hitting a man who'd tried going for a weapon. He headed for the kitchen where Courtney and another goon were having a conversation. The goon went for a knife, but Marcus was quicker, the butt of his shotgun crushing the man's jaw. He crumpled to the floor. Marcus aimed the weapon at Courtney.

'Sit down.'

'Tall-Man, what the hell are you doing? You can't rush into my house like this,' said Courtney, his eyes wide, locked on the shotgun.

'Sit down, or I'll sit you down,' replied Marcus. He heard scuffling sounds and moved position to allow him to see the door. Courtney waited a beat, then slid into a seat, his hands and lip trembling.

'What is this about?'

'Who sent shots at Shorty's spot? Mess me around, and we'll kill all of you.'

'You wanna start another war? You know who I am? You'll all die.'

Marcus's eyes bored into Courtney's. Courtney broke eye contact a moment later, sighing.

'We've known each other for years. You know how I get down, and you know I don't care who you send after me. Who sent shots at his spot?'

'Look, he's called Goodison. He went after Brandon's people, then he sprayed Shorty's yard. I didn't tell him to do it.'

'We spoke. You knew that Shorty had nothing to do with Neville getting stabbed, and you still went against me anyway?' Marcus cocked the shotgun.

'Tall-Man, please! On my mother, I had nothing to do with it.'

'You didn't stop it. Gimme his number and a location. Now.'

Courtney scribbled the address on some paper and gave it to Marcus. Marcus put it in his pocket, keeping his eyes on Courtney as he did so.

'I'm gonna take care of Goodison. You're gonna put the word out that Shorty had nothing to do with what happened. Understand?'

'You think you can tell me what's gonna happen? I am an elder, and you're a kid. You cannot come into my house and start telling me what I'm going to do.'

'If you don't, I make a call and put a kill-squad into play. They'll kill everyone connected to you, family or not. If you wanna do the same to me, then cool. I'm ready to die,' Marcus again met the older man's eyes. 'Tell me if anything in my face suggests I might be joking.'

There was a long silence, punctuated by whimpering sounds from the living room. Marcus tightened his grip, wondering if his team had been overwhelmed, and if he would need to fight his way out. Courtney finally nodded, letting out a deep breath.

'I'll put the word out. People will know that Goodison went into business for himself. We will not harm Shorty.'

Marcus surveyed the man, wondering if he could trust him. He considered just killing him right there, to send a message to the rest, but gave him the benefit of the doubt. He wasn't joking about the kill-team. They would murder Courtney's family first, and save him for last if it came to it.

'I hope we can work together in the future. Put your hands on the table.'

Marcus searched Courtney for a weapon, then checked the unconscious goon and made to leave the room when Courtney spoke again.

'What about Brandon? You protecting him too?'

'Brandon who?' said Marcus, leaving the kitchen. Half a dozen men were laid out on the living room floor, Sharma and Charlie securing them. Marcus grabbed their weapons and put them into a sports bag.

'This shit ends here. Me and your boss have spoken. Don't violate and make me come looking for every one of you.'

Marcus walked out first, followed by the others.

* * *

FRIDAY 7 SEPTEMBER 2001

Lamont was in the passenger seat as Shorty drove, rapping along to some mediocre tune that he couldn't get enough of. It had been a few weeks since the strife with the Yardies. Courtney kept his word and put it out that Shorty had nothing to do with Neville's stabbing. It had been touch and go, but the Yardie gunman had survived, and was now in recovery. Brandon was abandoned and left to deal with the Yardie's. His death was messy and highly publicised.

Lamont had spoken with Marcus, and they had organised a loose truce for now, both sides agreeing to back away. Delroy and a few other influential kingpins had helped to give it a sense of credibility, and for now, there was peace. Lamont didn't know how long it would last, but he was making the most of it.

Delroy had spoken with him a few days ago, wanting to know if Lamont changed his mind about working for him. He'd also wanted to make sure there wouldn't be any further problems between Lamont and Reagan.

'We're here.'

Shorty and Lamont climbed from the car, and Lamont followed his friend into the garden. They knocked, and Bill's wife answered, her considerable cleavage packed into a tank-top. She smiled at Lamont, but her eyes lit up when she saw Shorty. Lamont resisted the urge to roll his eyes when they hugged. He didn't know what they were playing at, but it was foolish.

'Bill's waiting.'

Lamont and Shorty made their way to the office, and Bill's wife returned to what she was doing after grinning at Shorty. Lamont elbowed him, causing Shorty to scowl.

'What was that for?'

'You know what it was for. Don't do anything that will jeopardise this arrangement. Please.'

Shorty kissed his teeth, shooting Lamont a dirty look as they knocked on the office door. Bill was alone which was a surprise. Normally his brother Jonny watched his back. Lamont filed that information away. Bill had his feet up, a beer in his paw, eyes on a large football screen. He didn't even move when he saw them.

'Nice to see you lads. Enjoying the weather?'

Lamont and Shorty both nodded. They didn't need the small-talk. Lamont had been wary of their supplier ever since they'd watched him beat one of his workers half to death. Lamont didn't understand why he'd wanted to send them a message, but he'd ensured that Marcus knew where the supplier lived, just in case.

Lamont truly hoped there were no pending issues. The supply was excellent; they paid promptly, and there was always a healthy reserve in case they needed more. He had other suppliers he could work with as a backup, but Bill and Jonny were convenient. He didn't want to ruin that flow if he didn't have to. Business had exploded, and everyone was making enough money to where they didn't need to kill each other. It wouldn't last. It never did, but it was enough for now.

'I don't like it when it's too hot. The missus always wants to go to the beach and all that crap. I keep telling her to just go on holiday without me, but she keeps talking bollocks about *romance*. Do you know what I'm on about?'

Shorty laughed.

'My missus keeps trying to get me to go away with her. No time for that shit.'

Lamont didn't reply. Women came in and out of his life, and he made no effort to keep them. From time to time he thought about Layla, wondering if he should have admitted how he felt. The fact she had a boyfriend irked him, but the man was lucky. There was something special about Layla, and Lamont knew she would go far.

'What about you, L? A pretty boy like you must have the women going crazy.'

'I'm afraid not. Just looking for Ms Right I guess.'

Shorty snickered, and Bill shook his head.

'Make sure you're not spending too much of all that bloody money you're making on them. Anyway, let's get to business. This shit with the bloody Jamaican lot. What's going on?'

'There was a beef between them. It was sorted.'

'So why were people shooting at your mate there?' Bill jerked his thumb toward Shorty, who had tuned out the conversation, watching the football.

'He was in the wrong place at the wrong time. It's sorted. That I can assure you.'

'Those guys are crazy. They robbed one of my spots and stole five boxes. That's five kilo's I now have to make up for, you know what I mean? I'm running a business, same as you. I can't be doing that all the time.'

'Bill, I understand your concerns, but I'm confused about why you're talking to us about it.'

'I'm talking to you because you're my link to those guys. When I hear about shootings and stabbings and people thinking they're gangsters and trying to do silly drive-by's, I'm gonna run it by you lot, especially if you're in the middle of it.'

'There are no problems anymore. It was a misunderstanding that spiralled out of control.'

Bill flicked off the TV, causing Shorty to kiss his teeth. He turned to Lamont.

'I like you, L. So I'll take your word for it. I'm gonna need you to take two extra boxes though, to help me out.'

Lamont and Shorty exchanged a look, then Lamont replied.

'Fine.'

* * *

'Shorty, find a buyer for the extra drugs. I want them moved as soon as possible.'

'I'll sort it. Do you wanna explain what that was all about?'

'The Yardie's targeted Bill, and he was sniffing around to see if we're involved.'

'Why would he think that?'

'Because the Yardie's are black, and we're black, so he's lumping us together. I don't know if he has any other black people he deals with, but he's assuming we're all connected. He gave us the extra drugs to see how we'd react. It could even be a sweetener so we call them off.'

Shorty mulled that over as they pulled up at the red light.

'Do you like dealing with him?'

'He's convenient. On a personal level, I don't like him, and I think he knows it. Speaking of personal, what are you playing at?'

Shorty cut his eyes to Lamont. 'What are you talking about?'

'I'm talking about you hugging up on Bill's wife and making eyes at each other. Have you slept with her?'

'Nah, we're just messing around and flirting,' replied Shorty. Lamont noticed he didn't meet his eyes though.

'Please keep it that way. I don't like to tell you what to do, but you can understand why fucking the wife of the man who supplies us might be a bad idea, right?'

'L, it's cool. I'm not daft. I won't mess with that woman. Stacey would kill me anyway.'

'Okay. Drop me at my place then. I've got a meeting with Martin tomorrow.'

* * *

'Everything is going well.'

Lamont sipped a cup of coffee and listened to Martin drone on. They were in Martin's office, and it was sweltering, the cramped quarters causing both men to sweat. On the desk between them were various pieces of paper highlighting profits and graphs.

'What about the houses? Are we ready to invest?'

Martin nodded. 'Are you sure about the location? With the way things are in your neck of the woods, investing in property may be a bad idea. You've got a bloody gang war.'

'The gang war is over,' replied Lamont.

'How do you know?'

Lamont had no intention of sharing this information. Martin was aware Lamont was connected to crime, but didn't know the full extent.

Lamont trusted Martin, and they had made money together since their initial introduction, but there was a limit.

'Just take my word for it. I want to invest in Chapeltown, so make it happen.'

'I will. You're the boss, and I'm here to help you stay rich. You're talking about a massive investment, however. You have a good thing going. You're invested in a few businesses, and they're steadily making a profit. The barber's especially has taken off over the past year. But, is it worth the risk?'

Lamont wasn't sure. He understood Martin's position, but he'd had the idea to invest in property over a year ago, and he'd taken his time, doing his research, imploring Martin to do all the legwork. Now, he could do so.

Lamont was investing over two hundred thousand pounds. This was a large portion of the money he had earned in his life as a drug dealer, and if he lost it, it would cripple the way he currently led his life. Martin was right to be cautious.

'Yes. It's worth the risk. If it works, it'll set me up for everything else I need to do. Is the company in place?'

'Yes. I've registered the company, and the office space and address are all sorted. Levine has looked over the figures and paperwork, and you can't be touched on this. Have you spoken with him about your plans to invest?'

'He's my solicitor, not my money manager,' Lamont replied. He had in fact spoken with Levine, and like Martin, the man felt that he shouldn't invest his money in such a manner. It concerned Lamont that two of his pillars were so against him doing it, but he had to try.

'Okay. I'll get the ball rolling and start buying up houses.' Martin wiped his forehead with a handkerchief. Lamont slid to his feet and patted the man on his damp shoulder.

'Stay in touch.'

Lamont left the office, saying goodbye to Martin's secretary. The suit he wore was too tight, but he liked to make the right impression when he went to see Martin, and blending in was essential.

When Lamont left the premises, he took off the suit jacket, then unbuttoned the top two buttons of his shirt and loosened his tie. A woman walking by smiled at Lamont and he returned it.

The rest of Lamont's day was free and clear. He needed something to distract him from Martin's warnings, deciding to get a drink. Heading to a nearby coffee shop, he ordered an iced tea and took it outside. He'd taken a seat at one of the coffee shop tables when he glanced to his left. He froze.

Layla was walking along the path, hand in hand with a smiling man. Layla hadn't seen Lamont, too busy giggling at her partner and leaning into him.

Lamont felt a rage take over him, the likes of which he hadn't felt in years. He forced himself to stay seated, keeping his head down and gritting his teeth as Layla floated by. He knew she had someone, but seeing it firsthand was something different. He wondered if seeing her was a sign he shouldn't invest his money. Layla had moved on, and Lamont fully knew that he could have made her his woman if he'd asked. Layla had liked him, but Lamont had been in too much of a funk to see what was right in front of him. Now it was gone.

He glanced up at them, watching them walk down the path, icy rage still filling his veins. Lamont's jaw clenched, and he sipped his drink to distract him. Nothing worked though. Layla was more beautiful than ever, and he didn't know if it was because he couldn't have her that he felt this way, but there it was.

Finally gaining his composure, Lamont dialled a number, holding the phone to his ear.

'Shorty? Wanna go out tonight? I need to drink. A lot.'

CHAPTER TWENTY TWO

Friday 17 May 2002

'ARE YOU ENJOYING YOURSELF, L?'

Lamont sipped a glass of champagne and smiled at Martin.

'Yeah, I'm good.'

Martin smiled nervously, drinking his own drink.

'Good. Tonight is all about you.'

'No. This is your thing,' Lamont insisted, taking another sip. He wore a light grey shirt with trousers and expensive shoes. His hair was neatly lined up, and he was clean shaven, save for his tapered sideburns and moustache. Lamont was the poster boy for a man who had made it. He had on a Rolex he had treated himself to, and some Calvin Klein aftershave. He felt fresh, but out of place.

It had been a long year for Lamont. The drama on the streets fluctuated from calm and happy to end-of-the-world critical. There was little middle ground, and some crews seemed to look for any reason to fight each other.

Lamont had focused more on legitimate ventures, making a great profit with his housing venture. This was only blighted slightly by a failed investment in a pub. On the whole though, Lamont had no financial concerns.

Martin had organised a party to celebrate their latest venture, a gym. Lamont didn't know any of the people Martin had invited. Apart from Xiyu, none of Lamont's people were there. He didn't know who to talk to, so he'd spent most of his time skulking in the corner, nodding to the music.

The party was in the backroom of a club on Call Lane. Martin had booked it and organised everything from the liquor to the DJ. Lamont liked some songs, but he wasn't feeling the vibe. There were women scattered around. Several had made eye contact, but Lamont wasn't interested. He wanted to be by himself, not surrounded by people he didn't know. He felt strangely flat. Xiyu had been next to him, until he had spotted a woman and promptly disappeared with her.

Draining his glass, Lamont placed it on the bar and made for the exit. Martin stopped him.

'L? Where are you going? You still need to say a few words.'

'Relax. I'm just getting some fresh air.' Lamont moved through the main room, nodded at the bouncers and stepped outside.

It was almost midnight, and the cool air was refreshing. Lamont leaned against the wall and looked at the sky. He liked the moment. The moon was out, but the sky was bereft of stars. Shrieking laughter brought Lamont back down to earth. Spotting the cause, Lamont froze.

She was more conservatively dressed than back in the day, wearing a pair of tight-fitting trousers with a navy blue top. Her hair was straight, just how he remembered it, and her face was flawless. She was laughing at something one of her companions had said. Maybe she felt his eyes on her, but she looked straight at him. Her mouth parted into an almost comical *o* shape. She stopped where she was. Her friends noticed. There were two of them. Both pretty. Both vivaciously dressed. Next to her, they were wallpaper.

'L?' She stepped toward him. Lamont did his best to look cool, but his heart hammered in his chest. It had been five years, but she looked as good now as she had then.

'Hey, Rochelle.' Lamont met her eyes, still trying to portray confidence. This was a woman that had seen his inner depths though. She had crushed him in a way no woman ever again could.

Lamont had often wondered how he would handle seeing her again.

He'd considered tracking her down, seducing her, leaving her in the lurch as she had done him.

Now though, face-to-face, he regressed back to that pathetic kid he had once been. Lamont felt the deep shame as he recalled the time he had stood on her doorstep, watched Ricky Reagan putting his arms around her. He could still see that door closing, and took a deep breath.

'What are you doing here?'

'I'm in there,' Lamont pointed at the club. 'We're having a party. It's a business thing.'

'*Business thing* . . . what kind of business thing?' Rochelle was trying her hardest to sound non-committal. Lamont sensed that now. He could pick things up in her body language that he'd been too inexperienced to pick up on before.

'We opened a gym. Guess you could call this a launch party.' It surprised Lamont at how easily his words came. He was on autopilot now. Her friends looked from the pair to each other, trying to work out what was going on. Lamont doubted Rochelle had ever mentioned him. *Why would she?* He had been unmemorable.

'That's great, L. That's really great,' Rochelle said brightly. Lamont noticed she still hadn't introduced him to her friends. He met their stares, then turned back to Rochelle.

'How have you been?'

'I've been well. Just working hard. You know how it is.' Rochelle ran a hand through her hair, then rubbed it against her trouser leg.

'Yeah, definitely.'

One of Rochelle's friends coughed. Rochelle picked up on it.

'Sorry. Lamont, these are my friends, Bronie and Tenika. Girls, this is an old friend, Lamont.'

'Old friend, huh?' Tenika looked Lamont up and down, her eyes suggesting that she knew exactly the type of friend Lamont had been.

'It's nice to meet you both.' Lamont evaded her stare. There was another moment of silence, everyone watching the other.

Outside a bar across the road, a woman was screaming at a man as the bouncers tried to separate them. Despite not knowing what the situation was about, Lamont seized the distraction, watching as the bouncers moved the commotion down the street. He mentally tried to compose himself. He needed to be in control. Seeing Rochelle had changed his night. He needed to put some distance between them. Fast.

'Do you want to come in?' Lamont motioned to the club. He could have kicked himself for blurting it out. Rochelle blinked.

'We shouldn't. It's your party.'

'I don't mind. Stay and have a drink.' Lamont motioned for them to follow, his head and heart not on the same page. Martin was chewing his nail when Lamont walked in.

'Where the hell were you? What's going on?' he eyed the women.

'I told you I went for fresh air. Ladies, this is Martin Fisher, my business partner and close friend. Martin, this is Bronie, Tenika and an old friend of mine, Rochelle.'

Martin shook hands with the trio. He led Bronie and Tenika to get drinks, leaving Rochelle and Lamont stood, trying not to look at each other. Lamont couldn't help it though. Some women never lost their mystique and Rochelle was one of them.

'L, while we're here, I want to say sorry, for—' Rochelle started.

'Don't worry about it.'

'No, I have to—'

'No. you don't. I made an error, and I learned the hard way.' Lamont didn't want to drag up the past. Rochelle looked at him for a long moment, then nodded.

'I understand.'

'Did you ever pursue the teaching gig?' Lamont changed the subject. Rochelle shook her head.

'I had to grow up. I was promoted, but I'm still working for the same company.'

'Well, we all have to work,' Lamont said, not knowing what to say. 'How's Mia?'

'She's doing really well. She's engaged, and she has a son. He's two years old.'

'That's good. Are you seeing anyone?' Lamont didn't know what possessed him to ask. Rochelle blinked, but recovered quickly.

'Not at the moment.'

Lamont nodded. 'I see.'

'You don't believe me, do you?' Rochelle's eyes narrowed. Lamont shrugged.

'It's none of my business. Doesn't matter if I believe you.'

'Fair enough. How's Marcus?'

'Still doing what he wants, when he wants.'

'That does not surprise me. I'm glad I don't have to listen to him screwing my little sister anymore,' Rochelle laughed. Lamont laughed with her, enjoying the moment.

'Those were some awkward nights.'

'Plenty of awkward nights back then.' Rochelle met Lamont's eyes. He felt himself relax. Rochelle was beautiful, but she was equally nervous. That gave him strength. Tenika walked over with a drink for Rochelle, and they talked.

The rest of the night was a blur, but Lamont didn't leave Rochelle's side, and she didn't seem to want to leave his. Before he knew it, they were both drunk. Lamont's shirt was sticking to him and he had to keep moving his arms to avoid the perspiration showing. Rochelle was next to him, smiling goofily, looking more like she had back in the day. He put his arm around her waist, pulling her close, pleased when she didn't move away.

'Where are you going after this?' he slurred in her ear.

'I don't know . . . Home I guess.' Rochelle whispered back.

'Yeah. Whose home?'

Rochelle giggled. 'Don't think you're gonna get me drunk and take advantage.'

'You're already drunk. So there's no need,' Lamont countered. Rochelle nudged him.

'You're trouble, L. you were always trouble.'

Rochelle beamed, and Lamont laughed. Tenika watched them both. She walked back over, Bronie trailing.

'We're gonna take off now. Are you coming?'

Rochelle hesitated, and Lamont made a split-second decision.

'Ring her later. I'll make sure she gets in.'

Tenika looked to Rochelle, who giggled.

'Make sure you look after her though. I know who you are,' Tenika warned. This piqued Lamont's interest, cutting through the alcohol haze.

'What do you mean?' he asked. The pair were already walking away though. Rochelle linked arms with him.

'What now then?' she asked, eyes twinkling.

* * *

They took a taxi back to Lamont's, not speaking. The taxi driver tried to make conversation, but they ignored him. Giving the driver a tip, Lamont led Rochelle inside.

'This is a nice place.' Rochelle remarked, sitting in the living room. It was decorated in shades of light blue. There was a TV/video player with an extensive collection. In the room's corner was a Hi-Fi, and a large amount of CD's.

'Thank you. Can I get you a drink?' Lamont offered. Rochelle shook her head.

'I think I had enough.' She crossed her legs. Lamont watched.

'You haven't changed a bit; I thought you would have learnt how to be subtle.' Rochelle giggled. Lamont shrugged. He headed to a wooden drinks cabinet and poured some brandy. He finished it and placed the glass on the table.

'I never thought I'd see you again.' Lamont looked directly at Rochelle. She shifted in her chair, but maintained his gaze.

'And now you have.' Rochelle laughed again, but it sounded forced.

'I was determined to put you behind me, but, I always wanted to speak to you. To find out about what happened that day,'

Rochelle didn't speak.

'Do you remember which day I'm talking about?'

'Did you bring me here to rehash the past?'

'What if I did?'

'If you did, then I think I should go home.'

'You're not going anywhere.' The authority in Lamont's tone unnerved Rochelle for a second. It was the same attitude he'd displayed the night they slept together.

'Are you going to keep me here against my will?'

'How could you sleep with Ricky? He's a prick.' Lamont ignored Rochelle and poured himself another drink.

'You don't even know him.'

'Of course I know him. I didn't then, but I do now. I know all about him. You picked him over me.'

'What are you talking about? I told you I had baggage, but you kept pursuing me anyway. Yeah, I had something going with Ricky, and it was awkward, it was all-consuming, and it made me that miserable bitch you used to stare at on the sofa. But that was then. I don't want to go through it all again. Can you understand that?'

Rochelle sighed loudly, closing her eyes. Lamont finished his drink, then licked a stray drop of alcohol from his top lip.

'I'm sorry. I just, that day . . .' It was Lamont's turn to sigh.

'Can we just forget it? Please?' Rochelle's voice was almost pleading now. He nodded.

'Consider it forgotten.'

They sat awkwardly in complete silence. Rochelle fidgeted with her handbag whilst Lamont stared at the empty glass on the coffee table. After a while, Rochelle rose.

'I'm going to go. This was . . .' Rochelle was about to lie, but couldn't. Instead, she gathered her handbag and started for the door, expecting Lamont to stop her. He didn't though, still analysing his glass. Shaking her head, Rochelle was at the front door when Lamont spoke.

'I loved you.'

The words were barely above a whisper, yet Rochelle heard as if he had shouted in her ear. She paused, her hand resting on the front door handle. Turning, she re-entered the room. Lamont was still looking ahead.

'What did you say?'

Lamont glanced at her now, his eyes wet and slightly bloodshot.

'I said, I loved you. I was a stupid kid, but I loved you. When I saw Ricky at the door, it crushed me.'

'You loved me?' Rochelle sat back down without realising.

'I did. I don't think I even knew until you closed the door on me that day. I had nothing to compare it to.'

'I didn't—'

'Of course you didn't know. I was a mess. I had nothing going for me. You were extraordinary. I wanted to tell you I wanted a relationship. Figured you'd laugh, but I was going to do it anyway.'

'Why?' Rochelle's voice was hushed.

'Because even if you'd rejected me, even if you laughed, at least I would have had closure. I suppose that piece-of-shit answering your door was closure too.'

Rochelle's eyes glistened.

'I'm sorry,' she whispered.

Lamont smiled. 'You have nothing to be sorry for. I was a silly kid. I learnt a lesson that day. About giving too much of myself to someone. I owe you for that.'

'That's not a lesson, L.'

'Really, then why are you single?' Lamont countered.

'There's nothing wrong with being single,' Rochelle snapped.

'When you look like you though, it makes a man think; makes him wonder what damage someone could have done to that woman.'

'I'm leaving.' Rochelle again stood, but this time Lamont grabbed her arm.

'Let go of me.'

'No.'

'I'll scream if you don't.'

'Scream then,' Lamont pulled Rochelle towards him. 'Go on then . . . scream.'

Rochelle struggled but Lamont was too strong, holding her arms tightly by her sides.

'Let go of me!'

Lamont paid no attention, his eyes calmer now. Gazing at Rochelle, he pressed his lips to hers. A delicious electric tingle shot down Rochelle's spine. She was no longer resisting. It took a moment to realise Lamont had let her hands go. His hands grasped her hips, and he slowly darted his tongue deeper into her mouth. They broke away, panting, eyes meeting, hearts frantically beating.

'Like I said; you're not going anywhere,' said Lamont, and then he kissed her again. This time, Rochelle was more than ready. She let out a gasp as Lamont slammed her against the wall but she didn't break the kiss. Her soft hands cupped Lamont's cheeks, tilting his head as she kissed him deeper. Lamont's hands travelled down her back, palming her ass.

Rochelle's body felt like it was on fire. This was not the Lamont she had dealt with previously. The awkward teenager whom she'd guided was gone. In his place was an assertive, worldly man who knew exactly what he was doing.

Lamont attacked Rochelle's neck with a viper's precision, leaving a tingle everywhere he touched. The pair writhed on the floor now, undressing each other. Holding Rochelle's arms above her head with one hand, Lamont traced her body with the other, his mouth engulfing a delicious breast. He dipped lower, his tongue touching her belly button, then going beneath her pelvis. Kissing at the insides of her thighs, Lamont took his time. Rochelle's head snapped back with such force it banged against the wall. She tried to cry out, but her voice caught in her throat.

As Lamont explored her with his mouth, a whirlwind of emotional pleasure cascaded over Rochelle. She couldn't believe this was happening. She grabbed Lamont's hair, her fingers tangled in his coarse black curls. She felt it manifesting, bubbling to the surface and until, finally, Rochelle exploded with an earth-shattering, ear-splitting climax.

CHAPTER TWENTY THREE

Saturday 18 May 2002

MORNING CAME. Rochelle opened her eyes, taking a moment to gain her bearings. She didn't recognise where she was immediately, light snoring to the left startling her. Lamont was laid half on his side in a deep sleep.

Rochelle watched him, thinking about the night before. The sex had been spectacular. After they had caught their breaths, they had headed upstairs to repeat the act. They had taken their time, exploring one another's bodies.

Last night it all seemed perfect. Sleeping with Lamont had seemed the most natural thing in the world. Now, she felt awkward.

Climbing from the bed, Rochelle quickly dressed. She had everything on but couldn't find her shoes. silently cursing, she hurried downstairs. The shoes were next to the table. Rochelle was about to put them on when she sensed another presence.

'Going so soon?' Lamont stood in the doorway clad only in some brown pyjama bottoms, his arms folded. Rochelle hadn't even heard him enter.

'Busy day, lots of things to do. You know?' Rochelle said in a fake, hearty tone she didn't recognise.

Lamont nodded. 'I understand.' He smiled, but there was no

warmth in his tone or eyes. Rochelle knew that Lamont sensed what was going on. She didn't need to break it down for him. Instead, she just stared. The vulnerability again flared in Lamont's tired eyes. Rochelle opened her mouth to speak, but she couldn't get the words out.

'How's things ended with us . . . I'll always regret it, L.' It wasn't quite what was on her mind, but it was true.

Lamont nodded.

'Call me if you ever want to talk,' he said listlessly. After putting Lamont's number in her phone, they walked to the door and shared a brief hug. Surprising herself, Rochelle leaned in for a kiss, only for Lamont to angle his head so she caught his cheek. She could smell herself on him and for a second, she squeezed tightly.

'Take care,' Lamont's voice was mechanical. Rochelle didn't know who she was seeing now. She'd thought sneaking out would be best for Lamont. He had truly changed though. Lamont wasn't that sensitive little boy anymore, and it was because of her. With a regretful smile, Rochelle left.

* * *

TUESDAY 21 MAY 2002

Lamont drove home, switching lanes as the sky slowly turned from amber to black. The day had been a busy one of running around making sure that everything continued running smoothly. Louie though, had been silent.

Since Lamont began working with Bill and his brother, he hadn't seen Louie as much. He still supplied him, and had even sent Shorty to have a word with the kids working for him, making sure they didn't take liberties. Dialling Louie's number while stopping at some lights, the phone rang but there was no answer. As the light turned green, Lamont called Shorty.

'Send someone to see the old man.'

'For what?' scoffed Shorty. Lamont could hear voices and loud music in the background.

'We haven't heard from him or his team. They should be done with their work by now.'

Shorty kissed his teeth. 'I'll send one of my gunners round. You better hope he's not in there watching *Quincy*, because I'll smack him up personally if he is.'

Laughing, Lamont hung up and headed home. Inside, he checked his phone for messages and changed out of his clothing. After a quick shower, he made himself a cup of coffee and plopped down on the sofa, picking up the book he'd started reading earlier. His mind was too wired though. It was common nowadays.

Even when Lamont was at home, away from all the drama, it was difficult to switch off from the streets. He put the book to one side, watching the end of a football match while he finished the coffee. He made food, then just picked at it for a while until he finally put it to one side.

Lamont was antsy and didn't know why. He was insulated, and he had a good team working for him. Financially, he was fantastic.

Lamont could have laughed. He had money and respect. Mostly, people left him alone, but it felt hollow sometimes. Lamont thought back to the second-hand clothes and the constant ridicule. Now, he had the world at his feet. Maybe it was time to act like it.

Heading upstairs, Lamont put on a new pair of jeans and a black designer t-shirt. He looked down at his dad's old watch for a moment, feeling strangely confident, as if the old man's strength was flowing through him. Spraying on some aftershave, Lamont headed outside to the taxi he had pre-ordered.

As always, the town centre was heaving with people out on the prowl. Lamont slipped through the crowds into a bar, ordering a glass of whisky. He sipped it quickly and ordered another, his eyes flitting around the bar looking for a distraction. He caught the eye of a few girls and thought of Rochelle for a moment. He wondered if he had done the right thing in dismissing her, resolving that he had. A girl that had been watching him since he walked in, again caught his eye, motioning for him to walk over. Shrugging, Lamont did.

'Lamont,' he said straight away. She smiled, appreciating his forwardness.

'Kari.'

'What are you drinking?' Lamont led her to the bar. She was nearly as tall as him, with a lithe frame and short, dark hair. She ordered a glass of white wine, sipping it as she met Lamont's eyes.

'Who are you with?' Lamont asked. Kari giggled.

'I'm by myself tonight. I just wanted to do something different.'

'I can sort of relate,' admitted Lamont. They sat in a corner of the room by now, the pulsating House music slightly muffled.

'Are you in here with anyone?'

Lamont shook his head. 'This was very spur of the moment. It's not like me.'

Kari made a face, 'Are you one of those people that plans out every moment of their life?'

'I can be. Last thing I want is to end up slipping.'

'How's it working out for you?' Kari surveyed him over the rim of her glass.

'It feels weird,' Lamont shook his head again. 'Forget it. We don't need to get this deep.'

'I want to.' Kari sidled closer to Lamont. She smelled amazing. Some women just had a naturally adult scent that made him think of rough sex rather than flowers.

'Everything in my life is going well. In terms of financial security and job security, I'm set. I've made some big moves that have put me in a good position.'

'And what? Now you're waiting for the other shoe to fall?'

Lamont nodded.

'Maybe you just need to relax.'

'Why do people always give that generic advice? It means nothing,' snapped Lamont. Kari made a face.

'Sorry, I wasn't trying to annoy you.'

'Nah, I'm sorry. Wigging out on the prettiest girl in this place won't make me feel better.'

Kari was all smiles now.

'I'm glad you realised it.'

'Realised what?'

'That I'm the prettiest girl in this place.'

They locked eyes. Lamont felt the pull, two parts of his brain arguing with each other. One side was telling him to put the moves on Kari. The other told him to go home and get his thoughts in order. Lamont didn't know which side to listen to.

Kari continued staring. She had a pretty face. Thick, luscious lips, the sort Lamont hated in his younger days but cherished now. *He was definitely a mouth man*; he realised.

She wore a dark shade of lipstick that seemed to shine under the club lights. He was going for it. Lamont moved towards her, only to be cock-blocked by his vibrating Motorola. Mumbling a swear word, he pulled out the phone and answered.

'L, where you at?' Shorty's voice boomed over the speaker, causing Lamont to move the phone from his ear for a moment.

'You don't need to talk so damn loud. I can hear you.'

'Where are you? This ain't a drill.'

Lamont stood.

'What's going on?'

Kari looked up at Lamont, confused.

'It's Louie. Meet me at your place. We need to talk.'

* * *

Shorty was pacing up and down outside Lamont's house as he climbed from the taxi. He glared at Lamont, Blakey hovering nearby. The pair blended in with the night sky around them in their dark attire. Blakey nodded at Lamont, who returned the gesture.

'Did you find him?' asked Lamont.

'Yeah, we found him all right,' Shorty's tone was sulky.

'If you think I took the piss in the taxi, I—'

'Fuck the taxi. He's dead.'

Lamont blinked foolishly, 'Who's dead.'

'Louie.'

'What?'

Shorty rubbed his face.

'Sent Blakey and one of my other dudes, like you said. They banged on the door for a bit, shouted through the letter box, but no one answered.' Shorty shot a look to Blakey, who took it as his cue.

'We were about to jet, but Larrie thought he heard the TV. We kinda broke in, and—'

'You broke into his house?' interjected Lamont.

'We wore gloves. Don't worry. Anyway, when we were inside, it smelt funky. We went into the living room and there he was.'

'How did he look?'

Blakey made a face. 'How do you mean?'

'Did he look like he died by himself?'

'There was no one else there,' said Blakey, completely misunderstanding.

'He means, did someone else kill him, you fucking prat,' sniped Shorty. Blakey hung his head.

'Nah. He looked like he was sleeping. We couldn't see nothing out of the ordinary, but we didn't stand around having a look.'

'Did you call an ambulance?' Lamont continued his questioning.

'We just kicked out. He was dead, so we just hurried out of there.'

Lamont held Blakey's stare for a moment, then motioned for them to come inside. He strode into the living room, reaching for his phone. He stared at it for a second, mumbled something, then picked up his keys, passing them to Shorty.

'Drive to a phone box. Can't make this call from the house.'

Shorty started Lamont's engine and flew down the street, ignoring Lamont's request to slow down. A few minutes later they found a phone. Lamont rummaged around in his pocket, then looked at his companions.

'Either of you two got any change?'

'I don't carry copper,' said Shorty, as if this were an adequate response.

'Here,' Blakey reached into his pocket and pressed a damp fifty pence piece into Lamont's outstretched hand. Lamont thanked him and hurried towards the phone box. He spoke for less than a minute and then went back in the car. Shorty drove them back to Lamont's.

'Marcus is gonna tell one of his guys to make the call. He's gonna check first, make sure there's nothing connecting him to us.'

'Bloody hell, I didn't even think of that,' said Blakey.

'Shut the fuck up. We're talking now,' Shorty snapped. Blakey's mouth immediately shut.

When they were back at Lamont's, he took out a bottle of brandy and poured three shots, handing the other glasses to Blakey and Shorty. Without a word, they held them aloft a moment, paying silent respect to Louie, then drank as one. Wiping his mouth, Lamont poured another.

'You're driving us back, B,' said Shorty, holding out his glass. Lamont topped him up, and they repeated the procedure.

'When was the last time you saw him?' Lamont asked Shorty.

'A month ago. I didn't even deal with him direct anymore. I left his people to K-Bar and Maka. My man was just collecting his money, really.'

'I haven't seen him since the last time we were there,' admitted Lamont, wondering why he felt guilty. He thought back to the first conversation he and Louie shared; where they admitted they were there because of women. Lamont wondered if it would upset Auntie when she heard the news about her ex.

Kari flitted into his mind then. She'd gone out looking for a good time and he'd ducked her without even getting her number. Some lucky guy was probably with her now.

'No reason for you to, I guess. He was a nobody. Everybody knows that.'

'Still, he got us started. Who knows where we'd be if it wasn't for him.'

'We'd have got somewhere regardless, fam. You can't keep hungry dudes like us down.'

'Damn right,' said Blakey.

'Shut the fuck up. We're talking here. In fact, go wait in the car. I don't need you repeating shit to impress little girls in town.'

Abashed, Blakey slunk out to the car without protest.

'Why do you talk to him like that?'

'Who? Blakey? He likes it. Do you think Louie will have anything connecting us?'

Lamont shrugged. 'My instincts tell me no, but it's worth it to double check. You just never know.'

Shorty nodded. 'I get you.' He again topped himself up. Lamont wasn't sure if it was Shorty's third or fourth glass, but he still clutched the bottle.

'What's up with you?'

'What do you mean?' Shorty made a face as he guzzled down the liquor.

'I mean if I didn't know any better, I'd think you were grieving.'

'Grieving for who? Louie?'

Lamont said nothing. Shorty kissed his teeth.

'Fuck him. Yeah, he started us off, but so what? We were running him by the end.'

'Then, why are you upset?'

'I'm not fucking upset!' bellowed Shorty. Lamont glanced at him, his eyebrow slightly arched. A second later, Shorty took a deep breath. 'It's just . . . That was how it ended for him. Dead on a mouldy sofa in a piece-of-shit house.'

'So?'

'So, that's not how I wanna go out. I ain't saying I wanna live forever, but I wanna leave in style.' Shorty poured yet another drink, topping up Lamont after. They both drank in silence, no more words needing to be said.

CHAPTER TWENTY FOUR

Friday 7 June 2002

IT WAS A POOR TURNOUT.

That was the main thought on Lamont's mind as he hung around after the service for Louie ended. He was with Shorty. No-one else from the team bothered to show. None of the kids Louie dealt with had turned up. Just a few old people probably looking to get drunk now that the service was over.

Louie had a sister who had organised everything. Lamont offered to help, but she hadn't let him, saying it was something she needed to do. He hadn't even known Louie had siblings. Lamont had learned Louie's parents were also dead. The similarities between the pair were uncanny, and Lamont was trying not to look too deeply into it.

Shorty had been subdued throughout the service, not speaking to anyone and even now that the service was over, remaining by Lamont's side. After they had found Louie's body, Shorty had admitted to Lamont that they'd found money at Louie's place. Thousands of pounds, which appeared to be profits from the drugs sold. He'd done nothing with the money. By the sounds of it, he'd stopped doing anything, no longer wanting to take care of himself. Lamont had initially suspected foul play, but no-one else had a hand in Louie's death.

'Are you all right?' Lamont asked.

'I don't like funerals,' said Shorty.

'Who does?' Lamont recalled his parent's funeral. He and Marika had sat stiffly up front with Auntie as the service had gone on. Everyone looked sympathetic but mostly it seemed staged, like the so-called mourners were just acting for non-existent cameras. They told him how sorry they were, patting him on the head.

Lamont had told himself he wouldn't cry during the service and he kept his word. Even when Marika had cried, shouting *mummy* when she heard her mother's name mentioned. Lamont had held her, feeling her tears soak his suit.

The after-party was full of debauchery. Some of the same faces that had told Lamont how sorry they were, now drank liquor and danced like they were at a party.

Auntie had been right in the middle of it, shimmying away to catcalls and wolf-whistles. Lamont had been relegated to the corner to watch as she lapped up all the attention. He had seen a gleam in her eyes that night that he hadn't understood.

'This though . . . this is pathetic. There's about twelve people here if you don't count the alcoholic crowd that are just waiting to get drunk. Look at them.'

Lamont spotted them. The laggers. Shuffling around in borrowed suits. They looked shaky, eyes darting all over place, constantly licking their lips. This little service would be the highlight of their week, and the chance to get a nice drink.

'I know. It's sad.'

'Damn right it is. Don't let me go out like this, L. When you bury me, make sure there's music and people dancing and shit. *Tupac* or summat.'

'*When?* Are you planning on going somewhere?'

'You never know.' Shorty shrugged. Lamont was about to question this, when a car pulled up outside the church and three men climbed out. Lamont recognised one of them. It was the same man he had seen looking at him at Shorty's party last year.

The men glanced in Lamont's direction, then made a beeline for Louie's sister. The man at the front spoke to her for a few minutes, his face full of concern. Lamont was too far away to hear, but she was sniffing and nodding. The front man gave her a brief hug, then headed in Lamont's direction.

He was surefooted, his back straight, wearing a white shirt, khaki trousers and boots. His dreads were even longer than K-Bar's and his face was thinner than his frame, his cheekbones almost jutting out at sharp angles. He glanced balefully at Lamont, then shook hands with Shorty, his goons following suit.

'Nice to see you here, Shorty.'

'You too, Leader. Didn't know you and Louie were cool like that.'

At the mention of the name, Lamont stiffened. He was looking at the man who had murdered Craig and destroyed Levi's life. He fought to keep his face neutral as Leader turned now, his hand outstretched.

'You must be the one they call *Teflon*,' he said in his heavily accented voice. His eyes glittered.

'That's me.'

'I've heard a lot about you. Heard you're a good person to know.'

'I don't know about that,' Lamont replied, not breaking eye contact.

'He's chatting shit,' Shorty interrupted. 'Teflon is the man out here. Get to know.'

Leader nodded at Shorty's words, a look passing between his men.

'Maybe we can all do some business. I knew your people. Years back. You probably don't even remember.'

'I remember.' Lamont hadn't taken his eyes from Leader.

'Sometimes you have to put people in their place, make sure they don't step out of line,' Leader smirked. 'I'm sure you understand that.'

'I'm sure I do.'

Leader nodded.

'I'll see you both around. Give my love to Levi when you see him.' Leader strolled away, laughing with his goons in tow.

'What was that about?'

'You tell me,' snapped Lamont. 'Since when did you get so pally with him?'

'Leader? I wouldn't call it pally saying hello to the dude at a funeral.'

'Do you remember what he did?'

Shorty kissed his teeth. 'You still crying over that shit that happened years ago? L, this is the game we're in. Craig was a fool, and so was Levi.'

'So they deserved what happened to them?'

'They rolled the dice and fucked up. You can beat yourself up about it, but they knew what they were doing. We all play this game. You need to realise that, because you can't pick and choose. Leader gets that. That's why he's around and they're not.' Shorty moved from Lamont, leaving him standing alone.

* * *

Shorty had accumulated a few different hideouts over the years. He had a main spot where he stayed most of the time though. It was a mess, with computer games, pirated DVD's and CD's everywhere, along with the lingering smell of weed.

As if on cue, Shorty lit his spliff when he took a seat, sighing loudly. With his freehand, he unbuttoned the top two buttons of his funeral shirt, dumping the suit jacket on the sofa next to him.

'You need to hit this. It's better than the shit we used to put out.'

Shrugging, Lamont took a small burn, coughing slightly. He hit it again then passed it back to Shorty, who laughed.

'Fucking hell, didn't think you actually would. What's the drill?'

Lamont laughed himself. He'd indulged in a few drinks at the after-party, and his head swam. Thinking back to when he first met Louie, he spoke.

'Remember a few years ago, when we first started, and you heard me and Louie talking?'

Shorty frowned. 'Summat about a girl, wasn't it?'

'Her name was Rochelle. She was the sister of a girl that Marcus used to deal with. Dunno if you ever met her.'

'Wait a sec, are you talking about *Bad Rochelle* from the ends? You smashed that?' Shorty's mouth hung open. Lamont again nodded. 'Gimme some skin!' he yelled, slapping hands with Lamont. 'Why didn't you tell me?'

'I didn't tell anyone. Marcus only knew because Mia told him. It didn't end well. Turns out she was fucking Ricky Reagan. I stopped by to talk to her and saw him there.'

'Wait, so she played you?'

'We were never a proper thing. I was just into her. Probably more than she was.'

'Is that why Reagan wigged out on you at my party that time?'

'I doubt he even remembered me. I was a nobody.'

Shorty killed the spliff and cracked open the bottle of brandy, half-filling two glasses, then topping them up with Coca Cola.

'Why are you telling me this now?'

'Because I need to talk about it. That funeral hit me harder than I realised. Louie left nothing behind. No-one cared. Even his sister just went through the motions. You're one of my best friends, and I needed to get it out. I saw Rochelle recently in town, and I slept with her again.'

'Why would you do it to yourself?' Shorty kissed his teeth.

'I needed closure.'

'*Closure?* Are you a girl?' Shorty rolled his eyes. Lamont laughed. It was typical Shorty.

'I was serious about her. I brought her back to my place, and we fucked. The next day she left.'

'Just like that?'

Lamont nodded.

'I'm surprised you didn't propose to her.'

'I'm not that bad.'

Shorty continued laughing, his drink shaking. Things grew hazy after that.

*　*　*

Waking with a groan, Lamont found himself face-down on Shorty's sofa, his head pounded. Closing his eyes again, Lamont swallowed down the nausea, then gingerly rose. Stumbling to the bathroom, he splashed cold water on his face until the cobwebs cleared, looking at his bleary reflection in the bathroom mirror.

Wiping his eyes, he left the room. His phone rang. Lamont checked the low battery, intending to charge it when he got home.

'Yeah?'

'Lamont? It's Paul. I live next door?'

'Hey, Paul. What's up?'

'I'm not sure if you're aware, but it looks like someone has broken into your house.'

'Are you serious?' Lamont pressed the phone to his ear.

'The front door is definitely open, but I'm not sure. I've called the police anyway, so get here as soon as.'

'I will. Thanks a lot, Paul.' Lamont hung up, glad he'd had the foresight to share his personal number with the neighbour. He headed to wake up Shorty, his mind racing. Shorty was already up and in the kitchen. He was staring into space, frown lines etched into his forehead.

'Bro, are you okay?' Lamont asked, forgetting his situation for a moment.

'Rochelle . . . I started putting pieces together when I woke up. Didn't really register when you were telling me last night.'

'How do you mean?'

'She's thingy's bitch.'

'What do you mean? Who's thingy?'

'Leader. Rochelle is his girl.'

'Bollocks,' scoffed Lamont. 'She works in an office. How would she even know Leader?'

'She's from the Hood. If she knows Reagan, why wouldn't she know Leader?'

'Even if she does, what's that got to do with anything?'

'Leader approached you yesterday. Remember? When he was talking shit?'

'Yes, I remember, but you're not making any sense.'

Shorty sprang to his feet, rubbing his forehead. Lamont watched him in disbelief. He didn't have a clue what was going on.

'She fucked you because of him.'

'What?'

'Leader told her to get close to you. It's so obvious. He's after you. That's why he was at the funeral.'

'He was paying his respects to Louie.'

'Are you hearing yourself? No one respected Louie!'

'Why are you shouting?'

'Because I'm vexed. That dude is coming after you. He's supposed to respect this shit. He knows who I am.'

'So this is about you?'

Shorty again kissed his teeth. 'It's about all of us.'

Lamont blinked, wetting his lips, still trying to catch up.

'Rochelle wouldn't do that.'

'What, like she wouldn't fuck you and Ricky Reagan at the same time? Grow the fuck up, L. This is the street,' Shorty paused. 'Wait, did you say you took her back to your place?'

Lamont froze, realising exactly why Shorty was asking.

'Yes,' he replied, his voice subdued now. 'A neighbour rang me just now. Someone broke in.'

'Leader was behind it. He expected you to be there. C'mon, I'll call K and we'll go over.'

* * *

Lamont was deep in his thoughts as K-Bar drove them to his house.

The connection between Rochelle and Leader seemed ridiculous. He and Leader had spoken for the first time yesterday. Leader had left after mocking Lamont though. The more Lamont considered things, the more twisted things became. He recalled seeing Leader at Shorty's party last year. That alone added weight to Shorty's words.

How would Rochelle have engineered a meeting though?

Lamont's stomach twisted in a knot. His phone vibrated and when he looked at the screen and saw Rochelle's name, he thought he was dreaming. Hesitating, he answered.

'L?'

Lamont didn't speak.

'L? Are you there?'

'Why are you calling me?' The phone shook in Lamont's hand as he tried to control his growing anger. He hadn't learned a thing, even after all these years.

'Look. I . . . what happened . . . I'm sorry. Please believe me. This thing with Leader is complicated. He found out I knew you and he was asking questions, and then he found out we slept together.'

'You told him?' Lamont wanted to trust Rochelle's words, but they were lost in his growing rage.

'No! Bronie told someone who told him. I swear, I haven't been like that with Leader in years.'

Lamont laughed. He could feel Shorty looking.

'You should be pleased.'

'Pleased? Why?'

'Even after all these years, your bargaining tools are still working. What are you after now? Money? You fucked me once, and now you've screwed me over once again.'

'No! I swear this is the truth.'

'No, this is the truth; you made one mistake. I am not the little punk you slammed the door on four years ago. When you run into your boyfriend, tell him that.' Lamont hung up, breathing hard. Shorty surveyed him, but didn't speak, a tense silence lasting until they arrived.

Lamont saw people milled around his house. K-Bar remained, but Shorty came with Lamont and they strode toward to the house. The front door was wide open and visibly damaged. An officer in the garden was making notes in his notepad when he saw Lamont. He blocked his path.

'Can I help you, sir?'

'No, you can't. I live here, officer,' said Lamont. This piqued the officer's interest.

'You're Lamont? *Lamont Jones?*'

'That's correct. What happened?'

'I was hoping you could tell me. One of your neighbours heard a disturbance and called us. They advised they saw men running from the premises and climbing into a large car.'

'Can I get inside please? I would like to see the full damage.'

'And I would like you to please answer my questions.'

'You haven't asked me any questions,' snapped Lamont. 'Also, you don't have the right to stop me entering my own premises.'

The officer cleared his throat. He was young, probably a fresh recruit, with sparse blonde hair around his chin and grey eyes. He sized Lamont up, watching Shorty in the background.

'I haven't established who you are,' he said, as if he'd scored a telling point. Instantly, Lamont showed the officer his driving licence.

'Satisfied? Now, move out of the way.'

'Watch your tone, mate.'

Shorty stepped forward.

'Did you hear what he said? Move out the damn way so he can see the damage.'

'This doesn't concern you, sir,' the officer said to Shorty.

'Nah, it doesn't concern *you*. He wants to see the fucking damage.'

The crowd watched the exchange. Already at boiling point after his talk with Rochelle, Lamont was just as ready to fight as Shorty. Thankfully, an older officer wandered over.

'What's going on?'

'This is Lamont Jones, sir,' The younger officer gestured to Lamont. 'He wants to get inside.'

'So, let him. It's his place.'

His face reddening, the officer moved. Lamont and Shorty hurried inside, their feet crunching on broken glass. Lamont went straight to the living room, his stomach plummeting when he saw his CD's and DVD's all over the place.

He knelt down and began picking up the chess pieces that had spilled to the floor. He'd collected all the black pieces when the older officer walked in.

'Any idea who could have done this?'

'I was out all night. I have no idea,' replied Lamont. He rushed upstairs. Thankfully, there was no damage.

'We'll need some details, and you'll need to come to the station to give a full statement,' the officer said when Lamont came back downstairs.

'No.'

'What do you mean?'

'I'm not pursuing any charges. I don't know what happened. You can see I was out. There is no reason for me to go to the station.'

'But . . . Mr Jones, sir, don't you want us to catch the guys who did this?'

'I doubt you could,' said Lamont scathingly. He hadn't meant to be so harsh, but he was barely keeping hold of his temper by now. The older detective scowled. He stowed his notepad and made for the door.

'Fine then. You're on your own.'

* * *

Shorty waited while Lamont got his things together. Blakey had been summoned, and would stand guard until Lamont's door was fixed. Lamont's mind was all over the place as he stuffed clothing and essentials into a sports bag he used for the gym.

Rochelle's betrayal stung. Lamont was sure that the night had meant more. To find out she was setting him up, was galling. It wasn't until they drove away, that Shorty finally spoke.

'Blakey will drive my car back. You need to ring Rochelle back.'

Lamont shot him a blank look.

'Why?'

'To get answers.'

'About what?'

Shorty's brow furrowed. He glared at Lamont.

'About Leader. This is war now.'

* * *

'She's not answering.'

Lamont and Shorty stood by a phone box in the Hood. Lamont had tried ringing Rochelle three times, but she wasn't picking up. After the way he had flipped out on her, Lamont wasn't surprised.

'Right, come on. We're gonna drop off your stuff, then we're gonna go out looking. I'm ringing Marcus.'

* * *

Later, Lamont and Shorty headed out and hit the gambling spots. It was evening now, and the games were just getting started. People would be there the rest of the night, hoping to take the tables. In a back room, Lamont and Shorty smelled fried food being cooked. The ever-present stench of weed and alcohol was in the air, but the pair barely noticed. Shorty stopped to question an acquaintance. Lamont made his way to the furthest table, tapping someone on the shoulder.

'Can I have a quick word?'

'What is the problem?' Trinidad Tommy asked.

'Leader,' said Lamont, once Trinidad had left the table with him. A man moved straight away to take Trinidad's place, sitting at the table and picking up the cards. 'I need to find him.'

'Why?'

'It's important.'

'Leader is nasty. You should stay away from that kind of person. He will get you in trouble.'

'I know what I'm doing,' said Lamont, which was a lie. He kept recalling the way Leader's guys had thrown the chessboard to the floor. The chessboard his father gave him. Lamont still felt the rage coursing through his veins. He wanted to hurt Leader and Rochelle for what they had done to him.

'I don't think you do. I know what you are, and what you're not. Don't let people get you into something you're not ready for.' Trinidad looked past Lamont at Shorty.

'Thanks for your time,' Lamont held out two twenty-pound notes to Trinidad.

'What is this for?' he looked offended.

'For your time. I made you lose your place.'

'I don't want your money. I just want you to listen,' said Trinidad. Lamont folded the money and stuck it in Trinidad's shirt pocket.

'The money is the only thing I can guarantee. Thank you for your time.'

CHAPTER TWENTY FIVE

Thursday 13 June 2002

'You hear anything?'

Shorty and Lamont were on Grange View in Chapeltown. Shorty slouched in the car, Lamont leaning against the bonnet talking to Marcus Daniels. Marcus stifled a yawn, his face ravaged with tiredness. Lamont didn't know how long Marcus had been tracking Leader, but he hadn't found anything either.

'Leader's people are being quiet. I've got contacts but all they're telling me is that Leader is shady and no-one's really fucking with him.'

'How can none of them have fucking seen him? Someone's lying,' interjected Shorty.

'Maybe. If they are, no-one is saying anything.'

'What about that bitch you used to lay with? Nothing there?'

Marcus shook his head. 'I haven't seen Mia since I dumped her. I went by the house, but Rochelle doesn't live there anymore,' Marcus rubbed his forehead. 'I can't believe she's involved in this shit though. Never expected it from her.'

'Did you know she was with Leader?' Lamont asked. He had a feeling Marcus always knew Reagan was in the background. It wasn't worth bringing up though.

'It's not a secret.'

'You should have told me.'

Marcus laughed.

'How was I supposed to know you were gonna bang her again?'

Lamont couldn't argue. No one had expected to see Rochelle, least of all him. He wondered how she learned about the event, and how she would have approached if he hadn't stepped outside.

'Anyway, I'm gonna keep looking. I'll get with you later.' Marcus touched Lamont's fist, nodded at Shorty, and left.

'Back to square one then I guess,' said Shorty. Lamont wasn't listening though. He had a plan.

* * *

'I hope you're here to take me up on my offer,' were Delroy's first words as Lamont was shown into his office. It was a small house at the top of Louis Street that was heavily protected. Delroy had turned the living room into his office, which had a desk, chairs, a sofa and a large TV. There was a computer in the corner but Lamont was positive Delroy didn't even know how to turn the thing on.

'I'm here to talk about something else.'

Delroy signalled to Lamont to take a seat.

'You're wearing that watch well. Your dad would be proud.'

'Thank you,' said Lamont humbly, looking down at the battered watch and feeling his heart swell for a moment. He focused on Delroy.

'You called this meeting. I don't think it's because you just wanted to chat.' Delroy waved his hand.

'Do you know Leader?'

'I know a lot of Yardies.'

'So, you do.'

'Why are you asking?'

'I need to find him.'

Delroy coughed.

'Why?'

'I need to finish something he started,' replied Lamont. Delroy digested that one.

'I'm gonna send someone to get food. Proper homegrown stuff. Do you want some?'

'I ate before I came.' Lamont recognised a stalling tactic when he saw one.

'Fair enough. So . . . You're after Leader. Must be big. You look different from last time.'

'How did I look last time?' Lamont was intrigued.

'On top of the world. Focused. I've been keeping tabs on you, Teflon. I'm sure you expected that.'

'I did.'

'This Leader thing. I've got a lot of influence over that side. One phone call to the right people, and I'd find him.'

'But?' Lamont prompted. Delroy smiled, but it didn't meet his eyes.

'But, you rejected me. As much as I respect the way you do business, helping you doesn't benefit me.'

'So, let's make it a business deal. Name a price.'

'I don't need money.'

'I bet that if your workers started giving you less profit, you'd have something to say about it,' Lamont pointed out. Delroy chuckled.

'Let me put it another way then; I don't want *your* money. I want you to work for me. If you can't do that, you're useless to me. Good luck though. I'll tell Winston you asked after him.'

'Please do.' Lamont clenched his fists, taking a deep breath. He shook Delroy's hand and moved toward the door.

'Teflon?'

Lamont paused. Delroy grinned.

'How does it feel to not be winning anymore?'

Lamont left.

* * *

Days passed. Lamont remained indoors, everyone else coordinating to keep things running smoothly, and hunt the renegade Yardie.

Lamont had made enquiries into where Rochelle could be, but she had disappeared. He recalled their conversation. He had ripped into

her on the phone, and though he didn't regret what he said, he wished
he'd shown more patience. She could have led him to Leader.

Pausing the *Sopranos* episode, Lamont went to freshen up. He was
tired of sitting around. Shorty had left him a loaner, and old Peugeot
that belonged to an associate of theirs. Shorty was driving Lamont's
Lexus to keep up appearances.

Driving to the Hood, Lamont parked around the corner from
Shorty's hideout and walked in. Downstairs, all the lights were off, but
Lamont could see lights coming from upstairs along with the sound of
soft music.

'Shorty?' he called. 'Are you about?'

Knocking once on the master bedroom, Lamont entered. He heard
TLC playing in the background at the same time he saw the bare
breasts of Bill's wife. She gave a gasp when she saw Lamont and
covered herself. Lamont's eyes flitted to Shorty, shirtless and grinning.
No-one spoke, as TLC crooned about a *Red Light Special*. Lamont
shook his head, but couldn't think of the words.

'I'll be downstairs,' he said finally, 'when you're done with your
business.'

* * *

'What the fuck are you playing at?'

Half an hour later, Bill's sheepish-looking wife had been sent home
in a taxi. Shorty reclined on the sofa, smoking a spliff and looking
pleased.

'What did it look like?'

'It looked like you pissing around and fucking things up, that's what
it looked like!'

'Why are you shouting?' Shorty frowned.

'Why are you screwing the connect's woman is a better question?'

Shorty grinned again. 'It just happened.'

'No, it didn't. How long has it been going on for?'

'I've hit it twice. It's nothing.'

'And Bill? The second you get bored with her — which we both
know you will, she'll run and tell him.'

'Fuck Bill.'

'For a guy who loves money so much, you love to fuck with business.'

'This is about business is it?' Shorty let out a harsh laugh.

'Of course it is.'

'Business is messed up because of you. You got played by that bitch Rochelle, and now the team are chasing Yardie ghosts.'

'Leader planned this. Not me. No-one saw it coming.'

'You sure? Because Leader knew what he was doing. He saw that you were pussy-whipped and sent her to get you.'

Lamont's temper flared. He was determined to wipe the smug look off Shorty's face.

'I've been cleaning your messes for years. You would have been in prison years ago if I hadn't held your hand and kept you out of trouble,' he snarled.

Shorty opened his mouth to reply, but Lamont's phone rang, distracting them. Seeing Rochelle's name on the screen, Lamont's stomach plummeted as he answered.

'What do you want?'

'I heard you've been looking for me?' cackled Leader, his voice muffled on the line.

'I have.'

'You should have stayed at your spot then. I went to see you and you weren't there.'

Lamont remembered the scattered chess pieces. His hands shook with humiliation and rage. He was still furious from the argument with Shorty, and now he had to deal with this fool.

'Tell me where you are. I'll come to you.'

'Stop talking. Your bitch lent me her phone,' Leader paused and Lamont heard whimpering in the background. 'You wanna come get her, it's gonna cost you five hundred thousand.'

'Go fuck yourself.'

'That's your choice then.' Leader hung up. Lamont flung down the phone. He rubbed his face.

'What happened?' Shorty asked.

'The joker wanted half a million for Rochelle.'

'When he rings back, talk nice. Try to set up a public meeting, and we'll take him out.'

They sat quietly, the tension from their short argument abating. Lamont thought about Rochelle. He'd definitely heard a female in the background. Leader could have been screwing with him, but Lamont was sure it was Rochelle. He was kicking himself for not negotiating. He was incapable of staying calm and was allowing emotions to cloud his judgement.

Rubbing his face again, Lamont blew out a breath.

'Shorty?'

Shorty glanced at Lamont.

'I'm sorry. I shouldn't have said that stuff to you.'

'You're my bro. Don't worry about it. We both said shit we shouldn't have.' Shorty patted Lamont on the shoulder, and they settled in to wait.

Hours passed with no call back. Shorty ordered enough Chinese to feed several families. Evidently screwing Bill's wife had left him with an appetite, because he tore his way through the food whilst Lamont picked at his, drinking two glasses of brandy. His head was pounding from the stress. Laying on the sofa, Lamont began drifting off when his phone rang again. He answered it without checking.

'Yeah?'

'L, where are you?' Marcus sounded worried.

'I'm with Shorty, why?'

'I . . . Look, I'm gonna give it to you straight. Police just found Rochelle in Harehills, with her throat slit. She's dead.'

CHAPTER TWENTY SIX

Thursday 20 June 2002

LAMONT SAT, drinking, hiding from the world. No matter what had transpired. No matter what Rochelle had or hadn't done, her death had left a hole. He had believed he was over his feelings, but the sorrow over her death, manifested with the guilt, was driving him over the edge.

Shorty and Marcus were out trying to find Leader, publicly slapping people around to put their point across. Lamont no longer cared. He didn't care what people thought. He could have talked to Leader, negotiated, arranged a meeting, asked for her to be left out of it. She could have left the Hood; free to pursue her dream of becoming a teacher. It wasn't meant to be.

In the two days that passed since her death, the police had questioned Lamont. They'd searched her phone and seen the call to Lamont before she was killed.

At one crucial point during the questioning — which was a medley of *no-comment's*, they showed him a picture of Rochelle's body, her head practically decapitated. The image stayed with him, plaguing him along with a single question: *Was he an effective boss, or was he too weak to lead?*

Lamont kept thinking of the world he'd willingly strode into. That had been because of Rochelle too. It all related to her. The desire to be better than Reagan had led Lamont to where he was. Right now, he couldn't stand any of it.

* * *

Another day passed. Lamont ate food and consumed cups of the horrible instant coffee that Shorty kept. He was going crazy sitting inside. Showering and throwing on some clothing, he made some calls and located an address for someone he needed to speak with.

* * *

'L?'

Mia gawped, surprised to see Lamont. It had been far easier to track her down than her sister. Mia had changed from the old days. The beauty was still there, but it was buried under too much makeup and clear signs of grief. Her eyes were heavy and her black clothing was rumpled.

'Hello, Mia.'

'What are you doing here?'

'I wanted to give my condolences. I'm sorry about what happened to Rochelle.'

'Come in.'

Lamont took a seat while Mia made them hot drinks. Soon, they were sat in awkward silence. The living room was cosy, stuffed with furniture, kids toys and family photos. Lamont studied Mia's partner, but didn't recognise him.

'Why is my sister dead?'

Lamont considered what to tell Mia. The police had interviewed him, but he didn't know if they had spoken with her.

'Do you know Leader?'

'What does Leader have to do with anything?' Mia froze.

'He killed your sister. Don't ask why. You can't tell anyone about this, especially the police. I'm telling you because you have a right to know.'

'What am I supposed to do, L? You can't drop a bombshell like that and then not say anything! You're talking about my family here.'

'The police won't catch Leader. He's too clever for them. I promise you, he will be brought to justice, one way or another.

Mia ran a hand through her hair, putting her untouched drink on the table. Lamont did the same.

'Remember the old days? The four of us in that living room, talking shit and drinking?'

Lamont nodded.

'You were so good for her, L. I'm not just saying this. Rochelle was never happier than in those moments when she'd be sitting and talking with you.'

Lamont swallowed down the lump in his throat.

'She broke my heart back then.'

Mia glanced at him, her eyes tearing.

'She broke her own heart too. Now, she's dead.'

Lamont held Mia as she cried, determined not to shed his own tears. The need for vengeance grew. Leader was responsible for so much sorrow. Levi had ended up in prison, Craig and Rochelle had lost their lives because of him. Lamont made a silent vow to end him by any means necessary. It had gone far enough.

* * *

'Nice to see you again. Heard you had a bit of trouble with the police,' said Delroy as Lamont sat down in the office. Lamont nodded. His face was drawn, and he was in no mood for small talk. Delroy recognised this and straightened up.

'I want Leader's location.'

'We've been through this already. I want—'

'Help my people find him, and I'll buy exclusively from you instead of my current supplier.'

Delroy took his time replying, a telltale gleam in his eye.

'Are you sure about this?'

'Do you agree?'

Delroy scratched his lip.

'Wait there, let me make a few phone calls, and we'll talk numbers.'

* * *

'He's in there.'

Lamont was in the back of the car, Shorty next to him, Marcus and K-Bar in the front. They were parked down the road from a terraced spot in Keighley.

Delroy had acted swiftly, finding Leader's location and stressing that he moved around a lot, so they would need to hurry. Lamont rounded up his people, and they had put the plan into place.

No-one replied to Marcus's redundant statement. This time, there would be no escape.

'Should be any minute now.'

As Marcus spoke, a black van pulled to a stop outside the spot, and four men surged toward the house. From their spot, they heard multiple bangs and loud noises, then watched as they dragged Leader from the spot, struggling. Lamont's jaw tensed. He wanted to jump from the car and attack the man that had caused so much trouble, but he waited.

'Drive to the spot. We'll meet them there.'

* * *

Lamont didn't like the fact that Leader wasn't scared. They were in the basement of an out-of-the-way spot that Marcus had set up. It was soundproofed and packed with weapons and tools designed to coerce information from people.

The floor of the basement was covered in plastic. Leader was trussed to a chair, his glittering eyes focused on Lamont.

'You got lucky.'

Shorty smacked Leader in the face, the hit making a dull slapping sound. Leader's head jerked back, but he kept smiling, showing blooded teeth.

'Does the truth hurt?'

'Maybe I need to hit you this time.' Marcus stepped toward Leader, but Lamont stopped him.

'You're going to die.'

The room was quiet, all eyes focused on the Yardie killer. He stared insolently at Lamont, blood trickling down his mouth, staining the t-shirt and tracksuit bottoms they had found him in.

'I don't fear death.'

'I think you're lying. Regardless, it doesn't matter. These lot are going to rip you apart, and you're going to know that it wasn't worth it.'

'I took what you loved. That makes it worth it. Teflon . . . the love-struck boss, happy to fuck *Shelly* after so many years. You loved her, but her pussy belonged to me. Nothing can change that.'

When Marcus moved forward this time, Lamont didn't stop him. The power of his uppercut toppled Leader's chair. Leader jerked on the floor, coughing, moaning in pain as K-Bar and Shorty steadied his chair before punching him multiple times in the stomach.

The tools came out. Lamont was desensitised to the sounds of Leader shouting in pain, or the retching sounds. He didn't care. The image of Rochelle's battered body was prevalent in his mind.

'Stop.'

Leader hunched over now, saliva and blood covering his clothes, his right eye closed and his lips bust. He glared at Lamont, no longer speaking.

'When you die, the world will forget you. Straight away. No one will avenge you. You killed the woman who loved you. Your team betrayed you. You got the better of me, but I still won the game. Enjoy your last few moments.'

Signalling to the others, Lamont stepped back as they pulled guns. Leader's screams were louder now, yet drowned out by the sounds of the bullets. They shot him in each leg, then Marcus put his gun to Leader's stomach at point-blank rage, firing twice. Leader's body jerked, then he was still. With a glance to Lamont, Shorty put his gun to Leader's head, and pulled the trigger, ensuring the job was finished.

For a few minutes, no one spoke. Lamont kept his eyes on Leader, waiting, hoping the image of his destroyed body would replace Rochelle's, but it didn't. Finally, Marcus spoke.

'K, take L home. We'll clean up here. Make sure someone is watching his spot, then we're all gonna lay low after this.'

* * *

MONDAY 24 JUNE 2002

Lamont lay on his sofa staring up at the ceiling when there was a knock at the door. Lamont opened it, surprised to see Xiyu. He carried a six-pack of Red Bull energy drinks in one hand, and two bottles of water in the other. Lamont led him into the house. Xiyu handed Lamont a drink, opening one himself. They drank silently for a moment.

'How are you doing?' Xiyu asked.

'I'm fine.'

'You don't need to lie. I spoke to the guys. I know about Rochelle, and I know she meant a lot to you.'

'I got her killed.'

'No, you didn't.'

'I should have negotiated with Leader.'

'Leader would have killed her, regardless. He wanted to get to you. Rochelle knew what she was doing.'

'I slept with her and it was magical. To me, anyway. It felt real, everything about that night. The emotions. All of it. When I think of her acting through all of that, it makes me feel sick.'

Xiyu was quiet for a moment.

'Maybe she was being real. I don't know the specifics of why she dealt with a man like Leader, but things could have played out differently. This might have been Rochelle's way of being with you again.'

Lamont thought about that. He wasn't sure he believed it, but it sounded good. For the first time since it all started, Lamont felt himself smile.

'You know what's funny?'

Xiyu shook his head. 'Tell me.'

'It's amazing how much of my life revolves around women.'

They both laughed.

'There is something I need you to do.'

'I'm listening,' said Xiyu.

'Set up an information network. I want it to be as intricate as possible. Pay whoever you need to pay, but put something in place so that in the future, we're not playing catchup, or forced to make deals. I want to know everything about everyone. No matter the cost.'

Xiyu surveyed Lamont for a long moment before he replied.

'I'll handle it.'

EPILOGUE

Friday 5 July 2002

LAMONT SCANNED the room as if through someone else's eyes, hands clammy.

A single thought resonated around his head: *What would he have become if he had gone into Rochelle's house that day?*

Lamont had often tried to put himself in that mindset, trying to wonder what would have happened if Reagan hadn't looked at him like dirt on that day, reminding Lamont that he was superior. *Teflon's* future had begun that day. It was as if that was where the tape had started and no matter how robust his efforts, Lamont couldn't look past that.

And now he didn't need to.

Leader's death was a story for a while, but rival's quickly filled the void he left behind, carving up his interests and manpower. No-one approached Lamont about the murder, but the right people knew what had transpired, even if they didn't know why. It had boosted Lamont's reputation, giving him and his team more street credibility.

Outside, a horn beeped. Splashing cold water on his face, Lamont tidied himself and sprayed aftershave before leaving. A new model BMW 4x4 idled at the curb. Even before he reached the ride, Lamont heard the pulsating music.

'Yes, Tef!' Shorty said over the music. Marcus slouched in the passenger seat smoking a large spliff. He nodded at Lamont, then closed his eyes.

'Are we ready?' asked Lamont as the driver set off.

'Everyone's waiting for us,' said Marcus. Satisfied, Lamont looked out of the window as the whip rumbled down Spencer place. Lamont recalled the days when he had struggled to sell drugs around this very street. He saw the scuzzy women on the game strolling, trying to entice passing cars to stop.

Nearby were other local pushers. They seemed younger than Lamont had been when he started. They were dressed similarly; dark hooded tops, tracksuit bottoms, and expensive trainers.

Lamont could see the hunger in their eyes as they eyed the Beemer. He wondered if any would ascend, or if they would stay on the bottom rung forever. He rubbed the scar on his chin, wondering what level he would finish at.

Shorty nodded his head to the beat and Marcus looked so still, he seemed asleep. The ride was void of words, and Lamont liked it. It wasn't often the two juggernauts were quiet.

Climbing from the ride, the trio walked toward the restaurant, dressed to turn heads. Lamont wore a sharkskin grey suit with a charcoal shirt, brown tie, and black shoes. Shorty and Marcus had ditched the suit jackets, wearing white shirts, black trousers, and shoes. People stared at the trio as they sauntered by like movie stars.

Inside, they were shown to a private room. K-Bar, Xiyu and several other faces waited, dressed in their finery and drinking champagne. They rose when the three entered.

The seat at the head of the table had been left for Lamont and he stood next to the chair with the regal arrogance of royalty. Reaching for a glass, he took a small sip, wetting his throat.

'Years ago, we banded together to try something new. The streets are no joke, and it all intensifies when the task is to build something real,' Lamont paused, looking into the eyes of every man present. 'We're stronger than we've ever been thanks to the efforts of everyone in this room, and all our people out of it. That's why I wanted you all here. To thank you for staying loyal, even when things grew difficult lately.

'As long as we keep going, the money will keep flowing. Let's continue to show everyone who the dominant team is,' Lamont saw the pride etched on all the faces of the men. 'Let's eat some of this good food, smoke some cigars, and go get drunk!'

As each man held their glasses aloft, Lamont prepared himself for the future.

TARGET

CHAPTER ONE

Wednesday 31 July 2013

LAMONT JONES STOOD outside the room, listening to two men discuss killing him.

'Del, he's a problem,' the first voice kept saying. It belonged to a man named Ricky Reagan.

'He's pure profit,' a second, more accented voice replied. This one belonged to Delroy Williams, a kingpin on the streets of Leeds. 'Do you realise what we make from *Teflon?*'

'He's too big. Everyone wants to buy more from his people than ours.'

'We control his supply. That means they're still buying from us. We control him.'

'Teflon's sneaky. You think he'll be satisfied behind you? He wants your crown,' said Reagan.

'He does? Or you do?'

Silence followed. Lamont pressed his ear closer to the door.

'What are you trying to say?'

'Maybe you're not happy with the way things are,' Delroy paused. 'Maybe you think you deserve a bigger slice.'

'It's not about me. It's about Teflon. Gimme the word and he won't last the night.'

'What, you wanna kill him in my office now? Is that smart?' Lamont could hear the amusement in Delroy's tone.

'You're a gangster, not a businessman. Why do you need an office?'

'I'm both. That's why I'm rich. Teflon realises that. You never have.'

'Are you saying he's better than me?'

'I'm saying there's no profit in killing him. Learn to work with Teflon instead of against him. I want you on your best behaviour when he arrives.'

Lamont had heard enough. He moved from the door and moved back down the draughty hall. The bribe he'd paid Delroy's people at the door had been worth it. He cut back around, knocked on the door twice and entered.

The office was old, particles of dust visible in the air. A large table dominated the room. The smell clung to Lamont's nostrils; stale cigarettes littering the overflowing ashtray, and the eye watering scent of white rum.

There were two chairs in the room. One, an oversized throne-like leather chair. The other, a metal contraption more suited for a torture chamber, faced the desk.

Reagan leant against the wall, feral looking and wild-eyed. His afro style hair was uncouth, his facial hair neater. He eyed Lamont, nodding. Lamont returned the gesture.

'Good to see you, Teflon. Take a seat,' said the dark-skinned, dread-locked man in the big seat, Delroy Williams. Born on the Island of Grenada, Delroy had fled to Britain after a murder in his home country. He had ascended to power in the prosperous, bloody Eighties, resting at the top of the Chapeltown hierarchy ever since. He eyed Lamont with a toothy smile not reflected in his eyes.

Lamont sat on the hard-backed metal chair. Reagan bristled behind him. Lamont ignored him, focusing his attention ahead.

'How's business?' Delroy continued, his chair creaking beneath him. From his own seat, Lamont noticed the buttons straining on the short-sleeved shirt the kingpin wore. Other than a shimmering gold watch on his right wrist and numerous rings on his thick fingers, Delroy showed no signs of wealth.

'Business is business,' said Lamont. It was an ambiguous reply, but he wanted to learn why Delroy had summoned him. They were both high enough up on the food chain that they worked through people. Lamont couldn't remember the last time he'd spoken face to face with Delroy.

'Business is important, don't you agree?' asked Delroy.

'I suppose I do.'

'Good,' Delroy's mask vanished. 'Tell me why I've heard things about your team then?'

'What have you heard?'

'You don't know?'

'He probably told them to say it,' said Reagan, interjecting himself into the conversation.

'You don't need to talk about me like I'm not here, Rick.'

'Don't talk like we're friends,' Reagan grumbled.

'I'm talking to your boss, not you.' Lamont wasn't even looking at him. Reagan's mouth twisted.

'You fuc—'

'Stop.' Delroy didn't raise his voice, but it silenced the pair. Agitated, Lamont tapped a slender finger on the table as Reagan stewed, breathing hard.

'Don't take me for a fool. Do you know or not?' Delroy continued.

'Stop talking in riddles. Just be straight up,' replied Lamont. Delroy studied him. His dark eyes flickered towards Reagan for a moment, then back to Lamont.

'Do you want a drink?'

Lamont didn't. He recognised the intent however and nodded. Delroy poured the remnants of the rum into a cloudy glass and handed it to Lamont. Lamont wiped the glass and drank.

'Reagan, wait outside.'

'What for?' Reagan's voice rose.

'I'm trying to talk business with Teflon.'

Reagan didn't move.

'I should be in the room when you're dealing with this sneaky motherfucker.'

'Why? Because you can handle me?' Snapped Lamont without thinking.

'What—'

'Ricky, go.'

Reagan stomped from the room, slamming the door behind him.

'I dunno why you're always aggravating him,' said Delroy, wiping his eyes. He looked tired, sounding less confident than he had earlier. Lamont wondered if it was an act.

'He's emotional. It's not my problem.'

'Until he makes it your problem. I dunno what it is with you two, but Ricky hates you. I don't think you're his best friend either.'

Lamont shrugged.

'Your people are talking shit about the goods. They're saying the supply is weak,' said Delroy, realising they were finished discussing Ricky Reagan.

'Do you have names?'

'It's not about names. I don't want that crap out there, so get your people in line and sort it. Got that?'

Lamont continued to assess Delroy. The kingpin scratched at his face with a paw-like hand, leaning backwards.

'I said, got that?'

'I suppose I do. Anything else you want to discuss?' Lamont asked. Delroy eyeballed him.

'We've got something coming in a few days. Save it for the drought. We'll tell your people when it's here.'

* * *

'Someone's been talking.'

Lamont slumped in the passenger seat as Shorty drove away from Delroy's at speed, loud music pumping from the ride. It was a new mixtape by some brash kid Lamont wasn't familiar with. All Shorty's music sounded the same though.

Lamont could feel a headache coming. The car was stuffy and the smell of weed was overpowering. He turned off the music.

'Oi! What are you doing?' said Shorty.

'I'm trying to talk to you, I don't want to shout over whatever rubbish this is.'

'Ask then. Don't just reach for my shit,' said Shorty. A small peanut shell coloured tank of a man, he would bring drama to anyone who wanted it. He was brutal, animated, and kept himself in ferocious shape by spending far too many hours training and working the bars in the park.

'Listen then, please. The big man's upset that we said his product was weak.'

'It is, so what's he crying about?'

Lamont shook his head. 'That's not the point. I don't want people talking out of line.'

'People are feeling the pinch, L. We're not making the same off this weak shit. You need to run that to Delroy.'

'Leave the supply to me. While we're paying wages though, I want no one talking out of turn. Sort it.'

Shorty cut his eyes to Lamont, not liking the bite in his friend's tone.

'Fine. It's handled.'

'If anyone complains, tell them we'll make it up on the next go around,' said Lamont.

'How? With more crap?'

Lamont didn't bother responding.

* * *

'Same old then?'

Shorty had dropped Lamont off at the Park Row apartment of Xiyu Manderson. Known as *Chink*, Xiyu's nickname came from his light eyes and facial features, inherited from his part-Chinese mother.

Chink grew up poor in Meanwood. Bullied by the tough kids of his neighbourhood, he learned to stay out of sight, developing a skill with numbers and gaining recognition as a proficient mathematician.

Chink and Lamont had become friends in their teens, and he had followed Lamont into the drugs game, using his talent for figures to help them gain a foothold.

Chink was smart with his money, and his home represented this. It was spotless, bereft of even the slightest dirt. The furniture combined *The Baroque* with a few modernists pieces such as Andy Warhol. The windows were wide, all-encompassing, the walls various shades of white and cream. A solid bookshelf displayed hundreds of titles of self-help books and history tomes.

'The quality will be shit again.' Lamont rubbed his eyes, sinking into the plush, linen sofa. Chink watched him.

'You need to sleep.'

'I will. I thought you needed an update,' Lamont said, stifling a yawn.

'And Shorty-The-Little-Wardog couldn't tell me? Where is he anyway? Outside smoking ganja?'

Lamont grinned. Shorty and Chink worked alongside each other, but their differences were clear. Shorty was rough and tumble; he was direct and kept himself immersed in the streets. Chink moved behind the scenes, weighing up the profits and flushing them through careful investments.

Chink thought Shorty was a thug, and Shorty believed Chink was a spineless pretty boy. Lamont did his best to keep them apart unless necessary.

'He dropped me here. He had something to do.'

'It was his people spreading those rumours. You know don't you?' said Chink.

'I know.' Lamont was fully aware it was Shorty's guys talking loosely. Shorty didn't respect Delroy or his team, and it was filtering down to the lower ranks. The thought of the drama made Lamont's head hurt more. He hoped he had suitable painkillers at home.

'So, tell him. Make him run his crew better.'

'Shorty's fine. Be on hand to coordinate,' said Lamont.

'I know the drill. We're overpaying for crap gear though. It barely stands up to a cut, and Shorty's people aren't the only ones with complaints. Clients aren't happy.'

'They're still buying though.'

Chink's eyes narrowed. 'Yes, they're still buying. Is this how it's gonna be? We let Delroy keep diluting the product and wait for our clients to go elsewhere?'

'I've got it covered,' Lamont muttered, irked with Chink's attitude.

'Do you? Because we already had one venture fuck up. Or did you forget Party in the Park?'

Lamont hadn't forgotten. The plan had been to set up a team of dealers to distribute drugs in the Park, and to supply after parties that sprung up after the annual event. Lamont had everything in place, but the weak product meant that the buyers copping the drugs opted to work with different dealers.

'Chink, I said I have it covered,' Lamont repeated. He rubbed his head. The headache felt worse now.

'What is with you?' Chink asked.

'Nothing.'

'You look like shit. Something's happened.'

Lamont took a deep breath. 'I got into it with Ricky Reagan.'

Chink grimaced.

'Was that smart?'

Lamont shrugged.

'Did you tell Shorty?'

Lamont smiled. Chink had a habit of asking questions to which he already knew the answer.

'What happened?'

'He kept interrupting when I was talking to Delroy, so I put him in his place.'

'You and your vendettas.' Chink shook his head. Lamont didn't want to talk about Reagan. He didn't want to talk about Shorty or any of it, even though he needed to. He needed to stay on top of the situation, but he couldn't bring himself to care right now.

'I'm tired, Chink.'

'Sleep.'

Lamont looked at him, 'you know what I mean.'

Chink sighed. 'Why do it then?'

Lamont pondered Chink's question. It gnawed at him daily. He took a deep breath, marshalling his thoughts.

'People depend on us to get paid. We used to control everything.

Now, it's like a fucking machine. And we're just going along without that power.'

'You don't have power?' Chink raised an eyebrow.

Lamont shook his head. 'That's not what I'm trying to say. I can't keep making excuses for the life I'm living though. Something has to change, and soon.'

'Like?'

'People used to listen,' said Lamont, needing to get the words out. 'Now they don't. The world used to be about money. Now everyone has something to prove.'

'Didn't we too? Maybe that's the problem, L. You made it. Cars, money, that mini-mansion you've got. There's nothing left to prove.'

'How can I live like that though? How can anyone live like that? With nothing to prove. With the people who used to be listening, not listening,' Lamont paused, his voice filled with emotion.

'What happens if I stopped playing by the rules? What happens to our people then? Does this thing we built fall apart?'

'Is that why you do it? To stop it all tumbling down?' said Chink.

Lamont couldn't answer.

* * *

That night, Lamont struggled to relax, drifting into a fitful sleep just after four. When he woke, his head pounded. He dragged himself to the shower and stood under it, letting the scalding water beat down on his head and shoulders. He closed his eyes, willing the thump of his brain to cease. It was to no avail though. He could have stayed in the shower all day, but readied himself instead.

Lamont had several missed calls from his sister, Marika. He stowed his phone and drove to his makeshift office, the backroom of a barber shop on Chapeltown Road. It was almost eleven now, and the barbers was in full flow.

The premises were reasonably sized, with four barber chairs and a tidy waiting area with weathered leather seats. The walls were adorned with flashy pictures of the different hairstyles available, along with a handwritten price list. There were magazines, and an entertainment system in the corner. Sky Sports News results flashed along the bottom of the muted TV. Loud reggae music played and several of the older guys waiting were nodding their heads along to the music.

Lamont greeted them, taking the time to talk to a few. Trinidad Tommy, the manager, approached him, his lined face cracking into a smile.

'Trinidad, everything good?' asked Lamont. The man nodded.

'The crowd will be here soon. You sleep? You look tired.'

'I'm fine.' Lamont excused himself to his backroom office. It was much smaller than the main area, with only a heavy wooden desk, computer chair and several filing cabinets. Lamont looked over the paperwork from his legal ventures and met people to talk business here. Cautious, he ensured it was swept for listening devices, just in case.

Lamont sank into his chair and opened the drawer, taking out an open packet of Pro Plus. He dry-swallowed two, glancing at the most valuable thing in the room as he wiped his mouth. It was a battered old chess set. The board was marked, the pieces chipped. He loved it though. It reminded him of the good times.

Lamont fingered several pieces, then started to work. He pored over several statements, his mind drifting in no time.

'L?'

Rough hands shook Lamont. He woke. Trinidad Tommy stood over him, concern in his eyes.

'Are you okay? I was seeing if you wanted any food.'

Lamont stood, yawning.

'No thanks. I'll get something from Rika's.' He wiped his eyes.

Before leaving, Lamont took another two caffeine tablets. As he started his car engine, his eyeballs throbbed. He blinked, pulled out and drove to Marika's.

Marika lived in Harehills, but wanted to move after several incidents with her neighbours. Lamont parked outside and strode in. Marika's place was small, but comfortable, the living room stuffed with toys and pictures of her children, Keyshawn and Bianca. The professional photographs were probably more expensive than the drab furniture. As always, the place was clean.

'Oh, now you wanna turn up?' Marika looked up from the show she was watching on TV. 'I've been ringing you all day.'

'Have you got any paracetamol?'

Marika fetched him water and a few pills.

'Coffee?' she asked him. Lamont nodded.

'Please. Black, no sugar.'

Lamont plopped on the sofa, closing his eyes. Minutes later, he heard the cup being placed next to him.

'Do you want any food? I can warm something up.'

'Sounds good.'

Lamont closed his eyes again, relaxing to the sounds of his sister clattering around in the kitchen. When the food was ready, they ate, talking as they did so. They had their difficulties, as all siblings did, but the love was still strong.

'Why didn't you reply before? I rang you loads of times.'

'I had things to tie up. How much do you want this time?'

Marika pouted.

'How do you know I want money?'

'Don't you?'

'That's not the point.'

Lamont laughed, putting his plate on the coffee table.

'If you say so.'

'I know you've got it, anyway. You lot are killing it on the streets,' said Marika.

'Says who?'

'Everyone. Keisha was telling me the other day that Ricky Reagan kept calling out your name.'

Lamont's stomach plummeted. During the day, he had fleetingly thought about the conversation he'd overheard. He'd always known Reagan didn't like him, but the fact he was so open about killing Lamont was unsettling. It remained another reason to make sure he had all the angles covered.

'Is he trying to beef with you?'

'Don't worry about Reagan,' Lamont said, wondering if he could take his own advice.

* * *

Shorty sat in the dingy gambling house drinking straight glasses of Hennessy. He'd procured a table in the corner, enabling him to see all the comings and goings.

The gambling house was rife with the pungent smell of sweat, mingled with weed and beer. It was nearly midnight and loud, the music playing in the background drowned out by people talking. It comprised four playing tables, and a few smaller ones. Men crowded these tables, seated on wooden chairs with ripped, cheap leather seating.

There was a backroom with a pool table where the younger crowd congregated. In his corner spot, nobody troubled Shorty. He wanted it that way.

Lamont took a few steps into the gambling house before greetings and requests from all around besieged him.

'Lamont!'

'Yes, L!'

'You good, man?'

Lamont had to buy the bar before being allowed to move. He trudged across the room and sat across from Shorty.

'Bloody vultures,' he muttered.

'You love it. How come you wanted to meet here? This ain't your scene.'

Lamont drunk his beer and ordered another one.

'Not like you to drink and drive,' Shorty added. Lamont was a stickler for rules.

'I took a taxi. Dropped my car off.'

'What's going on then?'

Lamont sipped his drink, froth gathering around his mouth. He rested his elbow on the table which creaked under the weight.

'Did you talk to your people?' he asked. Shorty expressed his disapproval by kissing his teeth.

'Why are you stressing? Forget Delroy.'

'Shorty, we talked about this.'

'We don't work for that fat motherfucker. We can say what we like.'

'While we work *with* Delroy, we stay quiet. Things are going on in the background. There's a plan in place.'

'What plan?'

A heavy hand clapped down on Lamont's shoulder before he could reply.

It was Reggie, one of the old crowd. Once a big deal in the streets, he was now an elderly man whose clothes hung on his frame. He had never planned for the future and had no money saved. It was a sad reality.

'Lamont! How are you?' said Reggie. His hearing was going, meaning he tended to shout.

'I'm doing well, Reg. How about yourself?' Lamont shook his hand.

'Life is hard. These young ones don't respect their elders. Not like you, Lamont.'

'Sit down with us. Have a drink.'

Reggie indulged and Lamont slid to order him a white rum from the bar. Shorty glared at the old man. Reggie had clutched the same pint for hours. Shorty had seen it too many times. Reggie would stay all night for free drinks now.

They listened to Reggie's tales of the old days, his peeves about life and its disappointments. They started a game of dominoes, Reggie and one of his pals versus Lamont and Shorty. The wily pair decimated the two of them. Shorty was decent, but Lamont was useless and Shorty wasn't pleased about it.

'Stop messing about. You'd be trying harder if it was chess!' he kept saying.

They left, drunk and poorer. Reggie and his pal had taken them to the cleaners. Shorty wouldn't shut up about it.

'We didn't win a single round man. That's ridiculous. You need to stop reading all the time and practise,' he said.

'Piss off. You made me pay for it, anyway. Reggie and his white rums cleared my pockets too.'

'Dunno why you even bother with him. He's washed up. We can't use him anymore,' said Shorty.

'He's an example of how not to turn out. There's a lot to learn from Reggie and his era.'

'Sounds daft. You're always talking nonsense.'

Lamont didn't reply straight away, watching as Shorty tried to light a cigarette.

'Whatever. Where are you going now?'

'I've got a girl on Hamilton Avenue I'm gonna wake up,' Shorty touched fists with Lamont. 'I'll get with you tomorrow.'

Lamont watched him stagger down the street. 'Catch you then.'

CHAPTER TWO

Friday 2 August 2013

LAMONT SAT in the back of the barbers, reading a newspaper and trying to ignore the raucous laughter coming from the shop floor. Shorty was supposed to be stopping by. An hour and a half later, he was nowhere in sight. Lamont yawned, stretching.

Trinidad Tommy poked his head around the door.

'That white boy's here to see you,' he said in his strong accent.

'Which one?'

'That loud one. Terry.' Trinidad kissed his teeth. Lamont sighed.

'Send him through.'

'Teflon, how's it going my mate?' Terry strode into the office. Behind him, Lamont saw Trinidad Tommy shaking his head as the door closed.

'I'm living. What's new?'

'Mate, life is bloody good. I'm all over. Can't rest. Everything's happening. I'm trying to get my piece of the pie. Got these dudes in Halton Moor, right, they wanna buy—'

'I don't wanna hear that,' said Lamont. The office was swept for listening equipment, but he stayed vigilant.

Terry was a few years older than Lamont and had been dealing drugs forever. Big money had passed through his hands over the years.

Stupid decisions meant he still needed to hustle day in, day out to stay ahead though. Lamont recalled Terry driving flash rides and throwing money around. Now he was struggling.

It was a lesson in how not to play the game.

Despite Terry's obvious flaws though, Lamont liked him. Terry could spin a story and draw a whole room in with his tales. He was the quintessential rich-for-a-day, broke-for-a-week type with a pound in his pocket and a dream in his eye.

'Tef, what do you take me for? I swear you act like I'm police or summat sometimes. You wanna check me for a wire?'

Lamont gave Terry an icy glare.

'You don't need to run your business by me. Got time for a game of chess?'

When he was concentrating, Terry gave a good game.

'Not today, mate, it's boiling. Let's go for a drive.'

'I'm meeting Shorty,' said Lamont.

'Let the little munchkin wait. I bet he was meant to be here about three hours ago. Go on, tell me I'm wrong.'

Lamont laughed.

'Where are you parked?' he asked.

'Behind you. C'mon, we'll drive up to Roundhay, get a spot of lunch at the pub.'

Lamont nodded. He was hungry and Shorty was AWOL.

'Lead the way.'

* * *

Terry drove, talking a thousand words a second, turning up the radio, trying to shout to Lamont over it. Lamont stared out of the window, struggling not to laugh at the absurdity of the situation. Terry's gleaming blue Audi was a recent acquisition. Lamont wasn't fooled. Terry was up to his eyes in overhead and trying to live beyond his means. The Audi had been purchased with profits and now Terry was struggling to sell it. He had no idea Lamont knew.

Terry's BlackBerry pinged like crazy but he ignored it, determined to tell as many tales as possible. He locked the car and the two of them headed into The Deer Park in Roundhay, procuring a decent table.

Terry wanted to order a bottle of wine but Lamont vetoed, not wanting to get drunk.

'Anyway,' Terry was still talking twenty minutes later, pausing only to sip his drink and shovel forkfuls of fish pie into his mouth, 'I've got orders going all over the place. Mikey B's moving pills like a bloody pharmacy too! Reckon I could see twenty grand after everything's sold. Not bad for a week's work.'

'What's going on in Halton Moor?' Lamont asked, ignoring Terry's lies.

'Everyone wants a slice don't they? I'm telling ya, I've got a good feeling about the future. Who knows, I might be in your league soon.'

Lamont cut into his steak. It wasn't the best, but it was decent for the price.

'This is good,' he said.

'Yeah, yeah. What's your plan though?'

'For what?' asked Lamont.

'Life. We never talk about you. What's your goal? Ten million?'

'One day at a time.' Lamont cut another piece of steak and chewed.

'Bet you've already got ten, haven't you?' pressed Terry. Lamont didn't understand why his situation was so vital to him. He shrugged.

'Well? What's the crack?' Terry was trying to hit Lamont up for a loan and as usual, the wannabe kingpin was being evasive. Terry needed start-up capital to get his schemes moving. That was why he'd invited Lamont to lunch. He had ruined it though. Instead of just asking straight up, he'd made up a story about Halton Moor.

The only element of his story with any truth was the part about Mikey B; he was moving a lot of ecstasy. He'd dropped Terry as a partner though and was making all the money without him. Terry needed to get back on his feet.

'I'm okay,' said Lamont. Terry wanted to reach across and slap him. He treated Terry like an alien entity, good enough to sit and play chess with for hours on end, but second-class, undeserving of knowing his secrets and thoughts. Terry believed Lamont was the most guarded person on the planet, and he despised and respected this mindset.

'Whatever then. How's your love life? Have you banged anyone good?'

Lamont laughed. Terry always brought the conversation back to women.

'Nothing serious,' he replied.

'Mate, you need to get out there. Tell you a story. Met this bird in town right. Cracking lass, dead bubbly, tits you could set up a fucking home on. I take her home to my abode right, and . . .'

Lamont tuned out, finishing his meal as Terry rambled on about the filth he and the woman had got up to. Terry liked to talk and Lamont liked to listen. It was another reason they got along. As Lamont was wiping his mouth, his phone rang.

'Hello?'

'Where the fuck are you? I've been here for ages,' said Shorty.

'Just eating lunch. Won't be long.'

Shorty hung up.

'Let's hurry, Terry. Business awaits.' Lamont waited for Terry to pay the bill.

* * *

Ricky Reagan drove through Chapel Allerton in a tinted Vr6. Rap music blared from the speakers, announcing his status to all around. Even in the current heat wave Reagan rocked a gilet, t-shirt and converse sweatpants. He was armed and ready for any situation. In this game, he had no shortage of enemies.

A lit spliff hung from Reagan's mouth as he gripped the steering wheel one-handed. On the passenger seat was a bag of cocaine he was on his way to sell. Delroy had forbade him from doing this, insisting he work through their network of distributors. Reagan wasn't paying unnecessary middleman fees though. He could handle his own business.

Screeching to a halt, he exited the ride, eyes flitting in all directions looking for anything out of the ordinary. Nothing sprang out though. He banged on the door.

'Ricky mate,' The man said when he saw Reagan standing there.

'Terry.' Reagan pushed past him into the living room, dropping the baggie on the table.

'Get my money,' he ordered. Terry hurried to do his bidding, his face pink. He returned with a stack of money, handing it to Reagan.

'There you go mate.'

Terry reached into the baggie, scooping out a small amount of the powder with his little finger and snorting it, breaking into a coughing and sneezing fit as the coke hit his sinuses.

'Top stuff!'

Reagan didn't respond, focused on checking his money was correct. Terry watched him, his lip quivering from cocaine and paranoia.

'Do you know Carlos? That DJ in town? I'm cool with him. You ever need tickets for his shows, I'm your man.'

No reply. Terry took a deep breath, noticing his hands shaking.

'He's got this half-Brazilian girlfriend too, mate. I'd do all kinds of shit to her. She—'

'Shut up. I'm gone. Bell me when you need more,' snapped Reagan.

Terry nodded and waited for Ricky to leave. He then locked the door behind him and hoovered two lines of cocaine, his heart hammering.

* * *

Reagan smiled as he jumped back in his ride. He had Terry right where he wanted him. Soon he would force Terry to take more drugs from him, extending him credit and dragging him further into the hole. Terry was a victim. People like Reagan bled victims. That was the game.

Reagan pulled onto Francis Street. He spotted K-Bar, one of Shorty's lieutenants, holding court on the road with some of his people. Reagan cruised by, winding down the window and grilling him. To his credit, K-Bar didn't turn away. He met Reagan's gaze with a steely one, not backing down as Reagan vanished around a corner.

* * *

Shorty and Lamont hopped out of Shorty's Golf. They were parked on a nice street in Oakwood that screamed *family*. Lamont always felt a sense of peace when he looked at the large houses with their spacious gardens. He followed Shorty, who knocked hard on the door, kissing his teeth and knocking again when the owner didn't answer.

The door swung open, and a woman faced them, panting as her auburn hair fanned her face. She looked at the ground for a moment, taking a deep breath before addressing them.

'God, Shorty, why can't you wait? I've told you before about knocking like that.' She ran her fingers through her hair, pea green eyes boring into him. Both men stared before coming to their senses.

'Answer quicker next time then,' Shorty pushed past her. 'Where is the most beautiful girl in the world?'

'Daddy!' A tawny bundle of joy charged from the living room and into Shorty's arms. He smothered her with kisses, carrying her back into the room.

'I'm trying to get her settled. Don't get her excited,' said Amy. When Shorty gave no sign he'd heard her, she turned to Lamont, hugging him in greeting.

'How are you, L? It's been ages.'

'Too long. I'm good, Ames. You?'

Amy and Shorty had been high school sweethearts, their affair far from conventional. She had been the intelligent, studious type, Shorty more hot-headed and streetwise. Their dalliance shouldn't have worked but had. The relationship was torrid and rocky, mingled with affection and a lot of passion.

After school, they had lost track of one another. Shorty had hit the streets, getting another woman pregnant when he was twenty one. After reconnecting with Amy years later, Grace was born.

Nowadays, Amy worked for a large marketing company. She made a good living, but with the money Shorty threw at her, she didn't need to. It was yet another reason Lamont admired her. She had character.

'I'm good, L. Just working hard and looking after that little madam,' said Amy. They both smiled now, hearing Grace giggle as Shorty tickled her.

It amazed Lamont to witness Shorty's transformation whenever he was around Grace. The street goon persona diminished, he became much happier, more carefree, dominated by the will of a curly haired four-year-old with an infectious smile.

Lamont understood that Shorty was making up for not seeing his son, who had moved away with his mother, by being there for Grace. Along with giving Amy money, he spent as much time with Grace as he could.

After playing with Shorty, Grace held out her arms to Lamont, and he gave her a hug and kiss.

'Hello, Gracey-Wacey. Shall we go to the shop?'

Grace nodded, 'I want a Ribena, Uncle. L.'

'C'mon then. Back soon, you two.' Checking to see if they wanted anything, Lamont left, swinging Grace up onto his shoulders. Amy and Shorty could hear the pair singing as they pranced down the road.

'Lamont should have one,' Amy remarked.

'One what?' Shorty glanced over at her.

'A kid. I think he's ready. He has that look when he's around Grace.'

Shorty snorted, dismissing her words. 'L's all about his money. He doesn't need a kid fucking up his flow.'

Amy's brow furrowed, her forehead crinkling. Her mouth opened and closed as she impaled Shorty with a glare. As she spoke, she folded her arms.

'Does Grace *fuck up your flow?*'

'Course not. Me and L are different though.'

'Maybe. I think he needs it though,' Amy paused. 'Don't you think he looks . . .' she hesitated again.

'Looks what?'

'He looks exhausted, don't you think?'

'What are you on about?' Shorty resisted the urge to yawn.

'He looks lonely and tired.'

'Lonely? L can get it whenever he wants. He's not lonely.'

Amy shrugged, exposing her neck. Shorty's laughter abated as he took in the beauty of his daughter's mother. As much as Amy irritated him, the attraction surged within, and he couldn't fight against it. She felt Shorty's eyes roving her body. Despite her instincts screaming not to, she met his gaze. He invaded her space, capturing her mouth in a vicious kiss, their bodies close enough to feel the others thudding heartbeat.

'Shorty, they'll be back in a minute,' said Amy, moaning. Shorty ignored her and kissed her pale neck, sending desire shooting down Amy's spine. Before they could take it further, Shorty's phone rang.

'Fuck off,' he grumbled, reaching for it. 'Yeah?'

* * *

Lamont and Grace headed back to the house with enough treats to fill a confectionery. Lamont opened the gate and arched an eyebrow at the sight of Shorty and Chink waiting in the garden, not looking at one another. Grace ran to Shorty.

'What are you doing here?' Lamont slapped hands with Chink whilst Shorty led Grace inside.

'I couldn't get hold of you, so I rang Shorty. I have news.'

Lamont checked his pockets, 'must've left my phone in the car. What's up?'

'I've got us a meeting. You remember my boy Marrion?'

Lamont did. Marrion was an associate that Chink had brought up from Manchester a while back to boost their ranks. Lamont had met him once or twice. He disliked the people Marrion hung with and had resisted bringing him into the inner fold.

'The Manny guy. Yeah, I remember.'

'He said Akhan's guys were keeping tabs on him. I've taken the initiative and reached out,' said Chink.

'Have you heard anything?' Lamont leaned forward. Akhan was a powerful supplier with links everywhere. He had interests in Leeds, but remained selective about who he worked with. Chink had been working on an introduction, and if Marrion's intel was correct, this would help.

'Not yet. It sounds promising though. Marrion's seen them around a few times now. He thinks they're interested.'

Lamont mulled it over, not wanting to take the word of someone he didn't trust.

'Put more feelers out. See what you can learn and keep me posted.'

Chink nodded, walking to his car. He drove away as Shorty came outside.

'Amy's gonna kill you for getting Grace all those sweets.'

'She'll have to catch me first.' Lamont grinned.

'Whatever. Where did Chink scurry off to?'

'To get us a new connect.'

Shorty frowned. 'You what?'

'Unlock the car and I'll explain. I think my phone's in there too.'

CHAPTER THREE

Sunday 4 August 2013

LAMONT SLOUCHED BEHIND the wheel of a nondescript Nissan. The car wasn't his; he never went to meet people regarding business in his own ride.

Chink had asked Lamont to come to a warehouse out of town they owned. It comprised a large, open space with a table and assorted spindly chairs. Shorty and Chink were waiting when Lamont arrived, Chink staring at the floor while Shorty messed about on his phone.

'Give me something good,' said Lamont.

'Akhan's people have a spot. Near that old mosque in the Hood. Do you know where I mean?'

Lamont nodded.

'Hares Avenue. It's a good spot. Police stay away from there. They're scared of pissing off the Muslims.'

'Exactly. They have invited us to see Akhan there,' said Chink.

'When?' Shorty asked.

'Tomorrow evening. Eight pm. Me and L will go in. You drive and wait.'

'Are you daft? I'm not waiting in the car.' Shorty crossed his arms.

'It's a meet-and-greet. Why do you need to be there?'

'Why do *you* need to be there?' Shorty's voice rose.

'I want you both there. We'll meet beforehand to prepare. Shorty, make sure K-Bar's on alert, just in case,' said Lamont. Satisfied, Shorty nodded. Chink raked his hands through his dark hair, his mouth tightening. Lamont watched them climb into their cars. He needed to ensure their egos didn't ruin a potential goldmine.

* * *

The next night, Lamont, Chink and Shorty headed to the meeting in another borrowed ride. Shorty drove, eyes darting between mirrors as he kept a lookout for the law.

When they pulled up on Hares Avenue, two Muslim men stood outside a house, smoking cigarettes on the otherwise deserted street. Lamont, Shorty and Chink walked past them, approaching the house.

Out of nowhere, half a dozen men surrounded them. Lamont glanced at Shorty, silently warning him to keep composed. After being frisked, the men led the trio upstairs into an opulent study. The room was quiet, a hint of incense in the air. Behind a smooth wooden desk, Akhan waited, perched on his seat. His elbows rested on the desk, hands locked, forefingers pointed outward towards the trio. His midnight-dark eyes assessed them, unyielding, his dark suit unruffled, head tilted to the side.

Chink and Shorty positioned themselves at opposite ends of the room. Akhan motioned for Lamont to take a seat opposite him, and they shook hands.

'You are Teflon,' he spoke softly, traces of an accent in his voice.

'I am. You must be Akhan,' replied Lamont, meeting Akhan's eyes.

'I'm pleased to make your acquaintance.' Akhan's expression softened, recognising Lamont's intent.

'Likewise. I believe we can be of some use to each other.'

'I concur. We've both done our research. I know this. You, Teflon, are exactly the person we want to deal with.'

Lamont hid a smile, pleased it was going so well. It was this easy sometimes, especially if each party knew what the other brought to the table.

'I'm glad to hear it. For any deal to work though, it is imperative the product remains consistent.' Lamont didn't want the same problems that plagued his relationship with Delroy. He held his breath, knowing Akhan's reply would make or break the deal.

Akhan inclined his head a fraction. 'Our product is solid, I guarantee this. Let's discuss a price.' He scribbled a figure on a piece of paper, passing it to Lamont.

Lamont studied the number, hiding his surprise. It was much lower than he had expected.

'This is very generous,' he admitted.

'If you require credit, I can offer bail on up to ten boxes.'

'I can pay up front.' Lamont appreciated the offer though. Akhan was offering credit for up to ten kilos, which was a huge upfront commitment.

'When you wish to do business, call this number and quote the code, *Mr J*. My men will provide you with the details and a sample as you exit,' said Akhan. Lamont assumed they were finished, and stood to leave. Akhan raised his arm, halting him.

'I also wanted to give you something else; a small token of friendship.'

'You've done more than enough,' said Lamont.

'Please, allow me to present you with this gift.' Whilst Akhan spoke, one of his men placed a black box laced with gold trim in front of Lamont. He felt Akhan's eyes on him as he opened it, stunned by the box's content.

'I'm led to believe you are partial to this brand.' Akhan, smiled at Lamont's shock.

It was a bottle of *Centaure de Diamant*. An expensive cognac. Lamont held it in wonder, transfixed by the mahogany colour and elegance of the diamond-shaped bottle.

'I don't know what to say, Akhan. Thank you for this. It's *too lavish*,' Lamont's tone was hushed. Akhan shook his head again, implying it was nothing. Lamont gave the bottle to an equally impressed Chink to hold.

'Thank you for agreeing to meet. I think we'll both see the benefits of this arrangement.'

'It's a win-win situation.' Akhan shook Lamont's hand, and they left.

* * *

'That was a result!'

Shorty was driving, bopping his head to the car music like a madman. There were moments when he could be joyfully childlike. His infectious mood caused Lamont to laugh too.

'Let's not get ahead of ourselves,' said Chink.

'We're sorted now. Those Asians are fucking large,' said Shorty, forgetting his dislike of Chink in his elation.

'Not in the car,' said Lamont, not wanting to discuss business while they were driving. Shorty scowled.

'Can I taste the sample?'

'No you can't. Take us to Tek's,' said Lamont.

Chink waited in the car. He and Tek had their issues. Lamont knew of them and didn't press it. Tek opened the door to Shorty and Lamont, grinning at the pair like they were long-lost family. He was a middle-aged burnout former chemist with a knack for drugs. Rail-thin and tattooed, he always seemed to have a spliff resting between his lips.

To most he was an unreliable cokehead, but to Lamont he was a genius who'd never reached the heights he should have.

'Tef, thought you were dead, mate!'

'He may as well be.' Shorty brushed past the pair.

'Ignore him. Are you busy?' Lamont asked, leading Tek into the house at the same time.

'A few peeps are coming over. What's the crack?'

'I've got summat for you to sample,' said Lamont.

Tek lit his spliff and inhaled before offering the joint to Lamont, who declined. Shorty took it.

'Follow me.'

Tek led them to a back room. When he switched the light on, they were in a room dominated by huge, scientific-looking machines.

'What do you have for me then?' Tek asked.

'Shorty. Give him the ting,' said Lamont. Preoccupied with the spliff, Shorty flung the pack at Tek, who caught it, and opened it with a small pocket knife. He placed the crystal-white powder into a glass vial, mixed up a solution, and added this to the same vial, before placing it into a large machine at the far end of the room.

'What the fuck is that?' Shorty asked.

Tek didn't reply. He hunched over the machine, pressing buttons and staring at several lines and equations that had appeared on the screen.

Shorty glanced over at Lamont, who watched Tek, his curiosity piqued. He had brought Tek product to test before and never had it elicited this reaction. Lamont strode over to see the screen which displayed a complex-looking graph. Tek was gazing at this, mumbling gibberish that only meant something to him.

'Go on, what does it mean?' Lamont asked.

'This beauty is a mass-spectrometry machine,' Tek gazed at the graph. 'It separates the individual components and identifies the chemical signature of the substances within the sample you provided.'

'What does that mean?' Shorty spoke louder now, annoyed at Tek for ignoring him.

'It means, you're looking at cocaine that is around seventy percent pure,' said Tek.

'Fuck off!' Shorty's eyes widened.

'There are other tests, but it's fantastic. The last stuff you guys gave me, I could barely get a reading.'

Lamont smiled to himself. If Tek was correct, and he believed he was, the product Lamont had was better than anything else in Leeds. He could cut the cocaine four, maybe five times and still have the best merchandise. His excitement bubbled. Life was about to change.

'L, may I?' Tek motioned to the rest of the sample. They were in the living room now, remnants of dinner on the coffee table, mingled with several cans of lager. Cigarettes and weed stench hung in the air mingled with Lynx. Lamont nodded. Tek had earned a taste.

'Me too,' said Shorty, crowding over the coke Tek had now placed on his coffee table.

'Be careful, this is strong shit,' Tek warned as Shorty scooped a large amount on the end of his car key. Shorty snorted the powder, his head jerking back as he spluttered.

'It's not all that,' he said, his face twisting. Lamont watched him. Shorty's nose was dripping, and he hadn't realised.

'L, you need to bang that at least four times,' Tek scooped a small amount up with his pinkie finger and ingested it. 'You'll kill someone otherwise.'

Shorty had cottoned on to his nosebleed, stemming it with a piece of tissue as he paced the room. Lamont beckoned him over.

'Get the word out. We've got some new shit. Get it pinging.'

'Say no more.' Shorty left the room. Lamont knew the drill. Shorty would relay to K-Bar, who would arrange delivery and figures. The operation was fluid, large in scope and well-structured. Akhan's drugs would launch it into another stratosphere.

'Tek, we're leaving,' Lamont motioned to the coke. 'Keep that.'

'Cheers. Stay and meet my mates before you go though. They'll be here in a sec.'

Turning to the window again, Lamont looked out at Chink. A car pulled in behind him.

'Chink's waiting,' said Lamont. Tek replied but Lamont didn't hear a single word he said. A man climbed out of the second car, but the woman stepping from the passenger seat distracted Lamont.

The world behind her melted. Raven-haired and long-legged, her pronounced curves were untamed by the conservative khaki jumpsuit she wore. Lamont's eyes blurred, unable to blink, unwilling to tear his eyes away.

'Tef! Are you listening?' Tek's voice rose.

'Sorry. What did you say?' Lamont remained glued to the window.

'What's Chink's problem? I paid him back.'

She had entered Tek's garden now. Sensing Lamont's presence, she looked up. For a moment, chestnut eyes met his rosewood own, then she was in the house. Lamont stepped back. Tek played host, his conversation with Lamont forgotten.

'Tone, good to see you mate. Can I get you a drink? A line?' Tek rambled, his mannerisms more vivacious under the influence of the drugs. 'Jenny, how're you doing, lass? Haven't seen you since we got stranded down in Brum that weekend.'

'L,' Shorty walked in the room before Lamont could hear Jenny's reply. His nose had stopped bleeding now.

'Is it sorted?'

'K-Bar's on top of it. Who is *that*?' Shorty leered at Jenny.

'Your guess is as good as mine,' said Lamont.

'She's tasty.'

Lamont frowned, but marshalled his irritation.

'Calm down, player. We need to leave.'

Before they could move, Tek led his friends over to them.

'Let me introduce you. Tone, Jen, these are my good friends, Lamont and Shorty. You two, these are my long-time compadres, Tony and Jenny.'

Lamont and Shorty shook hands with them, lingering a second longer with Jenny. Close-up, she stole Lamont's breath; she wore a touch of makeup, hair flowing past her shoulders with loose bangs either side. It suited her.

They spoke for a short while, Lamont learning that Tony worked in a bank, whilst Jenny ran her own florists. Lamont couldn't tell if the pair were together. If they were, Lamont decided it wouldn't stand in his way. Jenny was extraordinary.

Chink glared at the pair as they climbed in the car a while later.

'What took so long? It's freezing in here.'

'You should have come inside then. Tek was proper hospitable.' Shorty wiped his nose again.

'Whatever, cokey.' Chink's lip curled as he glared at Shorty. Shorty ignored him and tried to start the engine, still dazed from the cocaine.

'I'll drive.' Lamont saw Shorty was confused. Chink watched them switch seats.

'How are we looking then?' he asked.

'I think you'd better order more benzocaine.' Lamont flashed his friend a large grin.

* * *

Once home, Lamont headed to his drinks cabinet and added the bottle of cognac to his collection. He gazed at it, touched by both the gift and the gesture itself. Akhan had found out what Lamont enjoyed, which appealed to his ego.

During the meeting, Lamont had noticed not just power, but also the casual elegance only the wealthy possessed. He thought of Delroy, who had money but didn't use it with the same panache Akhan did. The timing was perfect.

There was more money to be made, and Lamont resolved to delay his departure a while longer. Lamont fixed another drink and smiled to himself as he fantasised about his future.

CHAPTER FOUR

Tuesday 6 August 2013

TERRY WORTHY DROVE along the quiet street looking for a parking spot. His clammy hands gripped the steering wheel as he turned down the thumping hip-hop song he'd been listening to.

Two youngsters waited for him, clad in dark tracksuits. One of them towered over the other. Terry could see the lining of his muscle through his Nike top. His companion had a ratty smile on his pointed face. Terry signalled for them to get in.

'Let's make this quick.' He reached under his seat, handing the boy the drugs. The kid looked at the packet, passing it to his ratty associate. He went to open the passenger door, but Terry grabbed his arm.

'What the hell are you doing? Where's my money?'

'Inside,' the boy pointed at the house. 'I'll be two minutes.'

'I said I wanted to be quick,' said Terry.

'It will be, man. Chill. Like I said, two minutes.'

'Don't fuck me about,' Terry warned. The boy nodded, not meeting his eyes.

'Yo, I know who you are, Terry. I wouldn't mess about a top boy like you.'

Terry smirked, satisfied that the kid knew his rep. The youngsters climbed from the car and hurried into the house. Once they brought his money back, he would clear one thousand pounds in profit for little work. Terry checked his watch a few minutes later when the kids didn't return. He grumbled as he climbed from the car and hurried towards the house. He knocked twice on the door, but received no reply.

Panicking now, he burst into the derelict house. A cool breeze coming from the kitchen led Terry to an open back door. He reached the gate in time to see a taxi speed away.

'OI!' Terry shouted, but it was too late. The youths had vanished and so had his drugs.

* * *

'I can't believe how easy that was.' Timmy Turner laughed from the taxi. His plan had gone off without a hitch. He had played to Terry Worthy's ego, counting on the old relic thinking he feared him. The ounces they robbed would pay for their night, and they would have money left to flip.

'Told you. Terry's not gonna do shit,' said Ben, his thick-lipped, ratty-looking accomplice. He looked up to Timmy and followed him, trying to make money and get laid in equal succession. He failed most of the time but Timmy liked him. Ben was entertaining in his own way.

'Where are we going?' the driver asked. Timmy gave him the address and pulled out his phone with a smile. Business was on the up.

* * *

Reagan stormed down the street, mobile phone in hand and danger in his eyes. He'd built an impressive reputation over the years, yet people still seemed to try him. Terry hadn't repaid him yet for drugs he'd received on credit, and now he was ducking his calls. Reagan could almost hear Delroy's voice in his head, telling him *I told you so*, lording it over him as he stuffed his fat face with yet another meal. As always, Reagan would leave one hell of a message and remind the streets why they feared him.

With two phone calls, Reagan had Terry's new location. A group of teenagers chilled on the road, laughing and joking, listening to music on their mobiles. Reagan quickened his step, pushing through the kids. No one protested. Some knew him by face, the rest by reputation. There was nothing they could do.

As Reagan approached his destination, a figure climbed from a parked car and fell in sync with him. Younger and almost as ruthless, TC had worked with Reagan for years. Reagan kept him close, using him for missions and to send messages.

Terry was a buffoon, but he was cool with Teflon, and some of his sneakiness may have rubbed off. Reagan wasn't taking any chances. TC was armed and had no qualms about using his weapon. The pair of them climbed up the steps. At a signal from Reagan, TC kicked the door in. They charged into the living room, startling Terry.

'Ricky, mate—'

Reagan didn't hesitate. A single blow cracked the bridge of Terry's nose. He toppled to the ground, the air driven from his lungs as Reagan stomped on his ribs. TC stood back and watched with a smile on his face, keeping an eye out for intruders as Reagan kicked Terry again.

'You think I'm a prick? Thought you could take my shit and not pay?' He kicked Terry a third time. Terry curled into a ball, retching and moaning, holding his ribs.

'Ricky, mate, I got robbed. Please—'

'I don't give a fuck. Get up.'

Terry froze with fear.

'I said get up,' said Reagan. Terry struggled to his feet.

'Now, tell me how you're gonna get what you owe me?'

'Mate. I'm fucked. I've got nothing.'

Reagan signalled to TC, who drew his gun and aimed it at Terry.

'That's not good enough.'

'I've got a mate doing pills. I'll get the money from him, I promise,' pleaded Terry, mucous mingling with the blood and tears. Reagan glared at him, breathing hard, smarting fists still clenched.

'You've got until tomorrow night. Don't think about running. I tracked you once and I'll do it again. TC,' he turned to his accomplice. 'Teach him a lesson before we go.'

* * *

Mikey B was a former doorman turned pill seller. He'd stumbled into the game after door work dried up, and he was doing well. On the scale of things, Mikey seemed like an ordinary decent guy. He kept himself in shape and had shovel-like hands that resembled *The Hulk's*. He had taken his hits, grinding to get into a solid financial position.

Now, Terry sat, trying to hit him up for money.

They were at Mikey's place. He'd moved from a spot in Cottingley to a bigger place in Moortown. It was a quiet area, and he liked it. As the pair spoke, classic *Britpop* played in the background. Mikey took a deep swig from a bottle of Coors, facing the mess in front of him.

'I need you mate,' said Terry.

Mikey sighed, putting the bottle down. Terry was his friend, but the guy gave new meaning to the word *fuckup*. He owed Ricky Reagan money and had no hope of paying it back in the time given.

'Please, Mikey. Gimme the five grand. I'll pay him and that'll be the end.'

'How would you pay me back?' Mikey asked.

Terry hesitated. 'I could work it off.'

'You got yourself into this position because you couldn't slang the drugs, but I'm supposed to believe you're gonna pay me back? Do you think you can rip me off because we're mates?'

'I'd never rip you off! The difference is you won't kill me if I'm late. Reagan is serious. He will murder me if I don't get his money. I need five bags. I know you've got it.'

'Yeah, I've got it. Worked hard for it too. Why can't you ask Lamont for the money?'

'Are you serious? He'll set me up on some payment scheme, then Shorty will rip my head off if I miss it. How is that any better?'

'Who ripped you off?' Mikey hated the part of him wondering if Terry was making the whole thing up.

'Some youngsters. Do you know little Timmy Turner? Black lad, well built.'

'You mean Shorty's little cousin?'

'Timmy's related to Shorty?' Terry was slack-jawed, eyes widening from the information.

Mikey shook his head. 'You can't be serious.'

'The sneaky little shit. I can't believe he skanked me.'

'I can't believe you let him. Speak to Lamont. Get him to make Timmy give you the money back.'

Terry hesitated. Mikey resisted the urge to smack his friend. He had no problem asking Mikey to loan him money, but baulked at the thought of asking someone else for help.

'Take your chances with Reagan then. Either way, I'm not giving you the money, so there you go.'

* * *

Carlos was lounging around at home, trolling on the internet. He was a smooth-skinned man with traces of Asian and Irish blood in him. He was about his music and was popular and outgoing.

Zoë was making them dinner and dancing to some music. They were both so engrossed that at first they didn't hear the door until the person knocked louder. He kissed his teeth and went to open it. When he did, two men dived at him, pinning him to the floor. They laid into Carlos with punches and kicks, subduing him.

Zoë heard the commotion and ran towards them, screaming. One caught her with a vicious backhander. She hit the carpet with a tremendous thud and lay still.

'Zoë!' Carlos tried crawling to her.

'Shut up. We'll deal with your bitch later. This is about you,' One of them snarled. Through woozy eyes, Carlos recognised the man as Ricky Reagan. He had seen him in town and knew he was a big deal.

'Ricky? What the fuck man? What is this about?'

Reagan grinned. 'You know me then?'

'Course I know you. Everyone knows you. Why are you doing this?'

The grin hadn't left Reagan's face. 'Ask Terry Worthy when I'm finished.' He hit Carlos again, knocking him out. He and TC turned their attention to Zoë, still sprawled out in the middle of the living room.

'Go lock the door,' Reagan ordered.

* * *

Lamont watched the crowds of people as the taxi approached a busy street, teeming with clubs and loud music. Still buzzing from the meeting with Akhan, Shorty wanted to celebrate. Lamont was reluctant, but was talked into it. He'd spent his day dealing with an issue that had cropped up.

Terry Worthy had stupidly done a deal with Shorty's younger cousin, Timmy. He'd ripped Terry off, which Lamont found amusing. He didn't want to be associated with skanking however, so Shorty had forced Timmy to give Terry the drugs back, issuing his cousin with a stern warning.

The pair made their way to Normans Bar on Call Lane. It was an elegant nightspot, with a pure white ceiling, thin, dark brown pillars, comfortable purple booths, and a well-stocked mahogany and glass partitioned bar. Loud R&B music was being spun by the resident DJ and the crowds were feeling it.

Shorty and Lamont fought their way to the bar and ordered bottles of beer. They were well-dressed and turning heads, but none of the females were biting yet. Shorty had his phone out and was making call after call, trying to get anyone else to come out.

'Losers,' he kissed his teeth. 'Everyone's moving soggy. Wanna go somewhere else?'

'I'm following your lead,' said Lamont. Shorty glared and was about to retort when he spotted something. His eyes narrowed.

'Back in a minute.'

Lamont sipped his drink and watched Shorty disappear. He spotted a petite blonde stood nearby, wearing a short black dress and heels. She was pretty but wore too much makeup. As she swayed to the music, she grinned at Lamont. About to go in for the kill, a movement by the entrance held Lamont's attention.

Jenny had entered, flanked by two other ladies. She wore a sleeveless top and loose-fitting trousers and was striding across the bar with her people like she owned the place. He stared at her, transfixed. His new friend sensed Lamont's attention wavering. She shifted closer, but it was futile. Lamont took a deep breath and stepped forward.

* * *

'It's too packed in here,' moaned Kate. Jenny's best friend since their younger days, she was a cocoa-skinned woman with sultry features and an hourglass figure. She stared around the bar with barely veiled contempt, her glossed lips smacking together.

'Don't worry. We'll have a drink and go somewhere else.' Jenny led the way when a hand touched hers, halting her. Startled, she turned to protest when she realised it was the dealer she'd met at Tek's place, *Lamont*. The corners of his eyes crinkled as he grinned.

'Jenny, right?'

'You're Lamont. Tek's friend.' Jenny could feel her friends staring, so she kept her attention on Lamont.

'That's right. What are you drinking?' He motioned to the bar. A blonde girl stood there, shooting daggers at both Lamont and also Jenny, who picked up on this.

'It's fine. We can buy our own.' Jenny wanted to put distance between herself and Lamont. The last thing she needed was trouble.

'I insist,' Lamont looked past her at her friends. 'Apologies, I didn't catch your names.'

'I'm Kate,' Kate replied.

'Michelle,' The other added.

'Nice to meet you both. You look gorgeous,' Lamont said. They beamed, pleased with the compliment. 'What are you drinking?'

Neither hesitated in ordering. With reluctance, Jenny did the same, unable to see the jilted girl now.

'Here you go.' Lamont passed their drinks, then paid with a fifty pound note. He held out his glass.

'To exquisite company.'

Their glasses clinked, and they all took a sip.

'Are you by yourself?' Kate asked Lamont. He shook his head.

'My mate's around somewhere.'

'What about that girl?' said Jenny.

'Which girl?' Lamont frowned.

'The blonde one by the bar giving me dirty looks.'

'She's nobody. Don't worry about her.' Lamont didn't even bother looking for the girl. His dismissive arrogance irked Jenny. She let it slide though, watching him charm her friends with ease. She sighed to herself.

'Are you okay?' Lamont asked.

'I'm fine.'

'I'll get you another drink. Who's up for champagne?'

Before they could answer, there were loud voices and screams. Lamont moved into a better position, unsurprised by what he saw.

* * *

Amy was on a rare night out. Since having Grace her social life had dwindled. Amy's friend had dragged her out tonight, insisting she needed it. After picking out a dress and sinking several glasses of wine to calm her nerves, Amy complied. She'd missed it more than she thought. Guys were all over her and she enjoyed the attention.

Amy was dancing with one of her admirers when a voice made her freeze.

'What are you doing here?'

Amy whirled around. Shorty stood there, his face twisted with fury, his nostrils flaring.

'Hey, Shorty,' she said.

'Where's Grace?'

'At the bar where do you think?'

'Don't play with me,' said Shorty. Amy could see his muscles straining against his dark t-shirt, his eyes red.

'She's with my mum. What's your problem?' Amy fiddled with her bracelet. Shorty's eyes flitted to her dance partner.

'Leave. I need to talk with my girl.'

'Shorty, I am not your girl. we were just dancing. It's no big deal.'

'Mate, I don't want any trouble.' The man was already backing away from Amy.

'Move then. Fuck off.'

'Shorty, please just go. We can talk about this tomorrow.' Amy sighed when a bouncer waded over, sticking his chest out.

'Is there a problem over here?' He asked her.

'Yo, this is between me and her,' Shorty barked at the bouncer.

'Calm down, pal.'

'Fuck you.'

'That's it. You're out. Let's go.' The bouncer tried grabbing Shorty, but he shrugged him off. Two more bouncers stormed over. The music had turned down, and everyone watched the standoff. The trio surrounded Shorty, but he didn't seem fazed. They grabbed for him and he tussled with them.

'Get off him!' screamed Amy. Shorty continued to struggle, but they were overpowering him.

'Stop. That's enough.' Lamont was in the mix now. One bouncer paused.

'That you, L?'

'I need you to cut him loose,' said Lamont. 'Are you okay?' he asked Amy, who nodded, taking a deep breath. The bouncers let Shorty go. After a glare from Lamont, he walked out, not even looking back at Amy. Debbie appeared at her side carrying two Amaretto and Cranberry drinks.

'What happened?' she asked, sensing tension.

Amy stared at her friend, feeling tears pooling in her eyes, suddenly wanting to go home.

* * *

The next morning, Lamont woke early. Instead of getting up, he lay back and assessed the night before. He'd calmed Shorty down and stuck him in a taxi, thankful Shorty hadn't ended up arrested or hospitalised.

By the time Lamont re-entered the club, Jenny had disappeared. Lamont found his thoughts drifting towards her. He visualised her big brown eyes, long legs, her penetrating glare, and imagined what it would be like to watch her come *undone*.

With a flourish, Lamont climbed out the bed and hurried to get ready. He had a plan.

* * *

Tek stumbled downstairs, half-naked and grumbling. The loud banging at the door had ruined an otherwise perfect lie-in.

'I'm coming. Chill,' he shouted, tripping over a pair of stray Converse trainers by the door. 'Shit.'

Locating the key, Tek unlocked the door and glared at Lamont.

'L, man. What gives? It's proper early.'

'I needed to see you. Make some coffee and wake up.'

'This is my place, not yours,' Tek grumbled as he headed to the kitchen. In the time since Lamont had last been, the house was no cleaner. The ashtray on the coffee table was cluttered with weed roaches and cigarette butts. Lamont perched on a chair and opened an energy drink he'd bought on the way, gulping it.

'What's up? Got another sample for me to test?' Tek took a hopeful sip of coffee.

'I'm not here about business.'

'Go on then. What's on your mind?' Tek made himself comfortable.

'That girl from the other night. What's the story?'

Tek laughed, spilling his drink. He ignored the billowing liquid staining his sofa as he sniggered.

'Surprise, surprise. I saw you eyeing her.'

'I'm curious, that's all.'

'When aren't you? Bloody hell, L, you run through these birds like Usain Bolt,' said Tek.

'Stop messing about.'

'I'm not. C'mon, you think you're the only one? Jenny's got a lot of guys chasing her.'

'What do I need to know?'

'How the hell would I know? If I knew, I'd take a run myself.'

'I saw her last night. Do you have a number for her?' Lamont pressed. Tek drained his cup and got up.

'One sec,' he stomped upstairs, returning with Kate. She had a duvet wrapped around her body and a tired smirk on her dishevelled face. 'This sexy queen might help. Usually finds her way here after a night out.'

'He means he *took advantage* while I was drunk,' Kate's tone was glib. 'Nice to see you again, L.'

'Likewise. Where'd you lot go last night?'

'Down to Greek Street. You didn't think you had Jenny after one drink, did you?' Kate raised an eyebrow. Tek giggled. Lamont glared at him.

'Jenny's a tough nut to crack. You want her, you need to surprise her,' Kate continued.

'How?'

'She needs a driver,' Kate said after thinking for a minute, 'to do deliveries. She's advertising for it. Take her work number. The rest is up to you.'

'That works.' Lamont smirked.

* * *

Mikey B sat in Terry's tatty flat, watching his friend knock back another beer.

'Mikey, I fucking love you mate.'

The drugs Timmy had brought back rested on the table next to two empty bottles.

'You've saved my skin! I can give these to that psycho.'

Mikey B shook his head. 'That's not gonna work. Ricky doesn't want the drugs, he wants his money. Have you got anyone else you can move it through?'

'Yeah, course. I've got loads of connections,' said Terry, as if he hadn't been ripped off. Mikey had to hand it to him; he didn't stay down for long. Whatever disappointment life threw at Terry, he took it.

'Why did you sell to Timmy then?'

Terry struggled to answer.

'He's a wrong sort. Why deal with him over someone else? You know what these youngsters are like.'

'I had plans, and I was in a hurry,' Terry scratched his face. 'It's cool now though. I'll flip this work, pay Ricky and that's the end. When I'm done, maybe we can talk about —' Terry's phone rang. He answered, listened for a minute, then stumbled to his feet.

'I'm on my way. C'mon, Mikey! We need to go.'

* * *

The scrap of paper with Jenny's number burned a hole in Lamont's pocket as he lounged in his home, eyes closed as the sounds of John Legend's *Get Lifted* album filled the room. Lamont grabbed the number, gazing as if it held the answers to a test. He smirked, laughing out loud at the absurdity of his situation.

Lamont had things to set up, plans to take his game to the next level, yet here he sat, scheming to get a date like some horny teenager. Jenny had him though. Lamont was no stranger to the fairer sex, but few had ever captivated him like she had. Lamont had a sudden brain-wave whilst he made a cup of coffee. Before he could stop himself, the phone was in his hand.

'Jenny Campbell speaking?'

Lamont froze.

'Hello? Is someone there?'

'I'm calling about the delivery job,' he said, altering his voice.

'Excellent. Let me jot down details. I need your name and the best contact number please.'

Straight to business. Lamont liked that. He gave her a fake name and arranged a meeting for the following day. Determined to make a better impression, Lamont had a sure-fire way to accomplish his goal.

* * *

Terry stood near the door, watching Carlos sob.

'What happened?'

Carlos glared at Terry, his tears dissipating.

'I'll tell you what happened. That psycho Ricky Reagan came to my house, beat the shit out of me and raped my girl. Because of you.'

'Mate, I—'

'Did you tell him about Zoë? Because he said I needed to blame you. Is that what you did?' Carlos' voice rose.

'Mate, you've got it all wrong. I said I could get him some tickets to a show. I never told him to do this.'

'Don't you get it? He sent you a message because you mentioned me. Because you always have to be the fucking big dog. Because you always have to talk yourself up and make yourself seem like the main attraction. All because you're an insecure little prick.'

'Steady on pal, I know you're upset, but—'

'Upset?' Carlos pointed upstairs. 'They raped the woman I love. She hates me. As far as she's concerned, it's all my fault, because I've got friends like you.'

Terry hung his head. He stared at the floor, feeling Carlos' pain, knowing how much Carlos loved Zoë. Terry couldn't even explain why he had brought her into his conversation with Reagan. He hadn't even thought the thug was listening. Now, Reagan had retaliated in the worst way.

'Carlos, I'm sorry,' He said, his voice thick with emotion.

'Get the fuck out of my house. I hope I never see you again.'

* * *

Terry was quiet as they left Carlos' place. Mikey drove along, listening to the radio. After a few minutes he turned it down and faced Terry.

'You need to shift this gear sharpish and get that crazy cunt off your back. Okay?'

Terry didn't reply.

'Oi,' Mikey raised his voice. Terry looked up. 'I know you're upset, but you need to sort this. I'll stay with you until it's done; we'll give him the money together, make sure that this is all done with.'

Terry nodded, feeling a profound guilt over what had happened to Zoë. She was a nice girl, and he had shouted his mouth off about her for no reason.

Mikey was on his phone now. With a single phone call, he had a buyer for the product and they were on their way to meet him. The only downside was they were selling cheap, killing Terry's profit.

Never had Terry felt so far behind the pack. Mikey moved pills, yet with ease had secured someone to take the cocaine. Resigned to whatever happened, Terry stared out of the window.

* * *

Reagan met Terry outside a barber shop in Harehills. He leant against a Mercedes Benz in a designer tracksuit, looking pleased with himself. His gundog TC watched the pair, his eyes lingering on Mikey, sizing him up.

'Terry! Good to see you. You got that then?' said Reagan. Terry handed Reagan the money without meeting his eyes.

'Summat wrong, Tezza? You're not your usual gossipy self. No stories for me?'

Terry didn't reply, watching Reagan thumb through the money. They were standing in public and he was a known criminal, but he didn't seem to care.

'Got any more links? The last one you recommended, she was everything you said she would be. Isn't that right, T?' Reagan turned to his soldier.

TC nodded, licking his lips. 'Dead right. She was delicious.'

Terry looked up then, his eyes blazing with fury. Reagan noticed and his attitude changed. The playful manner dissipated in seconds. He dropped the stack of money through the open passenger side window.

'You got summat you wanna say? Go on, say it,' he said. Terry didn't speak. Mikey stepped forward.

'I've got summat *I* wanna say,' he started. 'You may think it's cool to rape a bird, but it's not. You've got your money. Stay away from Terry now. This is done.'

Reagan frowned. No one spoke to him like that. He stepped forward. Mikey had two inches and some size on him. Reagan met his glare, his eyes narrowed.

'Who do you think you are?'

'I'm the one who tells you what others won't. Rape isn't cool. It's not summat to brag about.'

Reagan shook his head. 'You don't wanna get on my bad side. I can promise you that.'

'You don't scare me. Like I said, you got your money. Your business with Terry is over now. That's the end.' Mikey B stared into Reagan's eyes.

'Is it?' Reagan's voice was full of malice. TC watched the exchange, debating whether to get involved. He had seen Mikey in the company of some heavy faces. It wasn't worth the aggravation.

'Rick, we've got that meeting. Let's deal with this later,' he said. Reagan nodded. Not taking his eyes from Mikey, he climbed into the passenger seat. TC started the engine, and they motored off down the street.

CHAPTER FIVE

Thursday 8 August 2013

JENNY'S DAY WAS NON-STOP. A spate of summer events meant that she had worked hard to meet orders whilst interviewing for a new driver. They were more like meet-and-greets, but Jenny felt burnt out. She didn't want to hire the wrong person. The right driver could take her business to the next level. Jenny was getting more opportunities from other cities. Her arrangements were unique and people loved them.

The interviewees so far were awful. The first didn't have a licence but had expected Jenny to give him a job *driving*. Another had been a horny lorry driver, who had spent the entire meet staring at Jenny's chest and not-so-subtly rubbing himself. It was revolting.

Now, Jenny was in her office checking that she still looked professional. She had put an apron over the blouse she wore and smoothed her hair. She noted the bags under her eyes. The door to the shop clanged. The next applicant was here.

'One moment,' she called. Jenny composed herself, then walked out to a huge shock.

'What the hell?'

Lamont Jones stood by the door. He nodded at Jenny, watching her with appraising eyes.

'Nice to see you again.'

'Lamont, I'm working.'

'Correct.'

'I'm expecting someone.'

'Walter right?' Lamont mimicked the voice from the night before. 'I'm here about the job.'

Jenny looked him up and down. He wore a plum coloured, crease-less shirt, black trousers, expensive looking shoes. In his right hand he clutched a ring binder. The cocksure expression on his face annoyed her so much that she called his bluff.

'Okay then, *Walter*. Follow me and we can begin,' Jenny locked the shop door and led Lamont to the office. She slid behind her desk and motioned for him to take a seat.

'Let's get started,' she picked up a pen, ready to take notes. Her face was composed and her manner brisk. 'Can I see your CV?'

Lamont handed it to her. She scanned it, impressed by the layout.

'Full name?'

'It's right in front of you,' said Lamont. Jenny scowled. 'Sorry. Lamont Jones.'

'Age?'

'Thirty-two years and six months.'

'And what do you do? Are you in employment?'

'This and that.'

'Care to be more specific?'

'Okay. Supply and demand,' said Lamont with a wink. Undeterred, Jenny wrote his responses.

'Do you have a valid UK driver's licence?' She continued. He nodded.

'I will ask a few work-related questions, just to allow me to see what kind of worker you would be.'

'Fire away.'

'Why do you want the job?'

'It has great benefits.'

'Such as?'

'A *stunning* work environment.' Lamont met Jenny's eyes. She held his gaze for a second then continued.

'What skills do you bring to the workplace?' Her tone remained unchanged.

'I make a good cup of coffee, I entertain, I have flawless speaking skills, people skills, humour,' Lamont counted the traits on his fingers. 'Do I need to continue?'

Despite herself, his reply tickled Jenny. To her surprise, Lamont rose to his feet.

'Wait, don't answer that. I'll do a practical demonstration.'

'W—What?'

'I'll make you a kick-ass cup of coffee.' Lamont took two mugs from the cupboard and added coffee to them. Jenny watched, feeling like she was losing control of the situation.

'Aren't you going to ask how I want it?'

'Nope. I'm gonna *tell* you how to take it,' He winked again. 'Assertiveness right?'

Jenny didn't respond. Lamont's dismissive arrogance in the club had irritated her. Now, he seemed wittier than she had given him credit for. Before she could ponder any further, he placed a cup in front of her.

'Drink it.'

'It needs milk.'

'No, no. Take it black.' Lamont smiled again and sipped his own coffee. *He was playing games.* Jenny sipped the drink. It was strong, but not bad.

'It's good right?' Lamont watched her face.

'Let's press on. What do you have in the folder?'

'Apart from the CV, I've got my birth certificate, NI number, CRB form, driver's licence, qualifications, references, blah blah.' He pushed the folder towards her.

Jenny looked through the paperwork, again impressed by the layout. Lamont had gone to a lot of trouble to impress.

'Who is Martin Fisher?' She looked at his references, noting the contact number.

'My boss. He owns a small gym. I work there from time to time.'

'You said earlier that your business was supply and demand.'

'I work recreationally. I *demand* my clients work their hardest to achieve their goals and I *supply* the workplace, motivation and overall fitness expertise.'

Jenny hid a smile at the speed of Lamont's responses. He talked a good game.

'What are your hobbies and interests?'

'I like to play chess, I read—thrillers mostly. Slight film buff. I follow sports. I—'

'Like to drink champagne in clubs,' Jenny interjected. Lamont laughed.

'I'm isolated, but sometimes I need to be social.'

'Are you good at chess?'

'I know my way around the board. Do you play?'

Jenny nodded.

'We must play together sometime.' Lamont's rosewood eyes burned into Jenny. She looked away.

'Let's push on. If I was to call you in the middle of the night and ask you to deliver to Birmingham, would you be able to do it?'

'I have *no problem* working through the night.' Lamont let the double entendre hang in the air. Against her better judgement, Jenny grinned.

'Okay. Wait—what's the time?'

'Quarter to six.' Lamont checked his watch.

'Really?'

'Time flies when you're having the time of your life.'

Jenny studied him, 'you don't give up do you?'

'There's no fun in giving up. When are you gonna let me take you out?'

'I don't date employees, Mr Jones. I have a strict policy.'

'So I have the job then? Because I'll quit to uphold the sanctity of your policy. I swear I will. Scout's honour and everything.' Lamont placed his hand over his heart. Jenny laughed. He watched, pleased by the effect he was having on her.

'It makes sense, Jen. We get along. What's one little date gonna do?'

'Fine,' Jenny sighed. 'If it gets you to leave, I'll do it.'

'Splendid. I'll need that personal number and I'll be on my way.'

Lamont eased to his feet. The corners of Jenny's mouth twitched as she wrote her number on the corner of his CV. Tidying his paperwork, she closed Lamont's ring binder and handed it to him.

'Don't be ringing me at two in the morning about a booty call.'

'I'll try. If you get the urge though, I'd be very chuffed if you acted on it.' Lamont held out his hand. 'Thank you for taking the time to meet with me. I'm sorry I wasn't suitable for the role,' he deadpanned. Jenny shook Lamont's hand, impressed by his firm grip. She held it longer than was necessary, letting go once she realised this.

'I'll see you soon, Lamont. You drive safely.'

'I will.' With a mock-bow, Lamont left. Jenny gazed after him. When she realised she was staring at the door, Jenny walked back into the office. She still had work to do.

* * *

Timmy Turner and Ben stood in a queue in town, waiting to get into a club.

'I hope there's fit girls in here,' said Ben. Timmy scowled, but didn't reply. He was still sulking about having to give Terry Worthy his drugs back. Shorty had been furious about what happened, and Timmy had been lucky to avoid a beating.

The queue inched forward and they reached the front. Timmy and Ben were ready to step in and party when two beefy bouncers crossed their path.

'Not tonight lads,' One of them said. He forced them to the side, then let the people behind them straight in.

'We queued for ages though,' said Ben. The bouncer glared at him.

'We're only letting mixed groups in tonight. Get some lasses and try again.'

'C'mon, mate, there's only two of us. We're not here to cause trouble. We wanna spend money,' Timmy tried negotiating. For a second the bouncer looked receptive.

'Oi,' Ben prodded the bouncer. 'Your boy just let them three white boys in. That's tight!'

'You're not dressed right. Try again another time.'

'Prick,' Ben mumbled. Quick as a flash the bouncer grabbed him by his shirt and dragged him away from the crowds.

'Think you're a big man? I'll break your neck.' His massive fist was raised.

'C'mon man, he's sorry,' Timmy tried calming the bouncer down. Ben was annoying but he couldn't stand back and watch him get hurt.

'Shut it or you're next,' The bouncer wrapped his hands around Ben's neck. 'I'm sick of you little black bastards. You sell a few drugs and suddenly you think you're hard men. Well, not around here.'

Ben's arms flailed as the bouncer choked him. Timmy looked around for something to strike the larger man. He would have to use his fists. A voice stopped him mid-lunge.

'Timmy?'

Timmy turned, surprised to see Chink's friend, Marrion Bernette standing there. They had met before, and Timmy had noticed then how charismatic the Manchester man was. Timmy was bigger than most of his peers, but Marrion towered over him. He wore a white shirt and grey trousers with tan coloured boots. Timmy didn't recognise the men with him.

The bouncer released Ben, who leant against the wall coughing.

'You know these lads?' The bouncer shook Marrion's hand.

'That's Shorty's cousin.' Marrion pointed at Timmy. The bouncer paled. He knew who Shorty was. If word got out he had manhandled them, he was dead.

'Fuck. I didn't know that.'

Marrion smiled. 'Now you do. They're with us.'

The club was filled with scantily clad women of all races and sizes. As the quintet made their way to the bar, Timmy and Ben stared in all directions.

'Put your tongues away,' Marrion said, laughing. His people ordered two bottles of Dom Pérignon. 'Where's Shorty at?'

Timmy shrugged. Marrion nodded, seeming to understand.

'Drink up anyway. Everything's on us tonight,' he motioned towards his crew, pointing at a tall, light-skinned man, and a shorter man. 'That's Antonio, and Brownie. You two, this is Shorty's cuz Timmy and,' Marrion nodded at Ben. 'What's ya name boss?'

Ben replied with his mouth full of vintage champagne. He had drunk two glasses already.

'Chill,' said Brownie, watching him pour a third. 'It's early yet.'

It was a lively night after that. They hit several clubs, spending big money in each. Timmy had two hundred pounds in his pocket. Marrion and his people had spent double that in the first club. He couldn't remember having a better night.

Dawn loomed when Marrion draped his arm around him.

'You're all right, kid; didn't think you'd keep up. How old are you again?'

'Eighteen,' Timmy slurred, drunk from all the high-class alcohol.

'You've got potential. Tell your cousin it's time you got a bump up. And a pay rise.'

'I'm trying,' said Timmy thinking of all the times he had pleaded with Shorty to elevate him.

'Give it time. Take my number. I wanna talk to you when we're not so drunk. I'll put money in your pocket.'

'You've done enough,' Timmy's words tumbled out. 'You lot paid for everything and—'

Marrion silenced him with a hard stare. 'If a man wants to give you money, take it, but make sure you find out what he wants in return.'

'Well, what do you want?'

Marrion watched Timmy for a long moment.

'Friendship.' He looked past Timmy to a group of attractive girls who were studying the pair with interest. 'Let's go make summat happen with these slags.' He dragged Timmy towards the girls.

* * *

Lamont lounged in a café the next morning as Jenny entered, owning the room as always. She spotted Lamont, slid opposite him and greeted him with a wide smile.

'I'm surprised you wanted to meet here,' admitted Jenny, noticing the puffiness under his clouded eyes.

'When the company's right, where you are doesn't matter. What are you drinking?'

Jenny called the waitress over and ordered a bottle of elderflower water, requesting a glass and some ice. Lamont couldn't take his eyes off her. She wore her work attire, just like last time they had been together. Even when she wasn't trying, she still looked spectacular. She wore a touch more makeup and a dash of red lipstick this time.

'You look beautiful.'

Jenny beamed again.

'Thank you.'

'Tell me about your work; why flowers?' Lamont asked as the waitress brought Jenny's drink over.

'Not much to tell. I always had a fascination with flowers and art. As I got older, I put more into it.' Jenny twirled a stray lock of her dark hair as she sipped her beverage.

'How did you get started?'

'Worked hard. Borrowed money from my parents and rented a dingy shop. The rest is history.'

Lamont gazed as Jenny spoke, taking in the slight curve of her eyebrows, the hint of pearly white teeth beneath those sensuous lips. She was extraordinary.

'And you? How did you get into *personal training* was it?' Jenny made air quotes with her fingers. They laughed.

'I was in the right place. I'm personable and I have a knowledge of how the human body works.'

'One of these days, we will talk about your real job.' Jenny met his eyes.

'I look forward to it,' Lamont drained his coffee. 'Can I get you another drink?'

Jenny shook her head. 'You shouldn't drink so much coffee.'

Lamont wiped his eyes, acknowledging Jenny's words with a nod.

'Are you okay? I wasn't going to bring it up, but you seem tired,' she continued.

'Too many late nights, that's all.'

'Lay off the coffee then. Drink water.'

'I will. I do.' Lamont tripped over his words.

'Good. Make sure you do. Filtered if possible.'

'You seem to have quite an interest in my wellbeing.'

'Just making conversation,' said Jenny. Shrugging, she glanced out of the window, the atmosphere chilled.

'I'm gonna get a bottle of water,' Lamont scratched his ear as he headed to the counter. Lamont tried to make small-talk again after he returned with his drink. Jenny reciprocated, but it seemed stilted. Lamont was sure he had blown it, but kept up the conversation. Soon, Jenny looked at her watch and reached for her handbag.

'I need to go. I left my assistant in charge,' she stood. 'This was nice.'

'Agreed. You're good company.' Lamont slid to his feet. Jenny surveyed him.

'Would you like to go for a proper drink tomorrow?'

'Pardon?' Lamont hadn't heard her.

'Kate and I are going for drinks. Would you like to come?'

'What time?' Lamont didn't even try playing it cool.

'We should be there for nine.' Jenny's features seemed to glow now, and they both smiled. Lamont left a tip and followed her outside.

The sun rested in the sky and there were no clouds in sight, a testament to a surge of good weather. It was too warm now for the jacket Lamont had brought, so he held it in his hand as they stood on the pavement.

'Can I give you a lift to your office?' he asked.

'I'm parked nearby. Thanks for the offer.'

'I guess I'll see you on Saturday then.'

'Friday,' Jenny corrected.

'Just checking,' leaning over, Lamont kissed Jenny on the cheek. 'Take care.'

'You too, Lamont,' said Jenny. With that, she crossed the road. Still grinning, Lamont watched until she was out of sight.

* * *

'Fam, it's the best thing to do. We need to step up.'

Timmy sighed. It felt like he'd only slept for two minutes before his mum was waking him, saying that Jerome and Ben were waiting for him. He'd dressed and staggered out to meet them. They sat in Potternewton Park now, passing a spliff around.

Jerome was older than Ben and Timmy. He was unruly, the type of person you wouldn't let in your house even if you knew them. Known for being shady, the streets shunned him, and he'd taken to running with Timmy because of this.

'Jerome's right, T. We need to make something happen,' added Ben. He kicked a stray can around, making more noise than was necessary. Timmy and Jerome both scowled.

'Leave that damn can alone,' Jerome told him.

'Fine. Chill.'

'We can make it happen. Let's make our case,' Jerome continued.

'Teflon's funny. He doesn't like people just creeping up on him.' Timmy had heard Shorty talking occasionally and he had been clear on one thing; Teflon didn't like surprises.

'Trust me, this'll work. You're Shorty's cousin. He's waiting for you to step up to the plate. At your age, Shorty was moving kilos.'

Jerome's words hit home. Timmy remembered the times Shorty would stop by his house when he was younger. He always had fresh gear and always looked the part. Even at a young age, it had triggered something. Timmy wanted to walk Shorty's path. He wanted people to clamour towards him when he entered a spot. He wanted to be the main man.

Maybe Shorty had mentioned him to Teflon? Maybe they wanted him to take the initiative?

'Okay. Let's stop by and see him. He'll be down the barbers.'

* * *

'Checkmate.'

Ken kissed his teeth, staring at the board in frustration.

'How did that happen?'

'Easy. I sacrificed the Castle and forced you to commit the Queen. It was simple after that.'

'You think like an old man, I swear,' Ken laughed. He was a balding black man in his early sixties, full of stories about the old days. He spent most of his time sitting in the barbers, soaking up atmosphere. Lamont liked him. Ken was a fun guy who lived life and had taken full advantage of England after coming over from the West Indies in the sixties.

'I play to win,' said Lamont, hoping Ken would take the bait and challenge him to another game. He was about to reply when three kids walked in. Lamont recognised the one in the middle, but his phone rang before they could speak.

* * *

'You want a cut?' A barber motioned to the empty chair when he saw the youths.

'Nah, he does though.' Timmy pushed Ben forward. He tried protesting but sat in the chair after a look from Timmy.

While the barber asked Ben what style he wanted, Timmy and Jerome both stared at Lamont. He had looked at them for a second when they entered. Timmy thought he was about to speak, but his phone had rung. Lamont remained on the call, doing more listening than talking.

Timmy gawped. Lamont was the main man. Like Marrion Bernette, he exuded power. He sat in the chair, well-dressed, aware of his surroundings. Timmy felt his mouth drying.

'Go on, go and speak to him.' Jerome elbowed him. Timmy stumbled, but maintained his composure and glowered at Jerome. Lamont had finished on the phone, now gazing at the chessboard.

'Erm, Teflon?'

Lamont's head rose. He regarded Timmy with mingled curiosity and irritation. Timmy's hands were clammy now. He was out of his depth.

'My name is Lamont. You're Shorty's cousin. *Timmy*,' his words were clipped. Timmy hung onto every word.

'I was wondering if I could chat to you for a minute?'

'Do you play chess?'

'Nah, I don't.' Timmy made a face.

'I see. What do we have to talk about?' Lamont's question wasn't meant as a slight, but Timmy wished the ground would swallow up. *This was a crap idea.*

'I . . .' Timmy's mind had gone blank. Lamont's expression was mild but his eyes were a different story. They were boring into Timmy's. Timmy looked at the floor, unwilling to meet the gaze.

'Spit it out,' said Ken, annoyed at Timmy's stammering. The whole shop erupted into laughter. Everyone but Lamont chuckled.

'I wanted to say sorry for what happened with Terry.' Timmy got his words together. Lamont said nothing. His eyes implored for Timmy to continue.

'Me and my people just want an opportunity to grow.'

Lamont stared at him for a few more seconds.

'Okay,' he said.

'You what?' Timmy was sure he hadn't heard.

'I'll give you an opportunity.'

Timmy's face broke into a wide smile.

'Really?'

'Have you ever cut hair before?'

'Cut hair? What are you on about?'

'I thought you wanted a job?'

'Yeah, but not working in here, I wanna . . .' Timmy realised his mistake. Lamont would not talk business with him. He was toying with him.

'Sorry,' he mumbled, hurrying from the shop. Jerome followed him.

'Yo, wait for me!' Ben called from the barber's chair to no avail.

'Kids nowadays,' said Lamont. Everyone laughed again.

* * *

'I can't believe we did that.'

Timmy punched the wall in frustration. He had been humiliated in front of Teflon and the locals in the barbershop. With his failure, the plan seemed ridiculous.

'It's cool,' said Jerome. They sat outside an old shop on Louis Street in the Hood. 'You're on his radar now. He'll be watching you.'

'Don't be thick. I shouldn't have done it.'

'Trust me, it's cool. Can't believe we ducked Ben like that though.'

Before Timmy could reply he heard the screeching of tyres. Shorty's car pulled up, and he leapt out, eyes bulging with rage. Timmy opened his mouth, but Shorty raised his arm, silencing him.

'Don't say a word.' He turned to Jerome. 'Get out of here. I'll deal with you later.'

Jerome didn't need telling twice. Shorty glared down at his cousin as Jerome ran away.

'Stand up.'

Timmy did as Shorty demanded, aware of the throbbing pain in his hand. With no warning, Shorty slapped him hard in the face, sending his young cousin staggering. Anger flared up in Timmy and dissipated. Shorty would kill him if he tried to flex.

'Are you stupid?'

Timmy stared at the floor, his face and hand smarting.

'Yo, it was dumb, I—'

'Damn right it was dumb. This isn't *The Sopranos* you little prick. Did you think you were gonna walk up to Teflon, talk your talk, and he would give you a box of coke to move? You don't know how close I am to cracking your head open. First you rip off Terry, and now this. How daft are you?'

Shorty had stopped by the barbers. When Lamont told him about Timmy's stunt, he'd gone ballistic. Timmy wanted to run with the wolves but he wasn't ready yet. This proved it.

'I'm gonna tell you this one time; stop letting that fool Jerome put ideas in your head. He's where he is because he's a snake and a fuckup. No one trusts him with work. Why d'you think he's hanging around you? You need to cut him and that little prick Ben loose and get a better calibre of friends before you try to make power moves.'

Timmy still didn't speak. The slap had mollified him.

'Get in the car. You're not working tonight. Don't fucking go anywhere either. Stay in and think about your next step because I'm tempted to slap you again. Get in. Quick.'

Timmy climbed in, his face burning with humiliation. He was glad that his people hadn't seen Shorty telling him off. As soon as Timmy's door closed, Shorty sped away.

CHAPTER SIX

Friday 9 August 2013

LAMONT ROLLED OVER, wiping his eyes and yawning. He reached for his phone. When he saw the time, he vaulted out of bed, cursing. He was supposed to meet Jenny at nine pm. It was already half nine. His body yearned for more sleep, but he needed to do this.

Lamont hurried to the bathroom, turned on the shower, then stripped out of the clothing he had fallen asleep in.

As he stepped into the scalding shower, he soaped himself, thinking about the things that needed to change. Number one was the sleep pattern. He couldn't do this anymore. People respected Lamont for being reliable. Falling asleep in the middle of the day wasn't reliable, and it wasn't productive.

The shower was quick. Lamont hurried to the closet and picked a pair of jeans and a long-sleeved top. He fastened his watch and slipped on a pair of shoes. His hair was a mess as always. He'd run a comb through it but it had resisted the bristles. He looked at his face. His eyes were bloodshot and he could do with a shave. It would suffice though. As he dialled a taxi, Lamont hoped it wasn't too late.

The taxi driver was stoic, which Lamont appreciated. Already sweating from the muggy heat, Lamont climbed from the taxi and almost collided with an overweight drunken man bellowing at the top of his voice and staggering.

There was a queue to get into the bar, lengthened when a couple kicked off near the front when the bouncers said they weren't dressed right. After the wide-boy threatened to come back for them and the bouncers laughed it off, Lamont entered the bar, navigating his way through a mass of bodies. Lamont felt the old-school vibe, the crowd dancing to *Mary J Blige*. The bar was a modern monstrosity, lots of chrome and glass. Everyone was out in their finery.

Lamont made his way through the crowd, looking for Jenny, hoping she hadn't left. He was halfway to the bar when he saw her sitting in the corner, smiling as a guy talked to her at length. Kate was there, but didn't look as happy as Jenny. Lamont ordered a gin and tonic from the bar and walked over.

'Sorry I took so long.'

'Lamont. I thought you'd stood me up.' Jenny's face was unsmiling.

'Something came up. Let me make up for it by getting drinks.'

'No need. Tristan took care of us,' said Jenny. Lamont gave the man his attention. He had a square head and a similar build to Shorty, looking like he spent a lot of hours in the gym. They sized each other up.

'Nice to meet you, Tristan.'

They shook hands. Lamont turned his attention to Jenny. She wore a blue Peplum dress and black heels, her hair coiffed and teased, skin shimmering in the low lights of the bar. It was the first time Lamont had seen her so dressed up, and he struggled to avoid staring.

'Sensational,' he murmured. Jenny smiled tightly.

'What about me?' Kate piped up.

'I was getting to you,' said Lamont, laughing. Jenny's face remained impassive. She spoke to Tristan again, and the man shot Lamont a smug smile.

'Why were you so late then? Tell the truth?' Kate kept up the conversation. Lamont appreciated the distraction.

'I haven't been sleeping well. I dozed off and overslept.'

'Don't let Jen hear you say that. She'll have you doing yoga and meditating before the night ends.'

'I'll bear that in mind.' Lamont glanced around the room, unable to understand the exclusivity of the bar. Apart from the music, there was no theme. The floor was sticky under his feet and the bar staff were rushed off theirs.

'What do you think of this place?'

'Chrome isn't my thing,' admitted Lamont. He kept his eyes on Kate, trying not to think about Jenny growing closer to Tristan. He glanced in Lamont's direction as he swaggered to the bar.

'My friend wanted to start a bar. He couldn't get the funding though.'

'You should have sent him to Tek for a loan.' Lamont winked. Kate laughed.

'What are we talking about?' Jenny stood between them now, brushing her arm against Lamont's. The fleeting movement warmed his stomach.

'Lamont was giving his opinion on this bar. He thinks it's tacky.'

'It is. I was telling you this last time,' Jenny said. 'Why did we pick such a pretentious place?'

'Because we wanted to show Lamont how upscale we were.'

'Lamont's a man of mystery. We went on a date and he took me to a greasy spoon,' said Jenny. She was clicking her fingers to the beat as she spoke.

Lamont's ears pricked. 'That was a date?'

Jenny gave him an appraising glance as Tristan came back with three drinks.

'Sorry, Lamont. Didn't know what you were drinking.'

'No problem.' Lamont took another sip of his gin and tonic, his eyes surveying the bar. He spotted a stunning honey-shaded woman near the bar with her friends. She kept looking in Lamont's direction and smiled when she caught his eye. He grinned back, then continued drinking his drink.

'You seem to find them every place you go, don't you?' Jenny watched him.

'What do you mean?'

'I think you know.'

'I'm just here to drink with you, Jen. Don't worry about any other ladies.'

'I didn't say I was.'

Kate, Lamont and Jenny talked for a while. Tristan felt squeezed out and skulked away.

'So, L, what do you like about my girl Jen?' Kate asked. Lamont looked at Jenny to see her reaction. Her face was unreadable though.

'She opened my eyes,' admitted Lamont. He could see from their reaction that his answer had surprised them.

'How do we know you're not just trying to bang and tell your friends?' said Kate. Lamont wondered if they had planned these questions before he turned up.

'Because I'm a grown man who doesn't need to run and tell the world my business.'

'Can you get girls? Or is it only when you buy champagne for them?' Kate wasn't pulling any punches.

'I do okay. If I need to,' said Lamont.

Kate glanced around. 'So, if I said to talk to any girl here, you could?'

'If I needed to.'

'Do it then.'

'No.'

'Why not?'

'Because Jenny's opinion means more.'

Lamont and Kate locked eyes, neither backing down. A third voice piped up.

'Do it.'

They both looked at Jenny. She stared back at the pair.

'What?' Lamont gaped. Jenny looked amused though, her eyes sparkling.

'I want to see if you walk the walk. If you do it, I'll give you a kiss.' She met his eyes for a moment. Lamont felt the desire for this woman surging throughout his veins. He didn't care who saw. Jenny's eyes continued to twinkle as she waited.

'A kiss?'

'That isn't enough?'

'It'll do. For now. Pick a girl.'

They did. A round-faced, smooth-skinned black girl twirling a straw in her drink sitting in an adjacent booth. Lamont sauntered over. The girl didn't sense his presence, engrossed with dipping her straw in her drink.

'You seem sad,' he noted.

'I'm not interested.' She didn't move.

'In what? *Happiness?*'

Now she looked up.

'You're going to make me happy?' she asked.

'I'm going to buy you a drink, stop you from drowning that straw. Any drink you like apart from champagne,' said Lamont.

'Why not champagne?' She looked intrigued now.

'I realise it sends the wrong message. Makes me seem like a prick who throws money around.'

'Maybe you can't afford it.'

He laughed, 'there's always that,' he held out his hand. 'Lamont.'

'Robin,' she responded.

'Well, Ms Robin, what can I get you?'

'Who's this?' A man had stormed over during their conversation, his face shiny, eyes narrowed. He towered over Lamont, broader and almost bristling as he stood over the booth.

'Hey, babe. This is Lamont.'

'What's he doing here?' The man's eyes hadn't left Lamont's. Lamont stood.

'I was just talking to a new friend. Don't worry about it.' He walked away, defusing the situation. Jenny and Kate laughed as he took his seat.

'Nice try. I guess your skills weren't good enough,' teased Jenny.

'That's not fair. She had a man.'

'Doesn't matter. You failed.'

'Guess I better get another round in.'

Later, they left the bar. Lamont's head spun from the buzz of the liquor. He hung close to Jenny, his hand skimming her waist as he guided her outside.

'Where are we going now?'

'We're meeting friends. I'm not sure where you're going,' said Jenny, laughing. Lamont gazed, thinking about what he wanted to do to her, watching her in her sexy dress. He gathered her into his arms, pressing her body close to his.

'Don't keep me waiting,' he whispered.

'I'll try not to.' With a nibble of Lamont's ear, Jenny broke the embrace and sashayed away with Kate. Lamont watched them with a grin. He hadn't worked so hard in years. Jenny had him hooked, and worst of all, she knew it. Turning, he went to hail a taxi.

* * *

'You're just teasing him now.'

Kate and Jenny walked towards Brooklyn Bar. The cool air sobered them as they navigated past groups of drunken guys whilst avoiding being groped.

'I'm just making him work for it,' said Jenny. Kate rolled her eyes.

'Are you serious? Didn't you see the way he looked at you? Lamont wants you, Jen. You can see it in his eyes. He's jumped through hoops to get close to you.'

'We both know what he does though,' Jenny sounded concerned. Kate was quiet as they crossed the road.

'Lamont seems decent, and you're a good judge of character. Don't make him wait forever though. Either you take it further, or you don't.'

Jenny didn't reply. She knew Kate had her best interests at heart. They were always honest with each other. Lamont was in a dangerous business and she didn't understand why. He seemed to have everything going for him, yet Jenny sensed a vulnerability emitting from him. The more she was around Lamont, the more drawn she became towards finding out what he was all about.

'Let's see how it goes.' Deep down, she knew she had to decide.

* * *

The next night, Lamont went to see his sister. He noticed a Mercedes parked across the road as he approached the house. Lamont had seen it before but couldn't think where. He shrugged it off and opened the front door, startling Marika in the hallway.

'You scared me, bro.'

'Let's go for dinner. My treat. Are the kids in?'

Marika shook her head. 'They're at Clara's house.'

Lamont almost asked if Marika ever looked after them. He held his tongue.

'Me and you then. Anywhere you want to go.'

'We've already cooked. Auntie's here.'

Lamont took a deep breath, resisting the urge to leave. His stomach lurched as he followed Marika to the living room. Auntie Carmen sat there like she owned the place. She was their father's older sister. Lamont hadn't seen her in years, but she remained the same; overweight and beady eyed with a shit-eating smirk.

'Lamont. How are you?' She tapped her cheek. Lamont held his breath as he kissed it. She'd only done this because Marika was around. To say Lamont and his Auntie didn't get along was a colossal understatement.

'I'm fine, Auntie. How are you keeping?'

'Are you still in that barbers pretending to work?' Auntie ignored Lamont's question. He took another deep breath, controlling himself. Just then Marrion Bernette walked out of the kitchen, stopping when he saw Lamont. An awkward silence ensued. To his credit, Marrion didn't appear alarmed. Instead he studied Lamont.

'Nice to see you again, Marrion,' said Lamont. Marrion nodded, seeing the game Lamont was playing.

'You too, Lamont. Hope everything's cool.'

'Cooler that the Arctic. I assume you're staying for dinner?'

'He cooked, and we invited him. Unlike some people,' said Auntie.

'L, you don't mind chicken do you?' asked Marika before he could respond.

'Chicken is fine.' Lamont took the seat furthest from Auntie. She watched him with her piggy eyes, desperate for him to say something else she could rip apart. Lamont wouldn't give her the satisfaction. He stared at the TV, pretending to be interested in the mundane reality show on the screen. The tension thickened.

Later, the four ate the tasteless food in silence. Lamont twirled his fork around on the plate, not wanting to chew the rubbery chicken, wondering about the pair. He had never introduced them. He didn't know how they had met and that unsettled him.

Lamont didn't like having his worlds so close together. He knew Marika wanted him to ask about the situation and for once, he played right into her hands.

'What's going on here?' He laid his fork down. Marika and Marrion looked at one another.

'With what?'

'You two. Am I missing something?'

'What do you want me to say? We like each other,' said Marika.

'How do you even *know* each other?'

'We met in town.'

'Is that a problem?' Marrion wanted Lamont's answer.

'It's nothing to do with him. It doesn't matter if he has a problem.' Lamont shot Auntie a venomous glare.

'Eat your food. No one's talking to you.'

'Don't talk to her like that,' said Marika. Auntie waved her off.

'It's fine baby. He doesn't scare me. He's a miserable little boy still trying to control his sister after all this time. It's pathetic,' she spoke to Marika, but looked straight at him. Lamont felt the rage building. He shot to his feet, needing to leave before he exploded.

'That's it, run off. You're nothing but a poor excuse for a man. Your parents would be ashamed of the person you've become.'

The room went silent then as Lamont froze, glaring into Auntie's smug, satisfied face, his hands shaking.

'Don't talk about my parents,' he said, trying to get himself under control.

'Touched a nerve have I?'

'L, don—' Marika started.

'Stay out of this,' Lamont's eyes hadn't left Auntie's. 'You wanna talk about touching nerves? How about the stories about you in the gambling houses? The things you did? You're nothing but a gold-digging con woman.'

'L!' Marika said as Auntie's face paled.

'I said, stay out. She started it. I'm finishing it,' Lamont turned to Marika, then focused on Auntie again. 'What have you ever done? You're a sad, twisted harpy of a woman who can't face it that life left her behind.'

Auntie's mouth opened but she couldn't speak. Tears pooled in her eyes. Marika jumped to her feet.

'Get out of my house, L.'

Lamont didn't bother to argue. He heard Marika comforting Auntie as he stormed away. Lamont had started the engine when Marrion hurried outside.

'Lamont, listen, I'm sorry about the ambush.'

'I don't have time for this.' Lamont sped off, driving through the streets like a mad man. Lamont regretted losing his temper. He had allowed Auntie to get into his head. The crocodile tears she put on for Marika's benefit had worked like a charm. Despite her roughness, Marika had a vulnerable interior. Auntie was an expert at exploiting this.

Once home, Lamont grabbed a bottle of vodka and a glass, ready to drink his anger away.

After the successful meeting with Akhan and the time he had spent with Jenny, Lamont wondered if tonight was a sign that his luck would change. His instincts were all over tonight. He had played right into Auntie's hands by not leaving the second he saw her.

The first glass went down smoothly. Lamont poured another and downed that one too. There were too many bad memories where Auntie was concerned. He loathed her; her nature, her attitude, her appearance and above else, her ability to make him feel like a helpless young child whenever he was in her presence for more than a few minutes.

The bad times in Lamont's life all began when he was forced to live with Auntie after the deaths of his parents. There was no preparation, and life after that was shaped for him. He closed his eyes, taking a deep breath.

Another glass, then another, and another. By the time Lamont passed out on his sofa, only a trickle of liquor remained in the bottle.

CHAPTER SEVEN

Sunday 11th August 2013

LAMONT STOOD in front of his parents' gravesite, staring at their names etched on the front of the marble headstone. His shoulders shook as he laid some flowers down.

The argument with Auntie had brought Lamont today, but he visited at least twice a month, sometimes with Marika and the kids, most times without. He switched his phone off on these occasions. Business didn't exist.

Lamont had loved his parents; a redundant but necessary statement. They had grown up in poverty, working hard to rise above it. They were well-liked and bound by their words and values. Without realising, they had instilled similar morals in their eldest child, morals he had adapted to make the drugs game work for him.

Lamont wondered if they would be proud of him, and the way he too had battled through poverty.

A slight chill spread through the cemetery and he pulled his jacket a little tighter. How long Lamont stood there, he didn't know. He reached down and touched the marble, feeling a single tear run down his face.

'I love you both,' he whispered, turning to walk away. As Lamont started the car and switched his phone on, it rang.

'Hello?'

'Mr Jones. Are you free later?'

Lamont gripped the phone closer to his ear, startled. Saj was Akhan's point-man. Lamont had spoken with him after the initial meeting with Akhan, finding him to be funny and personable.

'What time?'

'Nine pm.'

'Where?'

Saj gave him the details and hung up. Lamont drove away from the cemetery, wondering what Akhan wanted. Saj hadn't mentioned him by name but it was obvious he had called on Akhan's behalf. Lamont would call Shorty and give him the location, just in case.

* * *

Timmy rose early. He wasn't working, so he took his time. After getting ready he threw on a t-shirt and tracksuit bottoms and hit the block.

Timmy nodded to a few familiar faces and strolled around the streets. Chapeltown had been his home as long as he'd been alive. He couldn't imagine living anywhere else. Timmy knew everyone. They knew him and his family. Nowhere exuded the same energy as Chapeltown.

Even with the violent reputation it had cultivated in the eighties and nineties, it was a community, and Timmy pounded the concrete pavement with a personal sense of pride. He saw Jerome and Ben when he turned onto Frankland Avenue. Ben watched for police while Jerome dealt with a sale.

Timmy waited until they finished before walking over.

'Yes, Tim,' said Jerome. He pocketed the money and slapped hands with him.

'What are you two doing apart from looking suspect?'

'We're on our grind, fam. You know how I do it. I don't rest; I need to follow that money.' Jerome wore a black tracksuit with the hood up. Timmy didn't understand him. Any police cruising would know what he was doing.

'Whatever. What's the plan then?'

Jerome shrugged. 'I'm looking to go out tonight but my funds are low. Why do you think I'm here?'

Timmy laughed. Jerome was always broke. He had to buy product from whoever was around. Usually he got ripped off, but had to take it. Timmy felt sorry for Jerome. Without Shorty, he would be in the same position. It gave him food for thought.

'Ben, is your mum around? We can go smoke at your house later,' said Timmy.

Ben shrugged. 'Doesn't matter if she's round or not. She'll fuck off to her room if we're there.'

'That's a bet then. We'll buy a bottle and a draw.'

'By the way,' Jerome interrupted, 'did you know about Reagan? He smacked up Terry. You know Terry Worthy, the one who's always talking shit.'

Timmy and Ben shared a glance. They had ripped Terry off, but hadn't known someone had beaten him up over it.

'Is he okay?'

'Yeah. Must have paid his debt too because he's still alive. Heard Reagan went on extra though. You know Carlos, that DJ in town? Word is that Reagan ran up in his yard and raped Carlos's girl in front of him,' said Jerome, cackling with laughter.

'That's not funny.' Timmy glared at his friend.

'What's not funny?'

'You can't be laughing about raping someone. That's disgusting. What if it was your sister he raped?'

'I'd put a hole in his head. Terry's a pussy. So is Carlos. He's always playing that dead Funky House shit. No wonder he laid there and let it happen.'

'Even if he did, you're a piece of shit for laughing.'

'Miss me with all that sensitive talk. You're a nobody. You only get status because of your cousin. Where would you even be without him?'

'This isn't about Shorty.'

'It's about you. This game is cold. You wanna run around feeling sorry for all the pussies, go work for Oxfam.'

'C'mon you two, let's chill. We don't need to be arguing,' said Ben.

'Shut up. Everyone knows you're Timmy's bitch. Just stay out of the way.' Jerome's remark stung Ben, and it showed. Timmy was about to support him when his phone rang.

'Yeah?'

'Damn, someone's in a bad mood,' A voice laughed on the other end.

'Marrion?' Timmy moved away from Ben and Jerome, both of whom continued to bicker.

'No names, kid. Where are you?'

'I'm in the Hood. Something wrong?'

'I'm gonna send someone to scoop you up. Meet them at the Petty Station at the bottom of Roundhay Road. Just you.'

'Okay.' Timmy hung up, turning to Ben and Jerome. They were nose to nose, shouting at each other but not doing anything.

'I'll get with you lot later,' he said. Both boys stopped shouting and looked at him.

'Where are you going?'

'Yeah. We're meant to be chilling.'

'Summat's come up.' Timmy hurried to the petrol station, mooching around near the pumps. A few minutes later, a midnight blue BMW pulled up. Brownie motioned for him to get in and they drove off.

'What's happening, kid?' Brownie pulled into traffic, turning up the volume on his CD.

'Nowt, B. What does Marrion want?'

'Relax. It's all good.'

Timmy wasn't convinced. Brownie seemed cool but Timmy didn't trust him. His eyes were like flint. Even when he was trying to be reassuring, it made Timmy more anxious. He stared out of the window until they reached the destination, a house on Bayswater Terrace.

Brownie parked up, and they climbed from the car. Two youths sat in the living room, playing Fifa on the PlayStation 3. They nodded at Brownie, paying no attention to Timmy.

Marrion waited for them in the kitchen. He grinned when he saw Timmy and touched fists with him.

'Yes youngster. Good to see you again! What's new?' he asked.

'Same old; just doing my thing,' said Timmy. Something about Marrion made him tongue-tied. He didn't want him thinking he was an idiot.

'You're probably wondering why I called you up. I wanna put some money in your pocket, like I told you. I want you to do a few drop-offs for me. Easy money.'

'That's cool, but I work for—'

'Teflon. I know you do. I'm not stepping on toes. When you're not working though, you can always get money with me. No law against that.'

Timmy thought it over. He could learn a lot from Marrion and accepted because of that. The money was a bonus.

'Okay, I'm down.'

Marrion grinned again.

'Good man. Antonio'll get you straightened out. I've gotta jet. I'll be back later.'

* * *

Lamont entered the restaurant where he had arranged to meet Saj. He had been before, always enjoying the layout. On entry, there was a large stocked bar area with a smooth black wood finish. Solid beams of light resonated from the middle of towering marble pillars.

As Lamont was shown to the table, he noted the soft jazz music being played on the stage, patrons nodding their heads along with the instruments.

In the main area, there were dozens of round gold-topped tables. As he approached, Akhan and Saj were drinking glasses of water and talking in genial tones. They were dressed in black suits with crisp white shirts. Lamont shook hands and took a seat.

'Nice to see you again, Teflon,' Akhan spoke first.

'You too, Akhan. Thanks again for the gift.'

'It's nothing. As I may have mentioned, I don't drink, but I'm told that brand is exquisite. Have you tried it yet?'

'I'm saving it for a special occasion.'

Akhan smiled. 'Don't save it for too long. Would you like to order a bottle for the table?'

Lamont shook his head. 'Water will be fine.'

While Lamont looked at the menu, Akhan again studied him, reminded of the feedback he had received from his sources. Trinidad Tommy and Ken were respected men Akhan had known back in the day when they were all young Turks. Both agreed that Lamont was a force. His people worked hard for him and lived well.

Once they had ordered, and the waiter had gone, Akhan's manner changed. He no longer smiled, now businesslike. Lamont straightened in his seat.

'Where do you see yourself in five years, Teflon?'

Lamont hesitated. Akhan sensed his uneasiness, impressed by how guarded he was.

'I promise you, I have no ulterior motive. This is for my interest.'

Lamont nodded. 'I see myself in a position of power.'

'Are you not in one now?'

'You tell me. You're the one asking the questions,' said Lamont. Akhan acknowledged this with a small smile.

'Do you have any close family?'

Lamont was sure that Akhan already knew the answers to these questions, but humoured him.

'I have a younger sister.'

'What does your sister do?' Akhan's eyes hadn't left Lamont's face.

'She's trying to find herself.'

'And you're helping her?'

'In a manner of speaking.'

'What about friends? Do you have friends?' Akhan switched gears.

'I have friends and I have acquaintances.'

'How do you differentiate the two?'

'Sometimes I don't. Some I work with. Others I socialise with.'

'You're most likely wondering why I am asking all these questions,' said Akhan with an almost self-deprecating smile.

'I presume you're trying to get to know me, to understand what makes me tick.'

Akhan smiled again, wider this time.

'Why do you do it?' Akhan didn't have to explain what he meant. Lamont understood the question. He had expected it earlier.

'It's easy money if you know what you're doing,' he said.

'And do you?'

'I'd like to think I do. I'm sure I could do more, but there are ways I could do worse.'

Akhan smiled, impressed with his answers.

'I hear good things about you, Teflon. It's why I wanted to work with you. You could go far in this business.'

'I don't know about that.'

'I have been in this game far longer than you, and I've seen many people and a lot of things. You have all the traits.'

'I won't be doing this forever. As soon as I'm able, I'll walk away.' This was the first time Lamont had shared this with anyone outside his circle. Saj glanced at him but Akhan seemed unmoved by the statement.

'What would you want to do instead?'

'Live off the money. I don't want the risk forever.'

'No one does. That's why you buffer yourself from the operation. With the right backing, a man like yourself could earn tens of millions.'

When Akhan said the words *tens of millions*, Lamont felt a tingle. He loved the idea of having that much money, but he was sceptical. The game was played for keeps. He had done well to navigate it but he knew he couldn't last forever. No one could.

'I'm not greedy,' he said.

'It's not about greed. It's about worth. Why be rich when you can be wealthy? I'll get you where you want to be. Scratch that: where you *need* to be.'

Before Lamont could reply, he noted a familiar party. Delroy Williams sauntered into the restaurant, followed by his son Winston, Reagan and another man whom Lamont knew was called *Mack*. Delroy faltered when he saw them. He and his entourage were shown to a table near to theirs.

'Are you okay?' Akhan noticed Lamont's distraction.

'I'm fine.'

Lamont could see the table shooting him looks. Delroy stood up then, scraping his chair. Winston whispered something, but his father ignored him and approached the table.

Lamont waited for the explosion, the inevitable scene that Delroy would cause. Lamont hadn't reloaded with him and now sat in a restaurant breaking bread with a new supplier.

To Lamont's complete surprise, Delroy ignored him and approached Saj with his hand held out. Saj studied Delroy, then shook his hand.

'Good evening, Delroy. How is everything?'

'Everything is well. Just treating the troops to some food.' Delroy waved his hands toward his table of goons, all of whom were glaring at Lamont. Lamont sipped his water, gazing at each man.

'That's good. Keeps the morale high,' said Saj. Akhan had not paid Delroy any attention. Delroy looked over at Lamont for a second, then turned his attention to Akhan. Akhan met Delroy's eyes for a moment, nodded, then picked up his drink and spoke to Lamont as if Delroy wasn't there anymore. Delroy's mouth tightened, but he maintained his composure.

'Enjoy your meal anyway,' he said, sitting back down at his table.

Lamont continued to make conversation with Akhan but in his head he was analysing the exchange he had just witnessed. He had known Delroy for years, and he had never seen another man humble him. Lamont allowed the events to process in his mind as he sipped his water.

＊ ＊ ＊

'He's taking the piss.'

Delroy and his men camped in Delroy's office. After running into Lamont, Delroy insisted they eat and leave.

'You can't deny it now, Del. I should have stabbed the cocky prick with my fork. He disses our people then steps out with a new supplier. It's bullshit.'

'Reagan's right. You've supported that little shit, now he's violating? Del, gimme the okay and I'll take care of him,' added Mack, another of Delroy's lieutenants.

Winston watched his father smoking a cigarette. His fingers twitched. Winston wasn't used to him looking nervous, and it made him uneasy.

'I don't give a fuck who he's working with now. These are our streets. We can't let him get away with disrespecting us. Every day that little prick seems to grow bolder. Let us off the leash,' demanded Reagan.

Delroy shifted in his seat.

'No.'

'What the fuck do you mean?'

'Do nothing to Lamont. I mean that. He is now off limits.'

'Why?' Reagan was beside himself. Mack looked just as incensed. Delroy couldn't believe he had to explain it.

'Do you know who Lamont was with?'

'Yeah. Two flash Pakis. So what?'

Delroy shook his head at Reagan's stupidity.

'That was Akhan.'

Winston sat up now. He had heard his father talk about Akhan, but had never met him. He hadn't looked like much, but looks were often deceptive in their world.

'So what?' Reagan shrugged.

'Do you know who Akhan is? Don't you think it was strange that he was meeting with Lamont?'

'Nah I don't. He looked sneaky. I know for a fact how sneaky Teflon is. We should chop the pair of them.'

'Shut up and listen. Akhan is an entity. He doesn't meet with just anyone. This could be terrible for us. If he's working with Lamont, then it could be catastrophic.'

An awkward silence and blank stares greeted Delroy's statement. Lamont had leapfrogged Delroy. He had been outmanoeuvred, and it didn't sit well.

On some level, Delroy agreed with Reagan. He was the boss though, and he had to decide accordingly. This went beyond drugs. Akhan had his fingers in many pies. If he was cutting Lamont in on his action, then this would make him a bonafide rival.

'Catastrophic how?' Winston spoke first.

'It would give him access to tremendous power. Akhan is more than a drug dealer. He's a warlord with dealings in every city. We have to be careful. The other gangs would never sit back if they believed we were doing anything to disrupt the rhythm of things. They would come down on us hard,' Delroy paused, as if confirming his decision. 'We need to wait on this. The blow must flow.'

CHAPTER EIGHT

Monday 12 August 2013

LAMONT SAT IN THE BARBERS, listening to the chatter of locals while reading a newspaper. There was a buoyant atmosphere in the air, the warm weather bringing out the joy in everyone.

Lamont was so engrossed that when the door banged open, he didn't pay attention until the room fell quiet. Lamont glanced up, folded his paper and slid to his feet.

Mack stood in the middle of the room, his bodyguard bringing up the rear. Everyone in the room knew Mack and the overall trouble he brought to the table. He was an incorrigible criminal who had never learned to be subtle. Because of this he made money, but never achieved success.

When Mack glared at Lamont, he knew that his lazy day had ended.

'Teflon, me and you need to talk.'

'Nice to see you, Mack. Are you hungry? We were about to get food.'

Mack's mouth twisted. 'No, I'm not hungry. Don't try showing off for these idiots because I'll finish you.'

All eyes were on Lamont. He remained placid as if talking sports rather than being threatened by a goon.

'How can I help? Does Delroy need something?'

'I'm here for me, not him. He likes you. Me, I think you're a fake, up-his-own-ass pretty boy. You think you could test me back in the day?'

The tension kicked up a notch. Lamont noted Mack's insecurity; his desperate need to prove himself a tough guy. It was pathetic.

'Mack, I don't know what your problem is, but that was then,' he replied. Mack glanced at Spinks, who stifled a yawn, then turned back to Lamont.

'I'm putting you on notice, Teflon. You've had a good run, now you need to pack it up. If you don't, it's over. You won't make it to your next birthday.'

A smile flitted across Lamont's face, taking everyone by surprise. Mack needed a reason to make a move. It was obvious. Now more than ever, Lamont wondered what Delroy had told his team. He hadn't heard from him since the scene in the restaurant. The product Akhan had given them was off the scale though, and they had almost sold out in two days.

'Why the fuck are you smiling? You think I'm taking the piss?'

Lamont shook his head.

'No, I know you're serious. Why don't you give me time to consider my options?'

'You think this is a joke? You know what? Get this idiot, nephew,' Mack ordered. Spinks stepped forward, only to find his path blocked by two tough-looking local goons. Lamont recognised them as some of Shorty's associates. Spinks stared them both down. Behind him, Trinidad Tommy picked up a nearby razor.

'It's time for you to go,' said Lamont. Mack's eyes were blazing.

'Big mistake, Teflon. I'll be seeing you.'

They left. Lamont watched through the window as they tore through traffic in a Land Cruiser.

'L, are you all right?' Trinidad Tommy asked after a minute. Lamont grinned, expertly hiding his annoyance with Mack and his antics.

'Why wouldn't I be?'

* * *

In the heart of the Hood, Shorty chilled in a garden, a spliff to his lips. The heat had sapped the energy from him, so he was content to smoke and move only when he needed to. K-Bar was out handling business, but a few of his crew were alongside Shorty, cracking jokes and talking nonsense.

'Shorty.'

Everyone looked up when Blakey, Shorty's affable errand boy, jumped from his car after it screeched to a halt.

'Sup, B?'

'Have you heard about Lamont?'

'What about him?'

'He had a run in with Mack.'

'What? When?' Shorty sat up now.

'Mack was talking reckless about an hour ago, going on about how Lamont's not gonna make it to his next birthday. Spinks tried amping, but our people backed it.'

Shorty kissed his teeth, flinging the joint to the floor. He found his phone and called Lamont.

'Why didn't you tell me?' He barked as soon as Lamont picked up.

'Hello to you too,' replied Lamont.

'Don't joke. Why didn't you tell me?'

'It's not a big deal.'

'Course it is. It's a violation.'

'Don't overreact. It's the desperate move of a desperate man. We'll speak later.'

'Fuck,' snapped Shorty when Lamont had hung up.

'What did he say?' asked Blakey.

'He's a prick. I swear, he doesn't get it. He thinks life's like them fucking books he's always reading. Mack punking him isn't good for anyone.'

Most of the crew shared looks. They had never heard Shorty talk so viciously about Lamont before.

'What are you gonna do?' Blakey spoke up again. Shorty's veins protruded in his thick neck as he clenched his fists. Sometimes Lamont overlooked the power of reputation. Shorty didn't.

'I'm gonna get with the Tall-Man and we'll handle this shit. B, you can drive me.'

* * *

'Want me to come in?'

Blakey pulled up outside a house on Hillcrest Avenue. It was nondescript and looked no different to the surrounding houses. The small, boxy garden was home to a few plants, but mostly it remained barren.

'Nah, I won't be long,' said Shorty. He knocked once on the door before entering. He paused in the living room. Two youngsters sat, both aiming guns at him. When they recognised him, they lowered the weapons.

'Tall-Man about?' Shorty asked.

'Course I am,' A voice said from behind Shorty. He flinched, turning.

'Fuck man, you scared the shit outta me.'

Marcus smiled, his obsidian eyes darker than coal as he greeted Shorty.

'Nothing scares you. What's the deal though? You don't just stop by.'

'We've got a situation. Someone's messing with *The President*.'

Marcus's attitude switched from pleasant to cold in an instant.

'Go wait outside,' he told the youths. He motioned for Shorty to sit down, remaining on his feet. 'What happened?'

'Mack threatened L. Said our boy wasn't making it to his next birthday.' Shorty watched Marcus's face as he explained.

To people in the Hood, Marcus Daniels, aka *Tall-Man*, was a certi-fied legend. He was a musclebound maniac who cared for little in the world and terrorised those who crossed him. Not only was he vicious, he kept a stable of like-minded goons who would carry out whatever degrading task he gave them.

Most of all though, Marcus allowed no one to trouble Lamont and Shorty. Mack was in for a rude awakening.

'Mack said that? Delroy's Mack?'

'Yeah. His people have been out of pocket for a while. It's like they wanna start something.'

'Okay. We'll sort it,' said Marcus, his tone neutral. Shorty wasn't fooled though. Marcus was more dangerous when he was quiet.

'Cool. I'll put L up on what we're doing.'

'No. Leave him. Meet me here tonight. We're gonna go hunting.'

Shorty smiled. He and Marcus worked well together and had handled business in the past.

'You got it, fam.'

* * *

After speaking with Shorty, Lamont drove to Marika's house, happy to see Marrion's car wasn't there. She lounged in the garden, drink in hand, watching the children playing.

As soon as the kids saw Lamont, they shouted his name. Bianca dragged Lamont towards the paper shop. They returned laden with sweets and drinks. As Bianca showed her mother the spoils, Marika smiled at her brother, but said nothing.

'Can we talk, sis?'

Marika nodded. While the children argued over sweets, Marika and Lamont moved to one side.

'I'm sorry about the other night.'

'I hate that you can't get along with Auntie. We're family. We have to stand by each other.'

Lamont's jaw tightened. His experiences differed from his sisters with their aunt.

'I know,' he said.

'Can't you try? Do you hate her that much?'

'Yes.'

'Apart from my kids, you two are the only family I care about. How do you think it makes me feel that you can't get along?'

'It's not about you. You know that.'

'It's shit, L.'

'Just leave it.'

'I can't,' said Marika. The kids glanced their way for a second. 'Anytime I try to talk about it, you won't. Auntie's the same. What happened?'

Lamont hugged her. 'Rika, you're better off not knowing.'

Marika made a noise of disgust.

'Forget it. C'mon, let me make you a cuppa. I'll tell you all about Marrion.' She got one last shot in, leading him inside.

* * *

Mack sat in *Jukie's*, a gambling spot in the Hood. He had been there all evening, making loud remarks about Lamont as he grew drunker.

'Tell you one thing, Juke,' he said to the barman and mild-mannered proprietor of the spot, Jukie. 'We've been too easy on this new breed and let them get away with too much,' Mack paused, taking another hearty swig. 'It's all good though, I'm gonna sort the lot, starting with that flash cunt, Teflon; the weak little prick who's never done an ounce of time in the nick.'

Jukie nodded and smiled, the whole time thinking how foolish Mack was. Jukie heard about things in Chapeltown as they happened, and he knew about Mack threatening Lamont. He had also heard Lamont had got the better of Mack, and he wasn't surprised.

Though some of his regulars spoke enviously of the youngster, Jukie recalled the fire in Lamont's eyes when he first sold drugs. He had risen to a higher level than many had imagined. Mack was allowing jealousy to cloud his judgement.

Jukie would keep his opinion to himself though. Mack was a friend and a paying customer.

'Can I get you another?'

'Nah. Think I've had enough. Spinks,' said Mack, interrupting his nephew's game of pool he was having in the corner. 'Get the car.'

'Can't I—'

'Now.'

Spinks glared, but heeded the command.

'Kids nowadays,' Mack called after him.

Spinks fumed as he stomped down the quiet road. When his uncle had first suggested he work for him, Spinks had figured it was an easy way to get rich.

Now, he realised he was wasting his time. Mack was cheap and too focused on petty vendettas to teach him anything worthwhile. He took liberties and one day, he would push too hard, and Spinks would end him.

Spinks stomped toward the Land Cruiser. He'd paid a crackhead a fiver to watch it, but she had absconded and not done the job. He would slap her when he saw her.

Spinks was about to climb in when he heard footsteps and sprang into action. Spinks pivoted and blocked the hit of his assailant. He swung and tried to hit his opponent in the face but missed.

They tussled, seeking to overpower the other. Spinks hit his attacker with two body shots, then cocked his fist back to deliver another blow. A hand of iron snatched his. Surprised, Spinks turned and was caught with a vicious uppercut. His eyes rolled back in his head and he crumpled to the floor.

Marcus surveyed the young man. He had held his own with Shorty and for that, he had earned Marcus's respect.

'Prick,' Shorty kicked the unconscious Spinks in the head. 'The tosser got me in the stomach. I should blast him.'

'Forget it. He's not gonna be helping anyone. Stick him in the boot and we'll handle his Uncle.'

* * *

After leaving Marika's, Lamont headed home to unwind. His eyes burned, but he had gone through this pattern a lot. If he tried to sleep, he would only lay in bed. It was pointless.

Lamont fixed himself a glass of gin. Mack's threats had unnerved him. Like Reagan, Mack could cause trouble without thinking. Lamont needed to watch out for him and keep Shorty calm at the same time.

Before he could even consider walking away from this life, Lamont needed to ensure his pathway was clear. It was vital if he ever wanted to live. That meant doing something about Mack.

Lamont picked up the book he had started re-reading, *The 48 Laws of Power*. He'd absorbed the lessons years ago, but liked to refresh his memory.

A sudden knock at the front door caused Lamont to slide to his feet, frowning. Few had his address, and the ones that did wouldn't turn up without phoning. Lamont's brain was in overdrive as he hurried to the door. He opened it and paused at the sight of Jenny.

'Surprised?'

'Very,' admitted Lamont. 'Come in.'

Jenny followed Lamont. She'd had an image of what she'd expected Lamont's place to look like, and it exceeded expectations. The walls were a light brown colour, the furniture dotted around a similar shade. Soft music played from a tasteful dock resting above a marble mantelpiece. There were several paintings on the walls, an old chessboard and various paperbacks and pieces of paper scattered around the coffee table.

Based on the mahogany drinks cabinet in the corner, Lamont seemed to enjoy the best of everything.

'I'll be back in a minute. Have a seat.' Lamont left the room and hurried upstairs. A door slammed, but Jenny thought nothing. She continued her assessment of the room until he returned, looking a little more relaxed and refreshed.

'Sorry about that. What are you drinking?'

Jenny picked out a bottle of red wine. He poured them each a glass. They toasted and sipped. She took another sip, enjoying the thick, fruity texture. Lamont observed her. She met his gaze.

'You want to ask me something.' It wasn't a question.

'A few things. How did you get my address?'

Jenny smiled, not in any hurry to answer.

'Does the name *Frankee* mean anything to you?'

It did. Frankee was a girl Lamont had known years back.

'Frankee told you where I lived?'

Jenny shook her head. 'I asked around.'

'Why?' Lamont wondered why she had mentioned Frankee's name.

'You said not to keep you waiting. You learn more about a person when you turn up.'

'There's truth there,' Lamont admitted.

'Every time, you always seem so together. I wanted to catch you off guard.'

'You succeeded. Is that the only reason you came?'

'No. I was horny too,' said Jenny. They laughed.

'It happens. You might want that booty call.' Lamont played along. Jenny bit her lip, but didn't respond. Lamont sipped his drink, feeling more awake and enjoying the company. As attractive as Jenny was, he appreciated her humour more than her looks at the moment.

'Did you find a driver?'

'Yes.'

'Bet he didn't make half the impression I did,' said Lamont with a wink. Jenny giggled.

'You think a lot of yourself, don't you?'

'Is that a bad thing?'

'There's a fine line between cockiness and confidence.'

'I'm aware of where that line is.'

'I'll bet. You're too smart for your own good. That's why you've got such a rep,' said Jenny. Lamont shifted in his seat.

'Okay, so what's my rep?'

'You're a player. You're not interested in settling down and having a relationship.'

'That's not entirely true. It's just not my main priority right now.'

'What is? Selling drugs?' Jenny blurted before she could stop herself.

'Amassing wealth.'

'And you don't care how you make that wealth?'

'I didn't say that.'

The awkward tension hung in the air. Jenny wondered again what was going on in Lamont's head, what drove him. He was keeping something hidden from her and the more Jenny was around him, the more determined she became to uncover it.

'I didn't expect you to live here,' she admitted.

'Why not? Too out of my league?'

'Yes.'

That got a laugh out of Lamont.

'It's quiet out here. I can relax.'

'Must impress the ladies too.'

'Are you trying to imply something?'

'Why would I do that?'

'If I didn't know better, I'd say you were jealous.'

'Good thing you know better.' Jenny picked up Lamont's book.

'You were slamming doors upstairs before. Hiding something?' she asked as she put the book back.

'A state-of-the art, all-purpose drug lab.'

'Unsurprising.'

'Did you come here to assassinate my character?' Lamont rolled his shoulders, his face playful. Jenny stuck her tongue out.

'Sorry. Sometimes the comebacks have their own mind.'

'You're forgiven. For now. Can I top you up?' He gestured to the bottle.

'Trying to get me drunk?'

'I don't need you drunk to get what I want.'

'Oh?' Jenny raised an eyebrow. The whole vibe had changed now. Her voice was amused, tinged with a sexy huskiness.

'Trust me.' Lamont rose to his full height. Jenny stared up at him, daring him to make the first move. Jenny didn't resist as Lamont kissed her, slowly at first, then gathering momentum. Lamont's arms enclosed her, crushing Jenny's breasts against his hard chest as he brought her towards him. Jenny felt his arousal pressing into her and she grinded against it, eliciting a moan. Lamont couldn't take anymore.

Before he could act further, Jenny slipped from his embrace, adjusting her clothing.

'I'll be leaving now,' she said, her breathing ragged.

'Are you for real?'

'Yes, I am.'

'You can't leave me like this.' Lamont pointed to his crotch.

'Watch me.' Jenny blew a kiss and left. Lamont stood still, breathing hard, horny beyond all normal reason. After a moment, the corners of his face stretched into a smile.

Game on.

* * *

Mack staggered out of the gambling spot, trying to light another cigarette with shaky hands. The night air jolted his senses, sobering him as he tottered down the street and turned the corner. The Land Cruiser was there, but Spinks was gone.

Mack muttered under his breath, then reached for his phone. He relaxed at the sound of footsteps and prepared to tear his Nephew's head off.

'Where the fu—'

Mack's words stuck in his throat. Shorty, one of Teflon's top guys, stood in front of him, staring at him through cold eyes. Mack backed away, looking for a weapon or distraction. He knew what time it was. He knew what Shorty was capable of.

'We don't need to do this,' he blurted. 'Teflon's making a mistake.'

Shorty ignored him. A twisted smirk appeared on his face, illuminated by the streetlight and making his features appear grotesque. His dark eyes looked beyond Mack at something behind him. Mack turned, his stomach dropping at the terrifying sight waiting.

'Fuck.'

Marcus Daniels loomed, blending with the night. The doleful look on his face worried Mack far more. He knew of the devastation that Marcus was famous for and never imagined they would catch him slipping.

'Listen, you know what Delroy will do if you touch me,' Mack continued to talk as the two fearsome enforcers approached from either side. He backed away until he was against the door of his car. 'This is bad business. That thing in the barber shop, it—'

Shorty caught the older man with a wicked hook. Mack's face shot to the side but he stayed upright. Marcus blocked his escape, and Shorty hit him with vicious flurries. He tried to rise and fight him off but Shorty was an animal. A knee to Mack's stomach caused him to throw up, the vomit barely missing Shorty's trainers.

This seemed to anger him and the last thing Mack saw before things went black was Shorty's trainer heading towards his face.

CHAPTER NINE

Tuesday 13 August 2013

A FIERCE KNOCKING at the door ruined Lamont's sleep the next morning. He climbed from bed, checking he hadn't dribbled in his sleep and went to open it. Chink stood there, sunken eyed, gripping his phone, jaw clenched.

'Thanks for waking me up. Do you want a coffee?'

Chink followed Lamont into the house.

'We've got a situation.'

'I gathered that. Coffee?'

'L, this is serious.'

'I need a coffee. I'm knackered. Gimme five minutes and tell me all about it.'

Chink held his tongue, nodded and sat down, flicking through the channels to the news. Lamont fixed himself a cup of black coffee and joined him.

'Okay, I'm listening.'

'Mack's in hospital.'

Lamont put his coffee down.

'What happened?'

'He and his bodyguard got jumped near Jukie's place. Marcus and Shorty did it.'

Lamont closed his eyes, trying to control his emotions. This wasn't good.

'Did Mack threaten you yesterday?' Chink watched him.

'Yeah,' admitted Lamont. Chink's mouth twisted, scarlet blotches tinging his porcelain features.

'Did you order them to attack him?'

'Course not. Have you spoken to Delroy's people?'

'Not yet. They'll be in touch though. That's a given.'

'You're right. I'm gonna go get ready. Track Shorty down.' Lamont hurried from the room.

* * *

Shorty lounged in his living room, smoking weed and drinking Hennessy from the bottle as an old *Jeru the Damaja* track played in the background.

Mack's assault had been the highlight of his week. Delroy's crew had always thought they were untouchable, and now they had been humbled. Shorty grinned at the memory of kicking Mack in the head and raised the bottle again.

A hard knock at the door startled him. He reached under the sofa cushion, came up with a gun, and cut the music off.

'Who is it?'

'Me.' Lamont's tones were clipped.

'What's up?' Shorty opened the door and touched fists with Lamont. Chink brought up the rear. He didn't acknowledge Shorty.

'Shorty, you know what's up. What happened?' Lamont got to the point.

Shorty sat back down and relit his spliff. The pungent aroma wafted through the air, upsetting the eyes of both Lamont and Chink.

'What do ya want me to say?'

'I want to know why you thought it was feasible to put one of Delroy's top guys in the hospital,' said Lamont. Shorty shrugged.

'You know why I did it. That's what I do; I hurt people who step out of line.'

'Do you think Delroy's just gonna sit back and take this? He's been around for years. What do you think's gonna happen next?'

'I'm ready for whatever. You already know that. We weren't gonna let Mack think he could talk to you like a prick in public.'

'We? Who's *we*? You and Marcus?'

Shorty just looked at Lamont without replying.

'This is gonna be bad. Don't you realise that? Delroy can't let this slide.'

'It'll be big,' Chink piped up for the first time. 'Delroy's people will retaliate.'

'So what? I'm not scared of him or his people. That's a fact,' said Shorty.

'The fact is that you did something stupid and now we'll all suffer. It's not about fear; it's about recognising that beef doesn't make us money. How can we get paid through the streets if we're at war?' Chink continued.

'Listen, you've never gotten your fucking hands dirty so miss me with the *we* shit. It's my ass on the line, not yours,' said Shorty.

'Is that what you think? Let me tell you what will happen. Delroy's gonna come for the lot of us. It won't matter who has shot people and who hasn't. You made the wrong call.'

'Whatever. You'd have let Mack get away with it and he'd be debting you an hour later. You're good with numbers, Chink, but you know fuck all about the streets.'

Lamont felt the situation escalating.

'It's pointless to argue. Shorty, sober up. Chink, get Winston on the phone. Tell him I want to see him.'

Both nodded their understanding. Lamont yawned, debating where he could get an energy drink or some Pro Plus. Carnival was close. He had the potential to make an explosive amount of money in a short period. It was essential he and his team did whatever was necessary to toe the line.

* * *

'What are we gonna do then?'

Reagan was ready to act. He stood in front of Delroy, watching the old prick dither over something that needed no thought. Teflon and his crew had violated them again, and he was ready to lay waste to the lot.

Delroy sat at his desk, chain-smoking, stubbing each cigarette into an oversized marble ashtray.

'Wars cost money,' he said.

'So does losing respect. What will people say if you let Teflon get away with slapping one of your guys about? You think crews are gonna wanna reload with us? They're gonna jump on Teflon's dick and deal with his people. We need to retaliate. Now.'

Delroy sighed. Reagan was right whether or not he wanted to admit it.

'Okay. Get Chink.'

'*Chink?* We need to get Teflon, Shorty at least.'

'Eye for an Eye. We do to Chink what they did to Mack, and then we let them make a move,' said Delroy.

Reagan scowled. It was better than doing nothing. With a defiant nod, he went to put the word out to his team. Chink was finished.

* * *

That night, Shorty chilled with a few of his guys, enjoying the dark atmosphere of a club on Briggate, in the city centre. He needed it after the day he'd had.

Shorty hadn't liked the way Lamont and Chink had approached him. They didn't understand the streets like he did. You had to go above and beyond to protect your rep sometimes. Lamont was skilled, but he'd had it easy because of the things Shorty and Marcus did to people who violated.

Shorty poured himself another glass, making a mental note to send someone for energy drinks from the bar. He was lagging after being up for two days. Scanning the room for talent, Shorty jolted when Blakey leaned in close and got his attention.

'Check out who just walked in.'

Shorty glanced up, surprised to see Ricky Reagan heading towards him. TC flanked him and another big-headed dude that Shorty didn't recognise. Several nearby locals aware of the situation watched, awaiting drama. Shorty noted the wide grin on Reagan's face. A prickle of unease ran through Shorty's body.

'Shorty, what's happening?' Reagan held out his hand. Shorty shook it, playing along.

'What can I do for you, Ricky?'

'Just thought I would stop by, show love to you and your team. This whole beef thing, it could get outta hand. It's nice that we can just step out like this with our teams and relax.'

Reagan's words were soft, but Shorty detected the obvious malice beneath them. He was letting him know he was coming for him. Shorty appreciated Reagan's balls, but he didn't like the disrespect. He promised himself right then that Reagan would fall, no matter what Lamont said.

'Glad to hear it. B, get bottles for Ricky and all his crew. Make sure it's the good stuff too,' said Shorty. Blakey hurried off to carry out the order. Reagan's smirk was still in place.

'Teflon about? I wanted a chat with him,' he started. Shorty shrugged. 'No bother. Maybe he's with that little thing we've seen him with. I'll catch up with him another time.'

'I'm sure you will. Some advice though.'

'Go on.'

'Take the bottles and go, before you and your whole team get dropped.'

Reagan burst into mocking laughter, 'Is that a threat?'

'Yeah it is. Come for Teflon or any of us, it's gonna get bad for the lot of you.'

'Oh yeah?' Reagan's mask of civility slipped.

'Yeah. Tell that fat prick you work for that the clock is ticking on his ass too. It's open season on all of you.'

'Let's go now then.' TC stepped forward. Reagan put his hand out to calm his friend. He had noticed what TC hadn't. Shorty's people slowly surrounded them. There were at least half a dozen; too many to take on.

'I'll pass it on. I guarantee I'll see *you* before you see *me* though.

Keep your flat-ass drinks.' Reagan nodded at Shorty, leading his team away. Shorty's people watched Shorty, expecting a reaction.

'Fam they were out of line,' snarled K-Bar. He had wanted to wipe the smug look off Reagan's face while he was talking.

'Yeah, they were. We came to have a good time, and that's what we're gonna do. Business can wait until tomorrow.'

* * *

In another part of town, Chink stood outside a bar, smoking a cigarette. His new minder, a Birmingham goon named Polo, was watching out for him. Chink couldn't see him, which was the way he wanted it. He didn't think Delroy's goons would try anything in such a public place, but it was best to safeguard against it.

Chink finished his cigarette and lit another. A drunken girl tottered over, asking to use his lighter. He obliged. The girl thanked him, trying to make small talk, but he blanked her. She was a mess, two or three drinks away from hurling. She called Chink a prick and her friend dragged her away.

Chink smirked and finished his cigarette. His patience paid off. A woman walked towards the bar, surrounded by friends. Chink smirked again, allowed her to enter, and followed.

Naomi swept through the club like she owned it, curves hugging the fitted black dress she wore, eyes fierce and lips full. Guys tried talking to her, but she ignored them.

'Lots of fellas in here tonight,' said Adele. She was pretty in her own right but her beauty paled next to Naomi's.

'Bunch of posers, nothing worth hyping about.' Naomi turned to the bar to order her drinks. Before she could, the barman was placing a bucket with a bottle of champagne in front of her.

'Who is this for?' she asked.

'I was told to give it to the beautiful lady in a black dress,' the barman grinned. 'I think that's you.'

'Who sent it though?'

'Dunno where he's gone. He gave me one hell of a tip though.'

'What did he look like?' Naomi glanced around.

'I don't check out other dudes. I'm about women,' the barman licked his lips like *LL Cool J's* long-lost brother. 'Speaking of which, why don—'

Naomi turned her back, dismissing him. Adele and the others had poured themselves glasses of the champagne by now.

'Thanks, Naomi! Didn't know you were planning on buying champers.'

'I didn't,' she said. They weren't listening though. When she scanned, Naomi noticed a man watching her this time. Straight away she sensed he had bought the champagne. His hair was styled in a disconnected undercut fashion, his eyes hard, a smirk permeating his lips. He held a glass, standing still as people danced and chatted around him.

Naomi felt like she was the only girl in the room. She smiled. He drained his drink and walked towards her. She studied him as he did. He wore an open-collar charcoal shirt, jeans and shoes. She noted the watch on his wrist. It looked like a Breitling.

'I guess I should thank you for the champagne,' said Naomi when he was closer.

'You don't need to.'

'Good, don't think you can win me with some bubbly.' Naomi expected Chink to wither and slink away, but he laughed.

'What would it take to win you over?'

'If I told you, it'd be no fun now, would it?'

'Good answer,' said Chink held out his hand. 'My name is Xiyu.'

'That's an unusual name.'

'I've been told that before. What's yours?'

'Naomi.'

Chink took Naomi's hand and led her away from the dancers. She didn't resist.

'Where are you taking me?' she asked.

Chink ignored her and led them to an empty booth. He signalled the bartender and ordered more champagne. His assertiveness impressed Naomi. His tone and the way he carried himself was a big turn-on.

For the next half an hour, they talked, learning more about each other. Chink told her about himself, most of which was nonsense. It worked though.

Women like Naomi always had guys trying to get them into bed, so Chink disregarded that and focused on her mind. He was skilled with wordplay; one minute he stared into her eyes and smiled when she spoke, the next he was reserved, staring into space. Finally, Naomi had enough.

'What is it?' she asked.

'What's what?'

'Do you like me?' Naomi's cheeks burned.

'Yeah. I think you're cool.'

'That's not what I meant. I meant do you *like* me?'

'I think you're spectacular. But,' Chink hesitated, then shook his head. 'Forget it.'

Naomi sat up. 'Forget what?'

'It's not important.'

'I want to know. Please.'

Chink pretended to think it over.

'I think you're high-maintenance,' he said.

'You what? I'm not high-maintenance!'

'It's just an opinion. I've only known you a short amount of time.'

'You're up your own ass,' said Naomi. To her surprise, Chink grinned.

'You're not wrong. I'm confident, I won't deny that. I'm my own man and I call things as I see them. Not everyone can handle that.'

'What happens when they can't?'

Chink looked into her eyes, his expression becoming sombre.

'They miss out.'

'I'm sorry I said you were up your own ass, Xiyu. I lash out sometimes.'

'Why?'

'Why do I lash out?' Naomi struggled to keep up.

'Yes. Did someone hurt you?'

Naomi turned away. 'No one can hurt me.'

'Because you distance yourself, avoid getting close?'

'Is that what you think?'

'I watched you swanning around, ignoring people. You don't want anyone to get close. I think it's because you were hurt.'

Naomi took a quick, sharp breath. This never happened. She called all the shots, did everything on her terms but now here she was, desperate to make him like her. She stood, her head spinning.

'I should go.'

'It was nice meeting you.' Chink picked up his glass.

'Is this fun for you? Are you trying to mess with my head?' Naomi spat.

'Not at all. I want to know what makes you tick, what inspires you. I want to learn it all,' said Chink. Naomi took her seat. She wanted to believe him. It was complicated though. Things were happening in her life. Some she had control of, most she didn't.

'Why couldn't you want to fuck me?' she smiled.

'Who said I don't?' said Chink. They laughed. He slid his phone towards her. 'Put your number in there.'

* * *

Lamont entered his home, bone-tired from the day's excursions. Neither he nor Chink could get hold of Winston Williams. Lamont checked with a few associates, but none had heard from him. He needed Winston before he approached Delroy. Delroy was the leader, but Winston was much more level-headed than his father. He could bridge the gap.

Not wanting to overthink things, Lamont traipsed upstairs and was about to lie down, when his phone vibrated. When he saw the number, Lamont sighed, knowing his night wasn't over yet.

Jukie's was heaving when Lamont entered. He kept his head down, dodging the locals. The man he'd come to see hunched over his drink in a corner. Lamont took a seat.

'Are you drinking?' Marcus didn't look up.

'No. What's so urgent?' said Lamont. It irked him that Marcus was drinking around the corner from the spot where he had almost killed a man.

Marcus looked up, his huge scarred hands dwarfing the glass of

Hennessy. He wore a grey t-shirt, stretched tight over his muscles, cargo trousers and boots. His leather jacket was slung over the back of the spindly wooden chair. Marcus was so old school that Lamont wondered if he had ever left the 90's.

'You're pissed off, aren't you?'

'Disappointed.'

'That's worse. It had to be done though. Mack took the piss,' said Marcus.

'It did not have to be done. You should have discussed it with me.'

'There's time for talk, and a time for action. You would have talked us down.'

'That's because I look beyond pointless violence.'

'And we don't?'

People glanced at the pair, but turned away.

'If you did, Mack and his fool nephew wouldn't be in hospital.'

'No, they'd be planning to make sure they ended you. These aren't local wannabes. Mack is a force, and you needed to take him seriously.'

'You think I didn't?' said Lamont.

'Course you didn't. You think you can sit and talk like a damn diplomat.'

'My talking has got you out of plenty of spots in the past, or have you forgotten?'

'No I haven't. I think you've forgotten all the times my fists have helped you though.' Marcus drank more of his drink.

'Bullshit. All I want is to profit. Everything with you and Shorty is about protecting rep. Mashing up Mack wasn't about me; it was about your egos, and now I have to pick up the pieces. I have to placate Delroy, which means he has the advantage.'

Marcus rubbed his eyes, breathing hard now. Lamont fiddled with his watch and resisted the urge to continue.

After taking Lamont and Marika in, Auntie had filled her pockets even more as a foster carer. A rough kid named Marcus Daniels had been her first and only case. He was uncontrollable, prone to fits of rage, with eyes that unsettled even the most experienced care workers.

When he had first joined Lamont and his sister, Marcus wouldn't speak or play. He only ate and slept. Lamont recalled the day they got along:

School had finished for the day and Lamont had done his chores. He was about to read a book when he heard a piercing scream from upstairs.

Marcus had Marika against the wall, his hand around her throat. He was screaming in her face.

'Oi! Get off her,' said Lamont.

Marcus whirled around. The look in his eyes was one of utter lunacy. Lamont held his ground though.

'She's a thief.'

'What did she take?'

'Something that didn't belong to her.'

'I said let her go. We can talk about this,' said Lamont.

Marcus released Marika, giving Lamont his full attention. He was twelve and already built like a grown man. Lamont had heard him at night doing press ups when he thought everyone was asleep. Marcus took a step towards him.

'It's nothing to do with you.'

'That's my little sis,' Lamont turned to his sister. 'Say sorry.'

Marika had recovered. Her face twisted with rage.

'He's crazy. All I did was look at that silly photo of his ugly parents,' she exclaimed.

With another snarl, Marcus turned and lunged for her. Lamont tried to get Marcus in a headlock and was shrugged away like a dandruff flake. Marcus swung for Lamont, who ducked and hit him in the stomach. he doubled over, and Lamont struck him in the back of the head. With a mad yell, Marcus took Lamont down, swinging wildly. Lamont kept coming back. Marcus was too strong though. Lamont hit the floor hard and didn't get back up. Marcus stood over him, wheezing.

'You're crazy.'

'That's my sister,' Lamont lifted himself up, wincing. 'She's all I've got left.'

Marcus thought this over for a moment. He held his hand out. Lamont shook, and from that day forward they were the best of friends.

. . .

'Say the word, and I'll bring you Delroy's head.'

Marcus brought Lamont back to reality with that statement. He was serious too. He was capable of a level of violence that Lamont had never seen in another person. Marcus dominated on a good day. On a bad one, the results were downright frightening.

'That's unnecessary,' said Lamont. Marcus drained his glass and stood.

'Make sure you're ready when it pops off. I will be.'

He left, leaving an annoyed Lamont behind.

CHAPTER TEN

Wednesday 14 August 2013

CARL AND TC sat in Shadwell. Across the road from them was a pristine apartment building. In the car park they could see Chink's grey Jaguar.

'Nice area,' said Carl. He was a short man with light brown skin and a jovial attitude. 'Bet Chink's sitting on bare money. I've heard he's got a place in town too. Park Row or summat.'

'Who gives a shit? Let's go get the little Chinese fuck.'

'Cheer up.' Carl didn't like the way TC spoke to him. He was always on edge and since the word had come down about the problems between Delroy and Teflon, he was even worse. Carl respected TC, but didn't like him. This was business though.

They climbed from the car and hurried across the road. The main door was locked. Minutes later they were inside the building. They traipsed the stairs, approaching Chink's door. They were armed, but the guns were only to scare Chink. Their orders were to kidnap and work him over. That would send a message to Teflon and to the streets that they played for keeps.

After breaking in, the pair of them tore through the flat. Chink was nowhere to be seen.

'Shit. Where the fuck is the little prick?'

'I'm right next to you. How would I know?' Carl's reply was flippant. TC ignored him, distracted.

'C'mon, let's go tell Ricky. He's gonna flip.'

* * *

Chink watched from his vantage point as Reagan's soldiers hurried back to their car. He had rented another flat in the building opposite his, one of his old flings staying for appearances.

Reagan and his team were after him, and Chink understood their thinking. He was the easiest of Lamont's inner circle to capture. It would send a message if they could take him out. He had a better plan though.

'They're pulling out now,' he said into the phone. 'Follow them. I want to know where they go, and who comes and goes.' Chink hung up, observing Reagan's men driving away, Polo now on their tail.

* * *

Shorty was at Amy's house. It was risky to come and see Grace with a war brewing, but he had two of his guys sat outside just in case. He'd dozed off whilst putting Grace to sleep. After he shook himself awake, he padded downstairs.

Amy was washing up in the kitchen. She looked relaxed, humming a tune he couldn't recognise. Desire skittered in Shorty's belly. He slipped his arms around her waist and kissed her neck. Amy shuddered and leant into Shorty's embrace, then composed herself and pulled away, leaving soap suds on Shorty's top.

'Shorty, not now.'

'C'mon, Grace is asleep.' Shorty moved towards her again but Amy held off.

'We can't keep doing this.'

'What do you mean?'

'You can't try it on with me every time you come round. I'm not just some plaything for you to mess about with.'

'Amy, why are you getting serious? This is how it is with us,' said Shorty. He forced a laugh.

'Maybe that's the problem. I want a proper relationship. I would love to have it with you, but I know who you are.'

'Amy—'

'No. Shorty, I love your bond with Grace, but it's either all or nothing. I won't be like your other baby mother. I have other options.'

'Options? Like what?'

'Like Chris.'

Shorty gritted his teeth. Chris Hart had been smitten with Amy since day one. Even after Shorty had impregnated her, Chris still hung around on the friendship tip. Shorty detested him because he was competition. He told Amy all that empowering crap about herself that she wanted to hear, and then Shorty would have to talk her round when she talked shit. *Like now.*

'So that's how it is then? That pussy pays you attention, suddenly you're too good for me?'

'No, Shorty, it's—'

'Fuck it. I don't have the time.' Shorty stormed off.

* * *

Lamont was sleeping the morning away when his phone rang. He ignored it until it stopped ringing. There was no reprieve though. As soon as it stopped, it started again.

'Yeah?' he said, picking up.

'It's me,' said Chink. 'I need to see you. Now.'

'Okay. Come through.' Lamont tossed the phone and hurried to shower. He was on his second cup of coffee by the time Chink arrived with Polo. It was the first time he had met the goon, and Lamont felt an instant unease. By the frown etched on Polo's face, he felt the same. Chink turned to the guard.

'Wait outside,' he said. Polo complied.

'Drink?' Lamont asked. Chink shook his head.

'Reagan's people were at my place.'

'How do you know?'

'I recognised them. It was TC and that goofy one that drives them around.'

'So, where were you?' asked Lamont.

'Nearby. I expected this. I'm the obvious target.'

'Is that why he's watching your back?' Lamont glanced at the door. Chink nodded.

'He's useful. I had him follow TC. Him and Carl went to a house in Harehills. We've got eyes on them wherever they go now,' he said.

'Good. We might have to use that. For now, I'll give you keys to a spot. You'll be safe there.'

'L, this isn't what we signed up for.'

'I know,' said Lamont, stifling a yawn. 'We're in it though, so we have to control it.'

'It would be different if the *Dynamic Duo* took responsibility for what they did. This is their fault and they don't even care.' Chink was sick and tired of Shorty and Marcus's attitude. They had been starting fires for years, and everyone allowed them to get away with it whilst putting out the flames. It was frustrating.

Not only was Shorty refusing to accept responsibility, he wanted to escalate the beef.

'I had words with Marcus. He stands by what he did,' said Lamont with a sigh. Chink glanced at him.

'You look wrecked, L.'

'I'm fine. Just didn't sleep well.'

'Me neither. Did you hear about Reagan and Shorty getting into it in a club? I must have had calls from about twenty people. We need a handle on it—' Chink's phone rang. He spoke then hung up, 'That was one of Delroy's people. He wants a meet. Today.'

'Ring Marcus and Shorty. Tell them I want them here now.'

* * *

Delroy Williams hunched over a plate when Lamont entered the cafe, his security team posted around. Lamont slipped into the seat opposite Delroy. Marcus and Shorty perched nearby.

'What the fuck, Tef?' Delroy got straight to the point, not even bothering to chew the egg in his mouth. He'd picked the table that allowed him to see the comings and goings. The table was sticky. Lamont glanced at a menu smeared with something that looked like a cross between syrup and egg yolk.

A grey haired woman limped over, asking if he wanted to order. Lamont shook his head.

'What am I supposed to say?' he said when the woman left.

'Did you allow them to go at Mack?' Delroy jerked his thumb at Marcus and Shorty.

'Yes,' Lamont lied. Delroy took a swig of his drink and carried on. 'That was stupid. You know I can't let that slide. There has to be a comeback.'

'Let me ask you something. Did you tell Mack to come into the barbers and make threats?'

'Course not. Mack went solo.'

'He threatened me on my turf, in public. How was I supposed to handle it? What would you have done differently?'

'You should have talked to me first.'

'How does me running to you look? It's all about reputation. I have to work on these streets too.'

'Fuck's sake!' Delroy shouted. He lowered his voice. 'I respect you. You know that. This is bad though. Reagan wants your head. He wants to take out the lot of you.'

'Can you control him?' asked Lamont. It was a loaded question, and they both knew it.

'Can you control those two over there? These psychos we keep seem to do what they like. Reagan's hated you for years. He's been waiting for this excuse.'

'I'm not scared of Ricky. Do I need to watch my back with you?'

Delroy rubbed his face. 'Have you listened to a single word I've said? This isn't just gonna blow over.'

'I'm sorry to hear that. Let me tell you something, just so there are no misunderstandings. Send your people at Chink or *any* of my guys again, and I will take it as an act of war.'

Delroy's eyes narrowed. His mouth opened, but no words came out.

'You're gonna take it as an act of war? What do you call kicking Mack's teeth down his throat?'

'Retaliation. He made threats. There was only one response.'

Delroy pointed a shaking finger at Lamont, struggling to hold back his anger. It was obvious he wanted to reach across the table and rip his head off.

'Tef, I respect more than anyone what you've carved for yourself. I've done this longer though. I've had my back to the wall. Have you? I know you've had little beefs but you've never been in *real warfare*. It's no picnic. Recognise,' he said, his Grenadian tones coming through now. Lamont didn't flinch.

'Mack violated. It's as simple as that. You wanna talk about warfare; there's a reason I never needed to. Just like there's a reason you made this little meeting rather than just striking. You don't want war.'

Delroy assessed Lamont's words.

'Give me ten grand. I give that to Mack and maybe this thing goes away,' he replied

Lamont got to his feet. 'I'll get back to you. Take it easy, Delroy.'

CHAPTER ELEVEN

Thursday 15 August 2013

'Ten grand? Are they high?'

Lamont, Shorty and Chink were back at the base. Marcus had gone to get his people in order.

'It's a fair deal. You and Tall-Man almost killed Mack. I'm surprised he didn't ask for more,' Chink was saying to Shorty, who was still protesting.

'He's stalling.'

Chink and Shorty paused, looking at Lamont.

'What do you mean?' asked Chink.

'He won't settle for ten. It's a smokescreen,' said Lamont. There was silence then as they considered his words.

'How do you know?'

'His body language. Something is going on.'

'So what now then?' Shorty piped up.

'Chink, stay out of sight and focus on the money. Shorty, you coordinate with Marcus. Get word to everyone to be on alert. After that, we wait.'

* * *

'We need to move on them.'

Delroy and Reagan had been in deep discussion for the better part of an hour. Winston Williams sat in the corner of the room texting on his phone.

'You think so?'

'I know so. We missed our shot with Chink but we'll get him next time,' said Reagan.

'Chink is guarded now. Teflon didn't even bring him to the meet.'

'Someone else then.'

'I'm still thinking about it.'

'Mack's laid in a damn hospital breathing through tubes. Every second of every fucking day we do nothing, we lose respect,' said Reagan.

'We can't rush on this.'

'Rush on what? You're acting like we're warring with some equals. Teflon can't test us on the battle field. You know the soldiers I'm rocking with.'

'You're underestimating them. Just shut up and let me handle it. Run your little team and I'll continue steering the ship. I fucking told you last time, this is big. Akhan is big. We cannot piss him off.'

Reagan stared at his boss. Winston noted the rising tension and positioned himself. Reagan scoffed and slid to his feet.

'You handle it then, *Captain*.'

* * *

When Reagan left Delroy's, he wore a scowl. Delroy seemed to make little decisions more difficult.

The whole situation was spiralling out of control and it was because Delroy was too indecisive. Reagan didn't care about Akhan or what Delroy thought he could do.

Reagan drove to a small house in the heart of Harehills. Ten minutes later he slouched on TC's sofa drinking Hennessy.

When Reagan brought him onto the team, the first thing TC did was get a place of his own. It wasn't much, but the rent was cheap and it was his.

'What are you thinking then, T?' Reagan asked. He had told him about his talk with Delroy.

'Simple. Let's get them.'

'Just like that?'

'Why sit around? If it was anyone else, we would've gone at them by now.'

'Exactly,' said Reagan. This was why he loved talking with TC. He cut through the bullshit.

'Teflon's got soldiers, but so do we. Let's bump. This sitting around shit is pointless. Makes us look soft.'

'I tried calling Marcel about that money he owes. It's been two days, and he hasn't called me back yet,' said Reagan. TC shook his head.

'People are thinking we're weak. It's gonna get worse.'

'Chink is out of sight now. We missed our shot.'

'Shorty's always with that dickhead K-Bar. He'll still be easier to get. Tall-Man's like the fucking wind,' said TC.

'Put two people on Shorty. Mack's people will help. They're pissed off about what happened. We'll watch him, then we'll strike. Get on it ASAP.'

* * *

Lamont stared at his phone, willing it to ring. Since Jenny's impromptu visit, they had messaged each other a few times. They would flirt, but every time it got to a certain level, she would pull back and leave him hanging. It was a strategy, but with everything going on, Lamont didn't want to play games.

With that in mind, he called her. She answered within seconds.

'Hey, Jen. It's me.'

'How are you, Lamont?'

'I'm fine. Do you want to do something tonight? We could go to dinner.'

'I'm busy tonight, I'm afraid. Someone else is taking me out.'

'Kate?' Lamont asked, wishing he hadn't. There was a moment's pause.

'No. Not Kate,' Jenny didn't have to say anymore. Lamont was smart enough to know what Jenny was trying to avoid saying.

'I see. Well, enjoy your date,' he said.

'It's not a date, Lamont. It's—'

'You don't have to front.'

'I don't have time for this. I'll call you, okay?' without waiting for Lamont to reply, Jenny put the phone down. He fumed for a moment, then dialled another number.

'It's L. Listen, what are you doing tonight?'

* * *

That evening, Lamont led his date into Moreno's, a Moroccan restaurant on the outskirts of the city. They had stopped off at a bar in town for drinks. Lorraine was a gorgeous caramel-skinned beauty with a penchant for shopping and gossiping. The white dress she wore complimented her skin. As Lamont pulled the chair out for her, she sat down with a smile.

As well as Moroccan cuisine, Moreno's served a plethora of steaks and fish, along with an excellent tapas bar. Stained glass light fittings hung from the ceiling. On the walls were several obscure paintings, the seating tables small and intimate.

They ordered drinks and studied the menu. The waiter brought over a bottle of red wine. Lamont tried a sample and nodded his approval. The waiter then poured two glasses and took their orders.

'You know your way around this place,' Lorraine tasted the wine. 'This is good.'

'I've been here twice. The service is always great.'

'Who with?'

Lamont impaled Lorraine with a look.

'Don't start.'

'Start what?'

'I've been here before. Let's leave it at that,' said Lamont. Their relationship was one of convenience. Lorraine did her thing on the side and Lamont never questioned her about it. He expected the same treatment.

'Fine. Whatever. I only asked a question.' Lorraine pouted. He shook his head. He never learned. Lorraine tended to start arguments over silly things and he had no time for it.

'Let's forget it then. How are things? What have you been up to?' she continued.

'Same old. Are you still doing the modelling?'

'When I can. It's slow nowadays. I do lots of promos for clubs right now. How's Shorty?'

'Shorty's Shorty.'

'Is he still with his baby mother? I've got a friend he'd like. Is it true he has a tattoo on his dick?'

'It's not something he's ever mentioned,' said Lamont, avoiding the question about Shorty and Amy altogether. He almost laughed at the absurdity of this situation. Lorraine was cool, but he didn't have that kind of vibe with her, which was causing him to ask himself a tough question; *why the hell had he invited her to dinner?*

Lamont watched as a member of staff showed an attractive couple to their seats. The dark haired woman looked familiar. As they drew closer, and she glanced in his direction, the penny dropped from both at the same time.

Jenny looked sensational. Her hair was wavy and styled, and she wore a plum coloured dress that clung. Lamont couldn't take his eyes from her. Jenny regarded him for a second, then took a seat opposite her date.

Lamont hated him already. He was average height, looked like he did yoga and seemed to have good fashion sense. His hair was ridiculous though, the same bowl cut that Javier Bardem rocked in the movie *No Country for Old Men*. He gave Lamont a quizzical look then turned back to Jenny.

'Lamont?'

He turned back to Lorraine.

'What?'

'What's up with you?' she asked.

'Nothing. I'm just hungry.'

Lamont doubted he could eat anything. He wanted to ditch Lorraine and whisk Jenny away to finish what they had started last time. Most of all, he wanted her date to choke on the cork of the bottle of champagne the waiter was opening for them.

'I'm hungry too but you don't see me snapping at you.'

'Sorry.' Lamont's eyes darted over to Jenny's table again. She was deep in conversation and looked happy. *What was she playing at?*

'L?'

'Yes?' He had to fight to make his voice sound normal.

'Who is she?'

'Who's who?' Lamont was still staring.

'That girl you can't take your eyes off.'

'Just someone I know. No big deal.'

'Do you like her?' Lorraine sounded hurt.

'I told you; it's no big deal,' said Lamont. Lorraine heeded his tone, falling silent until their food arrived.

* * *

'Who is he?'

Jenny resisted the urge to roll her eyes.

'Who?'

'That guy who keeps looking over.'

'What do you want me to say?'

'Do you know him?' Max sounded part-intrigued, part-pissed off.

'Yes, I know him.'

'So, who is he?'

'He's someone I know. Just leave it.'

Max grumbled, but heeded Jenny's request. She sipped her champagne, debating whether to get steaming drunk to ease the awkwardness of the situation she was in.

After the way the conversation she'd had with him had ended earlier, Jenny hadn't expected to see Lamont.

Max was a friend who had tried to get a date with Jenny for years. He was nice, but he didn't intrigue Jenny the way Lamont did. Lamont had the potential to get close to Jenny and turn her world upside down, which was hard to accept.

He looked good tonight, and Jenny wondered about the attractive woman with him. *Had Lamont screwed her? Would he screw her tonight?* Jenny drank more champagne, wanting to avoid further thoughts.

* * *

Soon, Lamont was ready to leave. The food was nice but it diminished his appetite. Lorraine had done her best to make conversation but his answers were curt. They ate, Lamont left a generous tip with the bill and they departed without giving Jenny or her date another glance.

* * *

Shorty pulled his car to a stop near some flats outside the Hood. He was in war mode and paranoia was setting in. He suspected he was being followed, so he parked away from his base. Shorty traipsed up the stairs to his flat, unlocked the door and strode into the front room.

'Your fridge is empty.'

The overhead light switched on. Ricky Reagan aimed a gun at Shorty.

'You meant to be some kinda Bond villain?' Shorty snorted. Reagan slid to his feet, never once taking his eyes from him.

'Cocky little shit aren't you?'

Shorty shrugged his shoulders, aware there were guns stashed all around the room.

'Do what you're doing. I don't give a fuck.'

Reagan smiled. 'Course you give a fuck. You said you were gonna get me.'

'Doesn't matter. You can't hide forever. My people will finish you.' Shorty needed to keep Reagan talking.

'*Hide?* Who am I hiding from?'

'Tall-Man and K-Bar will wrap you and your shitty team up like Christmas presents' Moving quicker than Reagan expected, Shorty dove to the floor as bullets thudded into the wall behind him.

This was his domain. As Spartan and impersonal as the space was, Shorty knew every inch. He was up now, gun raised, two shots in Reagan's direction causing the man to take cover.

Shorty hurried to the back room, flinching as a bullet exploded into his shoulder. He staggered, searching for something he could use. It was one on one, Reagan had been stupid to take him alone. As Shorty thought this, TC charged out of the backroom with his gun raised. Shorty froze, trapped.

More gunfire erupted. Then silence.

CHAPTER TWELVE

Thursday 15 August 2013

LAMONT BROODED in his living room, drinking and trying to read. He was alone. Even after the disastrous evening, Lorraine had still hinted at coming back with him before he put her in a taxi.

Lamont felt the buzz now, the wine and brandy playing havoc with his stomach and senses. Being tipsy seemed easier than being sober. Lamont felt foolish. He needed to think clearly. He had the potential to lose everything, and yet he was lamenting over Jenny. It was ridiculous.

When the knock sounded at his door, Lamont was so deep in his own world he almost didn't respond. He rubbed his eyes and strolled to answer.

'Trying to surprise me again?'

'No need. I already did that earlier.' Jenny swanned inside, still wearing the purple dress. She sat without being asked.

'Where's that prick you were with?'

'If I didn't know better, I'd say you were jealous.'

'Jealous of what?'

'Are you going to pour me one?' Jenny pointed at Lamont's glass.

'Do it yourself.'

Jenny smiled. 'You're in a proper mood aren't you?'

'Don't flatter yourself. It's just been one of those days.'

Jenny fixed herself a glass of Amaretto. 'In that case, I'm surprised your little friend isn't here relieving your tension.'

'I might give her a ring.'

'Oh and she'll come running will she? Real credit to the female race,' said Jenny.

'Maybe she doesn't believe in games like you do.'

'We all play games. Maybe she thinks you'll invite her to *Bachelor Heaven* if she plays nice.' Jenny motioned around the room.

'Maybe I will.'

'Maybe you should. Times like this, you need someone looking after you.'

Lamont tried hiding a grin at the thought of party girl Lorraine waiting on him hand and foot.

'About time you smiled. So, why isn't she here?'

'I didn't want company.'

'Do I not qualify as company?'

'You . . .' Lamont broke off, poured another drink.

'Me . . .'

'You intrigue me. You already knew though.'

Jenny sipped her drink, looking at Lamont.

'Good.'

'What were you doing with that dickhead?' asked Lamont, more relaxed now.

'Same thing you did with that slut.'

Lamont laughed, tickled by the speed of Jenny's replies. He recalled the last time Jenny was with him, how she had left him hanging. Lamont had been consumed by the same lust enveloping him now, threatening to twist his usual logical thinking and make it cruder, sexual.

'How do you know Lorraine's a slut?'

'With a name like that she's one.'

'Who was that moron you were with? *Cedric? Leonard? Paul?*'

'Max.'

'What a twit.'

'Max is okay. He's safe.' Jenny faltered.

'And what am I?' Lamont inched closer to her.

'You're—'

Lamont saw his chance. He pulled Jenny close, their mouths meshing, driving his tongue down her throat, causing her to drop the glass with a loud crash. They paid no attention.

Jenny teased Lamont's tongue with her own, wondering what had taken him so long. This would be no repeat of last time. There would be no escaping, no more games. And so she surrendered to every hot kiss on her neck, every soft caress, and when Lamont stripped her dress off and pierced her with those fiery rosewood eyes, Jenny was every bit as willing, every bit as ready as he was. He lowered himself onto her, and then his phone rang.

* * *

Chink lay in bed smoking a cigarette. Naomi was next to him.

'Is this your thing then?' She took the cigarette and put it in her own mouth. 'Preying on innocent girls and getting them to sleep with you?' she exhaled.

'Depends what's on TV,' replied Chink. Naomi laughed.

'You're shameful. I never thought I'd like a little posh boy like you.' Chink took the cigarette back. 'You think I'm posh?'

'You talk like you're royalty.'

'I was born and raised in Meanwood. I'm anything but posh.'

'So you just talk posh?'

'Not posh. Educated. I grew up hard. I decided early on I wouldn't live like my parents. College and university were my way out,' said Chink.

'I never expected that; you seem so in control.'

'I have to be,' Chink's practised cool appeared to dissipate. 'Loss of control is a failure.'

Naomi snuggled closer to him Chink was like her; guarded and putting up a front. There was more beneath the surface. Naomi kissed his cheek and sashayed naked to the bathroom.

* * *

K-Bar stood outside the house, smoking a cigarette and watching Lamont approach. It was late but the night air was warm. Lamont had dressed quickly and was regretting picking a sweater.

'Safe, family.' K-Bar flicked the cig away and greeted him.

'How's he doing, K?'

'Come and look for yourself.' Turning on his heel, K-Bar walked into the spot. Lamont followed, hearing loud music, the slamming of dominoes, and voices coming from the kitchen. The stench of weed stung Lamont's nostrils.

Shorty lounged in the master bedroom, smoking a spliff and watching TV. The vest he wore made it easy to see the stitching on his shoulder. He looked up at Lamont and nodded.

'Nice to see you, Bossman,' he said. Lamont regarded his friend for a second before speaking.

'Give us a minute, K.'

K-Bar nodded. 'I'll be downstairs.'

'What happened?' Lamont asked as soon as K-Bar closed the door.

'What did you hear?'

'I heard Reagan blazed you.'

'Well, I'm still here.' Shorty pounded his chest for emphasis, looking higher than a kite.

'Reagan went after you though?'

'Prick was waiting at one of my flats. Almost got me too,' Shorty yawned.

'Where is he now?'

'Underground. Guess shooting your boy in the head makes you wanna hide.' Shorty laughed.

'Run that one by me again?'

'Ricky shot TC in the head.'

'On purpose?'

'Course not. He tagged me on the shoulder and I took off. TC jumped out the bathroom. They had the drop, but I was stumbling cause of the gunshot. Ricky's next shot missed me, caught TC right in the face.'

'Are you serious?'

'Always. He put him down for the ten count. I jumped out the bathroom window and dipped.'

'Sounds like you got lucky.'

'For real. I sent a man to clean up. A Professional.'

'Is the flat in your name?'

'Don't be daft. One smoker in the Hood rents it.'

'Will they be a problem?' Lamont was in damage control mode now.

'Nah, he's tight. Don't worry.'

'Shorty, they tried to kill you.'

'Yeah, but they failed. We won't. TC and Carl are down, Ricky's gonna follow.'

'Carl? What do you mean Carl's down?'

Shorty smiled. 'Didn't you hear?'

* * *

Marcus traipsed the roads of Harehills with purpose. It was late evening, and he watched for anything out of the ordinary. It was his way of making sure he made it home when the job was done.

Marcus stopped outside a house. The gate looked like it would make a noise if he touched it, so Marcus scaled the fence, heading to the back of the house. He broke in with minimal effort. It was a skill from his robbery days that had always served him well.

The house was quiet apart from noise coming from upstairs. Marcus followed the sound, which became clearer once he reached the top. It was the exaggerated noise that came from bad porn movies. The door was ajar. He tiptoed into the room, gun at the ready.

An overweight black man perched on the edge of his bed staring at the screen, pants around his ankles. Marcus crossed the room and put his gun to the man's head.

'Enjoying it?'

Carl froze. His right hand was still wrapped around his shrinking penis, but he didn't dare let go.

'You understand why I'm here?'

Carl was too scared to speak.

'Nod if you understand me.'

Carl nodded.

'Do you realise why this is happening?'

Carl nodded again, tears streaming down his face now.

'I won't explain then.' Marcus pulled the trigger twice. Carl crashed to the floor. He was dead on impact, but Marcus fired twice more to be on the safe side, then left the house and climbed into a waiting car.

*   *   *

There was a knock at Lamont's door early the next morning.

'Lamont Jones?' Two suited men stood there. *Police.*

'Who wants to know?'

'We're just here to talk. This is DS Myers and my name is DS Sinclair,' Both men showed identification. 'Can we come in?'

'Am I under arrest?' asked Lamont.

'This is just a chat,' said Sinclair. His tone was soothing.

'Do you have a warrant?'

'No.'

'Then to answer your question, no you can't come in.'

Sinclair shrugged.

'We can do it here then. I assume you heard about Tommy Carter's murder?'

'Sorry to hear about that. I don't know them though.'

'You might know him by his street name. *TC.*'

'Doesn't ring a bell,' said Lamont, looking the officer in the eye as he did so.

'I'll enlighten you then. TC works for Ricky Reagan,' Sinclair paused, expecting a reaction. He continued, impressed with Lamont's composure. He was up to his neck in street beefs but he hadn't even blinked. 'There was a big shootout last night.'

'This is a fascinating story, Mr Sinclair. Why share it with me?'

'Wanna play dumb? Your choice. We know what's going on. Mack threatens you, the next day he ends up in intensive care. Ricky shouts his mouth off about your crew. Suddenly, two of his people die. This is bold stuff, *Teflon*. Do you think you can take on Delroy Williams? You think he's just going to roll over?'

'*Delroy Williams;* is he a footballer?'

'You think you're so fucking clever don't you? Drug dealing, criminal fuck. Do you think we'll lift a finger when Delroy sends a team to murder you? I'll shake that fuckers hand myself. I promise you that.' Spittle flew from Sinclair's mouth.

'Gents, this has been awesome, but I'm afraid I have a busy day ahead of me. You should write that tale you told me. You could sell it and make us all rich,' said Lamont, closing the door with a smile. He needed to shower and wake up. Police attention was never good. Trouble was on the horizon.

* * *

'Reagan needs to fucking go, L.'

Shorty, Lamont and Chink were in a safe house. It was a little spot they had in Calverley. Shorty's stitches were holding well, but he was irritable and out for blood.

'I don't even know why we're discussing this. The motherfucker tried killing me in my spot. I'm not taking that.'

'He tried getting me too,' Chink said to Shorty. He kissed his teeth.

'Fuck Delroy. Let's fucking drop him too and end this shit instead of giving them time to reorganise.'

Lamont still hadn't said a word. A cup of coffee was in front of him, untouched, as he went over the variables in his head.

'L?'

Lamont looked at Shorty.

'What the fuck? Are you gonna sit and stare into space, or are you gonna give us some guidance?'

'You don't want guidance; you want me to tell you it's okay to kill Reagan,' said Lamont.

Shorty shrugged. 'So what? Am I wrong to?'

'Yes.'

'For fuck's sake,' said Shorty, his frustration getting the better of him. 'What are we even doing here? We're at war and we need to strike back.'

'We are striking back. Why don't you calm down and stop screaming and shouting? Listen for once.'

Shorty grumbled, but held his tongue.

'Reagan will expect us, you, to retaliate. It's a foolish tactic.'

'Do you have another way?'

'I do. Me and Chink have already worked on it,' said Lamont.

'You and *him?*' Shorty jerked his thumb at Chink.

'Chink, tell him about your new friend.'

Chink did as he was bidden with a smile.

'I've been banging Reagan's woman.'

'Since when?'

'I spoke to L a while back. He told me to pursue her.'

'And you got her, just like that?'

'You think you're the only one who can get girls?'

'This isn't important. The fact is, Reagan went too far, so now we destroy him,' said Lamont.

'But, you said—' Shorty started.

'Not by shooting him. Follow what we're saying. We will destroy his reputation.'

'What the hell will that do? This is the streets, fam. No one cares about stories.'

Lamont and Chink shared a look.

'Do you trust me?' Lamont asked Shorty.

'Course I do.'

'Then relax, heal that shoulder, and let us handle it.'

* * *

The very next day, the games began. Lamont started by instructing Chink to ring a well-placed source in the Hood. That source went to several barber shops, then to Jukie's, then the streets, telling stories about Ricky Reagan.

Within hours, the streets were ablaze with tales he had murdered his comrades after refusing to pay them, plotted against Delroy

Williams, and that he was financially crippled. There were elements of truth, which had the desired effect. In no time, Reagan's credibility plummeted.

* * *

'Winnie, fucking ring me back when you get this. We need to talk.'

Reagan flung the phone on the sofa next to him. He was sure Teflon's people were behind the rumours, but he couldn't prove it. Reagan couldn't believe anyone would think he would murder his own team. He and TC had been like brothers.

Reagan had been in hiding ever since the shooting had gone wrong. He blamed himself. He had had the element of surprise, but Shorty's lack of fear had surprised him. Now, Reagan's name was mud. No one in Delroy's organisation would speak to him.

'They'll fucking pay,' mumbled Reagan to himself, sipping a bottle of Red Stripe. 'No one fucks with me like this.'

As sure as Reagan was of Teflon's involvement, there was no proof. The smearing was flawless, and the lies ingrained at street level. No one could say for sure where they had generated.

Reagan was in fact broke. He hadn't publicised it, but he lived from move to move and never thought of saving. Whilst in hiding, he couldn't hit the streets to make money, and if that fat bastard Delroy and his links were turning their backs on him, it would be an absolute catastrophe.

Reagan's phone rang. He snatched it up, hoping it was Winston or Delroy, but didn't recognise the number.

'Yeah?'

'Go on Star's profile on Facebook.'

'Hold on, who's this?'

The person had already hung up. Reagan logged into a fake account and typed *D.J. Star's* name into the search bar. He was directed to his page and when he saw the latest photo they had posted there, it stunned him.

Chink was in the photo, dressed in his expensive clothing. Reagan had assumed Chink was gay, but in the picture he was draped all over

Reagan's girl. His eyes narrowed as he saw Chink with his arms around Naomi, kissing her neck.

Reagan's blood boiled. Naomi didn't look distressed in the slightest. Her eyes shone as she looked into the camera, and she appeared at ease.

'Bitch!' Reagan flung the phone across the room. He couldn't believe she would betray him. He had poured money into her pockets, and this was how she had repaid his love.

Reagan was beyond furious now. The picture had told him all he needed to know. Teflon and his team were behind this, and they would pay.

CHAPTER THIRTEEN

Friday 16 August 2013

FOR JENNY, work had been one disaster after another. She had kept her composure, but now, nestled in the safety of her own home, she was happy to let the stress overwhelm her. As Jenny placed her cup on the table, a sharp knock at the door surprised her.

She unlocked it and stared out at Lamont Jones. He was smiling, smelt good and wore a fitted navy sweater, corduroy trousers and clean trainers.

'Can I help you?' asked Jenny.

'May I come in? I'm not accustomed to doing business on the doorstep.'

Jenny shrugged, allowing him in. Lamont took his shoes off and sat down in the living room. It was very spacious, with various shades of red furniture and porcelain white furniture.

Similar to his own place, there were books and papers resting on the cherry oak coffee table. Lamont placed his phone and wallet on the papers, leant back and steepled his fingers. She watched, amused.

'Can I get you a drink?'

Lamont gazed at her, lingering on her body. Her face grew warm. Apart from a hasty apology, Jenny hadn't spoken to Lamont since he'd all but forced her from his house.

'Jenny?' Lamont's voice brought her back to earth.

'Sorry. Did you say something?'

'I asked what the choices were.' He met her eyes.

'Choices for what?' Jenny was flummoxed. Lamont smiled again.

'You offered me a drink. I was enquiring what was available.'

'Right. Juice. Tea. Coffee. Water. Wine.'

'Do you have green tea?'

Jenny nodded.

'I'll have some of that please.'

Jenny headed toward the kitchen. Lamont's words stopped her.

'I guess you were right,' he said.

Jenny turned. 'About what?'

Lamont was in front of her now. He drew her in close, kissing her skilfully. She allowed the moment to continue, kissing him back harder. Lamont broke the embrace.

'You learn more about a person when you turn up randomly.'

'I'm glad I inspired you.' Jenny kissed him again. The pair of them swayed in the middle of the room, green tea and other troubles all but forgotten.

Later, they lay in bed amongst messy, damp, sheets.

'That was unexpected.'

'Was it?' Lamont's cocky response tickled Jenny. She poked him in the ribs.

'There's no way you knew what would happen.'

'I'm a man of many talents, Jen.'

'Pity sex isn't one,' Jenny giggled at Lamont's splutter. 'Kidding. Maybe.'

'That was low,' Lamont laughed, squeezing her. 'You're gonna give me a complex.'

'I'll try not to. How did you find my address?' Jenny asked.

'Like I said, many talents.'

'I'm serious. You weren't having me followed, were you?'

'Course I wasn't. Kate told me.'

'What happened last time? Why did you leave?'

'Business.' Lamont's whole manner cooled in an instant.

'*Business* could mean a lot of things.'

'True. I can't say anymore though.'

Jenny had so many responses ready. Lamont seemed to turn his emotions on and off. She felt as if she was playing catch up. The pair were engaged in a game and for the first time, Jenny wasn't sure she was winning.

'Fine. Keep your secrets.' She nibbled on Lamont's bare chest, closing her eyes.

'We do what we need to, to keep the intrigue alive,' said Lamont. The low rumble of his voice made Jenny shiver.

'Is that what we're doing?'

'I think we're trying to analyse a situation that is still morphing and changing for the pair of us.'

'Where is this situation at the moment?'

'With me and you?'

'Yes,' said Jenny.

'I think we're good together.'

Jenny smiled, ignoring the warning at the back of her mind. Lamont had a reputation, and Jenny didn't want to be involved in a messy situation. She trusted her gut though and it was telling her to see where this went.

'I'll make you that drink now.' Jenny tried to get up, but Lamont stopped her, his mouth claiming her own.

'I'm not thirsty. Yet.'

* * *

Since his trouble, life had changed for Terry Worthy. After his disastrous dealings with Ricky Reagan and Carlos falling out with him, he had become subdued. As a peace offering, Lamont had given him some drugs at a knockdown price, allowing him to make a decent profit.

Back in the day, Terry would have done the rounds, buying champagne and entertaining whatever gold-diggers were swayed by his wallet. He was deflated now though after being ripped off by kids, almost killed by a maniac, and Carlos' termination of their friendship.

Terry had fallen out of love with the game. He had no other skills in life though, and he lacked the drive and ambition to start again, he was stuck.

On this night, Terry had come from the pub. He was almost at his front door when there was a flurry of footsteps and someone pressed a gun to his back.

'Open the door,' muttered Reagan. Terry complied. Reagan pushed them in, locked it, then frogmarched Terry to the sofa. 'Sit down.'

'W-What's this all about, Ricky? I thought we were cool.'

'Shut up, before I smack you up again,' said Reagan. It surprised Terry how rough he looked. His hair was tatty, there were noticeable circles under his eyes, and his clothing looked rumpled.

'You're gonna help me with summat,' Reagan started. He rubbed his nose before continuing. 'I've got two boxes of white. You're gonna sell them for me.'

'Why?'

'Because I said so, that's why. You tried to fuck me over and I ain't forgotten that.'

'I paid you though. I gave you the money.'

'Did you hear what I said?' Reagan's voice rose. Terry swallowed and nodded.

'Good. Shut up then. I don't give a fuck what you or that fat bastard you were with last time says. You work for me now.'

* * *

Two days passed by in a cocaine and weed-fuelled haze for Reagan. Before meeting Worthy, he had robbed one of Delroy's smaller spots, stealing the two kilos of cocaine he'd given to Terry.

After getting away, Reagan had been on the move ever since, never staying in the same spot for longer than twelve hours. He was crawling up the walls, but it was a temporary measure.

When he got the money back from the drugs, he would take it and leave Leeds. The more time spent running, the less time he had to plan. Reagan would build up and then rain down on anyone who doubted him.

By the time Terry Worthy got in touch, Reagan was slouched on the sofa with his eyes closed, listening to an old *Mobb Deep* album with a loaded gun digging into his hip. Without even turning the music down, Reagan picked up the phone.

'What the fuck took so long?'

'Sorry mate. This wasn't easy though. It's proper hot out here, and—'

'Have you got it or not?' Reagan cut Terry off.

'Yeah, I've got it. Shall I come to you?'

Reagan considered this. He didn't want to leave his latest hideaway, but he also didn't want Terry knowing where he laid his head.

'No. I'll come to you. Make sure it's all there.' After Terry gave him the address, Reagan hung up and headed out of the door.

* * *

'Where the fuck is he?'

Marcus Daniels stewed in the passenger seat of a stolen 4x4. He had two of his guys in the back. From their position they could see Terry Worthy's Audi. It was late evening, and the night was a warm one. They had been sitting in the cramped car for over an hour and they were sick of waiting.

'Check with the other guys,' said Marcus.

'Sharma, can you lot see anything?' Victor, the driver spoke into a disposable mobile phone.

'Nah, it's clear down here,' Sharma's voice spoke back, a slight static in the background.

'Worthy must have fucked it up, the useless prick,' said Marcus. He snorted as his phone rang. He answered, but sat up in his chair after listening for a few moments.

'I'm on my way.'

* * *

Lamont Jones sat in his office in the barbers, poring over legal documents. He'd procrastinated for over a week, and the massive pile in front of him was his legal partner's way of sticking it to him. The boxy room was quiet, save for the soft Motown hits playing in the background.

Lamont kept checking his phone, waiting for confirmation the job was complete. He took a deep breath. Marcus always got results in this line of work. It was the one certainty the behemoth shared with Shorty.

The main room was silent. Lamont assumed Trinidad and the other cutters had finished. He cleared his mind and worked through the paperwork, filing it away in his drawer. He would have a copy sent to Martin in the morning.

Downing the coffee, Lamont washed out the flask and left it to dry in the kitchen. He yawned as he strolled to the main floor, then reared backwards in shock.

Trinidad Tommy lay motionless on his stomach, hands secured behind his back. The shutters were down, and Lamont saw the key in the door.

'Just the man I wanted to see.'

Ricky Reagan sat in one of the leather barber chairs as if waiting for a haircut. His eyes glittered as he stared down Lamont.

'Shut that door behind you. Me and you need to talk.'

Lamont hesitated as he saw Reagan's gun pointed at his chest. A fresh jolt of fear resonated through him.

'Just me and you, Tef; How does that make you feel?'

Lamont tried to marshal his fear.

'Did you kill him?' He pointed to Trinidad.

'Fuck the old man. This is about you. Thinking you're the smartest guy on the planet. Did you think you could get the drop on me?' Reagan's wild hair was nappier than normal, and his clothing looked slept in. He was a killer though, and Lamont had no doubts about the man's ability to pull the trigger.

'Am I supposed to understand what you're talking about?'

'Don't play dumb. That snivelling little shit Worthy contacted you after I threatened him. I counted on that. Who's waiting for me at the bullshit meeting? Shorty? Tall-Man?'

Panic rose in Lamont.

'You left yourself open, didn't you? You've never taken this shit seriously. Always left it to those pieces of shit working for you,' Reagan spat the words out. His hand shook. Lamont considered charging at him for a moment, but didn't think it would end well.

'Now though, I get to take my time with you,' Reagan placed his gun on the counter, never taking his eyes from Lamont. 'This has been a long time coming.'

Lamont turned to escape through the back but Reagan was faster. He grabbed Lamont by the back of his top and flung him toward one of the barber chairs. Lamont's back hit the chair and he fell to the floor.

'Fight back, you pussy,' grunted Reagan. He struck Lamont in the face, sending him skidding along the wet floor. Lamont eyed the mop and bucket in the corner. Trinidad must have been cleaning when Reagan took him out.

Reagan drew back his foot to kick Lamont, but he grabbed his leg and took him down to the floor. He hit the lunatic once before Reagan head-butted him. Lamont reared back, one hand to his nose trying to stem the sudden flow of blood. Reagan kicked him in the chest and straddled him, hitting him with slow, deliberate punches to his unguarded face.

'You're a pussy,' Reagan hissed. 'You've always been a pussy. Even back in the day,' he hit Lamont again, panting now, undisguised relish in his voice. 'You're nothing without your people. When I'm done with you, I'm gonna split, and everyone will know.'

Lamont was dazed and bleeding. He couldn't afford to lose, but each blow weakened him. Reagan stood in front of him, smug, self-satisfied. He was gearing himself up to finish this, Lamont could sense it. Heart pounding, with nothing to lose, he charged Reagan, slamming the maniac into the main worktop, causing him to cry out in pain.

This was Lamont's chance. He groped, fingers closing around a straight razor. He jammed it into Reagan's leg just as the man straightened up. Reagan screamed out. Lamont didn't let up as he pulled the razor from Reagan's leg and thrust it into the man's stomach with the last of his strength. He fell back, spent.

Reagan's eyes bulged. He spat out blood, trying to stem the torrents of blood billowing from his stomach. Lamont watched him, panicking, scared he hadn't done enough. Reagan's eyes met Lamont's for a moment. He jerked and was still.

* * *

Marcus didn't know what to expect as he pulled up to the barbers. He hurtled to the back door and wrenched it open, gun by his side as he cut through the makeshift kitchen to the main floor. Marcus paused then, his mouth agog.

Usually tidy, there were various shavers, hair products and wires all over the barbershop floor. Trails of blood led to the prone body of Ricky Reagan.

Marcus's eyes flicked to Lamont. He slumped in the corner, drinking from a bottle of Red Label whisky. His clothing was speckled with blood and his face was bruised.

'Your first?'

Lamont nodded.

'Thought Shorty might have brought you in on one of his jobs,' Marcus continued. 'You did good.'

'It's nothing to be proud of.' Lamont wiped his mouth and took another drink.

'Reagan had to die.'

Lamont stared at the blood on his hands, then at the majority tarnishing the floor. It was revolting. He could smell the stench of death. Marcus had his phone out now. He was telling someone they had a *situation*. He hung up, glancing at Lamont again.

'Get undressed. Take everything off.'

Lamont stripped to his boxer shorts, wincing as he took his shirt off. Marcus glared at him.

'I said everything.'

Lamont removed his shorts, covering himself. He didn't argue. He was in Marcus's world now.

'Do you have any spare clothes here?'

'No.'

'We'll get some brought over. Until then, go sit in your office,' Marcus noticed Trinidad slumped in the corner. 'Is he alive?'

'Reagan knocked him out.'

'Little prick. Sharma and them lot are still waiting at the lockup. I'll let them know about the change of plan.'

'Keep my name out,' said Lamont. He didn't want everyone knowing what had transpired.

'Why? You should be proud, L. Reagan was a prick. He fucked a lot of people. Hold up your head, man.'

Lamont knew Marcus meant well, but he took no pleasure in what he had done. He'd hated Reagan for years, but ending his life felt dirty, like the despicable acts Lamont had tried his hardest to pretend weren't associated with his world. He kept telling himself it was necessary.

'No one can know, Marcus. I mean that.'

Marcus shrugged.

'It's your call,' He looked to Reagan. 'We need to sort this quick though. Trinidad was a witness. What are we doing about that?'

'What do you mean *what are we doing?*' Lamont's eyebrows rose.

'I mean if you don't think he'll stay quiet, we can clean up two bodies.'

'We're not killing Trinidad. I'll talk to him.' Lamont was horrified at the suggestion.

'Fine. Whatever. Go to the office now. People will be here soon.'

CHAPTER FOURTEEN

Monday 19 August 2013

DELROY SAT IN HIS KITCHEN, annihilating a plate of food. His wife had left early that morning without saying where she was going. Delroy hadn't complained. He had a lot on his mind.

The streets had been in absolute bedlam. The Lamont situation was bad. Delroy's people were looking at him sideways over his lack of counter. Lamont and his team had stepped up, and with Akhan in his corner, Delroy's hands were tied.

To add to a torrid situation, Reagan's name had been in the streets, connected with everything from TC's murder to a run for Delroy's crown. Reagan hadn't helped when he had robbed one of Delroy's stash spots a few nights back.

Delroy had a team looking for him, with orders to put him down. He hadn't surfaced, but Delroy remained confident, upping his home security and placing guards around his multi-million-pound home.

After finishing his meal, Delroy was about to summon his driver, when his phone rang.

'Yes?'

'We need to talk.'

'Tef?' Delroy's grip on the phone tightened.

'The green place. One hour.' Lamont hung up. Delroy stared at the mobile in disbelief. He didn't know why Lamont was calling, but he knew he wouldn't like it.

* * *

'This must be him.'

Lamont and Chink stood in the park, watching Delroy and Winston make their way towards them. Delroy looked as imposing as ever. As he drew closer, Lamont sensed in Delroy's eyes what he'd noticed when they were at the restaurant with Akhan; uncertainty.

Delroy and Winston shook Lamont's hand. Both ignored Chink.

'What do you have to say?' asked Delroy.

Lamont looked at Chink before he replied.

'Reagan isn't coming back,' His words were blunt and had the desired effect. Winston glanced at his father. Delroy's eyes hadn't left Lamont's.

'Why are you telling me?'

'This thing we have going on. It's over,' said Lamont. Delroy's eyes narrowed. He didn't like the authoritative tone Lamont was taking with him.

'Tef, who do you think you're talking to?'

Lamont stared him down. Something had changed. Delroy could sense it. Lamont's face was bruised, but it wasn't that. He seemed surly, more aggressive than he had previously.

'I understand you lost two boxes of food,' said Lamont. 'Later, my people will ring Winston and arrange for someone to pick them up. There's no need for further conflict.'

Delroy weighed up his words before he responded. Reagan was dead. Lamont was dealing from an option of strength, and Delroy found that more galling than anything.

For a fleeting moment he wondered if Lamont had killed Reagan. He dismissed this though. It was impossible. Lamont had killer instincts, but he didn't have the nerve or the skill. No. It was likely Marcus. Or Shorty. Getting the drugs back would help though.

'And if I feel otherwise?' He asked. Lamont walked away.

'You don't, so no point answering. Be easy, Del.'

* * *

Marrion Bernette leant against the hood of his rented Volvo, adjusting his shades as he let the intense heat from the sun waft over him.

In the driver's seat, Antonio sat with the car door open. He wore a t-shirt and cargo shorts with a pair of pristine white high-tops. He checked his phone, mumbling to himself. Marrion ignored him and stared ahead.

A short while later, a blue Ford Focus rolled into view and pulled up a few yards away from the Volvo. Shorty glided from the car with his usual swagger. He wore a heavy chain over his crisp, white t-shirt. Blakey remained in the car.

'You good?' asked Shorty, slapping hands with Marrion.

'I'm living. Have you got that?'

'Wouldn't be here if I didn't.' Shorty signalled to Blakey, who climbed from the car clutching a Morrison's carrier bag. He handed it to Antonio.

'If this is like the last batch, you'll need to return quick. That's my word,' said Marrion.

'Cool. Ring me or Blakey. We've got it to give.' Shorty's eyes darted around the quiet backstreet as they spoke.

'This street shit; I can help with that too. I've got people of my own I can call up to do the dirty work. No cost to you or Teflon.'

Shorty considered Marrion's words for a moment.

'We've got that end covered, bro. Ain't no more warring. Get at me when you want more.' He nodded at Antonio and ambled away.

* * *

Antonio and Marrion drove back to the base. They stuffed the drugs under Antonio's seat. Antonio held the wheel one-handed and put a CD on, which Marrion turned off. Antonio frowned.

'Shorty's a cold bastard, man.'

'Shorty's mellow. His boss is the cold one.' Marrion glanced out of the window as they drove down Chapeltown Road. As he watched the usual's congregating outside the Landport building, he felt a longing for his own Manchester streets.

'*Boss?* Thought they were partners?'

'Teflon keeps them close, but he's the one in charge.'

'Why do you think he isn't keeping you close?'

Marrion scowled. 'Fuck knows. Either way we're making money.'

'We could make more though. Those lot are killing it. Do you think it's because you're banging his little sis?'

Marrion shot his friend an angry look. Antonio was oblivious to it though.

'How did you get in with her, anyway? You kept that on the low for ages.'

'No one needed to know,' said Marrion. 'I met her on a night out ages ago; we chilled and shit grew from there.'

'You like her then? Usually you're gone by now.'

Marrion didn't reply. He did like Marika Jones. It had started as something physical, but Marika was as stubborn as a firecracker, different to the norm. His brow furrowed as he thought about Antonio's words. He was being kept in the cold.

The product was off the scale. People couldn't buy enough. Chink had told Marrion he would grow rich moving to Leeds, but this had never seemed truer than it did now. There was more to earn though, and he wanted all of it.

Marrion's phone vibrated then. He read the text, smiling.

'Brownie messaged me. He said Timmy got that chain I copped for him.'

Antonio made a derisive noise and kept his eyes on the road.

'You got something to say?' Marrion said to him.

'I don't get what you see in that kid.'

'He's got potential.'

'Potential to do what though? He's Shorty's cousin.'

'He comes from a solid bloodline. He's got skills we can use.'

Antonio shook his head. 'I don't see it.'

'I didn't ask you to. Just drive the car and leave the thinking to me,' said Marrion. The rest of the ride continued in stony silence.

* * *

After meeting with Marrion, Shorty dropped Blakey off, then headed to Chink's Shadwell apartment. Shorty entered the spot. It was decorated similarly to Chink's town place, but to Shorty it seemed over the top.

As he walked through to the main room, he saw Lamont stood on Chink's balcony looking out. Lamont turned, holding a glass of wine in his hand and nodding at his comrade. He wore a tan short-sleeved shirt, chinos and a pair of tasselled loafers.

Shorty spotted the slight bruising around Lamont's eye and mouth. He didn't comment.

'Drink, Shorty?' Chink called out from the kitchen.

'Yeah, go on then.'

Chink brought him a glass of white wine. Shorty shook his head.

'Why are we kicking back drinking wine? Ain't you got any beer or brandy?'

'I'll remember for next time,' said Chink.

'Whatever. I dropped a box on your boy from Manny.'

'A full box?'

Shorty nodded. 'He's getting quick with the return too.'

'He does a lot of business outside the Hood.' Chink was fully aware of Marrion's moves.

'If he's opening new markets, maybe we should give him more work.' Shorty considered his pockets. He received a healthy share of profits, but wanted more.

'It's worth talking about.' Chink straightened up.

'What are we doing about Terry?' Shorty asked, steering the conversation to other business.

'He's part of the team.' Lamont glanced over the balcony again. Shorty glared at him. He was pleased Delroy had backed off, but didn't like the sneaky way they had gone after Reagan.

'You what?'

'He works for us now. Nothing major. He's gonna be in charge of a team and report to you,' said Lamont, turning back to face Shorty again.

'You've gotta be fucking kidding. Why would we want that loser on our squad?'

'He could be an asset to us. As long as he's working for someone, he's fine. Keep your foot to his throat and he'll make us money.'

'He's loud, and he knows too much about the setup. We need to eliminate him. I'll handle it if you don't wanna be involved.'

Lamont waved Shorty off.

'Forget him. I've got other news to share with you.'

'Cool. Afterwards though, we're gonna talk about this Terry situation,' said Shorty.

Lamont took a deep breath. It was time.

'I'm walking away.'

Silence ensued. Chink chuckled to himself. Shorty looked stunned.

'From what?'

'This. What we do.'

'What are you talking about? You can't walk away.'

'My mind is made up. I'm transitioning towards it now. By the time Carnival ends, you two will run the show.'

'You've squared it with Akhan?' Chink spoke up.

'Fuck that,' Shorty turned on Chink. 'You can't agree with this. He's talking about breaking up the team!'

'L's a grown man. We can't talk him out of something when he's made his mind up.'

'Fuck you too then. You're a punk. When we started, you were too pussy to even join us.'

'You're mad at me for getting an education?' said Chink, laughing.

'Don't flip this,' Shorty turned back to Lamont. 'This is about you. Has this got anything to do with that girl you met at Tek's; the one you're grinding?'

Lamont gazed at his friend, his expression neutral.

'This is nothing to do with Jenny.'

'Bullshit. It's always about some girl with you. Ever since we were young, you've always lost your shit over some female.'

'I told you it's nothing to do with her. I've wanted this for a long time. You should see it as an opportunity to grow.'

'You wanna sell out for pussy, fine. Don't make out like you're doing me a favour.' Shorty stomped away.

Lamont sighed and poured himself another glass of wine.

'That could have gone better.'

'I'd say it went just as expected,' Chink surveyed Lamont. 'You're doing the right thing. You don't look as haunted anymore.'

'I feel better,' Lamont admitted. What he had done to Reagan was front and centre in his mind. It was self-defence. Reagan had tried killing him and Lamont had defended himself. The world was better without him.

Lamont had spun a story to Trinidad Tommy about an argument growing out of control. He suspected Trinidad knew he was lying, but the old man had nodded and gone along with it.

'I'll sort things with Akhan. Shorty will be fine when I'm gone.'

'You think so?'

'I hope so.' Rubbing his eyes, Lamont took another sip.

* * *

Marcus Daniels sat in Jukie's spot sinking glasses of white rum, soaking up the smoke-filled hangout area. He'd tried his hand on the card tables earlier, losing a few hundred.

After sorting Lamont's mess, Marcus had slept for a full day. When he'd got up, he had come to play. Now he was getting bored. He drained the glass and climbed to his feet, unsteady for a second. After he collected himself, Marcus headed out and clambered into his ride.

He'd only driven a few streets from Jukie's when he was surrounded by flashing lights. Tempted to bulldoze his way through, Marcus calmed down when he realised he had no weapons in the vehicle. He assessed the surroundings. There was a police van and two Corsa's. A legion of officers had climbed out.

Unafraid, Marcus stared at them. Two of them appeared at either door, cutting off the possibility of escape.

'Marcus Daniels?' One man asked. He was broad with a pencil-thin moustache and dry lips.

'Who the fuck is asking?'

'We need you to come to the station and answer questions.'

'About what?'

'Climb from the vehicle and I'll tell you.'

'I'm tired. Come back another time.'

'You're being charged with murder, so that will not happen. Marcus Daniels, you do not have to mention when questioned . . .'

Marcus shot daggers at the officer as he read the rights, the raging inferno in his eyes making the man step back. He climbed from the ride, eyeballed the contingent of officers, then put his massive hands behind his back.

CHAPTER FIFTEEN

Wednesday 21 August 2013

CHINK RECLINED AT HOME, drinking a bottle of water. He was reading over the specs for a potential investment and thinking about his own future. Chink had earned a lot of money over the years but once he stepped into Lamont's shoes, this would skyrocket.

The only problem was Shorty. It was clear from his reaction that Shorty didn't want to work with him. The idea didn't please Chink either. Shorty was stubborn and brutish. Without Lamont to guide him, Chink didn't see how it would work.

For now though, he was focusing on his profits.

'Wow, that painting looks old!'

Raised voices startled Chink from his papers. He frowned as Naomi and another girl staggered into the room, laughing.

'Oooh, is this him then? You've done well, Naomi. He's gorgeous,' the girl slurred. She was an attractive pecan skinned girl with sultry lips and hazel eyes. Her crooked eyebrows looked ridiculous though and once he saw them, Chink couldn't take her seriously. He turned to Naomi, who leant against the wall, giggling. The stench of vodka, weed and cigarettes filled the room. Chink wiped his nose.

'What are you doing here?' he said to Naomi. The dress she wore clung to her curves but was too short for Chink's liking.

'Town was dead, so we thought we'd have a few drinks here,' said Naomi as she sashayed to the kitchen. She returned with a bottle of red and two glasses. 'This is Adele by the way. Adele, this is my boo, Chink.'

'Nice to meet you. You're fit,' Adele said.

Chink nodded at her, his eyes boring into Naomi's.

'You never said you were coming.'

'So, you're my man. I shouldn't have to say when I'm stopping by. You got another woman here or something?'

Chink shook his head. 'Don't be silly. I'm working and I didn't expect to see you tonight.'

'Oh crap.' Adele had opened the bottle, which had slipped from her grasp and spilled on the plush cream carpet, staining it scarlet.

'You clown,' Naomi giggled again. Chink whirled on her so quickly she took a cautionary step back.

'What is so bloody funny?'

'She's an idiot. She's always doing stuff like this,' said Naomi.

'I want her gone. Now.'

'Wait a second—' Adele started. Naomi stopped her.

'I'll sort it, 'Dele,' she glared at Chink. 'That's my best friend you're trying to kick out. She goes, then I go, and you'll never see me again.'

Adele smiled at Chink, drinking wine from the bottle. The smile vanished from her face when he took her by the arm and ushered her from the apartment. Chink slammed the door and faced Naomi.

'What are you doing? Go let her back in.'

'She never comes again. In fact, as long as you're here, never bring anyone you associate with again.'

'*Associate with?*' Naomi's face twisted. 'Listen, you don't tell me what to do. I'm leaving.'

'Sit down,' said Chink. Naomi glared at him. Shaking her head, she moved to push past him. The crack as Chink's palm lashed her cheek was like a gunshot. She toppled to the floor, shocked. Chink was so slender Naomi hadn't expected him to pack so much power. With shaking legs, she stared up at him.

'You don't come into my home with degenerates and make messes. Remove that dress, then clean this carpet.'

Naomi's mouth hung open. She wasn't seeing the generous, attentive man she had been sleeping with. His face was red, his eyes bulging and his fists clenched. Naomi was a warrior. She had allowed no guy to dominate her but in this moment, she didn't want to try Chink. She slunk from the room to do as ordered.

* * *

Marcus sat in the interview room, glaring at his arresting officer.

He wanted to rip his head from his shoulders, but calmed himself down. He had been in the police station for over twelve hours and it was cramping his style.

The police had arrested him in connection with the murder of Carl Coleman. Marcus didn't know how they had connected him to the crime, but the police had ways.

The solicitor Lamont hired looked confident, which gave Marcus reassurance. Marcus had refused to answer their questions when they had booked him. They had sent him to a cell and now they were trying again.

'Interview recommencing at eleven eighteen am. Present are DS Sinclair, DS Myers and the suspect, Marcus Daniels and his legal counsel.' Sinclair assessed Marcus, searching for weakness. He was a closed book though. He put out a powerful vibe and Sinclair resisted the urge to shrink back.

Sinclair knew all about Marcus Daniels. He was legendary in the Hood and had been on the police radar since his teens. Sinclair had heard the stories, the rumours of murders he had committed, people he'd had maimed. If they could put him away, it would be a powerful statement.

'Marcus, can you please confirm your whereabouts on the night of Thursday Fifteenth of August 2013?'

Marcus didn't take his eyes from Sinclair. 'No comment.'

'Do you know a man named Carl Coleman?' Sinclair tried again.

'No comment.'

'Do you know a man named Ricky Reagan?'

'No comment.'

'How about Delroy Williams?'

'No comment,' drawled Marcus.

Sinclair paused again.

'How long have you been friends with Lamont Jones?'

'No comment.'

'Is Lamont your boss?'

'No comment.'

'Did Lamont give the order for you to murder Carl Coleman?'

'No comment,' said Marcus.

'Did you murder Carl Coleman?'

Marcus hesitated. Sinclair thought they had him, but a second later he was proved wrong.

'I don't know Carl Coleman. I don't know Ricky Reagan or a Delroy Williams. Anything that might've happened is not my business. That's all I'm gonna say.'

'If you didn't murder Carl Coleman, would you be able to say who did?' Sinclair was reaching, and he knew it. The solicitor answered before Marcus could.

'My client has asserted his innocence, and I am recommending for the record he make no further comment during this interview.'

'Do you sell drugs for your friend, Lamont Jones?' Sinclair ignored the solicitor.

'No comment.'

'Has Lamont fallen out with Delroy? Is that why Carl was murdered?' asked Sinclair.

'No comment.'

'Where is Ricky Reagan?'

'No comment.'

Sinclair shared a look with Myers. It had been risky to bring Marcus in but they had hoped to get lucky. He wasn't breaking yet though. They would have to find another angle.

'Interview ended at eleven thirty six am.'

* * *

'Keyshawn!'

Marika's son hurried into the living room at the sound of his mum's voice. She held his Xbox 360 controller, scowling. Marrion, his mum's new friend, lounged on the couch. He held out his fist and Keyshawn touched it in greeting.

Keyshawn liked Marrion. As far as his mums' friends went, he was an okay dude. He never tried telling him what to do, and he treated his mum nice. He had even bought him a new game for his computer.

'Don't you hear me talking to you?'

'Sorry,' said Keyshawn, not meaning it. He didn't understand why his mum was like this. Even when she had company, she still yelled at him.

'Why is this pad lying around? What have I told you about tidying up after yourself?' Marika flung the pad at him. He caught it before it could hit the floor.

'Careful! That's expensive.'

Marika narrowed her eyes.

'You're telling me it's expensive like you paid for it. You don't pay for shit, so next time just do as you're told and stop leaving your fucking things around the place, or you'll find them in the bin.'

'I didn't leave it down here. Bianca must have moved it from my room.'

'I don't care who moved it. Get it out of my sight and stop answering back,' said Marika. Keyshawn glanced at Marrion who gave him a sympathetic look. Turning on his heel, the little boy trudged from the room.

'Make sure your room is tidy too,' she yelled after him one last time. Marrion chuckled, causing her to turn on him.

'What are you giggling at?'

'You. Why are you flipping out on your kid like that? All he did was leave a pad on the floor.'

'I didn't ask you for your opinion so just stay out.'

Marika was spoiling for a fight.

'I like to have an opinion.' Marrion's smirk infuriated Marika more. Marika trembled with rage. Lamont had always told her she had an anger problem, but she never paid attention. The world couldn't handle strong women.

'I don't need you to have an opinion on me or my kids.'

'Well, I'm going to. Deal with it.'

Marika gave him her most withering glare, but it seemed to have no effect. She looked him up and down. It annoyed her she couldn't get Marrion to bite. Every time she snapped at him, he never rose to it. As much as it aggravated her, she knew it was one of the biggest reasons she was still interested.

Marika had a low attention span with men. If they couldn't provide, they were useless and sometimes even when they could, she was happy to back off when it became too real.

Marrion was different. He was making strides in the game, and he was strong. Marika hated bitchy men. Marrion had no interest in arguing with her but he was decisive.

Marrion stared at Marika with a half-smile on his face. Marika Jones was the sexiest woman he knew. It was more than just looks. She was a tiger. She didn't back down, and she always had an opinion, a refreshing change from the wishy-washy women he dealt with.

You received what you expected with Marika, but underneath she had a vulnerable side. It was worth braving the volcano for the warmth within.

'Why are you always so highly strung? Come here and relax,' he said.

'No I'm not gonna relax.'

Marrion stood up, towering over her. She scowled, pissed off yet pleased with the image her man presented. Marrion's clothes hung just right and Marika knew what was underneath was even better. She allowed him to kiss her on her neck. It was a sloppy kiss, but she was wound tight and in her state, was enough to do the trick.

Soon his hands were running all over her body and Marika couldn't even remember why she was so mad. She told him to slow down in case Keyshawn walked in, but once she felt his arousal, she decided against it and pushed him towards the sofa.

* * *

'What did they say?'

Shorty, Marcus and Lamont were in Lamont's office. They had released Marcus on police bail. He wore the same clothes they had picked him up in. His face was lined and his eyes were bloodshot, but alert.

'They were asking if I knew Carl, Reagan's boy.' Marcus lit a cigarette.

'Someone's talking then,' Shorty spoke up. 'How else would the Feds make that connection? You wore a mask, right?'

Marcus's silence answered the question. Shorty shook his head.

'Are you for real? How could you go barefaced?'

'I wasn't planning on leaving witnesses,' said Marcus.

'Doesn't matter. You wear a mask so little bitches that see you, can't run to the police and tell them. That was stupid.'

Marcus cut his eyes to him. 'I don't need a lecture.'

'I'm not giving you one; I'm telling you you're an idiot.' Shorty didn't hold back. Marcus's eyes blazed with anger, but he remained seated. Shorty was right. In the heat of the moment, Marcus hadn't considered covering his face. He hoped the mistake wouldn't cost him his freedom.

Whilst they argued, Lamont stared ahead, not getting involved in the conversation.

'I'll handle it. Don't worry,' said Marcus.

'You better do,' kissing his teeth, Shorty stood up. 'I swear, it's like I'm the only guy keeping it real.'

'What's up with him?' Marcus asked Lamont when Shorty had left.

'He had bad news.' Lamont filled Marcus in on what he had told Shorty and Chink.

'How the fuck can you be ducking out?'

'That's not important, Marcus. We need to focus on keeping you out of prison.'

'I'm not going to prison,' said Marcus.

'Did they mention Reagan?'

'They know nothing. They'll never find him,' said Marcus. 'Fuck it. I wanna hear more about your plan, and I wanna meet this girl of yours too.'

'Marcus—'

'Tonight. Just for one drink. I'll bring Georgia.'

Lamont didn't want to go. Shorty had already fallen out with him though; if a few drinks kept Marcus sweet, it was a small sacrifice to make.

'Tonight it is then.'

* * *

That night, Lamont and Jenny met Marcus and Georgia at a bar near the train station.

'He's massive,' Jenny whispered to Lamont. They were waiting as Marcus and Georgia made their way across the room towards them.

'You're the girl who won my brother's heart then?' Marcus said to her as a greeting.

'You can just call me Jenny,' she said, laughing. Marcus hugged her, Georgia by his side. Lamont had met her several times, and found her nice enough, but quiet. She was short, blonde, blue-eyed, and curvy. She and Marcus had been on and off for almost ten years.

Lamont made small talk with her, and then the four of them sat in a booth in the far corner of the room, ordering drinks.

'Where did you two meet then?' Georgia asked Jenny, whom she had formed a bond with.

'We met through friends,' said Jenny with a smile, sharing a look with Lamont. He grinned and sipped his gin and tonic.

'You're feeling her, aren't you?' Marcus said to him. Lamont nodded.

'She's a special woman.'

'Is she the reason you're quitting?'

'I don't know.'

'You'd walk away over a chick?'

'I'd walk away if I thought it was the right thing to do,' Lamont corrected him. Marcus was about to reply when his eyes narrowed. Lamont turned, noticing two dudes walking in their direction. They were young, well dressed, laden with jewellery, and flanked by an entourage consisting mainly of women. One youth was stocky, dark skinned and bullet headed. The other was the same height, but chubbier.

As they walked by the booth, the bullet headed one grinned at Georgia. She didn't respond, but Marcus picked up on it.

'Oi!' he called, half the bar staring now.

'You talking?' Bullet Head asked, looking back.

'Don't scope my girl like that.'

'Don't tell me what to do.'

Marcus was on his feet then, 'are you on something?'

'Are *you?*' Bullet Head wasn't backing down.

'Marcus, chill.'

Marcus ignored Lamont and focused on Bullet Head.

'Little man, don't try me.'

'Whatever, *old man*. Step off before you get hurt,' taunted Bullet.

'Who's gonna hurt me? You?'

Bullet Head shrugged. Marcus moved towards him but the bouncers were all over it, swooping in, trying to calm the situation down.

Marcus was yelling at Bullet Head to follow him outside while Bullet Head and his people shouted insults at him. Lamont was helping the bouncers calm Marcus, who had gone ballistic. They got him outside.

'I'll fucking kill them. I swear down I'll fucking kill them.' he punched the wall, cursing out loud one minute, mumbling under his breath the next. Lamont was stumped.

'Marcus, let's forget it and go,' he said, still trying to talk sense into his friend.

'Lemme back in there.'

'Marcus, please. Just forget them and go. Please baby,' Georgia pleaded.

'Lamont, please take me home,' Jenny whispered in his ear. She looked terrified.

'Marcus, c'mon, we're going. Get in a taxi with us.'

Marcus took one last look at the bar, kissed his teeth and followed Lamont.

CHAPTER SIXTEEN

Wednesday 21 August 2013

LAMONT AWOKE the next morning tangled up in a mix of sheets with Jenny. He tried kissing her neck. She skated out of his reach and got to her feet.

'What's wrong?' asked Lamont.

'What happened last night?'

'Don't worry about that. Lie back down.'

'L. Your friend needs help.'

Lamont sat up now and sighed.

'Marcus is just Marcus. He overreacted.'

'Overreacted? He was ready to fight all those men by himself because one of them looked at his girl. How primitive does that sound?'

'Jen, you wouldn't understand.'

'Course not. I don't even understand you, and you're meant to be normal,' said Jenny. Lamont's eyes narrowed.

'What do you mean by that?'

Jenny ignored him. She grabbed her clothes, hurried to the bathroom, and shut the door.

Lamont watched the door for a moment. Marcus was too much for most people. He was intense. He should have prepared Jenny for it rather than assuming she would be all right.

'I'm sorry,' he said through the door. There was no reply.

'I'm not the most forthcoming guy, and my friends are fucked up. Me and Marcus grew up together though. He's just stressed.'

Nothing. Lamont shrugged, then headed downstairs and made himself a cup of coffee. Jenny came downstairs a while later, her hair still damp from the shower. She sat down and he poured her some.

'Are you hungry?' He asked. Jenny shook her head.

'I'm trying, Jen. I know it wasn't ideal for you last night, but I promise you, Marcus just had an off night.'

Jenny smiled at him. 'Your lifestyle just worries me. I try not to let it, but I can't help it.'

Lamont pulled Jenny to him and kissed her on the head. He hadn't told her of his plans yet.

'Are you busy tonight?'

'No. Do you want to do something?'

'A friend of mine is holding a fundraiser. Want to come with me?' asked Lamont.

'I'd love to.'

Lamont grinned, pleased she had said yes.

'I'll pick you up about sevenish then.'

* * *

'You sure this is the spot?'

It hadn't taken long for Marcus to track down the perpetrators from the club. The mouthy one was a dude on the rise known as *Maverick*. The other was known as *Scheme*. He would show them what happened when they fucked with him.

'Yeah, boss,' said Victor. He was a rough-looking meathead loyal to Marcus. 'This is where they base. You wanna rush it?'

'We don't need to.' Marcus pointed out of the window. Maverick was strutting down the road towards the house, looking pleased with himself.

'Wait here.'

Marcus climbed from the ride and approached Maverick.

'Still wanna talk shit?'

'You again. What the fuck do you want?' Maverick looked unafraid.

'Do you know who I am?'

'You're that washed up knucklehead from the Hood, so what? You and your whack crew had your time, and this is ours,' said Maverick, holding his ground. Marcus struck, almost taking his head off with an uppercut.

'Still wanna talk shit?' he repeated. He punched Maverick in the mouth.

'Fuck you, you're a fucking joke.' Maverick spat blood on the floor. Marcus kicked him in the head, knocking him out.

'Now who's the fucking joke?' He stalked back to the ride rubbing his knuckles.

* * *

The fundraiser took place in the Town Hall, in the heart of Leeds city centre. The organisers, hoping to attract deep pockets, spared no expense. It had a smart-casual dress code, and was invite only.

Jenny and Lamont entered the building after the party started, accompanied by Lamont's business partner, Martin Fisher and his fiancé. Jenny liked the vibe. From the moment they had arrived, people had clamoured towards Lamont and he had handled them with a lot more tact than Jenny had expected.

Lamont could be cold and just switch off, but he seemed in his element tonight. Jenny was by his side, sharing in this energy. For almost an hour, she and Lamont navigated the crowds, talking to people from different walks of life. He had gone with Martin to get drinks when Jenny became distracted by shrill laughter.

Jenny ignored the rumbles from the crowd and looked over, seeing a group of women laughing at something a stocky man in a tight shirt and jeans had said. The man glared at her with sullen eyes. When he did, Jenny realised it was Lamont's friend, Shorty. She smiled, then frowned when he shot her a hateful glance.

'Here you go.' Lamont handed Jenny her drink.

'Thank you. Your friend is here.' Jenny motioned towards Shorty, who still looked over.

'Oh yeah. So he is,' said Lamont. He and Shorty eyed one another now. Both men nodded.

Jenny watched, enthralled.

'What was all that about?'

'You'll have to be more specific.' Lamont sipped his drink. Martin and his lady were talking at length to another couple, so Jenny gave him her full attention.

'Have you fallen out with him?'

'Shorty? Nah, we're just going through some stuff,' said Lamont. It was a vague answer, and Jenny found it unsatisfying.

'What kind of stuff?'

'Differences in opinion.'

Jenny glanced back over at Shorty, who was shooting Lamont looks so ugly, they sent a shiver down her spine.

'He looks like he hates you.'

'Shorty's intense. I expect it.'

Jenny, frowned, forcing her mouth shut. Lamont surrounded himself with dangerous people, then seemed to placate them when they displayed any signs of aggression. She wondered if he feared his friends.

Before she could retort however, a thin, dreadlocked man in a blue shirt and trousers seemed to materialise out of thin air next to Lamont.

'You weren't even gonna say anything, were you?' the man said to Lamont. Jenny clutched his hand.

'I figured you'd drag yourself over here,' said Lamont, his eyes as hard as the man's. Jenny held her breath. A moment later, she gaped as they both laughed.

'It's good to see you, L! For real. Didn't think you'd come tonight.'

'I wouldn't have missed it,' said Lamont. The man turned to Jenny.

'L's not going to introduce us, so I guess it's up to me; my name is Kieron. Everyone calls me *K-Bar*.'

'Nice to meet you Kieron. I'm Jenny.'

'Likewise. Jen, I'm just gonna borrow L for two minutes if you don't mind?'

'That's fine.' Jenny watched K-Bar lead him over to Shorty and his harem of women. It seemed frosty, but Shorty and Lamont touched fists, K-Bar smiling in approval. Jenny turned to Martin, leaving Lamont to his business.

* * *

'Guess who I found?' K-Bar interrupted Shorty as he whispered in the ear of a woman.

Shorty and Lamont regarded one another. They had not spoken since he had shared his news. The girl Shorty had been flirting with was still standing there.

'Leave,' K-Bar told her. The girl made a derisive noise and didn't move. K-Bar's eyes darkened. 'You don't want me to repeat myself.'

The girl cut her eyes and stomped away. Lamont and Shorty half-glared at one another. K-Bar smiled at their stubbornness.

'I dunno why you two are fronting, acting like you ain't got love for one another. Bury this and move on.'

'He'd know all about moving on.' Shorty jerked his head towards Lamont, who smiled.

'Shorty, we're family. Even if I'm not in the mix, I'm always gonna be around.'

'It's not the same. You're leaving us to struggle, L. For a chick.'

'Struggle? Shorty, the team is stronger than ever. You have the best product, no Reagan or Mack to handle. Work with Chink and you will prosper.'

'Fuck Chink.'

'He's one of us, and he worked hard to destroy Reagan. You owe him respect for that if not anything else.'

'I don't owe him nothing. I've been watching out for his sneaky ass since day one. He owes me,' said Shorty.

Lamont rolled his eyes, not wanting to stand and argue. He was about to go back to Jenny when he noticed Marrion Bernette, followed by Timmy.

'What the fuck is he doing here?' said Shorty.

Marrion ambled over, Timmy trailing behind.

'Why are you here?' Shorty said to his cousin.

'He came with me, bruv. Hope that's not a problem,' Marrion spoke first.

'Get outside now. I want to talk to you,' Shorty ignored Marrion and addressed Timmy.

Timmy headed outside as Shorty stalked him. Marrion looked tight at being snubbed, but hid it well.

'What was that?' he asked Lamont and K-Bar. They shrugged.

'Shorty looks after his cousin,' said K-Bar, as if that explained everything. He was looking at Marrion with intense dislike. Lamont noted this as Marrion turned to him.

'Can we talk?' he asked.

'The floor is yours,' said Lamont. He would not make it easy for Marrion.

Without being asked, K-Bar left them.

'You don't like me, do you?' said Marrion.

'That's irrelevant.'

'That's a yes then?'

'Like I said, it's irrelevant,' replied Lamont.

'Things could have been different with you and me, and I should have stepped to you like a man about your sis. I care about her though.'

'It's nothing to do with me.'

'You're Rika's older brother. I've got sisters back home, so I get the role. I don't wanna step on toes, I just want to be with her.'

'Then be with her, and leave me out of it,' said Lamont, turning his back on him and heading over to Jenny, now standing by K-Bar. Marrion watched him, fury etched in his face.

* * *

'What the fuck is wrong with you?' Timmy said to Shorty. They stood at the bottom of the concrete steps leading up to the building.

'I'm doing the talking. Why are you here?'

'Marrion invited me. What's the problem?'

'You've got no business being around Marrion. You don't know him.'

'I know him more than you. He treats me like family. You treat me like I'm an outsider.'

'I'm not debating with you. Go home. Now.'

'No,' said Timmy, squaring up. Shorty slapped Timmy in the mouth, stunning him.

'Recognise who the fuck I am and go home before I leave you laying here!'

Timmy wiped the blood from his mouth and glared at Shorty for a moment, then stormed off.

* * *

Marcus smoked a spliff, a slow, heavy rap track playing in the background. He had been stewing all evening, ignoring his phone and brooding over Maverick's barbs.

Since he was a child, Marcus had grown used to people fearing him. Maverick had squared up, unintimidated though, and it wasn't sitting well.

Marcus wasn't like Lamont. He didn't have portfolios and investments. He spent money as it came in and for the first time, he was worrying about his future.

Over time, his money streams were drying up. It was getting harder to extort money from people, and everyone and their mother seemed to do loans. It made more sense to take a chance with one of the less experienced loan sharks than someone with his violent reputation.

In the back of Marcus's mind, he realised if he told Lamont he was struggling, Lamont would give him the money in an instant. Pride stopped him though.

Marcus had always looked after himself, however. He couldn't let Lamont see his weakness.

'Can you turn that noise down please?' Georgia entered the house and wrinkled her nose at the pungent stench of weed. She stood in front of Marcus with her hand on her hip. He ignored her, placed the joint in a nearby ashtray, then closed his eyes.

'For God's sake, Marcus; couldn't you open a window?'

Marcus again disregarded Georgia. She meant well, but he was in no mood for her nagging. He had his own place but when he wasn't working, he spent most of his time at Georgia's.

'I'm talking to you.' Georgia raised her voice.

'Piss off. I'm not in the mood.' Marcus waved her away.

'You piss off! This is my home, not yours. I've had a hard day and if you can't respect that, leave,' said Georgia.

Marcus snarled. Moving so quickly Georgia never stood a chance, Marcus slapped her with enough force to lift her off the ground. Georgia crumpled in a heap, tears of shock and pain filling her eyes.

'I told you I wasn't in the fucking mood,' said Marcus, glaring at her as if it was her fault, before storming out. Georgia touched her bloody mouth as the door slammed, crying now.

CHAPTER SEVENTEEN

Thursday 22 August 2013

TIMMY HEADED to Ben's house in a taxi. He plastered a smile on his face when Ben's mother answered the door.

'Timmy! You okay?' She swayed on the spot.

'Yeah, Mrs Skelton. Ben about?'

'He's upstairs. Go on up,' she slurred. Timmy stomped upstairs into Ben's room.

'Yes, Tim.' Ben was on his bed smoking a spliff. Jerome sat on a nearby chair, pouring Alizé into a paper cup.

'Where are you coming from?'

'This thing in town,' replied Timmy.

'Should have brought us in,' Ben held up the joint to him. 'What happened to your mouth?'

'Got into a little scuffle.' Timmy wouldn't mention Shorty. He took a drag of the joint.

'Where d'you get that chain from?' Jerome noticed the heavy belcher piece around Timmy's neck.

'Marrion gave it to me,' said Timmy. The chain had been a random gift. The gesture had touched him, and after the argument he'd had with Shorty, Timmy wondered why he was even bothering to stay loyal to his cousin.

'That must have cost a bomb.'

'Marrion's loaded,' Ben piped up. 'He was paying for top-notch champagne and everything when we were with him.'

'Is he rolling like that?' Jerome had a greasy expression on his face. 'We should rob him and take his shit.'

'Marrion rolls with killers. It's not worth it.'

'Yo, fuck him and anyone else coming out of Manchester. This is Leeds, fam. I say we fucking kidnap him. Make his team pay to get him back, or we pop him.'

'You'd do that?' Timmy asked Jerome.

'Course. I've got a piece at home.'

'You try stupid shit like kidnapping, you'll have to kill Marrion and his team to survive.'

Jerome didn't like Timmy disagreeing with him, and it showed.

'I ain't scared of that Manc prick,' he growled, frowning. Timmy saw how pointless the discussion was. There was a reason Jerome would never succeed; he was trapped at the bottom rung, and he didn't have the smarts to rise in the game.

'Go on then, J; do it.'

'Do what?'

'Kidnap him.'

'I will!' Jerome declared. 'Have you lot got my back though?'

'I'm not robbing him. That's snake shit.'

'I see how it is; my man buys you a little chain and suddenly you're on his dick? Fuck you then. I'm gone.' Jerome snatched the bottle of Alizé and stormed off.

'Should we go after him?' asked Ben.

'No. Leave him. He needs to cool off.'

* * *

Lamont sat at home, thinking about the loose ends he needed to tie up. Carnival was close, and he had everything ready. He always made money from the event, but he was taking it to an audacious level.

On the legitimate front, Lamont had been spending more time at the office with Martin, learning exactly where the money went. This also meant more sessions with his accountant, which he had pencilled in.

Everything was well, yet Lamont felt uneasy. His sleep had been reduced to two or three hours a night again if he was lucky, and no matter how much he analysed, he couldn't figure out where the feeling was coming from.

Lamont recalled the fundraiser, and how much he enjoyed being out with Jenny. He had felt almost normal. He only hoped he and Shorty would get back to their old relationship now.

A knock at the door interrupted his thoughts. Lamont assumed it was Jenny and opened the door.

'Mr Jones.'

Lamont was startled for a second, but recovered.

'Saj, nice to see you again. Come in.'

Akhan's second-in-command followed Lamont into the living room and perched on the sofa.

'Can I get you something to drink?'

'Some water, please,' said Saj. Lamont fetched him a bottle and sat opposite him, waiting. The indication was clear; Akhan was telling him they could find him.

'This is a lovely place.'

'Thank you.'

'Did you do the decorating yourself?'

'No, I paid someone.'

Saj smiled, placing the bottle on the coffee table.

'I'm here to talk about this conflict you are waging in the streets. Your altercations bring unnecessary attention. You see this.'

Lamont nodded. 'The conflict is over though. Delroy and I have ceased our drama.'

'What about Marcus Daniels?'

Lamont's cool slipped for a second. He'd had no idea anyone else knew of the arrest.

'Don't be surprised. We couldn't do our business if we didn't know everything about everyone. The police questioned Mr Daniels about a murder. This is a worry.' Saj's tone remained solicitous.

'I appreciate the concern. Marcus is a rock though. He won't talk. No matter what.'

'And you would put your reputation on the line to guarantee this?'

It took Lamont only a second to reply.

'Yes.'

* * *

'Why are you asking?'

Lamont was at Jukie's gambling spot. Once Saj left, he had driven down to the Hood.

Saj's comments had triggered something with Lamont. He'd learned titbits about the things Marcus was doing a while back and ignored them.

Lamont felt awful, but he had become immersed in Marcus's problems in the past, and he had no desire to do it again.

Jukie learned everything in his spot. Lamont's relationship with Shorty was tenuous at the moment, so he couldn't go to him. He and Jukie went back far enough for Lamont to learn that he could speak to Jukie in confidence. A man in Jukie's position couldn't afford enemies like him.

'You're a pillar of the community. People speak around you,' Lamont stroked the older man's ego, and it worked. Jukie grinned and spoke.

'Your boy is up to his neck in it.'

'How bad?'

'He's in here every night, L. Playing cards, betting big. High and drunk. He's—'

'How bad?'

Jukie swallowed. 'He's into me for fifteen grand. I don't know the ins and outs, but I'm not the only one he owes.'

Lamont gritted his teeth, annoyed at Marcus's carelessness. If he needed help, he could have come to him rather than gambling. He hid the anger from Jukie though.

'Have you approached him about paying?'

Jukie shook his head. 'You don't get heavy with Tall-Man like that. Last time he got in deep, he paid a few weeks later.'

Lamont digested the information. Marcus had always lived hand to mouth, and no amount of advice to save could dissuade him.

'L, are you that worried about him?'

'I'm not sure, Juke. Thanks for your time though,' he said, handing the man some money.

'I don't need your money, L. The info's free.'

'Nothing is free. Take it.' Lamont didn't raise his voice, but there was an insistence that made Jukie take heed. He thanked Lamont and limped inside.

'Fuck.' Lamont allowed his rage to take over for a second. He had vouched for Marcus, but now there was more. As Lamont started the engine, someone called his name. He cursed as he watched the person grow closer.

* * *

Chink stopped outside Georgia's place and killed the engine. He checked his reflection in the wing mirror, then knocked on her door.

'Who is it?' She called. Chink didn't answer, knowing curiosity would bring Georgia to the door.

'Xiyu? What are you doing here?'

Chink noted the bruise on Georgia's face she'd tried to cover with makeup.

'I've been trying to get hold of Marcus. Does he have a new number?'

'Not that I'm aware of.' Georgia's voice shook.

'If you speak to him, tell him I'm looking for him.'

Georgia burst into tears then, unable to maintain her composure.

'What's he done?' Chink led her into the house and closed the door. Georgia was in near hysterics now, unable to answer. He made her a hot beverage and forced her to drink while he stood over her.

'T-Thanks,' she said when she'd calmed down.

'What did Marcus do?'

'He's been stressed. I pushed him too far.'

'Don't blame yourself. He's wrong,' said Chink.

'He does. It's just been hard for him.' Georgia felt compelled to defend Marcus. Chink didn't like it.

'Stop making excuses. Just stop it. You're better than that.' He sat next to Georgia now, taking the half-drunk teacup from her hands and putting it down.

'Xiyu—' Georgia started. Chink hushed her with a finger to his lips.

'No,' he said. 'I love you, Georgia. I've always loved you.'

'Xiyu—' Georgia tried to stop Chink, but it was too late. He pressed his mouth to hers, and all the doubt and anguish seemed to leave her in a lustful rush. The walls she had built after straying with Chink the last time crumbled and she kissed him back with fervent gusto.

'I love you,' he repeated, as he unbuttoned Georgia's blouse. Like the last time, she succumbed.

* * *

'Little Lamont,' said the man, shuffling towards Lamont's car. Old Man Charlie was one of Auntie's more prominent suitors. The sight of him filled Lamont with rage as he remembered the turbulent childhood and thoughts he hoped to forget:

Lamont was eleven years old. He'd come home from school early. Auntie was in the living room, lording it up.

'What are you doing here?' Her words were harsh.

'I didn't feel well. Got sent home early.'

'Make yourself useful then. Go sweep your room,' said Auntie. Lamont didn't move.

'Are you listening?'

'Why are you wearing that?'

'Wearing what?'

Lamont pointed at the jewellery around Auntie's neck.

'None of your business.'

'It's not yours. That's my mum's necklace.'

'It was your mum's necklace. She left me in charge.'

Auntie's man bounded into the room. Charlie Mullen was overweight with bad breath, coarse skin and a rotten attitude. He glared at Lamont like he was the intruder. Lamont's eyes shifted to his wrist, recognising the gold watch as his dad's.

'What are you looking at?' said Charlie.

'That's not your watch. That was my dad's,' Lamont told him.

'It's mine now. Get out of here. Your Auntie told you to do something.'

Again Lamont didn't move. Charlie's eyes narrowed.

'Did you hear what I said?'

Lamont continued to glare at Charlie, feeling an infusion of hatred towards him and Auntie. He couldn't tell him what to do. He was nothing.

'Lamont, Uncle Charlie told you to do something.'

'He's not my Uncle.'

Charlie's palm shot out, lashing against the side of Lamont's face. He tumbled to the floor. Charlie picked him up and hit him in the mouth. Lamont tasted blood and felt the sting of salty tears falling down his face. Auntie watched, not saying a word.

'If I have to tell you again, I'm gonna give you something to cry about. Now go!'

'Look at you, boy; you got big,' said Charlie, exposing his worn teeth when he smiled. Lamont eyed him, self-consciously rubbing the watch on his wrist. 'Do you remember me?'

'How could I forget?' Lamont wound his window down, his voice dripping with sarcasm.

'Long time. You're not a little boy no more,' Charlie laughed, expecting him to join in. 'I'm fucked, champ. Don't suppose you could lend me something to get me back on my feet?' he added. Lamont shook his head.

'You've got to be kidding me.'

'I'm desperate. I've got info. We could do a trade,' said Charlie, his words quicker now.

'You've got nothing I want. Get away from my car.'

'Lamont, let the past go. I gave you some licks, but they made you strong. Help me out.'

'Are you deaf?' Lamont's fists clenched.

'Levi. What about Levi? Are you interested in him?' Charlie had Lamont's attention now. Lamont froze, the name he hadn't heard in years triggering more memories he wanted to forget.

'What about him?'

'I'll tell you where he is, if you help me. Please, man. I'm sick.'

Lamont pulled out two twenty-pound notes.

'Talk.'

* * *

Marcus drove to Georgia's house, wiping his eyes and popping two pieces of chewing gum into his mouth.

After leaving in a rage a few nights back, he had holed up, smoking rocks with some delinquents from the old days. He had come to his senses that morning, when he awoke to find himself face down on a wooden floor, missing a boot and surrounded by fiends. Marcus had thought of Georgia, feeling like shit for hitting her. He climbed from his ride and pounded on the door.

'Georgia,' he called out. 'Let me in please. I want to talk to you.'

'Bloody leave her alone!' The next-door neighbour opened her own door and poked her head out. 'She doesn't want you.'

'Fuck off, you fat bitch,' snarled Marcus. Georgia's neighbour, Mandy, was a squat woman with big hands who looked like she could handle herself. They had always hated each other, and as long as Marcus could remember, she had been trying to convince Georgia to leave him.

'You fuck off. I chuffing live here. I'll call the police if you don't leave.'

'Just because you can't get a man, doesn't mean you can interfere in my business.' Marcus was close to losing his top and head-butting her.

'I'd rather be alone than shackled to a loser like you,' said Mandy. Marcus ignored her and knocked again.

'Please, Georgia. I want to talk.'

'Mate, I think you should leave,' A neighbour across the street weighed in. That was it. Turning, Marcus was about to deal with the interferers, when Georgia opened the door.

'It's okay, Mandy; I can handle this.'

Marcus saw the bruise on Georgia's face and felt worse than he already did.

'Fine. Don't come crying next time though,' said Mandy. Marcus waited until she was inside, then turned back to Georgia.

'I'm sorry,' he whispered.

'You can't keep doing this, Marcus. I don't deserve it.' Georgia choked back a sob.

Marcus closed his eyes. The weight of his woes, the life he was living and the risk of prison all caught up with him. Tears pooled in his eyes. Marcus tried wiping them away but he couldn't stop them falling.

'You're right. I need help. I need you,' he mumbled.

Georgia stared at Marcus and her heart melted. She had never seen him cry. This show of emotion mixed with the guilt she felt over Chink, caused her to forgive him.

'If you ever hurt me again, we're through. For good. Okay?' she said. Marcus nodded, sniffing. 'Do you wanna come in?'

He nodded again and followed Georgia inside, shutting the door behind him.

* * *

Lamont stood in front of a ramshackle house that wouldn't have looked out-of-place in 2003 Iraq. The grass in the garden was over-grown and littered with weeds and refuse. The front and upstairs windows were boarded. Two grubby looking youths had watched him get out of his ride. Lamont ignored them and knocked at the door.

A living corpse of a woman answered. She was thin, with lank blonde hair, dull eyes that were too big for her face, and dry lips.

Lamont resisted the urge to flinch as she glared at him.

'What do you want?'

'Let me speak to Levi,' said Lamont.

'Who?'

'I'm an old friend.'

'Levi 'ant got no friends.'

'You know him then?'

While the blonde zombie verbally tripped over herself, a movement by the dirty window caught Lamont's attention.

'Move.' Lamont pushed past the woman. The volley of curses thrown at him dissipated when he locked eyes with the man sitting in the middle of the derelict living room. *Levi Parker.*

'You got past Siobhan then.' Levi laughed so hard he coughed.

Lamont took a step forward but stopped himself. He was trying to spot the Levi he'd known, the carefree, well-groomed ladies' man. That image wouldn't stick though. It never would again.

Now, all he would see was the shrunken remains of his friend. Levi had lost a lot of weight. His eyes had that lifeless sheen Lamont had seen too many times before.

'L, man, you look good.' Levi finished coughing, speckles of blood around his mouth, and hugged him. He stank but Lamont withstood it.

'Sorry, babe; this rude prick pushed past me,' said Siobhan, storming into the room. Levi cut his eyes to her.

'This is my oldest friend. Piss off upstairs.'

'But—'

'Just do one.' Levi didn't raise his voice. She flounced from the room mumbling under her breath. A door slammed upstairs, followed by a shout.

'Sorry about her. She's a horrible cunt,' said Levi. 'I can't believe you're here. How's everyone doing?' he sounded like the excitable kid Lamont once knew.

'Everyone's good.'

Levi grinned, showing brown teeth. 'You're killing the streets. Everyone knows your name.'

'I'm just living.'

'Bollocks. You're sorted. I saw your clothes, and the whip when you pulled up.'

'Things aren't always as they seem,' said Lamont. 'I can't live like this forever.'

'You're a fool. I could.' The hunger, the undisguised envy towards the lifestyle his friend was living was clear in Levi's voice.

'Why don't you?'

'What?' Levi was startled.

'Get straightened out. I'll pay. Get clean, then work with me.'

Levi didn't reply straight away.

'No. I'm not good enough.' He hung his head.

'If I can do it, you can,' said Lamont.

'L, look at me,' Levi grabbed his yellowing t-shirt for emphasis. 'I'm a pissing crackhead.' He was in tears.

'You can get help. I've got more than enough money,' Lamont insisted.

'No, I'm too far gone. I tried, L. It always wins though.'

'Levi—'

'Just go, L.'

'Levi, —'

'I'm serious,' Levi's voice was stronger. 'Go, man. Don't come back. Please.'

Lamont nodded. He reached into his jacket pocket and dropped an envelope on the coffee table.

'Use that. Buy yourself whatever you need.'

Levi snatched the cash and gave it back. 'I'm not taking your money, L.'

'C'mon, Levi.'

'No. I'm not taking it.'

Lamont stared at him, once again seeing the excitable, ambitious kid Levi had once been. The image faded to Levi's tear-streaked face the day his big brother had been murdered in the streets. Lamont snapped back to reality, understanding how things could have turned out for them both.

'Take care of yourself, brother.'

They shook hands, two young soldiers of the street, cut from the same harsh cloth yet at two opposite ends of the crime pile. Lamont walked out.

Siobhan hovered near the top of the rickety steps in the hallway and scowled at Lamont.

Outside, he glanced at the window. Levi watched him. Not taking his eyes from his friend, Lamont tossed the money onto the doorstep, climbed into his car and started the engine. A lone tear pooled in his eye. Brushing it aside, Lamont drove away.

* * *

Jenny had finished work for the evening and was on her way to Lamont's. They had arranged to meet, but she hadn't spoken with him today. She saw his car parked in the drive, but the house lights were off.

Jenny's heart raced as she called Lamont's phone again. There was no answer. On a hunch, she tried the front door, surprised when it opened.

The sweet sounds of *Stevie Wonder's Innervisons* album filled the house, and Jenny's insides shifted. Lamont was cheating on her. She wanted to flee, but she was stronger than that. She wanted to catch him in the act.

Jenny stormed into the bedroom, then stopped short. Like the rest of the house, the room was pitch-black, save for a small patch of light coming from the dashboard of a Mp3 dock. Jenny switched the light on and noted with stunned relief that Lamont was alone. His eyes were closed and turning the light on hadn't startled him in the slightest.

'L?' she called. He opened his eyes.

'Hey,' he said.

'Are you okay?' asked Jenny. It looked like Lamont had been crying. He sat up in bed, wiping his eyes.

'I had a rough day.'

'What happened?'

'I ran into an old face. Someone I allowed myself to forget when I shouldn't have.'

'Who?'

'A friend. I abandoned him, Jen, and now he's a fucking drug addict,' said Lamont. He laughed. Jenny didn't know what to say. She had never seen Lamont so unglued. It was strange to witness him lamenting over an addict, considering how he made his money.

'Levi and me were friends in our younger days,' Lamont carried on.

'Levi had an old brother selling weed. He offered to set us up.'

'Did you?' asked Jenny. Lamont gazed into her beautiful eyes and decided it was time to let her in.

'My parents died when I was a kid. In a car crash. It's how I got this,' he pointed to a thin scar on the underside of his chin that Jenny had never noticed. 'After they died, me and my sister had to live with my Auntie.'

Jenny nodded, listening to the story.

'We were struggling, so I did what I needed to do.'

'Wait a second; you're saying you sold drugs because your parents died?'

'I did what I needed to do,' Lamont repeated. Jenny scoffed. She had held back what she wanted to say to Lamont about his life, and she wouldn't anymore.

'How can you use your parents as a cop-out for doing something you know is wrong?' she said. 'It's illegal, L! You sell poison. The two areas do not mesh. How do you think they would feel? How would your parents feel if—'

'Who the fuck do you think you are?' Lamont hadn't raised his voice, but the effect was like a gunshot. Jenny stopped speaking. She had never seen this side. Lamont seemed to radiate some innate power. His rosewood eyes blazed. She froze on the spot.

'You . . . grew up in comfort. You don't have the slightest idea what my life was like, so don't you dare knock me for trying to survive. Judge me on me, not on what I do.'

'I'm sorry, L. Please, tell me,' Jenny found her voice. Lamont took a deep breath, then spoke again.

'Auntie betrayed us. The little money left to us, she spent on herself.'

'All of it?' Jenny gasped.

'I didn't realise straight away. She hated me. I was her slave. She abused me, her and whatever boyfriend was hanging about,' he said. 'I was sent to school in whatever clothes Auntie could scrounge up. I was laughed at, bullied and ostracised. We were broke, Jen. We went from happy to hell. Marika didn't remember. She was too young when our parents died. She grew up used to being poor.'

Lamont paused, then continued.

'I played it straight until my teens. I worked hard, wanting to get a good job so I could get me and Marika out, but I reached my breaking point.

'Levi's brother fronted us. We were up and running and making decent money. It didn't last though. Levi's brother got into it with another crew. They murdered him.'

'Oh God. That's awful.' Jenny's hand went to her mouth in horror.

'Levi attacked Leader, the head of the crew. Stabbed him. Ended up going to a young offender's prison. When Levi got out, he avoided us.'

'What about Leader?'

'What about him?'

'Is he alive?'

'No. Someone killed him,' said Lamont. Something about the way he said it sounded strange to Jenny. Lamont's tone was the same as it had been when she'd confronted him about the bruises on his face a while back. Lamont's tone had been vague, almost disconnected then too. She didn't dwell though.

'What made you visit Levi?'

'Someone pointed me in his direction. He left Leeds after all that trouble. I wasn't aware he was back.'

Jenny sat next to Lamont, holding his hand, feeling like she had a broader understanding of him and why he did what he did. She stroked his fingers, enjoying the closeness.

'What now, Lamont?' She whispered.

'Now, I walk away,' Lamont sounded more confident now. 'The plan has always been to leave. I never wanted to do this forever. I was waiting for the right reason to leave,' he gripped Jenny's hand. 'And I've found it.'

Tears of happiness sprang to Jenny's eyes.

'I love you, Lamont,' she let out the words she had been holding back. He blinked once before replying.

'I love you too, Jenny. You've saved me.'

They continued to hold one another then, having embarked on a new phase of their relationship.

CHAPTER EIGHTEEN

Saturday 24 August 2013

Shorty sat in a club knocking back liquor, sad and angry. Earlier in the day, he had hosted his annual pre-carnival barbecue. It wasn't a huge event, but the turnout was always good. Shorty and a few others would cook and play music while people hung out.

Everything had gone ahead like clockwork, apart from the noticeable absence of Lamont.

For the past five years, he had run the event with Shorty. He had called the day before to apologise and say he couldn't make it.

It was a sign things were changing. Lamont was already making his transition. It was rarer to see him in the streets these days. Instead, he was with Jenny, or schmoozing potential business links at *Épernay* or other high end spots.

Shorty wanted to be happy for Lamont, but he didn't see how they would stay tight if they were in two different environments.

To add to Shorty's mood, he had taken Grace to Amy's after the barbecue, stunned when her front door was opened by a man. What hurt the most was Grace yelling *Chris* and jumping into the man's arms for a hug. It showed familiarity, and he had been forced to keep his composure in front of his daughter.

Everything was changing. Only Shorty remained the same.

Shorty shrugged away the thoughts and ordered a glass of tequila. He drank and whilst surveying the room, spotted a girl named Kimberley from the roads. She seemed to be arguing with a group of girls.

As he watched, the biggest of the girls slapped Kimberley. The rest of the girls joined in the assault before Shorty hurried over and pulled the biggest one off.

'Oi, who are you?' She got in Shorty's face. He didn't recognise her but her accent was a Manchester one.

'She's cool. Fuck off and leave her alone.'

'Who the fuck are you though?' The girl shoved Shorty. Part of him wanted to walk away, whilst the rest of him screamed for action. He didn't need it tonight though. Shorty stepped around the angry girl and helped Kimberley. She had a couple of cuts and scrapes but apart from that she looked okay.

'You good?' Shorty asked, ignoring the hateful glares of the other girls. Kimberley nodded.

'I'm fine.'

'Come. Let's sit you down.'

'It wasn't my fault. They started on me. I've never met them.'

'You know what these out-of-towners are like,' said Shorty. They were walking away when the angry girl cut him off.

'Who are you, dickhead?' She was wild.

'Take your drunk ass back to Manny.' Shorty turned his back on her and led Kimberley over to his table. They had just sat down when Kimberley grabbed his arm.

'She's coming.'

Shorty watched the girl approach. She was bigger than him, her shoulders bouncing. He imagined she could hit hard.

'Go on, who are you?'

'You need to back off. I ain't gonna treat you like a woman if you start.'

'Fuck off.'

'I'm not gonna warn you again.' Shorty remained seated as the loudmouth stood over him. Her friends gathered around, giving her confidence. She raised her arm to strike Shorty. A second later he was on his feet and the girl was on the floor, out cold.

The punch had come out of nowhere, a blistering uppercut that had crunched her jaw, snapping her head back. Shorty sat back down, picking up his drink without another word.

* * *

In another part of the club, a gang of guys from Manchester were getting loose on Grey Goose vodka and other liquor. The leader of the group, a man named Solly slouched in the middle of the booth.

Solly earned good money in Manchester and had women queuing because of this. He was about to order more bottles when he saw one of his girls hurrying towards him.

'Solly, you need to handle one guy! He's going on reckless,' she said, getting the attention of the six-strong group.

'Zona, what are you on about?'

'This little guy knocked out Jasmine. She's out cold.'

'What?' Solly stood up. Jasmine was a prick, but she was from his area, and he was cool with her brother. 'Who hit her?'

'This cocky little fuck. We were just dancing, and he spazzed out,' said Zona. Solly flexed his muscles.

'Let's go handle this dickhead. Zona, show me where this prick is.'

* * *

'We need to leave.'

Shorty ignored Kimberley. He wasn't letting his night get ruined by a couple of rude out-of-towners. The girl was gone. Shorty had no idea where they had taken her, but if he saw her again, it would be worse.

'We're not going anywhere. She started it.'

'I can't believe you hit her so hard.' Kimberley glanced at the dance floor, as if expecting to see the bully laying there.

'She deserved it. No one fucks with one of my girls,' said Shorty.

'Please, I haven't been your girl in a long time. You're Amy's property.' Kimberley shook her head.

'You must be high,' said Shorty, putting on a front. Before he could add more, there were loud voices. The remaining women were yelling and pointing in Shorty's direction, followed by at least half a dozen angry-looking guys.

'Oi, mate, what do ya think ya playing at?' The smallest guy started in a Manchester accent. He was stocky and looked like he could handle himself. His team were surrounding him like bodyguards, each eyeing Shorty with dislike. The mouthy girls stood to the side, waiting.

'Do I know you?' said Shorty.

'Nah. You've been threatening my girl and her people though. Think you're tough, sparking out a woman?'

'You've got it twisted. They jumped my girl. That other bitch tried swinging, so I sat her down.'

Solly looked to his people, annoyed at Shorty's complete lack of fear.

'Are ya taking the mick? Do you know who ya fucking with?'

'If you wanna do something, then let's do it.' Shorty stood. Solly looked to his people again, taking a step forward. He was about to rush Shorty when a voice halted him.

'What's going on?' Marrion Bernette strode over, flanked by Brownie and Antonio. His eyes assessed the situation. Shorty looked bored, Solly ready for combat.

'M, this dude's talking reckless. I'm gonna do him in.' Solly eyed Shorty.

'No, you're not.'

'You what?'

'You heard,' Marrion turned his back on Solly and touched fists with Shorty. 'Sorry about this mess, fam. My guy's out of line, but he's all right.'

'He needs to watch himself.' Shorty's eyes remained on Solly.

Marrion nodded. 'You're right, fam. Oi barman,' he addressed the bartender who was bringing more drinks. 'Three bottles of champagne. Quick time.' Marrion dropped a handful of notes in his hand. Shorty glanced at Solly and his people, but didn't gloat.

'C'mon, let's have a drink,' said Marrion.

'Fine. This is my home girl Kimberley.'

Solly watched as they drank champagne and chatted like the best of friends. Marrion was from his ends and he was a big deal. Knowing he was around, Solly had figured it would be a wrap for the cocky little prick.

Now, not only was Marrion buying the bar with the dude, he had talked up to him. Shorty was a big deal, and this irritated Solly more. He grew angrier as he thought about the time he and Marrion had gone partying in Manchester. Marrion had bought one bottle of champagne for the group to share. Now, Shorty and his girl comfortably sat with three.

'Let's go,' said Solly.

'What?' Zona spluttered, wanting to see Shorty get his comeuppance.

'Now. Fucking come on.'

* * *

'Yo, sorry again about my boy.'

'It's squashed. Don't worry about it.'

Half an hour had passed and Marrion was still trying to apologise for the situation. Shorty just wanted to drink in peace.

'Yo, I'm living good here. Last thing I want is some of my people from home fucking it up,' said Marrion. 'It's bad enough that Teflon already doesn't like me. This is about money. I don't want anything to stop that.'

'True.' Shorty was half-listening.

'Teflon cool but he makes it tough, don't you think?' Marrion had been waiting for this opportunity. Chink had mentioned that Lamont and Shorty weren't clicking. 'I mean, I treat Marika good. She could be messing with some trampy dude who'd mess her around, but I've got her living pretty.'

'Yep.' Shorty sipped his drink.

'Trust. I mean, Tef can be a stuck-up little prick sometimes. He's lucky I—'

'You need to end it right there,' Shorty slammed his glass down. 'L's my brother. I dunno what you think is going on but if you violate, it's a wrap.'

'I didn't mean it like that,' Marrion back-pedalled. 'He needs to chill.'

'Nah, *you* need to chill. You seem cool, but you're moving way too fast for some people. Furthermore, I'm not feeling the way you've got my cousin running around after you. Focus on your money moves and when the time is right, you might get brought to the big table. Get me?'

'I get you,' said Marrion. He gritted his teeth, but said nothing else.

Shorty turned to Kimberley in time to catch her studying him. He moved closer.

'You want a top-up?' He motioned to the bottle.

'You had this mapped out didn't you?'

'What are you on about? What thing?' asked Shorty.

'You knew your mate was here didn't you?'

'I'm not a criminal mastermind. I didn't know he was in the club.'

'Whatever. Why else would you start with that guy and his people?'

'Because I'm crazy. Why else?' Shorty sized her up. Apart from the scrapes, Kimberley looked like pure sex in her wrap dress and heels. 'Fuck, you look good, Kim.'

'Don't start,' said Kimberley. She couldn't deny the chemistry though. Shorty was a thug, but you knew where you stood with him. He had earned big points with her too. He'd had her back and had even fought someone over her.

'I'm not starting, I'm *stating*. Drink up. It's gonna be an even longer night for you, I guarantee it.'

'If you say so.' Kimberley smiled, taking a mouthful of her drink.

* * *

The next morning, Lamont chilled in Roundhay Park.

The area was quiet, save for the usual visitors to the park. Everyone in his community minded their business. It was easy to lose himself, to blend right in amongst the doctors, solicitors and bankers he had for neighbours.

To them Lamont was another smiling businessman they saw on their way to and from work.

'Why do we have to meet here?'

'Because it's nice,' said Lamont.

'You live like five minutes away though. We could have met at your place, or you could have driven to the Hood.'

'I didn't want to drive. Enjoy the weather and relax.'

Shorty plopped down on the grass, yawning so hard Lamont almost copied him. He had bags under his eyes and looked irritable.

'What was so important?'

'I heard there was trouble.'

'I was chilling in one club; couple' girls started with Kim, so I pulled them off her,' said Shorty.

'Which Kim? The one you used to grind?'

Shorty grinned. 'Yeah. This big bitch tried hitting me, so I sparked her. A couple of Manny goons got involved, but Marrion squashed it.'

Lamont didn't like this. He was wondering if it was coincidental that guys from Manchester had started with Shorty, only for Marrion to play the saviour.

'You need to chill,' he warned. 'Scrapping in town is short-sighted. There's CCTV and snitches everywhere.'

'Just leave it, L. I'm not feeling a lecture right now. My head's banging and I'm stressed.'

'Fine. Did you sleep with her?'

'Who?'

'Don't play dumb.'

'Who, Kim?'

'Yeah. I remember how loved-up you were.'

'Fuck off; you're the master of being pussy-whipped. Look how open Jenny's got you,' said Shorty.

'Whatever. Still haven't answered my question though.'

Shorty grinned. 'She tried playing hard to get, but after that hero shit, she was all over me.'

'You seeing her again?'

Shorty shook his head. 'She knows how it is. She said some slick shit about Amy owning me.'

'So? She's not lying.'

'Amy can fuck off. I dropped Grace off yesterday, and she had that prick Chris answering the door, playing daddy,' said Shorty.

Shorty had mentioned Chris before. Lamont hadn't met him, but respected the man's bottle. Shorty had intimidated more than a few guys who had stepped to Amy. Chris seemed immune to it though.

'You can't get mad at her for moving on. She's waited years for you. What did you think would happen?'

'What the fuck did I say about a lecture!' Shorty exploded, causing people to stare in their direction. Lamont didn't even flinch.

'I'm always gonna keep it real with you,' he said, meeting Shorty's angry eyes. 'You've taken the piss. Step up, or let her go.'

Shorty sighed, the anger abating. Lamont was right. Amy had given him plenty of chances to commit, but he'd assumed she would always be around. The thought of them playing happy families sickened him to his stomach.

'Did you know Levi was back in Leeds?' Lamont sensed Shorty didn't want to talk about his love life anymore.

'Yeah. He's living up Seacroft sides.'

'Why didn't you tell me?' Lamont couldn't believe Shorty had kept it from him.

'For what? So you could play hero like you did with Terry and put him in our thing?' Shorty made a face. 'He's a gimp, and he's on that stuff. He's done with.'

Lamont said nothing. Even in their younger days, Shorty had despised Levi. It had been foolish to bring him up.

'Speaking of fiends; everything is sorted. All the work has been distributed.'

'How many paid up front?' Lamont asked.

'The dudes you'd expect. Have to admit, you planned this nice, L. I thought you might have ordered too much.'

'I anticipated the drought when I spoke to the man,' said Lamont. He had ordered far more product than normal. It was harder to get drugs at this time of the year, and Lamont had contingencies in place. Not only was he putting out the best product, he was making it available at the time when it was needed. If all continued to plan, Lamont would profit hugely for only two days' trade.

'I feel you. Can't imagine there'll be much spillage. Streets are fucking hungry.'Shorty looked wistful for a moment. 'Guess this is the last time we do this shit.'

Lamont watched him, but said nothing. Shorty stood up.

'Gonna jet anyway. Business.' He slapped hands with Lamont and walked off.

* * *

Marrion sat outside Marika's. Brownie and Antonio were with him, drinking and watching the world coast by.

'We all sorted then?' Marrion asked Brownie.

'Shorty's people dropped off the work this morning so we're chopping that up. We should be ready.'

Marrion shook his head. '*Should be* ain't good enough. I need more than that. This is the chance to make some fucking real money. Antonio, make sure we can place everything. At a profit.'

'On it. What was happening last night though? Solly was vexed,' said Antonio.

'He needs to calm himself down. The guy stepped to Shorty like he was gonna fight.'

'Solly's crazy. All that sniff has messed up his head,' said Brownie.

'Damn right. About to fight over Jasmine of all people.'

'*Big Jasmine*? Why would she need anyone to fight over her? She's a fucking monster,' said Antonio.

Marrion gave him the low down on the fight from last night. Antonio chuckled again when Marrion described how Shorty had knocked Jasmine out.

'About time. She's a lairy bitch.'

'Yeah. Solly's girl instigated, trying to get Shorty rushed. Shorty backed it though,' said Marrion.

'Shorty's fucking proper. We could work with him. He's legit.'

Marrion frowned. He didn't like the way Brownie was fawning over Shorty. His pride was still hurt from the way Shorty had dissed him last night. Marrion had stopped him getting jumped, and he hadn't appreciated it in the slightest.

'Look who it is,' said Antonio. Marrion glanced up at a tracksuit-clad Timmy Turner. The youngster touched fists with the three of them then handed Marrion a bunch of notes.

'That's everything. Stevie tried running his mouth, but he paid up.'

Marrion smiled, handing him five crisp twenties. He gave the rest of the money to Brownie.

'Good lad. You're a fucking asset, Tim. I mean that.'

Timmy beamed with pride at his praise.

'I'm happy to help, fam.'

'Hopefully people will realise it in time too, and the next bump will be yours. It was close this time.'

Timmy's eyes narrowed.

'What bump? Who got promoted over me?'

'Can't remember his name. Some young dude whose hustle Shorty liked. I thought for sure he'd pick you,' said Marrion. He could tell by Timmy's body language that his story had worked. 'Don't worry though, kid,' he continued, hiding his smile. 'Stick with me and I'll make you rich.'

* * *

Marcus pulled to a stop in his 4x4 but kept the engine running. He could see the Jaguar X-Type parked in front of him, and he waited for the man he was meeting to get out.

Chink oozed from the car in a dark blue suit, salmon coloured shirt and tan shoes.

As he sauntered towards Marcus, the giant resisted the urge to shake his head. Chink was cool, but nothing ever came simple with him. He was like Lamont in that way. Chink shook hands with Marcus and handed him a leather case.

'There's twenty there, and one hundred in an account in your name. The details are all inside.'

'I only asked for one hundred,' replied Marcus, frowning. He put the case in the back seat.

'The extra cash will tide you over. I'm good for it. After this weekend, I'll eclipse that.'

Marcus smiled. 'Carnival weekend is always a big one.'

'Why don't you get involved? We can front you a box and you can get paid.'

Marcus shook his head. 'I've survived this long without shotting. I can survive a bit longer,' he motioned to the money. 'Safe, Chink. When I've paid off my debts, I'm gonna spend the rest on Georgia.'

When Marcus said her name, Chink's insides turned to ice. He hadn't spoken to Georgia since they had spent the night together.

Chink hadn't meant to fall in love with Georgia, but years ago she was upset with Marcus over some fuckup. They had slept together in secret a few times before she ended it. Now, she had done the same thing again.

'You gonna buy her something nice then? I can get you a line on some jewellery,' Chink said. Marcus shook his head again.

'She's got fuckloads of jewellery from me for every time I've fucked up over the years. I'm thinking something different. I'm gonna take her away somewhere hot. Bahama's or summat. She'll like that.'

It was almost hurting Chink to keep the fake smile planted on his face. He wanted to reach across and strangle the giant where he sat, but that would be suicidal.

'I'm sure she will. I need to go anyway. Loads of last minute meetings.'

'Cool. Thanks again, Chink. You're a good dude.'

Chink's bad mood lasted all the way back to his house. He parked up, slamming the car door with more force than necessary and headed into his building.

When he entered his apartment, Naomi slouched on the sofa watching television. She sat up, her eyes widening. She had been like this ever since he had to discipline her over her friend's behaviour.

'Get me a drink,' he said.

'What do you want?'

'Surprise me.'

Naomi hurried to the kitchen, returning with some lemonade. Chink sipped it and made a face.

'I don't want this.'

'What do you want then?'

Chink sat up in his chair. His eyes on Naomi the entire time, he poured the drink on the floor, dropping the glass with a resounding crash.

'Clean it up.'

Naomi glared with traces of her old defiance. Chink hid a smile. He could almost see the gears turning in her head; the tug of war between standing up for herself and remaining subservient. She mumbled an apology. He grinned, the smile almost reaching his ears.

Chink padded to the kitchen. Naomi was on her knees under the sink looking for a cloth.

'I like you on your knees,' he said, causing Naomi to jump. 'Sorry babe, did I scare you?'

Naomi looked away from him, then tried going back to the living room.

'Where are you going?'

'I'm gonna clean up the drink before it sets.'

'Forget the drink,' Chink looked her up and down. Even with her spirit crushed, Naomi was still spectacular. The skimpy shorts she was wearing highlighted her bronze legs and the sleeveless top showed off her toned arms. 'Have I ever told you how sexy you are?'

Naomi didn't speak. Ever since Chink had struck her, she wondered how she had ever given him the time of day. He had seemed so harmless. Beneath that veneer though, Chink was a monster. A Jekyll with a Hyde within.

'I asked you a question.'

Naomi recognised the danger in Chink's voice and planted a smile on her face.

'Yeah, you've told me. I like hearing it though,' she said.

'Did Ricky tell you how sexy you were? I bet he did. I bet you did whatever he told you to do whenever he told you to do it.'

Naomi was silent.

'Am I right? Did you run around cleaning up Ricky's messes too? Did you fetch him drinks?' Chink asked, a creepy half smile on his lips.

'I—'

'Forget it. It's not important,' Chink looked at the rag in her hand. 'Put that down.'

Naomi did it without even thinking.

'Now, go upstairs and get in bed. Take all your clothes off. I'll be there in a minute.'

Naomi left the room, hoping that Chink couldn't see her knees shaking. Chink watched her walk away. The control aroused him more than she ever could. Grin etched on his face, he sauntered upstairs to have his way with Naomi.

* * *

In a dingy spot on the outskirts of the Hood, three rough-looking goons sat around, poring over a coffee table laden with guns. The crime film, *Rollin' with the Nines* was playing on a widescreen TV but the youths paid no attention.

'It's going down tomorrow,' one of them said. 'Our guy will be at the park. The job needs doing then.'

'Won't the park be busy?' another of the goons said.

'Doesn't matter. We've already got half the funds, so we're doing it tomorrow.'

'Why's this guy getting dropped?'

'Who the fuck cares?' Raspy-Voice waved his gun at the wall like he was in an action movie. 'We're getting a shitload of cash to handle it, so that's what we're gonna do. Get ready.'

CHAPTER NINETEEN

Monday 26 August 2013

Carnival rolled around in a flurry of good weather and great cheer. Carnival first took place in Leeds in 1967.

Forty-six years later, it was still going strong, holding its own against other large bank holiday events such as Notting Hill Carnival.

The main event was the parade, where dance troupes would make their way through the streets of Leeds, playing music and steel pans. Huge, garish floats moved along at a slow pace with people aboard, drinking, dancing and having a good time. The parade would proceed to Potternewton Park where a stage was erected for artists. The card was normally made up of local performers, but the organisers would sometimes book a superstar.

Lamont and Jenny strolled through the park. Apart from some out-of-town goons and a smattering of hard faced local youths, everyone was in good spirits. They had eaten fried fish and drunk bottles of Guinness punch.

Lamont was content. He had enjoyed talking about the history of the event, telling Jenny tales of going to the park with his family years back. They were debating whether to take another lap of the park or sit down when someone called his name.

'Lamont! Lamont Jones!'

Lamont turned, spotting a figure from the past striding towards him. He was an elderly black man with salt and pepper hair and powerful looking forearms displayed in a bright, short-sleeved shirt.

'How long has it been?' The man asked, growing closer.

'A long time. Too long. How have you been?' Lamont shook his hand.

Nigel Worthington was a local coach from his football days. A talented player, Lamont had used the pitch to display the confidence he didn't have in the rest of his life. Nigel brought him back to earth by teaching Lamont to play within the team, rather than on his own. They had learned to work together and had developed a mutual respect.

'I'm thriving. My son has brought the kids up to visit. I'm on my way to see them,' said Nigel. 'Is everything going well?'

Lamont assured Nigel he was fine, introducing him to Jenny. Nigel made small talk, then turned back to Lamont.

'Can I speak to you?'

They walked a short distance away and stood close, wanting to hear one another over the pulsating calypso beats.

'How are you really doing?

'I told you. I'm doing well.'

'Are you still doing that drugs stuff?' Nigel lowered his tone.

'I do what I need to do. Same as ever.'

Nigel looked disappointed, and his clear disapproval bothered Lamont far more than he wanted to admit.

'Do you need to do it? Even after all this time.'

'I don't need a lecture,' said Lamont.

'No, you need a beating. You were one of the most promising talents I ever trained, Lamont. You instantly picked up things it took the other kids weeks to learn. To watch you settle for this half-life? It's a waste. A complete and utter waste.'

'It's my life.' Lamont had heard similar sermons from Nigel before and didn't want them again.

'I know it's your life,' said Nigel. 'I walked in your shoes a long time ago. I did what I needed to do when I was broke, but you made a career from it. That's the part that sickens me.'

'I told you already; I do what I need to do. No matter the circumstances I stick with my decisions. Sorry if you can't accept that.'

'You suffered with your Auntie, L, but you're a bigger man than
that. That beautiful woman waiting for you,' Nigel jerked his head
towards Jenny, who had her back to them, watching the stage. 'Focus
on her. Don't define yourself by hatred for your past, or you'll never be
happy.' Nigel held his hand out, regret clear on his face. Feeling almost
childlike, Lamont shook it and Nigel left.

Dazed, Lamont walked back to Jenny.

'Are you okay?' she whispered.

'I'm fine, Jen.' The mask was back up now.

* * *

Shorty, K-Bar, and Timmy chilled at the top of the park, near a group
of large music tents. People were out in force, dressed in colourful
outfits. Carnival was a day for everyone to show off and out-stunt each
other, rocking their best gear and jewellery. Dressed in a sweat suit and
fresh trainers, Timmy nodded his head to the beat as he sipped from a
bottle of Coke mixed with Disaronno.

K-Bar was all-business with a phone glued to his ear. Most of the
time he was nodding as someone on the other end updated him, but
occasionally, his voice would raise when he received news he didn't like.
After every call, he would whisper in Shorty's ear.

Timmy was resentful. He wanted to be part of whatever the plan
was. It was definitely big. There had been rumblings of hot product
hitting the streets, but he wasn't in the loop.

Timmy scanned the crowds as a distraction, grinning when he saw
Marrion and a large crew walking towards them. One, a stocky man
Timmy hadn't seen before, glared in Shorty's direction. When Shorty
noticed, he mugged the man right back.

Marrion sensed the tension and nodded at Shorty, who reciprocated. After touching Timmy's fist, he kept it moving. K-Bar hung up,
eyeing the Manchester contingent as they continued past.

'Was that dude eyeballing from the other night?'

'Yeah,' Shorty's eyes also followed the crew. 'He was the one acting like Nino Brown because I sparked that bitch.'

'Why's he with Marrion then?' K-Bar's instincts told him something wasn't right.

'Fuck knows. I don't give a shit either. We need to focus on business, not those small-timers. They'll be gone by tomorrow.'

'True. We're solid anyway. I'm getting good news back. A few people have sold out. Everything's lovely.' K-Bar gave him the latest.

Shorty grinned. Lamont's planning was perfect. Even with the police presence and undercover officers masquerading as civilians, everything had gone off without a hitch.

He was about to speak when a gunshot ripped the air, followed by another. Screams resounded in all directions, unable to drown out the claps of more gunfire. Shorty was low now as was K-Bar.

'K, can you see anything?' He shouted over to his friend, scrambling back to his feet. Shorty's people were looking in all directions, trying to determine who was shooting. Timmy looked petrified.

'Can't see a fucking thing. Too many people running about,' K-Bar yelled back.

Shorty saw a cluster of people gathering around the grassy section ahead of them. Police were there. With a sickening feeling nestling in his stomach, Shorty hurried towards the crowd with K-Bar on his heels.

* * *

Lamont and Jenny walked through the park. He was deep in thought, wishing he had told his former coach he was walking away instead of letting his remarks affect him. Nigel had given Lamont structure when he needed it, and he would always be thankful for the attention the coach had shown him.

Lamont wished Nigel had more faith in him. He was successful after all.

They were close to a smattering of funfair rides above the embankment in the park now. Lamont was about to ask if Jenny wanted to move closer to the stage when a small figure hurtled themselves at him.

'Uncle L,' screamed Bianca, as he picked her up and twirled her in the air. Marika headed towards him, flanked by Keyshawn and to his surprise, Lorraine.

'Princess Bianca.' Lamont kissed the little girl on the cheek and set her down. He gave his sister a hug and nodded to Lorraine.

'You okay, sis?' he asked Marika, who looked worn out.

'I'm knackered, and these kids have been stressing me. You wanna take them for a bit?'

'I would, but we have somewhere to go after this,' Lamont put his arm around Jenny. 'Rika, this is Jenny. Jen, this is my sister Marika, my Niece, Nephew and Rika's friend.'

'You gonna pretend you don't know my name?' said Lorraine.

'Don't start,' Lamont's voice hardened. Lorraine grumbled and turned away. Marika hadn't taken her eyes from Jenny.

'So, you're the one who has my brother whipped?' she said to her. Jenny smiled.

'We're whipped over each other.'

'Make sure you take care of him. You mess him around, and I'll deal with you. Got it?'

'Rika—'

'Your girl can speak for herself, L.' Marika cut her big brother off.

'I can, and I like that you're looking out for him. I love Lamont, and he loves me. We don't need to mess each other around,' said Jenny. Lorraine snickered under her breath, but Jenny ignored it. Her eyes were fixed on Marika as the two dominant females sized one another up.

'I'll see you later, L. Come up and I'll cook you dinner,' said Marika.

'I will. Here, take this for the kids.' Lamont handed her twenty pounds.

'What about me?' she made a face. Lamont shook his head and handed her two more twenties, then walked away arm in arm with Jenny.

'So, that was your sister,' remarked Jenny.

'Yeah. I hope she didn't upset you.'

Jenny glowed. 'She didn't. She cares about you. You can tell. Your niece is gorgeous too.'

'She takes after her Uncle,' said Lamont.

'She has another Uncle? I want to meet him.'

They were both giggling. Fifteen yards away, Jenny spotted Marcus and Georgia. Marcus had his arm around her, and they seemed more content than they had previously.

'L, Marcus is over there. Shall we go over?'

Before Lamont could reply, a scuffle broke out nearby. Some local youths were tussling with each other, but Lamont recognised none of them.

Marcus had noticed. He locked eyes with Lamont, his eyes then narrowing as he focused on something beyond his friend.

Turning, Lamont froze, seeing a familiar face holding a gun. Maverick raised it in Lamont's direction, his bruised face twisted with hatred. Lamont heard Marcus's voice, then the crack of gunfire.

* * *

Marcus and Georgia roamed the park. Victor was nearby, giving them enough room to breathe. The day so far had been uneventful. Marcus had been with Georgia since the night before, and they were getting along better since sitting down and talking.

Marcus was taking it slow. Chink had loaned him enough to clear his debts, with some left to tide him over until his next hustle. It wasn't the first time Marcus had been broke, but this latest encounter had shown him he needed to put something away for the future.

'Are you okay?' He asked Georgia. She shook her head, feeling like shit. Marcus had made such an effort to straighten out, and the guilt of sleeping with Chink was eating away at her. Georgia enjoyed the sex, but it felt dirty now. Marcus wasn't Mr Sensitive, but she had known from the get-go, and it was no excuse for being unfaithful.

'I have to tell you something,' her voice shook. Marcus looked at her, distracted by angry shouts as some kids fought. Lamont was watching the brawl.

With a jolt, Marcus saw the kid he'd beaten stalking towards his friend. He reacted and knocked Georgia to the ground, reaching for his gun. Someone spotted it and screamed. People ran, impeding Marcus's vision.

'Move!' he roared. It was too late. A bullet thudded into his stomach. Marcus stayed on his feet, kept upright by his massive size, and fired once, watching with painful relish as Maverick fell to the ground, just behind Lamont.

It was short-lived; one of the scuffling youths sprayed a Mac-10 that cut Marcus down like a giant redwood. All around, people were panicking, tripping over themselves to escape.

'MARCUS!'

Lamont tried running to his fallen friend, but Marika grabbed his hand, stalling him. He hadn't even seen her approach.

'Let me go!' he shouted, watching in terror as Maverick struggled to his feet and limped towards Marcus, who was trying to sit up. Maverick smacked the giant across the face with the gun, then held the weapon to his head.

'I fucking told you. Your time is done,' he said, his finger tightening on the trigger.

Before he could pull it, another shot rang out. Maverick dropped, dead from the headshot. Victor tried shooting the second gunman, but he dropped the machine gun and disappeared into the wild crowd.

'Marcus!' Lamont wrenched free of his sister and charged towards him, grabbing his hand. 'Marcus! Fight! C'mon! Stay with me!'

Marcus couldn't speak. He was gasping, his tongue lolling out, blood dribbling from his mouth as he tried to breathe. His eyes were dimming. The crowd watched in horror. Jenny was holding Keyshawn's hand whilst Marika wrestled with a hysterical Bianca, fighting to get to her beloved Uncle.

Georgia was on her feet now, rooted to the spot as she watched Marcus take his last breath. His grip slackened in Lamont's hand, his eyes half-closing.

'NOOOOOOOO!'

Lamont's moan of anguish rent the air, mingling with the piercing noise that erupted from Georgia's mouth. Victor stared at Marcus, tears filling his eyes, smoking murder weapon in hand. He hadn't been quick enough to save his friend.

'Armed police! Nobody move!'

As the police converged on Lamont and Victor, Georgia fainted.

CHAPTER TWENTY

Wednesday 28 August 2013

LAMONT SLUMPED IN DARKNESS, drinking. The situation felt surreal, like something from a movie. One minute he was sauntering around the park with the woman of his dreams. The next, he was surrounded by armed police and covered in the blood of his best friend.

Marcus had always lived his life a certain way, but it still shocked Lamont that he had died so brutally. He couldn't help but think if he had been swifter, Marcus might still be alive.

Lamont had been lulled into a false sense of security, and he had been unprepared for the ferocity of the gunmen. He saw with complete clarity how lax he had been, walking around as if retired, with no protection. It was his fault, and Marcus had paid the price because of it.

On the vintage coffee table were two empty bottles of gin. Ever since the police had let him go, Lamont had confined himself to this room. He hadn't eaten, had turned his phone off when it wouldn't stop ringing. Lamont wanted the anguish to disperse. He wanted the liquor to blot everything. He had asked Jenny to give him space, not wanting to suck her into his depressive vortex.

Amid his mourning, Lamont heard a rapid knocking on his door. He lurched to his feet and let Marika in. She glanced at his appearance and shook her head. Lamont could tell by her blotchy face she had been crying.

They sat in silence. Marika sighed when he made himself a fresh drink, but held her tongue, seeming to understand.

Lamont's stomach churned but he didn't care. He wanted to be free of his burdens. Marika made a sudden movement as if about to pick up the remote next to her.

'You seem nervous,' said Lamont, breaking the silence.

'I'm not sure what to say. You must be fucked right now.'

Lamont didn't reply. The gin tasted disgusting now, but he would not let that stop him.

'How are the kids?' he asked, realising they weren't with Marika.

'Keyshawn hasn't stopped bawling. Bianca thought you had been shot. And then the armed police . . .' She trailed off.

Lamont understood. The police had flung him to the floor, their weapons inches from his body, screaming at him to stay down. At the time, none of it sunk in, but Lamont could understand his niece and nephew's reactions.

Victor had been detained and would undoubtedly faced murder charges. Lamont had hired him the best solicitor he could find, but everyone had seen him shoot Maverick. He was protecting Marcus, but that wouldn't matter to the police.

Victor would stay loyal as long as his family was taken care of. As a solider, he knew the risks and if he stayed quiet, the people he loved would be bereft of financial responsibility.

'The police questioned everyone nearby,' Marika continued. 'They were asking if I recognised the shooters, but I didn't.'

Lamont didn't say anything.

'Did you recognise them? I mean, they were looking right at you. Did you lot have beef?'

'Yes, I recognised them,' admitted Lamont.

'Did you tell the police that?'

Lamont shook his head.

'Why not, L?'

'You know why.'

'Because of a code? L, Marcus was a brother to us. Don't you want to see his killer get what he deserves?'

'It's not that simple.'

'They killed him, L. That's as simple as it gets. One of them is still out there. Aren't you worried he'll come for you?'

Lamont wasn't. He had been mere yards away from Marcus. If the shooters had wanted him dead, they could have done it with minimal effort there and then.

'Auntie's upset too,' said Marika, not waiting for Lamont to reply. 'I stopped by before I came here.'

Lamont's temper flared at the mention of his Auntie.

'Who cares?' Lamont slammed his drink down.

'Don't start, L. She's an old woman. She raised him.'

'Like she raised us? Marcus was nothing but a cheque.'

'Auntie didn't have to take us in, L,' said Marika.

'She got rich off us. She screwed us over, yet you still want to love her. Why can't you see it?'

Marika eyes widened. Lamont was drunk and overcome with grief. The last thing he wanted was a conversation about the woman who killed his childhood.

'You're hurting, but it doesn't give you the right to crap all over the only family we have left. Everyone can grieve, not just you.'

'Piss off back to her then! Fuck off out of my house and go be with your conniving bitch of an Aunt. You're just like her; a fucking leech! No wonder you're always defending her.'

Marika flared up, then softened. Her shoulders slumped. Watching, Lamont saw the fight leaving her. Marika gazed at him, then walked out. He started after her but the door opened again and Shorty stood there, red-eyed and defeated. Lamont sat him down.

'We need drinks,' said Lamont. The bottle of *Centaure de Diamant* caught his eye. It seemed like a lifetime since Akhan had gifted it to him. Shorty sniffed and looked up as he carried it over.

'You sure? That shit's expensive,' he noted.

'I'm positive.'

Lamont poured them both a glass, and they toasted, then drank. Straight away, the explosion of taste assaulted Lamont's senses. It was like heaven in a glass; a smooth, rich experience. He watched Shorty, who wore a watery smile.

Shorty rummaged in his pockets for his weed bag and built a spliff, giving Lamont a look to check it was okay before lighting up. Lamont topped their glasses up. He sipped his again, savouring the vintage liquor and taking a long burn on the joint when Shorty passed him it.

'Fuck, I'm fucking done, Shorty,' said Lamont later. The weed and liquor had him on another planet.

'We're just getting started.' Shorty's tear-stained face remained determined. He wanted to celebrate Marcus with the only other person who cared as much as he did. Lamont closed his eyes, taking deep breaths. His head spun. Shorty was right though. This was their chance to reconnect. So they did.

For hours, they told Marcus stories. Lamont recalled the money Marcus used to give him when he was broke, and the disastrous time he had gone on a robbery with Marcus and Victor.

Shorty shared tales of missions he and Marcus had gone on, and how much he had learned. Both had heard the tales before, but that didn't matter.

'You saw him get shot, right?' Shorty asked. Lamont nodded. All the alcohol and drugs hadn't removed the scene from his mind; the blood Marcus had coughed up as his eyes dimmed.

'People are saying it was a little dude called Schemes who popped off with the machine gun,' Shorty continued.

'They argued in town. Maverick was clocking Georgia and Marcus didn't like it.'

'Marcus boxed him up a couple' days later. Victor told me.'

'Marcus fought him?'

'Yeah. Didn't wanna take the disrespect,' said Shorty.

It seemed strange to Lamont, even in his befuddled state, for Maverick to retaliate by killing Marcus in a packed park. It was extreme.

'Schemes is dead when I find him. I'll rip him apart.'

Lamont bowed his head. He was as angry as Shorty, but as much as he desired revenge, Lamont wanted to walk away, and he hated himself for that weakness.

'He's gone, L. They fucking took my brother.' Tears streamed down Shorty's face. Lamont gripped Shorty's shoulder, expecting him to recoil. Instead, he cried more. Lamont comforted him, keeping his own emotions internal now.

* * *

Jenny unlocked the door early the next morning, hoping Lamont would be in a better state of mind after some sleep.

The first thing that hit her was the pungent smell of weed. Jenny walked into the living room.

Shorty lay on his stomach, snoring, almost cocooned by bottles of alcohol. Jenny tiptoed past him, looking for Lamont. He sat in the kitchen with his head in his arms. A cup of coffee was in front of him, untouched.

'Hey, baby,' he murmured.

'How did you know it was me?'

'I smelled your fragrance,' Lamont lifted his head, his eyes sunken and drooping. 'Fuck, I feel rough.'

'I'm not surprised. How much did you drink?'

'Far too much. I need a shower.'

'Go get one. I'll make you some breakfast,' said Jenny.

Lamont stood, yawning and stretching.

'I'm not hungry. Don't go to any trouble.'

'Do as you're told.'

Lamont complied. He left the room as Jenny opened the fridge.

* * *

'Fuck.' Shorty opened his eyes, sitting up. His head felt cleaved. He stood up, blinking his eyes to clear the cobwebs. He heard noises from the kitchen and headed to investigate.

Jenny, Lamont's girl, was moving around, pouring orange juice into two large glasses. On the table were servings of grapes, strawberries and a medley of other fruit. She was putting the glasses on the table when she spotted Shorty.

'Morning. You're just in time. Lamont will be down in a minute. Have a seat.'

Shorty slid into a chair, sipping from a glass.

'Is this okay? I figured you would both want to eat something light.'

'Yeah, this is fine,' he popped a grape in his mouth. 'Thank you.'

'It's no problem. I'm sorry about Marcus.'

Shorty nodded, feeling the lump in his throat.

'Thank you,' he repeated, feeling a newfound affection for Lamont's lady. 'I'm glad you and L hooked up. You're the best thing to happen to him.'

Before she could reply, Lamont walked into the kitchen, looking refreshed. He slapped hands with Shorty, then greeted Jenny with a hug and a kiss.

'Finally, you smell human,' she said.

'Cheeky,' replied Lamont, a tired smile on his face as he sat opposite Shorty. 'This all looks good. Thank you.'

'It's fine. I have to go into work, but I'll finish early and we can go out to dinner?'

'I'll book somewhere. What do you fancy?'

Shorty watched Lamont and Jenny interact. They were so in sync, so compatible with one another. Shorty couldn't think of any woman he had that connection with, apart from Amy. That was the difference between him and Lamont though. Lamont could separate himself from his *Teflon* persona when he wasn't in the streets.

Shorty was always Shorty. There was no off-switch. Maybe that was the problem. Maybe that was why Lamont was leaving.

'Shorty?'

Shorty snapped back to earth. They were looking at him.

'Yeah?'

'Do you want to come to dinner with us tonight?' said Jenny.

'I've got plans. Thanks for the offer though.'

'It's fine. Speak to L if you change your mind.'

Jenny said goodbye hurried out of the kitchen. They heard her fussing until she left the house.

'She's a keeper, L.'

Lamont smiled, wiping his mouth.

'She's not bad.'

'Is she living here now?'

Lamont shrugged.

'She has a key.'

There was a moments silence. Shorty nodded and struggled to his feet.

'I need to get shit in order with the crew.'

'I need to sort the funeral.' Lamont felt a fresh jolt of grief hit his stomach with those words. It was his responsibility though. Marcus had no other family. Shorty headed for the door. Pausing, he turned back to Lamont.

'You can't leave now. You know that.'

Lamont didn't respond.

* * *

'Can you believe him?'

Marrion listened as Marika raged. She had been in a bad mood the whole time he had been with her. From what he could gather, Marika and Lamont had fallen out big time.

Marrion wasn't surprised. He had met Marcus once or twice, but knew of his reputation and how close Lamont was to him. Lamont was probably devastated, he surmised.

'He had the nerve to throw me out. I can't believe it. He's supposed to protect me, not mug me off because I don't agree with him on every little thing. It's bullshit,' Marika snapped.

Marrion kept his eyes on the TV. Keyshawn was plopped on the floor watching a video on his tablet with his earphones in. Bianca was sat in between Marika's legs, wincing as her mother plaited her hair.

'This is it though. He crossed the line. He basically called me a slag. And what he said about Auntie was unforgivable. I mean, she did everything for us. We would have gone into fucking care if it wasn't for her. He's a fucking slanger who acts like he's *Martin-Luther-fucking-King* or summat.'

Bianca looked confused. Marrion didn't like Marika swearing in front of her kids, but he couldn't say anything.

'It's all good though. We're done with him. You kids don't have an Uncle anymore. He's dead to you,' she said to Keyshawn and Bianca now.

The reactions were predictable. If Keyshawn heard, he pretended he couldn't. Bianca burst into tears and ran from the room.

'Get back here,' Marika shouted. 'Keyshawn!' she said to her son. He continued to stare at the screen. Marika stomped over and snatched the earphones from his ears.

'What are you doing?' Keyshawn yelled. He received a smack that jerked his head. He looked up at his mother with a quivering lip, wanting to cry, but unwilling to give her that satisfaction.

'What have I told you about running your mouth? Go look after your sister before I kick your fucking head off.'

Keyshawn glared, snatched his tablet, and stormed out of the room. Marika stood in the middle of the room panting. Marrion watched her. The way she lived, she would make herself sick soon.

'So, you and your brother are really done then?'

Marika took a deeper breath, 'he's hurting over Marcus. I can't forgive him speaking to me like shit though. He's done a lot for me. I'm not ungrateful but still, he violated.'

'You know what the problem is don't you?' Marrion picked his words, drawing Marika in.

'No. Tell me.' Marika sat next to him.

'He's jealous.'

'Jealous of what?'

Marrion paused for effect.

'You've got another man who can provide for you. Lamont's a controller. He liked having you in a position where you relied on him for money and now it's shifting, and he's still trying to control the situation.'

Marika nodded along with what he was saying, just as he'd expected. He continued.

'You two should be pulling together now that Marcus is dead. Instead, he's picking fights, saying all kinds of shit to you. Because he doesn't like you being with me,' said Marrion.

'You're right. He said some nasty shit to Auntie too that time.'

'He's already turning the kids against you. Check Keyshawn's attitude,' said Marrion. He didn't want to use Marika's son as a tool, but the opportunity had presented itself.

'He's too fucking smart for his own good sometimes, just like Lamont. I'm sticking with it. Me and my brother are done. I swear down.'

Marrion held Marika close, kissing the top of her head. He clutched her, a smile on his face. This was almost too easy.

* * *

Timmy Turner sat in his room, messing around with a plastic chessboard. After seeing Lamont with one at the barbers, he had bought one and often studied the pieces. He wanted to see what Lamont saw when he played. He had tried learning how to play, but it was a complicated game and he lacked the patience.

Marcus's death had Timmy reeling. To him, Marcus had been a cornerstone of the Hood. Timmy had heard so many stories about him that he was invincible in his eyes. That was over now though. Marcus was dead, and the streets grieved.

Timmy wanted to see Shorty, but his cousin was blanking his calls. He wanted to help. Schemes was on the run. Shorty wouldn't sit back and let him get away with murder. As always, Timmy was out in the cold.

Lashing out in anger, he knocked all the pieces over and reached for his PlayStation pad. The king piece shook for a moment, then tumbled.

* * *

Shorty stood in front of his crew. They were in the home of one of K-Bar's ladies, who had been told to wait upstairs while they spoke.

Shorty's face was lined, heavy bags under his eyes. He took a spliff that K-Bar handed him and inhaled, wiping his eyes. When he spoke, his voice was strong.

'I don't need to go into detail. People violated when they dared to touch Tall-Man. We're gonna rain down on them. I want the shooter. Alive.'

There were rumbles of approval from the crew. All of them had respected Marcus and wanted to make someone pay for killing him.

'Get the word out. It's ten bags for a location. Cash. I want everyone searching. Get on it,' ordered Shorty.

* * *

Schemes hurried along the streets with his head down. He'd been off the radar since the shooting, but he had been summoned. His contact waited by an expensive motor.

'You're late,' The man barked.

'So what? You didn't tell me that fucking Marcus would be strapped or that he'd have a bodyguard. I lost my fucking boy behind that shit, and—'

The man tossed Schemes an envelope. Schemes thumbed through the notes, then stuffed them in his pocket without a word.

'Any job comes with risks. You knew what you were getting into when you took it on. Make sure you stay out of sight, and keep me updated of your location,' the man said.

Schemes nodded, realising that complaining wouldn't work.

'Don't spend too much in the same place. Don't flash it around either. Understand?'

'I'm not dumb,' said Schemes. The man glowered at him.

'Don't get lairy. You did a sloppy job, but it worked out. Don't ruin it by getting left in a ditch somewhere.'

Schemes stared at the floor, mollified.

'Get out of here. Marcus was just the beginning. I'll be in touch.'

CHAPTER TWENTY ONE

Monday 2 September 2013

A WEEK after Marcus's death, a tribute took place at the West Indian Centre. An old building at the bottom end of Chapeltown Road, it had seen its fair share of memorial services. This one was no different.

People had come from far and wide to pay their respects to a certified Hood legend and child of Chapeltown. Despite what he became, Marcus Daniels had still come from the absolute bottom, born to addicts who cared more about getting high than caring for their son. Marcus had been a menace.

Despite his reputation, he was respected and in most circles, loved.

Shorty brooded in the corner of the room, dressed in a crisp white shirt, black trousers and a cashmere overcoat with black Ferragamo moccasins. His eyes were blank.

Mutely, he drank from the bottle of Courvoisier he was clutching. The devastation of his friend's murder sank in. Life would never be the same for Shorty. He often chastised others for showing weakness, yet he could have cried and not stopped.

Marcus had lived life every day knowing he might die. Many of them did. That didn't make it any easier.

Timmy Turner stood with Shorty and looked around the room, impressed at the turnout. Some heavy faces from other cities were in attendance. He'd seen Shorty shaking hands with them earlier and was irritated that he hadn't introduced him. With Marcus gone, he wanted his chance.

'Cuz, can I speak to you for a minute?' he asked Shorty, who kissed his teeth.

'I don't have time for your shit,' Shorty told Timmy, just as K-Bar tapped him on the shoulder.

'Check who's here.'

Lamont was hand-in-hand with Jenny. He wore a flawless black suit and a matching tie, looking like a high-powered banker. As soon as people saw him, they flocked like he was the Pope.

Lamont addressed everyone, showing a politician's savvy and relating to each on a personal level. Almost twenty minutes elapsed before Lamont made his way to Shorty. He saw the devastation etched on Shorty's face, aware the misery was mirrored on his own.

'How are you?' Lamont asked. Shorty took a swig of brandy. He swayed, but maintained his composure.

'Still standing. For now.'

'Relax. We need to keep our heads straight.'

'It's been a week, L. I'm not happy about this shit. I can't lie.'

Lamont didn't reply straight away. He focused on Timmy.

'Nice to see you, Tim. That's a nice suit.'

'Thanks, L.' Timmy was buoyed by the compliments.

'Don't mention it. Listen, can you take this beautiful girl of mine to get a drink? Get yourself one too.' Lamont handed him a crisp fifty pound note.

Jenny glanced at Lamont, but followed Timmy through the crowds.

'Where's that bitch that Tall-Man was grinding?' Shorty looked around the room.

'Georgia's in shock, Shorty. She's with her family.'

'What about Tall-Man's family? We're here. She should be too.'

'People grieve in different ways. She was right there. She saw him get shot.'

'How do we know she wasn't in on it?' Shorty's voice rose. People were staring.

'Shorty, calm down.'

'Fuck you.' The liquor had Shorty ready to fight. The room occupants continued watching, feeling the spike in tension. Lamont didn't react, gazing at Shorty. A moment passed, then Shorty nodded, calming down.

'Shorty, we'll find them. For now, we need to . . .' Lamont's voice trailed off. He had seen Marika. His heart soared when he saw the kids. Keyshawn held the hand of his younger sister. Their faces brightened, but they made no move toward him. Lamont glanced over at Jenny, then moved towards his sister.

'Can we talk?' he asked. Marika's face tightened. Beneath the anger, Lamont could see the pain in her eyes. He had said some harsh things. They were true, but he regretted them all the same.

'We have nothing to talk about,' said Marika. The hurt Lamont had just seen, dissipated in an instant.

'Rika, please—'

'No!' Marika shouted, drawing the attention of the room. 'You don't talk to me like that, then act normal. You don't.'

'There's no excuse. I'm not trying to hide from it, but you're my sister and I love you.' Lamont ignored the room, focusing on Marika. He noticed people straining to listen, but blocked them out.

'Go to hell, Lamont. We are done. Stay away from me and stay away from my kids.' Wrenching Keyshawn's hand, Marika led the children from the wake.

Lamont watched them leave, his expression unreadable to the audience. Without missing a beat, he walked back over to Jenny and ordered a drink.

'Are you okay?' she asked. People spoke again now, likely discussing the argument they had witnessed. Lamont forced a smile on his face and nodded, wondering if there was any way back for him and Marika.

* * *

Shorty staggered out of the wake, the heat killing him. For the past few days the weather in Leeds had been crazy to where you couldn't stay outside for too long.

Lamont had hung around for a while then slipped out with Jenny, leaving enough money behind the bar to satisfy the crowd. Shorty had gorged himself on rum when his brandy had run out. He was now leaning to another level. He gripped the wall and tried to steady himself, needing fresh air.

'Shit,' he said. Before he knew it, he was on his knees, heaving. 'Never fucking drinking again.'

'That's what they all say,' a voice chimed.

Shorty was upright now. 'Who the fuck are you?'

'Sorry, didn't mean to startle you.'

Shorty wiped his mouth, thankful none of the sick had reached his clothes. He glared at the familiar man. He was average height, big-bellied, wearing glasses and rumpled clothing.

'Whatever. Dig up now,' said Shorty. He didn't like looking weak.

'No need to be like that. I was just taking an interest.'

'I'm not interested, so back up,' Shorty told him. He was about to re-enter the wake, when the man spoke again, this time saying words that stopped him.

'Franklin, you grew up big.'

Shorty whirled around.

'What did you say?'

'I said you grew up big. Look at you,' said the man. He was smiling now. He looked proud. Almost like a—

No

'Who are you?' Shorty's voice shook.

'I'm your dad, Franklin. It's been a long time.'

There was a roaring in Shorty's ears. His knees weakened, but it wasn't from the drink. He stared at the man again, taking in his nose, eyes, cheekbones. They were Shorty's features. *It couldn't be though*. His dad was gone. Long gone. A figment of his past.

'No,' Shorty spoke out loud.

'I've got a lot—'

'A lot of what? Catching up to do?'

'Son—'

'You're not my dad. You're a mess.'

Trevor Turner was silent.

'What the fuck are you doing round here?'

'I was in Southampton. I came back and spoke to Serena,' said Trevor. Shorty's face tensed. He had spoken to his mother yesterday. She hadn't said a word about this.

'She tells me you've got kids of your own. I'm proud of you, Franklin. I didn't set a good example, but—'

'You didn't set *any* example. I wasn't even born yet when you ran off. Now what? You heard I'm rich and you wanna creep up on me? Fuck you. Get out of here.'

Trevor took a step forward. 'Son—'

Unable to hold back, Shorty lashed out. Trevor took the shot on the bridge of his nose. There was a sickening crack, and he dropped like a stone. Shorty raised his fist to hit him again, but when he looked down at the pathetic excuse for a man, he changed his mind.

Shorty spat on the floor next to his dad and walked away, sobered by the experience.

* * *

Chink knocked on Georgia's door, checking his reflection in the window. When her sister Angie answered, he put on his nicest smile.

'Hi, Angie. I wanted to stop by and see how she's doing,' he said.

'Nice to see you, Xiyu. Come in. She's in here.' Angie led him to the living room.

Georgia was drinking a cup of tea and watching TV. She paled when she saw Chink.

'Sis, Xiyu's here to see you. Isn't that nice?' said Angie. Georgia nodded, unable to speak. Angie appeared not to notice.

'I'm gonna go upstairs and finish sorting the washing. Can I get you a drink, Xiyu?'

Chink shook his head, 'thank you for the offer though.'

Angie smiled at the pair and headed upstairs, shutting the door behind her. Georgia broke the silence.

'What the hell are you doing here?' she hissed. Chink looked confused.

'I came to see how you were.'

'You can't be in this house.' Georgia's voice was low. She didn't want her sister to overhear the conversation. Angie would judge her. She would be justified too.

'Why not?' Chink asked.

'Because, it's wrong. Everything that has ever happened between us is wrong.'

'I still love you, Georgia. I can be here for you now. We can be together.'

'No, we can't, Xiyu. You and I will never be together.' Georgia was trying to remain strong. Chink's shoulders slumped, but he needed to understand where Georgia was at. When Marcus died, her entire world had crumbled, and she was struggling. She couldn't eat, and she barely slept. Chink was the last person she wanted to deal with.

Chink sighed, his sadness evaporating.

'I don't accept what you're saying.'

'What are you talking about?' Georgia felt sick.

'I appreciate the convenience of copulating with you,' he said, each word a dagger. 'It's imperative you maintain your status as the *depressed wifey*. I can help you. The alternative is everyone finding out you were cheating on the beloved Marcus Daniels.'

'I should have never done it. I won't do it again,' Georgia's words were said with a strength she didn't quite feel.

'I didn't come here to debate the finer points of our dalliance. I came because I want you.'

'You can't have me,' Georgia's voice rose.

'Correction, I can, and I will.'

'Tell people what you want. I won't do it anymore.'

'You will.' Chink advanced on her.

'I'll scream. I mean it.'

Chink was already undoing the belt to his designer trousers, 'I wouldn't advise it.'

'Chink, I mean—'

Chink was on top of her now, forcing his tongue down her throat, yanking her black leggings down and pawing her body. His eyes were full of lust but his face and movements were calm.

'Chink, don't—'

'I wouldn't recommend making too much noise. If Angie overhears, then I'll have to take measures to silence her,' warned Chink. He yanked Georgia's underwear to the side and entered her. She lay back, accepting his jerky thrusts as tears poured down her face.

He didn't last long. After climaxing and pulling out, Chink pulled his trousers back up and resumed his seat. When Angie walked back into the room, she saw Georgia was weeping.

'Sis, are you okay?' she asked.

'She's still struggling, Angie. I think she should have a bath and maybe try to sleep,' Chink's voice was full of false concern. He met Georgia's eye. Unable to take it anymore, she hurried from the room to be sick.

'I'm sorry,' Angie said to Chink. 'I don't think she's up for company at the moment.'

'No need for apologies. I'll leave her for now, but I'll be back soon. Give her my love and keep up the good work,' Chink said, trying to hide his smirk. 'You're doing a stellar job.'

* * *

Marrion was at Marika's place, laid on the sofa with her. A few nights had passed since the wake. Marrion knew of Marika's argument with Lamont but she had said nothing else, and he hadn't forced her.

In the streets, the grief over Marcus's murder was giving way to anger. Shorty had his people out, doing what was necessary to get answers.

Marrion knew of at least three people who'd been beaten and interrogated. It made the hustle harder, but no one complained. Everyone knew what the stakes were. Until Marcus's killer was located, people would just have to cope.

Over the bank holiday period, Marrion had done well with the product he had received from Shorty's people. After paying Shorty and Lamont their end, he was now waiting for the rest of his money to come in. When it did, it would be the most Marrion had made in a single flip since coming to Leeds.

'Do you want a drink?' he asked Marika, her head resting in his lap.

She shook her head. Marrion was about to make himself one when suddenly, gunfire erupted.

'Marika!' he pulled her to the floor as the windows shattered, bullets pumping into the walls and furniture.

'Keyshawn! Bianca!' Marika screamed, trying to break free of Marrion's strong grip to get to her children. He held her down until after an age, the bullets subsided.

'Let me go,' said Marika, wrenching free and vaulting upstairs. They were both in Keyshawn's room, quivering under the quilt.

'Mummy,' cried Bianca. Marika smothered them with hugs as she wept with relief.

* * *

'Do you want a top-up?'

Jenny smiled up at Lamont, holding her glass out. They were sat in the garden, enjoying the remainder of the sun. Lamont had foregone his usual routine and spent the whole day with Jenny. Earlier, they had gone to a museum, then for some food. Now they were sharing a bottle of wine.

Lamont refilled their glasses and took a seat. He didn't spend much time in his garden, but had a decent table and chairs set for when the weather was good. There was also a football, and various bikes and toys that the kids would use whenever they were around.

Jenny liked the garden, but it needed work. It was too impersonal. Nothing made it Lamont's.

'Thank you,' she said.

'You're welcome.' Lamont held his glass, watching the darkening sky. He felt at ease. The dark cloud that had hovered over him since Marcus's murder hadn't evaporated, but was becoming easier to deal with.

Lamont would always miss his friend, but the best way to remember Marcus was to work hard at leaving the life behind. He would make his friend proud, and then he would solidify his legacy.

'I've been thinking,' he started. Jenny looked up.

'What about?'

'What to do with my life.'

'Have you come up with anything?'

'I want to travel and have a break from Leeds. When I was little, I used to dream of journeying to places like Japan, Argentina and the West Indies. I told myself that if I had the money, I would go,' he paused. 'I have the money.'

Jenny was quiet, watching Lamont as he spoke, moved by his passion. Like most things he did, Lamont appeared to have given it serious thought.

'That sounds great, L,' she said. He smiled back.

'Would you like to come with me?' Lamont surprised Jenny.

'What?'

'I want you come with me. Wherever I go, I want you there.'

'L, I have a business to consider. If you're suggesting a holiday, I can arrange cover, but I feel you're thinking longer than a two weeker.'

'I don't know,' Lamont sounded deflated now. The last thing Jenny wanted was to stand in his way, but she had to be honest. How long they sat silently contemplating, neither knew. When Lamont's phone rang, it startled the pair.

'L? Where are you?' Shorty said.

'Home. Why?'

'Get down to your sisters. Now.'

'Marika and me aren't—'

'Someone shot up her fucking house.'

Lamont hung up.

* * *

The street was packed with people as Lamont strode up, having parked his car on the next street. He spotted neighbours mingled around, and the flashing blue lights of police cars.

Marika was in her garden, her arms around the children, who looked petrified. When Marika saw Lamont, her eyes flashed, and she leapt to her feet.

'What the fuck are you doing here,' she said. 'Feel good, do you?

Getting people to shoot at my fucking yard!' she tried lunging at him but Marrion held her back.

'What are you talking about?'

'Don't play dumb. You wanna put my kids' lives at risk, you piece of shit?' Marika was still trying to break free.

'Rika, let me handle this. The kids are scared,' said Marrion, still struggling. Marika heeded his words and dragged the two children inside. Before the door slammed shut, Lamont glimpsed Bianca's confused little face, and felt something twist within him.

'What is going on?' he asked Marrion.

'They're coming to stay with me, that's what. How could you put your niece and nephews lives at risk? Are you that desperate to control your sister?'

'I don't know what you're talking about.'

'I don't believe you, and neither does your sister. Marika picked me. She doesn't need you anymore, and you need to accept that,' said Marrion.

'Are you done?'

'You what?'

'I said, are you done.' said Lamont. His face shifted now, eyes cold. He looked more in control.

'I don't know what—'

'I had nothing do with this shooting, and you're an even bigger fool than I thought if you think otherwise,' Lamont paused, looking Marrion in his eyes. 'If I were you, I would think long and hard about who my enemies were, and which ones I owed money to.' Lamont noted how pale Marrion looked after hearing those last few words. He glared one final time, then left.

CHAPTER TWENTY TWO

Friday 6 September 2013

TIMMY SAT in the passenger seat of Shorty's rented Mercedes and stared from the window.

After hearing nothing, Timmy had been surprised when Shorty rang and told him to get ready. Now, he was keeping his mouth shut, wondering what Shorty wanted him to do and if he would get paid for it. He wanted Shorty to realise he was there for him.

Shorty and Marcus had been tight, and Timmy knew the death was hitting him hard. Every time he tried to start a conversation though, the words wouldn't come out.

After a while, they were in Huddersfield. Timmy hadn't been to the town for years, and when they drove to the affluent Fixby area, he sat up and paid attention.

Shorty pulled to a stop outside a semi-detached property and signalled for Timmy to get out. He looked around, taking everything in. The garden was well-tended, with a new model Audi in the driveway. Timmy figured they were meeting the connect, so he was shocked when a beautiful woman strode out.

'What are you doing, Franklin?'

'You know why I'm here.'

'You should have called first.'

'Is he in?'

'Yes. He's in. That's not the point.'

'Stace, I'm in no mood for your mouth. Did you hear about Marcus?' Shorty asked. Timmy realised why she looked so familiar. She was the mother of Shorty's first child. No one had heard from her in years. Timmy hadn't realised Shorty knew where she was.

'Stacey?' he blurted. Shorty glared at him.

'You've grown up, Tim,' said Stacey, smiling. Timmy had always fancied her. She had been stunning back then, and age didn't seem to have slowed her looks down any.

'Forget him,' Shorty said. 'Did you hear?'

Stacey's eyes glistened. 'I'm sorry, Franklin. I know how close you both were. But, Marcus dying doesn't mean you can swan back into my life. Things are different now.'

As she said this, both Shorty and Timmy noticed the ring on Stacey's finger. Shorty kissed his teeth.

'I don't care about your life. I wanna see my boy,' he said. Timmy hung back, still confused by the whole situation. *Why were they here? And why had Shorty brought him along?*

Stacey folded her arms and frowned. 'You can visit for a few minutes. He's just come back from football training.'

She led them both into the house. Timmy took everything in as he walked through. There were neat paintings and immaculate, snow-white furniture. Timmy stuffed his hands in his pockets and followed the others to the kitchen where a tall boy hunched over a book. He looked up when the adults entered.

'Dionte, there's someone here to see you,' said Stacey.

'You're massive, son. You take after me,' Shorty broke the silence, his tone heartier than normal. Dionte stared, not saying a word.

Timmy was shocked at the similarities between them. Dionte had to be eleven or twelve years old, and he was big for his age. Timmy hadn't seen him since he was a baby. One minute, Shorty was driving him and Stacey around, showing off his son. The next, they were both gone, and no-one was talking about it.

Stacey cleared her throat.

'I'll leave you guys to talk,' she said, walking from the room. Timmy started to go with Stacey, but then Shorty stepped further into the room.

'This is your cousin, Timmy,' Shorty pointed at him, and Timmy nodded at Dionte. 'You kick ball too then? I used to play. What's your position?'

'Up front,' said Dionte.

'Me too. I bet you're banging in bare goals,' Shorty laughed. He stopped when neither of the others followed his lead. Shorty looked bewildered for a moment, then seeming to come to his senses, reached for his phone.

'Dunno if your mum ever mentioned your little sis, but here she is.' He brought up a picture of Grace, and showed it to Dionte, who displayed no reaction.

'Yo, what's wrong with you? I'm trying to show you your sis, and you're acting like a fucking retard.'

'Shorty—' Timmy spoke up, noting the bulging veins in Shorty's neck.

'Shut up, Tim. I'm talking to my son. D, what the fuck is up?'

'You're not my father, and she's not my sister.' Dionte faced Shorty.

'You little punk. Who do you think you are? I dunno what ya mum told you, but there's two sides to every story.'

'What's going on in here? Why are you shouting?' Stacey hurried back into the room.

'Kill that. What have you been telling my son about me?' Shorty turned on her.

'I haven't told him anything.'

'Whys he so damn rude then? I tried showing him his sister, and he's running his mouth. You must have told him something. Don't lie.'

'Don't shout at my mum,' Dionte told Shorty, who looked stunned.

'Oh, so now you wanna talk?' Shorty's eyes narrowed. 'Don't be pushing your chest out like you're gonna do summat. I'm talking to *mummy* now, so sit down and read your fucking book.'

Dionte held his ground.

'I said, sit down,' Shorty's voice rose, but still Dionte didn't move.

'Did you hear what I fucking said?'

'Franklin, it's time for you to leave,' said Stacey.

'Nah, I'm talking with my son.'

'If you don't leave, I'm calling the police.'

'You'd call police on me, Stace?' Shorty's voice was low now, his eyes wide.

'I would do anything to protect my son. Think about why he might not want to talk to you, or why he might not want to see a picture of the little girl you clearly love more than him.'

'I don't—'

'It doesn't matter. Don't you see? You swan back after years, and expect your son, who doesn't know you, to jump into your arms. Would you have done that if it were your father?'

'Tim, we're gone.' Shorty stormed off, not wanting Stacey to realise how much her words had affected him. With a bewildered expression, Timmy followed.

* * *

Outside a home in the St. Martins area of Leeds, Lamont was steeling himself to do something he didn't want to do. He sat in his ride, gathering his courage. The meeting he was about to have was a necessary one though, and with that in mind, he climbed from the ride, his legs heavy. He knocked on the door.

'Lamont,' Auntie said his name with her usual malice, tinged with a hint of curiosity.

'Hello, Auntie,' Lamont was going to great pains to keep his voice level. Auntie was dressed like she had been cleaning. He remembered the way she used to tie her hair up, so as not to get it dirty. The memory filled him with no warmth.

'Marika isn't here.'

'I came to see you.'

Auntie studied Lamont, trying to gauge his reason for being on her doorstep. Curiosity won over, and she stepped aside.

Lamont stood in the living room, feeling ten years old again. Apart from the TV, everything seemed the same as it had the last time. Auntie took a seat, waiting for him to talk.

'You need to take care of Marika.'

Auntie blinked.

'What are you talking about?'

'Me and my sister have parted ways. If I can't be there for her, then you need to be.' Lamont's words were more lucid than he expected. He was shocked at his composure around a person he loathed.

'*Parted ways?* I didn't invite you in so you could talk a load of nonsense.' Auntie's words were laced with intense dislike. She coughed then, a hacking cough that seemed to disappear only when she put a cigarette to her mouth and lit it.

'We fell out. Properly this time, so Marika needs you. She's always needed someone,' said Lamont. He hated the smell of smoke but over the years he had become used to it.

'Why did you fall out?' Auntie seemed more chipper now, gleeful almost.

'I said things in anger that she took to heart.'

'She told me that someone shot at her house.'

'I heard that too.'

'She told me you did it because you were jealous over Marrion.' Auntie dominated the conversation now, and knew it.

'She *thinks* I did it. I would never harm my sister though, or her kids.'

'You've been harming her since day one. You never saw it, did you? Marika had a twisted dependence on you, and you revelled in it. Now, it's blown up.'

'Someone had to support us. You were never going to.'

'That's crap. You liked the control. You were always a messed up child. I tried straightening you out, but couldn't.'

Lamont's blood boiled. He was allowing Auntie to get to him.

'You're a horrible woman,' he started, taking a deep breath. 'You influenced my sister more than I ever could. Now though, it's all on you; you and Marika no longer have me to unite against,' Lamont hesitated, letting his words sink in. 'I wonder how long that will last.'

Auntie didn't reply. Lamont looked at her, trying to see past the hatred and view her as a human being. He remembered her beauty, the guys she made jump through hoops. He felt sad, thinking about how life might have turned out had she only loved him.

'Why do you hate me?' The words were suddenly out before Lamont could stop them. Auntie didn't hesitate.

'Because you should have died. Out of the three people in that crash, it should have been you.'

Lamont allowed her words to wash over him, finding they didn't hurt as much as they should.

'You have a good life, Auntie. I don't imagine we'll see each other again.'

Back in the car, Lamont found he was smiling. He felt a certain clarity after speaking to Auntie. He didn't resent her as much as he had. She was an unhappy woman, but no longer would he be influenced by her loathing.

His phone rang as he pulled away from the curb.

'Lamont?' Georgia blurted.

'Hey. How are you?' Lamont asked. He was surprised when she burst into tears down the phone.

'Georgia, what's wrong?'

* * *

Timmy sat in a house in the Hood, watching Shorty chain-smoke and mutter to himself. The drive from Huddersfield was tense. Shorty had almost started a fight with a driver whom he had cut in front of. After being threatened with more police action, Shorty had driven off, swearing.

Timmy didn't know what to say. He realised Shorty was furious at how things had turned out with Dionte. He wanted to leave but he couldn't. Instead, he sat and scrolled through Instagram, hoping for a reprieve.

'Where've you been?' The door opened and K-Bar sauntered in, drinking a bottle of Magnum tonic. He nodded to Timmy and took a seat.

'Away,' said Shorty.

'Where d'you go? I was looking for you.' K-Bar either couldn't tell Shorty was in a mood or didn't care.

'I was busy, okay?'

'Whatever then. I handled it anyway,' K-Bar turned to Timmy. 'Were you with him?'

Timmy nodded. Shorty brooded, jabbing his cigarette into a chipped ashtray.

'What's up with your cuz? 'It's only girls that can get him this worked up,' said K-Bar.

'It's not a girl,' Timmy said before he could stop himself. Shorty turned on him.

'Shut your fucking mouth.'

'Shorty, chill,' K-Bar defended Timmy.

'Stay out of it, K. I'm dealing with my family.'

'I didn't do anything. Don't take it out on me because your—'

'Watch it,' Shorty pointed a finger at Timmy. 'Don't say summat that will get you fucked up.'

'I'm not the enemy. I'm family. Why do you always treat me like shit?' It was out now and Timmy was taking it all the way.

'You're a fucking worker,' Shorty said, laughing. 'How do you think this shit's supposed to go? You think because we're blood, you should get a treat? You little dudes kill me.'

'Steady on, Shorty. You're going too far now.' K-Bar spoke again, seeing how livid Timmy was.

'You're never gonna grow, Tim, and do you know why? It's because your mind ain't right. You're a fucking follower. You're not built to lead. That's why you get nowhere,' said Shorty. Timmy jumped to his feet.

'What? You wanna go?' Shorty noted his clenched fists. 'I'll give you one free hit, and then I'm gonna put you in the hospital.'

Timmy glared at his cousin, seconds away from attacking Shorty and taking the swift beating that would follow.

'Fuck you, Shorty.' Timmy stormed away and slammed the door behind him.

* * *

Chink was reading a newspaper in his kitchen when there was a hammering at the front door. He answered, surprised to see Lamont.

'L? Is everything okay?'

Lamont's face twisted into a mask of anger as he struck Chink in the face. Falling to the ground, Chink tried to rise, only for Lamont to boot him in the ribs.

'You piece of shit.'

'What the fuck, L?' said Chink, trying to catch his breath.

'Get up. You either get up or I'll stomp on you. Get the fuck up. Now.'

Chink clambered to his feet, trying to get his bearings.

'What's this about, man? What's happened?' gasped Chink.

'You raping piece of shit.' Lamont swung for Chink again. This time he ducked and tackled Lamont to the floor.

They tussled, Lamont trying to damage, Chink trying to survive. Lamont brought his head back and caught Chink on the bridge of his nose with a stiff head butt. Chink's nose exploded. Instinctively, he covered his face. Lamont smashed him in the ribs, feeling something shift as Chink grunted in pain.

Lamont hit him again and leapt to his feet. He tried kicking him in the face, but Chink tripped him, determined to keep the brawl on the ground.

'L! Calm down.'

Lamont wasn't listening though. His eyes blazed, fists clenched.

'Marcus was our boy. He dies, and you think you can rape his girl?'

Chink kicked out, catching him in the groin. Lamont fell back with a grunt of pain, allowing Chink to scramble away. He leant against the wall, panting.

'L, it wasn't like that. She came onto me. I'm weak, but I'm not a rapist.' Blood streamed from Chink's nose. Lamont was also on his feet now, breathing hard but in better shape than Chink.

'You're a liar. You've always been a twisted fuck, but even this is beneath you. I swear, I'm gonna kill you.' Lamont tackled Chink to the floor again, throwing punch after punch at his former friend.

Chink's hands were by his side. Lamont was enraged. Never had he felt such anger. Chink's eyes glazed over. Lamont cocked back his fist to hit him again when a scream startled him.

Naomi stood in the doorway, watching the scene with frightened eyes. Lamont remembered she was once Reagan's girl. He was moments away from killing another person. The anger left him. He let Chink go and stood up.

'You and me are done. I never want to hear from you again,' Lamont told his old friend before leaving.

* * *

Schemes was a man on a mission as he stalked the streets of Harehills, searching for a phone box. He had done well to stay under the radar, but it was driving him crazy now. The money he had been paid for the shooting was almost finished, and he was tired of being patient. Locating a phone, he dropped in some change and punched in a number.

'It's me,' he said when his contact answered.

'I told you I'd be in touch. You better have a good reason for calling.'

'I'm fucking struggling, and I need to leave Leeds. That's my reason. I need more money.'

'You were given enough money. What you did with it is your problem.'

'My girl is pregnant. I can't be a fucking dad if I've got people shooting at me, can I?'

'Don't ring me again.' The contact hung up.

'MOTHERFUCKER!' Schemes slammed the phone down. He glanced around and saw a young black kid staring at him. 'What the fuck are you staring at?'

Mollified, the kid turned and scurried off. Still smarting, Schemes threw his hood up and stomped off back to his nearby hideout.

It never occurred to check if he was being followed.

* * *

Marrion was lounging at one of his spots. Since the business with Marika's house, he had moved her and the kids into his place, and he had his team watching his back in case there was another attempt on his life. His place was designed for one person so it was a tight squeeze at the moment.

When he got his funds up though, Marrion would move them to a bigger place.

'Whoa,' he said, surprised by who had walked in. 'What happened to you?'

'It's not funny,' said Chink, glaring at Marrion. He was flanked by Polo.

'The bruising gives you some character,' Marrion sniggered. 'Who put their hands on you? Shorty?'

'Lamont.'

'Lamont did that to you? I thought he was a talker.'

'Not important. What's important is getting things in place. People need to be removed. First up, Shorty. You need to handle it.'

'You sure you can't get him in line?'

'He's a thug, and he is dangerous. I won't have him or anyone else jeopardising my plan.'

'Get your boy there to handle it,' Marrion motioned to Polo, who scowled.

'I'm getting you to handle it, unless you want to go on that list too?' Chink asked. Marrion raised his hands in mock surrender.

'Okay, okay. I'm only playing. I'll get on it.'

'In the meantime, I will lock down our supply,' Chink told him.

'Have you got anyone in mind?'

Chink nodded.

'I have a meeting in place.'

Brownie entered then, holding two containers of food. He passed one to Marrion.

'I'll leave you to it.' Chink left without uttering a word to Brownie.

'What did he want?' Brownie said to Marrion. He didn't like Chink, and he was sure the feeling was mutual.

'We've got a job to do. Get Antonio in here.'

* * *

Later that day, Chink climbed from his car, heading to his next meeting. Touching the bruises on his face, he frowned, unhappy at his looks being marred. It wasn't ideal, but he needed to handle this situation.

Shown into the office, he stood in front of Delroy Williams, who appeared larger and more impassive than ever. Winston sat in the corner, watching Chink with intense dislike. Chink focused on Delroy.

'Thank you for seeing me.'

'What does Tef want?' Delroy ignored Chink's pleasantries.

'I'm here of my own accord. Lamont and I have gone our separate ways.'

If Delroy was surprised, he didn't show it.

'What does that have to do with me?'

'I want us to work together. I'm going into business for myself, and a supply such as yours will help me grow.'

'What happened to your face?' Winston spoke.

'Just a misunderstanding.'

'Yeah, I'll bet,' Winston chuckled. Chink pursed his lips. He didn't have time to dwell on the fight, but he was irritated with Winston for drawing attention to it. The last thing he needed was to appear weak.

'It's not important. What is important is the two of us making money together.'

Delroy scratched his chin with a chunky finger.

'You remember my prices?'

Chink nodded.

'Well, they've gone up. By two grand a box.' Delroy observed him, impressed when he didn't even flinch.

'Money is no problem. I'll want five for starters.'

Delroy almost smiled. 'That'll work. Winnie will be in touch.' He nodded over at his son, who crossed his arms and scowled. Chink beamed, shook Delroy's hand and glided from the room.

'What the hell are you playing at?' said Winston as soon as the door closed.

'Have you forgotten who you're talking to?' Delroy gave his son a thunderous look.

'I mean no disrespect, Pops, but Chink is a snake. You can't trust him.'

'I don't.'

Winston was surprised. 'Then, why would you agree to a deal?'

'So I could see his cards. Get Teflon on the phone. I think he needs to hear what his little lackey has been up to.'

* * *

Marrion still sat in his base drinking a beer. On the coffee table, his phone vibrated. Eventually it stopped, but then it started again. Marrion knew who was calling, but he couldn't talk to them yet. He didn't have control of the situation.

Back in Manchester, Marrion had been affiliated, but he didn't stand out. He was a rung above street dealer and resented it. Before moving, he had borrowed a lot of money from the wrong people.

He'd had every intention of paying the money back, but upon arriving in Leeds, Marrion had burnt through the money, flossing to build up his profile and woo Marika Jones. Now, he was in a bind.

Marrion needed a saving grace. He needed to deal with Shorty, then he could ask Chink for a loan to pay his creditors. The shooting at Marika's had been a warning. Next time, they would take his head. Marrion rubbed his eyes and looked up as Antonio and Brownie traipsed in.

'Well?' he demanded.

'Boss, he's too fucking para,' Antonio threw his hands in the air. 'Our guys can't keep up with him. He's always switching cars, or he's running red lights.'

'Fuck!' Marrion pounded his fist on the table. He hadn't expected tracking Shorty to be easy, but this took the cake. It had been twenty-four hours since Chink had given his orders. Marrion needed Shorty dead. He needed Chink's goodwill. It was his only way to win.

'Yo, we can get him, but it'll have to be some guerrilla-style shit. You'd have to get someone to run up on him and blast him,' Brownie pointed out.

'That's suicide,' said Marrion. 'No one's dumb enough to roll on him like that. Not in Shorty's own city, anyway.'

'Well then, tell Chink you're not doing it,' Brownie said. 'He wants him dead anyway, not you.'

Marrion didn't reply, still thinking. There was a bang from outside and Timmy burst in.

'What the fuck are you playing at?' said Marrion. He had jumped up, thinking his debtors had found him.

'Sorry. I'm just stressed.' Timmy slumped down.

'Why? What's happened?'

'I'm not working with Shorty anymore. He's a dickhead. I wanna work with you,' said Timmy. The final straw had come when he had turned up for work today, only for K-Bar to tell him he wasn't needed. Timmy knew Shorty was behind the demotion, and he fumed.

Marrion spotted the anger and realised Timmy could solve his problems. He planted a contrite expression on his face.

'I've been waiting for you to step up and join my squad,' he said. In reality, he had kept the kid at arm's length since Shorty had spoken to him. Marrion paused, as if he had just remembered something. 'I need loyal people though.'

'I'm loyal,' said Timmy.

'Are you ready to prove it?'

* * *

Shorty lay in a dark room, messing on his phone and trying to avoid thinking about his issues. He was still angry at his dad for trying to creep to him. The anger Dionte had shown him mirrored the way he had greeted his own old man, and he didn't like that.

Shorty had been locked up when Dionte was born, and his son's birth hadn't deterred him in the slightest upon release. He had carried on partying and giving Stacey money every time he made a raise. She soon saw the light and moved away.

Shorty had been relieved, even helping her pay towards the mini-mansion she was swanning around in. It had all backfired though. Dionte had outgrown him, and that hurt. Amy was moving on, Stacey already had. Shorty had been crushed when he saw the ring on her finger. He hadn't even known she was involved with anyone. There had been no hint of the affection she had once lavished on him, and it hurt.

Shorty sat up when his phone rang. He glanced at the screen and answered.

'What, Tim?' he said. He didn't have time for Timmy's whining.

'I need to see you.'

'What's going on?' said Shorty. Timmy sounded panicky, and that wasn't normal.

'Marrion's up to summat. I overheard him talking about you and L.'

'Not over the phone. Where are you?'

* * *

Shorty screeched to a halt outside a spot in Seacroft. If Marrion was moving against him, he would kill him, no questions asked.

'Tim, where the fuck are you?' he called as he climbed from the car. The street was deserted and his instincts were going haywire. Something wasn't right. Shorty rang Timmy's number again, which went straight to voicemail.

'What the fuck?' He murmured. The hairs on the back of his neck rose as he heard a shuffling sound, spotting a flicker of movement to his right. He ducked, a hail of bullets hitting the spot he'd stood in.

Shorty popped back up, gun in hand and fired twice, hearing a loud scream as he hit one of his attackers. There were more of them though, and they continued firing, keeping him pinned down.

'Oi badman. Why are you hiding?' a voice taunted.

Crouched behind a car tyre, Shorty recognised the Manchester accent as Marrion's idiot friend from the club in town. With a sickening feeling, he realised Timmy had set him up.

Even coked-up out of his head, Solly was amazed by Shorty's reflexes. They'd had the drop on him but Shorty had not only avoided the trap, he had taken out one of the two gunners Solly had brought along. He had assumed Shorty was all talk, but he had never seen anyone move like that.

Signalling to his remaining hitter to flank him, Solly watched the goon hurry forward. Shorty was ready, ventilating the man's head with another bullet. He was amped, eyes alight with rage. Solly was out of his depth, and he knew it. He dropped the gun and put his hands in the air, standing by a streetlight so the surrender could be seen.

'Chill! Chill! I don't have a gun,' his voice shook. Shorty stalked over, eyes flitting in all directions. He pointed his gun at Solly, his finger caressing the trigger.

'Marrion send you?'

Solly nodded, sweating and scared.

'Thanks.' Pulling the trigger three times, Shorty watched Solly's body drop, then hurried to his car and sped off.

CHAPTER TWENTY THREE

Wednesday 11 September 2013

LAMONT SLOUCHED IN HIS GARDEN. He had been here for hours, watching the dark sky lighten and the sun rise. His sleeping pattern was picking up, but last night's events had him wired.

There had been a shooting near Shorty's, and three people were dead. Lamont knew they were associates of Marrion. Lamont hadn't heard from Shorty yet, and that worried him. Shorty was hard enough to control but if someone had attempted to take his life, he wouldn't rest until he'd had his revenge.

Lamont had also received a phone call yesterday from Winston Williams, informing him of a meeting that Chink had with his father. He was surprised at Chink's swift manoeuvring, but going to Delroy had been a foolish move. Delroy had never shown much love for Chink and as he'd shown in past dealings with Lamont, he was all politics.

Even armed with this knowledge, Lamont had done nothing. As badly as Chink wanted to be his enemy, his plans were unchanged. The meeting with Akhan was in place. Lamont would plug in someone to take over distribution for the team and then go.

Lamont needed to clear his head. The tickets to Uruguay had been purchased. He would ask Jenny today when he saw her and hoped she said yes to going. He was banking on the trip convincing her they should travel.

It was selfish to expect Jenny to put her business on hold but he loved her, and he wanted her around him. Lamont checked the time and wondered if it was too early to call her.

* * *

K-Bar stood in the middle of a dank cellar. Known as *The Dungeon*, it was a secluded, soundproofed spot where violators were punished without the risk of interruption. Grimer, a brawny associate of Shorty's who loved dealing with the heavy work, was with him. K-Bar had called him especially.

The streets were red-hot. Shorty was off the grid. K-Bar was a loyal soldier, but even he didn't understand half the things that were going on. Chink had split and was doing his own thing. People said that Lamont had ordered a shooting at his sister's spot. It was ridiculous.

K-Bar assessed their battered victim, slumped against the cellar wall with his arms tied above him. He was naked from the waist up, and his torso and chest were covered with burn marks and various cuts.

'Where were we?' Grimer asked the victim with an evil smile. He was old school and couldn't believe the little shit in front of him had gunned down Marcus Daniels.

'Please, I don't know anything,' said Schemes through cracked and blooded teeth. They had caught him slipping after someone had tailed him in Harehills, then dragged him to the dungeon. So far the youngster had held firm, but it wouldn't last long.

'You know how to squeeze off a fucking Mac don't you?' K-Bar stood in front of Schemes now. 'Our people spotted you in the park, spraying bullets at fucking Tall-Man. You thought you were a bad man, didn't you? Well, now I'm gonna show you how a real bad man rolls unless you talk. Who hired you to do Marcus?'

'Nobody! I told you, he jumped Maverick. We were coming back on him.'

K-Bar turned to Grimer. 'Get your tools.'

Grimer reached into a nearby leather bag, removing a battered mini-sledgehammer. He swung it, testing the weight. Grimer delved into the bag again and pulled out a selection of nails. Turning to the kid with a smile on his face, he walked towards him. Schemes tried to rear back but there was nowhere he could go.

'No. Don't!' He screamed.

'Talk then. If not, it's gonna get biblical. We're gonna nail your fucking feet to the floor, and that's just for starters,' warned K-Bar.

'All right. All right!' said Schemes as Grimer raised the hammer.

'Stop stalling. Spill.'

'I don't know who ordered it,' said Schemes. 'Wait! I met one of his people—Always the same dude; white guy, big, flash whip.'

Bored, K-Bar signalled for Grimer to begin.

'Wait,' Schemes yelled again. 'The guy, he was a Brummie.'

K-Bar halted Grimer.

'What did you say?'

'The guy was from Birmingham! I recognised his accent.'

'You better not be fucking lying.'

'I'm not! The numbers in my phone. Ring it! It's the last one I called.' Schemes was crying with fear.

K-Bar found the phone and rang the number, holding his breath.

'Yeah?' said Polo. K-Bar closed his eyes.

'Oi, you little prick. I told you not to fucking ring again. You'll get the money when I say so.'

K-Bar froze and dropped the phone, unable to believe what this meant.

'What's up? Do you believe me now then?' Schemes asked. K-Bar smacked him in the mouth, causing Schemes to hit his head against the wall.

'Shut the fuck up. Tell me everything, and I mean fucking everything.'

* * *

'Yo, it's crazy. They're saying that Shorty blazed some dudes from Manny.'

'Why though?'

Ben and Jerome were chilling. Ben's mother was comatose some-where, meaning they were free to raid her liquor stash. Jerome was filling Ben in on the situation with Shorty. He had tried ringing Timmy, but he wasn't answering.

'There was beef at Carnival. Shorty beat up one girl, and she must have been linked to these Manny goons, because they ran up on Shorty. They flopped though, and he dropped them.'

'Shit. That's heavy. They'd never have tried that if Tall-Man was still alive though.'

Jerome snorted. 'Fuck him. He was all hype. He got fucking riddled. No one was scared of him.'

Ben shrugged, helping himself to more rum and mixing it with the bottle of Lilt resting between his legs. Jerome was knowledgeable, so Ben took everything he said as gospel.

'Yo, try Tim again.'

As Ben pulled his phone out, there was a loud crash from down-stairs and footsteps trudging towards them.

'What the fuck?' Jerome, jumped to his feet. The bedroom door burst open and Shorty stood there.

'Yes, Shorty. What's—'

There was a sharp crack as Shorty hit Jerome in the mouth with a left hook. Jerome talked a big game, but he crumbled like pastry from the blow. Petrified, Ben tried running to the door but Shorty stood in his way. Ben raised his hands, but he stood no chance. Shorty hit him with a ferocious two-hit combination, and he slid to the ground, prac-tically out cold.

'You little bastards better start talking,' said Shorty, pulling a gun. 'Where's Timmy?'

'W-We thought he was with you,' said Ben, moaning when Shorty smacked him with the weapon.

'I said, you better talk,' Shorty repeated. 'Oi, big man,' he kicked Jerome in the stomach. 'You think you know everything. Where's Timmy?'

The pair lay on the floor in a terrified heap. Shorty had always scared them but as Timmy's close friends, they thought that gave them a pass. They realised now how wrong they had been. Shorty looked deranged. He pointed the gun at them, his hand shaking with rage.

'We haven't seen him, I swear! We tried ringing him but he didn't answer,' Ben gibbered.

'You expect me to believe that?' Shorty laughed. 'You two are his fucking bum boys. He tells you lot everything. You probably knew all along.'

'About what?'

Furious, Shorty hit Jerome with the gun.

'Tell me where he is!' he roared repeatedly, but Jerome was unconscious. Shorty stalked toward Ben, who had urinated out of sheer terror.

'Your turn,' he said, raising the bloody gun again.

* * *

Grim-faced, red-eyed and unshaven, K-Bar climbed from a car and hurried into a house. Lamont waited for him. He took in his comrade's bedraggled appearance and sensed that it was serious. Lamont's first thought was that K-Bar would announce Shorty was dead, and braced himself.

'We've got big problems.'

'People have been calling. Have you heard from Shorty?' asked Lamont.

'No,' K-Bar sounded distracted. 'It's about Chink.'

'Chink?'

'He paid for the hit on Marcus.'

It was like a ton of bricks had toppled upon Lamont. Of all the things K-Bar could say, few would have had more impact. He closed his eyes, knowing why Chink had done it.

'Georgia,' he whispered.

'You what?'

'Chink is in love with Georgia. He took Marcus out because he wanted her to himself.'

'Snake,' K-Bar spat. 'He can't live. You know that, right?'

Saddened, Lamont nodded.

'I know.'

* * *

Shorty put his hood up as he crouched across the road from Amy's. He knew she was in. He needed to see her and more importantly, he needed to see Grace.

Shorty still clutched the blooded gun. He wanted to hide it, but his street senses screamed for him to keep it. He trusted no one at the moment.

Family had betrayed him. Timmy had lured Shorty to a meet, knowing he would be killed. Shorty would never forgive that and once the heat died down, he would end both Timmy and Marrion.

Shorty hurried across the road and knocked on Amy's door. He looked around, scanning for nosy neighbours.

'Shorty?' Amy was startled to see him standing on her doorstep. Shorty gazed at her. In his fatigued state, she seemed more beautiful than ever.

'I wanna see Grace.'

'Is that a gun?' Amy noticed the piece in his hand.

'Amy—'

'You need to leave. Police have been by twice already. They're saying you killed three people.'

Shorty kissed his teeth. He didn't have time for this.

'I wanna see Grace,' he repeated.

'You're holding a bloody gun. Is that how you want her to see you? She's asleep. It's late.'

'Just move! I have to hide, but I need to see her,' Shorty was almost pleading. Amy felt his sorrow and her heart went out to him. She was about to speak when another voice interrupted.

'What the hell are you doing here?' Chris Hart appeared at Amy's side.

'I'm here to see my kid. Stay out of it.'

'No, I bloody won't,' said Chris. 'Do you have any idea the aggro you've caused? Police went to Amy's work. They've been here twice because of you.'

'Chris—' Amy tried to speak, but he waved her off.

'He's a murderer, Ames. He killed three people, and now he's trying to implicate you and Gracey.'

'Get out of the way, or I'm gonna pop you too,' Shorty raised the gun. Chris looked scared now, but he didn't move.

'Just leave. They're coming for you.'

'Who? Who's coming?' Shorty asked, his question answered by sirens and flashing lights. Chris looked smug, so Shorty clocked him with the gun, turned to vault a nearby fence, and took off running.

* * *

Marrion hung up his phone and slammed it down. Everything had gone to shit. The hit on Shorty had gone awry, Solly and his guys were dead, and Shorty had to know he had been behind it. Now he would have to deal with the vengeful thug who had eluded the police so far.

Brownie was handling the latest mission but Antonio was waiting for Marrion at the spot, and would guard him. Worst was the news he needed to give to the woman he loved. Marika was cleaning in his front room when Marrion approached.

'Sit down a sec, Rika. I've got summat to tell you.'

'What is it?' Marika asked. If he was about to say he was leaving her, Marika would kill him. She knew he'd been seen with other girls in town and that was bad enough. She wouldn't deal with this too.

'It's about your brother.'

'What about him?' Marika hadn't heard from Lamont since he had turned up at her house after the shooting.

'I'm only telling you this to prepare you, but I've got conformation Lamont was behind the shooting at your place,' said Marrion.

'That fucking prick!' Marika couldn't believe Lamont would put her kids at risk like that.

'Yeah. He's a cunt,' said Marrion, launching into the next phase. 'That's why he's getting taken out.'

'W-What?'

'My people are on it. It'll be quick, and I promise he won't suffer,' Marrion held her close. He was shocked when Marika wrenched free.

'No. Stop them.'

'What do you mean? He tried to kill you.'

'If Lamont wanted me dead, he would have made it happen,' Marika shook her head. 'He's my brother. Just because we're not talking, doesn't mean I want him to die,' she clutched Marrion's front, tears in her eyes. 'If you love me, then you'll call it off.'

'For fuck's sake, Rika,' Marrion pulled away and stormed from the house.

Chink had been insistent that Lamont had to die, but Marrion loved Marika.

It was early evening now. Brownie would already be on route. He would have to be quick. Marrion climbed into his Mercedes, dialling Brownie as he started the engine.

Before he could move, a tinted ride screeched to a halt alongside him. The windows wound down and automatic gunfire erupted, spraying the Benz with bullets. As the car sped down the street, Marrion slumped over in the driver's seat, bleeding.

* * *

Polo sat in his car across the road from Naomi's place. Chink had been holed up for hours, and Polo was irritable. He couldn't even turn the radio on and the battery on his phone was low from the silly internet videos he had viewed.

'He's taking the piss now,' Polo said to himself. When his boss emerged from his bird's house, he decided they would talk.

Polo decided to risk urinating in the street when he spotted something. A man darted across the road heading for Naomi's place. Polo reached for his pistol. Before he could reach it, a gun was pressed against the back of his head.

'Don't move.'

Polo froze, feeling a devastating pain as the gun smashed into his kidney. He fell onto the pavement, bile rising in his throat.

Arms grabbed at him, relieving him of his gun and a knife, dragging him into a nearby garden.

'I thought we would have to do you in the car, mate,' said K-Bar, attaching a silencer to his weapon. Polo stared up at him, steeling himself to meet his fate like a man.

K-Bar aimed the gun, tilted his head, then pulled the trigger.

* * *

'I'll be back later.'

Naked on the bed, Naomi nodded at Chink's words, going back to messing around on her phone. Chink was tempted to knock it from her hands, but he didn't have the time.

There were still details to sort, and he didn't think Polo would wait outside forever. Chink was waiting for confirmation that the job was done on Lamont.

After failing to take out Shorty, Marrion was his last chance. If he messed it up, he was finished. Chink had no time for fuck ups. Shorty had escaped for now, but he couldn't hide forever. Chink would track him down and kill him.

When everything was done, Chink could focus on wooing Georgia. Only Lamont stood between him and the woman he loved. Chink smiled to himself as he buttoned his silk shirt.

'Clean this place up when I'm gone too. It's a mess,' he added. Naomi glowered. It was her house, and yet he saw fit to tell her what to do in it. Not liking the way she was looking at him, Chink glared at her.

'Is that a problem?'

'No.' Naomi stood up. Chink stared at her naked body, feeling himself grow aroused again. He was about to tell her to lie down when he heard a noise.

'What was that?'

'Shut up,' said Chink. The noises grew louder. He hurried to the window. What he saw made his heart race.

K-Bar crept through the garden with a gun in his hand, his face full of resolve. Chink felt his bowels churning as he rushed downstairs, sprinting through the rooms and lunging for the back door.

Before he could flee, Grimer appeared at the door. He backed Chink into the room as K-Bar charged in, his face resolute.

'Going somewhere?'

Chink raised his hands.

'What's going on, K? Is there a problem?' Chink tried talking his way out of the reaper's hands. He didn't like K-Bar any more than he did Shorty but he knew what K-Bar could do. He was a killer and if he was in the house, that meant Polo was dead.

'I think you already know,' said K-Bar, letting him know his words wouldn't cut it. There were more footsteps and Naomi stood next to K-Bar. She wore a dressing gown, the hateful expression on her face, and the penny dropped for Chink.

'Why?' he said to Naomi, eyes blazing.

'You should never have hit me,' she told him.

'You told them where I was?' he was flabbergasted. 'Fucking ungrateful—'

'Forget this,' said K-Bar. His gun was raised.

'K, I have money. Lots of it. I'll make you a wealthy man. All you need to do is walk away, pretend you never saw me,' said Chink. He was terrified but didn't want to show weakness in front of Shorty's pet wolf.

'I know all about what you did,' K-Bar's voice was low, tinged with controlled anger. 'You thought you could kill Marcus and get away with it.'

'That wasn't me. Marrion did it. He was behind the whole thing. He tried killing Shorty too. I swear!'

K-Bar fired his gun, hitting Chink in the thigh. He screamed and fell to the floor, clutching his leg and moaning.

'W-Whatever happens, Lamont dies too. You can't stop it, unless you let me go,' said Chink.

K-Bar, Grimer and Naomi stared at him with disgust, lying on the floor in his expensive clothing, pleading for his life.

'Hold these for Marcus.' K-Bar fired at Chink until his clip was spent.

'We need to go. Quick,' said Grimer, gazing at Chink's body.

'You're right,' K-Bar turned to Chink's girlfriend, who looked shaken. When he had contacted her through a third party, she had agreed to set up Chink for free.

'Do it.'

There was no time. Naomi realised what was about to happen and screamed. The bullet smashed through her right eye, causing her to sink to the ground. Grimer took two steps forward, looking at her prone form.

'No witnesses,' he mumbled, firing again.

'Let's go! L's in fucking trouble,' K-Bar was already by the back door. 'Call Maka and tell him to go to L's birds house. I'll give you the address.'

* * *

Lamont was outside Jenny's place. He had gone back home hoping Shorty would contact him. He hadn't though. Lamont left it as long as possible before heading out with a travel bag.

Jenny was waiting in the garden as he pulled up. Even in the night, he saw her eyes sparkle with a happiness that made his heart almost burst from his chest. She beamed and Lamont returned the grin. He was so engrossed in her that he didn't see them approaching until the last second.

'Jenny! Get inside,' Lamont said, a tremor of fear cascading down his spine when he saw the guns. *Not now*, he thought to himself. His eyes widened when he recognised one of the men.

'Timmy?'

* * *

'Shoot him!' Brownie shouted at the youth, who looked as petrified as Lamont. It was bad enough he'd set up Shorty, but now he was about to shoot the man who had employed him for years.

The gun Brownie had forced on Timmy was heavy, almost burning in his palm. He tried raising it, but when he saw the terror in the eyes of Lamont's girl, lowered it again.

'You useless little shit,' Brownie pushed him aside, aiming at Lamont and firing.

Time seemed to slow down. Lamont was aware of Jenny's

screaming before he felt the fiery pain as the bullet slammed into his chest.

The second shot tore into Lamont's stomach, sending him tumbling to the pavement. He gasped for air now, panicking as the blood billowed beneath him.

Jenny knelt over him now, covered in his blood. Lamont tried reaching out for her but his arms wouldn't respond.

Brownie moved forward to finish him but was distracted by the screech of tyres. Maka jumped from the Renault Clio firing, missing Brownie but catching Timmy in the neck and chest. The kid crumpled in a heap and Brownie turned tail, running for the car. He jumped in and sped off, bullets whizzing around him.

* * *

Jenny . . .

Never in his life had he experienced such pain. His body felt like it was on fire. He couldn't move his limbs, but his eyes were wide open, staring at her.

She was still with him. Saying words he couldn't understand. Tears streaming down her perfect face. His blood staining her sweater.

Neighbours converged. One of them clutched a phone.

He tried to speak, but his throat didn't work. Maybe he was dead already. He could feel the darkness coming. He tried to fight it but it was futile.

Meeting Jenny's dark eyes one more time. Lamont succumbed to the nothingness.

EPILOGUE

Wednesday 24th September 2014

AKHAN SAT IN HIS OFFICE, staring into space. The room was quiet. He liked it that way. Outside the window the trees slowly lost the green leaves for another year. Akhan was checking the time on his watch when Saj knocked and entered.

'He's here.'

'Show him in,' said Akhan. He sat back as Lamont Jones entered.

Lamont had recovered from the worst of his injuries, but he moved slower than before. The bullet to his stomach had gone straight through, missing his vital organs.

It had taken over a year for him to function, but now he perched opposite Akhan.

'You look well.' Akhan poured him a glass of water.

'I've been worse,' said Lamont. He sipped his drink and focused on Akhan. 'I received your gift. It was thoughtful of you.'

'Not a problem. You seemed pleased with the first bottle, so I thought more might suffice. How are you though?'

Lamont shrugged. 'Day by day I guess. It's all I can hope for right now.'

Akhan nodded. 'When will we be able to resume business?'

Lamont looked him in the eyes. 'Never.'

Akhan didn't speak straight away. Standing, he stared out of the window as if Lamont wasn't there. Lamont recognised the strategy. It was designed to make him uncomfortable, to make him talk first. He didn't take the bait. Instead he sipped his drink and stared at the unread books on Akhan's shelf.

'Why, Lamont?' Akhan said. 'We have done well together. Look how much we made over the Bank Holiday period. Imagine that over a year. Imagine it over ten.'

'Some things mean more.'

'Such as?'

'Such as life.'

Akhan rubbed his eyes. 'How much do you want to leave this life?'

'More than anything.'

'Then, are you willing to pay the price?' said Akhan, his words cold now. Lamont looked at him as if he believed he was being tricked.

'I paid the price. I was shot.'

'You also survived.'

'What's the cost then?'

'Everything, Lamont,' said Akhan. He paused, waiting for his words to take effect. 'The cost is everything. That is the cost to leave for good. You must ask yourself now, how much she is worth to you,' he smiled at the surprise on Lamont's face. 'Don't look so shocked. A man talks like this; It can only be because he is in love. Is this woman worth it?'

'Yes,' Lamont said without hesitation.

'So, your mind is made up then?'

Akhan was shocked at the intensity that appeared in Lamont's face. He was reminded of the powerful young man who had sat in his office over a year ago. There seemed to be no trace of his injuries now as he stared Akhan down and spoke.

'There's no choice to make. I see this life for what is; you have power, wealth and status, but you're a slave to the game. The choices you make are not your own, just like the choices I made weren't mine. You're not playing the game; the game is playing you.'

Akhan was silent. Lamont continued.

'It's lonely. This life. Never relaxing. Doing business with people you don't like, all to keep the wheel spinning. You have to put on an act. You can't do what you want,' A wistful smile appeared on Lamont's face. 'I've sampled another world, and I'm ready to immerse myself in it.'

Akhan shook his head.

'You're an impressive speaker. It's one of the things I admire about you, but you will do as I say.'

'No I won't.' Lamont was on his feet now.

Akhan smiled.

'I heard a story . . . Over a year ago. A story of a struggle in a barber's shop,' he paused, watching it dawn on Lamont's face. 'A man ended up dead. It was covered up, but I recall everything about this story.'

Lamont couldn't speak. His throat constricted. He sat back down without even realising.

'Lamont . . . Sorry, *Teflon*. I know what you did to Reagan. I understand why you did it, but it becomes my gain. If you leave this life, you will go to prison. It's as simple as that.'

Lamont felt faint as he groped for the glass of water and guzzled the clear liquid. He couldn't believe this was happening. He was so close.

'Let's talk no more of you walking away, Teflon. For you, this game we're both being forced to play, it's only just beginning.'

TARGET PART II

PROLOGUE

Tuesday 15 October 2013

THE STREETS OF HULME, Manchester were deathly quiet, a rattling wind shuffling the sparse leaves of trees. Only a few faces were out; kids in parkas and hooded tops mooching around, spitting on the floor and talking in loud voices. They were unaware they were being watched.

A car at the bottom of the street idled with its lights off. The passenger, a brawny dark-skinned man with closely cropped hair scarred features, turned to the driver.

'Are we gonna have a problem?'

The driver shook his head. He was a dreadlocked killer known as K-Bar on the streets of Leeds. He tugged on a pair of weathered leather gloves. The criminals wore black jackets, combat trousers and plain black trainers. K-Bar stifled a yawn, a gun resting on his lap. In the dark car it was hard to see the livid bags under his eyes.

'The right people know what we're doing,' K-Bar cocked the gun. 'We're gonna go through the back, nice and quiet.'

Grimer nodded. Black balaclavas securing their faces, they moved. The youths glanced at them but didn't speak. In silence they made their way to the back of a terraced house, Grimer keeping a lookout while K-Bar broke in. They checked their weapons and padded through the living room, silenced guns at the ready.

Grimer approached the stairs, K-Bar covering as Grimer tested the steps for any noise. They ascended, searching each room. Approaching the master bedroom, they saw a flash before gunfire ensued. K-Bar ducked, Grimer following his lead. The gun-smoke made it hard to see, but they had been in similar situations before and their movements were fluid. The shooter's aim was off, but they needed to be quick. Police were likely on route.

'Cover me!' K-Bar yelled, rolling into the bedroom. Grimer rose from his position, firing multiple shots in the shooter's direction. K-Bar spotted the muzzle spray and picked his shots carefully. He hit the shooter who dropped with a scream. Hurrying towards the prone frame, K-Bar kicked the gun away, training his own on the shooter. The shooter wheezed, staring up at the figures, unable to recognise them.

Grimer moved to flick on the bedroom light. They surveyed Brownie, gritting his teeth in obvious pain. They hadn't seen the man since he'd fled Leeds after almost killing Lamont. His frame remained stocky, but his face seemed thinner. Living on the run hadn't agreed with him.

'You're lucky we don't have time to get deep,' K-Bar snarled. 'We took out your shit crew. Marrion's gone, and Antonio squealed like a bitch when we put him down. You're the one we wanted though.'

'I don't give a damn. I ain't a punk,' growled Brownie, eyes watering from pain, blood trickling from his shoulder down to his t-shirt.

'Yeah, you are. You tried getting a kid to do your runnings, and you really thought you and that clown you worked for were gonna run our thing?' K-Bar laughed, Grimer chuckling in his booming voice.

'Fuck you. Go to hell.' Brownie spat on the floor.

'Let's forget the talking then. You can hold this for *Teflon*.' K-Bar fired, shooting Brownie twice in the head.

CHAPTER ONE

Monday 12 January 2015

IT DIDN'T FEEL real for Shorty. He was being driven towards the Leeds streets he'd always known, yet felt more disconnected than ever. There was no music playing, so he stared out of the window as Akeem drove in silence. Shorty knew nothing about the man, other than the fact he worked for Lamont.

Akeem was probably around six-feet-tall, with a sculpted beard, short cropped hair and dark eyes. He'd shaken Shorty's hand, asked if he was okay, then said no more. He was in the zone. Shorty knew the type. He'd been around street people all of his life. Shorty was sure there were hidden depths to Akeem; Lamont wouldn't have him around otherwise.

As the buildings and scenery melded into a blur, Shorty thought about Lamont. They hadn't seen one another in over a year, but Shorty knew everything. Lamont's shooting shocked him, but not much. They were at war, and Lamont had been an unfortunate, near-fatal casualty of events. The streets were temptresses. They lured fools with promises of riches and fame, but Shorty had seen many close to him fall, none more so than Marcus Daniels.

Marcus, Shorty, and Lamont were like brothers. Marcus was a giant of a man who feared no one and took what he wanted from life. He and Shorty were formidable; they fought and even killed together. When Marcus was gunned down, Shorty lost a part of himself. Everything that happened since had only added to that.

Shorty's eyes grew heavy. He tried to force himself to stay awake, but the car started to swim, his eyes drooping.

'We're here.'

A strong hand shook Shorty once. He jolted awake, following Akeem up a short driveway. Akeem firmly knocked three times, then walked into the living room of a detached house. The walls were a refreshing cream colour, the furniture smoke-grey. On the sofa staring into space was the man Shorty had come to see.

'You need anything?' Akeem asked. Lamont Jones shook his head.

'Not right now. I'll contact you shortly. Your time is yours until then.' Lamont didn't turn. Akeem nodded at Shorty and left. There was an awkward silence. Shorty examined the fixtures in the room. The layout was like Lamont's old house, but more colourful; fresh red and pink flowers, various plants and paintings of sunsets on the walls. Shorty assumed this was down to Jenny's presence.

'Would you like a drink?' Lamont glanced at Shorty, who looked away after a moment. Lamont had a habit of doing that; assessing a person until they confessed their deepest, darkest secrets.

'Brandy if you've got it.'

Lamont headed to his drinks cabinet. He removed two glasses, then reached for a diamond-shaped bottle. Shorty's eyes were immediately drawn to it. Lamont noticed.

'You don't mind, do you?'

Shorty shook his head. It was the drink they'd shared the night of Marcus's murder.

'That's fine.'

Lamont handed Shorty a glass and sipped his own, closing his eyes.

'Don't tell Jen. I'm not supposed to be drinking.' Lamont, motioned to his stomach as he took another deep sip.

'Is she okay?' Shorty asked. It had never been so difficult talking to his friend. He and Lamont hadn't always agreed, but they'd never struggled to communicate. Now, Shorty felt like he was playing catch-up.

'She's works a lot, trying to grow her business. She keeps busy.'

Shorty dumbly stood, not knowing how to prolong the conversation. Lamont sat, motioning for Shorty to do the same. Shorty slid into an armchair, wishing that he had a spliff, or a line of cocaine to make it all easier. He drank the cognac though, savouring the unique taste.

'So . . . You're out then,' said Lamont. Shorty didn't reply. He didn't need to. It was still a surprise. One minute he was facing twenty years in prison for murder, stuck on remand. The next, the charges had been dismissed, and he was free. Whatever that meant.

'Good looking out on them solicitors, man. They definitely earned their cash.'

'You don't have to thank me. I wasn't going to leave you languishing in there. I did everything I could to get you out.'

'I know, fam. I'm sorry that I wasn't around. When it happened.'

Another awkward silence engulfed the room. Marrion Bernette, a Manchester gangster with a grudge against both Shorty and Lamont had orchestrated Lamont's shooting. He and his team sought to divide them, sending shooters to end their lives. Shorty was forced to kill three people, and Lamont had been shot twice.

'You were running for your life. If you could have been there, I know you would have been. How are you feeling?'

The concern on Lamont's face touched Shorty. He shrugged, noting how fragile Lamont appeared. His arms and shoulders looked thicker, but there was a haunted look in his once powerfully intelligent eyes. It daunted Shorty.

'I feel disconnected, fam. Like I'm in my pad, looking at this shit through someone else's eyes. I thought I was gonna be in that cage for the rest of my life. I was prepared for that . . .'

'Amy's doing well. So is Grace.'

Shorty's heart soared at the mention of his daughter. He hadn't seen her since his arrest.

'Bet she's huge now.'

'Cheeky too. I tried giving Amy some money on your behalf, but you know what she's like.'

Shorty did. Amy was wilful. It didn't shock him she hadn't taken Lamont's money.

'I'm gonna get myself cleaned up, then see them in a couple days. They still at the same house?'

'We can see them tomorrow.'

Shorty shook his head. 'I need clothes, and my hairs all fucked up—'

'Everything you need is in the spare room upstairs. We can stop at Trinidad's first thing if you wanna get lined up.'

Shorty genuinely smiled for the first time in forever.

'You still always think of everything.'

'That'll never change, Shorty. You're more than welcome to stay until you get yourself sorted. Jen's fine with it.'

Shorty doubted that. He and Jenny had never cared for one another, and in her position, he wouldn't want a murderous thug around.

'It's cool, I'll go lay at one of my older spots. Thanks though.'

Lamont led Shorty upstairs, pointing to a door.

'Your clothing is on the bed. I guessed at sizes. There's a connecting bathroom, so take your time. You should have everything you need.'

Shorty thanked Lamont and headed into the room. It had a similar cream decor to downstairs, and a rich, white bedspread. On the bed were two pairs of black jeans, a pair of trainers, shirts, and t-shirts, along with other bits and pieces.

There was a thick envelope at the top, resting on the pillow. Shorty opened it, glancing at the stacks of notes. He tossed it back on the bed, then went to take a shower.

Lamont was leafing through a book when Shorty re-entered the room.

'You found everything?'

'Yeah, boss. Good looking out for that cash. I'll pay you back when I'm on my feet.'

Lamont waved him off. 'We're brothers. Consider it a portion of your cut. You must be starving. Let's go get some food, and I'll bring you up to speed.'

* * *

Jenny's fingers lingered on the laptop keyboard as she stared into space. The hairs on the back of her neck bristled. Jenny shook her head, trying to shake the visions plaguing her. She needed to concentrate on the email she was sending. It was an opportunity to lift her dwindling business from near closure, and she had to make the most of it.

'Can I get you a drink, Jen?'

Jenny shook her head. Nadia had been with Jenny for years. She'd had more staff, but was forced to let them go when business dried up. Jenny had built her business from scratch, establishing a name and a certain reliability that her clients respected. That went downhill when Jenny's partner, Lamont Jones, was shot outside Jenny's house the previous year. She cradled his body, sure he was dead.

The aftermath was a blur. Jenny recalled K-Bar, one of Lamont's soldiers, telling her everything would be okay, assigning men to guard her.

Jenny practically lived at the hospital, eating little, watching as the love of her life underwent multiple operations. She had been a quivering wreck, sure that someone would come and finish the job.

Jenny had taken an extended leave of absence from her florist business, leaving Nadia in charge. The poor girl had done her best, but there was too much going on, and the customers began to leave in droves.

By the time Jenny was back on her feet, the business was on its last legs. She assumed control, but it seemed an uphill battle. Jenny needed to bring the clients back, and she was struggling to think what to do.

A company had contacted her yesterday, requesting a large order for a charity benefit. Sensing she was desperate, they weren't offering much money, but it was a good cause, and Jenny needed the positive publicity.

Nadia closed Jenny's office door. Jenny let out a sigh. Lamont had offered to put money into the business, but Jenny had turned him down.

After leaving the hospital, it devastated Lamont to learn about the state of Jenny's business. Insisting it was all his fault, he begged Jenny to let him be involved, claiming that he could get his business partner

Martin Fisher to help her. Jenny refused, insisting she could do it herself.

Lamont left her to it and focused on the business of getting stronger. He went to the gym as soon as the doctor allowed it, hiring a personal trainer and pushing himself harder than both Jenny and his doctors had liked. He moved them to a new house and tried to buy Jenny a new car. Lamont seemed determined not to let his injuries sideline him, insisting he was okay.

And so, Jenny let him believe it. She pretended she couldn't see him wincing sometimes when he moved too quickly. She pretended she couldn't smell liquor when he would come to bed. They were both trying to find their way back, neither knowing how. For the past few months they had stumbled through.

Lately, Lamont seemed more tense. He insisted he was stressed with business, but Jenny didn't know if it was that simple.

It was dark outside by the time Jenny locked up her premises and climbed into her ride. She wanted nothing more than a long bath when she got home. Lamont's car wasn't in the drive, so Jenny entered the house, running a bath and pouring various oils and soaps into the piping hot water. When the bath was set, she warmed up some spaghetti from the night before, forcing it down along with two glasses of white wine. She grabbed a book she'd started reading, lit a candle, and sank into the bath with a sigh of relief, distracted from her mounting issues for a short while.

'Bring me up to speed then.'

Lamont sipped his wine, weighing up his words. They had gone out to a restaurant in Garforth, fancying a longer drive. The place was full of people, with low lighting, black leather chairs, and mahogany tables. Lamont was already on his second glass, Shorty sticking to water. They'd ordered steaks, sitting in silence until now.

'We took some hits. When I got shot, everything was up in the air.'

'What about the money side of it? You had Chink running it, so didn't that fall to pieces after he got slotted?' Shorty asked. Years back, he would have been animated, wanting the drama. Now, he was merely curious.

'We had contingencies in place. I moved a lot of things around after we fell out over the Georgia thing,' replied Lamont.

'Rapist bastard. I'm glad he's dead. Have you spoken to her?'

Lamont shook his head, his expression hardening.

'Why not?'

Lamont lowered his voice, though it was so loud with all the background conversations that it was impossible to overhear.

'She was grinding him.'

'Who was?' Shorty looked nonplussed.

'Georgia. She was sleeping with Chink. For years.'

Shorty's eyes widened. 'How the hell do you know that?'

Lamont didn't reply. As Shorty waited, comprehension dawned on his face.

'You didn't . . .'

Lamont sighed, 'I caught them kissing years back. I told Chink to end it, or I would. I thought he had until Georgia told me everything.'

'And you never told Marcus?'

'Do you think Chink would have still been breathing if I had?' Lamont finished his drink, ordering another.

'What about K-Bar? He tried to come see me while I was inside, but I wouldn't let him.'

'I heard. K did well to steer the ship. He had everyone watching, waiting for him to fail. He stumbled a few times, but we made it through.'

Shorty sensed from Lamont's expression that there was more unsaid. Certain things seemed off with Lamont. Shorty had put it down to his accident, but he wasn't sure. His friend seemed on edge, and Shorty wondered why.

Their food arrived, and both men ate in silence. Shorty sprinkled extra salt and black pepper on the steak and began to tuck in. Until now, he hadn't been hungry, but his appetite had returned with a vengeance.

'Maka was worried about you getting out.'

'Why?'

Maka was one of Lamont's lieutenants. He worked with his friend Manson, making good money for the team. He and Shorty had always been cool.

'The Timmy situation. He was worried that you might have something to say about it.' Lamont was being careful with his words. He watched as Shorty's face sagged, the devastation palpable.

Timmy Turner was Shorty's younger cousin. Desperate to walk a mile in Shorty's shoes, he had allowed himself to be manipulated into turning on them. He set up Shorty to be murdered by Marrion's shooters and had held a gun on Lamont. He was afraid to pull the trigger though and had been murdered by Maka in the aftermath.

'Maka did what he had to do. Timmy made his choice. I just should have shown him a better way,' Shorty mumbled. They continued to eat, listening to the low lounge music playing in the background. They were surrounded mostly by families enjoying their meals, laughing and joking. Shorty wondered why the atmosphere between them was so strained. He and Lamont had been friends since they were five-years-old, yet they were making stilted conversation, as if they didn't know how to be around each other anymore.

'Why are you still here?'

Lamont glanced at Shorty.

'Pardon?'

'Why are you still doing this? Why are you still in the life when you said you were walking away?'

Lamont looked at his friend for a long moment before he replied.

'Things change.'

'What does that mean?'

Lamont reached for his wallet. 'Let's just pay the bill. You can stay the night, and we'll sort everything tomorrow.'

Shorty's brow furrowed. He wiped his mouth, watching Lamont hand a black card to the waitress, genially making small talk. Shorty wondered if it was all an act. The waitress giggled, tossing her hair back as Lamont spoke. Shorty needed to work out what was going on. There was something he wasn't being told.

A red Mercedes was parked in the driveway when they arrived home. Lamont parked next to it, and the pair made their way inside.

Lamont flicked a switch and the pitch-black hallway filled with light. Shorty followed Lamont to the living room, watching his friend go straight to the drinks cabinet. He took out the cognac from earlier, pouring some into a glass as Shorty observed.

'You can sleep in the room where you found your clothes. We'll talk in the morning.'

Lamont slapped hands with Shorty. As Shorty headed up the stairs, he watched Lamont heading towards another room, clutching the bottle, his shoulders slumped.

CHAPTER TWO

Tuesday 13 January 2015

SHORTY RUBBED his eyes as he clambered from bed the next morning. He audibly yawned and stretched, feeling his bones creak. His nights sleep had been poor. The bed was comfortable, but his mind had refused to shut down.

Shorty was nervous about seeing Grace, and about what to do next. His talk with Lamont had been brief, and his friend was vague about what was going on in the streets. He hoped Lamont would have a plan.

Shorty had wanted to write to Grace when he was on remand, but shame kept him from putting pen to paper. He couldn't explain where he had been. There was so much to work on, and he needed to be on point.

Lamont's behaviour worried him. He'd always liked a drink, but Shorty couldn't recall seeing him indulge with such abandon. There was a sadness that Shorty couldn't put his finger on, but he would get to the bottom of it.

After a shower, Shorty dressed and headed downstairs, his stomach rumbling. He made his way to the kitchen, pausing when he saw Jenny already sat at the table, drinking a cup of coffee. She glanced up.

'Hey.'

'Hi. Sorry, didn't mean to disturb you.'

'Don't be silly. L mentioned you might stay a few days,' Jenny appraised Shorty and signalled to her cup. 'Do you want one?'

Shorty nodded.

'Sit down and I'll make it for you.'

Shorty slid into a wooden chair, watching Jenny pouring coffee from a fancy-looking coffee maker. She checked how he took it, adding milk and sugar.

'It must be weird for you, being out and about,' she remarked.

'Yeah, it is.'

'I'm sorry, I didn't mean to pry. L's still sleeping. I'm guessing you made a night of it?'

'We went for dinner then came home.'

Jenny's brow furrowed. 'Oh, I just thought . . . He didn't come to bed until . . .' She shrugged. Shorty took the cup with thanks, unsure how to prolong the conversation.

'How is he doing?'

'What do you mean?' Jenny blinked.

'L. Is he okay?'

Jenny smiled.

'It's hard to tell sometimes. He keeps a lot to himself. I don't think he's sleeping well. Ever since,' Jenny paused. 'Ever since the accident, I think he sees things differently. Like he's trying to find his place.'

'I know how that feels,' Shorty admitted. He sipped the coffee, nourishing the spike of energy the caffeine gave him.

'You know it's his birthday tomorrow, right?'

Shorty had forgotten.

'Is he doing anything?'

'I wanted to throw him a party, but he refused. I was going to take him to dinner. You should come.'

'Nah, you two go. You don't need me around.'

'Don't be silly. L will want you there. I'll make the arrangements.' Jenny made to leave the room.

'Jenny?'

She turned.

'Are you alright?'

Jenny stared for a moment before nodding.

'I'm fine, Shorty. I'm going to work, so I'll talk to you later. Help yourself to whatever you need.' She lingered for a moment, then left.

* * *

Lamont's eyes shifted open, and he immediately stifled a groan. Sitting up, he massaged his temples and checked the time. It was after ten. Jenny's side was empty. She would already be at work.

Showering, Lamont dressed in a black shirt, jeans and boots. He reached for his phone and headed downstairs to hunt for caffeine. To his surprise, Shorty sat in the kitchen, an empty cup of coffee resting in front of him.

'Hey,' said Lamont, not wanting to disturb him.

'You good?'

'Yeah. Did you find everything alright?'

Shorty nodded. 'Jen went to work.'

'She leaves early. I'm surprised you're up. I thought I'd have to fling water at you to get you up.'

Shorty grinned. 'I didn't sleep well.'

'Wasn't the bed comfortable?'

'Course it was. I just couldn't settle. Guess I'm nervous.'

'It's fine to be nervous.'

'Not for me it isn't.'

Lamont grabbed a cup from a cupboard.

'Nor me.'

Lamont made some coffee, Shorty declining a second cup. He remained standing, holding the steaming mug with both hands.

'We need to talk about your future.'

'There's a lot we need to talk about.'

'Like?' Lamont was watching Shorty again.

'Like, why you're up drinking at all hours of the night. What happened to the L that used to wake up at 5am every morning, rain or shine?'

'You're looking for problems where there aren't any.' Lamont ignored Shorty's question.

'Am I?'

'Yes, you are. Think about Grace and Grace only. She needs you.'

Shorty had nothing to say to that. He would re-address it another time.

'Do you think I need to bring her a present?'

Lamont shook his head. 'I think she'll just be glad to see you. You could always take her shopping.'

* * *

When they were ready, Lamont called Akeem, and they piled into a black Mercedes 4x4. Shorty settled into the leather seating, Lamont next to him. Akeem started the engine, and they rumbled towards Chapeltown.

Lamont stared ahead, but Shorty glanced out of the window all the way to Chapeltown like a child on a school trip, taking in all the changes. For the longest time, he had lived and breathed the streets, but now he felt out of touch. As they drove up Chapeltown Road though, he saw a few old faces, still posted up, doing the same thing.

Akeem parked near the barbers. He stuck close to Lamont, his eyes flitting in all directions. Shorty admired his skills. He was sharp.

The door clanged to announce their entrance. There were a few people sat around waiting for cuts. Loud reggae music blared from the system, a loud argument about football competing with the track. The oldest man in the room broke into a smile when he saw the trio. Turning the shaver he held off, he put it down and wiped his hands, then firmly shook Lamont's hand.

'Good to see you, L.'

'You too, Trinidad.'

'Shorty, it's good to see you out, son,' Trinidad shook Shorty's hand next before greeting Akeem.

'Thanks, Trinidad. How's tricks?'

Trinidad scratched the back of his neck. 'Old age, man. Joints are stiff with all that arthritis and that there settling in. I'm still living though, so I cannot complain.'

Shorty grinned. He'd known Trinidad since he was a kid. A lot of the youths chilled at Trinidad's barber shop back in the day. He would give out free haircuts if he knew you didn't have the money, more concerned with helping people than making a profit. This generosity led to him nearly losing his shop.

Lamont stepped in, lent him the money to pay his debts, then invested money into dragging the barbers into the 21st Century. All of a sudden, Lamont owned the barbers, but kept everything the same and made sure Trinidad felt important, which he was.

They settled into their seats, and Shorty spoke with a few faces that he recognised. Their words were friendly, but he could see from their eyes they didn't trust him.

'Oi, Trinidad,' One of them started. 'Any word on the next meeting?'

Trinidad shook his head. 'Should find out in the next few days. Stop by here and I'll let you know.'

'What meeting is this?' Shorty asked.

'Ask L. He'll tell you all about it.'

Shorty frowned, unsure why Trinidad was being cagey. Shorty let it go and told the man what he wanted. After Trinidad trimmed his hair, Shorty cleaned himself in the bathroom, then they said their goodbyes.

The sky was darkening as they packed into the ride. Shorty ran his hands through his shortened hair, clicking his seatbelt into place.

'Does Amy know that I'm getting out?'

Lamont hesitated. Shorty sighed.

'This is gonna be fun.'

* * *

Shorty took a deep breath as they pulled onto the familiar Oakwood Street. The same cars were parked as if he'd never been away. He climbed from the ride, wishing he'd consumed more liquor. This visit would have been easier if he was drunk.

The last time Shorty had been on this street, he'd clutched a bloody gun. He'd demanded to see Grace, knowing the police were after him for the murders of the Manchester contingent. He'd argued with Amy, his daughter's mother. She'd almost let him in, but her boyfriend called the police. They came for Shorty, but not before he'd clocked her boyfriend in the head with his gun. He'd evaded them long enough to ditch both the gun and his gloves.

The police caught him, but hadn't found the incriminating weapon. Shorty would make sure they never did.

Lamont hung back, letting Shorty take the lead. Akeem watched from the car as Shorty knocked on the front door.

'Shorty?'

Shorty's breath caught in his throat. Many a night in his cell, he'd fantasised about the fiery redhead currently staring open-mouthed. Her misty green eyes still entranced him, her figure as trim as it had always been. He forced himself to meet her gaze.

'Hey, Ames. Is Grace in?'

'When did you get out?' Amy ignored his question.

'The other day. Is she in?'

'You couldn't have given me some warning? You can't just—' Amy was talking to Lamont now.

Tutting, Shorty manoeuvred around her and went to the living room. Amy called after him, but Shorty ignored her. The channel was set to the news. The heating was on, and the room had a toasty feel. In the corner, writing at a desk, sat Grace Turner.

Shorty stared at his little girl, his heart about to explode. Feeling eyes on her, Grace looked up, gazing at her father. For the longest moment, they both stared. Amy and Lamont paused in the doorway, tentatively watching the moment. Shorty felt his eyes blur, but he didn't wipe the tears away. Grace's lip trembled. Then, she ran out of the room.

'Grace!' Amy hurried after her. Lamont watched as Shorty stood, crestfallen.

'Give her some time, bro. It'll still be raw.'

Shorty nodded dumbly, wanting to burst into tears. He yearned to hold Grace and tell her everything would be okay. She didn't even want to be around him though, and that was tough to stomach.

After a few minutes, Amy came back into the living room.

'Is she okay?'

'She will be,' Amy's voice was cold. 'You're out then? For good?'

'They dropped The charges. Can I see her?'

'She needs to adjust.'

'I just wanna see her. Please, Ames,' said Shorty, hating the pleading tone in his voice.

'Shorty, she needs time. You have to understand that she hasn't seen you in over a year. You know what she has seen though? The papers calling you a murderer. She's seen the police searching the house; for drugs, for guns. You need to give her time.'

Shorty swallowed, the sadness emanating from him. Lamont bowed his head, knowing his friend wouldn't want to look weak.

'Can we talk, Ames?'

'I'll never keep you from having a relationship with your daughter, but we have nothing else to say to each other. I think you need to leave,' Amy's eyes flickered to Lamont. 'Both of you.'

* * *

Shorty didn't speak as they made their way back from Amy's. He had expected resistance from Grace, but he hadn't expected her to run away. Lamont had patted him on the shoulder as they climbed into the car, but that was it. He hadn't tried to counsel Shorty, and Shorty appreciated that.

'L, K-Bar called. He wants a meet.'

Lamont flicked his eyes to Shorty. 'Are you up for it?'

Shorty nodded, hoping his old friend could distract him.

K-Bar waited outside a house on Leopold Street. He climbed into the ride.

'Fucking hell, Shorty. I knew you were getting out, but not so soon! What's going on?'

Shorty grinned at K-Bar's excitement. He had known Lamont longer, but he and K-Bar had struggled together, pitching weed out of a dirty flat, desperate to make money when no one else would give them a shot.

When they'd began running with Lamont, K-Bar played his position, working under Shorty and keeping the streets in line by any means necessary. He looked to have put on size since the last time

Shorty had seen him, judging by the ways his biceps bulged against the navy blue hooded top he wore.

'You know what I's like about keeping secrets. I missed you, fam.'

It was K-Bar's turn to smile. 'I missed you too. Where are you staying? We need to go out tonight and show everyone you're back.'

Shorty looked to Lamont, expecting him to veto the idea, but his friend's face was blank.

'Yeah, we can go out. You down, L?'

Lamont shrugged. 'I'll go for a few.'

'Won't Jenny mind?' Shorty asked. K-Bar shot him a confused look. Lamont's face remained the same.

'I doubt it. She wants to do something tomorrow night. I don't think she'll begrudge me having a few drinks. K, what's the situation?'

K-Bar's smile vanished, 'Hughesy came to see me. He doesn't want to buy from us anymore.'

'Did he say why?'

K-Bar shook his head. 'Just said he'd had a better offer. Summat's up though. He looked nervous.'

'We can't force people to buy from us, K. We're not that kind of operation.'

'He's not the first, L. Three people alone in the past two weeks have stopped doing business with us.'

'We're still the best party in town. If we have to raise the price on the people dealing with us, we'll do that.'

K-Bar ran his hands through his dreadlocked hair.

'Is that the right thing to do?'

'Unless you know who they're all copping from, there isn't much to be done about it. It's not a problem at the moment. We have the best stuff on the market. Don't forget that.'

'Those fucking do-gooders, man. They're not making things any easier with their damn meetings,' K-Bar mumbled.

'What meetings?' Shorty asked, remembering Trinidad's words at the barbers.

K-Bar scowled, 'There's this new community thing. They call themselves the *OurHood* Initiative. They formed last year and started preaching about making changes on the streets.'

'Those dickheads have always been around though.'

'Not like this, bro. They're growing all the time, proper well-funded and organised. Some poet prick is at the head of it. Can't remember his name, but people are acting like he's some future leader.'

Shorty mulled over that. He'd known people over the years who claimed to have the best intentions for Chapeltown. They started collecting money, saying they would keep kids off the street and in youth clubs, but they never seemed to go anywhere.

* * *

'Do you really think that's a smart idea?'

Lamont watched Akeem as the bodyguard paced the hardwood floor of the safe house. Mindful of conducting business in the home, Lamont had a spot he went to whenever he needed to talk. It was scanned for listening devices every day and closely monitored to prevent surveillance.

After they had left K-Bar, Shorty decided to stay at his own place. Lamont knew Shorty was upset over Grace's reaction, but he needed to wait it out. Once the shock wore off, Lamont believed Grace would want to spend time with Shorty again.

'I think it's necessary. We need to root out who is working against us and playing dumb is the best way.'

'I understand that,' replied Akeem, 'but why not bring K-Bar in on it? He's already operating from a position of weakness. You know the messes he's endured.'

K-Bar had taken charge when Lamont was in hospital, but he was a soldier, and people both in and out of the organisation tried to take advantage of that.

K-Bar was a logical thinker but not a diplomat. An argument with a small-timer who had wanted to make a name for themselves had led to K-Bar shooting him in the leg. The man threatened to press charges, but it had all been smoothed over.

'You're right, Akeem. I do, but this is better. The less he knows, the more convincing it looks. How is that other thing going?'

'I've got my best people on it. We'll find something. Are you sure it's smart to go out tonight?'

'A few drinks won't hurt. Make sure one of your people is amongst the crowd. I don't want any surprises. I need you on call.'

Akeem nodded. Lamont drank his gin and tonic in silence. The team was still making money, but it felt less secure than in the past. Every day it seemed new crews were starting up, trying to get their piece of the money pie by any means necessary.

Lamont had aided K-Bar in getting things back in order, but he was reluctant to divulge his full attention to regulating the streets. There was so much going on at the moment that he was playing catch-up. Having Shorty back could free him up, but he was fresh out of prison. The authorities would be furious that he had slipped through their fingers. They were likely watching him, and by extension, Lamont too. He finished the drink and wiped his mouth.

'Take me home, please.'

* * *

Shorty sipped his drink quietly, sitting in the VIP section of an exclusive club near Call Lane. Lamont, K-Bar and Maka surrounded him, sipping champagne. Lamont insisted on fitting the bill, and so far, he'd paid for everything, from transport, to the overly expensive bottles in the clubs.

Maka kept his eyes on the crowd, not looking in Shorty's direction. The pair greeted one another coolly, but hadn't spoken beyond that. Shorty asked K-Bar where Blakey was, only to be told he'd moved on. When Shorty questioned why, K-Bar admitted they hadn't seen eye to eye, and had left it at that. His dreadlocked friend was grinning, trying to get the attention of several barely dressed females, with little success.

Shorty glanced at Lamont. He was clutching his champagne with a faraway look on his face. Shorty had noticed how distracted his friend had looked the entire time they'd been out, but it was pointless trying to get Lamont to talk. Shorty would need to do some digging around on his own. As Shorty watched, Lamont seemed to come out of some sort of trance. He stood, holding his glass aloft.

'Gents, hold up your glasses, and let's toast to the little thug we all know and love, fresh out of prison, and ready to do his thing.'

They all toasted, their glasses clinking as Shorty grinned, despite himself. All day, he'd been thinking about Grace. Deciding to loosen up, he finished his drink and made his way out to the dance floor. VIP was cool, but he felt like an idiot sitting around as people gawped. K-Bar followed. Maka stayed where he was.

'Maka, you need to talk to him and bury this,' Lamont said. Maka nodded, but didn't move.

'It's not that easy. I shot his family.'

Lamont understood Maka's position; Timmy Turner had held a gun on him the day he'd been shot, and although Timmy ultimately couldn't shoot, Maka hadn't known this when he arrived at the scene.

'You saw a threat, and you reacted accordingly. Shorty would have done the same thing, and he knows that. Trust me, bury this early and don't let it fester.'

Maka nodded again at Lamont, but he seemed more animated now. Slapping hands with Lamont, he left the corded-off VIP section, leaving Lamont alone with his thoughts. He watched as K-Bar conversed with a few females, gesticulating wildly as he spoke. He seemed to be keeping his distance though, as if going through the motions. Tonight was about distracting himself as much as Shorty, yet Lamont felt more distracted than ever.

'Yo, can I approach, *boss?*'

A voice snapped Lamont out of his reverie. A man hovered near the VIP partition as a burly bouncer glared at him. He was light-skinned, with cropped hair and a slit in his left eyebrow. He wore a chain almost bigger than him, leaning slightly forward. A short distance behind him stood two men watching his back.

'Nikkolo, how have you been?' Lamont nodded to the bouncer who let Nikkolo through.

'I'm good, man. Just sampling some of these ladies in here. You need to get out there and make summat happen, bro!'

Lamont smiled tightly. 'My lady wouldn't approve.'

'What she doesn't know won't hurt her. Anyway, how's business on your side?'

'Everything is fine,' Lamont replied, his tone neutral.

'I heard people are leaving your camp.' Nikkolo's eyes danced with glee as he spoke to Lamont, but he couldn't get a reaction out of the kingpin.

'I don't get caught up in rumours. Say hi to your boss for me.' Lamont shook Nikkolo's hand, then left the VIP section. He did not notice Nikkolo glaring at his back.

Lamont made his way to K-Bar, still surrounded by women. The space was cramped, people moving and dancing all around. One of the women, a slim Asian woman with short black hair, smiled at Lamont. He smiled back, not wanting to be rude.

'L, lemme introduce you to my new frie—'

'I'm leaving, K. Here,' Lamont handed K-Bar a stack of notes. 'Watch out for Shorty.' Before K-Bar could protest, Lamont left.

* * *

Shorty closed his eyes, enjoying the feel of the body pressing against his as he swayed to the beat of the music. He was sure his dance moves were out of sync but it was the last thing on his mind.

The girl he danced with had tried talking to Lamont earlier, but had gotten nowhere. Being spurned had hurt her confidence, and Shorty hadn't worked hard to get a dance out of her. As the DJ switched songs, she grinned against him, whispering in his ear.

'Let's go outside.'

Shorty didn't need any persuasion. He followed the girl, unable to keep his hands to himself, kissing on the back of her neck as she giggled against the thumping tempo of the music. All those months on remand meant Shorty was backed up and in serious need. He was tempted to get a taxi home with the girl, but didn't think he could wait.

The pair stumbled around the corner, Shorty pressing the girl against the wall and roughly kissing her, letting her feel just how erect he was. The hairs on the back of his neck stood, causing

Shorty to jerk away from the girl just as he heard hurried footsteps.

'Yo, give it up,' a gruff voice sounded. Shorty faced the pair, two men. Furious with himself for getting caught out, he glared, causing one to take a step back.

'S-Shorty?'

Shorty peeked at the trembling man. He held a knife, wearing a black jacket, trousers and trainers. His face was half-covered by a bandanna like some wannabe bandit. Shorty recognised the younger man with a sudden jolt.

'Jerome?'

Jerome was a friend of Timmy's. A delinquent from an early age, constantly getting Timmy caught up in his foolish schemes.

When Timmy set Shorty up, Shorty went after his cousin through Jerome and another friend. Shorty had mercilessly beaten the pair with a gun, demanding to know Timmy's whereabouts, which the pair swore they didn't know. He'd beaten them into unconsciousness before fleeing.

When he was arrested, Shorty presumed the pair had snitched, but they never said a word to anyone.

'You know this guy?' Jerome's accomplice snapped. He was around Shorty's height, with a slim frame, his entire face covered by a bala- clava. He too had a knife, still pointing it in Shorty's direction. The girl had disappeared. Shorty knew the scheme. She'd meet them later to collect her share, but she would be disappointed.

Shorty had never allowed anyone to rob him, and he wasn't starting now.

'You don't know Shorty from Chapeltown? He's a killer.'

Years ago, Shorty would have smiled at the obvious fear in Jerome's voice, but he simply felt hollow.

'I don't care what his name is. He needs to give up the money and jewels before I poke him.' The other would-be thief wasn't backing down an inch. Shorty kept his eyes on Jerome, ready to hit him first. Jerome's eyes widened, and he ran just as K-Bar and Maka rounded the corner.

'What the fuck is going on here?' K-Bar lunged for the robber, hitting him in the nose and causing the knife to fall from the man's hand. Maka sailed in, smashing his fist against the kid's jaw.

'You think you can rob our boy? Are you crazy?' K-Bar snarled, throwing the kid into the wall next to Shorty. He slid to the floor, bleeding, Shorty looking at him in disgust. He yanked the balaclava from the kid's head, but didn't recognise him. He was lighter than Shorty, with curly black hair with blonde tips.

'Let him up. Get him out of here,' Shorty said. He couldn't help but think about his cousin. These silly robberies were the kind of thing Timmy used to do to get his rep up. As K-Bar slapped the kid and warned him not to show his face again, Shorty sighed, wondering if it was all worth it.

CHAPTER THREE

Friday 16 January 2015

'HOW HAS IT ALL BEEN GOING?'

Jenny looked around the office, procrastinating as always. It was how their weekly meetings started but she was never prepared.

The office was compact, Jenny perched on a neutral blue sofa. Amanda's chair was a murky brown colour and seemed less comfortable than Jenny's, but the woman's chocolate brown eyes projected their usual warmth. If there was any discomfort, it didn't show.

Jenny had been visiting Amanda for over a year, after the nightmares from Lamont's shooting became too frequent. She was referred by her GP, willing to pay the additional fees to speak with the councillor.

Opening up wasn't easy; the idea of being privy to an attempted murder didn't seem real. Jenny had witnessed someone die, and the fact Lamont nearly died from his injuries was a trauma Jenny hadn't known how to navigate. They filled a lot of the early sessions with gaps of silence that took time to overcome. There was a familiarity now and Jenny respected the elderly woman, but they weren't friends. She was paying for her time, and that loomed over each session.

Jenny took a deep breath. 'It's old ground we've trod repeatedly. It always comes back to being there in that moment. Me and my partner had everything to look forward to; he was getting away from negative influences, and then it happened.'

'How much influence did you have over your partners decision; did you pressure him?'

'I don't think I did. I just wanted to be with him, and he wanted to be with me. He said I saved him. And then suddenly there were men with guns. He was terrified, yet still told me to get away.'

'Why didn't you listen?' If Amanda was aware she'd asked the same question a dozen times, it didn't show.

'I froze. I've never been in that position. I never want to be again. I guess I hoped it was all a bad dream.'

'It wasn't though.'

Jenny ignored Amanda's remark, rubbing her eyes.

'Nothing is improving, that's the problem. He was shot, and I saw it, and I was covered in his blood, and I thought he was dead. After all this time, after all the effort he put into getting stronger, it remains as distorted as ever.'

'Do you think it's possible you're stuck in the past because you don't want to embrace the change?'

'Of course I don't want to embrace it. We went from real happiness, to this tentative awkwardness.'

'Do you love your partner?'

'I do. The problem is that we don't know how to act around one another anymore. We're walking on eggshells and won't admit it.'

Amanda paused. 'You said that you spoke to Lamont about seeing someone?'

'He shot the idea down,' Jenny scoffed.

'Why do you think that is?'

'Because he thinks it's a weakness to let people in. He didn't even want to let me in.'

'Why?'

Jenny shrugged. 'Childhood, I guess. I don't know. All I know is that we're stuck.'

'Other than your relationship, how are things going?'

'Work is still a massive slog. I lost a lot of clients, and I'm struggling to get myself out of the hole.'

'Why do you feel you have to do this alone? Your partner is a man of means, is he not?'

'That's irrelevant. It's my business, not his. I don't want his help.'

They sat in silence, Amanda watching Jenny's every move. Jenny stared back at the picture of competence sat in front of her; from the steel grey hair to the cream sweater and demeanour, it all spoke of tranquillity. Jenny remembered wearing a cream sweater the day of Lamont's shooting. She choked back a sob at the memory, tears streaming down her face. Amanda handed her a tissue.

'It will get better, Jenny. That I promise you. You need to embrace the possibility that things will not go back to how they were, and work with the changes.'

* * *

Akeem and Lamont reclined in Lamont's office at the barbers. Akeem had swept the room for bugs and locked the door. He sipped a bottle of water as Lamont ate some cornmeal porridge they'd picked up on the way, waiting for Akeem to speak.

'I've done some analysis,' the man began. 'I assessed the strength of the crew, and we're weak in certain areas. We're still recovering from 2013, and we lost a lot of key personnel. We ramped up with younger, less skilled soldiers and runners. Police activity has increased, and more of our people are being arrested. They don't know enough to implicate anyone, but it's an inconvenience.'

'What are you suggesting?' Lamont valued Akeem's opinion. He had known the man for five years, meeting when Lamont visited London to see an associate, Vincent. Akeem worked for Vincent and specialised in problem solving. When Vincent mentioned Akeem wanted a move, he'd taken the fixer into his team.

'We, and by that I mean *you*, need to decide what's going on. You've been out of sorts, and it's causing confusion. K-Bar isn't pleased with the running of things, and he has sway over the younger guys. They don't know you. They saw you very little before; they see you even less now. You need to placate K-Bar if you want to survive.'

'And the people wanting to do other business? You had thoughts on that the other day.'

Akeem shrugged. 'Replace them with new customers. We have the best product. The game is changing and making it harder though, so we need to change with it.'

Lamont thought of the man he'd seen in the club. He knew who Nikkolo worked for, but he wasn't aware it was public knowledge that he'd lost customers. Lamont hadn't mentioned it to Akeem, but he wondered if Nikkolo was sending a message. Akeem was right though. The money was lower than it had been in years, the morale terrible.

Lamont was in the game, whether or not he wanted to be; he needed to find his form.

* * *

Jenny sat in her work office, staring into space. Since Lamont had left the hospital, and they moved in together, it felt like they'd lived under a protective bubble. Everything had been idyllic. Lamont hadn't directly spoken of his plan, but Jenny knew he was leaving the life and she welcomed it.

Lamont had more than enough money. Marcus had been murdered. Xiyu (*Chink as Lamont and the others called him*) had been murdered in what police called a botched home invasion. Shorty had been arrested and accused of murder.

Jenny didn't know much about Lamont's business, but she knew they were the cornerstone of the illegal empire he had built. Now, Shorty was out, and Jenny had no idea what that would lead to.

The conversation with Shorty flitted to Jenny's mind. He seemed so different from the vicious, fiery man she'd glimpsed in 2013. There was an air of unpredictability around him then, but now he seemed haunted. Life appeared to have caught up with Shorty and quenched the flames of rage. Jenny didn't know how to feel about that, or about Shorty's presence in Lamont's life.

After a while, Jenny heard the ding of the door announcing a customer had walked in. Giving herself a moment, Jenny headed out to the front, smiling widely at the man standing there.

'Good morning,' she said. 'Are you looking for a particular arrangement?'

The man returned her smile. 'I am. Maybe you could give me a few pointers?'

'What's the occasion?' Jenny slipped into worker mode. The man studied her for a moment. It was a speculative gaze and though not a leer, Jenny felt the look.

'I wanted a nice arrangement for my mum. Maybe with a nice card. Do you do cards?'

'We do . . . Is it your mother's birthday?'

The man shook his head, 'I just thought it might be nice. She likes roses, so the arrangement could include those.'

Jenny ran a hand through her hair. The man looked to be around her age. His face was clean-shaven, aside from a moustache and some stubble around his chin. His eyes were dark. He smiled widely, wearing a black lightweight jacket over jeans and a grey t-shirt. The outfit was casual but Jenny had a trained eye. She could tell it was expensive, yet he wore it with a disdain that intrigued her.

The man slightly adjusted his shoulders. He was broad, towered over her, and looked like he worked out. Jenny coughed discreetly, focusing on the task at hand.

'We have roses in different colours. Red is the most popular. Does your mother have a favourite colour?'

'We both like purple,' the man replied. His words were as smooth as his skin, clipped with the slight hint of authority.

'What about purple, some base red, and maybe some raspberry shaded pink?' Jenny led the man over to the roses section. She wondered if he was checking her out, feeling an immediate stab of guilt. There was no reason to feel guilty though. She wasn't doing anything wrong. She was serving a man buying flowers for his mother. And a card.

But was he really? And why did it matter if he was?

Jenny dealt with different customers, and she imagined some bought gifts for significant others. Or mistresses. It wasn't her problem. Her only concern was growing her business.

Something about the man; the cocky smile, the arrogance that seemed to surround him, reminded Jenny of a time that seemed an age ago. Jenny had been in the shop by herself that day too. Lamont came in, pretending to be someone else. They went into her office and had a mock interview. Jenny tried putting Lamont on-the-spot with her questions, but he answered them smoothly, wearing the same arrogance this man had now.

Lamont's had been an act though. He intrigued Jenny enough that she agreed to go out with him, but it was only when Lamont revealed the inner pain he hid from the world that Jenny truly fell for him. He had trusted her enough to let in then, but wouldn't now.

Jenny blinked, focusing on the customer, watching as he studied the flowers. More customers came into the shop. Most were on-the-spot orders; customers who knew exactly what they wanted and were picking up flowers and gifts before work. One customer wanted a custom order delivered, which Jenny arranged, taking some details and an upfront payment.

When she finished, the man seemed to materialise in front of her.

'I'll take the roses we discussed, but I would also like a dozen lilies.'

Jenny nodded. 'Do you have a vase for them, or would you like to purchase one as well? We have a wide range of custom-made vases, candleholders, candles . . .' Jenny's voice trailed off again when she noticed the man smiling at her.

'I like your spirit. You're a right little hustler aren't you?'

'I'm a businesswoman,' said Jenny with more ice than she intended. The man was equal to it though. His maddening smile hadn't dissipated in the slightest.

'That's good. But, don't take me calling you a hustler as a bad thing. I like the spirit. It must be why your shop does so well.'

'It doesn't,' Jenny admitted, before she could stop herself.

'It should. I've seen the way you deal with people. You're efficient, smooth, articulate,' he paused, meeting her eyes, 'and beautiful. Don't forget beautiful.'

'I'm not sure what my looks have to do with anything.' Jenny frowned. The man shook his head.

'Looks are important.'

'Maybe I'm just not as shallow as you.'

'It's not about shallowness. If you were sixty-eight-years-old, smelling like cough sweets and old mothballs, I'm sure it would influence your business. I think you see that.'

Jenny rubbed her forehead, wanting to rid herself of this arrogant man. He was a customer though, so she tempered her annoyance.

'You said you wanted a card as well, right?' she asked. The man watched her again, slowly nodding.

'I didn't mean to offend you.'

'You didn't,' Jenny lied.

'Good. I've learnt it's always best to be upfront.'

'Is that so?' Jenny decided she would test the smooth-talking man in front of her.

'It's most definitely so.'

'Who are the flowers really for?'

The man looked puzzled, 'I told you. They're for my mother.'

'Why would you randomly buy bouquets of flowers for your mum? Are you sure they aren't for a girlfriend, or maybe a side chick?'

'Positive,' the man again met Jenny's eyes. 'Mum's been lonely since dad died. I think some flowers, a nice card, the loving attention of her son, should all help.'

Immediately Jenny felt her face heat. 'Oh, I'm so—'

'You didn't know.'

'How did he die?'

'Heart attack.'

'I'm sorry,' said Jenny. The man smiled.

'Don't be sorry, Jenny. Really.'

'How do you know my name?'

'It's on your name tag,' the man said. 'My name is Malcolm by the way.'

'It's nice to meet you, Malcolm,' said Jenny, her voice warmer now.

'Likewise. So, I'll take a lavender candle, candle holder, two bouquets, and one of these nice custom-vases,' said Malcolm. He helped Jenny carry everything to the counter.

'Regarding the card, would you like me to compose a message?'

'I think I can do that. I would like you to write it though. I imagine you have beautiful handwriting.'

'I'll try not to disappoint.' Jenny picked up a fountain pen and a fresh custom card. It was brown, with a heart on the front so dark it was almost scarlet. She held it up to Malcolm to make sure he was satisfied.

'What would you like it to say?'

Malcolm thought for a moment.

'I would like it to say . . . *Mum, thank you for being you. I will protect you. You are the source of my strength, and I hope I can remain as influential to you as dad was. Love your son and Knight.*'

Jenny was speechless. It wasn't just the words that resonated. It was the sincerity. She had seen the cocksure act come down for a moment and witnessed Malcolm's pain. She found herself wondering things; *how Malcolm had coped after his father's death? Had he handled the arrangements? Did he speak at the funeral?*

Jenny thought again about Lamont. When he had told her about his torturous upbringing, his eyes held the same pain. She remembered the funeral. Marcus had been gunned down in the middle of the Carnival event last August. Lamont had held him in his arms, just as Jenny held Lamont after his own shooting.

At the funeral, Lamont had given a moving eulogy, speaking of how Marcus was the best, most unconventional friend he'd had. He nearly broke down giving the speech, and people cried, Jenny included. Malcolm's words about his mother had moved Jenny in the same way.

'Jenny?'

Jenny blinked, focusing on Malcolm again. He looked concerned.

'Sorry about that,' said Jenny. She wrote the card neatly, then passed the pen to him so he could sign it. She noticed he put seven kisses.

'It's her lucky number,' he told Jenny. Jenny nodded. Her thoughts were all over the place, and she was aware of her heart hammering against her ribs. She didn't know why. Or maybe she did.

When Jenny had bagged everything, Malcolm took the packages, declined her offer to help, and moved fluidly towards the door. He faced her at the last second.

'Would you like to go for a drink?'

'I have a boyfriend.'

Malcolm shrugged. 'Beautiful women always do. Still, a drink doesn't mean we will end up naked and sweaty.'

'Do you have to be so descriptive?' Jenny felt herself redden again. Malcolm smirked.

'I'm a Poet. Being descriptive helps. One drink won't kill you. Bring your boyfriend.'

Jenny shook her head, 'I don't think that's a good idea.'

'You're probably right. I don't know what it is, but I seem to threaten boyfriends,' Malcolm's wide smile showed off sparkling white teeth. 'You take care of yourself, Jenny. I'm sure I'll see you again soon.'

Malcolm left then. Jenny went to the window, watching him climb into a grey Range Rover. She waited to see if he would look in her direction as he pulled away, but he didn't. His face focused straight ahead on the road as he zoomed out of sight.

Jenny sighed, closing her eyes for a moment, wondering why she felt such tremendous guilt. She had served a customer. That was all. He had flirted and called her beautiful, but she hadn't reciprocated. She had been nothing but professional. *So, what was it?*

Going back to the office, Jenny called Lamont, wanting to hear his voice, but it went straight to voicemail.

'Jen?'

Jenny gave a small gasp as a woman appeared in the doorway.

'Are you okay? You look flushed.' It was Nadia.

'I'm fine . . . Are you okay? Did you get Toby off to school okay?'

'Yeah, I had a quick word with his teacher and came straight here. I'll just wash my hands then I'll check everything's okay out there. Do you want a drink?'

Jenny shook her head, watching Nadia leave. She slumped down, picking up the pen and continuing with her paperwork.

* * *

Shorty pulled up on Leopold Street. He was travelling without music playing more these days. The ride he drove was one that Lamont procured for him. It was a blue Toyota Corolla that ran well. Lamont offered him a range of different cars, but Shorty picked a low-key ride. The last thing he needed was to have the police on his back.

Popping a polo into his mouth, Shorty slid from the ride. The terraced house in front of him had peeling paint on the fence, and the brown gate was worn and dilapidated. The garden, normally well-tended, was overrun with weeds. Making his way towards the front door, Shorty firmly knocked. A woman he hadn't seen in over a year peeked out at him.

'Hello, Auntie,' said Shorty.

'Franklin.' Shorty couldn't read his Aunt's expression. She was open-mouthed, protruding bags under her eyes. Shorty remembered his Aunt as a vibrant woman, and it hurt to see her so defeated. Shorty was sure she would reject him as Grace had, but she sighed and let him in.

Ten minutes later, Shorty clutched a cup of tea. His Aunt sat on her sofa, looking anywhere but at him. The tension was stifling. Shorty wished he had some weed to smoke. His nerves were always shot lately. He detested the feeling.

'How's it been going then?' Shorty felt foolish for asking. His Aunt looked at the ground.

'Some days are good, some bad.'

'I'm . . .'

'I know you're sorry. That doesn't help me though. My son is still dead.'

Shorty didn't speak at first. He couldn't heal his Aunt's pain. At eighteen, Timmy had his whole life ahead of him, but he was determined to walk a mile in his cousin's shoes. Timmy wanted to be known. He wanted a reputation like Shorty. He'd died failing to achieve it.

'I know, Auntie. I wish he wasn't.'

His Aunt stirred her drink. Shorty drank his own, glad for the distraction.

'All he wanted was to be like you.'

Shorty let her talk.

'He wanted to do everything you did. He wanted to have the same trainers, same tracksuits. You were his idol.'

Shorty's mouth was dry, and the lump in his throat felt like a golf-ball.

'I'm not trying to hurt you,' Auntie's voice quivered. 'I know you loved him. Lord knows the both of you needed your daddies.'

Shorty's body was racked with a feeling he'd rarely felt before; guilt. His Aunt had no idea of the situation, and exactly who murdered Timmy. Even Shorty struggled with it. To learn that Maka had ended Timmy's life was harrowing. Shorty understood the circumstances, but Timmy was his blood. He'd played the game and lost.

'I've got a bit of change to help you out, Auntie,' Shorty said. He'd never heard his voice sound so flat.

'You don't have to.' His Aunt shook her head.

'I want to. I don't need it, trust me. Let me help you.'

His Aunt sighed. Shorty put the cup and saucer on the coffee table, reaching into his pocket. He handed her the stack of money he'd brought. She looked at the amount and then at him; her eyes a question. Neither spoke as she placed the money onto the chair next to her.

'Your friend, the one who was shot a few years ago . . .'

'L?'

His Aunt nodded. 'He sends me money every month.'

That was news to Shorty. Even when they discussed Timmy, Lamont hadn't mentioned giving his mother any money. Shorty knew Lamont took care of the people around him, but Timmy had betrayed them. He colluded with Marrion and Chink and helped to set up both Shorty and Lamont.

'L's good like that.' Shorty wondered if Lamont felt guilty over Timmy's death.

Shorty stayed a few hours. He let his Aunt make him some food, then hugged her for a long time before leaving. As Shorty sat in his car, he tried making sense of the situation. The money he'd given to his Aunt would hopefully help, but wouldn't appease his feelings. All his life, Shorty had lived and breathed the call of the streets. It had brought him money, respect, fear, and now grief. After another moment, Shorty drove away.

* * *

After leaving his Aunt's place, Shorty headed to see the crew. Maka was posted up with a few younger guys. He glanced up when Shorty entered, nodding and looking back at his phone. One of the youths paused the video game when he saw Shorty.

'Yo, un-pause it.' His comrade reached for the pad. The kid held it out of reach.

'Long time no see, Shorty. You probably don't remember me.'

Shorty shook the kid's hand. 'You're Darren. I used to roll with your brother back in the day. How's Lucas doing?'

Darren grinned, touched that Shorty remembered.

'Still locked up. He goes in and out.'

Shorty nodded. Lucas Lyles, was a goon of the highest order. He robbed everything that wasn't nailed down and liked to hurt people when he did it. Lucas could be cool, but most of the time he was a complete headache to be around.

'Tell him to send me a V. O when you see him,' Shorty greeted the other kid. 'Shadow, what's happening?'

'Just waiting for this phone to ring. I've been chatting to this girl for a minute and I'm trying to roll through today.'

Shorty laughed. Shadow reminded him of when he was younger, running around trying to get with any girl he could. It seemed like a lifetime ago. Maka cleared his throat and slid to his feet.

'Shorty, can I have a word?'

Shorty followed Maka out to the garden. The pair stood in silence.

Life seemed to have improved for Maka. He wore a black designer tracksuit and grey Timberland boots. It was strange for Shorty; Maka was one of the few originals remaining. He'd been around for years, doing business outside the crew with his crime partner, Manson. The pair clicked in the same manner Shorty did with K-Bar, and they always made money. He knew what Maka wanted to talk about, but held his tongue.

'I'm sorry.'

Shorty waited for Maka to finish.

'I didn't mean to kill Timmy. He was working with Marrion, but I don't think he was gonna shoot L. I just started dumping when I saw L was down. I wasn't even aiming for him, I promise.'

Shorty studied Maka. His face was hard, his eyes full of something Shorty identified. It was the same guilt resonating from Shorty's eyes when he looked in the mirror every morning. Maka wasn't apologising out of fear. He was doing it because it was the right thing to do.

'I know how you feel, fam. Timmy violated and tried to get me killed. If I'd caught him in the mood I was in, I would have probably killed him too. I know you weren't trying to, but when you're on the scene and the President is down, you shoot.'

Maka nodded warily, surprised Shorty was taking it so well.

'No hard feelings, Maka. Timmy made his choice. I wish things turned out differently, but they didn't. Let's put it behind us. Cool?'

Maka grinned, and the pair shook hands. They spoke for a few minutes about some old acquaintances, then headed back inside. Darren and Shadow were still playing on the PlayStation.

'I heard Diego's been getting bare donations,' Darren was saying.

'Yeah, them *OurHood* clowns have been everywhere. It's like people are giving money just to shut them up,' Shadow replied.

'What do you lot know about this *OurHood* shit?' Shorty interjected, the reference reminding him of Trinidad's words.

Maka snorted.

'It's some bullshit. Just some do-gooders looking for attention.'

'I've seen them advertising everywhere. That kind of promo ain't cheap. Money's gotta come from somewhere.'

Maka shrugged. 'Probably. What's your plan though? Are you gonna come back and run shit?'

Shorty considered the question. He was tired of mooching around doing nothing and while he was sure the police would have an eye on him, he was smart enough to avoid getting caught. He'd spoken with Lamont though, and so far he hadn't said a thing about Shorty returning to his role.

Shorty received a substantial weekly wage, but it wasn't the same as hustling for his own money.

'I need to talk with the big man and see what he's saying.'

* * *

When Lamont arrived home, he was still contemplating Akeem's words. Lamont needed the crew to be strong while he considered the best course of action for Akhan. Lamont didn't appreciate being black-mailed into maintaining his position of boss. He needed everything running before he could proceed though.

For now, Lamont was content to play along and if Akhan saw him replenishing his team, he was sure the warlord would grow complacent. When he did, Lamont needed to be ready.

Lamont and Jenny picked at their dinner a while later. Jenny had cooked some fish, with rice and salad, yet neither had much of an appetite. Jenny stared at her plate, her knife and fork abandoned. Lamont stirred his own delicious food around on his plate, occasionally eating a portion.

Lamont watched the woman, as beautiful to him as the day he'd first laid eyes on her, and felt a tremendous guilt. He had irrevocably ruined this woman's life, and now he was lying to her about his intentions.

Lamont couldn't tell her about Akhan, or that killing Ricky Reagan with his bare hands had blown up in his face. He didn't know how Jenny would take it, so he needed to lie and keep her from knowing the truth.

'How was work?' He asked, his high-pitched voice making him cringe. Jenny looked up, hastily smiling.

'I caught up on my paperwork, and a few customers wanted custom orders, so hopefully that'll drum up some interest. I'm struggling with the social media side of things. Networking is harder than I thought it would be.'

Lamont cleared his throat. 'If it's an issue of money—'

'It's not.'

'I'm just saying, I can help. Martin would even back the investment so we could do it properly. I could just give it to you, even. I mean—'

'Lamont, I said no!'

Lamont stared for a moment, then nodded and picked up his fork.

'I'm sorry, L. I didn't mean to shout. It's been a long day. I had a session with Amanda this morning before work.'

Lamont reached out and squeezed Jenny's hand, his rosewood eyes full of concern.

'How was it?'

'Emotional. She has a knack of getting me to speak about things. She had the idea that maybe you could come for a session with me, and we could—'

'Thank you, but I'll pass.' Lamont cut her off. He wiped his mouth with a napkin and headed to his study. Jenny had tried so many times to get him to go to counselling, but Lamont had no intention of telling a stranger his problems. Pouring a tall glass of brandy, he resolved to grow stronger on his own, determined to be the person he used to be.

* * *

Nikkolo was all smiles as he sauntered into the spacious house on Potternewton Lane. Locking the door, he made his way into what was formerly the living room. Other than two leather chairs, it was devoid of furniture. The walls were grey, the flickering lightbulb giving the room a horror vibe.

Nikkolo bounced into the only available chair and cleared his throat.

'I spoke to Ronnie. He wants to borrow twenty bags. He's aware of the rates and said he can pay back within two weeks,' Nikkolo reached into his jacket pocket and handed a watch to the other person in the room. 'He gave me that as collateral.'

Lennox Thompson took the Rolex without a word, examining it for a moment before handing it back.

'What's going on with the other situation?'

Nikkolo scratched the back of his neck. He'd run Lennox's crew for years, yet the man still made him uneasy.

Lennox was wiry, with a thin face and fathomless dark eyes that stared holes through whoever was in the vicinity. He had a quiet presence that radiated malevolent force. It was a lot to take in and didn't grow any easier.

'Our people are saying Delroy has lost his heart. Ever since Teflon humbled him, he's lost a lot of respect. You know my view; we should strap up and take him out. We can get someone to run the drug thing for us and make more money.'

'We don't sell drugs, or did you forget that fact? You wanna be a dealer, go work for someone else.'

Nikkolo hung his head, abashed. Lennox paid him no attention.

'There are easier ways to destroy a person than charging in and trying to kill them. Delroy is soft. The people he keeps around are softer. Their only goal is to keep making money. Teflon and the other gangs are more of a threat.'

Nikkolo clapped his hands together. 'That reminds me. Did you know Shorty is out?'

'So?'

'I'm just saying. They must have been celebrating the other night. I ran into Teflon.'

Lennox looked up now, his hawk-like expression stilling Nikkolo.

'What do you mean you *ran into him?*'

'I just saw him at the club and I said hello.'

'What else did you say?'

'Nothing. I didn't even mention you or anything.'

'Tell me exactly what was said.'

'I said hello, he said hello, and then I mentioned that he'd lost a few customers. After that, I kept it moving.'

Lennox's expression remained unchanged, but Nikkolo felt the tension spike in the room. Lennox held his stare for over a minute before he spoke.

'Why did you mention Teflon losing customers? Did you not think that information wouldn't be public?'

'I d-didn't think—'

'You're right. Get out of my sight. I'll deal with you tomorrow.'

Nikkolo clambered to his feet and hurried from the room, a bead of sweat dripping from his forehead. As he unlocked the door with shaking hands, he noticed his knees were knocking together.

CHAPTER FOUR

Saturday 17 January 2015

WHEN LAMONT MADE his way to the kitchen the next morning, Jenny had already left. Lamont ate the breakfast she'd prepared, thinking about their discussion the night before.

Lamont couldn't fathom needing a counsellor. He appreciated Jenny's situation, but he was in a different predicament. It was hard enough to even comprehend Jenny spilling his secrets and telling some stranger about his life, but he held those thoughts at bay. He trusted Jenny, even if he was lying about his intentions.

Lamont made a cup of coffee, switching his business brain on. He had meetings today, and the aim was simple; he would get the crew back in line and remind people why they respected the name *Teflon*.

* * *

K-Bar rolled out of bed, away from the warm body laying there. He padded to the shower, quickly washing and dressing. Returning to the bedroom, he was spraying aftershave when his phone vibrated. K-Bar was tempted for a moment to ignore it, but he couldn't.

'Yeah?' He put the phone on loudspeaker.

'Take me off speaker. I can tell,' Akeem's voice boomed on the other end. K-Bar laughed and did as ordered.

'What can I help you with?'

'Meeting spot. We're avoiding the usual place. Meet us at *Number Three.*'

'I'll see you there.' K-Bar dropped the phone on the bed.

'You're up early.'

K-Bar turned at the sound of the voice. The woman sat up; the sheet slipping and allowing him to stare at her breasts, which he did until she scowled.

'Early bird gets that worm, babe.'

'Was that your baby mother on the phone? That was you didn't want her on speaker?'

K-Bar frowned. 'Are you silly? Couldn't you hear the dude's voice on the phone at the beginning?'

'Whatever. Who was it then?'

'You're damn nosey. It was your bro, okay? We're meeting.'

Marika didn't reply, her brow furrowed. K-Bar wondered if the pair would ever make up. As long as he'd known Lamont, he'd always gone all out for his sister. The traitor Marrion from Manchester had ruined that though, poisoning Marika's mind and turning her against her brother.

He remembered the dark days after Lamont's shooting. K-Bar had survived on caffeine and adrenaline, tracking down anyone who had anything to do with Marrion. Marika had called in hysterics, screaming about Lamont murdering Marrion outside her house. She said she'd already called the police, but was shocked when she learned of Lamont's shooting.

Marika had visited Lamont in hospital after the shooting, but only when he was unconscious. K-Bar supported her, giving her money and making sure she and the kids were okay.

The first time they had slept together came a month later. They'd both been drinking away their anguish and ended up in bed. After avoiding one another out of awkwardness, they began having sex regularly.

They couldn't define what it was between them, but it felt right. K-

Bar had considered telling Lamont, but he didn't know how his boss would take it.

K-Bar wondered what Lamont wanted. They had spoken the day before, and he knew Lamont had been locked in meetings with Akeem, but he wasn't privy to the inner workings, and he wasn't sure he wanted to be.

K-Bar had been thrust into leadership after Lamont's shooting. The crew had been leaderless and when Shorty's arrest came to light, people began positioning themselves to make a move against the crew.

K-Bar had taken the reins, meeting with Saj to ensure the supply was consistent, then letting people know the crew was still strong. He had tried to deal with all the politics and drama the best way he could, but K-Bar wasn't Lamont. He didn't think the same way; he had street smarts, could hustle, survive, plan and execute murders, but he wasn't the analyst Lamont was.

This led to him getting the short end of a few deals and even losing his temper with people. One wannabe gangster ended up in hospital with a bullet in his leg after pissing off K-Bar. He'd had to pay and threaten the man into silence, but it was worth it.

Lamont was back now, and as much as K-Bar would miss the money he'd made, walking in Lamont's shoes wasn't worth it. It was too difficult.

* * *

'Nadia, how are we getting on with completing that order?'

'It's finished, Jen. The husband is picking it up this afternoon. His payment processed.'

Satisfied, Jenny deeply exhaled. Sipping her cold coffee, Jenny brushed her hair from her eyes, trying to focus on the ponderous report in front of her. She heard the shop door open, but didn't think much of it until she heard Nadia laughing. Smoothing her hair, Jenny headed to investigate.

Nadia was by a selection of hand-made vases, her shoulders shaking as she giggled. There was a man next to her, but Jenny couldn't tell who it was. Nadia shifted to the right, and then Jenny recognised him.

'Shorty?'

Shorty grinned at Jenny, but it didn't extend to his eyes.

'Hey, Jen. Your lovely worker here was just showing me around.'

'That's fine. Is everything okay though?' Jenny hadn't known Shorty knew where her shop was. Shorty hesitated. Nadia noticed and smiled at Jenny before excusing herself to the back.

'Did L say anything about Grace?'

Jenny had to think for a moment, remembering that Grace was Shorty's daughter. She recalled Lamont saying something about him having a son too, but that he didn't see him much.

'No, he didn't. Me and L haven't really spoken, to be honest,' Jenny admitted. She noticed Shorty sizing her up, likely wondering what the issue was. 'What's up with Grace?'

Shorty shook his head. 'She didn't want to see me when we went over there. She ran out of the room.'

Jenny saw the pain in Shorty's eyes and her heart went out to him. She'd never given children much thought, but it was obvious that Shorty's girl had hurt him.

'I'm sorry to hear that.'

'I can't blame her. I was away, and she had to hear all kinds of rubbish about me. She's probably confused. Anyway, I wanted to buy her some flowers to leave with her mum.'

Jenny smiled. 'That's a great idea. Do you have any arrangement in mind?'

'I was hoping you'd handle that for me; I just want summat colourful.'

When Jenny had prepared the flowers and given Shorty his change, the pair awkwardly stood.

'How come you and L haven't been talking?'

Jenny opened her mouth but Shorty spoke again.

'I'm not trying to intrude. Summat's not right with L, and I can't put my finger on it.'

Jenny took a deep breath.

'Honestly, I don't know,' she glanced at Shorty, and then the words tumbled from her mouth. 'He's not all there. Hasn't been in months. First, it was the shooting, and then he nearly killed himself trying to get better because he didn't want to look weak in front of me. He kept straining himself and his personal trainer tried to speak to him and get him to slow down, but Lamont sacked him. He didn't want to hear what the man was saying.

'I tried getting him to speak to a professional, but he won't. He just broods, drinks, and tries to be strong. I don't need him to be strong though. I need him to be the man I fell in love with.'

There was a long silence when Jenny finished talking, her face red with exertion. Shorty wiped his face, placing the bouquet on the counter.

'L's that kinda guy. Even when we were young, he never enjoyed looking weak. None of us did. L took it to another level though; he didn't want people to see him angry, or sad, or anything. It was mad when you look back at it, but it made him who he is. It's difficult to shake that, even when you love someone.'

Jenny's mouth was agape when Shorty finished. She'd only ever viewed him as a thug and was surprised he could be so eloquent. He'd hit the nail on the head regarding Lamont. He viewed the controlling of his emotions as the ultimate tool.

Jenny felt herself smiling, musing that Shorty of all people was helping her with her thoughts.

'What do I do then?'

Shorty shrugged.

'I know fuck all about relationships. I guess you just need to remember how to talk to him. L's not gonna like being given advice. He likes to be the one to tell other people what they should do. You two have summat though; we all saw it back in the day, and I saw it the other night. Things are just different. It's a different world for every-one, and I think we forget that.'

Jenny wrapped her arms around Shorty. She felt him stiffen, before he returned the hug and quickly let her go.

'Thank you for listening, Shorty, I really appreciate it.'

* * *

Lamont and Akeem approached the takeaway restaurant on Roundhay Road, parking on the side of the road and walking straight to the back. On the way, they had seen no less than three police cars — one an undercover vehicle, driving around Chapeltown. Lamont felt their world shrinking. The police had an agenda and he couldn't predict how it would turn out.

As Akeem drove by them, Lamont considered bowing out for good, only to be reminded of Akhan, and his ultimatum.

'I need you to do something for me,' Lamont said as they settled into the office space. The smell of fried food was overpowering, but they wouldn't be long.

'What is it?' Akeem asked.

'Find out everything about Akhan and his team. I don't care what it costs. Just be discreet.'

'Consider it done.'

* * *

Shorty felt uplifted after speaking with Jenny. She had been right, he realised. He just needed to give things time with Grace, get her used to being around him. It wouldn't be achieved overnight, but it was achievable, and he had a smile on his face at the thought.

Shorty was ready to leave the past behind. Men had tried to kill him. Shorty put them down and paid a massive price. It could have been worse, but he needed to make the most of the situation.

After leaving Jenny's, Shorty showered, changed his clothes, then drove to Amy's. Parking up, he clutched the bouquet and a card he'd written, and walked towards the door. He knocked lightly and when he didn't receive a reply, he left them on the doorstep and headed down the drive.

'Shorty?'

Amy stood in the doorway, wrinkling her nose in confusion as she picked up the card and flowers, sniffing them on instinct.

'I didn't think you were in.'

'I was in the kitchen washing up; I needed to dry my hands. Why are you here?'

'I just wanted to ask you to give those to Grace,' Shorty's tone was polite, his hands jammed into his pockets as Amy scrutinised him.

'Grace isn't here. She's staying at a friend's house.'

Shorty nodded. 'It's cool. I shouldn't have just turned up. I just wanted her to get the flowers. I'll talk to you later.' He turned to walk to his car.

'Do you want a drink?'

Shorty sat in the kitchen, holding a steaming mug of tea and watching Amy fuss around, moving plates and cutlery.

'I'm sorry for turning up like I did the other day.'

Amy didn't speak.

'I wanted to see Grace so bad that I didn't stop to consider it might hurt her. I just thought she'd jump into my arms and everything would be okay.'

Amy took a moment before she spoke.

'Grace was terrified when it all happened. She asked about you for days, and I didn't know what to tell her. We tried to keep the police away from her; my mum had her, Diana had her. We didn't want her exposed to any of it.

'And then you handed yourself in, and it was in the paper. We told Grace you'd gone away, and she cried. We couldn't console her. The last thing we wanted was for her to know you'd been locked up. She's smart though. She saw the paper, or someone showed it to her. After that, she stopped asking about you.'

Shorty hung his head, his heart aching at the thought he'd caused his daughter so much pain. He didn't regret the killings. They were necessary, and the people he'd put down had come to murder him. They hadn't shown him any mercy, and he'd paid the three of them back.

'Give it time, Shorty. Grace will want to see you again, she's just confused.'

Shorty smiled, remembering Jenny saying something similar.

'I will.'

Amy blew out a breath.

'I still think about that whole situation sometimes.'

'Which?'

'That summer. Everything that happened; Marcus, you, Lamont . . . I still can't believe someone tried to kill him. Even Timmy,' Amy rested her hand on Shorty's shoulder for a moment. 'I'm really sorry about your cousin. I can't even imagine what things were like then. I don't know anything about what you were doing, and I don't want to. Timmy was your family though, and I know you loved him.'

Shorty could have told Amy why Timmy was shot, but he didn't. It wasn't worth it.

'You're right; that summer was a complete mess, and I think people are still coming to terms with it. I'm still glad I clocked your boyfriend with the gun though. He caused me a lot of shit.'

'He's not my boyfriend,' Amy stared into her mug. 'Chris and I ended things shortly after you were remanded.'

Shorty hid a smile. He'd never liked Chris, even before Amy began a relationship with the man. He'd called the police when Shorty had tried saying goodbye to Grace. Shorty didn't know the ins and outs, but he knew threats were made to Chris to force him to change his story. Chris eventually stated he never saw Shorty with a gun and refused to press charges.

'Are you seeing anyone else?' Shorty heard himself ask. Amy again paused.

'I'm dating, if that's what you're asking. Nothing serious, nor is it anything I want to expose Grace to.'

Shorty nodded, swallowing down the lump in his throat. He and Amy hadn't been a thing for years, but the thought of her being with anyone else still jarred him. He understood though, at the same time. Too much had happened between them for anything to blossom, and where that fact would have made him angry two years ago, now Shorty focused instead on the bigger picture; earning back the love of his baby girl.

* * *

When K-Bar arrived at the meeting, he greeted both men and slid into a seat. Akeem remained standing near the door, ensuring he could see anyone approaching.

'What's up then?' K-Bar rubbed the back of his neck. He didn't know what the meeting was about, hoping Lamont hadn't found out about him and Marika. He eyed Akeem for a second. He knew the man had a reputation down in London and wondered if he could move fast enough to take him if it came to it.

Lamont stared at K-Bar unflinchingly, as if he knew exactly what was going through his mind. He cleared his throat.

'Things need to change.'

'Which things?'

'The streets. Things have been in limbo for a while, and it's messing everything up.'

K-Bar bit back the words on his tongue. Ever since he'd taken over, everyone had a sad story to sing about K-Bar and how he was perceived to be running things.

The money wasn't the same as it was when Lamont was in charge, but the times had changed. The police were everywhere, more people wanted to do their own thing, and K-Bar couldn't take things in any direction because he didn't know what the intentions were. He was a soldier who watched over drugs and people, then dealt with anyone who stepped out of line. K-Bar wasn't ready for the big seat and when it was thrust at him, he had to deal with things the best he could.

'I don't blame you, K. You were dealt a shitty hand after I was hurt, and you didn't know if I was even gonna survive. You were still loyal though, and you dealt with the people involved, and I'll never forget that. We need to establish ourselves all over again now.'

'How?' K-Bar leaned forward in his seat.

'First things first, I need to you find all the people still owing us money, and get it back. There's too much leeway, and it stops now. People are far too comfortable, and that's affecting our name.'

'I'm down with doing that, L, but I need more people. We're running low on solid personnel. People moved on and some got locked up. I'm working with what I've got but if you're wanting to make moves, it won't be enough.'

'Make a list of capable people, and we'll bring them into the team if they can fit. Darren Lyles, he's still down with us, isn't he?'

'Yeah,' replied K-Bar, wondering how Lamont even remembered

him. Darren had been a kid when Lamont was last running the crew, and Lamont wouldn't have known him if he'd tripped over him in the street.

'I've heard he's a solid worker; would you agree?'

'He's one of the best we've got, that's for damn sure.'

'Let's do more with him then. Switch things up, get the money in line, and let's show people why we're the best team in town.'

* * *

Lamont headed back towards Chapeltown after the meeting with K-Bar. The killer seemed more buoyant upon leaving, which Lamont viewed as a success. He knew how much hassle K-Bar had put up with, simply because he wasn't meant to be in charge. They would get the ball rolling, replenish their funds and armies, and spread themselves out as they always did.

With a stronger, more focused team, Akhan would grow complacent, and Lamont would be ready and waiting.

As Akeem approached the barbers, Lamont noted a large crowd of people, some looking angry, others upset. The flashing lights of several police vehicles dominated the road, and there were scores of brightly clad officers trying to maintain the peace.

'What's happened here?' Akeem murmured. Lamont didn't answer, his eyes searching the crowd. When they parked, Lamont hurried towards the barbers, searching for Trinidad. Lamont's stomach soared when he saw Trinidad standing in the middle of the barbers, consoling a woman Lamont didn't recognise. She was sobbing loudly, her head buried into Trinidad's bony chest.

'Trinidad, are you okay?' Lamont asked, Akeem at his back. Trinidad looked at Lamont, every bit his advanced years in that moment. He stared at Lamont, the weariness resonating.

'I'm fine, L.'

'What's happened then?'

'Marilyn's son,' Trinidad motioned to the sobbing woman, who didn't appear to have noticed Lamont and Akeem standing there. 'The police badly attacked her son, and now he's in hospital.'

CHAPTER FIVE

Thursday 12 February 2015

THE STREETS WERE tense after more details of the violent incident came to light.

The situation transpired when a fourteen-year-old boy named Diego was stopped by the police. Diego was allegedly known to them. When they stopped him, they tried to pat him down for drugs or money. Diego resisted, claiming he knew his rights. The police overpowered him, found nothing incriminating, and began hitting him, claiming he was struggling.

Locals hurried from their houses, some recording the incident, others shouting at the police to stop. More people arrived and the police quickly called for backup, several of the younger officers losing their heads and attempting to fight with the crowds. It was many hours later before they diffused the situation.

Even now, the tension continued to linger.

Lamont sat at the kitchen table, reading about the incident in the Evening Post. He'd heard most of the story from Trinidad, but didn't know Diego or which crew he was affiliated with.

Even after several weeks, there had been organised protests and demands for the police officers involved to be sacked. The videos of the police violence had gone viral on social media, and the OurHood

Initiative had been the most outspoken, spending money on advertising and highlighting the issue.

A man named Malcolm Powell in particular had been vehement in his demands for action. Lamont had read an article the man had penned on the *OurHood* website:

We had an incident recently, with police storming into our streets once again without impunity, doing what they wanted and attacking our people without the threat of punishment. It's not the first time, and unless steps are taken, it won't be the last.

Whatever Diego Northwood may or may not have done, at this time he was innocent. He knew his rights, and that police had no right to profile him while he was walking through his own streets and doing nothing wrong. Even after the police found no evidence of wrongdoing, they still assaulted him.

I'd like to ask those officers involved if they feared for their safety to the point it took multiple officers to overpower a skinny teenager? Does it seem acceptable, because to me, it is galling. When did the lines become so blurred that police brutality was viewed as acceptable? When did we begin to question why wrongdoing was done, rather than condemn it happening in the first place?

Let's go back to Diego, because I refuse to let this incident rest. There has been much talk about him being a local drug dealer. Whether or not he was selling drugs, he likely wasn't working for himself.

Chapeltown has been synonymous with drugs for years and the increased presence stems from tit-for-tat violence. This is not a rare issue, people! Over the past three years alone, there have been scores of murders, robberies, even public violent attacks, all stemming from drugs and illegal activity.

I'm not saying anything most of us are unaware of. The money these criminals make is astounding, and with that amount of money on the line, guns and knives are used to increase the share of the market. So many good people in Chapeltown and other areas are suffering, scared to speak up for fear of being targeted.

We've allowed it to happen for too long, and to all the above, I say no more.

Lamont had read the article several times. It was well written, and the community had absorbed the message. He'd even heard from Akeem that their workers were openly discussing the article. Closing the paper with a sigh, Lamont went to make himself another drink.

* * *

Jenny was handing a customer their change when the door opened and Malcolm Powell stepped in. His eyes twinkled as he surveyed Jenny, but he waited for her to finish serving the customer before he spoke.

'Nice to see you again.'

'You too, Malcolm. Did your mum like the flowers?'

Malcolm grinned. He had a presence, Jenny realised. He appeared well-built beneath the expensive clothing, and his eyes resonated with a power Jenny had only seen in a few people.

'She loved them. She asked me to pass along her compliments. I'm actually here to discuss a larger audience. I'm hosting an event in two week's time, and I'd like you to help set it up.'

Jenny hid her surprise. 'There are people who can do a better job helping with that than me.'

'We'll have to agree to disagree. I think you'll be perfect for the role, and the money is good.'

'What's the event?'

'It's a community meeting to discuss the violent attacks in Chapeltown, and what we can do to prevent them in the future.'

'I heard about that. The young kid that was beaten by the police?' Jenny recalled Lamont reading an article on the internet that called out the police for the attack. She had read a few lines, and they gripped her, but hadn't read the rest.

'Diego spent time in hospital and as of yet, nothing has been done. Me and my organisation will keep up the pressure and ensure that he's not forgotten, like so many other victims.'

'How?' Jenny found herself intrigued. Malcolm spoke with passion, and the situation clearly meant a lot to him. She wondered if he had a personal relationship with the boy involved.

'We organise protests against the police, but we also look into the root of the cause, which is the stigma of drugs and crime that has plagued Chapeltown and other surrounding areas for decades. It's an infection passed on from generation to generation.

'I grew up in Chapeltown, and when I was in school, I was ostracised because other parents didn't want their kids playing with me, because of where I came from.'

'That's disgusting,' said Jenny, openmouthed. She wondered if Lamont had experienced this. She recalled their conversation when he spoke of his upbringing, and why he started selling drugs. Malcolm's passion reminded her of him.

'How did you avoid the streets?'

'I wanted more. There's no magical tale. Growing up, I was beaten up a few times by the local kids, because they thought I was a victim. I learned to fight back with my mind and skills, and I applied those to education and furthering myself.'

'That's amazing.' Jenny had grown up with the best of everything, and the financial support to do whatever she wanted. She'd rarely considered the opposite end of the spectrum; the need to fight and survive every day. Lamont had even called her out on it when she'd tried to lecture him, reminding her that she grew up in comfort.

'Look, whether or not you want to be involved, come along to the meeting. It's in two day's time, and you can get a feel for how people are reacting to the situation. Check out the *OurHood* Initiative. The website is on here,' Malcolm handed a gold and black business card to Jenny, who pocketed it. 'Hopefully I'll see you there. Take care, Ms Campbell.'

Malcolm swept from the shop then, leaving a thoughtful Jenny in his wake.

* * *

Lamont drove to the barbershop after leaving his house. He parked around the corner from the barbers, nodding at a few local people. To his surprise, an older woman pulled her jacket tighter, giving him a foul look as she stalked past him.

Lamont frowned. Normally, she was full of smiles and always asked about his family. Shrugging it off, Lamont approached the barbers. The shutter was up, but the closed sign was still on the door. Curious, Lamont tried the handle, finding the door locked. Worried now, he quickly unlocked it and hurried inside.

Trinidad was sat in his chair, smoking a cigarette, staring at the walls. He didn't even look up when Lamont entered.

'Trinidad? Everything okay?'

'Haven't seen you around lately.' Trinidad ignored Lamont's question.

'I didn't want the publicity. People see me close to the scene of an incident, they start thinking I'm involved,' Lamont said darkly, thinking about the woman outside.

'You're part of Chapeltown, aren't you?' Trinidad asked. His blunt tone surprised Lamont.

'I grew up around here. You know that.'

'Then that means taking the good with the bad. You should have been here, giving people hope, showing that you care.'

'I care, Trinidad. Never assume otherwise. Chapeltown will always be in my heart, but for me, caring doesn't extend to protesting, or sitting around talking.'

'Take action then!' Trinidad roared, startling Lamont. 'Tell people what they should do, listen to their problems and their issues. Help them. Don't just sit around while your workers take their money. That's foul, Lamont and I expect better from you.'

'I don't know why you're coming at me like this. I didn't hurt that boy. He doesn't work for me and I didn't tell the police to target him. You're mad at me for keeping my head down? Do I have to remind you what happened to me?'

Trinidad's face softened. 'I remember what happened. It broke my heart. I care about you. I believe you're a force for good. Always have. You have a lot of power and if you just used it in the right way, you could help so many people.'

Lamont was growing tired of Trinidad's tone.

'I've helped many people. I've given people money, funded ventures. Most of the time there was nothing to show for it. I never made a big deal about it, so don't you dare talk about me not helping people.'

'Help now then. Chapeltown made you rich, so stand with us. There's a community meeting and if you're there; if you speak and show people you care about what happened to Diego, about what is happening to so many of our kids, it will go a long way.'

'That's not how I do things, and I need you to respect that.' Lamont had no intention of going to the meeting. It was being held by the *OurHood* Initiative, and he would not sit silently while they made him a scapegoat. There was too much going on at the moment to be distracted, and he needed to be *Teflon* now more than ever.

Trinidad shook his head, extinguishing Lamont's attempts to stand up for himself.

'I know that you're dealing with your own things. You were shot, but you have to realise that the community needs you! This community made you a millionaire, and don't give me that shit about *not being that rich*, because I know differently. I may not know everything, but I know that about you. Help them, the way we helped you sling that poison.'

Lamont clutched his water bottle tightly, his jaw clenched.

'Don't try to give me some speech about morality, Trinidad, because it will not fly. I've made money in Chapeltown, but I wasn't the first, and I won't be the last.

'You wanna talk about what I've gained from these streets? Well, let's talk about what I lost too. I lost my parents, and I was sent to live with a monster. I lost friends to pointless squabbles right here in these streets.

'You think the money makes all that welcome? You think it excuses the pain I feel when I cry at my parents graves, wishing I could give up this money just to see them again? I came from nothing. You know that. I told myself that I wouldn't bend and scrape. I was going to do whatever I could to get what I wanted. I love this community, but before I started doing what I did, who even gave a fuck?'

'And that gives you the right to be selfish?'

'Not at all! I have things going on at the moment that you couldn't even fathom. I'm trying my hardest to navigate through, for me, for everyone else. Do I want what's best for Chapeltown? Course I do. But, I need to fix me too.'

There was silence. The old friends glared. Trinidad again shook his head, disgusted.

'I never thought I would see you as a sellout, L. A man that cannot get behind his people, is no real man.'

Before Lamont could reply, there was a sharp tap on the front door. Both men looked, seeing a young woman and her son. She pointed at her son's nappy head with a shy smile. Trinidad shuffled over and let them in.

Lamont smiled, then hurried to his office, shutting the door behind him. He took several breaths, trying to calm down. He knew why Trinidad was angry, but to blame Lamont was out of line. Lamont wondered if there was more he could be doing. He downed the drink, dropping the empty bottle on the table, staring at his desk.

Maybe he needed to be more involved. It was just another thing on his list, he supposed.

Taking another deep breath, he reached for some papers, switched on some *Charles Mingus*, and tried to lose himself in the soothing music.

There was something about a white Mercedes that made K-Bar envision success. Whenever he saw one, he had to stare, reminded of his childhood. He saw many a player driving them back in the day, rich-for-a-day fools with whatever young girl they could coerce into the passenger seat.

K-Bar had grown up. Life had been good to him to where even now, stuck in traffic, he could still appreciate the beauty as he sat in one himself, *Cadell* pumping from the speaker.

'Do you have to play that so loud?' his passenger complained. She was a slight woman, brown skinned with poise and tired beauty. K-Bar ignored her, still looking at the car, an older version of his. The kid driving was younger, nodding his head to some track K-Bar had never heard of. He had his own girl in the car. Mixed raced with big breasts barely contained in a sleeveless top. She noticed K-Bar, glaring at first, then taking in the jewels and the ride.

Fiona noticed her looking at K-Bar and shook her head.

'If only she knew.'

'Knew what?' K-Bar sped up, driving down Harrogate Road.

'That it's not all it's cracked up to be. Riding with a thug.'

'What are you talking about?'

'Is that how you like them?' Fiona was still looking ahead.

'Are you gonna tell me what you're on about?'

'You don't know?'

'Forget it,' K-Bar sighed, turning the music up. Fiona immediately turned it down.

'Don't you know?'

'Why are we doing this shit? Is this why you wanted a lift? So you could talk in riddles?'

Fiona looked at him blankly. K-Bar hated when she did that. That was his thing. Giving people the vacuous stare to keep them unbalanced, unsure of his true intentions. He didn't like it being done to him. Fiona knew that.

'I asked for a lift because I'm going shopping for your child. You think I care if you want to sleep with that slag, or if you want to slip your dick into Marika Jones?'

So that was what this was all about. K-Bar resisted the urge to roll his eyes.

'Me and Marika are friends.'

'Me and Dwayne are friends too.'

K-Bar scowled. Fiona and Dwayne were as on and off as she and K-Bar were. Dwayne made a slick comment once when K-Bar had dropped off his child, so K-Bar had sought him out a few days later and broke his nose.

Dwayne had wanted to press charges but Fiona — with help from Grimer, talked him out of it. Still, it was a low shot, and they both knew it.

'Why isn't he giving you a lift then? No petrol for his shitty little ride?' K-Bar snapped back. Fiona's eyes narrowed.

'Just because he doesn't sell drugs like you—'

'Shut up about what you don't understand,' K-Bar snapped He was past the Arena now, approaching the Merrion Centre. He pulled to a stop outside the Yorkshire Bank, keeping his eyes out for overzealous traffic wardens.

'How don't I understand? Just remember, I was there in the beginning. I remember when you were a little tramp eating crisp sandwiches for dinner. I still loved you.'

K-Bar couldn't deny that. Fiona had loved him. Unconditionally. No matter what rumours she heard about he and Shorty, she'd stood by him. Until he got too deep into the game, and cheerful hailings of 'Franklin' and 'Kieron' turned into hushed whisperings of *Shorty* and *K-Bar*.

'Are you gonna pick me up?' Fiona paused with her hand on the door handle. K-Bar handed her a twenty-pound-note.

'Get a taxi if you can't get hold of me.'

Fiona shot him an evil look, but took the money. She slammed the door and stormed across the road towards the Merrion Centre back entrance.

K-Bar stared after her, then sped down the road. He was tired of Fiona making slick comments about his relationship with Marika. Turning onto North Street, he headed back to the Hood, passing a blue Vauxhall Corsa near Francis Street.

* * *

Lennox noted the silver Mercedes cruising by him. He was idled at the curb in the blue Corsa, siting with Nikkolo as they staked out a red-bricked terraced house. It had an attached brown garage, and some sparse plants in the tiny garden. Though similar to the other houses, they knew it to be one of Delroy William's spots. He had an office in the area, heavily guarded, where he conducted business.

This house was used to house large quantities of drugs, something Nikkolo wouldn't shut up about.

'There's gotta be kilo's in there. Delroy only deals in boxes. I bet there's at least fifty. We could have a team in and out of there before anyone realised, Len. Say the word and I'll—'

'Be quiet.'

Nikkolo stopped talking. Lennox hadn't raised his voice, nor did he need to. After a beat, Lennox spoke again.

'As I keep stating, we're building, piece by piece. Everything has a purpose, and a silly robbery isn't part of that. This isn't about drugs, and we're not drug dealers. Remember that fact, because I'm tired of reminding you.'

Nikkolo nodded, keeping his head down. The unpredictable energy in the car was unnerving, and he didn't want to say the wrong thing.

'This spot is a weak link. We target weak links. I want you to put a man on Winston Williams. I want to know everywhere he goes, and who he associates with. Don't engage him. Just watch and report. Understand?'

'Yeah, I understand. I'll take care of all of that,' said Nikkolo. He sighed before speaking again. 'Teflon's spending more time in Chapeltown. That was K-Bar who drove by in the Benz. What do you think they're planning?'

Lennox knew Lamont's intentions. He'd sat idle for too long, and the reputation of his firm was dwindling in certain circles. Lennox was sure that Lamont would now rectify that and get things straightened out. Nikkolo was waiting for an answer, so Lennox gave him one.

'I don't know.'

'What about Shorty? He bust case on that murder charge and he's out too. Is him being out gonna affect anything for us?' Nikkolo froze at the ugly expression on Lennox's face. It was the dark eyes that held an icy glint that worried him, and Nikkolo wondered if he had gone too far.

'I'm not worried about Shorty, and you shouldn't be either. If he involves himself, I'll break him.'

CHAPTER SIX

Monday 16 February 2015

LAMONT SULKED for a while after his argument with Trinidad. He saw where Trinidad was coming from, but didn't appreciate him trying to put all the blame on Lamont. Chapeltown's problems had been there long before Lamont was around, and they would be there long after he went.

The most irritating thing for Lamont was the guilt he felt. People were looking at him differently, and he didn't like it. The old woman avoiding his path was only the start. When he went to local takeaways, or to buy things from local shops, he felt the angry glares. He needed to shrug it off and focus.

Driving into the city centre, Lamont parked, took his ticket, and headed towards a little restaurant near Albion Street.

'Can I get you anything else, sir?'

Lamont shook his head, tucking into the grilled chicken breast. He didn't think much of it, but kept his expression neutral, letting the conversation swirl around him.

'What does Kingsford think then?' His business partner, a doughy, bespectacled man named Martin Fisher asked whilst shovelling fillet steak into his mouth and washing it down with wine. The third, a diminutive hook-nosed man with balding hair and a five thousand pound suit, picked at his salad, arranging it on the plate. He sipped a glass of sparkling water.

'He thinks nothing. He's out.'

'How can he be out, Levine? I'm not sure if you remember the talks from last year, but he was our best bloody friend then! What's changed?'

'The climate, Marty. I'm just your solicitor, but I've plenty of contacts in the Kingsford camp. People have been whispering in his ear for months about Lamont's background, and with his unfortunate incident, and all the publicity, he got cold feet.'

Lamont didn't even raise his head. Martin still believed they could salvage a deal but Lamont saw the writing on the wall. From a business standpoint, he was damaged goods.

After his recovery, Lamont had looked over some news coverage from the shooting. He'd received near national exposure, with talk relating to the fact the shooting was tied to drugs.

With Timmy dead at the scene, and eye-witness reports of multiple shots being fired, the press were desperate to unlock the secret of who exactly Lamont Jones was, and why people wanted to kill him.

Thanks in part to the machinations of Levine, the story died down, but the men Lamont was in business with had long memories.

'Commitments were made and I — rather, we, want to see something for it, Levine. I don't think that's too much to ask.'

'I'm only here to counsel and dispense advice. Reach out if you feel it's necessary. Don't be shocked if you receive a cold reception, however. That local initiative is making a lot of developers wary about treading into Chapeltown.'

Martin, now red-faced, stabbed his fork into the remains of his steak. The loud clinking sound had heads turning in their direction.

'L, I know you're not enjoying the chicken that much. How about a little input here?'

Lamont glanced at his business partner. 'No one is forcing the Kingsford's. If they want out, I say we leave them to it.'

'I agree,' said Levine.

'That means leaving the potential to make a lot of money on the table,' argued Martin.

'If we can finance the housing initiative, we'll have an excellent foundation. The Kingsford's are formidable, but they're not the only game in town.'

Martin shook his head, but didn't reply. He could be short-sighted, but Lamont knew he would have to accept that the Kingsford's had been spooked. He checked the time on his watch.

'I'm going to have to leave you two. I have another meeting.'

'With whom?' Martin demanded. Lamont stared him down, silently imploring Martin to relax.

'It's personal, not business. Levine, I'll call your office in a few days and we can iron out the details.' Shaking hands with both men, Lamont left two fifty-pound notes on the table, ignoring the protests he didn't need to. He always paid his own way.

* * *

Jenny and Kate met for drinks after work. They headed to a bar they remembered from years back and ordered cosmopolitans. The music was low and the bar still fairly empty, meaning they didn't struggle to hear one another.

'So, what's new?' Kate sipped her drink, looking around the room before bringing her dark eyes back to Jenny.

'One day at a time. Martha's helping a lot. She wants me to face the fact things won't be the same, and roll with the changes.'

'So, basically the same thing that I was saying all along?'

'Yeah, Kate, you're great and always right. Can we move on now?'

Kate grinned. Jenny stirred her drink with her finger, listening to the music for a few minutes.

'Do you know much about Chapeltown right now?'

'Are you going to be more specific?'

'That *OurHood* Initiative. Do you know much about it?'

Kate shook her head. 'I've heard of it, but not in much detail. Why?'

'I was speaking to the guy that runs it. He came into the shop a few times, and he was telling me about the work they do. He's really involved in fundraising and organising events to raise awareness. He does a lot of writing and blogging about social issues. I was checking out his website and some of the articles are insightful. You should read them . . .' Jenny trailed off when she saw the speculative look on Kate's face. She'd seen the look too many times before, and it never turned out well. 'What?'

'You said he's come into the shop a few times?'

'Customers do that sometimes, Kate. So what?'

'And you spoke with the guy enough that he told you all this information about an organisation and interested you enough to the point you checked out the website yourself?'

'Yes, Kate. Are you going to get to a point soon?'

'I'm just asking questions, Jen. Don't be so defensive. What does he look like?'

'Why? I don't know. He's tall. Really tall. Looks like he trains, and he's black with these really dark eyes . . .' Jenny again trailed off as Kate giggled.

'Sounds like you've got a bit of a crush there, Jen. You went from *don't know* to describing his build pretty quickly.'

'You asked, and I answered. Malcolm's an attractive guy, but it's not like that. He's just interesting. I enjoy interesting people. Must be why I'm friends with your crazy self.'

'You're friends with me because I liven you up and give your life meaning,' Kate stuck out her tongue. 'How's L?'

Jenny sighed. Lamont was a tricky subject. They were happy around one another, but there was an undercurrent of forced interaction they were both aware of. Sometimes the most difficult thing was to sit at the table, or at a restaurant and make conversation. It used to come so naturally, yet now they seemed to have to try much harder. Even before they became a couple, they could always talk and bounce off each other.

Jenny hoped that the disconnect didn't continue, because she loved Lamont, and wanted nothing more than to be happy with him.

'He's not one hundred percent. Hasn't been since it happened. I don't know how to help him, I mean, I've suggested he visit my coun-sellor but he won't even consider it.'

'You know what L's like. He just wants to deal with it all and get better by himself.' Kate's voice was full of warmth. She'd always had a soft spot for Lamont and had helped to get he and Jenny together. 'He nearly died though, and that's gonna change anyone, especially an alpha male like Lamont. When you think about it, you two haven't been together long, and you've dealt with so much. I guess you just need to wait it out, even if that's not what you want to hear.'

They sat in silence. Jenny contemplated Kate's words, grudgingly admitting that her friend was probably right. She and Lamont had been together for under two years, and they spent a year of that time dealing with Lamont's recovery. It wasn't enough time to get a full understanding of each other.

Jenny sensed when she began seeing Lamont that he was guarded, but of his own accord he eventually let her in on his pain and inner demons. Maybe he would do the same now if she remained supportive.

Feeling a sudden warmth in her stomach, Jenny smiled and finished her drink.

'Hey, smiley girl. Have you seen who's just come in?'

Jenny followed Kate's eye, surprised to see Marika Jones and a few of her friends. She hadn't seen Lamont's younger sister since they'd spent tear-filled nights sitting by Lamont's bedside in the hospital. Lamont had still been unconscious, loaded with powerful painkillers and recovering from surgery. By the time he was coherent, Marika had stopped coming.

'Should I speak to her?'

'Yeah, go say hi. I'll get more drinks.'

Jenny slid to her feet and walked over to Marika, who was in conversation with one of her friends. Jenny didn't recognise the woman, but she was hard-faced and looked ready to break a chair over someone's head. She eyeballed Jenny and when Marika noticed, she turned, noticing Jenny. They stood awkwardly for a second before Jenny found her words.

'Hey, Marika.'

'It's been a while, Jen. Everything good?'

Remembering the tight, skimpy outfit Marika had worn when Jenny saw her at carnival two years ago, her new outfit was almost prudish in comparison. She wore a blue blouse and grey jeans with heels, her sparse makeup allowing her natural beauty to shine through. It was weird being around a family member of Lamont's that looked so much like him. The eyes were similar, the facial features, the way both could stare through a person. Their personalities were different though.

'Yeah, just went for a drink after work with my girl. Is everything okay with you?'

'I work part time now, which I'm kinda enjoying. It's good to get out and be around people sometimes. How's L?'

It was a loaded question. Marika hadn't spoken to her brother since before the shooting. Things had been said during heated moments that both struggled to recall. Lamont had implied that Marika was a leech, relying on him financially because she didn't want to do anything for herself.

Marika had let herself be manipulated by her ex-partner Marrion into thinking Lamont had tried to kill her. Even after all this time, they hadn't found their way back to one another.

Jenny knew that Lamont missed his sister, and especially his niece and nephew, but he didn't say much about it.

'He's good.'

Marika's smile was tight and didn't extend to her eyes. 'I'm glad he's doing well.'

Jenny thought for a second and came to a decision.

'Would you be open to making peace with him?'

Marika hung her head, 'I don't think it'll be that easy. The things we did to each other, you can't really come back from. I don't know if there's anyway back,' she smiled now. 'Take my number though, and me and you can talk. I should make a better effort to get to know my sister-in-law.'

* * *

Darren yawned as he sat in the backroom of a hangout spot, watching his runners playing on the Playstation. The stench of weed hung heavily in the air mingled with the smell of fried chicken and dumplings.

'D?'

Darren glanced around, startled at hearing his name. One of the youths handed him a phone, his brow furrowed.

'Yeah?' Darren held the phone loosely to his ear.

'Meet me outside in half an hour.'

Recognising K-Bar's voice, Darren hung up, hoping he hadn't done anything wrong.

* * *

'You weren't waiting long were you?' K-Bar asked. He and Darren were in a rented black Alfa Romeo. K-Bar wore a black bomber jacket over some dark jeans and a pair of black boots. His dreads spilled freely down his back, his eyes darting around the streets, always on the lookout.

'Nah,' lied Darren. K-Bar was an hour late, but it would be pointless bringing it up.

'Meeting ran on longer, but I think you'll like what you're hearing.'

'Are we talking here?' Darren gestured to the car. K-Bar cocked his head and smirked.

'Nah, we're going to a spot.'

Darren asked no further questions, listening to K-Bar speak about random Hood politics until they pulled up to a spot in Seacroft that Darren had visited once before. It was a ramshackle red-bricked terraced house crumbling stone steps leading up to a pale door. They headed inside, slouching into chairs in the makeshift kitchen.

'First up, here you go,' K-Bar reached into his pocket, slapping a wad of notes on the kitchen table. 'Enjoy.'

Wordlessly, Darren scooped up the money, thumbing through the twenty-pound notes with an awestruck look on his face.

'What's this for?'

'People have been noticing the work you're doing on the roads, so keep it up.'

Darren shoved the money into his pocket. 'Thank you.'

'Teflon sees summat in you. We all do. He wants you to be a big part of what happens next.'

'What's gonna happen next?'

K-Bar scratched his head. 'You know shit's been funny since Teflon's shooting, right?'

Darren did. The shooting of their leader, along with the murders of Marcus, Chink and Timmy had cast a negative spotlight on a crew known for keeping things low-key. Their inner conflicts had been thrust out into the open, leading to a notoriety that made it difficult to do business. They persevered, but there had been little growth and the crew were surviving rather than thriving.

'Yeah, a few people have noticed.'

'Course they have. People think we're weak, plus the Feds are just waiting for us to mess up. Fact is though, Teflon is back.'

Darren frowned. 'I thought he was leaving.'

'Who told you that?' K-Bar flinched.

'Heard it in passing.'

K-Bar sized up Darren.

'Anyway, he's recovered, and he wants a push on the streets. We need to re-establish ourselves and to do that, we need you in another position.'

'Which position?'

'For now, you're only gonna report to me. Your money goes up, obviously. You'll meet a few new people and you'll keep everything you hear to yourself. Cool?'

'Course it's cool.' Darren fought to keep the grin from his face. He sensed he wasn't being told the full story, but would not turn down more money or responsibility.

* * *

Lennox Thompson sat in the kitchen of one of his spots, drinking coffee and writing in a battered notebook. He heard the front door unlock and footsteps heading toward him. Checking his gun was within reach, Lennox resumed writing as Nikkolo bounced into the kitchen.

'What you doing, boss? You writing bars or something?' He chuckled. Lennox laughed.

'Yeah, I'm trying to start a career as a Grime MC. Can you imagine me up on stage with *Kano?*'

The pair laughed. Lennox sipped his drink and motioned for Nikkolo to sit.

'Is everything in place?'

Nikkolo nodded. Lennox knew Nikkolo wasn't on board with the plan, but he wouldn't dare to speak his mind on it.

'The police are there now. They got our little tip-off, and they raided the spot.'

'Any word on what they took?' Lennox had ordered Nikkolo to leak the address of Delroy's stash house, wanting to weaken Delroy's fledging power base.

'Only rumours from people who were hanging around, but there were boxes and boxes in there, and about twenty kilo's of weed. They had some fancy equipment to hide the smell. Couple' guns too. People are still talking about it.'

'Good. Make sure our people are discreetly out there talking it up too. I want everyone to see Delroy Williams for the fat, worthless weakling that he is.'

'I'll take care of everything.'

Satisfied, Lennox went back to writing his notes as Nikkolo poured a shot of brandy.

* * *

Lamont led K-Bar into his study and poured him a drink. They toasted.

'Surprised you didn't want to meet at the barbers,' said K-Bar, noticing Lamont's expression darken for a second.

'It's good to switch it up. This room is well-guarded. Akeem made sure of it.'

'You trust him, don't you?' K-Bar remarked.

'I trust both of you. You wouldn't be here otherwise. There aren't many people that know where I live.'

'Mostly women I'm guessing,' quipped K-Bar. They both laughed, which seemed to take some tension out of the room. K-Bar knew Lamont was right. It had been years since K-Bar had been to any of Lamont's houses. The fact K-Bar was here was a sign things were changing.

'Did you put that list together?'

K-Bar handed a crumpled piece of paper to Lamont.

'Are these guys available?'

'I've put out feelers. They're all willing to work for the right money. Jamal and Rudy in particular will get shit done. They knew Marcus back in the day and had good things to say about him.'

'Bring them all in, piece-by-piece, and put them to work. What about the other thing?'

'We have collected Most of the money you were owed. A couple people were funny about paying. Akeem went to speak to them and the money popped up like magic. A few others arranged payment plans as they didn't have the money in full, so we'll make interest off that.'

Lamont smirked. Akeem had already informed him about those people.

'Great.'

K-Bar shook his head. 'There's one little problem.'

Which is?

'Big-Kev is holding out. He's ducking out of paying, trying to avoid meetings, fronting about paying later.'

'What does he owe?' Lamont scratched his chin.

'Fifteen bags,' K-Bar replied, though he was aware Lamont already knew the amount.

'It's not a massive amount, but definitely enough that people may pay attention.'

'Agreed. You wanna meet with him, see if you can convince him to pay?'

Lamont finished his drink, pouring himself another.

'Kev is the one who shot up Rika's house, right?'

K-Bar nodded. Big-Kev had links in Manchester and had loaned Marrion a large amount of money. Marrion then skipped town and ducked paying Kev back. After a few warnings, Kev struck, shooting up Marika's house, then murdering Marrion a short while later.

Lamont's expression became cold, taking K-Bar by surprise.

'Meet with Akeem, and you two sort the situation between yourselves. Send a message and let people know that we're back in the game.'

CHAPTER SEVEN

Tuesday 17 February 2015

'I DON'T THINK it'll hurt him.'

Darren Lyles sat in the stash spot with Maka, watching a few of the young workers bagging drugs. They were deep in conversation about the raid at Delroy's spot.

'Del's been doing this for years, and I heard the police got like twenty boxes at the most. That can't hurt Delroy,' he kept saying. Maka was more reserved. He had been in the game far longer than Darren and read between the lines with certain situations.

'You think so?'

'Yeah. Twenty's a minor when you've got money like he must have.'

Maka shook his head. 'Lesson number one: never assume the other man has money. You don't need to count anyone's pockets but your own. I'm telling you as a man that's been around, that loss will hurt Delroy a lot. There's gonna be a lot of restructuring behind the scenes. It's the same thing K had to do when Tef was down.'

'What are you lot on about?'

K-Bar entered the spot and greeted the pair, ignoring the workers.

'Just the Delroy thing. Is everything good?'

'I need to talk to you.'

Maka and K-Bar headed to the garden. The cold was biting to the point both men wore large winter coats, hoping that the spate of bad weather subsided soon.

'What's going on then?'

'You hear about Kev?' K-Bar got straight to the point.

'I heard he was ducking L.'

'Well, now he's gotta go. Permanently.'

'For real?' Maka's eyes widened.

'Tef is back, bro. He wants people to know they can't take liberties.'

'That's a big move for him though. Shorty used to have to talk him into hitting people. Now he's ordering it himself.'

'Things change,' K-Bar shrugged. 'I'll handle the hit, but I want you to do the driving. Cool?'

'Let me know when. What about the slotting crews in Manny? Didn't Kev use one of those to shoot up Marika's house?'

K-Bar nodded. 'They're not gonna get involved. They're saying it's a personal issue.'

Maka scratched his chin. 'Tef must have given them something to make them step aside.'

'I doubt it was a small amount either. He's gonna have us back on top though.'

* * *

Lamont sat in his study, leafing through a file Akeem had given him. Akeem stood in the corner, waiting for Lamont to finish. Lamont took his time and when he finished, he placed the file in his drawer and locked it.

'Those are the people you could locate?'

Akeem nodded. 'Akhan is a ghost. I couldn't find an address without exposing what I was doing. He stopped using the office on Hares Avenue over a year ago. Another family appears to be staying there now, and I don't know what connection they have to him. It could be family, or random renters. It's hard to get a fix.

'His organisation is all over the place, which makes them harder to track. Saj was easy enough to tail, and through him, my people were able to find some others.'

'Looks like mostly low-level guys in that folder, so we've either grossly exaggerated how powerful Akhan is . . .'

'Or, he keeps his inner circle close to his chest,' Akeem was silent for a moment before speaking again. 'What's the move here? Akhan is blackmailing you, but you decided to keep selling drugs, regardless. What's the endgame?'

Lamont thought for a moment before he replied, appreciating the question Akeem had posed to him. When Vincent suggested Akeem come and work for him, Lamont had quickly taken to Akeem's way of viewing things. He kept his own counsel and spoke when necessary.

Lamont appreciated those traits. He'd been open with Akeem about Akhan's threats. Akeem listened, then asked what Lamont wanted him to do.

'I can't let Akhan have an edge. If he thinks he has me over a barrel, he'll take more liberties. It's how men in his position work.'

'And are you willing to risk the high quality drug supply to usurp this man?'

Lamont rubbed his eyes.

'Let's deal with one thing at a time.'

* * *

Jenny entered a coffee shop in the city centre and waited in the queue. After ordering a drink, she headed upstairs and saw the person she'd come to see. Taking a deep breath, she strolled over and slid into a seat opposite.

'When you asked for my number, I didn't think you'd use it,' she said to the person, who smirked over the rim of their own cup.

'I just thought we should talk. A loud bar in the middle of town wasn't the best place.'

Jenny nodded. 'It always tickles me to enter these coffee shops. My first date with L was in one, believe it or not.'

'I'd have expected him to pull out all the stops.' Marika laughed.

'I did too, but it was nice. Awkward at first. You know how it is when you don't quite have the right back-and-forth yet. Didn't help that every woman that passed us kept staring like they wanted to steal him.'

Marika laughed again. 'We have good genes in my family.' she ran a hand through her silky hair.

'Things got better from there though,' Jenny finished. Marika watched her.

'How is he?'

'Like I said, he's getting there. L doesn't like to let people in. He just bottles it up and hopes it will go away.'

'I think he learned that when we were younger. Has he told you about his upbringing?'

'He's mentioned your Aunt if that's what you mean.'

'I didn't see what it was he saw.' Marika took another sip.

'What do you mean?'

'Ever since me and L stopped talking, I've spent more time around Auntie, and she'll always find a way to bring up L; how horrible he is. How he doesn't take care of family. It's bullshit, because L always helped me out, and he helped other family members too. L's paid for funerals over the years, family holidays, given people money when they were sick.

'I think Auntie's issue is that L doesn't give *her* any money. He doesn't acknowledge her, and the family are all aware of it. I guess we were all avoiding the question staring at all of us.'

'Which is?'

'Why did L hate Auntie so much? L's not a bad guy. He's no angel, but still. He was a top student, never put a step wrong, did all the housework and cooking without complaint. How can you do all of that and still have your Guardian hate you?'

'Did you ever see it?'

Marika looked away a moment. 'I saw little things. Beatings here and there. She was always going on about L's appearance, but she bought him rubbish clothing. Mine was a little better, but she used to say that was because I was younger and my clothes were cheaper. I used to try to get him in trouble all the time.' Marika looked ashamed.

'Kids do that though.'

'It was worse. Auntie didn't need much provocation to punish

Lamont, and he just took it. He never stopped loving me, never mistreated me. I was his closest family member, and I revelled in it, even as we got older. I could always count on him for money, and my kids loved him. Still do.

'When we argued after Marcus was killed though, and he called me a leech and said all those horrible things, it broke me. He was right though; I took and took, and I definitely learned it from Auntie.'

'Is that why you stayed with Marrion?'

Marika wiped her eyes, her voice quiet now. 'He wanted to look after me.'

Jenny waited for Marika to continue.

'Marrion came out of nowhere and he was strong, and he dressed and talked nice. I guess I hoped I'd found someone I could build with; someone who would motivate me to do something with my life. He was a hustler who'd come up from nothing, just like my brother, and I imagined them working closely together and everyone making more money. Marrion had different goals though, and his agenda was nowhere near mine.'

'In what sense?'

Marika took a deep breath. 'Marrion was behind the shooting.'

Instantly, Jenny's blood ran cold, as her hands began shaking. She remembered the man who had screamed for Timmy to pull the trigger, before grabbing the weapon and doing it himself.

'Why?' She whispered after a moment.

'He wanted it all, and L was in the way.'

'L was walking away from the life though; surely he knew that?'

Marika shrugged. 'I honestly don't know. Marrion lied to me and said L was behind the shooting at my house.'

Jenny breathed deeply, trying to rid herself of the memories. Marika clutched Jenny's trembling hand. It was just for a moment, but it calmed Jenny.

'What shooting?'

'Turns out Marrion owed some people. They came looking for him and shot up my house with me and the kids in there. Luckily, no one was hurt.'

'How does this coincide with Marrion trying to kill L?'

'Marrion warned me that L would be taken out. I told him that L was my brother. I said that if Marrion loved me, then he would stop it from happening.'

'And then what happened?'

'He stormed out, and he was shot. Right outside the house. I heard about L's shooting afterwards, when the police finished questioning me.'

'That's why you came to the hospital . . .' Jenny realised. Marika nodded.

'Look after my brother, Jen. He's not as tough as he wants you to believe, and he needs you. Just help him get where he needs to get.'

The two women from opposite ends of the spectrum surveyed one another for a long moment. Jenny broke the silence.

'I will if he lets me.'

* * *

That night, Lamont and Jenny hosted Shorty at home. It had surprised Shorty to get the invitation. He had seen little of Lamont lately, focusing on catching up with old faces and getting the lay of the land.

Youngsters dominated the roads, with many of Shorty's age group leaving Chapeltown behind, or going legal and working jobs. It was a culture shock.

Shorty vaguely remembered the rise of social media just before he got locked up, but now all he seemed to see were youngsters on their phones. Even Darren and Shadow had posed for a photo the last time he'd seen them, claiming the ladies loved it. They'd tried getting Shorty to take one with them, but he had refused.

Shorty hadn't broached the conversation with Lamont about getting started again. He was still collecting money, but other than giving some to Amy, hadn't done much with it. He'd purchased some new clothing. Having been locked up during the summer, a lot of his clothing was unsuitable.

Back in the day Shorty would have blown the lot, then hustled up more, but he was wary of the police now, and didn't know how to get in contact with a lot of his independent links. He would need to take things slowly.

Jenny and Shorty spoke as Lamont prepared the food in the kitchen. Jenny offered to help, but Lamont refused.

They kept the conversation light, speaking about her business, his daughter, and the incident in Chapeltown still dominating the local news. Jenny didn't know much about the situation, but was open to the thought of more scrutiny being given to police officers.

They spoke about the *OurHood* Initiative, and Shorty was surprised when Jenny mentioned Malcolm Powell, whom Shorty knew was the driving force behind a lot of the work the group was doing.

When Shorty pressed, Jenny said he was a customer she'd met recently, leaving Shorty to wonder if she was being truthful.

Soon, they sat at the table consuming Lamont's food. He'd made grilled steak, baby potatoes with asparagus and green beans.

'I gotta say, fam, I forgot you could cook like this,' Shorty admitted, a massive grin on his face as he tore into the food.

'I like to cook once or twice a week at least, maybe more if Jen's tired. It's therapeutic.'

Jenny sent him a wide smile which he returned, squeezing her hand.

Shorty watched the pair, happy that they seemed to be getting along. It was the most time he'd seen them spend together since his release, and he recalled how high-strung Jenny was when he'd gone to buy the flowers. Lamont seemed more relaxed now, more like the old *L*.

'Have you two ever told me how you met?' Jenny asked. By now they had finished eating and were in the living room sipping drinks. Lamont disappeared to complete the washing up, then sat next to Jenny afterward. Shorty and Lamont laughed.

'How many years ago was that?' Shorty asked.

'Thirty, thirty-one at least. We were in Reception,' Lamont took over the story. 'I was nervous, trying to avoid everyone around me.'

'I was a little shit,' Shorty said. 'I was bigger than everyone else in the class, and I didn't know how to sit still. I remember seeing L sitting there, trying to read some little kiddie book, and I just started hanging around him. Stayed like that for a few years. People used to trouble him because he was quiet, and I fought them off.' Shorty paused, reminiscing. 'It was just like that, I guess. We lived close to each other, and I guess I liked that he was quiet. I didn't want anyone else getting more attention than me.'

Jenny smiled. The pair continued to tell stories of things they had done as kids. Jenny noticed the stories were all light-hearted and innocent, for which she was thankful. The last thing she wanted was to hear more stories of Lamont's criminal days.

Jenny was tempted to mention the meeting with Marika, but didn't know how. She stayed quiet and sipped her wine.

When Jenny went to bed, Lamont and Shorty retreated to his study, taking their glasses and a bottle of brandy with them. Lamont topped up their glasses, and the old friends toasted in silence.

'It was a good night. We'll have to do this more often,' Lamont started. 'You should bring a girl next time. You got anyone in mind?'

'Amy?' Shorty joked. Lamont grinned.

'They got along when they met. Amy came to visit me, and she and Jenny were talking. I think Jenny met Grace after that, but you know what she's like.'

Shorty grinned. Grace was wary around new people, something he was sure she had picked up from him.

'Amy's dating now, and I don't think we could ever go back to the way things were. I met a girl after I got out of prison, but that was just a one-night thing. I don't even know her name.'

'Typical you then. What about Kimberley?'

Shorty scowled. He and Kimberley had been on and off for years. The last time they had been together was the Bank Holiday weekend when Marcus died. Kimberley had gotten into an altercation with some girls, and Shorty had defended her. They slept together the same weekend, but in the aftermath of the shootings, Shorty had forgotten all about her until he was locked up. He'd tried reaching out and even wrote to her, but she never responded.

'I'd have to try tracking her down, see what's going on. She ducked me when I was in prison, but I could always get her to slip up one-on-one.'

The pair laughed, remembering some of the altercations Shorty and Kimberley had in the past.

'It really is good to see you out, Shorty. We haven't spoken much, but I never liked the thought of my best friend rotting behind bars. If shit hadn't gone down how it had . . . you wouldn't have stayed in so long.'

Shorty nodded, touched by the emotion in his friend's voice.

'How are you doing though? I bet it's dodgy trying to get used to everything.'

'The entire world has changed. There's so many people I remember from before I got locked up, and they're not even around anymore. There's people fighting each other who I'd never have expected. Even this *OurHood* shit, it's mad. Jen was telling me earlier that she knows the man behind it. Some dude called Malcolm. I'm assuming you do too.'

'I've never met him,' Lamont replied, his expression hardening. Shorty blinked and Lamont's face was blank again.

'Think he must have bought some flowers or something. Is that initiative affecting business?'

'Everything is affecting business at the moment. I'm taking steps to get things in order though. It won't happen overnight, but it's necessary.'

'About that,' Shorty started. 'Me and you need to talk, L.'

Lamont sipped his drink, topping himself up. He motioned to the bottle, but Shorty shook his head.

'I thought we were talking?'

'I want back in. Put me on so I can start hustling again.'

Lamont didn't reply straight away. The silence stretched, Lamont holding his glass and staring off into space. The longer the silence, the more antsy Shorty grew.

'Did you hear me, L?'

'I think you should stay under the radar for now. The police might still be watching you, and the last thing we need is to give them a reason to look too closely.'

'I know the game. I know how to hustle low key. The money is running low, and I need to step up so I can fund my kids. You know that.'

Lamont smiled. 'Shorty, you're my brother, and you never have to worry about money. I've more than got you covered with everything you need.'

Shorty felt his hands twitching as he tightened his grip on the glass

'Listen, I'm not Rika. I don't need a handout. I can earn.'

'It's not a handout. I want to help you, and I don't want you getting yourself in any trouble.'

'Then you need to have some fucking faith in me. It's a handout if you wanna keep giving me money and not have me work for it.'

'Do you not understand where I'm coming from, Shorty? You just got released from a murder charge. You weren't worrying about money when I was paying my solicitors small fortunes to defend you.'

'What does that have to do with anything?'

Lamont rubbed his face, his jaw tight.

'It means that if you hadn't been so foolish to get yourself arrested, I wouldn't have needed to protect you. You should have left the Manchester situation alone. I told you to be careful, but you didn't listen. You never do, and that's why I have to be careful before I put you back in.'

Shorty let out a harsh laugh. 'Protect me? What could you protect me from? You couldn't even protect yourself when you got dropped in the street like a coward!'

The tense silence that followed Shorty's words was palpable, both men scowling. After a while, the ringing of Lamont's phone punctuated the silence. He answered curtly, his expression changing as the person on the other end spoke.

'I'm on my way.' He hung up and leapt to his feet.

'What's happened?' Shorty asked. Lamont rubbed his eyes as he drained his drink.

'It's K-Bar. We need to call Akeem and go. Now.'

CHAPTER EIGHT

Wednesday 25 February 2015

K-Bar winced, gritting his teeth, his hand wrapped around a bottle of the worst-tasting whiskey he'd ever tried. He wasn't in a situation to be picky, resisting the urge to touch the bandages that swathed his upper body. He closed his eyes as footsteps bounded up the stairs of the safe house. K-Bar resisted the urge to go for the gun under his pillow as Lamont burst in, followed by Shorty. Both froze when they saw K-Bar's condition.

'What the hell happened?' Lamont found his voice first. K-Bar sighed.

'Things were dicey.'

'Dicey how?'

K-Bar took a swig of the whiskey, making another face.

* * *

K-Bar watched the surroundings from the passenger seat of the Ford Focus, wearing his all-black killing gear. In the driver's seat, Maka slouched, devouring a packet of crisps as he stared at his phone. The loud chewing was irritating K-Bar, but he shut it out. He needed to be in the zone.

They had been tracking Kev for days, eventually tailing him to a spot near Armley. They were parked nearby, monitoring the house.

K-Bar hadn't fired his gun in a while and was trying to slip into his mode of focus. The last time, he'd gotten into an argument a few months back with a cocky crew of knuckleheads. They were causing trouble, throwing their weight around, trying to make a name for themselves.

K-Bar had set up a meeting to get them to calm down. When the crew took his soft words and tone as weakness, they flexed and began threatening him. K-Bar had cleared his gun and shot the loudest one in the leg. While he was rolling around on the floor, K-Bar aimed the gun at the others, who now looked terri-fied. Eventually he'd called someone to see to the man he'd shot, warning all of them about the dangers of running their mouths.

When Lamont found out, he was furious with K-Bar, saying it made them look weak and out of control. He told K-Bar that if he was going to run things, he needed to learn to keep his temper.

Annoyed, K-Bar had taken the rebuke in sullen silence. The word was out though, and his actions had thrown the crew under a spotlight.

If K-Bar was honest, it was likely part of the reason people were stepping away from dealing with their crew.

K-Bar took a deep breath.

'Oi, put the phone away and make sure you're ready, okay?'

Maka nodded, wiping his mouth and slipping the phone into the pocket of his combat trousers.

'Make sure you're on point. If anything goes wrong, make sure you finish the job and get clear.'

'Got it, K. I know the drill.'

It was after ten when Big-Kev lumbered from the house. He was a moun-tain of a man, standing well over six-feet-tall with the weight to match. Even from his vantage point, K-Bar noticed his chins wobbling as he struggled to move forward. He had to be at least twenty stone.

'Right then, show time.'

K-Bar slid from the car. Kev was paying little attention as his accomplice rambled on about something, waving the keys in his hand excitedly as the Range Rover clicked.

K-Bar's black boots clumped over the frosted ground, making little noise. He raised the gun when he was close by, satisfied neither man had even noticed him. His finger caressed the trigger as Kev stopped short.

'Shit, forgot my—'

K-Bar's gun whistled, silencing the rest of Kev's words. His hesitation saved his life, K-Bar aiming for where he expected the man to be. The bullet whizzed past them as his accomplice yelled. Kev trudged back towards the house as his accomplice reached for something, but K-Bar was far quicker, a bullet lodging into the man's chest as he flew backwards.

K-Bar hurried after Kev, the large man already out of breath after a few yards. Three shots slumped into his back and Kev fell face-first to the ground with a grunt. K-Bar put his gun to Kev's head and pulled the trigger, finishing the job.

As he turned to find Maka, he was stunned to see a flash of metal, then felt the searing pain of the knife slashing against his chest. The accomplice he'd shot bore down on K-Bar, holding the blooded knife, his face contorted with pain. K-Bar could see the red patch on the man's sweater, but it didn't seem to hold him back. K-Bar tumbled over Kev's dead body and fell to the floor, the gun slipping from his hand. The accomplice raised the knife to finish the job, and K-Bar cursed himself for not making sure the man was dead.

Three shots rang out, and now the man was lurching towards him, the knife tumbling from his hand. K-Bar leapt to his feet, fumbling for the gun as Maka dropped his own smoking weapon.

'Come, man; we need to go!'

Maka helped K-Bar, and they stumbled towards the car.

* * *

'Why didn't you finish him in the house?' Lamont's eyes seared with fury.

'We didn't know how many people were in there. We figured we'd get him when he came out. It would have worked if he hadn't hesitated.'

'You should have made sure his guy was dead the first time, K,' said Shorty. 'You know to always clean your plate. You nearly got finished because you were sloppy.'

'I know, Shorty. I don't need to hear this shit right now though. My fucking chest is killing, and I just wanna drink until the pain goes away.'

'Did anyone see you?' Lamont asked.

'I don't know. I was too busy trying not to die,' snapped K-Bar. Lamont's expression softened.

'Fair enough. At least he's dead. That's one thing at least. I'll send word to the Manchester links that he's gone. Did you leave any blood at the scene?'

'I honestly don't know. There was no time to call anyone to clean up, but the Fed's won't be able to prove it's me, anyway. It was dark, and we burnt out the car we used. It's cool.'

Lamont nodded, sharing a look with Shorty.

'I'm gonna send Akeem to see if there's any possibility of a cleanup, but I doubt it at this stage. For now, lie low and speak to no one. I'll send word when it's cool to resurface.' Lamont swept from the room, with Shorty following.

'I expected better from K,' Lamont admitted, as they climbed into the ride. Akeem motored away.

'These things happen, L. He did the job regardless. If anything pops off, K-Bar will ride it. He's not gonna roll on us.'

Lamont shrugged, thankful that K-Bar's mission had distracted Shorty from their argument. He wasn't ready to let his friend back into the fold yet, but it was growing harder to keep him at bay. Lamont needed to sit down, think, and reinforce his next move.

* * *

Detective Inspector Rigby slumped, wiping tired eyes as he pored over a succession of papers on his cramped desk. It was late in the office, and very few were still working, other than the night shift.

Sipping his stone-cold coffee, he ran a hand through his greying hair as someone approached.

'Figured I'd find you here.' Murphy took a seat next to Rigby and glanced at the paperwork. 'This couldn't wait until tomorrow?'

'There was nothing to go home to.' Rigby shrugged. Murphy grinned, showing yellow teeth.

'Guess I'm staying here with you then. What do you have?'

'This Kev thing.'

'What about it?' Murphy had been placed on the case of the dead criminal, with Rigby and a few others. The name was one they knew. Big-Kev was a nasty man known for throwing his weight around and taking liberties with people. Murphy wasn't enthused about having to catch his killer, but it was better than the cases they'd had recently.

'It stinks, to be honest.'

'He was a scumbag everyone hated. Course it stinks,' Murphy pointed out.

'That's my point; everyone hated him, but no one ever made a move. He was a big deal, and he had a lot of connections, so no one could touch him. What changed?'

'I dunno, Rig. I don't see why you think it's so important.'

Rigby shook his head. James Murphy didn't get it. He had lost that desire for police work two marriages ago. Rigby still believed in the work they did, even in a sparse department, almost threadbare from the redundancies and recent cutbacks.

'Because it's an important part in everything that's happened recently. We've seen more murders in the past four years than the last ten years before that. Doesn't that shock you? Even when we had all the mess between the Yardie's and the local kids, it was never this bad. We need to pull the threads and follow them while we still have a city left to protect.'

Murphy wanted to argue, but held his tongue. It was hard to stop Clive Rigby when he was off on a tangent. He was the sharpest detective on the unit though, and as annoying and convoluted as his thinking could be, it bore results more often than not.

'Do you have a plan?'

* * *

Lamont washed and dressed the next day, ate a quick breakfast with Jenny and then left with Akeem. They had spoken earlier, Lamont calling Akeem from his PGP phone. Akeem was quickly mired in traffic.

'I'm assuming we couldn't get people up to Armley in time?'

'The police had the area cordoned off. Someone got close enough to see that there were two bodies. We should be okay though. Doesn't look like K-Bar left much mess behind and it was late, so it's less likely someone saw anything.'

Lamont was satisfied, for now. K-Bar was in hiding and would remain there until things calmed down. Lamont had used the situation to get Shorty to agree to back off. He wouldn't be able to keep him at bay forever, and he wondered to himself why he didn't want Shorty involved.

It wasn't a question of greed; Lamont paid his people well, and Shorty received a larger share than anyone other than Lamont himself. Skill-wise, Shorty was in a different league. He could shoot and maim enemies, but had the charisma to make people want to be around him; an essential trait for the role he'd held.

Lamont wanted Shorty to be safe though. The police loathed people getting away with murder, and Lamont didn't want them trying to put Shorty down for good. It wasn't the time to think about it though. He had work to do.

They reached their destination. Akeem led the way, Lamont following. The garden was unkempt. Weeds lived where flowers once rested, and the gate wailed as they pushed it, its rusty shell creaking. They knocked at the door, waiting.

'L?'

A powerfully built, dark-skinned man loomed over them. He wore a rumpled white t-shirt, grey jogging bottoms and was barefooted. His sleepy eyes brimmed with obvious confusion.

'Hello Sharma.'

Lamont didn't have many memories of Sharma. He, along with another soldier named Victor, did the running around of Marcus Daniels. Victor had lost his freedom trying to protect Marcus when he was shot. He was serving time. Lamont made sure he was looked after, but money was nothing compared to freedom.

Lamont realised this now more than ever.

'Come in, fam.' Sharma shuffled to the side to let them enter. Sharma had never made big money rolling with Marcus, and it was clear he was making even less with Marcus's death. There was a sofa in the middle of the room that looked like it had been left outside someone's house, some splinter-ridden wooden chairs and a TV. The floorboards creaked under the weight of the men.

Sharma hung near the door, suddenly abashed.

'Sorry about the mess. Wasn't expecting company.'

'How are you doing?'

'I'm getting by. Juggling here and there. You know how it is.'

'Definitely,' agreed Lamont. It had been years since he'd needed to scramble around to make money, as everyone present knew. He went along with it though.

'Ring K-Bar. Tell him I said to call. We'll find something for you.'

'You don't have to do that . . .'

'Marcus was closer than family. He trusted you, and I shouldn't have left you out in the cold. Blame the shooting.'

Sharma nodded, humbled.

'I need to ask you something though. I need you to be honest.'

'Okay, L. I will. I swear.'

'Reagan. Who got rid?'

Sharma swallowed audibly, his eyes darting between the pair.

'I was there, but Marcus hired cleaners. He needed to leave no trace, probably cos' of where it happened. He knew how much you and the old man loved the spot.'

'Do you know which cleaners?'

Sharma again hesitated. His eyes widened slightly, probably regretting opening his door.

'Some freelancers out of Gipton. They're trustworthy though.'

'Give me all the info you can on them. You can take down K's number too.'

Sharma rooted around for a pen and some paper. He stopped mid-search looking at Lamont, the fear and uncertainty dissipating.

'L, I just want you to know, Marcus loved you like a brother.'

'I need the name regardless, Sharma, but thanks,' replied Lamont, noting how empty the words made him feel.

* * *

'Are you really going to give him a job?' Akeem asked Lamont when they left Sharma's. Lamont intended to learn how Akhan had found out about Reagan's murder. There was a camera fitted above the barbers, but he and Marcus had checked the footage, erasing anything connected to the day Reagan visited.

Lamont thought back, recalling how nauseous he had felt after killing Reagan. He'd expected a massive outcry, but the work he and Chink had undertaken in smearing Reagan's reputation paid dividends. Most people assumed Delroy had him bumped off. The police asked a few generic questions, and then they'd buried the case.

That was why Akhan was able to blindside him, Lamont realised; complacency. He'd forgotten about Reagan until Akhan had brought him up again.

'Sharma is a good soldier, and he's loyal. If he cleans himself up, we can put him to work.'

Akeem nodded, focusing on the road again. They had called around, pinpointing the exact location. The cleaners were three men in their late fifties. They had experience in the army and had been cleaning up messes resulting from disputes for years. A friend of a friend had given Lamont the address of the ringleader. He lived in a nondescript semi-detached house.

As they pulled up across the road, Lamont could see a new model Vauxhall people carrier in the driveway.

'I guess he's in,' said Akeem.

'We don't want him to feel threatened. Say nothing.'

Lamont and Akeem made their way up the drive. Lamont knocked. A few moments later, a man with balding, silvery-grey hair and a ruddy face looked out at them with hawk-like green eyes.

'Travers?' Lamont spoke directly to the man who had answered the door.

'Yeah. Don't think we've met though, Teflon.'

'How do you—'

'I've been around enough people to know that you're a force. Do you need something doing?'

'I need information. Can we come in?'

Travers gave Akeem a long look, sizing him up. Akeem met the stare. After a second, Travers stepped aside.

'What do you need information on?' Travers picked up a can of beer, but made no move to drink from it.

'You knew a friend of mine. *Tall-Man*.'

Travers gave no indication that he recognised the nickname.

'He came to you for some work last summer, didn't he?'

'What if he did?'

That threw a loop into Lamont's questioning. *Sharma had already confirmed that these were the cleaners Marcus had used. What could he really learn from this conversation?*

'Tall-Man paid for a job. Wasn't the first time. We don't ask more questions than necessary,' continued Travers.

'How secure is it?'

'Excuse me?' Travers glared at Lamont now.

'Someone knows about the job . . . Is there anything to find?'

'No one could put that back together. Someone else must have given them the information. Otherwise, the person is lying.'

Lamont wanted to be relieved. If the cleaner was being honest, there was no tangible evidence of Lamont's misdeeds. It didn't explain why Marcus would speak to Akhan though.

'Has anyone else come to speak to you about this?'

Travers nodded now. 'This young Asian lad was here months ago.'

Lamont straightened in his seat. 'What did he look like?'

'Young, like I said. Lots of jewellery. Had a white Mercedes convertible. Tidy Asian bird in the front with him. She was stunning.'

'Did he give you a name?'

'Can't remember it. Summat with an R. Gave me five grand too. For my time.'

Lamont stood now, his head spinning with all the implications. The young man had to work for Akhan. He was sure of it.

'Thank you for your time. Someone will drop something on you later. For your co-operation. And your silence. Got it?'

Travers again nodded, and Lamont left.

* * *

Jenny mooched around a coffee shop, sipping a bottle of water and staring into space. She didn't want to go home. She and Lamont had eaten breakfast and sent vague texts through the day about potentially going out for dinner. Jenny hadn't heard from Lamont since and decided she needed some alone time.

Jenny had been to visit Martha several times since asking Lamont to attend a session with her, but the woman was sticking to the same line about Jenny leaving the past behind. Jenny wondered if that was what Lamont was doing.

The disconnect between them seemed to grow. Shorty had said that she needed to remember how to talk to him, but it was difficult with Lamont. He could close himself off in a way Jenny had never experienced before.

Ordering a scone and some jam, Jenny pulled out her phone and went onto the Internet. Remembering the business card Malcolm Powell gave her, she went onto his website, impressed with the black, gold and white layout. It was clear as she navigated that a lot of effort had gone into the design. She was surprised when checking out Malcolm's latest blogs that he had mentioned the name of her business and posted a photo he'd taken of the arrangement she had made for him.

Jenny smiled, distracted for a moment. She clicked on the most recent blog piece and settled in to read:

Another day, another home invasion.

Technically, this one occurred outside the home, but that shouldn't discount the message. Two men dead, shot multiple times, and the police have no clue. One of the men, Kevin Roberts, or Big-Kev to his cronies on the street, was an overweight gangster who like so many others, peddled misery. He was a loan shark who lent money to people and crippled them when they couldn't pay it back. He was immersed in this life and for a long time, no one touched him.

Now, he's dead, and while my thoughts go out to his family, I can't claim to be sorry for his brutal murder.

It ties back to what I'm saying; the criminals run this city of ours, and it goes much further than just pushing a few drugs and walking around in a new chain.

What if innocents had been caught up in the crossfire of the shooting? It wouldn't be the first time now, would it? When will someone hold the criminals so many of your children look up to, accountable?

It's not a good life! A life built on inflicting pain on others is never a good life, and should never be a measuring stick, nor should it be something to look up to. Yet, so many do! And they shouldn't. Respect your mums, dads, Aunties and uncles and other family members that are breaking their backs to provide for you.

I understand though; it's difficult, clawing from the bottom, with temptation and fast money on every corner. I'm talking from experience because I grew up among it. I wanted more though, and I type these words as proof that you can do it the right way.

In other news, Police recently seized a large quantity of drugs in the heart of Chapeltown. These were mostly class A drugs, and there were multiple kilo's, enough to do a lot of damage to the community.

I'm no friend of the police, and many of their actions relating to Chapeltown and other surrounding areas has been vile, but I applaud the seizure, and I hope it's a step in the right direction towards ridding Chapeltown completely of drugs.

I've heard people scoff and say it's impossible, because too many people profit from the drugs trade, and to them I say this; maybe you should stop them.

Jenny had to blink a few times after reading the piece, having forgotten where she was. She knew Malcolm could write, but this particular piece resonated with her.

As Jenny finished her scone in silence and made her way home, she was still thinking about his words, and the obvious passion behind them.

Lamont's vehicle was in the driveway when she pulled up. He sat in the living room staring into space with a glass of brandy in his hand. He looked up when Jenny entered and gave her a wan smile.

'Hey babe. Everything okay?'

Jenny nodded. 'I just went for a coffee after work. Everything okay with you?'

'Yeah, just chilling.'

'Do you want something to eat?'

'I already cooked. I left you some in case you were hungry.'

Jenny kissed Lamont on the cheek and padded to the kitchen. She found the pasta salad and warmed it up. When she'd finished, Lamont was still sat in his chair. She watched him from the doorway, noting how fatigued he looked. She wished she knew what was going on, but she hoped he would let her in.

'I read an interesting article about Chapeltown today.'

'Tell me more.' Lamont put his empty glass down.

'Someone named Malcolm Powell wrote it. Apparently he does a lot of work in the community.'

'*OurHood*, yeah I've heard of them,' replied Lamont. 'What did the article say?'

'Read it for yourself.' Jenny found the page and gave her phone to Lamont. He read quickly, his face expressionless as he handed the phone back.

'He writes well.'

'Doesn't he? I think growing up locally gives him more insight into what is going on. He's passionate.'

'You've met him?'

'He came into the shop to buy flowers for his mum. Do you know him?'

Lamont shook his head. Jenny watched him carefully, noting the tenseness of his jaw, and iciness of his eyes. Jenny couldn't believe it; Lamont was jealous.

'Are you sure you're okay?'

Lamont stood and hugged Jenny, kissing her on the forehead.

'I'm fine. Just tired. I'm gonna get an early night.'

Lamont trudged upstairs, Jenny's eyes on him the entire way. She frowned, thinking about Lamont's reaction to Malcolm, and wondered if there was more to it. Lamont had been in that life for a number of years, and it was possible he'd drawn comparisons between Malcolm and himself.

As Jenny collapsed onto the sofa, she wondered something else; *how could Malcolm write about street politics with impunity?* Everyone else was scared to speak out for fear of reprisal, but Malcolm not only seemed unconcerned, but appeared to go above and beyond to antagonise both criminals and people in authority.

Jenny looked to the door one more time, then picked up her phone to read more of Malcolm's work.

* * *

'What time did you ask him to meet us?'

Rigby and Murphy sat in Rigby's grey Skoda. Rigby was looking out of the window as Murphy kept checking the time on his watch.

'He'll be here shortly. Relax and stop drawing attention to the vehicle.'

They didn't wait long. A man approached the ride with his head down and climbed in the back, a hood and cap obscuring his face. He pulled the hood down, breathing heavily.

'Fucking hell. Dunno why I had to meet you lot all the way out here.'

'Maybe because you don't want people to know you're working with us, did you think of that?' Murphy spat. Terry Worthy waved him off.

'Whatever. What do you want anyway?'

'Don't whatever me, you little prick,' Murphy raged. 'Don't forget who you work for, and what we've got on you. You're the scumbag who got caught trying to sell ounces to an undercover, so remember that and speak properly when you're dealing with us!'

'This all doesn't matter,' Rigby weighed in. Terry's face was red with rage, as was Murphy's. He needed to take over the talking before his partner did something stupid. 'The focus here is putting the right people behind bars. Don't you agree, Terry?'

Terry nodded, shooting a dirty look at Murphy. Rigby grinned. They had caught Terry on a distribution charge and he had quickly begun working with them to avoid prison time. Terry was relatively low on the totem pole, but he had a relationship with Lamont and more importantly, he knew the rough shape of the organisation, which had helped them identify some key components.

'What do you know about Kev's murder?'

'I know he was a fat bastard who took liberties with people.'

'Tell us something we don't know,' said Murphy, still eyeing Terry.

'How am I supposed to know what you know?' Terry shot back.

'Fine. Was your boss involved?'

Terry seemed surprised by the question, scratching his patchy beard.

'Kev definitely owed Tef some money. Ten, fifteen, twenty grand maybe, and he wasn't rushing to pay it back. People said Kev was connected to some Manchester guys too, the same ones who shot up Tef's sister's gaff, so there was definitely bad blood.'

Murphy and Rigby shared a look.

So, who would Teflon use if he wanted to take him out?

Terry shrugged. 'I dunno. Serious. L never discussed that side of things with me. I couldn't even get him to tell me his favourite colour, never mind which slotting crew he was gonna use to take out some loser.'

'The last thing you want is us to think you're not being useful, Terry . . .' Rigby let his words hang in the air as Terry paled.

'What do you want me to tell you?'

'Who do you think L would use?'

'Fine, K-Bar, If I'm guessing. Happy now?'

Murphy and Rigby shared another look.

'We've got work to do.'

* * *

That afternoon, Lamont was surprised to get a phone call asking for a meeting. He made his way to a barbers near Harehills, Akeem at his back as he was led into a backroom.

'I see you're copying my style,' he said to the man waiting for him.

'Behave. I've owned this barbers for nearly thirty years. You've got a long way to go.'

Lamont chuckled. 'How can I help?'

Delroy struggled to rise to his feet, but Lamont pretended he didn't notice. He hadn't seen the Kingpin in over eighteen months. He and Delroy always had issues, almost going to war at one point, but there was always an undercurrent of respect. Lamont was shrewd enough to know Delroy could have made a lot of situations more difficult for him and was grateful to the man for showing restraint. It was why he was here.

Delroy shook hands with Lamont and Akeem, offering them drinks, which they declined. Delroy was by himself, which was a surprising sign for Lamont, and he wondered if he should take it in the spirit it was intended; Delroy trusting him.

'I have a proposition for you.'

'I'm listening.'

'I want you to run my team.'

'Haven't we had this conversation before?' Lamont didn't react. Delroy had tried many times to get Lamont to work for him, and even when Lamont was buying his drug supply directly from Delroy, he would still attempt to talk Lamont into it. Lamont enjoyed his position though and even when the offers increased to ridiculous monetary levels, he still refused.

'I'll pay you an up-front fee. You'll answer to no one, and I'll only be included when necessary.'

'Up-front fee?'

Delroy nodded. 'I'll pay you one million pounds.'

The offer was astounding, and far more than Lamont would ever expect Delroy to come up with.

'What's this really about, Del?'

Delroy frowned. 'Don't you think I'm good for the money?'

'I don't doubt you have the money, I just think it's a massive step. You must know about what happened to me.'

'You got shot. So what? You're still here, and I know you, L. Shit like this makes you better.'

'Still doesn't explain why you'd want me to work for you. The last conversation we had was basically us threatening one another.'

Delroy sighed, his face lined and older than ever.

'I don't know how much longer I can go on. I need someone to teach Winston the game.'

'You taught Winston though. He learned from you,' said Lamont, his brow furrowed. He'd grown up with Winston, and thought he was an effective manager, but soft, allowing people, Lamont included, to take advantage.

'The drug seizure was his fault.'

'You mean he set it up?'

Delroy shook his head. 'I mean that he should have been paying attention. I left the day-to-day to him. He knows that the main spots either get switched up, or you plant them somewhere to allow you to see everything coming, and protect the fuck out of them. He didn't do that. He left them the same, and people learned the pattern.'

'Do you think someone tipped off the police?' Lamont had spoken with K-Bar and Akeem regarding the situation, and both believed that Delroy had people in his camp working against him.

'I had three people in mind who I thought might be responsible. Natty Deeds, and Lennox Thompson . . .'

'That's two,' Lamont pointed out, as Delroy straightened in his seat and looked Lamont in the eye.

'The third one was you.'

'Fair enough,' Lamont didn't even flinch. 'Lennox doesn't sell drugs though. In fact, he's always been against them.'

Lamont had known Lennox Thompson through Marcus. He refused to sell drugs, but moved guns and loaned money amongst other things.

Lamont recalled him committing robberies all over the country, including targeting drug dealers. He'd done some time in prison, but had kept a tight grip on his crew.

Natty Deeds was a well-known drug dealer who had come into further prominence while Lamont was recovering. He couldn't argue with Delroy picking any of them. Delroy scratched his chin, mulling over Lamont's words.

'He's the one I believe's responsible. He's crafty enough not to come out and say he did it.'

'I think you're reaching. The police aren't stupid, so there's always the chance they just ran surveillance and got lucky.'

'Raids are nothing new, L. We both know that. I've never lost that amount in one sitting though. It wasn't about taking the drugs, otherwise he could have robbed me. I think he was sending a message, and I think if it pops off, Winston won't be able to deal with him. You can.'

Lamont sighed. 'I'm not heavy like that anymore.'

'I know about Kev, and I know people have been scrambling around trying to get money because *Teflon* came out of hiding and demanded repayments. You're ramping up for something. We can help each other.'

'I want to ask you something else,' said Lamont, disregarding Delroy's statement.

'Go ahead.'

'What is the deal with Akhan?'

Delroy didn't speak for a long time, tapping his fingers on the desk before smirking.

'Why?'

'I'm curious.'

'He turned up the heat on you, didn't he? That's why you're stepping up. You're moving against him.'

Lamont didn't reply, waiting for Delroy to continue.

'L . . . You're talking about an entirely different sort of power here. Those Asians are embedded, with shooting crews and men all over the place. He's a warlord, and he's got direct links to people abroad that will murder you and your entire crew in your sleep. How can you go up against that?'

'I never said I was.'

Delroy rubbed his eyes. 'You know he was the reason I backed off, don't you?'

'I worked that one out.'

'So, what does that tell you?'

'It tells me you take him seriously, but you haven't told me anything I don't already know.'

'Then let me tell you this; don't engage Akhan. Just keep working, making money, and let me know about my proposition. Stay in touch.'

* * *

'What do you think then?'

Rigby took a long swig of coffee. It was again late in the office, and he and Murphy were hunched over Rigby's desk, looking over files and making notes. Terry's information had been sparse, but it was enough for them to pay more attention.

'I think Teflon was definitely behind it. We know that Kev owed him money, and there aren't many people who could take him out without a backlash on the streets. Kev was definitely behind the shooting of Marika Jones's house back in 2013. That's been corroborated by several other informants. Kev was even a suspect in the murder of Marrion Bernette, who was also originally from Manchester. There's a definite connection here. Plus, there are those rumours from back then. You know which ones I mean.'

Murphy did. The time after Lamont Jones was shot was tumultuous. The police were terrified that there would be retaliatory shootings every day, understanding Lamont's power and the control he had over his crew. They had tried to penetrate the crew multiple times over the years, but Lamont and his men were smart and difficult to pin down.

The rumours were that shooters from Manchester had attempted Lamont's life, and that there was beef between the two cities.

'Exactly. There is a definite Manchester connection. Add in the fact that Shorty avoided a life sentence for murdering three other shooters from Manchester, we're definitely looking in the right direction.'

Murphy grinned. He'd wanted to lock up Lamont Jones for years and potentially recapturing Shorty was also appealing.

'Do we think Shorty was the triggerman?'

'I'm not sure. Reports suggest that's he's been lying low since his release. There's definitely enough for us to approach the higher ups though. We need to get an investigation into Teflon going, and then we need to take him down for good.'

CHAPTER NINE

Monday 2 March 2015

'Why are we doing this?'

Darren Lyles paced around his living room, his phone pressed to his ear as he spoke with his girlfriend. The argument was a familiar one that he had never learned how to navigate in the two years he'd been on and off with Clarissa.

'Because it's not enough. I thought you'd be done with what you're doing by now, and I'm sick of waiting around for you to give me more.'

Darren resisted the urge to swear. It was the second argument of this magnitude he'd had with Clarissa in the past week alone. He'd missed a dinner she'd set up because he was working with Maka, and she had thrown a fit.

Darren couldn't help it. Like others in the crew, he'd come from nothing, and he had the opportunity to live a certain life if he focused. That would mean he missed a few dinners now and then.

'Babe, I can't make you wait around, but you need to understand I'm doing this for us.'

'You're doing it for you. I see you posing for photos in town and popping bottles. You like the lifestyle, not me.'

'It's not about that. I make appearances with my people, but that's it. You're my girl, and you're the only one I care about.'

They went back and forth for another thirty minutes before
Darren told her he had to go. He wiped his face, annoyed with Clarissa
and her antics. Times like this he wondered why he even bothered.
She'd stuck by him though, he swiftly reasoned. Clarissa only acted as
she did out of concern for him.

The streets were deep, and the more entwined Darren became in
the game, the more dangerous it became.

A firm knock at the door jolted Darren out of his thoughts. He
jerked to his feet and stomped to the door, flinging it open. The words
on his tongue died as he looked at Akeem's inscrutable expression.

'We need to talk.'

* * *

Jenny was sipping coffee in her office when there was a knock on the
door.

'Hey, Nadia,' Jenny smiled warmly at her employee who stood in
the doorway. 'Is everything okay?'

Nadia nodded. 'That man is here to see you again. Malcolm.'

Malcolm was browsing the flowers when Jenny out. Smoothing her
hair, she headed towards him and shook his hand.

'Thank you for the mention on your site,' she said.

'Thank you for the email response. I'm glad you saw it.' Malcolm
wore a navy blue sweatsuit and white trainers. His hair appeared damp
and Jenny presumed he'd gone to the gym before coming to see her.

'It was sweet of you. You didn't have to do it.'

Malcom shrugged. 'I often do what I'm not meant to. I was
wondering if you'd let me take you for a quick coffee?' Jenny opened
her mouth to refuse. 'Nothing nefarious, I promise. Just conversation.'

Jenny mulled it over a moment. 'Okay.'

After letting Nadia know, Jenny climbed into the passenger seat of
Malcolm's Range Rover. They drove to a coffee shop in silence, the
sounds of *Slum Village* providing the melodic soundtrack.

Jenny thought about Lamont, wondering if he would mind her
being with Malcolm. She didn't think he would, and she didn't intend
anything to happen.

When they parked and headed inside, Malcolm ordered two coffees and they took seats. It was after eleven, and the coffee shop was fairly empty. A couple sat at a far end, and one other person pounded away on a laptop. Jenny noticed Malcolm watching the writer.

'Tell me about your business,' he said as he turned back to her. Jenny smiled.

'I don't know what to say about it, really. I like flowers, and I always wanted a career where I could develop it, and here I am.'

'What's the next step? Expansion?'

Jenny shook her head. 'I need to fix the business first. It's not going so well at the moment, so that means more hours and less profit.'

'What caused the switch? Having seen your demeanour, and having purchased some of your products before, I can speak for the quality. Is it your marketing plan?'

'My partner was involved in an accident. I put everything on hold until he recovered, and the business suffered.' Jenny gauged Malcolm for his reaction to her boyfriend.

'He must feel bad about that.'

'He offered to give me money to re-grow the business. He even offered to invest, but I turned him down.'

'Because you wanted to do it all yourself? I'm sure you know he was likely offering because he wanted to help, not because he assumed you needed it.'

'His heart was in the right place, but what happened couldn't be helped. It wasn't his fault, and the business is mine. He runs his own business, and I stay out of that.'

'What does he do?'

'He's an entrepreneur.'

'Sounds vague,' remarked Malcolm. Jenny flashed another tight smile.

'He wouldn't like me talking about his business. He's very private.'

Malcolm chuckled. 'How long have you been together?'

'Nearly two years.'

'And you live with him?'

Jenny tilted her head to the side. 'This is sounding suspiciously like an interview.'

'I have a curious nature, and I like to ask questions.'

'Understandable, with what you do for a living. There's not much to say though. We love each other, but I guess we just struggle to communicate.' Jenny paused, frowning, unsure why she had shared this information with Malcolm. If Malcolm noticed her hesitation, he didn't comment.

'I understand. Personally, I struggle in relationships because I can never switch off, and my work keeps me busy. Makes it harder to form connections.'

'How did you get started with that work? I was checking out some work on your website, and the pieces are engaging.'

Malcolm smiled. 'I tried to write fiction novels about people from the streets, but I could never seem to make them work. It depressed me for a while, then I started writing poetry and taking part in readings. I studied to be a copyeditor, got my degree, then ended up working a few free-lance roles. After that I stumbled into social commentary and blogging, I even co-produced a podcast and Internet show for eighteen months.'

'That's impressive,' Jenny admitted. Malcolm chuckled again.

'Sounds over the top, like I'm at an interview, but I enjoy my work and make a good living from it. I grew up in Chapeltown, and all my life I saw the good overshadowed by the bad. I decided to bring about change with the tools at my disposal, and here we are.'

It took Jenny a moment to realise Malcolm had stopped talking. She had become so enthralled in his speech and the passion behind it that it was overwhelming. It was a similar feeling to the one she experienced reading Malcolm's words online.

The most jarring thing for Jenny was that she saw elements in Malcolm that reminded her of Lamont. When Lamont spoke, you paid attention to the words, and they resonated with you. Malcolm was the same. She sipped her coffee, her brain alight with thoughts.

They spoke for a short while longer, then Jenny had to leave. Malcolm drove her back to the office, but stopped her before she could climb from the ride.

'I know you weren't interested last time, but there's a community meeting this evening at the church on Chapeltown Road. You don't have to speak, you don't even have to contribute. Just listen and we can discuss your thoughts another time. Bring your partner.'

Jenny mulled it over. She didn't have any plans, and she was curious about Malcolm's narrative and what he might say.

'Will you message me the details? If I can make it, I will.'

Malcolm grinned, exposing dazzling white teeth. 'That's not a problem.'

* * *

Darren sat in the passenger seat, wondering what had transpired to lead to this meeting. He'd kept his head down, focusing on business and avoiding the politics.

The crew was in a transitional period, and Darren wanted to be involved in the next steps. Teflon was back in the driver's seat now, and he'd already made moves, collecting unpaid debts, and wiping out Big-Kev.

Darren snuck a look at Akeem, who remained as unflappable as ever. He wiped his hands on his trousers, trying to look in control.

As they pulled up to a spot, Darren looked at the house. It was nondescript and white-bricked, a small garden and driveway leading onto a garage. Anyone could have lived here, which Darren supposed was the intention.

Akeem led the way into the house, and they entered the living room. This was much nicer than the outside, the floorboards varnished and immaculate. There was a Television that took up most of a wall, a few books and some magazines. Darren also noticed a chessboard hidden amongst various paperbacks and bits of paperwork.

In the room, Teflon assessed Darren from an armchair. He wore a pair of reading glasses and had a selection of papers resting lazily in his lap. Darren's mouth was dry, hands jammed into his pockets. He hadn't expected to be face-to-face with the boss.

'You know who I am?' Teflon motioned for Darren to come closer.

'You're Teflon,' replied Darren, his voice hushed. Darren had grown up in the same Chapeltown streets Teflon had, living with his mother in a small home with not much money coming in. His older brother

Lucas was in the life of crime and as Darren got older, he wanted to do the same. School was pointless. No one learned anything there. The streets were where it was at; people could grow rich overnight, turn themselves into legends and drive around in the fanciest cars.

Darren wanted all of that. Lucas had too, but when police caught him with drugs, they had sentenced him to years behind bars. He kept his mouth shut, and he was looked after. Because Darren was his family, he too was brought into the fold, working under the tutelage of Maka, and later K-Bar. Darren kept quiet, soaking in everything around him, and was eventually promoted to run his own team, receiving a percentage.

Now, he was stood in the same room with the legend who had cheated death.

Everyone knew about Teflon's shooting. He had been shot at close range. The people behind it were all dead. Teflon was still here, probably richer and more powerful. *He looked so normal*, Darren thought to himself. He was dressed similarly to Darren in a white long-sleeved top, jeans and trainers. His hair was unruly. The eyes and stature were powerful though. They assessed Darren with consummate ease, and Darren felt far more self-conscious than before.

'Call me L,' replied Lamont, holding out his hand. Darren shook. 'I've heard good things about you. There are things in the works now, that I want you to be part of. I want to ask you a few questions though. Cool?'

Darren nodded, not trusting himself to speak.

'You grew up in the Hood, didn't you?'

'Leopold Street. Lived there pretty much all my life.'

'Do you have a girlfriend?'

'For now.' Darren made a face.

'What's happened?'

'She's stressing. She knows what I'm doing, and she's worried that something will happen to me.'

Lamont smiled. 'Shows that she cares though. I guess you need to look at the positives.'

'You're right, but I'm doing this for me and her; so we can stack money and establish ourselves. This is all I know how to do, and that might seem shit, but it's all I want to do, and I think I'm good at it.'

'I do too. You wouldn't be here otherwise. For you and your girl, I guess you need to spend some time with her and let her know where your heart is. If she's gonna stress, at least let her understand the situation.'

Darren shifted, thinking about Lamont's words. He was buoyed at the fact that Lamont had received positive feedback about him. Lamont seemed to want to get to know him. Darren would be patient until he could figure out why.

'Back to you. You wanna stack money, and I can appreciate that. What's the endgame though? Are you trying to rise?'

'Definitely.' Darren didn't hesitate. Lamont rose from his seat more fluidly than Darren would have expected. He also noticed for the first time that Akeem had left.

'Do you play chess?'

'I haven't in a while, but I used to when I was little. My uncle taught me.'

Lamont smiled. 'We're going to have a game.' Lamont grabbed the chessboard and spread it out on the table. They positioned themselves on either side, and picked colours, Lamont white and Darren black. They played in relative silence, Darren making his moves quicker than Lamont, wondering why he was being so cautious. Before long, his pieces were routed, and he was swiftly checkmated. Lamont laughed as Darren stared at the pieces in disbelief.

'How the—'

'Chess is no different than life, Darren. Stay as many moves ahead as you can, and you'll be fine.'

Darren considered the advice and found he liked it. He didn't like to lose, but at least he'd learned a lesson. Lamont was light years ahead of anyone Darren had encountered, and the longer the meeting went on, the more Darren realised this. It was everything; the effortless panache with which he dressed. His expression. All of it banded together to make him what he was.

'I have a job for you.'

'What is it?'

Lamont paused, assessing Darren for a long moment.

'I need you to get close to someone. An Asian kid with solid connections. I want you to become his friend.'

'Okay,' Darren replied. If this would get him to the next level, he would do it.

'Don't agree without considering the facts. The man in question is connected. I'm talking power on a different level. Do you still agree?'

'Yes. What's the plan?'

'We're gonna test his greed, learn who his boss keeps around him, and see what he says about the people he works for. Akeem will handle it all. He'll give you the information we have and then it's up to you. He'll also give you some money so you can act the part, and you'll have access to whatever resources you need. Don't take the piss. Eyes will still be on you. Understand?'

Darren fought to hide the grin on his face. This was what he had waited for; the opportunity to prove himself.

'You'll report to Akeem. One more thing; you're going to get a driver. He used to work with Marcus. He's trustworthy, but don't say more around him than necessary.'

'Marcus as in *Tall-Man*?'

Lamont nodded.

'Which guy? Vic's still locked up. Is it Sharma?'

Lamont again nodded. Darren remembered Sharma driving Marcus around the streets. He hadn't seen the man in months, correctly assuming he was keeping a low profile after Marcus's death.

'Any more questions?'

'Nah. Thank you though. For giving me this chance.'

'I didn't give it to you. You earned it. If you pull this off, we will talk about something better for you. Okay?'

It was Darren's turn to nod.

* * *

Shorty rose from the barber chair and wiped the leftover hair from the back of his neck. He checked out his new trim in the mirror, satisfied with how the barber lined him up. Handing the man a twenty pound note, he instructed him to keep the change.

'You keep tipping these kids like you are, they're gonna be fighting over who does your hair.' Trinidad patted Shorty on the back. They laughed as he walked with Shorty to the door.

'You spoken to L?' Shorty asked, noting Trinidad's face sag. He sighed.

'Not since we argued. I kinda miss seeing him around here. He kept to himself, but it was still comforting.'

'Me and L argue all the time, Trinidad. I wouldn't even overthink it. L likes people to challenge him, and I think he's just getting used to being in the public eye again.'

Trinidad nodded, his eyes slightly brighter. 'You might be right. Did you hear about the police involved in attacking Diego?'

'I heard they got suspended pending investigation or something. Wasn't one of them in an accident?'

'He's in critical condition. He was in a car crash a few days after his suspension. Wrapped his car around a tree late one night.'

'Good, I hope he dies. I ain't got no sympathy for those devils, especially after what they did to the kid,' said Shorty.

'It's dangerous though. You know the police as well as I do; they'll come back stronger and make everyone suffer. There's got to be another way to deal with this mess.'

Shorty shrugged. 'I get where you're coming from, but I'm on that other side, old man. I'm in those streets doing what I need to. It ain't for guys like me to dictate where we go. No one's gonna take me seriously.'

'People know what you've been through, and you're still out here. You speaking up could help change the minds of some of these young kids that wanna be like you.'

Shorty mulled over Trinidad's words. He'd never seen himself as a role model, but he liked the fact Trinidad believed he could do it. Shorty had always gotten along with the old man, and while they weren't as close as he and Lamont, there was a mutual respect.

'I'm not trying to force you into anything, but there's a community meeting tonight down at Roscoe Church.'

'Is this to do with that *OurHood* shit?'

'They'll definitely be involved.'

Shorty scratched his jaw, the rubbing alcohol applied after his haircut beginning to itch. Going to the meeting wouldn't hurt and if he didn't like what he heard, no one could stop him from leaving.

'What time does it start?'

* * *

Lennox Thompson's face was unreadable as he strode into a room, several of his people waiting. They surrounded a man who was sprawled on the floor. The room itself was formerly a living room, now bereft of any furniture. The carpet had been torn away, leaving a grey flooring currently covered with plastic.

Nikkolo greeted Lennox with a nod.

'It was easy getting him, Len. He thought he had the drop.'

Lennox allowed a small smile, then approached the man, signalling for him to be turned over. Despite the livid bruising around his left eye and cheek, he was still recognisable.

'Spinks, how have my people been treating you?'

Spinks mumbled an inaudible reply. He had been stripped of his clothing and was trying to protect his modesty.

'You're the one they sent? They thought an idiot like you would catch me slipping? Delroy must be losing his marbles.'

The room filled with laughter and jeers as they humiliated Spinks. He tried to get to his feet, but was forced down.

'You haven't been the same since Marcus and Shorty nearly killed you. Your brain doesn't work right anymore. Hold him down,' Lennox ordered, laying into Spinks with deliberate, slow right hands, impacting the face and body of the beaten man. 'Gimme the bat.'

Nikkolo handed Lennox a baseball bat, which Lennox brought down repeatedly on Spinks's ribs, savouring the screams.

'You know how it goes. Slow . . . quick . . . it's all the same to me. I wanna know all about Winston and Eddie Williams. I want hangout spots, safe houses, where they get their pussy, what brand of baked beans they like. I want all of it.

'You're gonna give it to me, and if you don't, then after I've torn you apart, I'm gonna do the same to your family. Everyone you love. Anyone you've said hello to on the street. I'll destroy them all. Start talking. Now.'

* * *

Shorty slipped into the back of the church just as the meeting was starting. The cramped main room was almost full, with most of the attendees standing. As Shorty pushed his way forward, he was surprised when an arm brushed against his.

Jenny Campbell smiled at Shorty, but before they could speak, a man at the front cleared his throat. His name was Calvin Newton.

'I'm glad to see so many of us here tonight,' Calvin was a squat man with glasses and a quizzical expression, but he had a presence that reminded Shorty of Lamont. Looking around, he could already see people leaning forward in their seats, not wanting to miss a single word. 'I understand it's hard to get out to these meetings, and your support is invaluable,' Calvin waited for the applause that had started up to disperse before he continued. 'I know that we have several crucial issues to discuss, and I feel that we need to tackle the biggest one of all, which are the police, and their behaviours in our town.'

'They're damn-well out of control!' Ken barked. He was another man Shorty recognised; a regular in Lamont's barber shop who often took on Lamont in games of chess.

Shorty had seen the old man argue over football or one of Lamont's moves, but he'd never heard him speak with so much anger. 'They put Claudette's grandson in hospital, then tried to charge him with assault when the hospital released him.'

Calvin shook his head as the crowd began talking amongst themselves again. He looked pained and gave them their chance to speak before holding up his hands again.

'I believe they are out of control, but the police are nothing but a private army, bought and paid for. They've always come into Chapeltown with impunity, bringing drugs and drama with them, trying to arrest your brothers and sleep with your sisters. I want to clarify why though? Why are they suddenly coming in and terrorising people? What is their agenda?'

No one had an answer. Shorty watched Calvin, and he noticed the man stare intently at him for a second.

'We have had some terrible events take place that have rocked our community, and a lot of bad press that has people again vilifying Chapeltown, just as they did in the olden days. I feel that the police and their paymasters are using this situation to their advantage, and I believe it ties into funding. The police force across the country are facing heavy cutbacks. If you can justify certain areas appearing to be dangerous or even on the verge of rioting, you can justify your budget.'

'So, what do we do to stop them?' a man called out. Calvin looked that man in his eye, picking his words carefully.

'We all need to come up with that plan together. In light of that, I would like to welcome Malcolm Powell, who will share a few words. For those of you that don't know, Malcolm is a key member of the *OurHood* Initiative, and has organised several of the recent demonstrations that have taken place in and around Chapeltown. Malcolm, come on up.'

Shorty watched Malcolm approach the podium, people already clapping and shouting words of encouragement. Shorty felt he looked familiar and was sure he'd seen him around back in the day. He had a refined look similar to Lamont, but was broader, his facial features more accentuated.

Malcolm greeted the crowd with a smile as he adjusted the microphone.

'Good evening and thank you all for coming. Calvin asked me to say a few words, but honestly, he touched on most of it already. A lot of the recent events have been the catalyst for the agenda of those in authority, which is to subjugate by any means necessary. It goes beyond that though, and if you've listened to any of my recent podcasts or read my articles, the fault clearly lies with the criminal element that has dominated Chapeltown for decades.'

A hush fell over the room. Shorty felt several people looking at him, but willed himself to stay calm, keeping his eyes on Malcolm.

Malcolm surveyed the room, giving Shorty the briefest look and nod before he continued.

'Many criminals in and around Chapeltown profit from the sale of drugs. People have made excuses for them in the past; anything from a lack of education, to being unable to find work. I can't refute any of that, other than to say that I'm from Chapeltown; I grew up around the corner in a house that didn't have much money. What it had was plenty of love and support, and I used that as fuel to succeed.

'I went to college. I worked, I put myself out there and helped people establish themselves. I wanted it. The fact is, some of these criminals are lazy. It's easy money selling drugs, and they're making a lot, so why not continue? And if someone comes along trying to take your spot, why not murder and maim them? After all, the community will protect you, right?'

'It's not as easy as you're making it sound, brother,' a man stood. He looked to be in his late thirties, stout, dressed in a sweater and faded jeans. 'We have families to consider, and speaking out just puts a target on our backs.'

There were murmurs of agreement. Malcolm nodded along with them.

'Thank you for speaking up, sir. Again, you're not wrong. These people have the means to reach out and silence people. Since I stepped up my work, I've had death threats. I've had people approach me, giving me messages warning to shut all of this down. I'm in the same boat as you guys; I have family and friends at risk too.

'But, you know what keeps me in the game?' Malcolm waited a beat, aware all eyes were on him, waiting anxiously for his next words. 'I'm doing the right thing. It's as simple as that. For as long as we can remember and beyond, there have been people who have been oppressed and ostracised, while trying to make things easier for those around them. Without people stepping up. Without people doing the right thing despite the odds, we'd be nowhere.

'That is why I'll never give up, and you can't either. We succeed as one, or we suffer as one. No matter the consequences, I'm in this until the end. Thank you for listening.'

The applause that followed Malcolm's words was deafening, and even Shorty clapped. It went on for minutes, growing louder as the man stood on stage and smiled.

Shorty appreciated the guts it took to stand there and say the things Malcolm had. It was puzzling to him at the same time. Malcolm was walking around with no fear, saying what he wanted, and no one was stopping him.

Shorty appreciated his words, but he wasn't as invested as some others. He was a hustler. It was all he knew, and he understood the mind of people like Lamont and Natty Deeds. They were champion strategists, used to thinking on their feet and tearing apart plots and ideals that worked against them. If Malcolm thought he would unseat them, he would need to try harder.

Before Shorty could speak to Jenny, Trinidad hailed him, and they spoke for a few moments. Most people had cleared out of the church by then. Shorty saw Jenny approach Malcolm, and they exchanged words before she gave the man a brief hug and walked away.

Shorty's jaw tightened, his nostrils flaring. He wanted to attack Malcolm for violating, but the hug had been so brief, he couldn't bring himself to do it. Jenny noticed him and walked over.

'I didn't know you knew Malcolm like that,' Shorty said, hoping his voice didn't sound accusatory. Jenny grinned.

'Looking out for L's interests, are we?'

The comment was perfect for defusing the tension, and Shorty laughed, Jenny giggling at his reaction.

'Summat like that.'

'He bought some flowers from me, and I've been checking out his website. He talks a lot of sense. Are you walking out?'

Shorty followed Jenny outside, nodding at a few people he knew. He noted several others were avoiding his eye, and a brazen pair of women glared at him, mumbling under their breaths as he passed. Shorty and Jenny stood near the main road, illuminated by nearby streetlights.

'I haven't seen you around lately.' Jenny stuck her hands in her pockets to stay warm.

Shorty rubbed his forehead. 'Me and L kinda got into it the night of that little dinner we had.'

Jenny studied Shorty for a moment.

'I'm not going to ask what you argued about, but L needs you, so make up.'

Shorty grinned again despite himself.

'Just like that?'

'How long have you two known each other? You're closer than brothers, Like I said, you need each other.'

Shorty shrugged, knowing Jenny was right, but not wanting to admit it.

'How's Grace doing?'

'I've been to see her, but its early days.'

'And your son?'

Shorty sighed and closed his eyes.

'I acted like a complete prick the last time I saw him.'

'In what way?'

Shorty filled Jenny in on the circumstances of his last trip to Huddersfield. Timmy had been present, and Shorty had expected Dionte to be happy to see him. The lack of contact had made Dionte unapproachable though, and Shorty nearly attacked him out of anger. Since then, he'd heard nothing from either Dionte or his mother, Stacey.

'You should go and see him.'

'I thought about it, but I assumed he wouldn't wanna see me again. I decided to stay away.'

Jenny impaled Shorty with a sudden glare he was sure Lamont had been on the receiving end of.

'He's a child, Shorty, just like Grace. Personally, you seem a lot more centred than you did two years ago. Don't give up. Deal with your children, and your brother, because they all need you.'

Shorty felt uplifted by Jenny's words. She'd hit the nail on the head, and he was done with moping around and waiting for things to get better.

'Thanks, Jen.'

'Don't mention it. You can walk me to my car now. It's freezing out here.'

CHAPTER TEN

Saturday 7 March 2015

BUOYED from the conversation with Jenny, Shorty hit the motorway early one morning.

After a while, he entered Huddersfield, driving through the Fixby area. It didn't escape Shorty's attention that the last time he had driven through, he'd had Timmy with him. After his visit with his son imploded, Shorty had lost his temper with Timmy shortly after.

Shaking away the negative thoughts, Shorty drove up a long driveway, stopping in front of a neat, white-bricked stately home. There was a Mercedes parked up. Shorty parked alongside it.

Stacey waited in the doorway, hawk-like eyes watching Shorty's every move. She'd put on weight since they last saw one another, but it was well distributed. Her skin was a dark brown shade, and she wore her age elegantly the way some women seemed to.

'Hey, Stace.'

Stacey nodded. 'Are you okay Shorty?'

'Yeah. Thought I'd get here in quicker time, but the motorway was rammed.'

'I think there was an accident. Traffic probably got diverted.'

That was the extent of their conversation. They awkwardly looked at one another, then away. They were young when they'd gotten together. Shorty was on the streets building a reputation. Stacey was in the clubs taking drugs with her friends, trying to meet a big-timer. She wasn't prepared for Shorty though, and their tenure was rocky, filled with accusations of cheating — most of which were true — and violence.

Shorty was more volatile back then and had beaten up at least two men he believed were making eyes at Stacey. Finally, this culminated with Shorty being arrested for assaulting a taxi driver whilst under the influence of drink and drugs. He'd been sentenced, and a pregnant Stacey had seen the writing on the wall and moved away.

Shorty reached out to Lamont from behind bars, wanting to make sure his kid was provided for. Despite Lamont's objections, Shorty used most his stash getting Stacey the very house they stood in. He'd assumed that after his release, he would move out there with her. This backfired when Stacey made it clear that they didn't have a future and began dating a businessman. Shorty had wanted to blow the house up and kill the man, but Lamont talked him around, and Shorty had left Stacey alone.

'So . . . Is he in?'

Stacey smiled tightly, 'I told you he was. He's watching television in the front room. Can I get you a drink?'

'I'm good,' Shorty started towards the front room. He paused when he realised Stacey wasn't following. 'Aren't you coming?'

'This is about you and your son.'

Shorty nodded, his heart pounding as he walked into the front room. Dionte was playing *Fifa*, the same computer game Darren, and the others liked to play. Loud grime music played through a Sony speaker, and Dionte nodded his head in time to the beat as he clicked the buttons with dexterity. He looked up when Shorty entered, and his face changed. His eyes hardened, and he glared up at his father with the same surliness he'd last time.

'How are you doing, D?' Shorty started lamely after a minute, realising that his son would not take the initiative. Dionte stared a minute longer, not bothering to turn off the music. He unpaused his game and carried on playing.

'I'm fine.'

'You look fine. You're growing up to be a strong young man. That's good. Means I did something right.'

'You didn't have a thing to do with it,' Dionte told him. Shorty felt the familiar spark of annoyance, but controlled himself.

'You're right. I could have probably done more, but I guess I thought as long as I was throwing money at your mum, you would be all right. Do you wanna know why I randomly came to see you last year?'

Dionte didn't reply, but Shorty noticed he'd paused his game and turned the music down. Shorty took a seat next to his son.

'My friend died a few weeks before I came to see you. I was outside the wake, drunk, when a man approached me. I didn't recognise him, but he knew me. He knew my mum's name. He even knew I had kids. When I asked who he was, he said he was my dad.'

Dionte still didn't speak, but he looked at Shorty, imploring him to continue.

'I hadn't seen my dad since I was about four. He ran out on my mum, and he provided nothing. No money, no visits. He just ditched us. So, when he came out of the blue and started trying to be friendly, I knocked him out.'

Dionte looked like he was trying to hide a smile. His lip quivered, and there was more light in his eyes.

'After I knocked him out, I couldn't stop thinking about you. Not to say I didn't before, because I did. It was just easier to distract myself, and tell myself that you were okay in this big house with your mum and her man, and that I was doing you a favour staying away.

'That was wrong of me though. I should have attempted to come and see you and stay a part of your life. There's no excuse I can give for why I didn't. I just want you to know that I'm sorry about that, and that I'm sorry that our relationship is like this.'

More silence. Dionte's body arched towards his now, but he couldn't bring himself to speak. Shorty patted him on the shoulder.

'You're probably wondering why I'm saying all this crap to you, and the reason is simple; I never want to be that broken old man trying to speak to my son, and I never want to be the reason that you put your hands on me. You ever need anything, tell your mum to tell me, and I'll come to you. You have my word on that.'

Dionte turned back to his game and unpaused it, but his expression was different. He seemed sombre. Shorty stood and walked away, not wanting to push it. He almost bumped into Stacey, who stood in the hallway. She gasped.

'Sorry, I shouldn't have . . . I just wondered what you would say,' she admitted, smoothing her hair.

'It's your house. You don't have to apologise.'

'Come and have a drink in the kitchen. I want to talk to you.'

Shorty followed Stacey to the massive kitchen. The last time he'd been here, he argued with Dionte for not wanting to look at a picture of Grace. The room had the same wide surfaces and light worktops that had been commonplace previously. Stacey poured coffee from a fancy-looking filter. It was very Lamont-esque.

'I thought what you said to Dionte was sweet,' Stacey started. 'I'm not just saying that either. I've never heard you talk like that before.'

'Like what?'

'Honest. You've always been your own man, but I've never heard you speaking from the heart before. Even in the older days.'

'Shit's different for me now, Stace. You know some of the shit I've been through last year since Marcus died. It feels like everything in my world fell apart, and I'm just trying to pick up the pieces.'

'I heard about Timmy. I'm sorry, Shorty. I went to his funeral and spoke to his mum. She was sweet.'

'He should have never been in the life. He always wanted to be like me and look at the example I set. He should have been out going to college and trying to get laid, not running corners and selling drugs.'

'Shorty, the circumstances weren't the same. Timmy wanted that life. I don't think he would have ever gone to college. Sometimes we have to live our lives the way we want to, regardless of what other people think. Timmy did what he wanted to do.'

'I still could have done more. Do you ever feel like you're realising shit too late in your life to do anything, but you can't help thinking about it, anyway? Like, what might have been?'

'In terms of what?'

'What if I'd been more like L? Setting up businesses, thinking of the future instead of for right now. Things could have been so different. I could have been a proper dad to both of my kids.'

'Focus on the fact you're feeling these things now. That's the important bit. You can still change your life.'

Shorty nodded, recognising the truth in Stacey's words. He grinned.

'Thanks.'

'Don't mention it. I've never known this side of you.'

'I don't even know what this side of me is. I just know that I think about Marcus daily, and I think about how abrupt his murder was. The world moved on without me, and it feels like I'm struggling to catch up to everyone.'

'Like Lamont?'

Shorty again nodded. 'L was always ahead of me in terms of thinking. He's been preaching all this shit to me for the longest time, but it's only making sense to me now.'

'How is L doing? I can't believe he got shot!'

'Still the same. He's just still getting used to shit. I guess we all are. How's your man?'

Stacey gave Shorty a hard stare. 'Don't go back to being that guy.'

'What guy?' Shorty frowned.

'The guy that tries to flirt with me in my house.'

'I'm not flirting! I'm just asking you a question.'

Stacey laughed. 'Fine. I'll believe you. We're okay, I guess. Marriage is hard work, and we're both busy, so we sometimes struggle to communicate,' Stacey shook her head. 'I can't believe I'm talking to you about this.'

'I can't believe that I'm listening.'

They both laughed, talking for another twenty minutes. Shorty had another coffee, showing Stacey photos of Grace. After a while, Shorty said his goodbyes, giving Stacey a hug and departing.

As he was climbing into his car, Shorty looked back. He saw Dionte looking at him from the window. Shorty nodded, inwardly gratified when Dionte nodded back.

* * *

Jenny was tidying the work area when the door clanged and she was face to face with Lamont. The silence lingered until she broke it.

'What are you doing here?'

'Visiting my girl. I want to take you out tonight.'

Jenny grinned, raising her eyebrow. 'What's the occasion?'

Lamont laughed. 'There's a disconnect with us lately, and that's my fault. Some time away to recharge will do us both some good.'

It was surprising to hear Lamont openly taking responsibility for the awkwardness between them, and Jenny cleared the distance and planting a long kiss on Lamont's lips. They held each other for a moment, Jenny enjoying the strength of the man she loved.

'It's a great idea, L. We could go to a hotel, or we could just stay at home?'

'Your choice, so let me know. We can do anything you like.'

* * *

Shorty drove back to Leeds with a smile on his face. He'd never realised just how tense his situation with his son had made him until now.

For years Shorty had tried to make excuses about his lack of contact, blaming Stacey and her move away from Leeds. He saw now that she had done the right thing, and he was pleased with the life she had made. Dionte had grown up well and while he wouldn't be as close with Shorty as he'd like, being civil was enough.

Driving into the Hood, Shorty parked outside K-Bar's safe house and bounded inside. K-Bar was sat on the sofa. He looked better than the last time Shorty had seen him, but was still lying low. He nodded at Shorty.

'Where are you coming from?'

'Huddersfield.'

Shorty's answer surprised K-Bar.

'You went to see Dionte?'

Shorty nodded.

'Did Stacey flip out again?'

'I called ahead this time and arranged it. We had a long talk, I apologised, and then left.'

'Are you two cool now then?'

'We're talking, so I guess that's enough. Anyone else stopped by?'

'Darren did, but he's on a mission now.'

'What mission?' Shorty's brow furrowed. Darren had a good reputation, but Shorty couldn't imagine anyone letting him pick his own missions.

'I dunno, fam. It's summat for L, but he can't tell me what it is, apparently.'

'You try asking L?'

K-Bar nodded. 'He just said it was personal. You know what L's like. If he doesn't wanna talk about something, he won't. I just fell back.'

Shorty heard the anger in K-Bar's voice, relating to it. It still annoyed him that Lamont wouldn't put him back on the streets.

'I tried speaking to him about getting back in, but he wants me to keep waiting.'

'I see his point, but still, you're not an amateur. You know what you're doing.'

The friends sat in silence, neither in a hurry to break it. They had been friends for so long they recognised the other's mood. Shorty thought about Dionte again, wondering if he would try to go professional as a footballer, silently vowing to support him all the way if he did. It brought Shorty's attention back to Grace, and he remembered he still had a lot of work to do.

'We ain't chilled together much lately, have we?' He said to K-Bar, who scratched his stubbled chin.

'Different world nowadays, fam. When you were locked down and L was in recovery, the streets were on a different level. I had to step up in L's place. People turned to me because they were scared, but I didn't know what I was doing, so I had to do what I thought you or L would do. Everyone tried us. We took so many hits in a short space of time that they didn't think we would survive. No one did.'

'How did you?'

'L. The guy had all sorts of contingencies in place. After he got shot, and we were running around, I had people getting in touch, leading me to stash houses I didn't even know about. People were in place to do pickups, and everything on the business end was the same.

'The connect sent his people to speak with me, the boxes kept coming, and the money was sent where it was needed. I had to keep shit in line and stop these dickheads on the street from taking liberties. I couldn't just chill and play the background like I used to. People knew me and they needed me to sort shit out.'

Shorty was silent. He didn't want to praise Lamont, even if he agreed with K-Bar. Lamont had always been forward-thinking and Shorty was man enough to admit that the money he made with Lamont was more than he would have made hustling for himself.

As frustrating as Lamont was, Shorty appreciated his business head.

'What happened to Blakey?' Shorty recalled asking when he first landed, but never getting the full story.

'He quit couple' months after you got remanded, saying he'd had enough of the streets. He works in a bar in town on Greek Street.'

'Which one?'

'I'll remember when I see it. We can go tonight if you like?'

Shorty rubbed his forehead.

'I'll let you know.'

* * *

Winston Williams slouched on his sofa, dipping his hand into a packet of Big Eat crisps as he stared at the insipid action movie on the screen. He'd lost the plot of it thirty minutes ago, but it allowed him time to centre his thoughts.

There was a war on the streets, and Winston didn't know how they'd gotten involved in it, nor what the endgame was. Over the past few years he'd taken control of most of his father's business, with Delroy content to oversee.

Then, Lennox Thompson had made waves.

Lennox wasn't a drug dealer, so Winston hadn't understood. He'd tried reaching out anyway, and his offers were rebuffed. Lennox hadn't fired any guns or laid a hand on any of their workers. Winston was sure he was behind the raid on one of their spots recently, however; a raid that Delroy had chewed him out about. Winston had dropped the ball and not rotated the spots frequently enough, allowing the complacency to be taken advantage of.

The streets were looking sideways at the Williams empire, and several amongst their ranks were whispering about how bad things were going. The links were looking elsewhere, and the money was dwindling. Customers were holding back repayments, and Winston was working overtime trying to get things in line. He'd sent a man to track down Lennox, but no one had heard anything from Spinks.

Mack, Spinks' uncle, was in Winston's ear every day asking where he was, and Winston didn't know what to tell him.

Stuffing more crisps into his mouth, Winston nearly choked when he heard a loud bang from outside, followed by the smash of a car window. Leaping to his feet, Winston fumbled for his trusty baseball bat and charged outside.

'C'mon, you fucking cowards!' He yelled, tired of the neighbourhood kids and their antics. He saw a bunch of hooded boys running away. Winston jogged toward his Audi, panting. They had smashed the front and side windows, and the jarring alarm now pierced the quiet street. Out of breath, Winston again looked around the street, then trudged back inside to make some calls.

* * *

Darren poured another glass of champagne, acting like he was having the time of his life, doing his best to hide the nerves that were threatening to jeopardise his night.

Lamont's mission rang loudly in his head, and Darren was playing up to it. Lamont hadn't given him any sign of how long the task needed to take.

Darren was determined to do it properly, playing his position to the max. He'd quickly learnt the movements of Rashad. Akeem had complied a list of the young goons likes, dislikes and hangouts, and by checking out Rashad's social media accounts, Darren quickly built an image of the man. He knew that Rashad had responsibility within Akhan's team, similar to the role Darren had in Lamont's. He supervised a crew and did a lot of running around, picking up money and making sure things were smooth.

From what Darren could gather, Rashad seemed to be decent enough at it.

At present, Darren was in a club near the train station with some acquaintances who knew Rashad's people. They were serial ravers, so Darren had been going out with them for the past few weeks, trying to bump into Rashad.

This plan had been a bust so far. Rashad hadn't shown, but Darren had met some other people including some game women, getting laid twice in two weeks. That wouldn't pacify Lamont however, and Darren tried to focus. He hated what he was doing to Clarissa, but when the women were all over him, he couldn't resist.

He was in regular contact with Akeem, giving him progress reports and explaining his plan to the bodyguard, who seemed satisfied.

Darren remained worried though, which explained his nerves. He needed something to show for his efforts. He had killed himself to get noticed, but now he didn't know what would come next. Darren was no fool. He knew people had been murdered within the organisation.

Despite K-Bar's cleanup of Chink's murder, everyone knew that he'd been killed for betraying Marcus. None of it would deter him though. The plan would work out and if it didn't, Darren would tweak it to ensure it did.

'Next rounds on one of you lot,' Darren said, holding his champagne glass aloft. His beaming, half-drunk acquaintances followed suit.

Behind Darren there was a flurry of noise. His friend Nathan was shaking hands with a well-dressed man. Feeling a flutter of relief, Darren realised it was Rashad. He wore a fitted white designer t-shirt with tight-fitting jeans and white and gold trainers. He was laden with jewellery, wearing two white gold chains and a gaudy-looking Rolex. His arm was around the waist of a slim Asian girl with the most alluringly dark eyes Darren had ever seen.

'Rashad, this is my boy, D. D, this is Rashad.'

Darren shook hands with Rashad. He immediately sensed that Rashad was used to people flocking to him the way Nathan had.

'You good? There's champers if you and your woman want it.'

Rashad helped himself to a glass, leaving his woman to fend for herself. Darren filled her glass, and she softly thanked him. Nathan and Co were trying to chat up a group of girls now, leaving Darren free to talk with Rashad.

'Its too packed in here. I remember when only a few people knew about this spot.'

Rashad gave Darren a measured look.

'How long have you been coming here?'

'Years now. My people are deep in here, so it was a good little moneymaker. Still is sometimes, when people don't mess it up.' Darren saw the gleam in Rashad's eyes as moved away from his woman to speak to Darren. He noticed her scowl, filing this information away.

'What kinda business are you talking about?'

Darren looked around, checking they weren't being overheard. This was all for Rashad's benefit, and it seemed to be working.

'Can't really say, bruv. You know what's like these days. People talk too much. All I can say is that we were steady stacking. People are making it hot nowadays though.'

'Listen, I'm not any guy,' Rashad lowered his voice, talking into Darren's ear. 'I've got connections too, and I'm always trying to make money. Maybe we can work together.'

Darren paused, drawing Rashad in. He couldn't react too quickly. To do so would arouse suspicion. He glanced around the club, taking a sip of champagne, watching Rashad grow more restless. His woman was looking at her phone, occasionally throwing dirty looks at her boyfriend.

'Do you want a top up?' Darren motioned to the bottle. Before she could speak, Rashad interjected.

'Forget her. She's fine. Tell me about the business. Talk to your guys Nathan and them lot. They'll tell you I'm trusted, G.'

Hiding a smile, Darren spoke.

* * *

Lennox was staring into the bottom of a cup when Nikkolo entered the back room.

'The kids just reported in. It's done. Winnie came out and chased them with a bat. They were gonna stab him, but they remembered their orders.'

'Good. I don't want him touched.'

Nikkolo cleared his throat.

'People are saying Eddie Williams is lying low. Delroy has beefed up his security too. We've got a couple squirrels within their team letting us know their movements.'

'Good. Make sure everyone keeps up the pressure on all fronts.'

Nikkolo hesitated before speaking again.

'Boss, I have to ask; why aren't you just pulling the trigger? We took out Spinks and kept it quiet, and now we're vandalising cars like some amateurs. What's the point behind it?'

Lennox fixed Nikkolo with a stony glare, freezing the lackey where he stood. He held the look for over a minute. Nikkolo squirmed against Lennox's quiet force. He'd never in his life met a man that put out a vibe like Lennox Thompson. It was malevolent, but twistingly captivating.

'I don't pay you for your advice. Keep doing exactly as you're told.'

Nikkolo left the room without argument.

* * *

Lamont and Jenny were shown to their seats. Both had dressed to impress, Lamont wearing a tailored navy suit with brown brogues and a white shirt. Jenny wore a fitted black Peplum dress, her hair teased and wavy, eyes sparkling. Lamont allowed Jenny to pick the wine, and they stared into one another's eyes whilst waiting for their menus.

'This is a lovely restaurant. Feels like ages since we've been.'

Lamont nodded. 'It has been a while.'

'It feels like a while since we've done a lot of things,' admitted Jenny. Lamont tilted his head.

'Hopefully we can work towards changing that. So much has

changed in our lives, and I'm sorry for how I've acted. I've not been considerate and I promise you that's not the intention.'

Jenny reached squeezed Lamont's hand.

'I know, L. I've never doubted that you cared. We just seem at opposite ends sometimes.'

They sat in silence. Lamont hummed along with the soft jazz music. The place was packed, everyone in their finery and out to have a good time. After browsing the menus and placing their orders, Jenny spoke again.

'Have you spoken to Shorty lately?'

Lamont's face tensed, but he forced his features into a smile.

'No. We had a little falling out, but we'll be fine.'

'He said the same thing.' Jenny sipped her wine.

'When did you speak to Shorty?' Lamont tucked into his grilled fish with abandon, his brow furrowed.

'I saw him at that community thing I told you about.'

'Shorty was there?' Lamont scratched his chin after placing his fork on the plate.

'He walked me out. He was with the nice man from the barbers, Tommy.'

Lamont mulled it over. It made more sense now.

'How did he seem?'

'Less tense than when he was staying with us. I'm not sure if he agreed with everything Malcolm said, especially the parts relating to the criminal element, which is to be expected I guess. It was a good meeting though. Malcolm's words were inspiring. He really cares, you know?'

'That's good to hear.' Lamont hoped his words weren't as stiff as they sounded.

'I went for coffee with him. It's refreshing to hear about—'

'You went for a coffee with him?' Lamont's voice was low.

'Yes. He's an interesting man. Is that a problem?' Jenny's eyes rested on him. Lamont sighed, messing with the remaining food on his plate, feeling less hungry.

'No, course it isn't. Just be careful.'

'Don't you trust me?' Jenny glared. It was Lamont's turn to squeeze her hand.

'Jen, if there's one person I'll always trust, it's you. Malcolm is a target though; you said it yourself. He's playing with fire talking about reforms. I don't disagree with his methods, but even you can't deny that it's a worry.'

Jenny smiled, draining her wine.

'If you're finished, let's get out of here and head to the hotel.'

Lamont gave Jenny such a look that she shifted in her seat. Her face flamed, stomach tingling.

'Yes. Let's.'

Lamont paid the bill, leaving an exuberant tip. They took a black cab to the hotel, at the bottom end of the city centre, and checked into their room. The door closed, and Lamont forced Jenny against the wall, cupping her face and capturing her lips.

The kiss was slow and tender, and Jenny melted on the spot as Lamont applied more pressure. His hands skimmed her body, everywhere he touched seeming to flame. Jenny gasped and pressed her body against Lamont's. They spilled to the bed, Lamont rearing up and kissing Jenny's exposed neck, her dress askew and hanging from her shoulders. He pulled back, panting, his eyes still on hers as he undressed, flinging his expensive shirt to the floor and kicking out of his trousers. Jenny mirrored his actions and shimmied out of her dress, removing the black lingerie she had picked.

Lamont surveyed her entire body, his eyes gleaming. She was perfection, and he felt like the luckiest man alive. All the doubts about the future seemed to drift away as he drank in her features. Jenny stared at Lamont's ripped frame, the jagged scar from his surgery visible. Lamont looked down at it, then at her.

Jenny padded towards him, dropping to her knees and worshiping the mark with her mouth as Lamont hissed and gritted his teeth. When Jenny reached for him, Lamont came to his senses, pushing her back onto the bed and entering her with one fluid motion. They quickly found their rhythm, their mouths and bodies meeting as they pushed the world away for the night.

* * *

Shorty and K-Bar entered the spot on Greek Street, surrounded by bright lights and loud music. K-Bar quickly commandeered a table and started checking out the talent, Shorty bullying his way to the bar. They had phoned ahead to check Blakey was working. He was handing cocktails to a group of giggling girls who appeared very taken with him. Shorty made his way over.

'Yo, B?'

Blakey turned, recognising Shorty's voice over the music. He grinned, coming from behind the bar to greet Shorty.

'Fucking hell, bro. Look at you! You look healthy, man,' He shouted over the music. They moved back towards the bar.

'You too. Heard you were working here, so I thought I'd come check you. How's things?'

Blakey shrugged. 'I enjoy what I'm doing now, y'know? Feels less serious. After you went away, the game wasn't fun anymore. Too much blood, so I ducked out and went legit. K-Bar and everyone else needed to change and adapt to survive. I couldn't do it.'

'You need money or anything?'

Blakey shook his head. 'I had a bit saved up. I was dumb with my money, but I didn't spend all of it. I realised things about myself after I stopped hustling. I was never the same when you weren't around. I thought you were gonna go away for life,' he admitted.

Shorty nodded. 'Me too,' He didn't admit how much that thought terrified him. Freedom was something everyone took for granted, but Shorty had almost lost his for good 'I'm glad you're doing well.'

'Me too, bro. You look proper healthy though. You back working with Tef?'

'Sort of.' Shorty still needed to speak with Lamont and clear the air after their last discussion. Blakey was about to reply when a woman sauntered towards them, placing herself in the middle.

'Blakey, babe, can you get me and my girls more bubbly and bring it to the table please?' She met Shorty's eyes for a minute, and he didn't back down. She was an inch or so shorter, with milk chocolate skin and curly dark hair. She wore a black blouse and tight trousers, outshining everyone around her with ease.

'Don't worry, Sienna, babe. I'll get someone to bring it over,' Blakey noted that the pair hadn't taken their eyes from one another. 'Shorty, Sienna. Sienna, this is my day-one brother, Shorty.'

They smiled, still taking in the other's appearance. Blakey excused himself to fetch champagne for her table and Shorty continued speaking with Sienna. He learned that she worked in an office in town and that they'd met years ago at a party. Sienna laughed, saying that Shorty had been drunk and passed out in the corner, which tickled him.

They'd just exchanged numbers when K-Bar sauntered over, giving Sienna a hug.

'Easy, Sienna. Where are your friends?'

'At the table over there. They're all spoken for though, so leave them alone.'

K-Bar laughed. 'You're always spoiling my fun. Everything cool though?'

'I was just re-introducing myself to your boy here. I'll leave you both to it.' Sienna sashayed away, both men watching.

'I'm gonna smash that,' Shorty said, feeling the old hunger returning. He hadn't had sex since leaving prison, not counting the random girl from his second night out. He was attracted to Sienna and looked forward to getting to know her.

'You need to watch out. Her man doesn't play.'

'She didn't mention having a man.'

'They rarely do, bruv. You know that. Did you speak with Blakey?'

'Yeah, he's cool. Enjoying his life.'

'Good. Let's enjoy yours now. You can buy the first round.'

* * *

Lamont woke the next morning, Jenny's arms tightly pinioned around him. He grinned, remembering the activities the night before. They'd had sex since Lamont's recovery, but none he'd enjoyed as much.

They'd completely let themselves go in a way they hadn't since they first met, and he liked that.

Reality was looming though, and Lamont still had a mountain of business he needed to handle. He thought about Jenny meeting with Malcolm, annoyed. He remembered Jenny meeting with him at a coffee shop once and finding him interesting.

Lamont didn't believe Jenny was cheating, but the fact she wanted to spend time with another man made him jealous, and he hated that. Lamont wondered if Jenny had kept her meeting a secret because she was worried about how he would respond. It was galling. He was supposed to be bigger than that.

Lamont disentangled himself and went to take a shower. When he was finished, Jenny was awake. She smiled, but it seemed strained.

'Do you want to take a shower, or maybe order some breakfast?'

Jenny shook her head. 'I'll get a quick shower, then we can check out.'

The hotel ordered them a taxi, and they sat in silence the journey home. The energetic driver tried making conversation, but other than a few bland remarks, they stared out of their respective windows.

When they reached home, Jenny headed straight upstairs. Lamont watched, wanting to call after Jenny and say something. He understood her reaction though. A single passionate night wasn't enough to erode their problems, and he wondered if suggesting the night had been a good idea.

Sighing, Lamont trudged to his study, ready to close off from his world.

CHAPTER ELEVEN

Monday 9 March 2015

RIGBY AND MURPHY sat in the canteen, food untouched as they devoured the awful work coffee.

'K-Bar then,' Rigby said.

'People are saying he was the Head Chief while Teflon was laid up. He was making all the decisions and I'm sure he was behind Bernette's murder.'

They had looked into the Manchester murders of 2013. Marrion had been gunned down, then several of his associates were killed in separate incidents months later.

'Just Bernette's? Others were dropped during that period. Daniels, the other Carnival shooter. Schemes. The guys from Manchester that Shorty killed. His little cousin. They were all connected, right?'

Murphy scratched at his stubble, frowning.

'Chink was murdered too. He was Teflon's number two though, so hard to include him. Looks like we had a war between the two cities. The Manchester lot murdered Chink, that Polo character, Timmy, and the girl we found with Chink. Lots of tit-for-tat murders in retaliation. Teflon and Shorty were the main prizes though. Shorty killed his attackers, then Teflon nearly died.'

Rigby thought about Murphy's words. It was plausible, but they had no concrete proof.

'We need to talk with people; anyone connected with the murders. We'll shake a few bushes and see what we find. The chief won't like us going off base for long, so we better find something quickly.'

* * *

Shorty lifted the barbell in the air, breathing out as he held it up for a few seconds, arms straining under the large weight. He lowered it back to his chest and repeated the motion twelve times before stopping.

Shorty was spending more time in the gym lately, working off his frustration. They had cleared the air, but Lamont hadn't changed his mind, only choosing to give Shorty more money. He wasn't doing much with the cash. He purchased some new clothes and gave money to both Amy and Stacey. The urge to splash out like back in the day eluded him. He'd taken Sienna out for dinner and gone back to her place, but nothing transpired other than some kissing. Shorty didn't mind, which was a change. He enjoyed being around her.

K-Bar was back in business, the heat from Kev's murder subsiding. He and Lamont remained frosty, with more orders being relayed through Akeem.

Darren was progressing with his mission, but K-Bar and Shorty remained in the dark. Lamont was stuck on Shorty's arrest, hammering home the point that the police would loathe the fact they hadn't been able to put him away. Shorty understood, but resented the fact that Lamont believed him to be sloppy.

When he'd finished at the gym, Shorty went home and ate a quick meal. Slouching in front of the television, his eyes were closing when his phone chirped.

'Who's this?'

'It's B. Listen, have you been spending time with Sienna?' Blakey asked. Shorty sat up.

'Why?'

'Listen, her man has been around the club, asking people about you.'

'So what?' Shorty scoffed. Sienna had mentioned her ex's anger issues. Shorty wasn't phased by Lutel Forde or his so-called crazy reputation.

'He's a rugged guy, Shorty. He's not afraid to make a problem. Even knowing your rep, he's still not backing down.'

'B, I'm an easy guy to find. I'm not studying Lutel.'

'Okay. I just thought you'd wanna know.'

Shorty hung up, sniggering at the thought of someone asking around about him. He assumed people had seen him and Sienna at community meetings. Trinidad was another regular fixture, but Shorty hadn't seen Jenny since the first meeting. Dropping his phone on the nearby table, Shorty quickly fell asleep.

* * *

Jenny hurried through the doors of the nail salon, rubbing her arms from the outside chill.

'I'm sorry,' she said, spotting the person she was here to meet.

'Don't worry about it,' replied Marika. 'I haven't been here that long myself. Had to beg my boss to give me some holiday.'

Jenny grinned. She'd met with Marika several times, learning a lot about Lamont's younger sister. She worked part time in a contact centre and had taken an interest in finance, which made sense. She'd relied on Lamont to fund her for years and had seen the importance of managing her own money.

Marika had asked Jenny for financial advice, and Jenny did her best to help, but her situation differed. Struggling business aside, Jenny was born into wealth, and financially, hadn't struggled for anything.

'I'm glad you were able to persuade him. Have you looked into that thing we were talking about?'

Marika nodded, her infectious grin making her features shine. Jenny thought Marika was beautiful, but when she truly smiled, she was in a different league. Jenny noticed other patrons beaming at them. By now, they were being seen to, talking with one another as their nails were taken care of.

'I've seen a few online courses, so I'm debating between those, or going to a physical night school to get qualified. It'll take a few years, but I'll be more established, and I can think more about a career.'

'What about the kids?'

'Keyshawn can look after his sister. He's old enough,' Marika hesitated. 'Auntie is always a last resort, depending how many days a week I'd have to study, but the kids don't like her. The online course might be the best.'

Jenny smiled. 'I'm thrilled you're taking this step, Marika. It's never too late to start a career.'

'Thanks, Jen. I've always messed around, but money is kinda fun when you look beyond how quickly you can spend it. There's something I need to tell you though . . . it's kinda personal.'

'What is it?'

'I'm seeing someone.'

'That's great; who is it?'

Marika paused. 'K-Bar.'

'K-Bar as in L and Shorty's *K-Bar?*'

Marika shifted in her seat.

'How long?'

'A year, maybe longer.'

'Seriously?' Jenny's eyes widened.

'I know . . . at first he was just comforting me after Marrion, but then we started to like each other.'

'Does your brother know?'

Marika shook her head.

'You're the only person I've told. K can't really tell anyone, not in the position he's in.'

'He needs to talk to L directly about it if he's serious.'

Marika sighed. 'I know, but L's awkward. He hated Marrion because he was involved with me, and he and K-Bar have been close since they were teenagers. K doesn't want to jeopardise that.'

'I understand, but he needs to know, and he should hear directly from K-Bar.'

The pair changed the subject. They were preparing to leave when Jenny blurted something out.

'You should come for dinner.'

'What?' Marika shrugged into her coat and picked up her handbag.

'You and the kids should come for dinner.'

'What about L?'

'It's my house too, and it's time you started talking again. It's been too long.'

Marika opened her mouth to speak, then nodded. Jenny grinned. Lamont's reaction would be worrying, but she would deal with that when the time came.

* * *

Lamont parked around the corner from the barbers and strode toward the building, hands in his pockets. He nodded at a few familiar faces, all of whom gave him blank stares. It was a strange response, but Lamont didn't dwell.

The place was in full swing, with all four barber chairs filled, loud music and hearty conversation taking place. The noise dimmed a little when Lamont entered. Lamont nodded at Trinidad, who nodded back. He paused his hair cutting and handed Lamont a stack of letters. Lamont thanked him and headed to his office. He hadn't been since he and Trinidad argued, and there was a fine layer of dust on the desk.

Lamont dropped the letters on top of the desk, thumbing his old chessboard. The pieces were dusty, but holding them seemed to calm him. Lamont took a deep breath. It had become abundantly clear lately that he had no idea who he was anymore. He pushed ahead, struggling to focus on anything around him. He didn't know where to turn, or how he could stop.

All he'd wanted was freedom. That dream had changed to include Jenny, but now there was nothing but helplessness. Their relationship was precarious, and he didn't know what to say to fix things. Everything he had worked toward seemed to have imploded, and Lamont was struggling to deal with that fact.

'I've missed seeing you around here.'

Lamont looked up. Trinidad stood in the doorway.

'I'd have thought you'd prefer me not being around.'

Trinidad stepped into the office and closed the door.

'We both said some things. I don't agree with your actions, but I shouldn't have spoken to you the way I did. It's not your fault Chapeltown is the way it is. This is going back before you were born.'

'Even so, I respect your opinion. You're more than welcome to blow off steam now and then.'

Trinidad grinned. 'Glad you feel that way. Is everything good though? Would you like some food?'

'I'm alright, Trinidad. I'm just going to catch up on some work. How are you doing though? Everything good money wise?'

Trinidad shrugged. 'No complaints. I have money put away for my children, and I send a little something back home. All I can ask for, really.'

'How would you like to buy my share of the business?'

'What?' Trinidad's brow furrowed.

'Seriously, how would you like to buy me out?'

'You can't be broke?'

Lamont wanly smiled. 'I'm far from broke. You should have a business to leave to your children along with the money. I can help with that.'

Trinidad's eyes shone as he surveyed Lamont.

'I've always seen you as one of my children,' he mumbled. Lamont was speechless, touched by the words. They awkwardly looked around each other for a minute, before Lamont spoke again.

'I heard you've been a regular at the community meetings.'

'They're a great place to talk, and there's a lot of positive work in place because of them. I don't suppose I can get you to attend one?'

Lamont shrugged. 'Never say never. What about this Malcolm dude? Is he as cool as everyone thinks?' Lamont thought of Jenny, who had nothing but positive things to say about the man.

'He's a force,' Trinidad said. 'He lives and breathes what he does. He's always doing something, and he gives people hope when he speaks.'

Lamont nodded, feeling a twinge of what he suspected was jealousy at Trinidad's words. He wondered if it was worth attending a meeting to check Malcolm out. His phone rang, Trinidad leaving the room as Lamont answered.

'Hey, Jen.'

'I'm cooking a special dinner tonight, so make sure you're home for six, if that's okay?'

'I'll be there. Should I ask about the occasion?'

'No, you shouldn't. Bring wine please. Love you.'

Lamont dropped the phone on the table and closed his eyes for a moment. He needed caffeine. Deciding not to move, he allowed his eyes to droop and fell asleep in the chair.

* * *

Shorty rose from the gambling table with a smirk. He'd been playing cards and dominoes most of the day, making a small profit.

The gambling spot was an easy place to hang out. No one asked questions and Shorty liked the atmosphere. He'd had a few brandies and cokes, and was in the middle of a chat with another old head when he heard a commotion.

'Oi, Shorty; I've been looking for you.'

Shorty turned his head to the speaker, who towered over most in the room, his muscled build obvious against the black crew neck and bottoms he wore. He was clean shaven with closely cropped hair and beady hazel eyes. Shorty didn't recognise him.

'Who the hell are you?'

'I heard you've been sniffing around Sienna, and you need to stop,' Lutel growled. The room was silent, everyone watching the exchange with interest. There was no fear. The older generation frequented the spot and this kind of standoff was commonplace, especially where women were concerned.

'What's it got to do with you?'

'Sienna's my woman.'

'Forget the talking. You wanna do something, then step.'

Lutel lurched forward just as Shorty sprang from his stool. He swung for Lutel, who avoided the hit and caught Shorty with a looping blow that staggered him. Shorty kept his feet though, slipping inside Lutel's guard and smashing his ribs with vicious hits. He clipped Lutel's jaw with a nasty punch and flung the bigger man to the floor, kicking him twice in the head.

Reaching for a chair, Shorty smashed it against Lutel's face and shoulders, feeling the glorious rage. It had been too long since he'd laid into someone, and he repeatedly hit Lutel until Jukie snapped him out of his trance.

'Shorty, get out of here before someone calls the police!'

Shorty glared down at the barely moving Lutel, then left.

* * *

Lamont arrived home at a quarter to six, grabbing the bottle of red wine he'd bought on the way. He let himself into the house, surprised to see other voices. He entered the living room after taking his coat off, pausing when he saw Marika and the children sitting with Jenny. When Bianca saw Lamont, she hurtled into his arms.

'Uncle L!' She screamed as he lifted her into the air. He clutched his niece tightly, placing kisses on her face. Jenny and Marika watched, both wiping their eyes, overcome with emotion.

It took a while before Lamont released his niece, his eyes wet. He couldn't believe how big she was. Keyshawn sat close to Marika, regarding Lamont almost warily. Lamont nodded and patted him on the shoulder. He was trying to respect Keyshawn as an adult, and the teenager seemed to appreciate that effort, returning the nod.

'Hey, L.'

'Rika, how are you doing?' Lamont asked, his tone noncommittal.

'Jenny invited us to have dinner,' she said. Lamont flicked his eyes towards Jenny, whose eyebrows rose, daring him to say something.

'I wasn't aware you two were in touch.'

'We're friends,' Jenny spoke up. 'I thought you should talk. It's been far too long.'

Lamont handed Jenny the bottle of wine and faced his sister. Marika's hair was shorter; there were more lines under her eyes, but he begrudgingly admitted she looked well. He slipped onto the sofa, Bianca plopping on his lap and chattering nonstop about all her friends and school and everything else going on in her life. Lamont half-listened, keeping his eyes on his sister.

They sat for dinner, Jenny and Bianca keeping up a running commentary of their favourite films, songs, and everything they liked in the world. Keyshawn spoke sporadically, confirming that school was fine.

Lamont was surprised that Marika was working, but it made sense. He doubted Marrion had left her any money and she couldn't claim much from benefits, especially nowadays. When she spoke of studying, he couldn't hide his surprise.

'What's brought this on?'

Marika smiled almost shyly.

'I want to understand money,' she replied.

After dinner, Jenny put on some music and they retreated to the living room. They had some wine, and Lamont showed Keyshawn and Bianca around the house.

'Are we going to see more of you now, Uncle L?' Bianca looked up at Lamont with wide eyes. Lamont felt his heart crack as he stared at his beautiful niece.

'Yes, *Princess Bianca*. I'm not going anywhere.'

Lamont thought he saw a gleam in Keyshawn's eyes but when he blinked, it was gone. His nephew reminded Lamont of how he'd been in his younger years. Quiet, introverted and damaged. He cursed himself for not being around; for allowing his temper and circumstances to cost him good years with the few family members he cared about.

It was after nine when Marika and the kids left. Lamont paid for their taxi. When he'd seen them off, he locked the door and headed to the kitchen, rolling up his sleeves to wash up.

'I can do that.'

Lamont didn't even turn.

'I've got it covered.'

Jenny paused before she spoke again, entering the kitchen and standing close to Lamont.

'Don't keep it bottled up. Say what it is you've got to say.'

'You had no right,' Lamont mumbled.

'Pardon?'

'I said, you had no right to interfere in my family business!' Lamont snapped, surprising Jenny with the ferocity. He didn't turn, still washing a plate, but his shoulders shook with suppressed rage.

'Are you serious? I care about you, L. I want you to be happy. The only reason I invited Marika is because this whole mess has dragged on too long, and you're both too stubborn to make the first move.'

'That's not the point and you know it. It's my situation to work out. It doesn't need you forcing people together and trying to resolve things.'

'You weren't happy to see your family, is that it, L? Because you seemed really happy to see your niece, I can tell you that much.'

'Stop trying to twist it. My family, my problems. Stay out of it.'

'Don't tell me what to do, L. I'm your partner, I don't work for you, and I expect us to compromise on things.'

'There was no compromise, because you didn't tell me what you were doing. You didn't even mention it. Seems to be a common theme with you nowadays.'

'What do you mean by that?'

'Who else are you going on little coffee dates with? There's Malcolm, Marika, Shorty . . . who's next, *K-Bar*?'

'Is that was this is about? You don't like me being around Malcolm?'

'No, the problem as I clearly said, is you being around my sister and trying to force us together.' Lamont flung the plate to the side and glared at Jenny, soap suds adorning his hands. Jenny was red-faced, chestnut eyes alight with rage.

'I just want you to be happy, L. Is that such a bad thing?'

'I'd be happy if I was left alone to deal with my life. Don't speak to my family again without permission.'

'I don't need your permission. I'll do what I think is right. You're not dealing with your emotions properly. Why is that so hard for you to see?'

'Jenny, just shut the fuck up with all that, okay? I don't need help. I don't need you to fix me. I'm not as weak as you, so focus on your own problems with your fucking counsellor, and leave me out of it!'

The palpable silence stretched, Jenny's face whitening as Lamont's vicious words hammered into her. Without a word, she stormed from the room. Lamont glared at the space where she'd stood, trying to control his trembling hands. He wanted to run after her and apologise, but didn't move. When he heard the front door slam a few minutes later, he grabbed a plate and flung it against the wall.

Yelling, he began systematically destroying all the plates and cutlery he could see until he stood in the kitchen, surrounded by shattered kitchenware.

Lamont stared at his hands, breathing hard, wondering how he would get out of this latest mess.

CHAPTER TWELVE

Tuesday 10 March 2015

SHORTY HEADED to the barbers the next day. He'd missed the morning rush and when he walked in, Trinidad struggled to his feet to greet him.

'Are you okay?' Shorty noticed the stiff movements and pain in the old man's face. Trinidad waved him off.

'People have been talking about you all morning.'

'I bet they have,' Shorty's phone had been ringing all morning. Everyone wanted to talk about his fight with Lutel. Even Sienna had called. Shorty had said little, but he was already tired of talking about it. 'Have you seen L?'

'A few days ago, but not today. Are you sure you're cool though?'

'Why wouldn't I be?'

Trinidad squinted, rubbing his ear. 'Lutel is a madman. He's not gonna be happy that you whipped him in a room full of people. His reputation is on the line now, and he's dangerous.'

Shorty shrugged. 'I didn't start this. He did.'

'I understand, but you took it further when you embarrassed him. I just want you to be careful.'

Shorty growled, shaking his head.

'Trinidad, I'm the one people need to worry about, not that dickhead. Did you forget who I am? Did you forget what the hell I'm about? I don't avoid trouble, I end it,' Shorty swept a glare around the room, people cowering from the fire in his eyes. 'Any of you talk to that pussy, tell him I'm easy to find. He needs to worry about me, not the other way around.'

Silence ensued. Trinidad met Shorty's eyes, nodding slightly. He seemed almost relieved.

'Do you want a haircut now?'

Shorty nodded. 'Shape me up please, old man.'

* * *

Lamont raised the glass of brandy to his lips, looking at his phone as he slumped over the table in his spacious kitchen. He and Jenny's spacious kitchen. She'd packed some things and left the house.

Lamont had called Kate numerous times, but couldn't get anything out of her. Lamont wondered for a fleeting moment if Jenny was with Malcolm. He'd received a dossier of information about the man. Malcolm had distinguished himself at college and university level, and his online work was prominent. Lamont had even listened to some podcasts he'd produced without even knowing Malcolm was involved. He was direct and able to control his obvious intelligence without sounding condescending. It was easy to understand why Jenny would enjoy his company.

His annoyance rising, Lamont dialled Kate again.

'L, you've got to stop calling,' she answered.

'I just wanna know she's okay.'

'She is.'

'And I want her to know that I'm sorry.'

'She does.'

'And I want her to come home.'

'You need to give it time then. I know how you're feeling, L, but you can't rush this. Look after yourself and she'll be in touch, okay?'

'Okay.' Lamont dropped the phone on the table. He hurled the bottle against the wall with a resounding smash, the pieces of glass joining the destruction from he and Jenny's aborted dinner. Lamont picked up his phone to call her, but it went straight to voicemail. Nostrils flaring, Lamont called Akeem.

'Follow Malcolm, make sure Jenny isn't with him.'

'Okay.'

Lamont lurched to his study, locating a fresh bottle of brandy. He opened it, dropping the lid on the floor and not bothering to pick it up. He was about to drink when there was a knock at the door. Lamont left the bottle and wiped his eyes, smoothing his hair. Opening the door, he sighed when he saw Shorty.

* * *

Jenny pushed away her paperwork. There were orders she needed to sign off, but she couldn't focus. She kept replaying the argument in her mind. She didn't believe Lamont had meant the things he'd said, but it didn't make them hurt any less.

The argument need to happen. They had probed one another for months, walking on eggshells, avoiding the major topics until it imploded. The fact Lamont had referred to Jenny as weak was jarring, and it had Jenny thinking, wondering if going to counselling was the right action.

Should she have tried speaking directly to Lamont about her issues?

Maybe he would have confided in return. Now, they were both adrift. Lamont had tried contacting Jenny but she couldn't face him, not without knowing what she wanted to do.

Jenny slumped on the table, wanting to block out the outside world. She wanted to escape, leave it all behind. It was harder than it should be, and she had no idea where to start. Dimly, she wondered if that was how Lamont had felt the whole time.

'Are you sleeping?'

'You know I'm not,' Jenny said to Kate, lifting her head and watching her friend hover in the doorway.

'Good. I'm taking you to lunch.'

'It's three in the afternoon.'

'So what? Did you eat at lunchtime?'

Jenny didn't answer.

'Exactly. Get up and put your coat on.'

'I can't go to lunch, Kate. I have work to do.'

'You're not getting any work done, and we need a change of scenery. Let's go.'

They went to a local sandwich shop, Jenny picking at a Chicken Teriyaki wholewheat baguette. She sipped her water and waited for Kate to speak.

'Your man contacted me again today.'

Jenny was silent.

'He didn't sound good. He was slurring, so I'm guessing he's been drinking.'

Jenny's stomach lurched. She forced herself to eat the sandwich as a distraction, hating Lamont being in distress.

'What's your move? Are you breaking up with him?'

'I just need some space right now.'

'How do you think L's gonna take that? Do you think he's gonna stay away forever?'

'I don't know, Kate. I don't know about any of this, but if me staying with you is a problem, I'll check into a hotel or stay with my parents.'

'Go to Hell. I'm not letting you go anywhere. I need to ask these questions though. You know that.'

'We had an argument, and I can't help feeling that if we'd talked things out properly before then it wouldn't have happened. I mean, we had a great night out, and amazing sex. That would have been a great time to get everything out in the open, but we didn't. We went with the facade instead.'

'After the time you've both had, is it so wrong that all you craved was that facade for a while?'

'Look where it's lead us though?' Jenny replied. 'I'm staying with you and my partner seems comfortable drinking himself to death and ringing and texting me to the point I have to block him. He's not supposed to act like that, but he's broken and I'm not sure I know how to fix him,' She paused. 'What should I do?'

'It's your life and you both love each other. I guess you need to ask yourself if that's enough.'

'It shouldn't be so hard,' Jenny sighed. Kate squeezed her friend's hand.

'When the hell have you ever had it easy where L is concerned?'

* * *

'Can I come in?' Shorty wrinkled his nose. Lamont's eyes were bleary and his hair was more of a rumpled mess than ever. Lamont shakily stepped aside, letting Shorty in. He tottered back toward the study on unsteady legs. Staggering into his office chair he took a deep swig of brandy as Shorty watched. Lamont offered his friend the bottle, but Shorty shook his head.

'You're a damn mess, L. What the hell happened?'

'You don't know? I thought you and Jen were such good friends?'

'What are you talking about?'

'We had a fight, and she left.'

'What did you fight about?'

'Does it matter?'

'With you smelling like you bathed in brandy, it kinda does,' replied Shorty. Lamont mockingly clapped, the bottle slipping from his grasp, liquor billowing over the expensive carpet. Shorty grabbed the bottle and headed to the kitchen, hesitating when he saw the destruction. Glasses, plates and cutlery were nestled amongst dried liquids and broken glass.

Shorty was used to Lamont's space being devoid of any mess or dust, so it was a complete shock to see this state. He headed back to the study. Lamont was slumped over the desk.

'Tell me about the fight,' Shorty said, jolting Lamont from his stupor.

'She was seeing Rika behind my back.'

'So?' Shorty knew Lamont and his sister hadn't spoken in nearly two years, but still didn't understand why it was such a big deal.

'What do you mean *so*? You remember what Rika was like, right? How she picked that piece of shit Marrion over her brother? Her family, who supported her and paid for every single fucking thing she needed for years, without ever complaining? You think it's cool for

Jenny to go behind my back and then to invite her to our house without speaking to me?'

'L, Rika fucked up, but she's your little sis and you love her. Jenny did what she thought was right.'

'It's not Jen's place to sort things. She's struggling with her business, you know? Ever since she took time off to look after me, Jen's florists has been in the shitter. I offered to help; to give her the money and even treat it as a loan if she wanted, but she refused, so I let it slide. I watch her go into her office every day and come home a little more fucked up. It breaks me that she won't let me help, but I stayed away and let it slide.'

'Women are different, and you know that. They don't look at things like we do. Sometimes that's a bad thing. Sometimes it's good, but it's the way it is, and you can't really control the two.'

'Why are you here?' Lamont didn't want to discuss Jenny anymore. Shorty held Lamont's gaze for a moment before answering.

'I've waited long enough. I want back into the game, and I'm not taking no for an answer.'

* * *

Lennox Thompson parked up in Miles Hill and strode towards a door, knocking and entering. The man he'd come to see was in the living room, his face heavily bruised. He glanced up when Lennox walked in, but said nothing. Lennox surveyed the pitiful specimen, struggling to control his annoyance. He was about to speak when a woman sashayed into the room, handing Lutel a drink. Noticing Lennox, she beamed.

'Hey, Len. Is everything good?'

'Everything is fine, Nicole. Do you mind giving us a minute?' It wasn't a request and everyone in the room knew it. Kissing Lutel on the cheek, Nicole smiled tightly at Lennox and went upstairs. Lennox waited a moment before speaking.

'Are you suffering from some disease?'

Lutel frowned. 'What are you talking about?'

'I'm asking if you're suffering from some illness that stops you from listening. I specifically told you to stay away from Shorty. You can imagine how funny I found it when I heard that not only did you not do as ordered, you were also beaten unconscious in a room full of people.' Lennox clapped his hands. 'Well done.'

'My rep was on the line, Len. I needed to do it.'

'How?'

'Huh?'

'How was your rep on the line? You're not with the silly bitch you were fighting over anymore. You've moved on.'

'Shorty violated. He was warned not to step on toes and he did it anyway. Whether or not I'm with Nicole doesn't mean shit. You've never had two girls at once before?'

Without warning Lennox sprang forward and slapped Lutel, the sound echoing around the room. Lutel leapt to his feet with a roar, but Lennox didn't move. Coming to his senses, Lutel backed away, wincing.

'You're an emotional idiot. Look at you, jumping to your feet, ready to fight despite getting fucked up the last time,' Lennox gripped Lutel by the chin, his nails digging into the injured man's face. 'If your stupidity has messed my up plans, I'll have you pulled apart at the joints while your pretty little girlfriend upstairs watches. Understand?'

Lutel nodded. 'I'm sorry, Len. I got caught up but it won't happen again. I promise.'

'Good. It better not.'

Lutel sank back onto the sofa, looking up at his boss.

'What are we gonna do now?'

Lennox turned, looking out of the window for so long that Lutel started to wonder if he had even heard the question.

'You need to clean your plate. Get yourself sorted, then take out Shorty. Don't fuck it up.'

* * *

Lamont looked at Shorty, the determination etched into his friend's face. He rubbed his temples, trying to blot out the impending headache. His mouth was like sandpaper, and he felt the nausea of too much alcohol swimming around his stomach.

'We've already discussed this—'

'And I listened. I didn't agree with what you were saying, but I still followed orders and kept my nose clean. Now, I want back in. I can work with K-Bar.'

'Shorty, there's nothing wrong with being patient.'

'Don't give me that bullshit, L. You're just stringing me along.'

'You're letting emotions get away from you. Just like when you fucked up Lutel. Yeah, I heard about it directly from Jukie. You're lucky the police didn't come for you.'

'Fuck Lutel. I'm tired of hearing about him,' said Shorty.

'What about Lennox Thompson? Are you tired of hearing about Lutel's boss, because I bet you he knows about the situation.'

'I don't care. Lutel came for me, or did Jukie not fill you in about that part? He started it and unlike you, I defend myself when someone attacks me.'

'You're a fucking idiot,' Lamont slammed his hands on the desk. 'Is having multiple people aiming guns at me and being shot something to be ashamed of? What about you, *Big bad Shorty?* You got arrested and carted off to prison like some little runner. What does that make you?'

In the silence that followed, Lamont saw the veins in Shorty's thick neck throbbing. Shorty clenched his fists, nostrils flaring.

'You're a drunken mess, losing your shit over your woman like some pussy. You're not in the right frame of mind to lead, so stop preaching, and put me back in.'

Lamont took a deep breath, surpassing the urge to retort. His head was pounding, and he wished Shorty would leave so he could throw up.

'You can't aggravate things with Lennox Thompson. We're not in a position to fight that war. We've hired soldiers, but we're still getting everyone into shape. I need you to keep calm.'

Shorty rubbed his eyes.

'L, I can do it. Please, just put me back in, and I'll stay calm. I'll be distracted. Cool?'

There was another long silence, both men sizing up the other. Lamont broke it this time.

'Fine. You're back in. You and K-Bar can work out what's happening, but make sure I'm kept in the loop.'

Shorty grinned, looking ten years younger in an instant.

'Thank you, L. I mean that. For starters, let's get you some coffee so you can tidy up. You're looking like some drunken loser.'

* * *

Lennox and Nikkolo were clad in all black as they entered a restaurant near the Hood. When he saw them, the owner scurried into the back as the pair pulled guns, aiming them at the men in the room. Without warning they fired, two of the three men falling with cries of pain.

Lennox and Nikkolo were unfazed, focusing their guns on the other man, hunched over his plate of food. Lennox assessed the large man, respecting the fact that he was trying hard to hide his terror.

'You're an unfortunate casualty, Winston. Your daddy is at fault, but that falls on you now.'

Winston itched to reach for his pistol. Both men had him in their sights though, and the fact they had coldly dispatched of his guards showed they had no qualms about killing. He searched Lennox's blood-shot eyes, noting they looked devoid of emotion. There were tired lines around the man's face, but he seemed composed.

'You don't have to do this. We can still work something out. Kill me though, all bets are off. You'll be hunted down like a dog. You won't be able to make any money. My pops will see to that.'

Lennox nodded at Winston's words.

'You're not wrong, Winnie. I've respect the fact you always try to be practical. You're always looking at the big picture. Your daddy ain't the man he was twenty years ago though. The fact he thought he could point you at me proves that. He'll learn once everyone dear to him is gone. Please don't take what happens next personally.'

Lennox fired four times, each bullet slamming into Winston, his chair toppling backwards and sending the big man to the floor. Winston spluttered, his tongue lolling as he choked on the torrents of blood billowing from his mouth.

Lennox looked at him without pity, then signalled to Nikkolo, who put his gun to Winston's head and fired, finishing the job. Dropping the guns on the restaurant floor, they hurried from the premises.

CHAPTER THIRTEEN

Friday 13 March 2015

FOR DAYS after Winston's murder, Chapeltown awaited the explosion they were sure would follow. The murder was being investigated, but the police were simply going through the motions, trying to stop a war from escalating.

The owner of the restaurant had been questioned. No one had spoken with or seen Delroy. The streets suspected Lennox Thompson was responsible for the hit, but a small crew from Seacroft were stupidly claiming responsibility.

Malcolm Powell held court outside the health centre on Chapeltown Road, where he spoke at length about the drug war tearing apart the community. Speaking only to a few people at first, others quickly convened to hear what he had to say:

'Thank you all for coming. Another week passes, and there is more strife and bloodshed for us to overcome. What happened to the Williams family was a tragedy and my condolences go out to them. I don't condone their alleged business, but Winston didn't deserve to die.

'How many more though? How many more soldiers have to die in this point-less war, caused by greed and the sale of illegal goods. The same illegal goods that allow police to storm into our ends like overseers and beat us at will.

'This is all linked — a home linked to Delroy Williams was raided recently, *the largest drug seizure in years that I can remember. It all needs to stop, and we need to continue working together to allow that to happen. It needs all of us working collectively.*

'To Delroy Williams directly, I again apologise for your loss and if you see the light and wish to speak to me in confidence, contact me and I will do my best to help you, I promise.'

* * *

'It's only a matter of time until Delroy goes on the attack.'

Rigby and Murphy were eating a quick lunch consisting of wraps from a local bakery and containers of coffee. They'd worked through the night leading up to their current meeting. So far the progress had been pathetic.

'Was it definitely Thompson who took out Winston? Maybe Teflon got his hands dirty?'

'I don't think so. Teflon and Delroy get along, according to intelligence reports. They've definitely done business together, I'd stake my pension on that.'

'We need to speak to Holdsworth again. He's leading that investigation, and it's like he doesn't care.'

'He doesn't, Rig. You know that. We need to make sure it doesn't spill over. If you're finished eating, let's talk to our friend in there.'

The pair of them left the bakery and headed to an apartment building in the heart of the city centre. After announcing themselves and riding the elevator to the 6th floor, they knocked.

The woman warily stared at the pair. Rigby smiled, but this didn't seem to reassure her.

'Can we come in, please? We just have a few questions.'

'About what?'

'About your friend Naomi.'

This startled Adele enough for her to pull away from the door. The flat was one bedroom, but appeared lived-in and comfortable. They sat, pen and notepads out.

'What about Naomi?' Adele folded her arms, her eyes darting around the room.

'We're investigating a spate of incidents around the time of your friend's murder, so we apologise if it seems like we're treading old ground. Did anyone speak with you at the time of the murder?'

Adele shook her head.

'Do you know why it occurred?'

'Why would I?'

'Naomi was murdered with two other people. One of the men, Xiyu Manderson, was in a relationship with your friend, putting her in the middle of it.'

'That fucking cunt. It was his fault Naomi was involved. All of it was his fault.'

Rigby and Murphy shared a look.

'Why?'

'He broke my friend's spirit. Naomi was special; she was beautiful, and she had this quality that made her stand out. Chink . . . *Xiyu* broke that. She wasn't the same when she was with him.'

'How?'

'She was nervous. They argued a lot, and she was feisty and liked to run her mouth. Then she just stopped.'

'You think Xiyu was beating her?' Rigby realised. Adele nodded.

'I saw bruises once. I tried asking her, and she just looked right through me. Even when I suggested getting some help, she just ignored me. She wasn't even mad; it was like she'd shut down.'

'We're trying to understand the crime. Polo, an associate of Xiyu's who we believe was his bodyguard, was shot outside. We believe that it was a planned hit.'

Tears streamed down Adele's cheeks as she choked on her sobs.

'They treated her like trash. She was murdered for the sake of it.'

Rigby nodded. 'I agree. Your friend didn't deserve to be murdered just for being there.'

Murphy hung in the background, making notes and watching Rigby work. This was their thing. Rigby was better at making people feel comfortable. Murphy found it easier to intimidate. Adele was slowly becoming comfortable around Rigby. She slumped onto the chair facing him and he offered her a tissue.

'Why are you really here?' She softly asked.

'We want your help to catch the people responsible. You know about the situation, and I think you know why it happened. We'll find out everything. This lovely flat you've got; is it above board? We'll be thorough in checking everything, including finances. Help us out. Don't let Naomi's killers get away with it.'

Wiping her eyes and blowing her nose, Adele finally nodded.

'If you can guarantee my safety, I'll tell you what I know.'

* * *

Lamont waited for the electronic gates to open, allowing him access to a sprawling property on the outskirts of Leeds. Driving up a long, winding path, he parked in front of a multi-room mansion.

Even as he climbed from the car, Lamont spotted at least eight armed men patrolling the premises. Lamont was quickly patted down and led into the main room. Delroy and a woman Lamont recognised as his wife were sat there. Both were quiet, the grief far more obvious on the face of Delroy's wife.

Lamont gave Delroy's wife a hug and offered his condolences, yet received very little reaction. Delroy shook Lamont's hand, and they traipsed towards another room to talk. He poured two glasses of whiskey and gave one to Lamont without even asking. Silently, they toasted and drank.

'Winston shouldn't have been caught up in it,' Lamont finally said, clearing his throat as the hot liquor attacked his chest.

'I know,' Delroy stared into his glass. 'I wanted you to take over. Winnie didn't have the tools. Not for war anyway. Spinks went missing, and no one even noticed. Lennox probably forced him to share Winnie's routine. After Mack's attack, Spinks drove Winnie around. They were close.'

Lamont absorbed the information, going over every little point in his head. He wouldn't say it out loud, but Lennox had played a brilliant move. He had effectively weakened Delroy's position by killing his son, having already arranged for his spot to be raided.

The pressure was now on Delroy to strike back, yet looking at him, Lamont couldn't see it happening. Not effectively at least. Delroy wore every single one of his years on his face. He was finished, even if he hadn't yet realised.

'Where's Eddie?' Lamont asked. Eddie Williams was more in the mould of Shorty; he was a hothead who needed little provocation to cause destruction. The death of his brother would put him on the warpath. Delroy shrugged, refilling his drink.

'No one's seen him. Either Lennox got him too, or he's gone directly after Lennox. He didn't answer my calls, and he hasn't stopped by. Possible he doesn't know, but I doubt that. Word spread quickly.'

Lamont agreed. He'd had well over a dozen phone calls once the news hit the streets about the murder. A man in Eddie's position definitely had contacts.

'What now?'

'Are you going to take up my offer?' Delroy finally looked at Lamont.

'No.'

Delroy nodded.

'I've got a crew in place. They're gonna wipe out Lennox and the rest of his people,' Delroy held Lamont's attention, his lined face hard. 'You might wanna stay out of Chapeltown for a while.'

* * *

'It's mad.'

Shorty was tucking into some fish soup with K-Bar, Darren and Maka at a safe house. A stream of empty containers and carrier bags surrounded them.

Shorty was in his element, happy to be back in the life. He'd spoken with K-Bar and picked up right where he'd left off, but with a newfound calmness. Yesterday, he'd even spent time with Grace, under Amy's careful supervision.

Shorty was re-learning the ranks, but found he spent less time amongst the soldiers and more time analysing things from a distance. As he'd told Lamont, Shorty knew of the risk involved with the police. He had no desire to go back to prison. There was too much to live for.

'What is?' Darren asked K-Bar, wiping his mouth as he finished a dumpling.

'This whole situation. How the hell does someone get the drop on a man like Winnie? He's supposed to have security out of the ass.'

'Winnie never took it seriously. He was probably sitting in the restaurant stuffing his fat face,' said Shorty.

'He had one guard there with him; he was just a little slow on the draw,' replied K-Bar.

'Lenny was gunning at them. Winnie needed more people, or he needed to avoid being out in public. We've all done dirt before. We know the signs.'

No one could argue with Shorty. Other than K-Bar, Shorty was in a league of his own when it came to warfare. His track record spoke for itself.

'Either way, everyone needs to be careful. Delroy is old, but he won't sit tight on this. He's gonna have his people out there hitting back against Lennox. Lennox's people might not discriminate, so we need to have people out there when necessary.'

'Do you think L's gonna get involved?' Maka asked. No one spoke for a moment. All were aware of the weird relationship between Lamont and Delroy. At times there was a father and son vibe. At others, they were at each other's throats.

Lamont had mentioned an offer that Delroy made for him to lead his organisation, but no one expected Lamont to take it. Lamont wouldn't work for another person; it was the one consistent fact about him.

'I don't know, fam,' Shorty finally replied. 'I don't think so though. L's playing it different. He's not trying to take on someone else's drama. Not anymore.'

* * *

Lamont left Delroy's, his mind full of questions. The situation with Lennox was about to heat up. Lamont hoped Delroy's shooters were good, because he couldn't see them having many chances to take out Lennox Thompson.

Lamont was focused the future. He'd heard about Malcolm's speech on Chapeltown Road, but didn't know if Jenny had been there.

Long-term, Lamont could slide into Delroy's spot if Lennox murdered him. He had the infrastructure in place and it would help placate people if they were able to earn more money. The positive about the conflict was that it was keeping him from overthinking about his estranged girlfriend.

Reaching home, Lamont paused. There was a note pinned to the door. Removing it, Lamont noted it had a number to call. Sighing, he called the number.

'Lamont Jones?'

'Who's asking?'

'A car will pick you up in ten minutes.'

'The person hung up. Lamont called Akeem.

'Someone left a note at the house. A car's coming to pick me up in ten minutes to take me somewhere.'

'I can have someone at your place in five minutes. Go inside and lock up.'

'It's fine. I believe I know who's behind this.'

When the car arrived, Lamont was blindfolded and driven to a location. Despite the circumstances, he felt oddly calm. He was led into a building, and then the blindfold was removed.

'Hello, Mr Jones,' a familiar voice intoned. Lamont nodded, a small smile on his face.

'It's good to see you, Akhan.'

CHAPTER FOURTEEN

Friday 13 March 2015

LAMONT AND AKHAN stared at one another, neither man blinking. Lamont recalled their last conversation; when Akhan had calmly blackmailed Lamont under threat of Lamont's murder of Ricky Reagan becoming public knowledge.

Akhan looked the same; unflappably calm and fastidiously dressed in a shirt, trousers and dress shoes. Finally, he motioned for Lamont to sit down.

'Would you like a drink?' Akhan asked.

'Some water please,' replied Lamont. Akhan signalled for someone to fetch it.

'How are you?'

'I'm well,' said Lamont, keeping his words succinct. He was aware of the guards posted by the door.

'Our last meeting, things went in a different direction to how I'd intended.'

'I doubt that. You wanted to establish control, and you did.'

Akhan shook his head, his expression almost pained.

'I wanted what was best for you. The freedom you desire, it doesn't exist. Chapeltown needs you, especially with the current situation with Delroy and Lennox Thompson.'

'You know about that?'

'Delroy will lose. We both know this. Lennox is more organised, more logical, and he's utterly ruthless. He wants everything, and Delroy is in the way. Even before his son's death, he could not have won.'

Lamont rubbed his forehead, drinking the water, so he had something to do.

'Are you going to explain what this has to do with me?'

Akhan assessed Lamont for a long moment. The guards shifted slightly, but held their positions.

'Lennox is a problem because if he wins, he won't leave you unchecked. You're a threat, maybe the only one he has in Leeds. He doesn't think the same way as Delroy and he will not co-exist. You'll be taken out.'

'Why do you care?' Lamont understood Akhan's concerns, but the fact remained Akhan had blackmailed him, and that loomed over everything else the warlord said. 'You could do a deal with Lennox. He'd be forced to take you seriously. You don't need me for this.'

Akhan grinned. 'I meant everything I said, Lamont. It's only your unwillingness to really get involved that holds you back. If you looked at your whole city the way you do your crew, things would work better, and everyone would profit handsomely. Lennox is concerned only with himself.'

Lamont closed his eyes.

'If I take out Lennox, will you allow me to walk away?'

Akhan again gave Lamont a long look.

'Stay for dinner and let us talk of other matters. One more thing,' Akhan began as he led them from the study. 'Darren is to stay away from Rashad and any other member of my organisation. If he doesn't, he dies.'

* * *

Jenny played with the food on her plate, her appetite awol. She was in a trendy restaurant near Park Row, but her thoughts were scattered. She looked at the mobile phone resting on the table, thinking of

Lamont and what he might be doing. She'd had a lot of time to think about their argument and hated that things had grown so out of control.

Several times, she'd considered contacting Lamont and trying to work past things, but she couldn't predict where it would end. The future seemed murky, and Jenny had no idea how to navigate that.

'Aren't you eating?'

Jenny glanced at Malcolm and shook her head. He'd called earlier, inviting her to get some food. Jenny appreciated the distraction and agreed. Malcolm met her eyes, a strong, confident presence in the full venue. Women snuck appreciative looks at him as he ate his food but he paid them no attention, completely focused on Jenny.

'Starving yourself won't make things any better. You need to eat something.'

'I'll eat later.'

Malcolm looked for a moment as if he would argue, but shrugged and kept on eating. After a while he wiped his mouth.

'What do you know about the war in Chapeltown?' He asked.

'I try not to think about it. I still gave nightmares from what happened to my partner a few years ago.'

Malcolm's face was unreadable as he surveyed Jenny.

'You don't talk about him much.'

Jenny sighed. 'There isn't much to say. Sometimes, relationships are a struggle. I'm sure you've heard all the cliches before.'

'What does your boyfriend think of you spending time around me?'

Jenny made a face. 'Why would you ask that?'

Malcolm grinned. 'I'm a curious fellow. You won't eat, so I'm going to talk at you for a while and see how that works out. So, stop avoiding the question.'

'I'm not avoiding the question. Look, he's a private guy, and he's fantastic at hiding his emotions. If you're trying to ask if he knows about you, the answer is yes.'

'And, he said nothing at all about spending any time with me?'

Jenny thought back to the conversations she and Lamont had shared about Malcolm. Lamont had mentioned his name the day they'd argued. Malcolm was a good-looking guy; he was articulate and quirky, and Jenny enjoyed spending time with him. The fact he was a superb writer was an additional bonus.

Jenny saw him as someone she could confide in, and wondered if that would upset Lamont. She tried putting herself in his shoes. *If Lamont was speaking with another woman the way she spoke with and spent time with Malcolm, how would she feel?*

Seconds later, her eyes narrowed, and she shook her head to clear the thoughts from her mind.

'Where the hell were you just then?' Malcolm's eyebrow rose.

'Somewhere I'm not sure how to navigate,' Jenny admitted. 'To answer your question, no he didn't. He's a closed book.'

Malcolm rubbed his eyebrow. 'Let's talk about something else. What do you want to do with the rest of your life?'

Jenny's face crinkled in surprise. It was such a simple question, but it startled her.

'I want to grow my business. I can make it better than it was before, it's just going to take time. I often have to remember that and stop beating myself up.'

Malcolm nodded. 'I told you before that your passion was one of the things I liked the most about you. I know you're in a relationship and you're giving that your attention, but you should always put yourself first because quite simply, you deserve the best, Jenny. Whatever or whoever that may be.'

Jenny couldn't speak at first, moved by Malcolm's words. They were empowering and touching and warmed her in a way that it shouldn't.

They stared at one another for a long moment. Jenny's hands trembled, her stomach churning in a way that had nothing to do with nausea and everything to do with nerves.

'Have dinner with me. Tonight. I'll cook.'

Jenny's heart seemed to stop for a second. She thought again of Lamont, but Malcom was right. He was invested in her and wanted to spend time with her. With that in mind, there was only one answer to give.

'Okay.'

* * *

Lamont met with Akeem. They sat in the study, Lamont pouring drinks as he shared Akhan's words.

'We need a strategy for getting rid of Lennox. Delroy will struggle. He's got shooting crews in place but Lennox will see them coming. Lennox's team is solid, but he's the key.'

'He's powerful. He has people ready to die for him,' Akeem agreed.

'The police exposure at the moment won't make it easy either.'

'Shorty could kill Lennox?' Akeem suggested. 'K-Bar is still benched. The only other person I'd suggest is myself.'

'I don't want to use you for that. I've no doubt in your ability, but it's a risk, and I need you for too many other things.'

Akeem nodded. 'What's Akhan's game? He could go after Lennox himself if he thought he was a threat.'

Lamont didn't reply. He agreed that Akhan definitely had an agenda he hadn't shared with Lamont. He was playing a role, and Lamont couldn't predict what Akhan would do if he killed Lennox.

'I don't know. He seems determined to have me in place. Maybe he wants to keep me distracted? He knows about Darren getting close to Rashad, meaning Darren was sloppy, or Rashad told Akhan what he knew . . .'

'Or, Akhan knew all along and let it happen.'

Lamont flinched. He'd given thought to Akeem's theory, but didn't want to believe he could be outplayed in such a manner. He wasn't on top form though. Jenny occupied a permanent place in his mind; he was trying to listen to Kate and stay away, yet felt things would only grow worse if he did.

'For now, let's focus on Lennox. Akhan is the long-term plan. We have a few goons in place now. Let's at least get an idea of Lennox's team, and any potential weak links.'

'I'm on it, boss.' Akeem downed his drink and reached for his phone.

* * *

'I'm glad you've made up your mind.'

In the middle of doing her hair, Jenny turned to look at Kate, ignoring the wide grin on her friend's face.

'I don't know what you mean.'

'Sure you don't. You and Malcolm going on a date and you going over for dinner is a sign you and L are done, girl.'

'I'm in love with L, Kate. Malcolm is a friend, a good one who has stepped up when I needed someone. We're friends, that's it.'

'Whatever you say; you're wearing that sexy-ass black dress and those *fuck-me* heels. I haven't seen you like this in years, so you can save the *friends* shit for someone who doesn't know you.'

'L knows about Malcolm. He doesn't mind me having friends.'

'Course, and if the position was reversed, you wouldn't mind L going to dinner with a beautiful woman who wrote really well, would you?'

Jenny didn't reply. She didn't know where they were at, but her feelings were unchanged. She loved Lamont, but the confusion and his refusal to let her in were jarring. Deciding to put it out of her mind, she focused on finishing her hair, ignoring Kate's triumphant cackling.

* * *

Jenny's heart hammered. She knew why. She knew how she could stop it. *It's just dinner*, she kept telling herself. She took her car. A powerful red Mercedes. While Lamont was recovering, and she was driving him around, he'd insisted on buying it:

'I don't need a car, L.'

'I know you don't. You're happy with this one, and that's fine, but I want to buy you one.'

'And I don't want you to. Like I said. I have my own money.'

'I know you do,' Lamont smiled. *'We both have money. So, if you're not going to let me buy you one, then I'll treat myself. A nice cherry red Mercedes,'* he gently rubbed his stomach. *'But, with my condition and all, I'm going to need you to drive me around.'*

So, they both got what they wanted. Jenny got a car and kept her independence, and Lamont got to buy it for her. She quickly found a buyer for her old car, and it was never spoken of again.

Jenny wondered what Lamont was doing, but shook the feelings. She pulled into Malcolm's drive, parking behind his Range Rover. The house was detached and pale-bricked, with a sturdy looking brown door. Her chest fluttering, Jenny knocked at the door.

'You're right on time,' said Malcolm, beaming when he saw Jenny stood there. He wore a green polo shirt, tight around the biceps, khaki trousers and deck shoes. He showed her into the living room. The lights were dimmed low, the TV on, but muted, silently playing what looked like the Evening News.

Jenny was surprised at the organised clutter. Books, newspapers, notepads, pens and paper were all over, but haphazardly placed into piles.

'Can I get you a drink?'

'I'm driving, so just a glass of water will be fine,' said Jenny. Malcolm snorted.

'Glass of wine coming up. Take a seat.'

Jenny did as she was told. The comfortable sofa was a dark murky brown. She watched the news, hearing the music playing in the background. *Al Green*. She had owned several of his CD's when she was younger.

'Here you go,' Malcolm handed her a glass of red wine. 'Try this.'

Jenny sipped it. It was strong, but did a lot to ease her nervousness.

'So, how was work after our lunch?' asked Malcolm. Jenny glanced at him.

'Are we doing small talk?'

'If you want to go straight to bed, then that's fine with me,' replied Malcolm. Jenny laughed.

'I guess I asked for that.'

'Ask and you shall receive.'

'Is that why you've got *Al Green* playing?'

Malcolm shook his head, grin still etched on his face.

'I'm just a big Al fan. If you'd rather have something else on, I can play a bit of *Spice Girls?* Maybe some *Cher?*'

Jenny shrilly giggled. 'Al will do just fine.'

They spoke easily. Malcolm told Jenny a little about his latest projects. They ate dinner, a delicious chicken salad.

'I wrote something based on you,' said Malcolm much later. He was pouring them more wine. It was Jenny's fourth glass, and she was feeling light-headed.

'Did you now?'

'I did,' said Malcolm, all lightheartedness gone.

'Well, are you going to share it with me?' teased Jenny. Malcolm didn't smile. His eyes locked on hers, and Jenny faltered. As she wondered what was happening, Malcolm cleared his throat and began to speak:

The most beautiful thing about her isn't her beauty.

It's not her lips; lips that make you want to hold her, gently nibble, and seduce her.

It's not the body, highly sexual, molten fire from a volcano, though she does not flaunt it.

It's not the hauntingly intelligent eyes.

It's all the above, and the personality on top.

That of a humble woman who knows, understands, appreciates the world around her.

Yet still goes out and grinds for what she wants.

When Malcolm stopped, it took a few moments for Jenny to catch up. The wine glass was frozen in her hand. With a start she sat back. Malcolm remained unsmiling. His voice had been monotone while reciting, but Jenny was moved.

'Wow . . .' She said.

'You like?'

Jenny nodded. 'It's amazing. I don't think I'm worthy of the words though. You might have exaggerated. A lot.'

'You would say that, and that's what makes you so extraordinary.'

'You probably say that to all the girls.'

Malcolm drained his wine. His eyes were slightly red, but it didn't seem to affect him as much as Jenny.

'I'm no virgin, but I don't make it a habit of writing personal poetry for women I'm trying to get with. Usually I just use what I have on hand, and it does the trick.'

'Malcolm, I have a boyfriend,' said Jenny. His reaction was the same as always. He gave a snort and shrugged.

'So what?'

'So, I can't do anything.'

'Can't, or won't?'

'Both,' Jenny put her wineglass on the table. 'I love him, and I don't cheat. I've had it done to me before.'

'It's not supposed to be nice. Cheating is a way of life though I think you're wonderful. For all the words I said above, and for many more. You know why I invited you here. I know you know, because you're smart, and yet you came anyway. Why?'

'I—' Jenny couldn't speak. Malcolm was in her space now, his eyes dark, serious, predatory with their intent. She felt trapped, fighting against her desires, trying to remain true to Lamont.

Malcolm's lips were on hers now though, and it felt right. She went with it, forcing her mouth further against his as he stimulated her lips, determined to control what was undoubtedly a good kiss. Jenny summoned her strength and pulled away just as Malcolm snaked her waist.

'No!'

'No?' Malcolm breathed heavily, his face incredulous. Jenny's lips still tingled, a growing part of her wanting to continue what they'd started. It had gone far further than it should have, however. She would not do that to Lamont.

'We can't do this. I love my partner and I can't go any further with you. I'm sorry if I gave you any impression that I would.'

'Are you serious?' Malcolm's voice rose. Jenny glanced at the exit, ready to flee if he grew hostile.

'I am.'

'You love your damn drug-dealing kingpin of a boyfriend, right? Yes, I know,' Malcolm added when he spotted Jenny's stunned expression 'I know all about *Teflon*, and the misery he brings to the community that I love. He's tactless, more concerned with streets and waging war than seeing the beautiful, driven, perfect woman in front of him! Is that really what you want?'

Jenny's mouth was dry. She couldn't believe Malcolm knew of Lamont, and not just Lamont, but Teflon too. He'd known the whole time.

'You don't even know him.'

'I know more about Teflon than you could ever imagine. What did he spin you? That he was going legit? Did he blame his childhood? We all have our demons, but we don't all sling poison to the same people we're smiling at, day in, day out. He'll never stop doing what he does. He's too damn good at it, and while he keeps doing it, people will die. You need to get away, and I can help you. I want you by my side.'

Jenny felt sick, part of her hoping that the words Malcolm spat couldn't be true. The air between the pair was devoid of emotion now, the tension palpable. Shaking her head, Jenny hurried from the house before Malcolm could kiss her again.

CHAPTER FIFTEEN

Saturday 14 March 2015

SHORTY KNOCKED on Amy's door, glancing around as he did. He loved the area Amy lived in. Shorty was a child of Chapeltown. Even when he started making money, he'd always stayed in the Hood. This area had a peaceful vibe though. Shorty had noticed this in the past when he used to pick up Grace. Before he got locked up. Before everything in his world had changed for him.

After waiting a few seconds and hearing nothing. Shorty knocked again.

'Why do you always have to knock so loudly?' Amy finally swung the door open, glaring at Shorty. She ran her hands through her hair. Her eyes were narrowed and her face drawn, but Amy's natural beauty shone through. *She was so normal*, he thought to himself. Normal and very attractive. She had that in common with Jenny.

'I thought you might have gone out.'

Amy shook her head. 'I'm not feeling all that great, so I'm resting. What are you doing with Grace?'

Shorty had no idea. It had taken multiple phone calls and apologies just to get Grace to spend more time with him, and that tore Shorty apart. Before everything went wrong Grace had adored Shorty, and then he'd gone.

'I'm not sure,' he finally said.

'Don't get her all hopped on sugar wherever it is, please. She'll be down in a minute. She's just brushing her teeth.'

Shorty nodded, thinking about Dionte. They had spoken a few times since his trip to Huddersfield. Dionte still had his guard up, but it was a start.

Shorty didn't deserve a second chance from either of his children, but he would make the most of it. He wouldn't fail them like he had Timmy.

Shorty closed his eyes. He'd brought Timmy into the game, taught him the basics, then expected him to sit around and wait patiently, because that was the way it was.

It hadn't been that way for Shorty though. He'd gone from moving weed with K-Bar and Lamont, to selling Class A drugs and making real money.

Aside from Lamont, Shorty had never worked for anyone. He'd worked with people like Marcus and a few elders had schooled him, but he hadn't waited around. He wouldn't wait around. *Why would Timmy?*

'Are you okay, Shorty?' Amy looked concerned. Shorty nodded. There were more footsteps, and Grace Turner stood next to Amy. She glanced at Shorty, and his heart felt ready to burst. She looked so much like Amy, but he saw his sullenness in there. She gazed at him, a small smile on her face.

'Hey Gracey, are you ready to go?'

Grace nodded. Amy hugged her, kissing her on both cheeks.

'I love you, Grace. Be good for your daddy, okay?'

'Yes, mummy.'

Shorty held Grace's hand, settling her into the back of the ride, a Land-Cruiser he'd rented. He started the engine, cringing when the loud hip-hop music blared. Grace jumped. Shorty chuckled.

'Sorry, baby. I'll turn this off. We can put the radio on.'

* * *

Jenny was slumped on Kate's sofa, a blanket pulled around her as she stared at the television like a zombie. The kiss with Malcolm plagued her mind. Jenny had enjoyed it far more than she intended. It would have been easy to succumb further and sleep with Malcolm. At first, she'd dismissed Malcolm's parting words as a petty attempt to break up her and Lamont. They stuck with her though.

Lamont's attitude had changed, and she had put it down to the aftermath of the shooting. Lamont told her he would leave the street life behind, and Jenny had taken him at his word. When she thought about it, there was no proof that he'd done so.

'Have you been sat here all day?' Kate called out as she came through the front door. She kissed Jenny on the cheek and took off her coat.

'I want to give you some money,' said Jenny.

'For what?' Kate made a face.

'For letting me stay here.'

'You're my best friend and I'm not taking your money. That's the last I want to hear about it,' said Kate. 'I was going to ring you earlier.'

'Why?'

'Why do you think? I want to hear all about your date.'

Jenny shook her head. 'It wasn't a date.'

'Sure it wasn't. Anyway, tell me all about it.'

'Fine. He made me dinner, we talked, and he recited a poem he wrote.'

'A poem about what?'

Jenny paused. 'About me.'

Kate giggled.

'Wasn't a date, right? But the man crooned poetry to you? What happened after that?'

'He kissed me.'

'And you pulled away?'

'After a minute I did.'

Kate's eyes widened.

'Wow. I teased you, but I didn't actually think you had it in you. Was he a good kisser?'

'Yes.' Jenny still recalled how Malcolm made her lips tingle, and how badly she'd wanted to go further. She felt another crippling wave of guilt.

'What happened after you pulled away?'

'He started talking about L. He was saying all this stuff about Lamont murdering people, and how he was still a presence in the streets.'

'He convinced you, didn't he?' Kate watched Jenny now.

'I don't know. Do you think L is still selling drugs?'

When Kate hesitated, Jenny felt a lurch in her chest that had little to do with guilt.

'Fuck,' she whispered. Kate grabbed her hand.

'Look, I don't think L wants to, but I also don't think he can leave that life so easily. Not at the level he's at.'

Jenny didn't reply, staring at her hands, her eyes watering.

* * *

'Thanks for coming,' Lamont said to Darren when he entered the office at the barbers.

'No drama. K said it was important. What's the drill?'

'You need to cease contact with Rashad. Immediately.'

Darren's face fell.

'Did I mess up?'

'No. You played the role brilliantly. Rashad wasn't as careful as you were, and the wrong people found out.'

'Well, thanks for giving me the opportunity anyway.' Darren turned to leave.

'Would you like a promotion?'

Those words stilled Darren. He whirled around, staring at Lamont with abject disbelief.

'What?'

'I want you working with K-Bar. You'll have people reporting into you. Can you handle that?'

'Course I can handle it,' exclaimed Darren, forgetting himself in his excitement. 'Are you sure though?'

'I've been hearing good things about you for a while, and this just solidifies that. If you're interested, I'm happy to make the transition, and I know K-Bar and Maka will be too. Do you want it?'

'Yes, thank you, L. I mean that.'

'Don't worry about. Take the day off. Someone will contact you with more instructions.'

After Darren left, Lamont ate lunch and headed from the barbers with a quick nod to Trinidad. People were still distant with him, likely the results of Malcolm's speeches. The streets were quiet. Lamont was waiting for things to escalate after Winston's death.

Climbing into his car, Lamont drove up to Chapel Allerton, stopping in front of a semi-detached, cream coloured house. He headed through the well-tended garden, enamoured with the different coloured flowers. It was the type of garden Jenny would like. He knocked, smiling at the bespectacled brunette who answered. She returned the smile and invited him in after a small hug.

'Can I get you a drink?'

'Some tea, please. No sugar or milk.'

Soon, Lamont was perched on the sofa sipping his tea. The woman sat beside him.

'I'm sorry for not stopping by sooner. Life has grown extra complicated.'

'You don't have to apologise for living, Lamont. Do you want to talk about what has become complicated?'

'Not really,' Lamont admitted. 'I think I should though. After everything with the shooting, I've tried to do more on my own. Jen's been after me to speak to someone impartial about my issues. I didn't feel comfortable doing that. Things are happening in Chapeltown. They're making people look at me differently and I don't like it.'

'Are you referring to the thing with the police? Malcolm's been on a right tear with his writing.'

This surprised Lamont. 'You know Malcolm?'

'I've met him a few times at different writing events. He's definitely a character, but he has star power, if that makes any sense. He reminds me a lot of you, actually.'

'Great,' mumbled Lamont.

'Why is that an issue?'

'He's been spending time with Jen.'

'As in, your girlfriend?'

'The same one.'

The woman assessed Lamont. 'What aren't you telling me?'

'Jenny and I had a massive fallout. She's been staying with a friend.'

'Why did you fall out?'

'Life. My refusal to get help. I called her weak for speaking to a counsellor. She went behind my back and spoke to a family member I'd fallen out with, trying to force a reconciliation.'

'So, her intentions were pure at least.'

'Yes, but I flipped my lid and now we're on the outs. I have no idea how to even begin fixing it.'

'Start by talking to her.'

'I've tried.'

'Have you? Or have you tried telling her she should come home? You both need to sit down and talk about what the future is for you both, and if you will stay together. If you stay like this, it'll just fester.'

Lamont shrugged. 'No harm in trying, I guess. How's the book coming along?'

The woman rubbed her eyes. 'It's such a struggle. When I agreed to take this on, I had no idea what I was getting into. Justin's first book sold really well within the community and did okay within other cities. Trying to write more books from scratch is fun, but time-consuming. I've had to reduce my hours at work so I can keep up with it, which everyone tells me is stupid, but I have to do this, you know?'

'Justin left money though, didn't he?' Lamont asked. Justin Holmes had been a drug dealer on the rise years ago. After getting locked up, he was released, re-entering the street life. He'd had a desire to write, but he'd been gunned down two years ago.

His ex-girlfriend, Charlotte took up his mantle and began writing, setting up a publishing press in his name. She tidied his novel with the help of some professional editors, then released it. The book had been well-received, and Charlotte had continued writing. She and Lamont first spoke after Justin's death. After his own shooting though, Lamont had been less available.

'You're still running the business then?'

'I took on a business partner. They do most of the day-to-day stuff, but I manage the books.'

Lamont nodded, scratching the underside of his chin. Charlotte had given him a lot to think about.

The pair chatted a while longer, and Lamont knew he was just delaying the inevitable. Charlotte was right about one thing; the longer he and Jenny waited, the harder it would be to come back.

'Don't be a stranger, L,' said Charlotte as she led Lamont to the door. They shared a longer hug, and he kissed her on the cheek, happy he'd stopped by.

* * *

'Gracey!' Shorty's mum exclaimed as Shorty walked into the living room holding Grace's hand. Serena Turner was a short, fleshy woman with beautiful cocoa features and a big smile. She immediately smothered Grace with hugs and kisses, paying Shorty no attention. He left the pair to it, making a drink and checking his phone. He headed back into the living room. Grace sat comfortably on Shorty's mum's knee, giggling at whatever story her Nana was telling her.

'How could you take so long bringing this beautiful little thing to come and see me?' she demanded, finally acknowledging her son.

'I've been busy, mum. Sorry,' he replied. He hadn't told his mum about Grace not wanting to see him. It was too painful.

'Well, she's here now I suppose. That's better than nothing. C'mon, Grace. Come with me, I've got some things upstairs that I want to show you.'

* * *

Lamont thought about Charlotte as he drove home. He admired her putting everything on hold for Justin's sake. Justin was full of potential, and Lamont had wanted to work with him. Justin turned him down and ended up being murdered pursuing a silly street feud.

Lamont hadn't told Charlotte how much money he would give her, but he wasn't concerned about the price. Justin's words could help on the streets, and he knew Charlotte was the best person to get behind that. He would call Martin in the morning.

As Lamont pulled into the drive, he was surprised to see Jenny's Mercedes already parked. He stared at the ride for a moment, trying to evaluate what to do. After a minute, he took a deep breath and headed inside.

Jenny was on the sofa listening to music when Lamont entered. There was a long moment as they took the other in. Jenny was still the most beautiful woman in the world. He saw the changes though; the pinched tiredness in her face. He felt a wave of guilt, realising how much he'd impacted her life in a few short years.

Everything wrong with her was down to him, and Lamont freely accepted that.

'I've missed you.'

Jenny didn't smile. 'I've missed you too, L.'

'I'm sorry for the things I said. I don't think you're weak. The opposite in fact. You're one of the strongest people I know, and I know for a fact I wouldn't have been able to handle everything you have.'

'I appreciate what you're saying, L. But it's a bigger conversation than that now.'

Lamont wasn't surprised by Jenny's. The leaden feeling in his stomach expanded, but he steeled himself.

Jenny took a deep breath, tears pooling in her eyes.

'For my health and sanity, I need to leave you, L. I love you, but I need to do this for me. You're . . . in too deep. Even after the attempt on your life, you're still doing it. Don't deny it.'

Jenny watched Lamont for any glimmer of a reaction, but his face was like stone.

'Does any of this relate to Malcolm?'

'I find him appealing, and I've spent time with him. It's not about Malcolm though. I love you, but I can't be with you. I can't be with anyone.'

Lamont twitched with anger, furious at the thought of Malcolm spending time with his Jenny. The information Akeem had given him on Malcolm had yielded nothing. He controlled his rage, opening his mouth to reply, but his phone rang.

'This isn't a good time,' Jenny watched as Lamont's eyes widened, his mouth agape. 'Find him. Send people to the hospital. I'm on my way there and I want it locked down.' Lamont faced Jenny, his jaw tight.

'I need to go, Jen. Something terrible has happened.'

* * *

Shorty and Grace returned home. Grace held bags full of clothes and toys. After leaving his mum's house, they'd gone shopping. Shorty had bought her a quick burger from McDonald's, then they headed back. Since leaving town, Grace had become distant, content to stare out of the window and communicate with nods.

'Gracey?' Shorty stopped the car. Grace faced him. To try to make her smile, he'd let her sit in the front seat.

'I'm . . . Sorry it came to this. You're the only good thing that daddy ever did in his life. I know I left you alone, and I can never make that up to you, but I'm here now. I'm not going anywhere. Anytime you want daddy, all you need to do is tell your mummy, and I'll be there. Okay?'

Grace stared at Shorty for a long time. The doubt in her big brown eyes made Shorty want to cry. This wasn't supposed to happen. No child should ever be so disappointed by a parent.

Shorty blinked back tears, searching for the words to comfort her. He heard the sharp acceleration of another vehicle. Instantly, he knew.

'No!' Shorty lunged towards a stunned Grace just as brakes squealed, followed by the unmistakable roar of gunfire.

Shorty covered Grace's body with his own as bullets bombarded the ride, showering them with glass. Shorty's body jolted, a bullet grazing his shoulder. Grace was screaming. Shorty had no weapons, but even as that terrifying thought gripped him, the car was gone.

Shorty hurtled out of the Land-Cruiser in time to see a Vauxhall Astra pulling around the corner.

'Shorty?' Amy was hurtling the door open. Shorty whirled around as Amy's eyes widened.

'GRACE!' she screamed. Dumbfounded, Shorty looked down, his entire world shattering. At first, he thought she was sleeping. Then he saw the blood.

'No . . .' He gasped, frozen. Amy wrenched open the vehicle door, holding Grace, screaming her name, tears streaming down her face. Shorty still hadn't moved. His own tears harboured his vision now. He blinked, his entire body and mind on standby.

This wasn't real. This couldn't be real . . .

'CALL AN AMBULANCE!' Amy shrieked at Shorty. He dumbly reached for his phone, dialling the number, waiting for someone to answer.

'My daughter . . . She got shot . . . Please, send someone,' he said, his voice shaking when a woman answered.

People gathered on the street, wearing expressions of shock and disbelief. Amy hadn't stopped clutching Grace. Shorty heard the wailing of sirens, but he didn't dare tear his eyes from his daughter. He didn't know where she'd been hit, but she was deathly still. As the ambulance screeched to a stop, followed shortly after by two police cars, Shorty finally let the tears fall.

CHAPTER SIXTEEN

Saturday 14 March 2015

IT WAS easy for Lamont to shake away thoughts of Jenny as he strode through the hospital with Akeem at his side. The breakup hurt, but the present situation was far more important. People would die from the results of what transpired today.

Lamont ignored his ringing phone. Akeem was barking orders down his own, ignoring the onlookers. People were already in place, securing the perimeter in case of attack. Others were combing the streets for immediate answers.

Shorty slumped against a wall, his face tear-streaked, his agony almost palpable. Lamont had never seen him so devastated. Even after Marcus's murder, when they drank and cried together. This was different. The fringes of Shorty's sanity were on the verge of exploding; a pulsating aura of destruction. Lamont knew of it, and a quick glance to Akeem showed he sensed it too.

Amy tottered towards Lamont, pale and red-eyed, flinging her arms around him. He held her tightly, muttering pointless platitudes, telling her everything would be okay.

'I'm so sorry,' Lamont repeated, over and over again. He felt the wetness on his chest from her tears. After a moment, she released him. Lamont approached Shorty, placing his hand on his friend's shoulder.

Shorty didn't look up, but Lamont felt the resonating rage, his muscles almost vibrating.

'I don't even know what to say, Shorty. However you want to do this, I'm with you. The team, money, anything you need. We've got people out there now. They'll find something.'

'It was Lutel,' Shorty croaked. 'He's the only one who fits. The only one dumb enough to try to hit me when I'm with my girl.'

Lamont didn't argue. It made sense.

'Did you tell the police that?'

The vicious look Shorty gave was answer enough.

'I'll target Lennox's people until he comes forward. No one is gonna rest on this shit. I love Grace too. Do you know anything?'

'They've taken her in for surgery. Bullet hit her in the lung, she's barely hanging on. I don't know too much about all that technical shit, but she's fighting.' Shorty's shoulders shook. 'My girl's a fighter.'

'I know she is. Just like her parents. Stay here with Amy, and I'll take care of everything.'

'I'm coming too.'

'Shorty . . .'

'Don't fight me on it, L. You said however I wanted to do it. I'm no good here. I've already nearly scrapped with security and screamed at the nurses. I need to be out there making things happen.'

'I agree.'

Both men gave a start. They hadn't noticed Amy approach. Her face remained pale and drawn, but her blazing eyes kept them tethered to the spot.

'I want you to go, Shorty. I let you back into Grace's life, and now she's fighting for it. Go be you, do what you need to do, kill who you need to kill. You will never see her again.'

It was a testament to how devastated Shorty was that he didn't argue. His shoulders slumped and he let out a breath before following Lamont and Akeem from the hospital.

* * *

Grace's shooting sent a ripple through the streets of Leeds that it hadn't felt in a long time. There had been scores of incidents, murders, shootings and beatings, but nothing that matched a young girl being shot on a quiet suburban street. The fact it was Shorty's daughter only added to the tension.

Everyone on the streets began mobilising, and most people pulled back, content to wholesale their drugs for now. It was only a matter of time until the drama started.

Lennox and Nikkolo strode to Lutel's spot in Ebor Gardens. Lutel was watching a TV show with his feet up when they stormed into the room.

'It's fucked up that I missed, but—'

Lennox hit Lutel in the face, feeling the satisfying crunch of Lutel's nose breaking under his fist. Lutel fell to one knee and was kicked in the face, toppling to the ground. Lennox kicked him several times, not uttering a sound. Nikkolo watched in grim silence.

'Why do I bother?' Lennox finally said, over the sounds of Lutel's pathetic whimpering. 'You're an absolute liability. Missing Shorty was the worst thing you could have done, you cretin. I said *clean up*, not make a situation worse. Did you not understand your orders?'

'Listen, I panicked when I saw the little girl. I just let a couple shots go thinking I'd pop Shorty and done. I didn't mean to hit her.' Lutel coughed, holding his battered ribs.

'You're weak. Weak, petty and emotional. The girl is nothing to me. I care about one thing; ruling Chapeltown. I don't know if I've ever bothered to tell you why, but now I will; I'm the only one who can give the streets structure. I can stop the tit-for-tat, *my-strap-is-bigger-than-yours* nonsense. More money for everyone. Less police interest. No drugs. It makes sense. It benefits everyone, but now you have ruined that with your foolishness.'

'If you'd backed me earlier, none of this would have happened!' Lutel snarled, forgetting himself. 'If you just took Shorty out, there wouldn't have been any problems. But no, you just left him.'

Lennox stared at Lutel for so long that the man started to tremble. Even Nikkolo stepped back, marvelling at the quiet force emanating from Lennox. After a moment, Lennox scratched his cheek.

'Hide out until we can sort the mess. Nikkolo will get a spot for you.'

When they left the house, Lennox didn't speak until the pair were back in Nikkolo's car.

'Lutel is a loose end. Leak the spot to Shorty. He'll take care of it. It might even placate him.'

'Do you really believe that?' Nikkolo couldn't keep the scepticism from his voice. Shorty was a maniac. Lamont had kept him on a leash since he left prison, but that was done. Lennox ignored Nikkolo, already deep in thought.

* * *

'Let me know when you hear anything else.'

K-Bar hung up on Darren, putting his hands in his head. The streets were about to be locked down. K-Bar knew exactly how it would go. He'd spoken briefly to Akeem about the situation. They had dispatched men to find out the location of Lutel and whoever had driven the car.

K-Bar tried ringing Shorty, but his phone was unavailable, and Lamont was flat out ignoring K-Bar's calls. Marika wrapped her arms around K-Bar, kissing him on the cheek.

'Have you spoken with Shorty or L yet?'

'I can't get hold of either of them. I've got all kinds of people ringing me, trying to find out what's going on, and I can't say shit to them.'

'Good. People are too damn nosy,' said Marika, though she wanted to know what was going on just as much. 'What happens now?'

K-Bar pulled Marika closer, running his fingers through her hair as she leaned further into him. They stayed this way for a few moments. K-Bar was sure he was falling for Lamont's sister. It was dangerous, and he needed to speak with him before feelings grew any deeper.

K-Bar had no idea how the conversation would go, but he would step to Lamont like a man. There was no way around it.

'War, babe. That's the only thing that can happen. We all know what Grace is to Shorty. People are gonna die. Simple.'

* * *

Lamont left Shorty planning with Akeem, heading home. Two of Akeem's men followed in a separate vehicle. They were expensive, highly trained bodyguards, but Lamont wasn't thinking about cost at the moment. When the guns started going off, things would grow even more expensive.

Lamont had people watching out for Amy, Stacey, Shorty's mother and his Auntie. He hadn't asked Shorty if he wanted any of this, he'd just done it.

Lamont walked past Jenny's Mercedes, not knowing if she had left since he'd rushed away to the hospital. Hearing noises from the kitchen, he headed in that direction. Jenny and Kate were speaking in hushed tones. They stopped when Lamont appeared in the doorway.

'L, are you okay?' Jenny asked, noting how tired Lamont looked. His eyes brimmed with passion though and for a moment, Jenny was reminded of the dangerous man she had fallen for. Lamont hugged Kate.

'I'm fine, Jen. It's nice to see you, Kate. Surprised you're here though.'

'I heard about Shorty. Jen rang me after you rushed off, and I came over,' Kate looked from Lamont to Jenny. 'You two are through then?'

Lamont jammed his hands in his pockets, thinking about Shorty's situation to prevent his own from overwhelming him.

'It's for the best. Especially now.'

'Is Shorty okay?' Jenny didn't want to think about the breakup anymore than Lamont did.

'I can't discuss anything that's happening, or is gonna happen, Jen. I don't want you becoming an accessory. In fact, I'd appreciate it if you let me have someone guard you, just in case.'

'That's not going to happen.'

'Jen—'

'No, L. I'm not part of your world, and we're not a couple anymore. I'll be fine.'

'Grace isn't part of that world either, but she was still hit,' Lamont argued. It was futile though. Jenny's mouth was drawn and her eyes were hard. There would be no fighting her on this one.

'Forget it, L. I'm going to the letting agency when it opens in the morning.'

'You don't need to do that. I have plenty of places to stay, and I'd prefer it if you kept the house,' said Lamont. Jenny shook her head.

'I want a fresh start. You can understand that, right?'

Lamont could. A lot had transpired and he couldn't blame Jenny for wanting to be away from it all. The night started to catch up with Lamont, and he stifled a yawn, his eyes burning. He needed to be fresh in case there were any new developments.

'I'll sleep in the spare room. You have the bed, Jen. I need to get some rest.' Lamont bid Kate good night, surprised she'd stayed so quiet. He was halfway to the door when Jenny spoke again.

'L?'

He span around just in time to catch Jenny as she hurtled against him, her mouth finding his. For a delicious moment, all was well, Jenny's lips causing a whirl of desire to surge through Lamont's body as he gripped her closer. Jenny moaned in his mouth as the kiss deepened, but then pulled away, her legs weak with sudden lust and love.

'Be careful, L. I love you, and I'll always care for you.'

'I love you too, Jen, and I'm always careful.'

* * *

The next morning, a group of men sat in a meeting room in a local police station. Mumbled greetings were exchanged as tired hands stirred sugar in cups of coffee, needing the caffeine to get them through the torrent of mess in Chapeltown.

Rigby and Murphy were at the front of the room, ready to speak. At a signal from their superior, they began.

'Through careful investigation, we've linked Kieron Barrett, AKA K-Bar, to numerous murders from September 2013. He was responsible for the deaths of Paul 'Polo' Dobby, Xiyu 'Chink' Manderson, and Naomi Gateworth.'

'What *careful investigation* are you referring to?' A man asked. 'This all sounds very circumstantial. Does any of what you're saying connect to the mess on the streets, because if the intel is correct, we're going to have another gang war on our hands.'

'There's enough for us to bring in K-Bar and question him. A friend of Naomi's will testify in court. She was present when K-Bar approached Naomi and offered her five thousand pounds to set up Chink. Half the money was paid up front, the rest to be paid after. Instead, they murdered Naomi too.'

'We found Two different gun calibres at the scene if I recall; who else was there other than K-Bar?'

'At this point we don't know, but K-Bar could prove more forthcoming. There are several within Teflon's organisation with the reputation to pull it off, but we haven't narrowed it down at present.'

'I'm not sure about any of this,' another superior spoke up. 'Again, it all seems rather thin, even with the tie-in. K-Bar works for Teflon, who has money and a lot of political might behind him. We can't afford to fail.'

'Agreed. Adele being willing to testify is huge though, sir, as it offers motive. We believe it's connected to the murder of Marcus Daniels in August 2013, and that everything after was a direct result. Chink was behind the hit on Marcus in the park and was murdered in retaliation.'

'I thought Chink and K-Bar both worked for Jones? That's what the last report I read showed.'

Murphy and Rigby shared a look. They hated the whole show of having to justify every piece of police work they did. They understood the need for clarity, but as veteran officers, they knew the politics, and were always committed to putting together airtight cases. They wanted to catch bad guys and stamp out crime. That was it.

Neither was interested in climbing the police ladder, or getting recognition. It was simply the job. They had planned to brief their immediate superior this morning, but they had been blindsided and forced to present the meeting to half a dozen higher-ups.

'There was definitely a fall out. We believe Chink was engaged in a sexual affair with Marcus's girlfriend, Georgia Pearson. We tried to track her down, but she's left Leeds and no one has heard from her.'

'What about the more recent shootings? That's where we should be focusing. All the protesting and press from Chapeltown by that blasted organisation has caused a lot of issues. We need to be seen to be doing the right thing on this, and I don't know if that involves digging up cases from two years ago.'

Rigby tried to keep his annoyance clear as he replied.

'I appreciate what you're saying sir, but K-Bar is a key piece of Teflon's organisation. He's linked to several murders and ran the team while Teflon was recovering from his own shooting. If we can get him, he could be the key to unlocking the story behind numerous murders, past and present. The intel suggests Teflon was behind the recent murder of Big-Kev. K-Bar would have detailed knowledge of that.'

'We need a resolution, Detective Rigby. Simple as that. I want arrests, and I want to show people we're not sitting on our arses doing nothing. I suggest you get back out there and find more information.'

* * *

Shorty sat in a safe house, rag in hand as he cleaned a section of guns. Every time he thought about Grace's shooting, he grew angrier. She was in critical condition. The surgery was apparently a success, but the doctors remained tight-lipped about her chances of recovery.

Lamont had spoken with Amy and passed on the information. A few of Akeem's shooters were nearby, keeping their straps close as they waited. Shorty wasn't sure if they were guarding him or keeping him detained. It didn't matter.

Lennox hadn't been seen, nor had Nikkolo or any of Lennox's higher-ups. Shorty planned to smoke out Lutel. When he poked his head out, Shorty would annihilate him.

Shorty's phone rang. He was tempted to ignore the private number, but decided to let out some anger on the caller. He put the gun and rag down, picking up the phone.

'What?' He snapped.

'Is this Shorty?' A muffled voice asked.

'Don't play dumb. You wouldn't have called if you didn't know who it was.'

'The guy you're looking for, he's at a spot on Grange Park Road. It has a blue gate and a white door.'

'Who is this?' Shorty clutched the phone tighter.

'Don't worry about who I am. Check out the spot if you don't believe me.'

The person hung up. Shorty looked down at the phone, his mind alight. It was possible they were lying, or trying to set him up. Shorty weighed up the risks and decided it was worth it. Rising to his feet, he shrugged into a bullet-proof vest and readied his weapons.

* * *

'The call has been made. I already had the driver taken care of.'

Lennox nodded, approving of Nikkolo's initiative.

'Any word on Teflon?'

'People are definitely looking for us. They're connected to him, so he's working with Shorty on this. People are reluctant to talk to me though. It's like they think we're already finished.'

Lennox had expected this. As soon as he'd heard about Lutel shooting Shorty's child, he'd scaled back his war with Delroy Williams, refusing to get caught out on both fronts.

'Contact Teflon directly. Try to arrange a meeting on neutral ground. Use a go-between if you have to. Someone Teflon will trust.'

'Are you sure about this?' Nikkolo blurted. Lennox shot him a sharp look. Nikkolo sighed, then pulled out his phone to make another call.

* * *

Shorty studied the address he had been given, unable to see anything out of the ordinary. The gun resting on his lap had a silencer attached. He wanted to take his time with Lutel.

Shorty had no idea how many people were inside, but he'd called off Akeem's shooters, wanting to handle this on his own.

Pulling up his hood, Shorty climbed from the stolen car, strap held low. The street was deserted. It was early evening and the cold cut through Shorty's hooded top with ease. He ignored the chill and kept his head down. Shorty saw the blue gate and hopped the wall, landing stiffly on the other side, wincing as pain shot up his ankle. He tested his leg a few times and seemed to be okay. He saw lights on both up and downstairs, and the curtains were closed.

Disregarding the front door, Shorty headed to the side door and tried the handle, unsurprised to find it locked. Shorty had no tools to pick the lock. Stepping back, he kicked in the door, which smashed open with a satisfying crunch.

Shorty was inside, following the voices as he charged to the living room, spotting two men. The younger man went for his gun, but a bullet smashed into his throat, knocking him back with an awful choking sound. Lutel was slow to respond, giving Shorty ample time to shoot him in his right knee. Lutel fell with a scream. Shorty bounded over, hitting him three times in the mouth, kicking him in the stomach.

'Shut the fuck up. I don't wanna hear your damn mouth. Is there anyone else in the house I need to kill?'

Lutel hesitated, causing Shorty to shoot him in the other knee at point-blank range. His gloved hand covered Lutel's blooded mouth, muffling the scream.

'Answer me.'

Lutel jerkily shook his head, twitching in pain. Shorty aimed the gun at his face.

'Where's Lennox?'

Lutel didn't reply, trying to glare whilst grimacing.

'Talk, or I'm gonna make you.'

Still, Lutel said nothing. Kissing his teeth, Shorty dragged him by his leg to the kitchen. Turning on the stove, Shorty reached for a knife, heating it under the flame. Advancing on Lutel, he sliced at the man's skin, relishing the growing screams of pain. He poured table salt on the wounds, a demented smile on his face.

'Tell me, before I slice your nuts off!'

'Alright! Alright! L-Listen, he m-moves around, but he's got a main base near Cottingley. It's g-guarded, but he spends a lot of time there.'

'What's the address?' Shorty took his phone out. When he'd typed the address into a notepad and saved it, Shorty faced the cowering man at his feet.

'You would have died anyway, but when you went for my daughter, you violated.' He placed the gun to Lutel's stomach and fired once, feeling Lutel's body jerk. Straightening, Shorty fired the next bullet into his neck, watching Lutel's body twitch one last time. He breathed deeply. There was still a massive debt to be paid, and Lennox Thompson was next on the list.

CHAPTER SEVENTEEN

Thursday 19 March 2015

OVER THE NEXT FEW DAYS, Chapeltown played host to an increase in street violence. Fights and ambushes broke out all over the Hood, with doors being kicked in, people being interrogated, and several isolated incidents involving drive-by shootings on certain houses.

The *OurHood* Initiative held two meetings, but participation and attendance had dramatically dropped. No one wanted any part of the situation.

The body of Lutel Wood had turned up on the streets, his injuries consistent with repeated torture, followed by execution. The police had a host of suspects, including Shorty, but no one had seen him.

Lennox Thompson climbed from a navy Ford Focus, two goons with him, and strode into a house. The man he'd come to see was pacing around the living room mumbling to himself. When he saw Lennox, he paused, his eyebrows knitted together in a frown.

'What the hell is going on?'

Lennox went to the kitchen and put on the kettle. When it boiled, he added coffee then hot water to a cup, stirred for a few moments, and took an immediate sip. The man stood in the doorway, bristling with impatience.

'Are you going to answer me?'

Lennox studied the man, resisting the urge to smirk at his less than immaculate appearance. There were circles under his eyes, and he needed a haircut.

'Answer you about what, exactly?'

'People are saying you ordered the shooting of Shorty's kid, which led to Lutel's murder. How am I supposed to spin this?'

'You're the wordsmith, you tell me,' replied Lennox, his dry tone showing a lack of interest.

'Len, I run the meetings, and I can steer people towards certain perspectives, but even I don't know what I'm supposed to do with this one. Did you do it?'

'Does it matter? My name isn't even supposed to be in it. Blame it on someone else. Isn't that what I keep you around for?'

'Don't talk to me like that!' Malcolm snapped. 'You need me. Without my work out there, opening eyes and controlling the masses, all eyes are on you. You think you can get your little *Hood Utopia* if you make an enemy out of me?'

Lennox glared at Malcolm until some of the bluster went out of the scholar. He held the stare a moment longer.

'Understand one thing; you're a tool I use. You have no power. You're not a threat. You're only relevant because I gave you purpose and direction. You're a failed writer turned blogger, nothing more.'

'Bullshit! I was successful long before I met you, and the *OurHood* project is mine, not yours.'

Lennox smiled icily. 'You still don't get it. Without me, there *is* no project. Do you really not know what I was doing behind the scenes? People wanted you dead. You ranted with impunity, because of me. I intimidated everyone who wanted to silence you. If I made it known I was withdrawing my support, you wouldn't last twenty-four hours. If you want to look at it objectively, you failed.'

Malcolm had paled throughout Lennox's cutting tirade, but now he found his voice. 'How did I fail?'

'You were supposed to seduce Teflon's lady. You didn't do it.'

'I broke them up though!'

Lennox's smirked. 'Do you really believe they'll stay broken up?'

Malcolm didn't reply. Lennox continued.

'You got caught up in feelings and fell for a woman you could never have. Now, scurry back to your laptop and get to work. It'll be open season if I pull support. Remember that.'

Malcolm hurried to the door, wrenching it open. Before he left, he glared at Lennox.

'You'll always be nothing, Len, and that galls you.'

* * *

Shorty glared at the four walls of the living room of his safe house, coiled and ready to act on the information Lutel surrendered to him. Shorty had posted up on the spot, but hadn't seen Lennox yet.

His body ached with tiredness. Shorty hadn't slept, running on adrenaline and rage. He was tempted to ring K-Bar and Maka for backup, but they worked for Lamont. He wasn't sure Lamont would agree with his plan of action.

Trudging to the kitchen, Shorty made another cup of coffee. While the kettle boiled, he cracked open a Red Bull and chugged it, wiping his mouth and leaving the can on the worktop. He grabbed the cup and headed back to the living room, turning on his phone. Checking his messages, he saw one from Jenny, asking for Shorty to call. Without even thinking, he dialled her number.

'Shorty?'

'Hey,' he replied after a few moments.

'Where are you? Are you okay?'

'I'm fine. I'm safe.'

Jenny paused before she spoke again. 'Can I see you?'

'Why?' He sharply asked.

'I just want to make sure you're okay. If you want to talk over the phone instead, it's fine. I . . . guess I understand just enough to see why you might be paranoid.' Jenny's voice broke.

'Where are you staying?'

* * *

Jenny left the door unlocked for Shorty and he walked in, nearly tripping over a pile of boxes.

'Sorry about that,' said Jenny. 'I only moved in yesterday. Still getting all my things in order.' she led Shorty to the living room. He looked around. There was a CD player stuffed in the corner, an old coffee table, two sofas and an armchair, all of which looked like they had come with the house.

Jenny wore a black hooded top with leggings and thick socks. It tickled Shorty that she was so comfortable being casual around him, and it took away a lot of the tension.

'You look tired. When was the last time you slept?'

Shorty shrugged. 'There are more important things than sleep right now.'

'Like revenge?'

'Exactly.'

'That won't make Grace magically better, you know that right?'

Shorty wanted to shout at Jenny, but didn't. He couldn't. There was something keeping her out of the range of his wrath, and Shorty didn't quite understand it.

'This is me, Jen. This is what I do. They went at my daughter, so now they go. That's it. It doesn't get less complicated than that.'

Jenny didn't offer a response, and the silence lingered until Shorty spoke again.

'I'm surprised L didn't give you the house.'

Jenny smiled wanly. 'He offered. I said no.'

'Why?'

'I wanted to start again. I loved that house, but it had too many bad memories, mainly revolving around my deteriorating relationship with Lamont.'

'I get that,' said Shorty. 'No chance of y'all getting back together then?'

Jenny sighed. 'I don't see how we can. He's following his path. I'm trying to figure out what mine is. L said that I saved him once. That I made him see a future for us. I bought into that.'

Shorty didn't reply, absorbing the words. He remembered Lamont's change after he met Jenny, but if he was honest, the signs were there before that. Lamont had dominated the drugs game, but there had always been a reluctance to his actions. He'd carried himself differently, engaged with women differently, and played the game his own way.

It had taken a lot out of Lamont, Shorty realised. Jenny had been his salvation, but it hadn't lasted. The revelation reeled him, making him think about his own path.

'What does the future hold for you, Shorty?'

Shorty shrugged again. 'Honestly, I don't care. I'll murder Lennox. Beyond that, nothing else matters. I don't know if you get that, but it's about as real as I can be.'

No more words were said. They sat for a long time, both understanding the other's view. Shorty opened his mouth to speak, but held back. It wouldn't help the situation.

'I'm gonna take off, Jen. There's a lot to do.'

He stepped toward her and she met him halfway. The embrace was lingering, and they clung tightly as if the action was essential. Shorty finally broke the hug, kissing Jenny on the cheek.

'Good luck. I know you'll smash whatever you do.'

'Thank you, Shorty. Please, please be careful.'

Shorty had already closed the door on Jenny's pleas.

* * *

Lamont and Akeem entered the city centre club on high alert. The club was located on Call Lane, but currently closed to the public. A shot-caller who had links with Lamont and was deemed to be neutral territory owned it. The terms of the meeting had been outlined to both attendees: No weapons, no trouble. Lamont would not break the terms.

The man he'd come to see was waiting, sitting at a table overlooking the club with another man. Lamont made his way up, and they shook hands.

'It's been a while, L.'

'It has, Len.'

Lennox sent Nikkolo downstairs, and Lamont asked Akeem to go too. For a while, there was silence, the pair content to let it play out.

'I'm trying to remember the last time you and I needed to meet about something,' Lennox finally said.

'Marcus was alive, I know that. Wasn't it that thing with one of your guys trying a robbery, and some of my guys got involved, and we squashed it?'

Lennox shrugged, a half-smile on his lips.

'Might have been. We've both been doing what we do a while, through the difficulties. You've had a couple more ups than me, I think.'

'We're in different businesses; it's expected.'

'Yeah. You sell poison and I don't.'

'Indeed. You just kill and maim people instead,' replied Lamont, matching Lennox's calm tone.

'So did, Marcus, and you still cried over his body.'

'He was my brother.'

Lennox turned to Lamont. 'You can appreciate what I'm saying though, right? Your *brother* did the same dirt I did.'

'I didn't necessarily agree with him doing it either.'

'You allowed it though. Turned a blind eye, tolerated it. Any way you want to put it, facts are the facts.'

'Marcus was a grown man. We collaborated when necessary.'

'You have an answer for everything. I like that,' said Lennox, grinning. It was a grin with no mirth.

'I guess we're getting down to the reason we're both here?'

Lennox nodded. 'Do you mind if I start?'

'Not at all.'

'Chapeltown is in a funk; it needs more funding, there's a loss of community spirit and influence. The influence comes from the money, and the money comes from drugs. Drugs are the problem. Drugs bring in the police, other gangsters, and it needs to stop. I'm going to make it stop. That's my mission.

'You wanted to walk off into the sun and leave it behind, so do that. Leave the drug game to its death. Walk away, leave Delroy and Shorty to their fate.'

Lamont respected the strength of Lennox's words. This wasn't a ploy; Lamont sensed Lennox was being honest.

'You shouldn't have shot Shorty's daughter. That goes against everything you just said. There's no structure that involves the shooting of an innocent girl.'

'What about an innocent woman? Is that different? Because there are a few innocent women whose deaths are connected to your people.'

'I've never authorised the murder of anyone who wasn't in the game,' said Lamont. Again, Lennox grinned.

'That's not the point, and you know it. I agree with you about Shorty's little girl. Lutel fucked up and was eliminated because of it. I didn't authorise her shooting, and I didn't tell Lutel to get into a pissing contest with Shorty. As you know, my attention was focused elsewhere.'

'Meaning Delroy.'

Lennox nodded.

'Delroy won't stop, because his son is dead, and he needs to save face. Shorty won't stop, because he could never comprehend backing down. You've done all you can, L. You need to leave them to their fate.'

'Your plan is doomed, Len. There's too much money, and too many people depending on a wage from the drugs game for you to come in and stop things. You don't have that sort of power.'

'You just don't know. That's the problem.' Lennox's hands balled into fists. The eerie grin had vanished, replaced with a malevolent look.

'You *think* you know, Len. There are level's beyond you, and that lack of understanding will ruin you.'

'You know what the problem is, L? It's all about money to you. Money and the opinions of people you don't even like. I understand it. You came up hard, broke and disrespected by people you saw as beneath you. I was there, remember, chilling with Marcus, blasting people when you were in town buying drinks for girls you could never get without your status. It's everything to you, Shorty and all those other dickheads.

'Me, I'm about order. I want power and I want to be left alone, but you know what? That can't happen while you lot are moving powder and warring over turf. So, I need to take drugs out of the equation. I need to control the street so that the structure is there. One leader. Me. No drugs, no reason for police to patrol our territory. *My* territory.

'You're a threat to that, L. The biggest threat because you actually have a brain in that head of yours. You're flashy though. You have expensive tastes and you're influential enough to cause problems, so you're my enemy. But, it's nothing personal.'

Lamont remained calm through Lennox's words, but the atmosphere had changed. He noted Nikkolo and Akeem looking up at the balcony, both tense and alert.

'It feels personal. You won't disrupt the flow, Len. Simple as that.'

Lennox rubbed his hands together, his dark eyes boring into Lamont's.

'It's a game of sheep masquerading as lions. You're the only anomaly, and you don't even want to be in the game,' Lennox slid to his feet, no hint of a smile on his face. 'Leave them to their fate, or go down with them. Last warning.'

* * *

'They broke up?'

K-Bar was at Marika's, bored of hiding out. The noise surrounding Big Kev's murder had dispersed, but Lamont insisted on K-Bar remaining low key, which irked him. He understood why Shorty had been so tetchy. So much was happening, and few were as qualified when it came to killing and handling drama as K-Bar. He was relying on his people keeping him updated, but no one knew much, other than Shorty being on the warpath and dropping bodies to get to Lennox Thompson.

Now, Marika had dropped another bombshell.

'I spoke to Jen today. She's not living at the house anymore. She moved out.'

'Over what though?' K-Bar had been around Jenny and Lamont in the past and believed they were well-suited.

'She didn't say. When I went for dinner that time though, there was definitely tension. I think they argued after I went. Maybe L cheated on her? We know how he used to get down.'

'Maybe she cheated on him?' K-Bar felt compelled to defend Lamont. Lamont had indulged in his day, but K-Bar couldn't imagine him cheating.

Marika shrugged, 'Doesn't really matter, anyway. What's Shorty saying?'

'He's doing what he needs to do.'

'And L?'

'I dunno, Rika. Why are you asking me so many damn questions?' Marika jerked back, her eyes flashing.

'Listen, if you're gonna snap, fuck off to your own house.'

K-Bar took a deep breath. Arguing with Marika would fix nothing.

'Sorry. This shit just gets me mad. Lennox is out there doing what he wants, and people aren't moving against him quick enough. Shorty can't be expected to go up against a whole crew by himself. It's mad.'

Marika squeezed his hand and cuddled up against him. K-Bar kissed the top of her head, her presence calming him.

'I was running things, doing what I needed to do, then suddenly I'm just out. Everyone is leapfrogging me.'

'Do something about it then. When you think about it, Shorty might have the right idea.'

'What do you mean?' K-Bar shifted so he could see Marika.

'You know Shorty better than anyone. He doesn't really ask permission. He just does shit, and L kinda has to go along with it.'

K-Bar didn't reply. Marika had given him a lot to think about.

* * *

The next day, Shorty was playing *Blade Brown* as he completed sit-ups in his safe house. His arms burned from the press-ups he'd finished a short while ago, but he pushed through, determined to finish his workout. His phone ringing brought him out of the zone, and he snatched it with venom, pausing the music.

'What?' He snapped. The person on the other end spoke for a few moments, then hung up. Shorty tidied and waited for the coded knock on the door. He let in Akeem, who remained standing as Shorty slumped onto the sofa.

'What does L want?'

'He met with Lennox Thompson, but nothing was agreed.'

'What was the point of meeting him? He should have killed him instead.'

Akeem didn't respond. Shorty wanted to punch him in his stupid face. He was as non-committal as Lamont.

'To try resolving the situation with as little bloodshed as possible.'

'It's too late for that. He shot my girl.'

'Lutel shot at your daughter, and you took care of that. Lennox is much harder to get at.'

'I know where he is. I've got a location, and I've got a guy watching. I'm just waiting for the word that Lennox is at the spot.'

'I'm assuming you got the location from Lutel before you finished him,' Akeem started. 'It may have been abandoned, especially if Lennox feels it's compromised.'

'Lutel said he wasn't supposed to know about this spot. No reason for him to lie when he's about to die. That's the plan though. Once I get the call, everyone's gone.'

Akeem headed for the door. 'Do what you need to. Grimer, Maka and Rudy are available at your convenience. L said you would know the number.'

'L's authorising this?' Shorty scratched his head, trying to keep the surprise from his face.

'Did you leave him a choice?' Akeem asked as he left the house.

* * *

Another forty-eight hours passed before Shorty got the word. Lennox had turned up at the spot with Nikkolo. Shorty made the calls, got his people together, and laid out a plan.

Maka and Shorty drove to the spot in one car, Rudy and Grimer in another. They were communicating by Pay-as-you-go phones as they approached Cottingley. Shorty expected the roads to be busier, but the way the bodies had dropped, the police probably had no idea where to start.

The car was silent. Maka drove, but kept looking at Shorty and then looking away. Finally, he cleared his throat.

'How's Gracey doing then?'

Shorty was quiet for so long Maka thought he was ignoring him.

'She's had two operations. The survival rate in children isn't high, and the bullets fucked her up. That's all I know though. Her mum doesn't want me anywhere near the situation.'

'I'm sorry, Shorty. She doesn't deserve that shit. We'll take everyone out and try to leave Lennox to the end, so you can take your time. You clipped the shooter, didn't you?'

'Yeah.' Shorty's jaw tensed as he remembered ripping Lutel apart and slicing at his body.

'I'm gonna ring Zero, make sure Lennox hasn't left yet.'

* * *

The gang pulled up in their cars around the corner from where Lennox was holed up. The Cottingley area was quiet, which was a surprise. It was normally far more thriving, even in winter. Zero had already left.

'Right, we need to handle this quickly,' said Shorty, when the four of them were assembled. 'We're kinda close to that police station, so use silenced weapons. The cocaine and drink is on me when we're done here.'

Everyone grinned and checked their weapons. They all wore bullet-proof vests underneath their jackets. Rudy and Grimer would sneak around the back. Shorty and Maka would approach from the front and take care of any resistance. Shorty had an Uzi. Rudy the same. Maka had a silenced 9mm pistol, and Grimer grimly clutched a shotgun that had belonged to Marcus Daniels.

They split into their teams and moved. Shorty and Maka tread silently down the path, tense, looking for scouts. Timmy flashed into Shorty's head for a moment, but he put the thought aside, signalling for Maka to move forward. They'd approached the garden when all of a sudden, gunfire erupted.

Shorty dived for cover behind a nearby wall but Maka wasn't quick enough. He took a hit and went down, men emerging from seemingly nowhere, firing shots at Shorty. He popped up, hitting two of them with the same burst of gunfire, causing the others to back off.

'Maka! Get over here,' Shorty screamed, letting off cover-fire Maka stumbled towards him, clutching his chest and wheezing.

'Did it go through?' Shorty yelled, firing at the attackers. 'The bullet! Did it go through?'

'Nah,' gasped Maka.

'Good. Start fucking shooting then. We need to get back to that car.'

Maka took aim, sending a target spinning backwards with a well-placed chest shot.

'Now!' Shorty yelled, sprinting down the path towards the car. He expected to see more assassins, but the pathway was clear. He reached the car ahead of Maka, climbing into the driver's seat and starting the engine.

'Drive!' Maka shouted.

'Not without the others,' Shorty shouted back.

'They're dead, man! You heard them shots.'

Shorty didn't reply, but knew Maka was likely right. The gunfire had started at the back of the house. They hadn't done a walk-around. He didn't know what kind of cover was in the back garden, but if he hadn't been able to get behind the wall, he would have been a goner. They both would have.

Shorty's hands hovered near the steering wheel as Maka warily aimed his pistol out of the wound-down window. They had killed everyone attacking from the front. Acrid gun smoke was everywhere. Shorty's foot teased the gas pedal, and then he heard a shout and saw someone stagger around the corner, holding his stomach, followed by four more assassins. Shorty started spraying, cutting them down when he realised they weren't any of his people.

With another lurch, Shorty realised Grimer and Rudy weren't coming out, and sped away.

* * *

The mood of the safe house was only comparable to the night of Marcus's murder. Shorty swigged brandy from the bottle, perched in the corner. Lamont had summoned a friendly doctor to dispense painkillers and stitch up Maka. Luckily, the bullet that had breached Maka's vest only grazed his stomach. He'd lost some blood, but would be okay.

After the doctor had patched up Maka and collected his payment from Akeem, Lamont steepled his fingers.

'I don't know how Lennox laid a trap so quickly, but it's possible he was never even at the spot, Shorty. Where did the Intel come from?'

'Zero said he was there. He drove away afterward as arranged.'

'Have you tried ringing him?'

Shorty frowned. 'His phone was switched off.' Zero was an old acquaintance from back in the day.

'He was in on it. He sold you out,' said Lamont.

You don't know that, snapped Shorty, noting everyone else in the room giving him the same pitying look.

'Lennox wanted us to hit that spot, and he wanted us to hit it hard. He knew you would get to Lutel. He probably leaked that information. He's been a step ahead this whole time.' Lamont was about to add more when his phone rang. The number was blocked, but he knew who it was.

'Put me on speaker,' Lennox ordered. Lamont forced the swearwords back and pressed the speaker button without a word.

'I knew you lot would come, so I left some gifts. You're lucky my people only got two of you. You may have protected Shorty's family, but you know what, L? You didn't protect your main prize.'

Lamont's brow furrowed. He and Shorty shared a look, both saying, 'No!' at the same time.

'Lennox, don't do it. I mean it,' Lamont's voice shook.

'All the best, L,' replied Lennox, hanging up. Lamont and Shorty hurtled towards the front door.

'Wait!' Akeem yelled, leaping to his feet as Maka sat there, stunned.

* * *

Jenny turned up the *Definitely Maybe* album, debating running a bath to prepare. Her phone buzzed, but Jenny ignored it. It was probably Kate, but it was all about Jenny tonight, and Kate would understand that. She headed to the kitchen, not noticing the phone stop vibrating, and then start again straight away.

* * *

'Have you got hold of her yet?' Shorty yelled. They were in Akeem's ride, the bodyguard zooming through traffic like a madman.

'Does it sound like I have?' Lamont shot back. They glared at each other, then Lamont again dialled Jenny, hoping they were being paranoid. Lennox was a Child of Chapeltown, just like them. He wouldn't involve Jenny in their issues.

'She's probably working late. Tell Maka to send someone to Jen's work.'

Shorty clutched his own phone, glad to have something to do. Akeem warned them to brace themselves as he swerved around a corner. Lamont's breathing intensified, fear threatening to overwhelm him. Lennox wouldn't hurt her. It was probably a ruse.

'Maka's sent two guys to her work. They'll stay with her if she's there.'

Lamont's jaw clenched as he dialled Jenny's mobile a third time. Just as he was giving up hope, he heard a click.

'L?'

'Jen?' he gasped into the receiver. 'Where are you?'

'I'm home. I must have missed your other calls. Is everything okay?'

'Jen, there's no time. Get out. Now.'

'Excuse me? What the hell do you mean?'

'Look, people are coming. You need to leave.'

'L, wh—'

Lamont's stomach lurched as he heard a loud crash, then a blood-curdling scream.

'Jen? Jenny!' he yelled, Shorty watching. 'Jenny, answer me!'

* * *

Jenny leapt back as three men burst into the living room. She screamed when one of them lunged at her, instinctively smashing the wineglass against his face. He went down with a hiss of pain as the others grabbed for her.

'Jenny, answer me. We're nearly there!'

Jenny heard Lamont's voice, but she couldn't reply. One assailant held her wrists, but she was struggling too much. His partner tried to grab Jenny, but she kicked him in the face before flinging her head back. There was a crunching sound followed by a bellow of pain.

Jenny didn't hesitate. She sprang for the door but the man she'd hit with the glass gripped her leg, pulling her to the ground. Jenny struggled, but the man was too strong. He held her arms firmly, his full weight pressed against her, hot breath in her face causing her to gag.

'Keep still and we won't hurt you,' he grunted. Jenny kept kicking her legs until she could break free. She hurtled for the kitchen door which was closer, the man on her tail followed by the others.

There was a knife on the kitchen sink and she lunged for it as the man's hand clamped down on hers. She slashed at him with the knife, hearing him scream as he hit the floor in a flash of red. The remaining assailants slowly moved into the room.

'Get back,' hissed Jenny, her hair bedraggled as she tightly held the knife. 'Teflon will be here soon. He'll kill you all.' She was shocked at her words.

'Put the knife down, love. Come with us and nothing else will happen. We swear.'

Jenny didn't believe the man for a second. He wore a balaclava like the rest of them. She advanced toward them, noting with relish that they were backing up, not wanting to be stabbed.

'Get out of the way and—' Jenny's back arched and she staggered forward. The fist smashing into her kidney made her head spin, a wave of nausea crashing over her. The knife was still in her hand, but her weak thrust was parried. She was wrestling with the man she had stabbed. He was panting, but she couldn't even tell where she had struck him.

'Stop struggling,' he roared, but she wouldn't listen. Fear and adrenaline had taken over, and Jenny was beyond reason. The hand clamped over hers as she tried to jerk the knife towards him. There was a twitch, another jerk, and then more pain.

* * *

'Hurry!'

Lamont recognised the roads. They were nearly there. As they hurtled to a stop outside of Jenny's, he saw the front door wide open, along with the gate.

Jenny's car was still in the drive. Neighbours had converged, but had gone no closer. One of them was talking rapidly into his phone. Shorty was right there with Lamont, gun in hand. They charged towards the house.

'Jen! Jenny!' Lamont yelled, bursting into the house, and stopping short in the kitchen.

'NO!'

The heart-wrenching scream was uttered from both Shorty and Lamont when they saw the slender figure stretched out near the dining table, so still she could have been sleeping.

Lamont hurried to Jenny's side, turning her over. Shorty hung back, angrily blinking away tears.

'C'mon, Jenny, get up. C'mon, quick, babe. We need to go. We need to go away and be free,' Lamont babbled, paying no attention to the billowing wound near her heart. Her lifeless eyes were glassy. All around were signs of a struggle. There was blood near the kitchen door, but Lamont couldn't tell if it belonged to Jenny, or someone else.

'L, we need to go,' Akeem urged. 'Quickly before the police come.'

'No. I'm staying. You two go.'

'L—'

'I said go.' Lamont's tone brokered no argument. Akeem nodded once and left. Shorty stared at Jenny, his eyes red. Shaking his head, he ran after Akeem.

'Just the two of us,' Lamont said shakily, holding Jenny's cold hand. 'You want to be free. If you wake up, I swear I'll walk away. I'll tell you everything. I promise. I'll tell you why I had to stay. Just wake up and I'll tell you. I promise.'

Lamont's body shook as he held Jenny's frame to his. Tears splashed against Jenny and he closed his eyes, wanting only peace from the hell he felt, as he realised that Jenny was truly lost to him.

CHAPTER EIGHTEEN

Sunday 22 March 2015

LAMONT SAT in the police station. He hadn't requested to speak to his solicitor, or even uttered the words *no comment*. He'd clutched Jenny's body in a daze, tears staining his face until the police came.

They had taken Lamont to the station and given him a plastic cup of piping hot coffee, now lukewarm. Lamont still clutched it, lost in thought.

All his life, Lamont had tried to remain vigilant. He had guarded his heart and emotions. Now, Jenny was dead, and Lennox was his ultimate enemy. He would be hunted down and terminated. Him and his team would fall. Anyone foolish enough to get in the way would be dropped. To Lamont, it was as simple as that.

* * *

'Look at the poor sod.'

From across the room, Detectives Hardy and Murphy watched as one of the top kingpin's of Leeds sat on a chair, staring blankly into space. Hardy was a younger detective with good instincts. Rigby and Murphy liked him, and he looked up to the pair.

'From what I gather, their relationship was the real deal. Nothing concrete, but *Prince Teflon* over there was seriously sweet for her. Head over heels from day one.'

'It will be crazy on the streets. Whether or not Teflon goes psycho, bodies are gonna fall. We need to tell the boss not to let him go.'

'How are we going to do that?' Hardy asked. 'We have nothing to keep him here. It was a hit, but Teflon came afterwards. We've got his people on some traffic cams driving like madmen.'

Murphy scratched his face. 'Don't overthink it. We know that Teflon there is a criminal. When we have a criminal on our turf, we break them. C'mon.'

'We haven't even read him his rights,' said Hardy, aghast.

'So what? He's away with the fairies. Let's have a chat with him.'

* * *

They led Lamont into an interrogation room. He faced the officers blankly staring straight ahead. Hardy looked to Murphy, who had his eyes on Lamont.

'What happened then, L? Why did she end up dead?'

Lamont didn't reply. If he'd even heard Murphy, he didn't acknowledge it.

'We know you had a problem with someone. We know that you were in love with Jenny Campbell. Why did they knife her?'

Still no response. Hardy shifted in his seat. He didn't want the wrong people seeing what they were doing. Murphy was already on thin ice within the department, and Hardy didn't want to go down with him. He had been warned by Rigby about getting caught up, but hadn't listened.

'Tef, we all know that you wanted to walk away. We applaud that decision, but this is serious. An innocent woman is dead. A woman who had ties to you. Don't let her murder be in vain. Help us.'

Lamont didn't move Murphy's face twisted from fake pity to fury.

'Listen, you little prick. I'm talking to you. Do you understand me? Fucking answer me.'

Lamont's eyes flickered towards Murphy, but before he could

speak, a man strode into the room, still wearing an overcoat over his suit. He was red-faced and appeared agitated.

'Please tell me what you're playing at?' he snapped. Murphy glared at him.

'Who the hell are you?'

'I'm the legal counsel for Mr Jones. Please explain why my client has been arrested?'

'He hasn't. We were just talking about the circumstances of his little girlfriend getting knifed. Just a chat amongst friends.'

'Lamont,' Levine called to him. 'Let's go.'

Lamont shuffled to his feet and left the room without a word. Levine glared at the officers one last time, then followed his charge. Hardy sighed.

'Guess that didn't work out how we wanted it to.'

'It was worth a try though,' replied Murphy, revealing a yellow-toothed smile.

* * *

Shorty sat in a safe house, pounding shots of white rum. Jenny was dead. Lamont should have made sure she was safe, and he hadn't. That wasn't Shorty's fault, but the escalating issues with Lennox Thompson were. He hadn't heard from Lamont since leaving him, but he knew that Lamont's solicitor, Levine, had been called.

Akeem was in another room and Maka was upstairs making phone calls. Shorty's phone was blowing up, but he didn't want to talk to anyone.

When Lennox became a problem, Shorty hadn't allowed himself to consider the possibility of losing. Shorty knew the streets; he knew how to hurt people and get information out of them, so to envision loss was inconceivable. Until now.

Lennox was a terror. Worse, he was a terror who knew their moves, who had come up alongside Marcus and his crew, just like Shorty. He had previously done business with Lamont, keeping himself in the kingpin conversation despite his open refusal to sell drugs. No-one had ever got one over on him. Lennox had ripped apart the inner workings of Delroy's organisation with ease, then adopted similar tactics in luring Shorty into a trap.

Everything had been planned, Shorty now saw that. Lennox had leaked the location of Lutel's safe house, knowing he would give up the main location, and he waited patiently to spring the trap, causing their team to lose two good men.

Taking out Jenny was ruthless, the sort of move Marcus had done in the past, It was clear where Lennox had learned.

Shorty closed his eyes, tears sliding down his face. He angrily wiped them, not wanting anyone to see. He'd downed his fourth shot of liquor when he heard a key jangling in the lock. Shorty reached for his gun as Lamont trudged into the room. He looked a mess, wearing a faded grey sweater and jogging bottoms. His facial expression was the worst, however; he looked utterly devastated, and Shorty didn't know what to say. He settled for the obvious.

'Did they take your clothes as evidence?'

Lamont might have nodded, Shorty wasn't sure. He grabbed a second glass and filled it to the brim, handing it to Lamont.

'Here.'

Lamont took the drink and held it like he didn't know what to do. He collapsed into a chair, spilling a bit of the liquid, then downed the rest.

'L, I'm sorry, bro. Jen shouldn't have gone out like that.'

'It's fine.'

That was it. Those were Lamont's only words. He reached for the bottle of rum, but Shorty moved it out of his reach.

'Fam, she was your girl. It's not fine. It shouldn't have happened.'

'It did though. That's the game. It's the life we live, and I should have known that before I involved her,' replied Lamont. His hands shook as he closed his eyes, feeling them burn with the urge to weep, but he wouldn't do that. Not anymore.

'For fuck's sake, L! She was your woman. This isn't street shit anymore. Man the fuck up and stop trying to fight how you feel.'

Lamont turned cool eyes on Shorty. 'You wanna know how I feel? Really?'

'Yeah, I do.'

'All of this is your fault, Shorty. You let all of this happen.'

'What did you say?' Shorty's eyes widened.

'You wanted me to be honest? You couldn't just leave the situation alone, could you? God forbid Shorty ever back down, right?'

'Are you serious, thinking you can blame me? You've always been soft, hesitating over shit rather than taking action. We lost Marcus because of you. You were right there, and you did nothing. Everyone close to you ends up dead, or wishing they were.'

'Lennox got to Jenny because of you!' Lamont roared, silencing Shorty. 'Killing her was a shot at *both* of us. I had Grimer watching the house, until the point you needed him for your little suicide mission. You visited her, and I guarantee you that led Lennox's men to the house. I may hesitate, but you got Jenny killed. If Grace dies, that too will be your fault.'

Lamont regretted it as soon as he'd said it. Shorty's face was harrowing. He stared at Lamont as if he'd never seen him before.

For a moment there was a lull. Shorty broke it, letting out a strangled yell and diving at Lamont. Lamont expected it, but Shorty's mass still sent them toppling to the floor. Lamont was about to try to reason with him, but he saw the fury in Shorty's eyes. This was a fight.

Shorty struck first, a short jab to the ribs. He tried mounting Lamont, but he kicked Shorty off and sailed in with a knee, catching Shorty in the stomach. Shorty let out a moan of pain, grabbing Lamont around the throat and slamming him into the wall.

Lamont struck with his elbow, catching Shorty in the eye. He hit him twice more, sending his friend stumbling. Shorty came back though, dodging the next two blows, clipping Lamont's jaw with an uppercut, then hitting him twice in the ribs. Lamont sagged to one knee, but only for a second. When Shorty lunged again, Lamont evaded it, shoving Shorty into the wall. There was a noise behind him, then strong arms pulled him back.

'Enough.' Akeem stood between the pair. Lamont and Shorty breathed heavily, giving each other death stares. Something had shifted between them. They had argued many times before, but they'd never once raised their hands to each other.

'You're a cancer,' spat Lamont. Shorty tried to pass Akeem, but the guard was too strong. He pushed Shorty against the wall, keeping his eyes on Lamont.

'This isn't the way to deal with this.' Akeem's words fell on death ears.

'This is on you, Shorty. You're responsible for all of this. All you've ever done is weigh me down with your bullshit. I should have left you in prison.' Lamont used his jumper to stem the blood from his nose.

Shorty's eyes blazed. Lamont braced himself, expecting Shorty to try again. Instead, Shorty spat blood on the floor and stormed from the house, holding his gun.

* * *

'Blood, what the hell is going on?'

K-Bar didn't know what to say to Darren. His phone was ringing off the hook. There were rumours Shorty and Lamont had been murdered by Lennox, but K-Bar had spoken with Akeem, who had set him right before hanging up.

'I don't even know,' K-Bar admitted after a long silence. The pair were holed up, smoking weed and waiting for word.

'How is Lennox still breathing? I mean, he's got half of Leeds after him, so what's the drill?'

'I know they were moving on him last night,' said K-Bar, annoyed he'd been left out of the action. 'I dunno what happened, but it doesn't sound like they got him.'

'This is bullshit. I'm need to get hold of something, because I'm feeling vulnerable when I'm moving around. I can't even go see my girl because I'm shook that someone's gonna come for me.'

'You definitely need to be strapped,' said K-Bar. 'I'll get you one to hold and we can practise shooting to make sure you're ready.'

Before Darren could reply, they heard a voice shout *POLICE*, and then a boom as the door was smashed open. Officers surged into the room, ordering Darren and K-Bar to fall to the floor without giving them time to comply. The officers slammed them to the ground, restraining them and cuffing their hands behind their backs.

Neither man struggled. The safe house was clean. Police would find no evidence of illicit activity there.

'What's the charge, pigs?' Darren spat, only to have his face pushed further into the carpet. The leading officer, a greying man with a paunch and tired eyes began reading them their rights, but K-Bar tuned him out as they dragged him to his feet.

All across Leeds, there was a similar spate of activity, with fifteen people being picked up in coordinated raids. Some were part of Lamont's crew, and the others had similar crew affiliations.

Drinking in his living room at home, Lamont made sure Levine was aware of the situation, in case they tried to take him in. He had Akeem searching for Lennox, whereas Levine's team would represent his men and get to the bottom of the situation.

* * *

Lennox had his feet up at an out-of-the-way spot in Adel. He had mixed feelings about the current climate. People had been arrested in connection with various drug cases, but none of his men had been caught in the sweep.

The streets were all looking for him however, and Lamont seemed to be sparing no expense in having his killers prowl around the streets of Leeds. Lennox moved around when necessary, but refused to have security watching his every move. It slowed him down and Lennox couldn't afford that.

Deep down, Lennox knew they could have avoided the situation. He'd told his men to kidnap Jenny and bring her to him. The plan was to use her to force Lamont to back down, allowing him to deal with Shorty and Delroy unchecked. Instead, his team had panicked when Jenny fought back, and ended up killing her.

Now, Lennox would have to contend with a fully invested Lamont. Emotions aside, Lennox knew that Lamont wouldn't back down. One of them would end up killing the other. His people were organised and knew their roles. It was up to Lennox to engage.

'I can't believe you.'

Lennox looked up, seeing Malcolm framing the doorway. Malcolm's face was haggard, bags under his eyes, his hair unkempt. His hands shook as he stared down Lennox.

'What are you doing here? This spot is for emergencies only.'

'How could you do it?' Malcolm ignored Lennox's response.

'You'll need to be more specific.'

'How the hell could you murder her?'

Lennox resisted the urge to roll his eyes. He'd never understood how so many men allowed themselves to become enthralled by the women around them. Malcolm was no different.

'These things happen.'

'That's not enough,' Malcolm stepped further into the room. 'She was a good woman. She wasn't mixed up in your shit. You didn't have to kill her.'

'Shut up. You have no idea what's going on,' said Lennox scathingly. 'This situation is so much bigger than you. I don't have the time for sentimentality. I have an actual war to win.'

'A war? Who the hell do you think you are, Lennox? You're not a general. You're not some great revolutionary. You're a basic gangster, and that's it. There's nothing special or noteworthy about you. I'm sad it took me so long to realise it.'

Lennox was about to reply when a noise distracted him. He heard the click, then the pounding gunfire as he was knocked out of his chair. Malcolm was clipped twice in the neck and jaw and crumpled to the ground, unmoving.

Eddie Williams stepped into the room, aiming his gun at Malcolm and shooting him twice more. He approached Lennox, his jaw clenched and his eyes wide with fury.

'You're next, you piece of shit.'

As Eddie aimed the gun at Lennox, he surprised Eddie by lurching to his feet, gun in hand. Lennox didn't hesitate, popping Eddie in the head, then firing four more shots into the man.

Gingerly, he touched the bullet-proof vest beneath his hooded top. The bullet had hurt like hell, but at least it hadn't penetrated. Firing one more shot at close range into Eddie, Lennox snatched his phones and hurried from the house.

* * *

K-Bar stared ahead, not taking his eyes from the police officers. He was being interviewed and had been advised of the reason for his arrest. K-Bar thought he was being picked up on drugs charges, which were easy to fight without concrete proof. When the police told him he was being charged with murder, it completely blindsided him.

'Kieron Barrett, for the benefit of the tape, please tell us where you were on the night of Wednesday 11th September 2013?'

'No comment.'

The questions continued in a similar vein, with the police asking about his connections to Chink, Polo and Naomi. K-Bar *no-commented* everything, inwardly wondering who had given him up. Grimer was his co-conspirator, but he was dead. Unless he'd snitched while alive, K-Bar didn't understand where the police were going.

'Kieron, we know all about you. We know everything that has transpired over the past few years. We even know about the Manchester war, and the job you did on Big Kev. Make it easier on yourself and cooperate.'

K-Bar looked at his solicitor, but the man didn't seem to have a game plan. Lamont had been onto K-Bar for years about making sure he had a legal team ready just in case, but K-Bar hadn't taken heed. He had no rapport and very little relationship with the solicitor he'd hired, and it showed. The man was content to let the police control the interview.

'I have no idea what you're talking about.'

'We have a witness who has stated you paid Naomi Gateworth five thousand pounds to set up Xiyu Manderson, better known to you as *Chink*. She was given two and a half thousand pounds up front and agreed because of an abusive relationship she was in with Chink. You killed Chink's bodyguard, then you murdered both Chink and Naomi, thinking that was the end of it. Stop me if there's anything that I've gotten wrong.'

K-Bar's stomach was going haywire as he fought to keep his expression neutral. He didn't know how, but the police were spot on.

'We know everything. We know the meeting spot. We know what

was said between you and Naomi. You'll take the full force of the punishment, unless you start talking about the people you work for. Help us fill in the blanks about the time period. Don't go down with the ship when you don't have to. We know Teflon is behind this. You don't need to protect him.'

'Like I said, I have no idea what you lot are talking about, so you may as well just let me go.'

The officers shared a look with one another, then shrugged.

'Have it your way then; Kieron Barrett, we are charging you with the murders of Naomi Gateworth, Paul Dobby, and Xiyu Manderson. You do not have to say anything. But, it may harm your defence if you do not mention when questioned something which you later rely on in court. Anything you do say may be given in evidence.'

CHAPTER NINETEEN

Friday 27 March 2015

ON THE MORNING of Jenny's funeral, Lamont slumped in his living room, staring at a bottle of Red Label rum, debating whether to get drunk. He was already in his black suit, his tie dangling precariously over the bottle.

Lamont had considered skipping the funeral, not wanting to face a venue full of people who blamed him for Jenny's murder. If they didn't, they should. Lamont had been cleared by the police, but none of that did anything to blot the stain around his heart. Shorty was right; people around Lamont did end up dead.

Street activity was at its lowest for years. No one was making much money, and police were an almost permanent presence in the Hood.

No one had seen Shorty since his argument with Lamont, but Grace Turner was in recovery after several operations. Lamont had spoken with Amy who had been grimly pleased, stating there was a long way to go before Grace would be better. Amy hadn't asked about Shorty, nor had Lamont volunteered any information.

People had swept all of Shorty's known spots, to no avail. Lennox was also on the missing list, but Lamont and Delroy had teams dedicated to tracking him down.

The murder of Malcolm Powell was another talking point, as was the fact he'd been gunned down alongside Eddie Williams, a known gangster and son of Delroy.

There were rumours flying around about Malcolm's involvement, people believing he'd been associated with gangsters from day one. Lamont believed this. A person saying the things Malcolm had, shouldn't have been able to walk around with impunity. It was just another part of Lennox's diabolical plan he had to admire. The man had covered almost every angle, and Lamont saw now that the plan had been to destabilise Lamont on the streets, and to break up his relationship.

K-Bar remained on remand, charged with three murders. Lamont had been unable to contact him, and had no idea what he might have said.

Regardless, Lamont had a go-bag ready, just in case he needed to flee. Proper instructions had been meted out. There would be no messing around this time; everyone would know what to do if things went south.

The *OurHood* Initiative was still going, yet had floundered slightly in the death of its leader and public face. Figures such as Calvin were still prevalent, calling for harsh punishment for the drug dealers responsible for the wrongdoing. More civilians were beginning to cooperate with the police, who continued to make scores of small-time arrests. The public and the police were for a time, united.

Lamont was wholesaling his drugs, letting the younger, crazier outfits take the risk of selling during a police lockdown. He couldn't bring himself to care though. He sat around, mourning Jenny, waiting for the news that Lennox had been taken care of, but there was nothing so far.

With a start, Lamont clambered to his feet and went to finish freshening up. He had a funeral to attend.

* * *

As funerals went, the service was fairly brief. Lamont noted several people he recognised, including Jenny's friends. Kate was there, her face already wet with tears. Lamont didn't approach her. Nadia and several others who had worked for Jenny were present.

Even Marika had shown up, dressed in her black clothes and standing near Jenny's friends. She locked eyes with Lamont, but neither moved to speak.

Lamont spotted two people who could only be Jenny's parents. They were greeting several attendees, their faces heavy with their grief. Jenny favoured her mother, who had the same dark hair and cheekbones, but she had her father's eyes and nose. He was a thin man with a lined face, chestnut eyes and a slight Mediterranean tan to his skin tone.

Lamont debated whether to introduce himself, but decided against it.

He drove alone to the cemetery after the service, watching in silence as they buried the woman he loved. Lamont didn't move, even as others around him made their way toward a gathering being held at a prestigious hall in Shadwell. When people started to file away, Lamont noted one figure still stood by the graveside. He debated whether to approach.

'Hey,' he said, walking over. Kate glanced at Lamont, then turned back to the graveside.

'If there's one person on this planet who deserves to not be in there, it's her.' Kate's voice was full of the pain Lamont was internalising.

'I know.'

'She loved you, L. Even after the split.'

Lamont didn't speak. Kate looked back at him, her eyes swollen with the tears she'd already shed.

'Was it your fault?'

Lamont didn't hesitate to reply to Kate's loaded question.

'Yes.'

'Why couldn't you just walk away?'

'I wanted to, but I couldn't. Don't ask why.'

'Wasn't she worth it?' Kate's voice rose. A few stragglers looked over, but no one approached.

'Of course she was worth it! You should know that better than anyone. You were there. At the beginning. You saw how I felt about her. She was the first person in a long time that I thought could help me navigate away from the darkness.'

'So, what happened; the darkness won?'

'Does that answer your question?' Lamont pointed at the graveside.

Kate didn't speak, fresh tears rolling down her face. Lamont resisted the urge to hug her. He and Kate had been close, but it directly resulted from Jenny. Their only conversations had been about her, and she defined them.

Now, Jenny had been stripped away. She had been in the middle of a war and they'd all paid the ultimate price. The cool wind whistled through the cemetery.

Lamont jammed his hands into the pockets of his suit jacket, looking around. Akeem was a respectable distance away from them, monitoring the surroundings.

'I'll leave you to it.' Lamont turned to leave. Kate's words stopped him.

'Do you know who did it?'

Lamont met Kate's eyes. She had stopped crying, the recognisable fire back. He debated lying, just to spare her feelings.

'Yes.'

'You're going to kill them, aren't you?'

Lamont stared at Kate, gauging whether to reply.

'Yes, Kate. I'm going to eradicate them.'

'Good,' Kate smiled for the first time. 'Make them suffer.'

* * *

Lamont and Kate drove to the hall in Shadwell in silence. Declarations had been made, and Lamont had made a vow that he would see to fruition. Lennox would be torn apart. Lamont was putting money on the heads of everyone involved. He was tired of the waiting around.

Lamont led Kate into the hall, full of people milled around, telling stories in large groups. Lamont wanted to drown himself in the liquor but he remained composed, instead drinking water, ambling around the fringes of different groups, not getting involved in conversation.

He saw Marika watching and as she made her towards his corner of the room, he didn't move.

'Hey,' Marika said.

'Hey.'

The siblings stood in silence a moment.

'I'm sorry,' Marika started.

'I know.'

'Jenny was nice. She was good for you.'

'How do you know that?' Lamont stared at Marika.

'I saw you together. Everyone did. You were at peace when you were with her.'

It hadn't been peaceful when Marcus Daniels had been murdered in front of them, or when Lamont was almost killed, but he appreciated the sentiment.

'I'm not gonna ask about what comes next, because I know you. Just, be careful. Whatever is going on with us, you're still my brother and I love you.'

Lamont didn't respond, but Marika understood. She squeezed his hand, and for a moment, Lamont forgot his pain, remembering the bond they shared, and how much he loved her.

'Come by and see the kids sometime. I'll make you some dinner.' With that, Marika left Lamont to his grieving, and he'd never been more grateful to her.

The event crawled by. Lamont eventually spoke with a few of Jenny's friends, all of whom were nice, but in a guarded manner that told Lamont quite starkly that they blamed him for Jenny's death. Lamont felt they should and didn't argue the point. He saw Jenny's parents and couldn't avoid them any longer. Swallowing his courage, he forced himself to approach.

'Mrs Campbell, I'm so sorry for your loss. I . . .' Lamont didn't know what to say, and as fresh tears formed in Jenny's mother's eyes, his throat tightened. 'Your daughter shouldn't have died, and I wanted to tell you that. I loved her more than I can put into words, but this isn't about me. It's about you; your loss. I just wanted you to know that.'

Jenny's mother flung her arms around Lamont, tightly hugging him.

Lamont held the embrace, pouring all the anguish and emotion he felt into the gesture. When they pulled apart, both their faces were wet. Lamont sniffed, shaking hands with Jenny's father. He was about to leave, when he felt the man grab his shoulder.

'I'd like to talk to you. Come to our home when everyone leaves. This is the address.'

* * *

Lamont arrived at Jenny's parent's home, not knowing what to expect. He'd never met them before today, but Jenny had stated she got along with her mother more than her father. The pain of losing her hadn't diminished, but it fed the volcanic rage simmering within Lamont. He needed to absolve himself by murdering Lennox.

Perhaps Jenny's father wanted to shout at him about the murder?

Lamont wouldn't mind.

Shortly after knocking, Lamont was shown into a study. It was at least three times the size of Lamont's, filled with books, a fine leather sofa, a roll-top desk in the far corner, and a liquor cabinet. Jenny's father stared out of the window. He turned, motioning to the sofa. He sat in an armchair facing Lamont.

'So, you're the famous *L*?'

Jenny's father seemed dwarfed by the simple brown chair. Watery brown eyes and rumpled hair were the main signs of grief. Lamont had the impression he was a man who knew how to manage his emotions. Lamont could relate.

'*Lamont* is fine.'

'My daughter spoke of you. Mainly to my wife. I was always protective over her. But, I knew of you. She said you were special.'

'I think she was the special one, sir.'

'Call me Stefanos.'

Lamont nodded, but didn't try the name. Stefanos was testing Lamont, trying to gain the measure of him. It was a tactic Lamont had used in the past.

'Do you have a code, Lamont?'

'Pardon?'

Stefanos cleared his throat.

'Do you have a way of life that you adhere to?'

'I try to do what I believe is right in order to survive.'

Stefanos nodded. 'Survive. I like that. My daughter may have been right about you. From what I've gathered, you are a man of means. You dress well, you lived with my daughter in a large house that you paid the rent on. You drive nice cars. I can spot a pretender, but you're the real deal. So, how are you surviving?'

'I live in a world I shouldn't. I wanted to take the steps into another world with your daughter, but I wasn't able to do that.'

'Are you telling me it was your fault she died?' Stefanos's expression and tone were unchanged, which surprised Lamont.

'Yes.'

'How?'

'I brought her into my life and I shouldn't have. I realised a long time ago that people who grow close to me seem to end up broken. Like I am.'

'You're broken?'

Lamont met Stefanos' eyes. 'More now than ever.'

'Because of my daughter?'

'Yes.'

'So, why go after her? You wanted a pretty girl on your arm, to sit with in the clubs? To take lots of little photos with?'

'Are we speaking freely here, sir?'

'Stefanos, not *sir*.'

'Okay, Stefanos, sir. Are we speaking freely?'

'Yes we are,' Stefanos replied, his eyes glittering.

'You've had me checked out, which means you know I'm not the sort of person who sits in the clubs posing for photos. I went after Jenny, because she made sense.'

'Explain.' It was a request that came out as a command, and they were both aware of the fact.

'I was searching for the way out. Your daughter was that way out and when I first spotted her, I knew she was different. She didn't even have to open her mouth. She was extraordinary. I had to get closer to her. Jen didn't make it easy. She never made anything easy. I jumped through hoop after hoop to grow close, and I don't regret that.

'I don't regret telling her I loved her. I don't regret telling her my deepest secrets. I regret that I was stupid enough to bring her into my life, but not do everything in my power to keep her safe. I was at war. Still am. I know my enemy. I knew them before they became my enemy, but I still thought they would leave her alone. I'm still here. She's dead. I can't let that stand.'

Stefanos cleared his throat, but still said nothing. After a moment, he opened his mouth.

'I don't doubt that you loved her, Lamont. The fault doesn't lie with you. It lies with me.'

Lamont frowned. 'What do you mean?'

'Answer another question; do you know exactly who was responsible for my daughter's death?'

'Yes, I do. I will handle it.'

Stefanos didn't speak for a long time. Lamont strangely enjoyed the silence. It was comfortable, similar to the silences Lamont had shared with Jenny once upon a time.

'You have . . . ways of handling this situation?'

Lamont slowly nodded.

'I won't pry. Please, make sure you punish them, and leave with my blessing.'

Lamont's brow furrowed, but he rose to his feet, shaking hands with Stefanos. His grip was like iron.

'Hopefully we will speak again soon, Lamont. Stay safe and watch the surrounding angles.'

* * *

'What's the update then?'

Rigby and Murphy were in the office of their superior. They had been up most of the night, and it showed in their rumpled clothing and haggard expressions. Their cases seemed to grow harder every day, with little breakthrough, and it was causing the pair a lot of stress.

'K-Bar still isn't talking. We've remanded him and he hasn't tried to get in touch with anyone. He didn't even react when we read the charges.'

'Do you think he might be innocent?' Superintendent O'Hara asked. Rigby shook his head.

'He's definitely guilty. He's also loyal, and either doesn't think we've got a case, or he's more scared of the people he's working for than us.'

O'Hara rubbed his eyes, looking just as bedraggled as the men who worked for him. His job wasn't any easier than theirs at the moment. There was such a spotlight on Leeds and Chapeltown that the past year alone was a blight on their administration. Multiple assaults, riots, demonstrations and murders had made his role more tenuous than ever.

'No word on Jones?'

Rigby again shook his head.

'There hasn't been any retaliation for the death of Jenny Campbell, but it's coming. Unfortunately, our informant is low in the pecking order. He overheard just enough to get us to K-Bar, but Teflon is different. He's far more organised and hands-off, though the word is that he's depressed over her murder.'

'Wouldn't surprise me,' Murphy mumbled. 'Did you see his face when we had him in here? I've never seen a more broken man.'

O'Hara clutched his mug of cold coffee, staring at the liquid.

'Broken or not, he's one of the most dangerous men in our city, and must be taken down. Lamont Jones, *Teflon*, or whatever his name is, is key to this situation. He has the power, the clout, and a tremendous amount of resource. If we can smash his organisation, we can save our city, gentlemen.

'Get me something, anything that we can use to go on. Put more pressure on K-Bar, squeeze his people. He has a wife, a girlfriend, a brother, anything. Use it. All eyes are on us, and we need to make something happen, and quickly.'

CHAPTER TWENTY

Saturday 28 March 2015

LAMONT TRUNDLED OUT OF BED. Strangely, speaking with Jenny's father had helped. Lamont still felt the same level of guilt, but the fact Jenny's parents didn't outright blame him had boosted his mindset. After a quick shower and two cups of coffee, Lamont left his house flanked by Akeem. They drove toward Chapeltown.

'Anything?'

Akeem shook his head. 'We're slapping his runners and middlemen around. This is Lennox we're talking about though. He wouldn't tell them anything and even if he had, I'd think twice before acting on the information.'

Lamont mulled this over, knowing Akeem was right. Lennox had been one step ahead of Lamont so far. Lennox had been trained by Marcus, but had none of Marcus's obvious weaknesses. As far as Lamont knew, Lennox didn't take any drugs, and if he drank, it wasn't to excess. He couldn't think of any women Lennox had been linked to. That was a problem.

'Could you reach out to Vincent? Let's cast the net further if needed. There's no guarantee that Lennox is still in Leeds.'

'I'll make some calls down south and around, but Lennox won't leave Leeds. He's not hiding. He's waiting for something.'

* * *

'Is this how it's gonna be then?'

Darren continued ironing his hooded top. Realising she wasn't keeping his attention, Clarissa stood and turned him toward her.

'Watch I don't burn you,' Darren warned, placing the iron on the ironing board.

'Daz, please don't avoid the question.'

Darren sighed. He knew Clarissa cared, but he still had a job to do. With everything transpiring, she worried every time he left the house.

For the first time though, Darren had real responsibility. He had been picked up by the police along with K-Bar. The police interrogated him for hours, even getting a warrant to search his place. They found nothing, but the events scarred Clarissa.

The game was wide open though. Money was low, but it was just a period Darren was determined to ride out. Lamont had given some of K-Bar's responsibilities to Darren, and he was doing his best to act on them.

'Babe, I know you're worried, but you don't need to be. I'm fine, and I'm not moving sloppy out there. I promise.'

'People are dying though, Daz. You can't blame me for being scared that the same thing might happen to you.'

Darren finished ironing, then pulled on the hooded top. He held Clarissa, stroking her hair.

'All I can tell you is that I'm watching my back, babe. Why don't we go away somewhere when it blows over?'

'Really?' Clarissa's face brightened, and Darren felt a warmth in his heart as he realised how much he loved her.

'Start looking for places and we can go in May or June. Anywhere you like.' Darren kissed Clarissa's cheek, then gave her a lingering kiss on the lips. 'I've got to jet for now, but I'll see you later on.'

Darren left the house, a car already waiting. He scanned the street before he climbed in. Sharma pulled off.

'Don't you ever listen to the radio or anything?' Darren had asked Sharma the same thing previously, but he never said much.

Sharma shrugged as they turned onto the main road.

'Marcus used to flip out about it, saying we needed to be on point.'

Darren nodded. He'd never worked alongside Marcus, but he'd seen the larger-than-life man doing whatever he wanted around Chapeltown. Darren had been at Carnival when Marcus had been murdered, but in a different part of the park. He'd heard the gunshots, then run and hid with everyone else. There were always little incidents at Carnival, and even last year there had been several stabbings, but Marcus's murder had been a planned hit.

He'd since learned the internal situation and knew that Chink had planned it. He didn't know why he'd turned on Lamont, Marcus and the crew, but he was dead now because of it.

'You ever miss him?'

Sharma didn't reply straight away, his face unchanged.

'He was a cool boss. Crazy, but he always had your back if you were down with him. He put me on, paid me well, and never asked me to do anything he wasn't willing to do himself. He just let the women get to him. Some guys are just like that.'

'Nothing wrong with liking women,' replied Darren, his tone defensive.

'You can't make them your everything though, especially when you're doing dirt. People will use it against you. Look at L.'

Sharma's words made sense, and Darren considered Lamont and his reaction to Jenny's death. Everyone knew Lamont loved her, and Lennox had probably targeted her because of that. Darren wondered if he was doing the right thing with his own girl.

'You think L shouldn't have gotten with her?'

'I can't speak for L, but this life ain't made for wives and girlfriends. With how things are at the moment, it's gonna be worse than it was a few years ago.'

'Things have calmed down though,' replied Darren. The *OurHood* people were cooling off, confused, leaderless and arguing amongst themselves. Police were still neck-deep in Chapeltown, but they couldn't cause any further harm to Lamont's crew. K-Bar had taken the hit for that. 'All we need to do is clip Lennox and the job's done.'

Sharma smiled.

'Kid, learn to see all the angles. Lennox killed both of Delroy's sons and had the man on the ropes. He tried to take out Shorty, hit his daughter, and had Lamont's missus murdered. You think L's gonna get him easily?'

'Not easily, but he'll definitely get him. L's smarter.'

'No doubt. He's the smartest person I've ever met, but he's not perfect. He makes mistakes, and he's at the top, so those mistakes are bigger.

'Lennox is ruthless and has nothing to lose, especially with us picking away at his team and money,' Sharma pulled up outside the safe house, turning off the engine and again looking at Darren. 'All I'm saying is, watch your own back, think about your own moves, and don't expect your boss to sort everything out. He's hurting, and hurt people can make even more mistakes.'

* * *

Lamont sat indoors, music playing in the background. Lennox was still in the wind, and Lamont had no idea where to find him. Akeem was right. Lennox was probably still in Leeds, but any move he made would be on his terms.

Lamont had people in place, but the surge of arrests had made them wary. K-Bar remained in prison, fighting a murder charge. Lamont didn't know how the police had found evidence linking him to the murders of Chink and his people, but it was a massive loss to the team.   K-Bar was looking at a long stretch, and that affected everything.

A bottle of gin and a glass rested on the table in front of Lamont, but he hadn't touched them. He hadn't touched a drink since fighting with Shorty. Lamont regretted their fight, but understood why it happened. It had been coming for a long time.

Rubbing his eyes, Lamont decided to go to bed, the idea immediately expunged by the vibrating of his phone. He picked it up without even checking the number.

'Yeah?' His voice was toneless. There was no pretence at being in the zone. He needed to rest.

'It's me, Charlie?'

'How are you doing?'

'Better than you, from the sounds of things. Is this a bad time?'

Lamont wanted to tell her it was always a bad time, but he liked Charlotte. He didn't want to alienate her as he had others.

'It's been a long day. Listen, I haven't forgotten what we discussed. I'll have someone drop it on you.'

'L, I'm not calling about that. I heard what happened, and I'm making sure you're okay.'

Lamont laughed, staring at the alcohol again.

'I don't have a choice. I have to be okay.'

'I'm coming to see you. Give me your address.'

'Charlie, I—'

'Now, L.'

* * *

When Charlotte entered the house, Lamont was slumped on the sofa looking at the ceiling.

'Have you eaten?' She asked.

'Earlier.'

'Earlier when? You need to eat, L.'

'I'm not hungry.'

'You're certainly thirsty though.' Charlotte reached for the bottle of gin and the glass, moving them out of reach.

'I haven't even opened the bottle. Check the lid.'

Charlotte placed the bottle in the cabinet, then turned to face Lamont. She wore a hooded top under a blue jacket, and ripped jeans, her hair tied in a basic ponytail. Lamont received the full effect of her haunting grey eyes. It was nice, especially after everything else that had transpired recently.

'Do you want me to make you some food?'

'No.'

'I'm going to anyway, so I hope there's something to cook.'

* * *

Soon, Lamont was playing with grilled chicken breast and crispy vegetables. Charlotte eyeballed Lamont, waiting for him to eat. Tired of the messing around, he began eating the chicken.

'How was the funeral?' Charlotte asked.

'Difficult, especially considering the fact I put her there,' said Lamont, struggling to swallow. He closed his eyes for a moment.

'She was attacked. You had nothing to do with it.'

'When someone shot at King outside your house, did you feel he had nothing to do with it?'

Charlotte paled. 'How do you know about that?'

'There wasn't much I didn't know about back then. King needed to keep guys like me sweet in order to even ply his trade.'

'And Justin?'

'Justin was one in a million. He had everything. He could have done anything. He just couldn't let the streets go.'

Charlotte didn't reply. Lamont felt bad for bringing up King and Justin. Years had passed, but he couldn't imagine it was any easier for Charlotte to deal with.

'What's next?' She asked after a moment.

'Nothing that I can discuss with you.'

'Why don't you just walk away?'

'That's not an option.'

Charlotte was again silent. Lamont finished the rest of his food, then did the washing up, enjoying the mundane task. When he'd dried his hands, Charlotte waited by the kitchen door.

'Come here.'

Lamont moved to Charlotte, stiffening as she wrapped her arms around him. After a moment, he relaxed, and he tightly hugged her back, saying everything in the hug that he couldn't say aloud. Charlotte seemed to understand.

* * *

The next day, Lamont left the house with a protective cordon consisting of Akeem and several handpicked men. They climbed into a

4x4 and were about to drive away when Akeem's phone rang. He answered and handed the phone to Lamont after a few moments.

'Who is this?'

'A friend. I heard you're looking for some guys.'

'What about it?' Lamont had no time for nonsense.

'I have an address. Delete it once you've read it. You'll find something there.' With a click, the person was gone.

'Do you know who that was?' Akeem took the phone from Lamont, reading the address after the message buzzed.

'Not a clue. He said we'll find something at the address.'

'Could be a trap.' Akeem scratched his neck.

'It could be,' Lamont admitted.

'What do your instincts tell you?'

'That you and a few of your men should check out this address.'

* * *

Akeem parked across the road from the address. He had two men with him. Lamont was back at home and under guard.

Signalling for his men to exit the vehicle, Akeem checked his weapon, then followed. They kicked down the front door and surged inside. Akeem heard yells in the front room, but he was on top of the person there before they could move, driving his fist into their stomach and flinging them to the floor. His men searched each room, but found no one else.

'Get off me. You're all dead,' the man snarled. Akeem smiled grimly.

'Nice to see you, Nikkolo.'

* * *

Lamont hung up. Akeem had caught Nikkolo at the spot, and they had him at *The Dungeon*, where they would interrogate him.

Lamont racked his brain thinking about the caller. He had a few suspects in mind; namely, Shorty, Akhan, or Lennox himself. He couldn't see Shorty allowing someone else to kill Nikkolo, and he didn't see Lennox trying the same trick twice, which left Akhan. The more Lamont thought about it though, the less sense it made. He hadn't spoken to Akhan since the impromptu kidnapping. He would need to sit tight and see what came back.

* * *

Akeem came to Lamont a day later, grim-faced and unshaven.

'He's gone.'

Lamont felt nothing. He didn't care about Nikkolo's fate.

'Lennox?'

'Nikkolo knew nothing. Gave up some stash spots and safe houses. We found a lot of guns and some small-fry soldiers, but no Lennox.'

'Do you think Lennox planned this?'

Akeem shook his head. 'We completely took Nikkolo by surprise. He wasn't expecting to see us. He started speaking straight away.'

'We're back at square one then.'

'Lennox can't and won't hide forever, but if you ask me, I'd suggest letting some of the heat off. Concentrate on a few small areas, put money on his head, but let everyone else go back to work.'

'Do it,' Lamont replied.

* * *

Days passed. For the most part, Lamont's people were happy to be back at work. Lamont spent his time hanging out by the barbers and going to the gym. He heard little titbits about the *OurHood* Initiative, but nothing major.

On the Friday, Lamont was eating a sandwich when his phone rang. He didn't recognise the number.

'Who's this?' He asked, once he'd swallowed.

'Did you like the tip I gave you?'

'Who is this?' Lamont clutched the phone to his ear. This person was a potential link to Lennox.

'I'd like you to come and meet me. There is a warehouse near the

Canal. It will say *C&C* on the building. If you come, you will receive all the answers you need.'

'I don't even know who you are. That is a lot of trust to give some voice over the phone.'

'You operate within a volatile world, Teflon. You understand the need to take measures to hide one's identity. I won't force you, but I promise that without my help, you won't succeed. Hopefully, I will see you soon.'

The person hung up. Lamont stared at the phone, trying to piece together what he remembered from the person's voice. They sounded familiar, but he couldn't pinpoint where from. It was a tremendous risk, but Lamont didn't have any choice.

Taking a shower and throwing on some clothes, he arranged some paperwork that Levine had delivered that very morning. His will and effects had been updated, just in case. Nearly everything would be left to Marika and the kids, but there were provisions for other people. Lamont sighed, then shrugged into his jacket and left.

* * *

Lamont drove in silence. He'd chosen not to tell Akeem where he'd gone, and forbade the guards at his house from following him. Lamont couldn't help but wonder if he'd made a misstep somewhere down the line, relating to Lennox and Akhan.

The memory of meeting Jenny for the first time planted itself in Lamont's mind, and he felt tears prickle his eyes. He needed to focus. It was difficult though. Ever since Jenny's murder, Lamont had tried so hard to bury his feelings; to work through his anguish as he had when Marcus died, but it was too hard. Lamont wiped away the tears, blowing out a long breath.

'Get it together, you pussy,' he hissed to himself.

The warehouse loomed in front of Lamont, and he pulled into a private car park in front. There were men milled around, two of them wearing fitted suits, the rest wearing black bomber jackets and jeans. All carried weapons, and all were glaring at Lamont.

He froze after turning off his engine, wondering again why he'd chosen to come alone. He didn't even have a weapon. For the first time, Lamont realised he was truly alone. He had no Marcus, no Shorty, K-Bar, or any of the others who had always watched his back.

Swallowing down the fear, Lamont climbed from the ride. Immediately the men patted him down, then they led him toward the warehouse. Lamont owned several of his own, but none that matched the scale of this one. It was enormous, and Lamont was sure that his whole house would fit in the expansive space.

'Get in,' one of the men signalled to a buggy, similar to the ones used by golfers. Lamont did as he was told, and they drove toward an office on the other end of the room. The man who'd accompanied him, jerked his thumb toward the office, and Lamont walked in, preparing to die.

The room was occupied by two men. The first was an older Asian man whom Lamont had never seen before. The second was a more familiar face.

'Thank you for trusting me and coming, Teflon.'

CHAPTER TWENTY-ONE
Tuesday 31 March 2015

'WHAT THE HELL IS THIS?'

Jenny's father reclined on a black leather chair. His face seemed more lined than at the funeral, and he had dark circles under his eyes as he calmly assessed Lamont. The other man said nothing.

'This is you believing in my word. I trust Nikkolo has been disposed of?"

'Where is Lennox?' Lamont asked.

'He'll be taken care of once we locate him. I can assure you my resources are extensive. This meeting pertains to a more sensitive matter, and I need you focused, not distracted like you were at the funeral. Remember, I told you to watch the angles around you.'

Lamont took a moment to reply. If Stefanos was going to ignore the third man in the room, then he would too.

'*Who* are you?'

Stefanos smiled, the Asian following suit. 'I know you're having trouble with your supplier. That should give you a small clue about the scale of things.'

'If you're in league with Akhan, then we have nothing else to say to one another.'

'Please, control your foolish stubbornness. I know of Akhan. I've done business with him over the years. Here, this is for you.'

Lamont reached for the scrap of paper Stefanos held out to him. It had an address on it.

'What's at this address?'

'One of Akhan's main warehouses. Check it out first if you don't believe me. We don't need a repeat of what went down in Cottingley. Send someone either white or Asian though. Akhan and his men have a heavy distrust for blacks.'

'If Akhan is an acquaintance, then why would you give me this information?'

'You're sceptical . . . You still believe I'm trying to trap you, correct?'

Lamont didn't reply. Stefanos grinned.

'I promise you my intentions are above board. Do as you see fit with the information, but I promise you that all will be explained soon enough.'

* * *

'Can you trust him?'

It was midday, and Akeem and Lamont were in the back of the barbers. Lamont had filled in Akeem on his conversation with Jenny's father.

'I think so. He gave us Nikkolo's address, and Lennox murdered his daughter. I can't think of a single reason why he'd work against us.'

'If he worked with Akhan, why would he suddenly switch sides?'

Lamont mulled that one over. 'He thinks that we can help him more than Akhan, which means Akhan has likely overplayed his hand.'

Akeem looked at the address Lamont showed him, his dark eyes absorbing the information.

'If we're going to do this, we need to move quickly. We need numbers too, in case it's a trap. We're stretched thin at present with the hunt for Lennox.'

Lamont sipped a bottle of water, his brow furrowed.

'We need an insurance policy and some backup. I know where to get both.'

* * *

'I was sorry to hear about your girl.'

Lamont could only nod at Delroy's words. After a few quick conversations, they had arranged to meet at a restaurant near the city centre.

'Thank you,' he finally replied.

'I'm guessing you haven't found Lennox yet?'

'Neither have you. I'll settle up with Lennox another time. I'm here to talk business with you.'

Delroy gestured wordlessly for Lamont to continue.

'I need your help taking down Akhan.'

Throwing his head back after a stunned second, Delroy bellowed with laughter, slapping his legs, loud guffaws resonating around the room. Lamont waited.

'Fucking hell, L . . . I haven't laughed like that in years. Go easy on me. I'm an old man.'

'I didn't make a joke.'

'L, you've worked long enough with the guy to know how deep his reach is. You can't touch him like that,' said Delroy.

'Have you ever known me to plan poorly, Del?'

Delroy shook his head. 'I think this thing with Lennox is the first time I've seen you make the wrong call. That and not coming to work for me.'

Lamont assessed Delroy's words, silence hanging heavily in the air.

'Believe me when I say two things; Lennox will be eliminated, and I will take down Akhan.'

'How, L? You're not talking about a rival such as Lenny or even me. You're talking about a warlord. A man with unlimited resources. Even if we combined, we couldn't match up.'

'There are powerful forces at play, Del. Together we can win, against Akhan, then against Lennox. We both have a stake in this. He had my ex-girlfriend killed, and he took out two of your children. Not only do we have the green light to engage, but I know exactly how to damage Akhan's organisation beyond repair.'

It took Delroy only a few seconds to fully comprehend what Lamont had told him. He leaned forward.

'Tell me more.'

* * *

'Look at the size of that place . . .'

Akeem and Jamal were in a black Ford 4x4, watching Akhan's base of operations with binoculars.

They had picked carefully for the mission. Only ten highly skilled men had been selected, including them. They would work in two groups of four and were already scattered around. A few of the men were Akeem's, and the rest were from Delroy's hit teams. They were all dressed in black, carrying powerful automatic weaponry. If everything went to plan though, they wouldn't have to use it.

Stefanos had given them everything. He provided the layout of the base, along with blind-spots, camera locations, and the details of exactly who would be in and at what time. It was no coincidence they were here in the middle of the night. Only a skeleton crew would oversee at least one hundred kilo's of product.

They had staked the place out as best they could, not wanting the same problems that had befallen their attempt at storming Lennox's Cottingley base.

'Is everyone in place?' Asked Akeem. Jamal made a call on a disposable phone. He spoke for a few moments, then hung up.

'Everyone's in play.'

'Okay, let's move.'

The pair exited the ride, blending in with the night. The base was a warehouse on the outskirts of Bradford. It looked huge from the outside and had two cars parked in the small car park. The sign said something about textiles. They had learned Akhan's imports were hidden in the form of textiles equipment, which was an effective cover.

Sneaking around to the side of the warehouse, Akeem typed the code they had been given into the side door. There was a camera above the door, but it only turned one way. The security neglected to mention this to Akhan after a bribe, and the team were using it to their advantage.

Jamal entered the building, Akeem covering him. From their studying of the blueprints, they knew there were two control rooms; one twenty yards down the hall from them, and the other at the far side.

They made their way along the corridors to the control room at the far side. There was a man staring at his phone, laughing. He was the nighttime overseer, the man who gave orders to everyone else in the base during the night. Before he could blink, Akeem and Jamal had their weapons trained on him. He glared, but didn't move.

'On the floor. Now,' Jamal growled, the weapon pointing at the overseer's chest. He didn't look afraid, but slowly complied, lying face down on the floor. Akeem covered Jamal whilst he secured the man, tying up his arms and legs, then stuffing a rag in his mouth. They used his system to turn off the cameras. They saw four more people on the premises, bagging large quantities of cocaine in a room.

'Right, you guys can come in now. Go straight to Room B.' Akeem hurried from the room with Jamal at his tail. They heard yelling and movements, but no gunshots. They secured the other rooms, finding no resistance, then headed to Room B.

Akeem and Delroy's teams had secured the workers. Jamal's legs shook at the sight in front of him. He was no stranger to drugs spots in his time. This was on another scale though. There were bricks and bricks of product, all sealed and lined up. Some of it was already boxed up, the boxes hosting the same Textile insignia on the outside of the building.

'Are the trucks ready?' Akeem asked one of his men. The soldier nodded.

'Get all of this loaded up. You and you stay here and make sure this lot try nothing. No one will get hurt if they don't resist.'

* * *

Lamont was in his office drinking a cup of coffee when he got the call he had been waiting for. He paused a few beats, before answering the

PGP phone.

'Hello?'

'Where is it?'

Lamont took another sip.

'I'm sorry, who is this?'

'Teflon, I beg of you not to play games with me. My compound was attacked. Well-trained men made off with a tremendous amount of product. I want this back immediately. If I get it, there will be no further conflict. This is my assurance to you as a businessman.'

Lamont again waited. Akhan was on the back foot for once, and he relished it. The move on the warehouse had been a success. As per the arrangement, the drugs were being guarded by Lamont's people, with Delroy's men in reserve. They didn't have a final count, but there were well over one hundred kilo's, and that was just the cocaine.

Lamont grinned, realising this was the first time Akhan had made his own phone call.

'You're presuming that I know what you're talking about.'

'Teflon, I politely asked you not to play games. I want the product back. If I have to, I will tear apart Chapeltown and the surrounding areas to find it.'

'No you won't.'

'Excuse me?'

'Let's cut the shit and act like two men who know all about this business. Now, you want the consignment. I understand that. I'm willing to deal with you.'

'There will be no deals. I have told you what I want.'

'Are you sure? If I hang up on you now, I won't pick up the phone again. This I assure you as a businessman.'

There was an ugly silence on the other end. Lamont wanted to smile, but stayed in the moment.

'What do you want?'

'The same thing I always wanted. To walk away, free of all retribution. I also want the name of the person who betrayed me, along with all material relating to that situation. If I get all of this, then you will get your product back.'

'Done. We will meet in twenty-four hours and exchange the information. My men will have the videos and paperwork pertaining to your personal situation. You will verify that these are original, un-doctored copies. You will bring the product to the location, and we will both send our respective teams on their way. Is this a deal?'

'Yes. Now, who was it who told you what transpired with me last summer?'

There was a long silence, and then Akhan uttered one name.

'It was Chink.'

Lamont clenched his fists as Akhan continued.

'He approached me in an official capacity, wanting me to work with him. He proposed a great deal of money up front and as a sweetener, he gave me information about you, and what you had done.'

It all made sense to Lamont now. Chink was excellent at staying under the radar. It was his kind of move, and it might have worked, had he not been murdered.

'Are you still there, Teflon?'

'Yes.'

'Twenty-four hours, and we will end this for good. One last thing, in turn for the information that I have provided you with . . .'

Lamont finished his coffee. 'Name it.'

'Who told you where my drugs were kept? Very few people knew this information.'

'Lennox Thompson.'

'Nonsense. He is a bandit. There is no way he could have found out that information.'

'He's resourceful. He can find things when he needs to. He gave me the information before we became enemies. I held off until I needed to.'

'I see.' Lamont heard the anger in Akhan's tone, maintaining an indifference that he knew added credibility to his story.

'I would never try to tell you your business, but I would be careful going after Lennox Thompson. He's a dangerous man.'

'Don't worry about what I do, Teflon. We will speak again in twenty-four hours.' With a click, Akhan was gone.

Lamont placed his phone on the desk, a wide smile encompassing his face. He was almost finished. He was so close to the finish line and this time, there would be no stumbles. He hoped that Jenny was looking down, and that she saw the lengths he was going to in order to be free. He stared into space a while longer, then he rose to his feet.

There was still work to be done.

* * *

Darren frowned at his phone, sipping the bottle of Lucozade clutched in his hand. He was with Maka and Terry. They had been told that business was back to normal. There had been whisperings of things going on in the background, Delroy's men being seen with theirs, which Darren didn't understand.

'Guys, am I missing something?'

Terry glanced at Maka, then to Darren.

'About what?'

'Everything. We're smacking around Lenny's men, then we're not. Then we're back to business, now Delroy's people are around. I don't get it.'

Maka sniggered.

'Lennox made the biggest mistake of his life when he went at Tef's girl. Tef will murder him. That's a given.'

'It's mad though. We're warring because Tef's ex got killed?' Darren held up a hand before Maka could reply. 'I know, fam. He's the boss, and he calls the shots. He's done a lot for all of us. We're talking about war though. We could die or get locked up tomorrow. I guess I just wanna make sure I'm doing it for the right reasons.'

Sharma's words to Darren had made him delve deeper into the situation, looking past the money and responsibility. There was a price to be paid for his new success, and Darren was terrified about paying it.

'Don't worry, just be careful, because we've all got targets on our backs. I trust Tef though, and whatever he's doing, I know it's gonna be good for us,' said Maka. Before Darren could respond, one of Akeem's men entered.

'You two are needed outside,' he said, pointing to Maka and Darren.

'What about me?' Terry asked. A look from Akeem's man had him glancing at the floor. Darren and Maka followed the man, who signalled to a black 4x4 vehicle. They climbed in the back.

Akeem waited, dressed for combat, openly wearing a bullet-proof vest over a dark sweater. Darren felt his hands tremble as the reality of the situation started to sink in.

'Everything good?' He asked.

'Yeah, the lines are smooth. Pure dodgy things going on though. What the hell's up with Delroy's people?'

'That will be explained soon enough. For now though, Teflon needs you to front an important meeting. A deal of sorts.'

'What's the deal for?' Maka asked. Darren remained quiet, his heart pounding.

'You'll see. Meet me out here this evening at seven. You won't need anything. I'll speak to you then.'

'What was that all about?' Darren asked. Maka didn't reply, his jaw clenched as they watched Akeem drive away, wondering what would transpire next.

* * *

Lamont looked around Stefanos's garden. It was practically a field, seeming to stretch on as far as his eye could see. He kept his hands jammed in his pockets, his fleece coat and boots doing an excellent job of keeping out the cold. He wished he'd opted for a scarf though.

Lamont had always hated the cold with a passion. Jenny had liked winter, he remembered. It struck Lamont that they hadn't spent much of one together. Their first winter together had been fraught with Lamont's recovery from his shooting. He didn't even remember what he had done last Christmas, but he was sure it was done under the haze of painkillers.

'L.'

Lamont whirled around, shocked that Stefanos had managed to sneak up on him. Stefanos wore a jumper, fleece trousers, and shoes, a wide smile on his bushy face.

'I called out to you several times, but you were in your own world.'

'Sorry about that. I was just thinking.'

'About what, if you don't mind me prying?'

'Jen. I was remembering that she used to love winter, and I always hated it. The cold reminded me.'

Stefanos met Lamont's eyes, smiling sadly.

'She used to write long letters to Santa when she was younger, detailing exactly how good she had been, and why she deserved presents. Halloween, Bonfire Night and Christmas. She loved them all.'

'I never got to spend much of a winter with her . . . My recovery was long.'

'I heard. We will talk about my daughter in greater detail soon enough, but I have more information to relay to you. It relates to Akhan.'

Lamont straightened.

'What is it?'

'He will come for you. Regardless of how the exchange goes down later.'

'Let him,' said Lamont. He and Delroy's partnership would need to contend with Akhan's shooters.

'Akhan has a tremendous amount of resource.' Stefanos had a shrewd expression on his face.

'I know. I won't be subjugated, and I won't back down. I faced death once before, and I'm still here. Let him come.'

Stefanos was silent, looking out at the darkening sky.

'Come inside with me, please.'

Lamont followed Stefanos. Akeem knew where he was, but if this was an ambush, he wouldn't be able to reach Lamont in time. His heart hammered, but he controlled his emotions, looking for potential escape points.

'Take off your shoes in the hallway, please.'

Lamont unlaced his boots, expecting to feel a gun being pressed to the back of his head. No such action came though.

'Would you like to take your jacket off?'

Lamont shrugged out of his jacket, and Stefanos hung it up for him.

'Follow me.'

Lamont followed Stefanos down the hallway. They entered a room. It contained a small sofa, an office desk and computer. In the corner was a roaring fire, and on the sofa, a man sat. He was brown-skinned, with cropped hair and a tailored beard. He wore a black shirt, trousers, and had his shoes on. He stared at Lamont with fathomless dark eyes, a small smile on his ratty face. Lamont remembered seeing him at the warehouse with Stefanos.

'Lamont, this is Jakkar. He is a friend of our friend Akhan.'

Lamont shook Jakkar's hand. His grip wasn't as firm as Stefanos's, but Lamont still felt the strength of him.

'Nice to meet you, Lamont.'

'Tell me about Akhan.'

Jakkar's smile widened.

'You work with him, correct?'

Lamont nodded.

'How do you find him?'

Lamont considered this for a moment.

'Resourceful.'

It was Jakkar who nodded now.

'Akhan was bred for this life. I knew him growing up. He was skinny, frail, a magnet for the bullies. Like many smart people, he learned to use his weaknesses to his advantage. He was hungry and willing to do what needed to be done. These traits brought him to the attention of The Council.'

'Tell me about this council.' Lamont had never heard of them.

'One thing at a time. Akhan began working for the council. He was in place as a lackey but he waited, and he listened. He rose through the ranks until he was given control of the drugs at a local scale. He took this to England and worked to make it stick. Others were in play in different areas doing the same, but Akhan started showing the council a lot of return for their investment. They gave him more drugs. He was loyal, or so it seemed.'

'What do you mean?'

'In 1989, Akhan asked for permission to leave. He promised to pay a five percent tax for life, but wanted to work for himself. The council vetoed his request and Akhan attempted to go rogue. Fourteen of his men both here and in the Middle East were slaughtered. He returned to the fold, but he wasn't beaten.'

Lamont's heart hammered as he processed everything he was being told.

'When Akhan returned, he was seemingly loyal. But, he was moving money around and making his own connections. He invested in local housing in areas such as Chapeltown, where drugs and crime were rife. He sat on these properties and in the early 2000s, sold them and made a ton of money. His own money.'

Lamont saw where this was going. 'He was trying to establish his independence.'

'Akhan saw his way out as a purely financial one. He wanted to amass his own wealth so he could gain his freedom from the council. He began working many money schemes, ensuring the council was paid, but lining his own pockets at the same time. When funds were low, he blamed it on recession and promised to get things working.'

'He was skimming.'

'Millions of pounds, over a near twenty-year-period. He bribed many of the council's emissaries. Finally, they sent me.'

'Why finally?'

'I wanted to be the one to end this little reign. Akhan has run unchecked. I warned the council of his ambition and advised them to restrain him. Finally, they are listening to me.'

Lamont watched Jakkar. His eyes were hard as he talked of Akhan. He thought of Chink. Chink too had ambition. Even when they were dirt poor, he always planned to be rich. Lamont wondered what Chink would have become if he hadn't befriended him.

'So, it's your turn now. Why?'

'You'll have to be more specific.'

'Why do you want to bring down Akhan? You've become profitable under his charge.'

'I was profitable long before I met Akhan. He forced me into a servitude that I didn't want.'

'So it's freedom you desire . . .'

'Always.'

CHAPTER TWENTY-TWO

Saturday 4 April 2015

DARREN SWALLOWED DOWN HIS FEAR.

Akeem had briefed he and Maka. He knew the meeting involved their supplier, but that was all. They were outside a building, five of them in all. Maka was near a wall, staring at the ground. Darren had tried speaking with him about the situation, but Maka wasn't talking.

Darren motioned to the surrounding men to drop the bags on the floor. It was a simple drop-off. They had driven the consignment in a white transit van emblazoned with the name of a haulage company. If anyone was diligent enough to Google the company, it would bounce back with nothing.

Darren checked the time. The supplier's men had let them in. They seemed unfriendly, but hadn't been hostile so far.

Darren was shocked at the size of the building. It had various doors and sections, almost like an office building. Darren noted a camera pointing down at them, but noticed there was no blinking red light. He felt the hairs on his arms stand on end, his palm itching. There was a whirring noise as the metal gate by the entrance slowly rose.

A black panel van coasted into the main room, followed by a 4x4 vehicle. Men descended from both vehicles, eight in all, all armed to the teeth. Darren didn't look to Maka or the other men, but sensed their anxiety. They were outnumbered.

'Good of you to join us,' a man said, climbing from the passenger seat of the 4x4. Darren froze. He'd been briefed on Saj and knew he reported to Akhan.

'There's the stuff, we'll be on our way.' Darren motioned to the men with the bags. Saj grinned.

'There has been a change of plan I'm afraid,' Saj raised an arm and his men pointed their weapons at the group. 'Call Teflon. Tell him to come to this warehouse. If he does not come, or is delayed, then you will die.'

'What the hell—'

'There is a time for wondering, and there is a time for action. Make the call to your boss immediately, or die.'

Darren tensed, slowly reaching for his phone. He located the number with shaking hands and pressed the call button.

'Tef?' he said after a moment, looking at Saj to confirm Lamont had answered. 'I'm here now. Listen . . . Saj is here. Yes,' Darren paused, then grinned. 'They acted exactly as you predicted.'

Before Saj could react, Darren and the others hit the floor as doors all around the warehouse opened. Men armed with automatic rifles opened fire on Saj's crew. They tried turning their guns onto the invaders, but were too slow. They were cut down before they could let off a shot.

When the gunfire subsided, Darren motioned to the shooters to finish any survivors. As he and Maka left the building, they heard a few bursts of gunfire, then silence.

They changed into spare clothing hidden in the back of the van, placing the worn clothing into a single black sports bag. Once done, they climbed back into the van and drove away, leaving Akeem's hired killers to take care of the clean-up.

* * *

Lamont sat in his office with Akeem, waiting for the confirmation to come through. Lamont had suspected a double-cross. The first flag had been the need to wait twenty-four hours. It was too long for a man of Akhan's calibre.

Lamont had moved quickly, reaching out to Stefanos about more locations of Akhan's. Stefanos reported back with the best locations, and Lamont's men spread themselves trying to find the right one. When they'd seen Akhan's team setting up a few hours ago, they'd sprung the trap.

'You should have set the warehouse on fire with the bodies inside,' said Akeem.

'I wanted him to know that he couldn't beat me.'

'You're not thinking about the bigger picture. You are already becoming more of a target with the police. This display will only further propel your name out there.'

'Akhan has plenty of enemies. There's no reason my name should be the one people hear.'

'And, if he works against you with the police?'

Lamont rubbed his eyes. Akeem was giving him food for thought. He'd never contemplated the possibility of Akhan choosing to work with the police.

'We'll cross that bridge when we get to it.'

The pair sat in silence until Lamont's phone rang. He checked the number and put the phone on speaker.

'Yes?'

'It's done.'

Darren hung up. Lamont grinned at Akeem.

'How long do you think it will take for Akhan to ring?'

'I'm guessing about ten minutes.'

Three minutes later, Lamont's phone rang.

'Nice to hear from you, Akhan.'

'That was a mistake, Teflon. I'm sorry to say you won't live long enough to regret making it.'

'Just remember, you started this. All I did was retaliate.'

'You really think you can win against me?'

Lamont hung up. Akeem calmly assessed him, waiting for instruction.

'Put everyone on alert.'

* * *

Lamont had a fitful sleep, tossing and turning, drifting off after three in the morning. He was up by seven, showering and shovelling down some breakfast. He'd spoken with Delroy. They had all bases covered, waiting for Akhan's fist to come down. Lamont hoped he hadn't overextended himself.

Lennox was still a ghost, as was Shorty. Lamont didn't know if he would ever see Shorty again, and now that the anger had abated, that feeling hurt. Lamont rubbed his eyes. There was no time for sentiment. There were too many things going on. When everything died down, he would locate Shorty, and they would talk.

Lamont checked in with Akeem, who was on the frontline, organising both their soldiers and Delroy's. They hadn't decided how to distribute the drugs without upsetting the flow, so they were being kept in storage for now. The split would be fifty/fifty, and profits would be huge. Lamont was considering the idea of moving them out of town, but it wasn't his top priority.

Lamont started to doze off when his phone began ringing, startling him. He wiped his eyes and answered.

'Yes?'

'We need to see you.'

* * *

They were at Stefanos's home again. Lamont noted that he hadn't seen Jenny's mother either time he had visited, but shrugged it off. Jakkar waited in the study. He greeted Lamont with a smile and a handshake. Stefanos offered drinks, but they declined.

'Excellently done, Lamont. You played Akhan beautifully, but he will come for you with all his force now. He'll attack your men, your drug spots, your family. This is a very dangerous path you've undertaken,' said Jakkar.

Lamont shook his head. 'I know what he's capable of, but I'm the wrong person to back into a corner. He underestimated me, and it's cost him both money and men. My team are ready, no matter what direction he wants to take it.'

'Are you truly prepared to take it to the wire?' Stefanos spoke now.

Lamont already had his answer ready.

'Your daughter was my reason to leave. Akhan prevented that for his own ends, manipulating me into a position that meant I couldn't stop her murder. No matter what happens, he doesn't survive, nor does Lennox.'

'This will help you,' Stefanos fished into his pocket and removed a piece of paper. He looked at Jakkar before handing it to Lamont. Lamont glanced at the scribbled address. He looked up at both men, who were gauging his reaction.

'What's this for?'

'That's Akhan's home address.'

* * *

Lamont clutched the address tightly. His men had worked overtime trying to collate this information in the streets, bribing people and threatening others. Nothing had worked. Now, Stefanos had pulled this out of nowhere.

'Where did you get this?'

'It wasn't hard,' Jakkar spoke up again. 'It's sensible to keep a close eye on a dangerous subordinate.'

'And now you want me to do your dirty work for you,' replied Lamont, letting the pair know he was hip to the attempted manipulation.

'You stated you won't allow him to survive. We're simply helping you.'

'This has to benefit you in some way.' Lamont studied the pair, concentrating on their body language, looking for the slightest slip. They were composed though, almost amused by his attempts.

'It's up to you if you choose to do it. If you don't, this will be the last we speak of it.' Jakkar, slid to his feet. Stefanos followed suit, glancing at Lamont, who recognised it was time to leave. He shook hands with both men as Stefanos walked them to the exit. Jakkar lingered, smiling at Lamont.

'It was nice to meet you, Teflon. I hope this isn't the last time.'

'I'm confident it won't be,' said Lamont, as he left, the piece of paper with Akhan's address in his pocket.

* * *

Lamont headed home, staring at the address. He had in his hands the power to change his whole life. He couldn't comprehend Stefanos's motives, but Akhan had outlived his usefulness with them, and they were willing to let him die because of this. There were questions Lamont needed to be answered, but for now, he had to do it. He had to go to Akhan.

* * *

Akeem drove. It had started raining earlier in the afternoon, and the roads were slick. Lamont played with the leather gloves he wore, trying to imagine how Shorty, Marcus and the rest had done this so often. He thought back to his earlier days, when he'd gone on a job with Marcus, and how terrified he had been.

Lamont remembered the time he'd fought Ricky Reagan for his life. That murder had stained Lamont, but it was necessary. What happened tonight would also be necessary.

Akeem was armed. Lamont was too. He couldn't remember the last time he'd held a gun, but the 9mm felt comfortable, and he wasn't sure how to feel about that. Akeem pulled to a stop fifty yards from Akhan's house, turning to Lamont.

'Are you sure about this?'

'Yes.'

They were shocked at the location. Akhan lived in a simple semi-detached house in Bradford. There were no signs of wealth. A Mercedes was parked outside, but looked several years old. There was a single light on downstairs.

'Follow me, keep the weapon down until you need to use it. He doesn't look to have any security measures in place, but if he does, I'll disable them,' said Akeem.

Lamont expected sophisticated, state-of-the-art security, or at least guards patrolling. He saw the move for what it was though: arrogance. Akhan had never considered the idea that anyone would get close to him, and now he would pay for it.

Lamont blew out a breath, trying to calm down. His senses were on overdrive, sure that every sound was something harmful. Akeem disappeared around the side of the house as Lamont crouched in the garden, hoping he was well-hidden. He heard a sound to his left and his heart leapt in his chest as he raised his gun, but it was just a cat. In any other situation, Lamont would have laughed.

Akeem materialised next to Lamont after another minute.

'I've double-checked the perimeter. There might be an alarm when I break in, so move quickly toward the room with the light. If it looks bad, shoot first, ask questions later.'

Lamont nodded and Akeem took a tool from his pocket, and started fiddling with the back door. It opened and they slipped through. There was no sound, but Lamont crept into the house, listening to the rain tapping relentlessly against the roof and windows.

Soft piano music was playing from one of the rooms. Other than that, there were no sounds. No one else seemed to be in the house.

Lamont moved along the hallway, looking at the classical paintings on the wall, illuminated by the soft lighting, dotted along like an exhibit in a museum. Lamont followed the music, his heart hammering, hoping he wasn't walking into a trap. He paused outside the lit room, he could hear the music clearly now. It was *Mozart's Requiem*. He pushed gently at the door, then entered.

The room was larger than it appeared from the outside. It was full of books, a large desk, and two regal leather chairs. It reminded Lamont of his own study. The music blared from an old CD player against the wall. A Hitachi.

The room had large, Georgian-style windows. At these windows, Akhan stood, looking out at the rain, and giving no indication he'd heard the door opening.

Lamont stood and watched him, and for a few minutes, neither man spoke.

'Are you going to do it then?'

Akhan's voice startled Lamont. The elderly man faced him now. He wore an impressively white shirt, grey trousers and matching grey tie. His expression was impassive.

'I have to.'

'I know,' said Akhan. 'Everything is in order. I worked out what was going on when Stefanos stopped returning my calls. He had you do his dirty work.'

'No, he didn't.'

'You don't think so?'

'You forced this, when you forced my hand. You made me stay in this life and you cost me everything. For what? So you could make more money? How's that going to help you now?'

'This is your destiny.' Akhan, ignored Lamont's questions. His hands rested by his sides. Lamont raised the pistol. The cleaning team was already on standby. Lamont wanted to talk more. He wanted to question Akhan, but it had gone beyond that. Both men knew it.

'Just remember. One day, you'll be where I am, and you'll be staring down the gun. When you pull the trigger, you will never be free.'

Lamont nodded at Akhan's final words.

'Freedom is a myth. Thank you for teaching me the lesson.'

Then, he fired.

CHAPTER TWENTY-THREE

Monday 6 April 2015

LAMONT AWOKE THE NEXT DAY, feeling strangely light. The spectre of Akhan was removed. The cleaners had done their job, but Lamont had several alibis just in case.

As Lamont used the bathroom and washed his hands, his only regret was that Jenny wasn't there to enjoy it with him. Sadly, her murder had been the catalyst to force him to take action. Lennox was next.

Lamont spent a long time in the shower, then picked out a khaki polo shirt and black jeans. His phone rang as he was forcing breakfast down his throat. Akeem was outside. Grabbing his wallet and dumping the remains of the cereal, Lamont left.

'Stefanos wants to see you,' was all Akeem said, as Lamont buckled himself into the passenger seat, then busied himself looking out of the window at the fractured streets. Chapeltown was capable of so much more. With Lamont at the helm, spearheading the change, pumping money into the community, it could reach its full potential.

Akeem stopped outside a small office building. They climbed out and they were shown inside by a dumpy, grey-haired woman with olive skin and a sweet smile. Stefanos rose from his seat when he saw them.

Pumping Lamont's hand, then Akeem's, he signalled for both men to take a seat.

'Can I get you gentlemen anything to drink?'

They both shook their heads.

'That will be everything, Agatha,' Stefanos said to the elderly woman. She left with a swift nod.

'How are you feeling?' Stefanos asked Lamont.

'Well-rested.'

'I heard from Jakkar early this morning. He spoke of a home invasion. I have people in the local press who will write up that story. The killers will never be found. Akhan's family will bury him back home, and likely stay there. There is panic amongst the people who worked for him. They are worried about where the next meal will come from.'

'I'm sure Jakkar will plug the gap.'

Stefanos smiled slowly.

'He has a way to do this. You.'

Lamont tried not to let the surprise show on his face.

'What do you mean?'

'Jakkar wants you to take Akhan's place. He wants you to run the entire Yorkshire distribution for the council.'

'That's . . . ridiculous. I'm not even Asian,' spluttered Lamont. Stefanos allowed himself a wider grin.

'It's a brave new world, predicated on trust far more than bloodlines. You have done them a service, and they recognise your worth.'

Lamont shared a look with Akeem, his bodyguard's face blank. Lamont had always thought himself a decent poker player, but he was sure Akeem would best him if they ever played.

'Is this an offer, or a demand?'

A chill descended over the office. Every man in the room knew precisely where Lamont was going with the question, and Stefanos wasted no time answering.

'The days of you being forced to do anything against your will are over. There will be no attempt at blackmail. This is an opportunity for you to assume control of your destiny.'

'By answering to someone else.'

Stefanos shook his head, looking almost disappointed.

'Everyone answers to someone. But, this life we live is all about power. It's about ascending so we hold dominion over more and look up to less. You take this position, you will experience true power.'

'Like Akhan did?'

'Akhan was greedy. He sought to overthrow the council, and they took necessary action. I have more faith in you.'

'You believe I should take it then?'

'I do.'

'Why?'

'Because I need my daughter's death to mean something.'

Lamont's stomach lurched and for a moment he was back cradling Jenny's cold body against his. He would never be rid of the images that plagued his thoughts. Jenny shouldn't have died. Lamont still believed this with every fibre that remained of his heart.

'My daughter was touched by greatness. She hadn't even begun to utilise her gifts. I don't want you to waste your potential.'

'I wouldn't. I have money and investments in place. There's no risk of going to prison.'

Stefanos shot a look at Lamont. 'If you don't want to go to prison, then don't. You put together a formidable team on the streets. Everyone played their roles, and you all made money. This is the opportunity to do that on a larger scale.'

Lamont was quiet for a moment.

'I promised your daughter that I would walk away.'

Stefanos's eyes were gentle. 'I believe you meant it when you said it, Lamont. You were forced to break that promise though. You want to honour my daughter's memory? Do it by wielding power from the seat you earned.'

'I'm . . . Filled with so much guilt,' Lamont admitted, feeling the lump in his throat as the words tumbled from his mouth.

'About my daughter?' Stefanos hadn't taken his eyes from Lamont.

'About many things. My parents had high hopes for me, yet I picked a life that keeps me at the bottom. I pedal misery.'

'That's life. You may not be working a nine to five for *The Man*, but it's up to you how you affect your community. If you want to be a force for good, do it from a position of power,' Stefanos paused, his eyes alight with the passion of his words. 'It's all about power,' he repeated.

Lamont took a few moments to consider.

'I'll do it.'

Stefanos grinned. 'I hoped you would. I'll be in touch. We have much to discuss.'

* * *

Lamont left the meeting with a spring in his step. He would speak with Delroy about the situation later. For now, he had some other issues to resolve. As Akeem drove, he dialled a number.

'Hey, L. How are you feeling?'

'Will you go for dinner with me?'

Lamont heard Charlotte's breath catch. He waited.

'You want to go on a date?'

'Yes.'

'Why?'

'Because we get along.'

Charlotte didn't speak for a moment. He could almost hear the conflict churning within, but he wasn't worried.

'Okay. I'll let you arrange everything.'

'I'll be in touch.'

Putting his phone away, Lamont again thought about Jenny. He needed to let her go. He'd made his decision about the life, and he needed to be stronger than he'd been before. Charlotte had experienced the crime life with both Justin and King. He didn't know if things with them would go anywhere, but they could help each other.

Akeem drove to a spot in Moortown. Darren sat in the living room playing on a PlayStation. He hopped to his feet when he saw Lamont, dropping the pad.

'Teflon? What are you doing here? I mean, shit, is everything good?'

Lamont smiled at Darren's nervousness.

'I wanted to personally thank you for your recent work. You stepped up when I needed you to, and I want to reward that.'

Darren began protesting, but stopped speaking when Akeem gave him an envelope. His mouth widened at the array of notes.

'Akeem said you preferred cash to direct transfer. I'm different, but to each his own.'

'Thank you, man. I mean . . . there's thousands here.'

'Plenty more where that came from. A lot of change is coming, and our money will go through the roof. I want you to work with Maka and recruit. Don't rush it. We want capable men. Can you handle that?'

'Yeah, course I can, boss. Thank you.'

Lamont grinned.

'I know you were worried about how things would go. That's fine. I'd be more concerned if you weren't. Focus on your task and when the time is right, we'll discuss more.'

* * *

When Lamont left, Darren pumped his fist.

'Yes!'

Darren was elated. The rumours of an alliance between Delroy and Lamont were true, the team was on the rise, and Darren would be right there when it all happened. He dialled Clarissa, tapping his foot and waiting for her to pick up.

'Daz, what's up?'

'Book a holiday. Anywhere you like. First class even.'

'Oh my God, babe! Are you serious?'

'Deadly serious. Look, I'm gonna come and see you soon, but get looking. We're gonna do it big!'

* * *

Lamont stopped at Marika's. He'd called ahead and arranged it after realising he didn't know where she lived now. The house was off Roundhay road and appeared comfortable.

The gate squeaked as Lamont entered the garden, and the door swung open. Marika looked like their mother every time Lamont saw her, and it made his heart ache. He wasn't sure about greetings, but when Marika flung her arms around him, he clutched her tightly.

Minutes passed before they let go, neither looking the other in the eye, embarrassed over the show of vulnerability.

'Are you okay?'

Lamont nodded.

'Day by day. How are the kids?'

'Getting older. They want to do their own thing more, but still.'

'I'm glad you're doing well, sis. Sorry I haven't contacted you. I've been dealing with some shit.'

'I know. I saw how you were at the funeral. I really am sorry about Jenny. She was right for you.'

Lamont nodded, remembering his thoughts earlier.

'Thank you.'

'Have you heard from K-Bar?'

'My solicitors are working on his case as we speak. Why?'

Marika let out a deep breath.

'We're involved, okay?'

Lamont couldn't help it; he laughed. Marika glared, hand on her hip.

'Why are you laughing?'

'You just love the thugs, don't you?'

Marika grinned. 'K-Bar's not a thug. He just does bad things sometimes. I thought you'd be angry.'

'I don't have the right. I've made too many mistakes lately to judge anyone, sis. You wanna be with K-Bar, I have no problem with that. I'll get him out, no matter the cost.'

Marika squeezed Lamont's hand, and he smiled.

'Come with me. I want to take you to see someone.'

* * *

Lamont, Marika and Akeem walked along the hospital corridors until they found the correct room.

Amy was sat by Grace's bed, watching her daughter, still hooked up to complex machines. Lamont's heart lurched when he thought of the proud, wilful little girl who always made him take her to the shop. The little girl he viewed as a niece, just as Bianca was. Amy looked at Lamont, but didn't move. He kissed her on the cheek, noting how cold she felt.

'How is she?'

'She's still fighting, but she's not in the clear yet.'

'Is there anything I can do?'

Amy shook her head.

'I took a leave of absence from work. They understand the situation and there's no pressure to get me back.'

'Do you need money?'

'I'm fine, L. Even if I wasn't, your boy took care of that.'

'You've heard from Shorty?'

'No. Some money was transferred into my account, and I put the pieces together.'

Lamont glanced at Marika, remembering she was unaware of the fallout between him and Shorty. He would check with Stacey to see if she had too had received any money from Shorty. If possible, he would use it to track down his friend.

'I'll come back and see you soon, Ames. Please ring me if anything changes.'

* * *

That afternoon, Lamont and Akeem were at his home. They'd been planning strategy for several hours, and both were yawning from fatigue. It had been a trying period. Lamont was ready to leave Akeem in charge and take a break, but he needed things to be solidified.

'Lennox must have family; some kind of connection keeping him in Leeds other than revenge. Between ourselves and Delroy, we'll find it. For now, Darren and Maka will handle recruitment. You'll oversee them. My legal team are working with K-Bar and searching for Adele. She was the loose end K-Bar left behind. Police will keep her under wraps though. When we understand the new scope of the operation, we'll get into that aspect of it. My thinking is—'

Lamont's phone vibrated, and he snatched it up, annoyed.

'Who is this?' His eyes widened, and he stumbled towards the door, Akeem watching him in alarm.

'L?'

'We need to go. Someone blew up the barbers!'

* * *

Akeem's ride sped through the streets as Lamont made more phone calls, trying to find someone who could confirm if Trinidad was okay. He'd tried calling Trinidad's direct number, but couldn't get through. Panic gnawed at Lamont's insides. Trinidad wasn't involved in this. He wondered if it was Lennox, or if Akhan had orchestrated something before his murder.

There was a crowd already gathered. Lamont and Akeem pushed through them, but it was futile. Lamont saw the firefighters nearby, trying to put out the blaze. His building, the first one he ever owned. Akeem moved forward, asking about survivors, but Lamont knew it was too late. Trinidad would have been working. He never took days off.

With a lurch, Lamont thought about the only other thing he valued; his father's chessboard. Someone would pay for this, he decided, clenching his fists. Akeem headed back over.

'I spoke with the fireman, he said—'

There were two sharp cracks from a gun and Akeem toppled to the floor, unmoving. The shooter, a skinny teenaged kid looked at Lamont, grinned, then disappeared into the crowd.

People screamed, running to get away as Lamont stared dumbly down at his bleeding bodyguard, his building burning in the background.

EPILOGUE

R IGBY WAS in his office catching up on paperwork when Murphy bounded over.

'Rig, you're not going to believe this.'

'Can it wait? I've got a lot of paperwork to do.'

Murphy turned Rigby's chair so his colleague faced him.

'What the bloody hell is wrong with you? I just said that I've got work to do,' Rigby snapped.

'Trust me, you want to hear this. K-Bar's solicitor is trying to reach us.'

Rigby forgot about his paperwork in an instant. They had charged K-Bar but he hadn't received a court date yet. All attempts to speak with him had been stonewalled, and an expensive and tricky legal team were fighting his corner.

'Why?'

Murphy's yellow-toothed grin was full of gleeful malice.

'K-Bar wants to talk.'

TARGET PART III

CHAPTER ONE

Monday 6 April 2015

BEING a multimillionaire criminal engendered little community sympathy, yet as Lamont Jones stood on the tough streets of Chapeltown, he silently prayed for help. His eyes flitted from the bleeding man at his feet, to his burning building, as he tried desperately to think of a plan. He could hear the loud shouts of the firefighters and the screams of the people still brave enough to be standing there. The acrid stench of gunpowder stung his nostrils. Never in his life had Lamont felt more vulnerable. He didn't know if the shooter was still in the vicinity, or if there was more than one.

The gunman had given him a smile after pumping bullets into his bodyguard, Akeem. He couldn't take it. He was sick of all of it. As unnerved as he was, part of Lamont wondered what that sweet release would feel like for him.

For a second, Lamont closed his eyes, ready for it to be over.

A second later, he opened them, feeling foolish. He needed to be strong. Now more than ever. Lamont pulled out his phone and with only a split-second to decide between calling an ambulance or calling for backup, he made his choice.

'L, what's happening?' Asked Manson, one of his lieutenants, when he answered,

'There's a situation. The office got blown up. Trinidad is dead, Akeem got shot. I need people sweeping the Hood, looking for the shooter. He's skinny, short hair, light-skinned, wearing a black jacket and trackies. Question anyone you don't recognise. I need you to do this now.'

'Got it. Catch me up when I get there. I'll have people on route.'

Lamont hung up, again glancing down at Akeem before finally calling an ambulance, only to learn the firefighters had already called through. Akeem was unmoving, the pool of blood surrounding him growing by the second. He knelt down, trying to stem the bleeding. He didn't know what he was doing, or if he was making a difference, but he needed to try something. Marcus Daniels had died in his arms in similar fashion two years ago, and he hoped history wasn't repeating itself. Giving the ambulance five minutes to arrive, Lamont called again, stressing that they needed to hurry.

He sensed the crowd growing closer and instinctively concealed his emotions. The idea the shooter could be watching meshed with the rage he felt. Lennox had caught him off-guard, and given Lamont yet another reason to hunt him down.

'You're going to make it,' he said quietly to Akeem, his hands warm with the man's blood. The wet body armour had done nothing to stop the bullets. The crowd's murmuring grew louder. A man had his phone out, recording. A glance from Lamont and he put the phone away, mumbling an apology.

'Let me help you,' a woman he didn't recognise pushed her way through the crowd. 'I have medical training.'

Lamont stepped away, overcome with dizziness. Nothing about the situation seemed real, but it was. This was life for him.

The sounds of screeching tyres announced Lamont's people arriving in two cars. Manson jumped out, along with half a dozen other men. They hurried over, most of the crowd dispersing when they noticed.

'I've got people sweeping the Hood now. Which direction did he run in?'

'He ran toward Nassau Place,' said Lamont. Manson shouted instructions, and four men peeled off, hurrying back to the car and driving away. Manson looked from Lamont to Akeem, his face solemn.

'We need to get you out of here.'

'I'm not leaving him,' said Lamont immediately. He didn't know if the woman was helping, but she was checking airways, keeping one hand pressed to the bleeding area. She certainly seemed more composed than he was. Manson grabbed Lamont's shoulder, stealing his attention.

'You're too exposed out here. Trust me, you need to go.'

Still dazed, Lamont was bundled into the remaining car and driven away.

* * *

At home, Lamont waited for news about Akeem. Several hours had elapsed. Manson had checked in, saying they still hadn't found the shooter, and Lamont was racking his brain trying to work out who it was. Lamont had been right in his sights, and the shooter had left him alone. He couldn't work out what Lennox was thinking. The conflict that had escalated between them could have ended right there.

Was he toying with him?

The thought filled Lamont with both dread and frustration. It struck him that he knew little about Lennox's organisation. Even his assault on Nikkolo had only been possible because of the information he was given by Stefanos's contacts. It was something he would need to rectify.

A shooting in public would need an immediate police response and investigation. There was nothing in the building or on records that would negatively link Lamont to the business. The business he had helped Trinidad grow. Trinidad was dead, and it was all his fault. The nausea swam over him and he took several deep breaths, trying to control himself. Trinidad had died for his stupidity. He should have warned him of the danger, rather than leaving him to suffer.

Lamont paced the room, his temples throbbing. Trinidad had a family, and someone would need to contact them. The phone rang, and he scrambled to answer it.

'Lamont?'

It was his solicitor, Levine.

'Yes?'

'I don't know all the details of what you're involved in, but the police want to ask you some questions in connection with two murders.'

Lamont's stomach plummeted. He knew he had heard correctly, but still needed to check.

'*Two* murders?'

'A second man died on Chapeltown Road, and witnesses placed you at the scene. I want you to come to my office, and we will draft a statement together.'

Lamont didn't respond. Akeem was dead, and it hurt to hear. He closed his eyes, his shoulders slumping.

'Lamont. Are you listening?'

'I heard you. I will come to your office tomorrow.'

'Time is of the essence here. The police aren't looking to arrest you at this stage, but if I'm going to protect you, I need to know the facts.'

'I said, I will come tomorrow. Or did you forget you work for me and not the other way around?'

The coldness of Lamont's tone reminded Levine who he was dealing with.

'Tomorrow will be fine. I'll be in the office from ten.'

Lamont hung up without responding. There was no reason for him to react to Levine like that, yet he couldn't help it. The police wanting to speak to him was nothing important. He wouldn't be giving them any information that would help.

Sitting back down, he rubbed his temples and closed his eyes.

What the hell was Lennox thinking?

* * *

Lennox Thompson waited for news of his attack with no emotion. He had prepared his message with care. Teflon had located one of his hidden spots. He didn't know how, but it had rattled him, and needed answering in kind. The plan was simple. He would destroy Teflon's business. Everyone knew he owned the barber shop, and that Trinidad ran it for him. It would send a clear-cut sign that war wasn't a good idea. If he showed, his shooter, Sinclair, was to kill whoever was with him. He wanted Teflon to know he could get him whenever he wanted.

The spot Lennox was in was on Well House Drive, off Roundhay Road. He had several spots dotted all around and after Teflon had located one, he had instantly moved. It was spartan, with a television and a lumpy grey sofa, and simple table in the middle of the living room.

Soon, two booming knocks at the door alerted him. He slid into a seat and waited for a worker to let them in.

The pair traipsed into the living room. One was stocky, with straight brown hair, steely blue eyes, and hard features. The other, Sinclair, looked like a kid. He was twenty-four years old, but had the build and features of a teenager. Lennox signalled for both men to sit.

'Is it done?'

'Yes,' said the stocky man. He was Mark Patrick, and had been elevated by Lennox after Nikkolo's demise. He had served time in the army and had connections and experience with explosives. 'The owner bit it too.'

Lennox straightened in his seat. 'You killed Trinidad?'

'By the time we realised he was in there, it was too late.'

Lennox glared at him. 'You messed up.' He wasn't pulling punches.

'You wanted a message sent, and I sent it. He was an old man, and he was down with Teflon.'

'He was a civilian.' Lennox continued to stare Mark down. 'Watch how you speak to me.'

'You should have let me drop Teflon too,' Sinclair added, bored with the conversation. 'His bodyguard went down easy. He never even saw it coming.'

Lennox ignored the boasting. 'We have a primary target in place. What happened today was payback, and Teflon will realise that.'

'Do you know how they found Nikkolo yet?' asked Mark. Lennox shook his head.

'I spoke with everyone connected with that hideout, and no one gave anything away. No one stands out either. It's possible they just got lucky, but I doubt it.'

'What's the next step then? Teflon and his people are gonna be gunning for you.'

'Set up a meeting with Nicky Derrigan.'

Mark and Sinclair exchanged looks. They knew Derrigan by reputation, and it wasn't a move they expected Lennox to make.

'Are you sure you want to go there?'

Lennox's stare only intensified, and Mark looked away.

'I'll make the call.'

* * *

Detective Rigby waited in an interview room as K-Bar was shown in. His solicitor was with him, and they both took seats opposite Rigby. K-Bar appeared well for a man on remand. His expression remained as guarded as it had during the initial interview. He brushed a stray dreadlock from his face, not taking his eyes from Rigby, waiting for him to speak.

'You wanted to talk,' said Rigby after a long moment. He hadn't started recording. The conversation was informal at this stage, but for anything to be agreed, they would need to have it on record.

'I want to know what's on offer.'

'Do you have something to trade?'

K-Bar evaded the question. 'What do I get if I did?'

'What do you want?'

K-Bar smiled. It was the first bit of emotion he'd shown since entering the room.

'I'm innocent. I want to be released.'

'If you were innocent, you wouldn't be behind bars, would you?'

K-Bar's smile widened. 'Wouldn't be the first time you lot got it wrong. You don't have a clue what's really going on out there.'

Ignoring the jab, Rigby pressed on.

'You're looking at serious time, Keiron. If you want to spend your time dicking around, I'm sure you would be more comfortable doing that from your cell. You killed people — men and women — to further your interests. You're not innocent and your hands are not clean. So, you can help yourself, or you can go back.'

'Innocent until proven guilty.' K-Bar remained unruffled, though his smile had vanished.

'We have nothing but time. Time, and some key witnesses.'

'That saw me kill people? Can't be the case if I'm innocent, can it?'

Rigby shook his head. His temper crept up, and he couldn't stop it.

'Innocent? You've no shame, have you? You take away somebodies daughter, a lifelong friend . . . a life. Then you sit here giving it *innocent until proven guilty*. You'll see what we have when you're in court fighting for your freedom.'

Rigby was unsure how he expected K-Bar to react, but he hadn't expected his eyes to light up. A moment later, he was back to normal.

'I think I made a mistake. I changed my mind, and I don't wanna talk anymore. You're never gonna get what you want. That's a promise.'

'What do you mean by that?'

Shaking his head, K-Bar rose to his feet. His solicitor, who had remained silent throughout the exchange, followed suit. After directing an officer to take K-Bar away, Rigby headed back to his desk. Murphy immediately came over.

'What did he have to say then?'

'Nothing. He was fishing to see what he could find out.'

Murphy frowned. 'That's a shame. I'd have liked to stuff Teflon in the cell next to him.'

'We'll let K-Bar stew a while, then go for him again. He is the key to bringing down the whole crew.'

* * *

After Rigby left, K-Bar asked to speak with his solicitor. The officer was hesitant, but allowed it after a quick glance over his shoulder to see who was around.

'What was the point of that, Mr Barrett?' the solicitor started. 'You overplayed your hand with the officers, and it didn't help our position.'

K-Bar grinned.

'There was never a deal to be made. I just wanted to confirm something.'

'What could you have possibly confirmed from that interaction?' The solicitor frowned. K-Bar's grin only widened.

'We don't have long, but I need you to pass on a message for me.'

CHAPTER TWO

Tuesday 7 April 2015

DELROY AWOKE with his usual stiffness. After staring at the ceiling for a few minutes, he clambered from the bed to get ready.

When he was washed and dressed, he checked his messages, but they were all business. No one had contacted him that he wanted to speak to, and he felt his chest tighten.

Traipsing downstairs, he made himself his usual breakfast of plain porridge. He wasn't supposed to drink coffee anymore. Doctor's orders. Like many things in his life, he ignored them. He was an old man, and he had earned the right to live his life exactly how he wanted.

Delroy's kitchen, like everything in the house, had been designed by his wife, Elaine. She had taken control of all the decorations, so now he had a modern, ghastly, chrome nightmare. It took months to learn how all the various devices worked, but he had to admit, once he had, that they made things easier. He wondered what Elaine was doing. He hadn't spoken to her since shortly after Eddie died. She was still using his money. The credit card bills were proof of this, but something was broken between them. There was no fixing it. As far as Elaine was concerned, she had lost two children because of him. Because he was a criminal.

He couldn't make her understand.

Delroy had come from Grenada with a vicious reputation and boundless ambition. He had looked at the gangs that were established in Chapeltown and, even early on, had seen the potential in selling hard drugs.

That kicked off a series of wars, and Delroy was simply more vicious than the rest. By the time crack, coke and heroin were established, he controlled most of the flow in the Hood. Not wanting all the attention, he allowed little gangs to run wild, figuring they would keep themselves distracted and away from him. This action led to more police attention, as they couldn't ignore the rising drug trade in Chapeltown forever.

Things settled down after that, and Delroy consolidated his power, growing richer and more influential. Things changed a few years ago, but no one was a bigger example of that than Lennox Thompson.

Lennox had grown up around the Hood and was committing robberies from a young age. Charisma set him apart from the rest. He was a natural leader who planned tasks with absolute precision. Only his temper in his younger days held him back, leading to him serving serious time in prison. Like others, he used his time behind bars to cultivate criminal connections. Unlike most, Lennox didn't go the drug route. It was making everyone rich, but he didn't seem interested. Instead, he focused on extortion and robberies, working with other thugs like Marcus Daniels and Ricky Reagan.

Delroy had paid attention to him as he did all the interesting criminals, but Lennox wasn't a concern. He wasn't selling drugs, nor did he seem interested in anyone who was. Delroy put him to one side.

Until the attacks started.

No one picked up on the patterns at first. A dealer jumped in Bankside. Another in the Mexborough's. A few spots in the Hood robbed with no casualties. Delroy increased security, but the problem only grew, leading to one of his top distributors getting shot twice outside his home. He survived, but it was a true sign someone was out there.

Delroy mobilised his son and right hand man, Winston, to sniff out who was behind it. Winston was a great son. He took any opportunity to prove himself and was a born negotiator. He quickly unearthed that

Lennox Thompson was the man leading the charge, and this shocked everyone.

There had been no lead-up. No slights or crew issues. Lennox had just started attacking with no reason, and they had to respond in kind. No one imagined it would be difficult. Even in decline, Delroy's team was still the biggest in Leeds. They hunted Lennox's people, but they were well hidden. They picked off some smaller fruit, but they couldn't get anywhere near Lennox or his inner circle. Winston grew desperate and began sending men to infiltrate the crew. This backfired and led to Lennox tracking him. Winston and his bodyguard had been cut down with ease, the rumour being that Lennox had executed him personally.

The murder of his son devastated Delroy. His wife had been inconsolable, and his second son, Eddie, had gone off the reservation, swearing revenge against Lennox Thompson and his crew.

Delroy reached out to Lamont Jones, wanting him to assume control and take the fight to Lennox. Lamont refused, and Delroy had reluctantly taken control of the troops, restructuring the crew and setting up several teams focused purely on tracking Lennox. They hadn't come close to finding him, and with the increased police pressure and the surgical attacks by Lennox's people, Delroy was close to losing, and he knew it.

Then Shorty became involved.

Delroy and Shorty had never got along. Delroy respected Lamont, but not the people he kept around him. Shorty was too bloodthirsty for Delroy to ever like him. He had no respect for his power and clashed constantly with Delroy's men. Lennox's people took a shot at him, and hit his young daughter instead. She survived, but Shorty was enraged, and took the fight to Lennox, killing several of his men. Lamont backed his friend, and this cost him, when his girlfriend was murdered by Lennox's forces.

Lamont and Delroy had teamed up after this, with Delroy helping Lamont to spring a trap against the powerful warlord, Akhan, making off with his load of drugs. Lennox had quietened for a while, but had recently struck again, killing Trinidad Tommy along with one of Lamont's bodyguards.

The only way to get rid of Lennox for good was to kill him, and that was still Delroy's goal. He considered speaking with Lamont directly to come up with a plan, but no one had heard from him lately, and Delroy needed to do this. He hadn't earned his power by accident. He had fought for it every step of the way. Sacrificed for it.

If he couldn't defeat some upstart like Lennox Thompson, then what was the point of having it?

An hour later, he was being driven along Chapeltown Road, then down Newton Grove, a long, winding road with several semi-detached spots. Arriving at his destination, Delroy put his earlier thoughts to one side. He climbed from the car, surrounded by his men. They scoured the street, looking for anything out of the ordinary. Three youths stood outside the spot — a pale bricked house with a rusted black gate and a grey Mercedes that had seen better days parked outside. They straightened when they recognised Delroy, their eyes full of adoration and respect. Delroy nodded easily to them, then made his way inside.

Mack sat in the living room, smoking a cigarette and holding a phone to his ear. He wore a creased grey shirt and black trousers with a visible brown belt. When he noticed Delroy in the doorway, he stubbed out his cigarette and told the person on the phone he would call them back.

'Boss,' he said, his tone neutral. Delroy's men secured the spot, leaving Delroy alone with Mack. Neither spoke immediately. They had a long working relationship stretching back over twenty years. Mack had been instrumental to Delroy's takeover, using his viciousness to bring people around to the new regime. Over time he had grown more bitter, less pleased with the newer, upcoming gangs, in particular Lamont's. He had hated Lamont immediately and disliked the fact Delroy was fond of him. For his own reasons, he publicly threatened Lamont a few years ago, and the swift retaliation had kicked off a small conflict. Mack had been badly beaten by Shorty and Marcus Daniels, suffering a fractured skull amongst other injuries. He had spent time in hospital recovering and, in his own words, hadn't been right since.

The living room was cramped, a TV that was far too big taking up lots of space, along with two ghastly purple sofas that had been jammed into the room, regardless of how it would look. There were generic paintings on the wall, along with DVD's, empty bottles of liquor, and two ash trays plonked on the coffee table.

'Do you want something to drink?' Mack finally asked.

'No. What do you have for me?'

'Nothing you're gonna like. Lennox and his people are still underground. We can't even get at the little ones right now. Won't last forever, but for now, we're shooting at shadows.'

'Someone has to know something. What are the streets saying?'

'Everyone is talking about Teflon getting punked. Way I heard it, Lennox's shooter was right there in front of him, and he crapped himself like he always does. Lennox could have finished him right there.'

Delroy ignored most of Mack's bitter re-telling of the story. People got word to him as soon as it went down, and most said Lamont had tried to save his bodyguard, and had been whisked away by his men before the police could show. It made Delroy wonder about Lennox's end game. Lamont was exposed and vulnerable, and Lennox hadn't taken the shot. He had ruthlessly cut through Lennox's sons, along with attacking Shorty's daughter and Lamont's woman. He was ruthless and not afraid to kill, so it made even less sense to leave such a powerful enemy alive. Delroy pushed the thoughts away for now.

'No one is saying anything specifically about Lennox then?'

Mack shook his head.

'People are scared. He looks like the winning side right now.'

Delroy glared at Mack, but didn't refute his words.

'What about sales?'

'They're down. Police are still everywhere, and even though that *OurHood* crap is quiet, they're still out there, shutting down spots and targeting runners. Might be worth stretching further out if we want to sell. I've got people in Wakefield and Bradford crying out for more product. Just say the word.'

'Wakefield might be an idea,' said Delroy. He had high placed contacts in Bradford that wouldn't want him stepping on their toes. The last thing he needed was more people trying to kill him.

'I'll send a couple' men out there to see how things are. You decided what you're gonna do about those drugs yet?'

Delroy scratched his head. He was torn between sitting on the drugs they had stolen and waiting for the war to end, and moving them out of town. He had money tied up everywhere, but there were places he could move it to in a pinch.

'Not yet. That's a conversation to have with Teflon.'

Mack scowled and lit another cigarette.

'We should fuck him off and keep them all. What's he gonna do?'

'That would be silly. Teflon is a powerful ally.'

'He's a prick, and he's always been a prick, Del. You indulged him for far too long, and we lost face because of it.'

Delroy's face hardened.

'We lost face because you stupidly challenged Lamont in public, involving yourself in a situation you didn't need to. We lost face because you and Reagan could not see the big picture. You got your head cracked open and for what? What did it gain you?'

Mack's eyes flashed with rage, but he held his tongue. Delroy rose to his feet, furious at his subordinate for his stupidity.

'Make sure everyone knows what they're doing. Keep juggling the spots as often as you can and make sure I'm made aware of the new locations.'

'Fine.'

Delroy gave him one last look, then left.

* * *

'We were lucky, Lamont.'

Lamont was on his way back to Levine's office. The police interview hadn't taken long. Lamont had *no-commented* their questions, and the police had multiple witnesses who saw Akeem's shooting. They weren't pleased, but couldn't push it any further.

'I had nothing to do with what happened,' said Lamont.

'That's not my concern. You pay me to keep you out of prison. Whether or not you're involved, I don't care. It was your business that was blown up. You were right next to this other man when he was shot.'

'Are you ever going to get to the point?'

Levine shook his head. 'Just be careful. Don't give the police any reason to focus their investigation on you. In the meantime, I will keep working behind the scenes to learn how things are progressing.'

'Fine.'

Levine glanced at Lamont, who stiffly stared ahead. He had been Lamont's solicitor for almost a decade and had never seen him look so fatigued.

'Are you sure everything is okay?'

'I'm done talking about this.' Lamont coldly cut off Levine, not wanting to discuss it any further. He was onto other things now. It was obvious the shooter had escaped. He could be hiding out anywhere. Lennox had likely planned well, and would have had an exit strategy for him. The shooter was extremely young, likely only a few years older than Lamont's nephew, Keyshawn. It was a sobering realisation.

Thoughts of Trinidad again hit Lamont. It was a guilt that had slotted in next to his sorrow over Jenny's murder. Two innocent people he should have protected. Dead because of their association with him.

When Lamont left Levine, he drove back to his house, not feeling comfortable being out in the open. He called Maka whilst he was driving.

'L, is everything good?'

'It's fine. I want you to send someone to see Trinidad's family. Give them some money to help cover costs.'

'How much?'

'Five grand for now. Make it clear they only need to ask if they need more.'

'Are you sure you don't wanna do this yourself? I mean, you and Trinidad were close, fam. He loved you.'

Lamont closed his eyes for just a moment, conscious he was still driving. Maka wasn't wrong. It should have been him speaking to them, but Lamont couldn't face it. He had enough people in Chapeltown that hated him lately. He couldn't take seeing more angry faces right now.

'Just . . . make sure you send someone good. Get at me if there are any issues.'

'I'll send D. He's smashed it lately.'

Lamont hung and dropped the phone on the passenger seat. He took another deep breath, focusing on making it home. Lennox had a lot to pay for, and Lamont would make sure he did exactly that.

* * *

Nicky Derrigan was one of the few men that Lennox could claim to be intimidated by. He was brawny, beady-eyed, yet had surprisingly smooth features. His dirty blond hair was cut low, and he favoured simple crew neck sweaters and loose combat trousers. Lennox had known Derrigan for years and had used his services in the past. He didn't play sides and worked only with people who came recommended. Once you had his services, he was loyal until the job was done. The problem was that he was picky in the jobs he took.

When Lennox reached out, Derrigan had agreed to meet, providing he picked the location. It was risky for Lennox as he was in hiding. The only way to stay one step ahead was to control the surrounding people, and limit their access to him. Knowing Derrigan would play a vital role in his mission, he agreed.

They met at a lockup near Cross Gates. Lennox had fond memories of the area, and had laid a trap for Teflon's men here a few months back. He knew the area well, and had come alone, wanting to show Derrigan he was serious.

'Thanks for meeting me,' said Lennox, glancing around the empty lockup. It was damp and mouldy, and their voices carried around the empty place.

'We do jobs here,' said Derrigan. 'People keep their mouths shut. We bring people here and get what we need out of them.'

Lennox agreed. The locals kept to themselves and had allowed his men to operate in the area without involving the police. He didn't ask for details about the jobs. Derrigan liked to hurt people, but he was controlled, and that was the main factor. Lennox didn't need more idiots like Lutel lumbering around and making things worse. Lutel had been useful to a point, until he botched the hit on Shorty, instead shooting his daughter and uniting half the Hood against Lennox. It had taken some manoeuvring to regain the advantage.

'What's your schedule like right now?'

'Depends on the job.'

'It'll require your commitment for at least few months. I want you on retainer.'

'You know the drill. I don't come cheap.'

'If you do what I want, there's half a mill in it for you. Fifty thousand up front.'

Lennox had him. Derrigan had a poker face, but he couldn't hide the gleam when he heard the fee.

'What's the job?' He asked, an evil grin flitting across his face.

'You know Delroy?'

'Williams?'

'That's your job.'

Derrigan leaned forward. 'You think you can get him?'

'How much do you know about what's going on in Chapeltown right now?'

'I'm in and out of town, but I hear things. Lot more shootings lately. Teflon's people are recruiting, but they never contacted me.' He grinned again. 'No idea why.'

Lennox understood why. Derrigan was brutal, and he was hard to control. Someone like Teflon wouldn't be able to use him effectively. He'd had enough trouble keeping a leash on Marcus and Shorty.

Lennox recalled the stories of Derrigan in his younger days. A skilled boxer, he was destined for good things, until a bout went awry, and he killed his opponent, continuing to hit him even after the referee had called off the fight.

'Don't worry about Teflon,' he said.

Derrigan frowned. 'You know he's gonna come for you. From what I heard, you've messed with people close to him. He's not the guy to shake that off.'

Lennox didn't want to discuss Teflon. He kept his eyes on Derrigan, letting the silence play out.

'Delroy is my target. Either you can help, or you can't.'

'Talk me through it.'

'There's a war going on. I've done well so far, but Delroy is finally getting off his arse and fighting back. I've lost a few key pieces lately and I can't think of anyone better than you to restore the natural order.'

'He won't be easy to get to.'

'That's my problem to deal with. Are you in or not?'

The silence dragged on, but Lennox wasn't moved. He was skilled at playing this game, and no one had more willpower than him. Finally, Derrigan nodded.

'Tell me the plan.'

* * *

It was well after midnight. Lamont was on his sofa, staring into space.

The past few days had been draining, yet he'd attempted to sleep earlier, and it hadn't come. There were too many things in the air, too many threads that would need his work. He didn't know where to look for Lennox. People were making subtle enquiries on his behalf. He didn't know how long it would take, or whether they could sustain it. His organisation had taken some hits lately, and with Akeem's death, Lamont felt more vulnerable than he had in months.

For a moment, everything had worked. He had struck against Lennox, removed the threat of Akhan, and ensured an alliance with Stefanos and Jakkar. Now he was dealing with an attack in the heart of the community he loved, and the deaths of a father figure, and a man who had protected Lamont on more than one occasion. Both had given him wise counsel in the past, and now he was fighting through it alone.

No Akeem. No Trinidad. No Shorty. No Jenny.

Sighing, Lamont trudged to his kitchen, rooting around the cupboards until he found what he was looking for; a bottle of Wray & Nephew white rum. He hadn't had a drink since Jenny died, but right now, there was nothing stopping him. Grabbing a glass, he filled it to the brim and drank it, wincing at the harsh taste. Without thinking, he poured another and when that was finished, one more. When the room started spinning, he smiled for the first time in forever, desperate for the escape.

CHAPTER THREE

Wednesday 8 April 2015

WHEN LAMONT AWOKE, he was dazed, and his head was aching. Gingerly shaking the cobwebs free, he checked the time, noting it was after midday. He had slept for over twelve hours. When he made it downstairs, he gulped down some water to get rid of his dry mouth, then made a coffee, needing the energy boost. He groaned as he checked his phone, noting the multitude of missed calls and text messages. Darren was his first port of call.

'Hey L. You good?'

'I'm fine,' replied Lamont, feeling anything but. 'Maka said he gave you a job. Did you handle it?'

'Yeah. Dropped in on Trinidad's family. They wouldn't take the money.'

Lamont closed his eyes, staring out of his kitchen window for a long moment.

'L?'

'They just lost him. Can't expect them to be hugging and smiling.'

'It wasn't your fault. They need to recognise that.'

Lamont wanted to shout at his underling. He wanted to tell him it was his fault, and that Trinidad died because of his mistakes, but he didn't. Darren spoke again after a moment.

'What do you want me to do with the money?'

'Keep it.'

'Are you sure? We're talking five bags here.'

'Do something nice. Take your woman out.'

'Are you sure you're okay?'

'I already told you I'm fine.' Lamont's tone was icy now, and Darren recognised he'd pushed too far.

'Sorry, boss. I'll talk to you later then, if you don't need anything else.'

Lamont hung up, staring down at the phone. He'd made a mistake not going to see the family himself. He was so worried about facing them, that he'd made things worse by staying away. Maybe it was for the best, he reasoned. He wasn't at all liked in Chapeltown right now. Staying away was likely the best move.

Washing up his dirty cup and glass, Lamont forwent breakfast and traipsed upstairs to take a scalding shower. When he was fresher and dressed, he made a few calls, seeking information on Lennox Thompson and his people, promising to pay handsomely for good leads. Planning to speak with Maka later, his attention was taken by one of the people who had tried calling earlier. He hadn't paid attention to the call log, but his stomach jolted when he saw Stefanos's number.

Lamont's relationship with Jenny's father was a strange one. Jenny had died not knowing her father was more connected to the life of crime than Lamont or anyone he knew. They had first met at the funeral and ever since, he'd opened multiple doors for Lamont, and helped him remove a powerful enemy in Akhan. He called him back.

'Lamont. Are you well?'

'Had a rough night. Is everything okay?'

'I would like to speak with you as soon as possible.'

'Where?'

'Come to my home, please. I trust you remember the way?'

'I'll see you soon.'

* * *

Lamont left his house, realising he still needed to arrange some proper protection. He would either speak with Manson and get him to sort someone, or he would hire a personal team to look after him. It would be expensive, but far better than the alternative.

The ride to Stefanos's was quiet. His paranoia was high after the recent shooting. It could have been him. The thought kept resonating in his mind. Lennox could have ended his life right there, and he wouldn't have seen it coming. The more he considered it, the more stupid he realised it had been to rush down there. There was nothing he could do to stop the fire. Going after Lennox without protecting Jenny had been stupid. As Lamont settled into traffic, he wondered how many mistakes he could get away with, before he paid the ultimate price.

Stefanos's sprawling estate was a comforting sight. It was larger than Delroy's property, with large iron gates, an attached garage, and fields surrounding the perimeter. Lamont had only been a few times. He imagined Jenny spending time here, sitting out in the open, reading, or walking the grounds, taking in the scenery. He wondered if she had cultivated her love of flowers out here, then dismissed the thoughts as his heart clenched.

Stefanos waited for him, a wide smile on his face. He wore a navy jumper, well-pressed trousers and slippers. Lamont found it endearing the man was so comfortable in his own skin. They shook hands and Stefanos led him inside.

As they headed to the study, Lamont noticed a photo of Jenny on the hallway wall. She was smiling at the camera, eyes sparkling. Lamont paused in front of it. His heart wrenched in his chest. He couldn't take his eyes from her. Stefanos noticed Lamont stop, studying his reaction to the picture. It was one of a collection his wife had placed all around the house. The pain in the younger man's eyes was palpable. Putting his hand on Lamont's shoulder, Stefanos's eyes flitted from Lamont back to the photo, and he smiled for just a moment. After a few more seconds, he led him away and into the room.

The study remained as luxurious as ever. Stefanos had an oak desk, several comfortable looking chairs, and an array of photos on the walls.

Lamont tore his eyes from another picture of Jenny, only to find Stefanos already observing him.

'You look tired, Lamont.'

'Rough night, like I said.'

'You need to take care of yourself. You're still a young man. I'm sorry about Trinidad. He was a good man, and a pillar of your community.'

'How do you know the things you know?' Lamont asked. It was unnerving just how much influence Stefanos seemed to have. Stefanos shrugged, pouring himself a glass of whiskey after offering Lamont one.

'Information is always useful.'

It was a vague answer that only made Lamont more curious, which he supposed was the intention.

'I trust there's a reason you wanted to see me?'

'Jakkar asked me to speak with you.'

Lamont had expected this. Reclusive by nature, Jakkar represented a powerful council back in the Middle East. The same council that had subsidised Akhan when he moved to England to sell drugs. They had links everywhere, and Lamont had stumbled into an alliance with them through Stefanos. Recently, they had made Lamont an offer, wanting him to take over Akhan's distribution ring in Yorkshire and the surrounding areas. It was a tremendous opportunity, and he had accepted.

'I see.'

'No one is pleased about the situation on the streets. Less money is being made, and there are more police in Chapeltown and Hare-hills. When Jakkar made his offer, he assumed you could deal with this.'

'The police presence was stifling long before Jakkar made his offer. I didn't start any of this.'

'That being said, he has high hopes for you, and expected you to deal with it. What happened on Chapeltown Road shouldn't have happened.'

'I agree. Trinidad was a good man.'

Stefanos shook his head. 'That isn't what I'm talking about. You were out in the open with only one guard, a guard who is now dead.

Add to that you travelled here today without a bodyguard, putting us both at risk.'

Lamont grew annoyed. He didn't like the way Stefanos was speaking to him.

'It might mean nothing to you, but Trinidad didn't deserve to die, and frankly, that's more important than what might have happened to me.'

'That's grief talking. You are a powerful man, Lamont, and you are destined for great things. Use this conflict as a chance to show everyone what you are made of.'

'Lennox was responsible for the death of your daughter, Stefanos. You helped me track Nikkolo and Akhan. Help me track Lennox, and I can finish this.'

'I've spoken with Jakkar, and we don't want to get more involved than necessary. He has resources you can use, but only in defence of your drug routes.'

Lamont couldn't believe it. Akhan had multiple teams of killers that he'd used when necessary, and Lamont had hoped to have use of them, along with their extensive information network.

'Your daughter died. What the hell does that have to do with Jakkar?'

'Focus on the tasks we have given you. Finish Lennox, or the promotion will vanish.'

The meeting was spiralling out of control, and Lamont found he didn't care.

'Lennox is dangerous for everyone. He's ambitious and ruthless, and he won't stop. Nikkolo gave us nothing major about him or his organisation, but I know he was behind the *OurHood* Initiative, and used them to discredit myself, amongst others. He should be stopped as soon as possible.'

'Stop him then. We have faith that you can do this.'

'Faith, but no genuine support. What the hell is it with you and Jakkar. How does a Greek entrepreneur get involved with a Middle Eastern drug ring?'

Stefanos gave a momentary smile. 'All the product in the world is useless if you can't move it. They use my shipping resources and tankers to move their product wherever they need it. It gives me a modicum of influence where they are concerned, and we make a lot of money together.'

'All while the people responsible for your daughter's murder walk around free. Excellent.'

Stefanos's smile vanished, and his eyes were like flint as he stared down Lamont.

'Do you want me to judge you as responsible for my daughter's murder too, Lamont? After all, her involvement with you got her killed. I put that aside because it was right, but if I hadn't, you would be dead. Instead, I remember my daughter in the best light, and respect the choices she made. I helped you remove Akhan because of that. I suggest you keep your mouth shut where it pertains to myself and my daughter, and get back to work.'

There was nothing Lamont could say to this, nor did he try. They held all the cards, and nothing good would come from making enemies of them too.

'No problem.' Lamont slid to his feet and held out his hand. Stefanos shook it, and Lamont turned to leave.

'Lamont?'

He turned at the door and faced Stefanos. The man's face was unreadable.

'Good luck.'

* * *

The tense conversation had given Lamont a lot to think about. He couldn't help noticing the shift in tone between the last meetings he'd had with Jenny's father. His attitude had changed, and Lamont wondered what sort of pressure Jakkar and his people were putting on Stefanos. It was a complex world of politics and subtext that he didn't have the energy to sift through.

The bottom line was that he would receive no help from them with Lennox, and he would have to go at it alone.

* * *

Derrigan stood in a garden in St Martin's, smoking a cigarette and enjoying the soft night breeze. He'd been standing there for the better part of thirty minutes and didn't mind. Many in his line of work suffered from impatience; they liked to charge in and make things happen, whereas Derrigan had no problem waiting if needed.

Delroy's men were not lying down and taking their defeat. As of late, they were attacking with a vengeance, hunting down spots where Lennox could be hiding with ferocity. None was making a bigger dent than the man Derrigan was waiting on.

Solomon was skilled and well-liked by people. A few nights ago, he had tracked down two of Lennox's couriers, executing both. Lennox wanted Derrigan to make an example out of him and with the money he was paying, Derrigan was happy to do so.

Finishing his cigarette, he heard a noise behind him and turned, but it was nothing. He had worried the family whose garden he was hiding in might stir, but they hadn't. One of his guys was watching the street, sitting in a parked car. He would ring Derrigan if there were any hiccups. Other than that, he settled in to wait.

Another hour passed by before a black BMW pulled to a stop outside a house. Two men climbed out. One was gangly and slightly balding. The other — Solomon — was shorter, with a powerful build and fluid grace. Solomon and the other man stood in the street talking, then Solomon lit a spliff, the smoke from the joint wafting around him. Derrigan was itching to go after him, but there was no way to take Solomon without the other man getting the drop on him, and he didn't know how armed they were.

The pair stood outside for another twenty minutes, with Solomon answering two phone calls in that time. He didn't know why they weren't going in the house, but it wasn't worth speculating. The night was pleasant, and there was nothing strange about enjoying it. Quietly, he stretched, watching the pair for any signs of weakness. He sent his spotter a text message, telling them to follow the BMW if it pulled away with Solomon inside, but then he had a reprieve. The other man touched Solomon's fist, then climbed back in the car and drove away.

Derrigan grinned to himself, waiting for the car to drive out of sight before he made his move. Reaching down, he grabbed the small length of pipe he'd brought, padding across the road. Solomon was almost at the door before he realised Derrigan was on him. He turned but wasn't quick enough, as Derrigan slammed the pipe against his ribs, then jabbed him in the stomach before he could scream. Solomon toppled to the floor, Derrigan looming over him, smiling. He hit him twice more, hearing his right arm crack, then his kneecap. No words were necessary. He let the pipe fall to the floor, working Solomon over with his gloved fists, hitting him with powerful, vicious blows to the face. When he grew tired, he grabbed the pipe again, bringing it down on Solomon's skull.

Derrigan breathed hard, pleased with the attack. It would send a message to Delroy and his men that they could be picked off. He stalked off, leaving the destroyed gunman in his wake.

CHAPTER FOUR

Friday 10 April 2015

LAMONT, Maka, and Manson met at a safe house in Harehills. The spot wasn't one that was used regularly. It was stocked with food and emergency supplies, but had a musty odour from lack of use. Two soldiers waited outside, with another sat in a car. They were the first line of defence in case of an attack, but still Lamont was wary. Being out and about was more of a calculated risk each time he did it, and he had yet to secure adequate protection. He'd given the matter some thought and would hire a personal bodyguard team. The last thing he wanted was to take resources from the crew when they were stretched thin as it was.

Maka and Manson weren't sure what to expect from the meeting. Neither had seen Lamont since Trinidad's shooting, but quickly noticed how tired and drawn he looked. The usual glint of power in his eyes was missing, and they appeared dull. The pair shared a look.

Despite the odour, the living room was comfortable. There was a plush brown sofa that Maka and Manson were currently sitting on, along with an old-fashioned armchair that Lamont was using. Several glasses were on the coffee table, along with a bottle of Courvoisier. Lamont wasn't partaking, but Manson had poured himself a glass, sipping it as they waited.

'Has this spot been checked?' Lamont asked. Manson nodded.

'My people checked it earlier, and then I went over it afterwards. It's clean.'

'What do we know then?'

'I dunno which of Lennox's people got to Solomon, but they did a number on him. Beat the shit out of him outside his house.'

'Is he still alive?' Lamont knew Solomon by reputation, and he was good at what he did. Back when they'd had their scuffles with Ricky Reagan's crew, he'd hoped Delroy wouldn't involve Solomon, and thankfully, he hadn't. To hear of him being brutalised was another stark reminder that no one was safe in this conflict.

'For now. Doesn't look good. People are saying he's got internal bleeding, broken ribs, fractured skull. Whatever they hit him with split his skull wide open.'

'No one's claiming yet?' Lamont didn't want to think about Solomon with his skull split open. Manson shook his head.

'Lennox isn't gonna claim it. People know what he's doing, and that's enough.'

'Forget that for a minute.' Lamont focused on Maka. 'Are you sure you're well enough to be here? You got shot.'

'The bullet barely grazed me, L. I'm good. It's not like I'm running a marathon.'

'Make sure you take care of yourself, Maka. Bullet wounds are no joke.'

Maka nodded, signalling for Lamont to continue.

'I've got feelers out about Lennox, but people seem reluctant to share information.' Lamont stifled a yawn, his rough nights of late catching up with him. He shook it off and continued. 'I'm willing to pay for proper information, but it isn't moving people yet.'

'People fear Lennox, L,' said Maka. 'He wiped out Delroy's kids. Add to that the moves he's made against you and Shorty . . . fact is that the longer he's out there, the weaker we look as a unit.'

'How bad is it out there?'

Manson blew out a breath. Lamont noticed the pair were practically taking it in turns to speak, but shrugged it off.

'Money is low. So is morale. Police are everywhere and even when they're not, people are running scared that they're gonna get shot. The Feds are making low level arrests, both in and out of our crew. Makes it harder to get runners out there and working.'

'That could be a job for Darren then. He's young enough to appeal to them, and we wanted him helping on recruitment, anyway. We need more runners and we need more shooters. We're running low on both, so let's make it a priority.'

'What about Shorty and K-Bar?'

Lamont didn't reply immediately. Both men would have been fantastic to have around in the current situation. He hadn't spoken with Shorty since their fight, and he wasn't going near K-Bar while the police had him in custody.

'I don't know what Shorty's doing, nor do I know where he is. I need to work on getting K-Bar released, but that's a job for my solicitor. I'm paying him a lot of money to facilitate it. The fact is, I want Lennox Thompson dead, no matter the cost.'

Maka and Manson nodded, and they sat in silence. Lamont was tempted to tell them about Stefanos's warnings, but held his tongue. It would only make things worse, he reasoned. There was enough pressure on them as it was.

Finally, he clambered to his feet, wiping his eyes.

'Use whatever funds you need to get people hired and make sure Darren is on board with the plan.' After saying his goodbyes, Lamont left.

Maka and Manson sat in silence for a few more minutes. Without a word, Manson refilled his drink, and poured one for Maka.

'What the hell was that all about?' he asked.

'He looked wrecked. All this shit that's going on is taking its toll.'

'What does that mean for the rest of us?' Maka shook his head. 'He's our leader, and he looks like he's cracking up. Do you think he's scared?'

'Course he's scared. None of us have ever had a challenge like this. Aren't you scared?'

Manson didn't reply straight away. 'I'd feel better if we had a proper plan in place. You saw the way L was talking. Feels to me like he doesn't even believe we can win. If Delroy's struggling, can we?'

'We have a better organisation than Delroy's crew. Always have.'

'Back in the day, maybe. Those people are gone. Dunno where the fuck Shorty is, but Tall-Man's dead. So is Chink. Even Akeem. We don't have Victor, or Grimer or Rudy. K-Bar's looking at life in prison. We've lost a lot, Maka.'

'We don't have a choice. We need to make our moves, unless you wanna just roll over and let Lennox win?'

Manson's eyes darkened. 'I don't roll over for anyone. All I'm saying is that L clearly isn't with it. That means we need to be.'

Maka met his friend's eyes. He went back the furthest with Manson, and they'd always had each other's backs, through thick and thin. They were closer than brothers. He finished his drink and patted his oldest friend on the shoulder.

'Tell me what you're thinking.'

* * *

FRIDAY 17 APRIL 2015

When the day of Trinidad's funeral arrived, Lamont hoped he was ready. He'd shaved and spent a lot of time examining himself in the mirror, unhappy with the man looking back at him. He looked haggard, with prominent circles under his eyes. Without liquor, it was hard sleeping at night, yet he didn't want to become dependent. Sitting in the kitchen in his expensive suit, he had some coffee to sharpen up, then finished getting ready.

After his conversation with Maka and Manson, Lamont knew how people were perceiving Lennox, but the way word had spread still shocked him. People spoke of Lennox with reverence, and it was even harder for Lamont's contacts to get back to him. As far as the streets were concerned, Lennox was winning.

When Solomon's death was confirmed, it sent things into over-drive. The fact someone could brutalise him on his doorstep made everyone wary, Lamont included. He'd spent a small fortune securing a bodyguard team. Several would guard his house, and the others would shadow him wherever he went. As he drove to the funeral, he had two with him.

As they arrived at the church, Lamont slipped inside, having timed his arrival so he would almost be late. Before he took his seat on the back row, he glanced at the coffin, and felt a wave of fury. It was a shabby excuse for a coffin; cheap, light brown, and as basic as could be. It didn't stand out, and Trinidad deserved better. He'd offered them the money to pay for a luxury service, and the family had turned it down. Apparently, they would rather snub him than ensure Trinidad got a good send-off.

The people on the row glanced at Lamont, taking in his expensive clothes and demeanour. He didn't recognise them, but they seemed to have some idea who he was. Ignoring them, he stared ahead, singing along tunelessly when called for, and silently listening to people tell stories about Trinidad. He wanted to do the same, but knew it wouldn't be welcomed.

At the cemetery, Lamont again hung near the back. His suit ruffled in the wind, but other than the breeze, the weather was calm. He could see people shooting him looks, but continued to ignore them. The funeral was almost over, and then he could go back to his home and wallow in peace. He already had the liquor ready.

'Lamont.'

He turned before he even recognised the voice, his bodyguards reacting instantly, positioning themselves around him in case of attack. He told them to stand down, moving forward to address Shorty. The pair stared one another down for a long moment. Shorty wore a black jacket over a shirt and black jeans. Lamont had seen him get dressed up for funerals before, and wondered why he hadn't for this one. He'd also shaved, however, and his hair was neatly shaped up. He seemed more like his old self.

Shorty was his oldest friend, and he regretted the fact they had come to blows. At the time, the grief over Jenny's death had been too much for Lamont to take. He missed Shorty and wanted his friend back in his life. The way Shorty was glaring, he had a sneaking suspicion that would not happen.

'Have you seen the light yet?' he asked.

'I came to pay my respects, not to get caught up with you.'

Lamont could have pointed out that Shorty had sought him out to speak, but didn't. Shorty never enjoyed being corrected in the past, and Lamont suspected that to do it now would only make things worse.

'How's Grace?' Seeing Shorty was a reminder Lamont hadn't spoken with Amy in a while. He hoped she was coping with everything that had happened, and that Grace's condition was improving. Shorty glared.

'Keep my daughter's name out of your mouth,' he said. Glancing past Lamont, he looked at the people surrounding Trinidad's grave. 'Another one died around you. When does it stop?'

Lamont's stomach lurched as Shorty's words hit him. The night they fought, he had said in his rage that everyone around Lamont died, and this was a fresh reminder that Shorty's words had some truth to them. Trinidad died over Lamont's stupidity, and there wasn't a chance he would get over that.

'Shorty . . .'

'Save it. I'm done here.' Giving Lamont and his bodyguard's one last glowering look, Shorty stalked away. Lamont watched, the ripples of guilt in his stomach growing. Nearby murmurs grew louder. Evidently, people had watched the exchange between the pair. The funeral was the last place he wanted to be, and he hated the idea of being the subject of gossip and entertainment.

'Let's go,' he said to his bodyguards. They were making their way back to the car when another voice stopped them.

'L.'

It was Ken, one of the old crowd who would frequent Trinidad's shop. Lamont had known him since he was a child. Ken would look out for him, giving him money to go to the shop. He was a bald-headed man in his sixties who looked good for his age. His dark eyes met Lamont's own, concern clear.

'Hey, Uncle Ken.'

'How are you doing? I know this can't be easy.'

'Do you really care? You're part of *OurHood*, and I know what that group has been saying about me.'

'I care about my community, L. I want what's best for our people.

Whether I agree with *OurHood* or not, we go way back, and I know how you felt about Trinidad.'

'If community is so important, why the hell was Trinidad buried in that matchstick box? He deserved something special. He was the heart of the community, but you buried him in that shitty coffin. How do you justify that?'

'It was the choice of the family, and they don't have much money.'

'That's bullshit,' snapped Lamont. 'Trinidad always provided.'

Ken chuckled despite the tension. 'I knew Trinidad all of my life. He wasn't a saver; more of the *can't-take-it-with-you* variety. He put his kids through university and sent money back home, but after that, they were on their own.'

Lamont shook his head. 'The community should have banded together to give him something special.'

'It's not that simple, L. You know that. Regardless, Trinidad was loved. It's not all about money.'

'It's about respect. Plain and simple.' Lamont dismissed Ken's words with vitriol. The older man surveyed him.

'You look tired, L. Noticeably so. That might be making you irritable.'

'I'm not a child, Unc. I don't need a nap. All I wanted was to make things right. I offered them the money for the service, and they turned me down.'

'If you want to make things right, speak with them.'

Lamont glanced past Ken. He could just about make out several of Trinidad's family standing near the coffin. After a moment, he shook his head, the guilt too much.

'There's nothing I can say to them.'

Ken let this go.

'What happens next, L?'

'What do you mean?' Lamont frowned.

'I mean, what do you want from life?'

'That's a pointless question,' Lamont scoffed. 'It means nothing.'

'It meant something to Trinidad. He respected you. Loved you like a son. He wanted you to be happy and he wanted you to be free.'

The words hit Lamont for six. He recalled his argument with

Trinidad a few months back, where Trinidad had been furious about Lamont's lack of role in Chapeltown, and his refusal to get involved with community conflicts. He felt emotional at the thought of the old man that wanted nothing but the best for him, and that emotion made him think of Jenny. She had also wanted the best for him. She too wanted him to be free of the streets and happy, and now she was dead. They both were. He wiped his eyes and lowered his head, not wanting Ken to see him so weak.

'I'll see you around, Ken.'

'Are you free, L? Happy?'

Something in Lamont's chest hitched, and he glanced back at Trinidad's family, making their way out of the cemetery. He hesitated, overcome by guilt and frustration. Their lack of respect for Trinidad galled him the longer he stood there.

'Go on, L. Speak to them. It's the right thing to do.'

Lamont made his way toward them, with Ken following and his bodyguards maintaining a respectable distance. He recognised Gloria, Trinidad's ex-wife and the mother of his two children, Graham, and Marie, both of whom were there, alongside a retinue of older women. Lamont found he couldn't look at the women for too long. Their grief turned his stomach and made him feel worse, if that was possible.

'I'm sorry for your loss,' he said, thankful his words were clearer than he'd expected. 'Trinidad was a great man and if there is anything I can do, don't hesitate to ask.'

Before they could reply, Trinidad's son Graham stepped closer, disdain visible on his face.

'Not sending your thugs to speak to us again then?'

Lamont forced himself to meet Graham's eyes. He was an inch taller than Lamont, though his suit hung far looser on his gangly frame than Lamont's tailored masterpiece. He had a look of his father, with hard eyes, pronounced cheekbones, and a solid jawline. Lamont and Graham had always got along, but those days were over. The resentment was palpable.

'I just wanted to help. Judging by what you ended up burying your father in, you should have taken the money.'

'We're fine with what we had.' Graham's family nodded their agreement. Lamont could feel Ken's eyes burning into him, but he didn't stop.

'Trinidad deserved more.'

Graham took another step forward, disdain replaced by clear anger. Lamont wondered if he was going to hit him, and whether he would stop him. Others inched closer, acting like they weren't listening.

'You wanna talk about what he deserved? He deserved not to die just because he was involved with some gangster who can't fight his own battles. If you truly respected him, Lamont, it wouldn't matter what his family buried him in.'

Lamont ignored the *gangster* jibes, and the muttering that followed from the crowd.

'Whatever I am, I never wanted to bring harm to your father.'

'You did a magnificent job of stopping that,' replied Graham, the sarcasm in his tone venomous. With a last look of disgust, he stormed off, his family following. Ken stood with Lamont as the crowd dispersed, not one person stopping to speak to him.

'That didn't go how I expected,' said Ken, breaking the tense silence.

'It went exactly as I expected. He should have taken the money. I stand by what I said.'

Lamont turned away before Ken could say anything. As he walked to the car, Trinidad, Jenny, Marcus, and all the others that had died around Lamont resonated in his mind, and he knew Shorty was right about his effect on the world around him.

He was bad for people, and there was no getting away from this.

CHAPTER FIVE

Tuesday 21 April 2015

SHORTY RAISED the cup to his lips and took a deep sip. He wasn't a fan of tea at the best of times, but Amy had offered and he couldn't refuse.

Since his fallout with Lamont, it had been a turbulent few weeks. He had left Lamont's place on a suicide mission, determined to go out in a blaze of glory by taking Lennox and as many of his goons as he could with him. He spent the next few days getting his money together, ready to leave it to his children. It was when he'd gone to see Amy that the problems had begun.

Amy was hunched over her kitchen table, pale and drawn. She looked up and immediately stifled a gasp.

Shorty stood over her, his face tense. He wore a black warm-up tracksuit with trainers. A woolly hat was pulled low, almost obscuring his eyes. On his hands, he wore a pair of black leather gloves.

'Shorty? What the hell are you doing here?'

Shorty didn't reply, staring Amy down.

'Are you listening? You can't be here. What if the pol—'

Shorty left the kitchen and came back in with a black hold-all. He dropped it on the table in front of Amy. She opened it, her expression quizzical. The bag was full of money. Notes of various denominations were stuffed to burst. Even as Amy opened it, several ten-pound notes fluttered to the floor, resting at her feet.

'What's this for?'

'That's it,' Shorty replied.

'That's what?'

'That's all the money I have left. After everything. All the shit I did. Thats all I've got,' Shorty explained. 'I want you to split it with Stacey. L's got her address, he'll—'

'Why are you talking like this?'

'Did you hear what I said?'

'Did you hear what I said?' Amy retorted. Shorty glared.

'You're smart. I breeded you for a reason. I wanted my daughter to be smart too.'

'What does me being smart have to do with anything?'

Shorty slid into the spindly chair opposite Amy and faced her. He took his hood down and peeled the woolly hat from his head, exposing unkempt, picky hair.

'You're smart enough to know why I've given you all my money.'

'Shorty, Grace is still alive. Whatever stupid thing you're planning, please don't do it,' Amy gestured toward the money. 'I know you think this is more important, but it isn't.'

'I've always provided for Grace. I always made sure you had money when you needed it. Don't tell me that isn't important.'

'As important as having you? Do you really think the money mattered to Grace when she cried herself to sleep night after night, wondering where her daddy was? Do you think it mattered when she sat in the room with her head-phones on because I didn't want her to hear the police badmouthing you as they searched the house? The money doesn't matter.'

'Don't tell me it doesn't fucking matter!' Shorty slammed his fist on the sturdy table, shaking it. 'You don't get it. The money is all I have. It opens doors for Grace. Means her having all the opportunities I didn't. Do you know the things I've gone through on these streets? To survive?'

'Don't kid yourself it was all for Grace, because that's not the truth. You love this. The life was more important to you than anything. Even me.'

'Once maybe, but Grace changed everything. Believe that or not.'

'It doesn't matter now.'

'I know.'

They were both silent now, breathing hard. Amy's eyes widened.

'You're not coming back, are you?'

Shorty was shocked to see tears in her eyes. He wouldn't let it slow him.

'There is no coming back from this. I'm going after anyone who had a hand in the shooting.'

'What will that achieve? They already shot our daughter. You going after them will only make things worse.'

'They nearly took the thing I care most about on the planet. They don't get away with that.'

Amy shook her head. 'You'd murder half of Leeds just to settle a grudge?'

'I would murder all of Leeds if it righted the wrong.'

'What happened to you?' Amy gasped. Shorty frowned.

'What are you talking about?'

'How can you justify it? How can you make out what you're doing is right? You kill—'

'So what!' Shorty thundered. 'You think I care? You think I lose any sleep over those fuckers who tried ending my life?' Shorty glared at Amy. 'What would you rather have? Them alive, or me?'

Amy stared back at Shorty, unable to reply. He wiped his eyes.

'This is what I am. I accept it. I'll do what I need to do.'

Amy stared at him. He wasn't sure what he expected to hear next, but he was still shocked.

'Is it over three?'

'Is what over three?'

'Have you killed over three people?'

'Yes.' Shorty didn't hesitate.

'I don't know what to say,' Amy said, minutes later.

'I never said I was Mother Teresa.'

'And you're sure you can kill these people?'

'I don't have a choice.'

'How can you be so sure you'll find them?' Amy ran a hand through her bedraggled hair.

'Because, I already know who gave the order.'

'How?'

Shorty again looked at Amy. Pale and drawn with worry, he still found her achingly beautiful. In another life they could have made it work, but in this one, he was just a killer.

'You really wanna know?' He locked eyes with his baby mother.

'Yes.' He saw her lean forward, ready for his words.

'I tracked down the shooter. He told me who hired him.'

'He told you just like that?' Amy's eyebrows rose.

'Course not. I got it out of him.'

'How?'

Shorty glanced at Amy again. She was clutching the table for support, but her eyes were lucid.

'You really wanna know?' He repeated.

'Yes.'

'I held a hot knife to his skin in his kitchen, then kept pouring salt on him until he cracked.' Shorty's words were utterly monotonous.

'And this man, the one who shot Gracey . . . Is he dead?'

After a long moment, Shorty nodded.

The pair sat in the kitchen with a bag of dirty money resting between them. It was the most peaceful moment the grieving parents had ever shared in their turbulent relationship.

'I spoke with Grace's doctors. They say she's doing a lot better. It'll take time and a lot of support, but it's not as bleak as it seemed even a few weeks ago.'

Relief washed over Shorty. Every day since his daughter's shooting, he expected to hear that she hadn't made it. She had taken two bullets to the chest and as a young child, he didn't think she could survive, but she had proved him wrong.

'That's fucking brilliant.' Shorty hung his head a moment, overcome with a wave of emotion. Amy waited for him to look at her before she spoke again.

'Is it enough?'

'What do you mean?'

'Grace is alive. With time, she will get better. Can you leave this vendetta of yours alone and not retaliate?'

'It's not that simple,' said Shorty, his eyes hardening. They had been over this.

'Have you forgotten our conversation last time, Shorty? I want Grace to have a dad. That is more important than what you feel you need to do.'

Shorty shook his head. 'You can't say that. This is something I *have* to do.'

'No, it isn't,' Amy's voice rose. 'You love Grace, Shorty. I had my doubts when I got pregnant, but you've proved me wrong every time, and she loves you because she knows how much you love her, and that you would do anything for her. You don't need to prove it to her, or to me. Why can't you just walk away?'

'Because this is my life. This is the man you met. I'm a gangster, Ames. Always have been, always will be. The fact of the matter is that you can't shoot at someone I love and get away with it. Walking away isn't an option. We're talking about dangerous people here. They killed L's missus, for fuck's sake.'

Amy paled. 'What?'

Shorty took a deep breath, regretting blurting it out like that.

'Jenny was killed on the orders of these people. As revenge against L.'

'How . . . Who the hell are you involved with?'

Shorty hesitated. Amy already knew far more about his world than he was comfortable with, but he trusted her. They had a child together, and she had never shown any sign of betraying him.

'Someone had a problem with me. We had a fight. I kicked his ass, and he tried to get back at me by shooting me, but missed and hit Grace.'

Amy didn't reply. Her eyes were wide and her face was even more pale than before.

'And this is the man you told me about?'

Shorty nodded. 'It's his boss that's the problem. He's the one going after everyone, and it's kill or be killed with this guy.' He saw how terrified Amy looked, and his face softened. 'I'm sorry, Ames. I'd have never asked to spend time with Grace if I'd known they would come back like that. I'd never let any harm come to her.'

'I know that,' replied Amy, her voice softer. 'I've never questioned your love for Grace. It was rocky after you got out of prison, but I was hoping your relationship with her would improve and be like it used to.'

'You and me both.'

Both parents sat in silence for a while. Shorty finished the rest of his tea, holding onto the cup just to have something to do.

'L must be devastated about Jenny's death.'

Shorty didn't respond.

'He came to see me at the hospital a while back. He was asking about you.'

'Right.' Shorty couldn't even muster any enthusiasm. He'd said his piece to Lamont at Trinidad's funeral, and as far as he was concerned, there was no further business between them.

'What's going on with you two?'

'Nothing.'

'Why would he ask me how you were then? That doesn't make sense.'

'Ask him.'

'Shorty.'

Shorty looked up, meeting Amy's misty green eyes.

'What?'

'Just talk to me, please. What's going on with you two?'

'We're no longer friends.' Shorty gave it to her straight, hoping it would shut her up.

'You two are like brothers. How could you have fallen out?'

'It's not important.'

It was Amy's turn to shake her head. She looked at him with folded arms and raised eyebrows.

'Our daughter was shot, and L's girlfriend was murdered, and you don't think it's important that you've fallen out with your best friend?'

'Just leave it alone. I don't want to discuss it.'

'But—'

'What the fuck did I say!' Shorty snapped, making Amy jump. Shooting to his feet, he stormed from the house, slamming the door behind him. Amy remained seated, shaking with fear. Sometimes it was easy to forget how dangerous Shorty was, and how much his temper remained at the surface. Realising after a few moments he wasn't coming back, she went to lock the door.

* * *

Several days after Trinidad's funeral, Lamont was called by Stefanos, who told him to be at a warehouse on Elder Road at ten o'clock the next morning. He gave Lamont the address, wished him well, then hung up.

The next morning, Lamont and two of his new bodyguards drove to the spot. From the outside, it was unimpressive. It was surrounded by a rusting metal blue fence, and the entire building had a bleak, greying colour scheme. A man stood outside, smoking a cigarette. He was short and squattish, with balding black hair and a pointed nose. When he saw Lamont, he nodded, taking one last drag of the cigarette and flicking it away.

'You must be Mr Jones.'

'Call me L.'

'Very well, L. call me Mustafa. We were told to expect you. I trust you found us without issue?'

'The instructions were excellent,' said Lamont.

'Fantastic. Ahmed is waiting inside for us. Your men can wait out here, or they can come with you. The choice is theirs.'

'Wait here,' Lamont said to his men. He followed Mustafa into the warehouse. Inside were several nondescript white vans, with men milled around each. They all wore grey overalls and looked up when they saw Lamont, sizing him up. He met the eyes of each man, then trailed Mustafa into an office at the far side of the room. The interior was cramped yet organised, and reminded him of his old office at Trinidad's. A man sat there, talking on the phone, his expression set in a frown. He had straight black hair, a flabby face, and dark eyes. He glanced up when Lamont and Mustafa entered, his eyes lingering on Lamont. Curtly telling the person on the other end to call back, he hung up.

'Teflon, I presume?'

Lamont immediately noticed that Ahmed didn't get up to greet him, and took it as a slight. Whatever camaraderie Mustafa had shown would not be replicated by this man.

'I guess you must be Ahmed.'

'Our friends have explained the situation and decreed that you are to run the operation. It is our job to assist you and help with the transition.'

It was clear Ahmed wasn't pleased with the arrangement. His demeanour was unfriendly, and he viewed Lamont with suspicion. Lamont skipped past all the posturing.

'I take it you worked for Akhan?'

Ahmed's jaw tightened. 'He was a great man. A great man and an even better boss.'

There it was. This was the reason Ahmed had a problem with Lamont. He had obviously learned through the grapevine that Lamont was responsible for the death of his beloved boss, and he could not do anything about it. It was a bitter pill to swallow, but it also wasn't Lamont's problem.

'I trust you understand why he is no longer your boss?' Lamont wasn't in the mood for playing around. Ahmed's brow furrowed.

'I'm going for a smoke. You can explain to him how things work,' he said to Mustafa, who looked embarrassed.

'Sorry about that,' he said when Ahmed left.

'Don't worry about it,' said Lamont. 'It'll take a while for us to get to know one another.'

'Still, Ahmed showed poor judgement. Whether we agree with a situation, proper respect should always be shown.'

'Sounds like you've known him a long time.'

'Ten years and counting. We both began working for Akhan and Saj at the same time.'

Lamont hadn't thought about Saj in a while. Saj had loyally served Akhan, including his attempts to serve up Lamont's crew to his master after the robbery of their drugs hub. He had been executed, along with every loyalist Akhan had working for him. Based on Ahmed's attitude, they had missed one. Lamont had liked Saj, but he allied himself with Akhan, and was determined to bring down their crew. He needed to understand if Mustafa shared the same views as Ahmed.

'What happened to Akhan . . . how does that sit with you?'

'I don't want to get involved in anything.'

'We're just talking. If we're going to work together, it's important we understand one another.'

Mustafa sighed. It was clear he didn't want to have the conversation, but to his credit, he didn't back away.

'Akhan was a good boss. He rewarded loyalty, and he always made it clear what he wanted. At the same time, he didn't play by the rules, and he knew what that could lead to.'

Lamont digested what Mustafa said. It seemed he was on the fence about whether to trust him, but he suspected he would have no problem accepting orders. Ahmed was another story, but Lamont would deal with him when the time came.

'Tell me about the play.'

'I'm sure you know most of it. We provide supply to multiple crews. Product isn't a concern, nor is the amount. We have people throughout Yorkshire and the surrounding areas, and we tend to over-order, ensuring there is a healthy surplus of product in case any of our people need it.'

'Do we work with minimum orders?'

'Nothing under five boxes a month. We cater toward the larger spectrum, your crew included.'

Despite everything, Lamont still enjoyed the fact his crew was one of the biggest. Mustafa carried on talking, and it was easy for Lamont to follow along. He remembered his initial meeting with Akhan, and how open everything seemed. By working with Jakkar and his ilk, he hoped he had made the right decision, but was determined to see it through.

'What about the *accessories?*' he asked. Mustafa gave him a blank look.

'Accessories?'

'Security. What if things go wrong?'

'We have specialist teams available to handle any issues. They are at your command, but if you abuse their use, someone above may have something to say.'

Lamont smiled. This was a good thing. He knew the killers that

Akhan had controlled, and if it hadn't been for Jakkar and Stefanos, he might have lost his life to them.

'Akhan had a knack for finding information. I presume there is a network I can tap into?'

Mustafa shook his head. 'The network is off limits to all but Jakkar.' He said it in a casual tone, but Lamont knew better. This was something that had recently been added. He was sure of it.

'Is that a new ruling?'

Mustafa looked away before he replied, 'I know nothing about it.'

Lamont let it slide. It wasn't a situation he could do anything about for now, so he would focus on making money and using his own considerable resources to track down Lennox Thompson.

* * *

Lamont left the meeting with more questions than answers. He wasn't concerned with Ahmed's petty vendetta, but the fact Jakkar seemed determined to curtail his access was jarring.

Lamont had long admired the information network Akhan had at his disposal and had wanted to use the same network to finish Lennox and his organisation. Instead, he would need to rely on his own, and it hadn't been well-manned since Chink's death two years ago. This meant a lot of the sources of information they had set up were obsolete.

Lamont was out of touch with the lower levels of the street. He could get hold of the big fish with a single phone call, but he didn't know who was running which crews on a local level, and that kind of information left him vulnerable. He didn't know if anyone had allied with Lennox, or how the crews felt about him, and he needed to. Lamont was at war, and information was vital. He would need to know everything in order to destroy Lennox.

Wiping his eyes, he stifled a yawn and shuffled to his feet to make more coffee. He was taking his first sip when his phone rang.

'Yes?'

'L, it's me.' It was Delroy.

'Nice to hear from you. How are things?'

'I think you know. I need to speak to you. It's important. Can you come to my house?'

Lamont's street instincts kicked in, but he forced them away. He trusted Delroy and didn't think he would have him killed in his own home.

'Can't give you a time, but I'll ring before I come.'

'Speak to you then.' Delroy hung up.

Lamont stood at the counter, staring at the dark liquid in the cup. He and Delroy had a loose alliance when they had worked together to take out Akhan, but it had stretched little further than this. Scalding his lips with a sip of coffee, Lamont let his brain concoct theories and scenarios while he stared into space.

CHAPTER SIX

Wednesday 22 April 2015

'Do you know what the meeting is about?'

Rigby busied himself, making sure his shirt was tucked in before he answered Murphy. Meeting with the bosses was never good, and he ignored them as often as he could get away with.

'No idea, mate. Let's get in there before she moans about us being late.'

Quickening their steps, they hurried into the meeting room on the second floor of the station. It was a classroom-sized space, with several hard-backed chairs and a whiteboard in the room's corner. Detective Chief Inspector Lisa Reid was already there, sipping a cup of coffee, a selection of files in front of her.

'Rig, Murphy. Thanks for coming.' She signalled to the seats in front of her. Rigby and Murphy sat down.

'I don't mind waiting if you both want to get a drink.'

'We're okay,' said Rigby. Murphy nodded in agreement.

DCI Reid had been transferred to their building six months ago. She was middle-aged, with light brown hair, glasses and a steely determination that had won her the respect of most of the station. Rigby was reserving judgement. He'd dealt with far too many manager types to be on board with her immediately.

'Good. We can get started then. You'll notice a distinct lack of supervisors. There have been some recent reshuffles, and suffice to say, I will be running the criminal teams for the foreseeable future. Now, Keiron Barrett . . . Also known as *K-Bar*. I understand he requested to speak to us recently after being on remand for some time.'

It was clear that Murphy would not talk unless specifically addressed, so Rigby spoke.

'Seemed like he was just messing around, Ma'am.'

Reid's eyebrow rose. 'Messing around?'

'We have K-Bar on a laundry list of charges. He arranged the meeting to see what he could get from us.'

'From what I've read, the paperwork we have is a little shaky. We have a witness that claims she knew about the setup of some gangland hits, but we have no weapons or any tangible evidence. I'm surprised this made it through CPS.'

'K-Bar is a shooter for Teflon. He's the second major arrest we've made, the first being Franklin Turner, also known as *Shorty*.'

'It's my understanding that Turner was released. Something to do with a lack of evidence?'

Rigby felt his temper rising, but kept his voice steady.

'These people have been operating a long time, and they're savvy when it comes to the law, hence the pressure.'

'What do Teflon, or K-Bar, or Turner, have to do with the shootings ravaging Chapeltown? We are putting more resource into the area, which is doing nothing to improve relations with the locals. We're the enemy, and we need to change that perception.'

'Maybe we should sack the officers that smacked around the kid then,' Murphy snarkily said. Reid shot him a look, then surprised them by smiling.

'I know that I'm fairly new to the case, but I've dealt with similar cases in other areas, and we need the locals to believe we're the good guys. That means stopping this gang war and involving ourselves with the local organisations and people. If Teflon isn't involved, we can't prioritise K-Bar. We'll take our chances with him in court, but I want you guys all over the conflict. Find out who the major players are and then plug it.'

'Look, Ma'am, I understand the pressures involved, but Teflon is a problem and if we don't strike now, he will continue to grow more powerful. He is connected to everything going on. K-Bar is highly placed, and he is our best bet at winning.'

'Teflon isn't involved in the gang war, Detective.'

'His girlfriend was stabbed a few weeks back. That was not an accident.'

'When you questioned him afterwards, what did he have to say?'

'He refused to answer. He was involved in a shooting in Chapel-town recently, however.'

'He was the shooter?' Reid's stare was unblinking.

'No. His bodyguard was shot, and there was a fire in a building he was linked to. He's involved, Ma'am. I know it.'

'Maybe so. And during your investigation, if you can piece him in, then go for it. For now, this is your priority.' Reid rose to her feet and headed for the door. 'Keep me updated.'

* * *

'How are we solving this gang war then?'

Rigby wanted to sulk after his meeting with Reid. He was tired of dealing with bureaucrats who only cared about stats and not quality policing. Rigby saw Teflon and his organisation as the biggest threat in Leeds. Delroy's crew was a bigger outfit, but there was something about the running of Teflon's crew that worried him. He didn't want to see a man with so much power, and they needed to do something about it. K-Bar was the best chance to do that, but he couldn't get Reid to see it. She either didn't know how, or didn't care.

Rigby and Murphy had spoken to Peterson, who had been assigned to make inroads into the gang war. To say he'd had nothing would be a gross understatement. He didn't know the major players, what they were warring over, or any major victims. It was no surprise Reid was getting antsy.

'We'll see what Worthy has to say, then shop around our other squirrels. It involves Teflon. I can feel it.'

'Are you sure you don't just want him to be involved so you can stick it to Reid?'

'She doesn't have a clue, and she won't last long in the job if she doesn't pull her finger out.'

'Fuck her, mate. We crack this war, we jog onto the next case. Don't worry about Teflon.'

Rigby didn't bother replying. No matter what Murphy or Reid thought, he felt in his bones that Teflon was connected to the conflict.

* * *

Shorty took a deep breath and squared his shoulders. Knocking on the door, he waited for Amy to answer. She gave him a small smile when she opened the door. He regretted storming off the way he had. Amy had just been trying to talk to him and he had overreacted and flown off the handle. Hopefully, it wasn't too late.

'Hey, Shorty.'

'Ames. Can I come in?'

They headed for the kitchen. Amy pottered with the kettle as Shorty slid into a chair at the kitchen table.

'Can I get you something to drink?'

Shorty shook his head.

'Is everything okay?' She continued.

'I wanted to say sorry for the other day. You were just trying to help, and I was being a dickhead.'

Amy smiled again, shaking her head.

'I've known you a long time, Shorty. I know what to expect from you.'

Shorty didn't want that. He didn't want Amy to associate him with losing his temper when he didn't get his own way. Not anymore.

'That's not me,' he said after a moment. Amy raised an eyebrow, and he hurried on. 'I don't want to be flying off the handle for no reason. Especially not with you.' When Shorty looked up, it was Amy's turn to look at the floor, unable to meet his eyes. The reaction puzzled him, but he put it out of his mind and continued. 'You deserve to know what's going on. I want you to know.'

Amy sat down and waited for Shorty to continue.

'Me and L fell out. Big time.'

Amy didn't even react. 'You've had arguments before. What's different?'

'We got into a fist fight and we both said some things. We're not cool anymore.'

Amy's hand went to her mouth, her eyes widening.

'Are you being serious?'

Shorty nodded.

'What caused that?'

Shorty told her about the fight after Jenny's murder, and the things they hurled at each other. Amy paled, but didn't speak until he had finished.

'I can't believe it. He'll need you though, Shorty. Now more than ever. You know that.'

'He made out like it was my fault his missus got killed. Even mentioned Gracey's name and said it was my fault.'

'You told him everyone around him died, Shorty. Is that any better?'

'Wait, so you're taking his side?' Shorty snapped. Amy held up her hand.

'Slow down, before you get annoyed and have to apologise again. Him using Grace against you like that is deplorable, and he definitely knows better. All I'm saying is that he was hurting over Jenny. You told me yourself it was serious. How many women have you known L get that deep with?'

Shorty said nothing. He folded his arms, his nostrils flaring.

'Exactly. There's all this stuff going on at the moment, and you two need one another. I'm not saying it'll be overnight, but you need to fix this.'

'It's not that simple.'

'Shorty . . .' Amy trailed off. He noticed.

'What?'

'It doesn't matter. It was silly.' Her face reddened, which intrigued him further.

'No, say it.'

'Were you sleeping with Jenny?'

'Are you serious? Where the hell did that come from?'

'I'm just asking. I won't be mad either way. Can't be, really. We're not involved like that. I'm asking because you two fought, which suggests it was really serious. What was going on you with you and Jenny?'

Shorty frowned, gathering his words.

'Remember a few years back, when I got mad about you and L spending time together?'

Amy nodded, understanding.

'After I got out, I stayed with them for a bit. I could see Jenny breaking down, and I saw something was wrong between them. I just couldn't put my finger on it. I considered her a friend, and she was someone I could speak to. About Grace. Even about Dionte.'

'L found out?'

'We weren't hiding it. It wasn't like that. We just all had our shit, and I wasn't clicking with L.' Shorty remembered those first few days of being out of prison. Going to see Lamont. Getting a stack of cash he'd saved for his return. Watching him go back to his office with a bottle instead of going upstairs with Jenny. His vague explanation about why he was still in the game. All of it contributed to the disruption of their friendship.

'Because you got locked up?'

Shorty rubbed his eyes. Talking about this was giving him a headache, but if there was anyone he wanted to confide in, it was Amy.

'L tried walking away before he got shot, and I thought he was doing it for Jenny. Then, Marcus died, people tried to kill us. We just never really found our way back.'

'Maybe now is the perfect time to do that. You're both hurting. You need each other.'

'I don't need him.' Shorty's breathing intensified. He didn't know why he was so angry. There was something deep between him and Lamont, but he couldn't put his finger on it. Women had added to the issue, but it was more than that. 'He got shot while I was on the run, and I dunno . . .'

Amy saw where he was going. '. . . You feel guilty that you weren't there?'

Shorty shrugged, but they both knew that was the case.

'Shorty . . . Grace is alive. She will get better. Surely that more than anything is a sign you and your best friend should bury the hatchet?'

Taking a deep breath, Shorty changed the subject. Amy smiled, knowing him well enough to know he was done sharing. She had given him food for thought, just as she intended.

* * *

As always, Lamont was impressed when Delroy's mansion loomed in front of him. It was a sign of his kingpin status. It had a long drive that led up to the property, with well-tended gardens and multiple luxury vehicles parked outside.

'Wait here,' Lamont said to his security, climbing from the car. One of Delroy's people approached, nodding when he recognised Lamont, leading him to a room where Delroy waited, slumped behind his desk.

'Drink?' he motioned to several bottles of liquor on the desk in front of him.

'Brandy, please,' replied Lamont. He wasn't driving and had no reason to hold back. Delroy shuffled to his feet to fetch glasses, moving even slower than he had the last time Lamont saw him. He seemed thinner and more drawn, and Lamont felt a pang of hurt that he was showing his age. Despite his stature, he wore his usual shirt and trousers combo, the shirt loose around the stomach. Delroy's eyes were full of a tired vitality that only the old could pull off.

'How are you?' Delroy asked when Lamont was seated opposite him, holding his drink.

'I'm fine.'

'You don't look fine. I'm not the only one who can see that either.'

'You pay more attention to what others think than me.'

'Depends on the person.' Delroy's features softened. 'I knew Trinidad for a long time. He was a good man. Loved you, spoke highly of you . . . when you invested in the shop, you changed his life. He might have gone out of business like a few other local businesses did around that time.'

'How come you never backed him?'

'Maybe I would have, if he'd come to me.'

Lamont accepted this, mulling over Delroy's words. They seemed familiar.

'Ken said something similar about Trinidad. Said he cared about me a lot.'

'Course he did. Ken's been around a long time too. Sees everything, even if he doesn't speak on it.'

'Did you invite me to speak about Ken and Trinidad?'

Delroy took a sip of his drink. 'Partly.'

'Why?'

'Trinidad's death wasn't your fault. It was Lennox's fault.'

'Did Ken tell you to say that?' Lamont tried for a smirk, but couldn't pull it off. He hated the idea that people were telling tales behind his back, and he definitely hated the idea they thought he was weak.

'He's worried about you.'

'Respectfully, he doesn't need to worry about me. Neither of you do. Lennox went for Trinidad because of me, and I should have protected him.'

'How?'

'I should have told him Lennox was a threat and made him hide.'

'Wouldn't have worked. Trinidad lived for his business and his family. He wouldn't back down from what he saw as a threat. Too much pride.'

Lamont didn't reply, so Delroy continued.

'Power, L. Power ain't easy. You're at a level few people get to in our game, and you need to let things go if you want to survive. Blaming yourself for everything in the world will only make it harder in the long run.'

Lamont couldn't believe what he was hearing from Delroy. It was a far cry from the conversations the pair had shared in the past. The earliest tenure of their relationship was Delroy subtly bullying Lamont into working for him. When that didn't work, Lamont was forced to accept his supply in order to get a line on a dangerous criminal moving against him. The thought made him smile for a moment. Sixteen years on, and he was still getting caught up in ridiculous drama.

'You've never let a grudge go in your life,' he finally said.

'I let it go when we had our problems a few years back. Things could have easily gone another way. You remember what I told you? When we met in the restaurant after Mack's beating?'

Lamont did, but rather than respond, he took a sip of the expensive brandy.

'I said war isn't a picnic. I stick to that. No matter how high we rise, we're not invincible. Someone else always comes along.'

'Is Lennox that someone?'

Delroy downed his drink and topped it up. He offered the bottle to Lamont, but he shook his head.

'I don't know what's gonna happen with him, if I'm honest. He's crafty, and he doesn't poke his head out often. My people are out there, and we've had a few wins, but nothing major. He took out Solomon, and that shook up a few of the people I had working for me. Solomon was good. Not in the league of Reagan, or Shorty, or Marcus, but he was well on his way.'

This was the conversation Lamont had been waiting for.

'Let me in, Del. Point my people in Lennox's direction and we can work together.'

'No.'

Lamont's eyes widened. Of all the things he'd expected Delroy to say, a blunt refusal wasn't even on the list.

'I can help you. We can pool our teams and get him together, like we did with Akhan.'

Delroy shook his head.

'You're worth more than succumbing to revenge, L. Leave Lennox to me and my people.'

'What the hell are you talking about? You're acting like I'm some helpless little shit. You talk about revenge, but why are *you* warring with him? Is it not because he murdered Winnie and Eddie?'

'This is my life, L, don't you get that?' Delroy suddenly roared, catching Lamont off balance. 'This is it for me. My wife refuses to live with me. My daughter hates me. All I have is my money and my reputation. Lennox is the only thing keeping me here. When I've killed him, I'm heading out to Grenada. Already got my tickets booked.'

'Why Grenada?' Lamont didn't know everything about Delroy's

history, but knew Delroy had fled his homeland when he was younger because of a legal situation that many speculated was murder. As long as he had known him, he'd never heard Delroy even mention the place he grew up.

'I can be free out there.' Delroy smiled. 'Never take freedom for granted, L.'

Lamont's eyes narrowed. He suspected there was a lot he was missing in the exchange with Delroy, and he hated feeling outmanoeuvred when dealing with anyone. He was still irritated that Delroy was refusing his help with Lennox.

'What changed?' he finally asked. Delroy frowned, signalling for him to continue.

'A couple of months back, you were willing to pay me one million pounds to lead your crew for you while you warred with Lennox. What changed?'

'The entire situation changed. More than that, *you* changed.'

'I haven't changed.'

'You have, and if you don't see it, that's even worse. You're tired, L. I don't want you crumbling under the pressure of people's expectations. Put that shit behind you.'

'You can't say that, not after everything that has gone down. The fact is, I have as much reason to go after Lennox as you do. He took people from me too.'

'This is bigger than that, and it only needs one of us.'

'I have my own resources. Whether you work with me, I'll go after him, regardless.'

'Drink your drink,' replied Delroy. It was the last thing Lamont expected him to say, but he complied, downing the drink and placing the empty glass on the table. It would help him sleep tonight.

'Del—'

'Let me just quietly enjoy your company, L,' said Delroy, his tone softer than it had been all night. 'No more talk about Lennox or revenge.'

Lamont blew out a breath. None of this conversation had gone how he expected, and he wondered, not for the first time, if he was truly losing his edge.

'So . . . Grenada then?'

Delroy nodded. Something he'd said earlier finally resonated with Lamont.

'Wait a second? *Tickets* . . . plural?'

'Two tickets. One for me and one for Elaine,' replied Delroy, as if it was obvious.

Lamont was surprised, remembering Delroy's earlier words about his wife.

'I thought you weren't on the best of terms?' He said slowly, trying to be delicate. Delroy's eyes softened for just a second.

'Guess I'm living in hope that she'll come back to me.'

Another silence descended. Lamont broke it after a minute.

'They offered me Akhan's role,' he said. 'The people backing him. After Akhan was killed, they asked me to step up.'

'I take it you did?'

Lamont nodded.

'It's an impressive role. Do you trust the people you're working with? You rushed to work with Akhan to spite me and look how that turned out for you.'

'Akhan is gone. It's irrelevant.'

'You're right. He is.' Delroy gave Lamont a knowing look. He didn't react to it, pressing on with his point.

'I trust they want to do business. Seems dangerous to go beyond that.'

Delroy grinned, showing worn teeth. 'Maybe you *are* learning something after all, L.'

'I have access to as much product as I need. All the best quality. If you switch your supply, I'll cut you one hell of a deal.'

Delroy's smile didn't fade. 'Maybe in the future. Not right now, though. I want things to remain as they are.'

Lamont didn't argue. They would revisit it at a later time. He allowed Delroy to top up his glass now, stifling a yawn. The old man had given him a lot to think about, but Lamont couldn't give weight to most of what he said. He had messed up, and his mistakes had led to multiple deaths. No matter what Delroy said, Lamont had got himself into this mess, and no matter the cost, he would get himself out of it.

CHAPTER SEVEN

Friday 24 April 2015

'WHAT DO you have for me then?'

Lamont had spent his morning working out. He'd taken to it after recovering from his shooting, and kept up with it.

Sharma sipped a Lucozade, his appearance much improved since Lamont last saw him. He'd worked for Marcus, and other than doing the odd job for Lamont, they had never hung out. Sharma had been loyal to Marcus, and competent. He'd done a lot of work with Victor, another henchmen of Marcus's who was currently serving a sentence for murder.

Lamont still felt bad that he had forgotten about him in the aftermath of Marcus's death, but consoled himself with the fact he'd been shot, and his recovery had taken almost a year. Sharma had gone under the radar until Lamont had gone looking for him, but he had kept him employed ever since.

'Thompson's people have completely removed themselves from the day to day, even the little fish. People think they're on the back-foot. Delroy's people have come back strong lately.'

Lamont thought back to his conversation with Delroy, and the resolve he'd seen in the man's eyes. Delroy had nothing to lose. Lennox had pushed him to the limit. His back was to the wall, and he was coming out swinging.

'There's a reason he's been on top for so long. Len's mainly into what, though? Protection? Loans? Guns? You can't hold down that racket without a street presence.'

'Why does that matter?' Sharma looked nonplussed.

'Lennox has fought a continuous battle for months. He has shooters. Safehouses . . . it's a lot. Unless he has a sugar daddy sponsoring him, I don't see where it's all coming from.'

'Len's been around longer than you, L. He was never one for spunking money in the club or buying new cars.'

Lamont stifled a yawn. The late nights were catching up with him.

'One thing I've learned about this lifestyle is that it's possible to make a lot of money, but the lifestyle costs.'

'Even when he was banged up, he had people running his rackets. Fact is, I remember Thompson when he was knocking around with Marcus, and he always had money.'

Lamont didn't reply, but Sharma was missing the point. Lennox had seemingly limitless funds in this battle, and unless he'd saved every penny he'd earned, it didn't seem workable. Drugs were still the principal source of income for criminals in the hood, and Lennox had been staunchly against them from the beginning. There was something Lamont wasn't seeing, and he was determined to do so.

He thought about *OurHood*, and Lennox's influence in that organisation. He'd used Malcolm Powell as his mouthpiece and had apparently funnelled money through the company. It was possible he was laundering money for other criminals and taking a cut, but even that was a reach. *OurHood* was a grassroots organisation, and there was only so much money they could hide before the authorities cottoned on.

'What do you want me to do now, boss?'

'Keep looking for his people. I want to know more about his money. Find me clients that he lent to. Punters that have dealt with him. Keep the info coming.'

Sharma nodded and left. Lamont closed his eyes and sat back. Having a nap now would only mess him up later, but he couldn't stop the sleep from creeping over him.

* * *

'Thanks for meeting me.'

Shorty nodded at Maka.

'Course I was gonna meet you. You said it was important.'

'It is. C'mon, let's get some drinks.'

The pair were in a club in the city centre. It was a large, flashy place, with small black booths dotted all around, and a VIP section overlooking the dance floor. Maka had called Shorty and invited him out. Shorty's social life hadn't exactly been rocking lately, and he agreed to come.

The club was on Albion Street and mainly catered to a younger crowd. It was just after nine pm, and most of them didn't come out before midnight. Shorty remembered the days of being young, drinking and taking drugs all night. It exhausted him just thinking about it.

After ordering their drinks, they found a booth to sit in.

'What did you want to talk about then?'

'You,' replied Maka. Shorty's brow furrowed.

'What about me?'

'What's your plan now? What are you doing?'

'I need to get at Lennox, but he's not an easy guy to track down. Other than that, I'm focusing on Grace.'

Maka's eyes softened. 'How is she doing?'

'She's not on death's door anymore. The doctor's say she's getting better, but I don't even know what they're talking about half the time.'

'I'm glad she's doing well, Shorty. What happened to her shouldn't have happened.'

'I know, fam. She's gonna get better though. Let's talk business.'

Maka blew out a breath. 'Where did it all go wrong with our crew?'

Shorty couldn't put his finger on it. The crew had run without issue for years. Even when conflict erupted, they had all the pieces in place to beat down any challenges. Somewhere down the line, that all changed, and everything became a lot more political. A gulf sprang between Lamont and Shorty, and people in the crew began going in their own directions.

'Guess we just all stopped communicating. We started beefing with Delroy and his people, and L wanted out. Marcus died. Chink snaked us, and we've been trying to catch up ever since.'

Maka drained his drink. Shorty hadn't touched his yet.

'Brings me onto my next point. What's going on with you and L?'

Shorty shrugged.

'Nothing.'

'Don't give me that, Shorty. I'm right here with y'all. We're all trying to keep our heads above water, but I need to understand what the situation is. People are saying some wild shit. They're saying you were nearly fighting at Trinidad's funeral.'

Shorty scowled. 'We had words and kept it moving. People need to keep out of my business, or I'll make them.'

'Fine. I'm not gonna push you if you don't wanna talk to me about it. We need you to be down with the crew though.'

'What does L think about that?'

Maka scratched his head.

'L's not around to ask. We're running the show at the moment. You know how he is right now.'

Shorty knew little bits. He'd noticed how destroyed Lamont looked at the funeral, but didn't know what was going on in his world. He still didn't understand why Lamont was still in the game. Maka had presented an intriguing offer. Shorty had helped Lamont build the crew. They had accepted Lamont as the leader, but if he wasn't stepping up, maybe Shorty needed to.

'L's gunning for Lennox. We need you back. Manson feels the same. Things haven't been clicking right for a while.'

'I thought everything was good?' Shorty recalled the stack of money Lamont had given him when he touched down after prison.

'K-Bar did his best, but he wasn't a leader. He's a street goon, not the guy that should make decisions about business. He put off a lot of people with his way of doing things, and the money dropped.'

Shorty understood. He'd known K-Bar longer than any of them, and he had his strengths. Leadership wasn't one. It was one reason he had always deferred to Shorty and Lamont.

'L took the reins again, as you know. Things got better. He had people collecting debts. He sent K-Bar to do that job on Big-Kev to send a message. Then all that stuff happened with Lennox, and then Akeem. Now, he's missing again, and we look weak. Spots are getting raided. A few smaller crews are getting brave and casing our spots. One of our runners got jumped the other night. We need to get back on track, and we need you for that, fam.'

Shorty shook his head.

'I feel you, but with the way things are with me and L, stepping back into the crew wouldn't be right.'

'I don't know what the things are with you and L. What I do know is that we need you, and you need us too. You can't take on all of Leeds by yourself. You've got skills, but you're not that good. I was there when we got ambushed, remember? I took a bullet.'

Before Shorty could reply, a third man approached the pair, beaming widely. He wore a salmon shirt with a navy waistcoat and matching trousers. His ostentatious jewellery caught the light, and Shorty glanced at the chunky Rolex around his wrist. Back in the day, he'd had a similar one. He didn't know what had happened to it, which made him realise how pointless buying one had been.

'Nice to see you both tonight. I thought you were coming tomorrow?' he said warmly. Maka shook his hand and Shorty followed suit. Naveed was one of Chink's old disciples. With Chink making a foray into the Leeds club scene years back, he'd cultivated people to do his running around. Naveed had been a significant find. He understood money, was charismatic and knew absolutely everyone, making him perfectly placed to step up after Chink's murder. Shorty hadn't seen him in years, but he still looked exactly the same. He a similar coiffed look to Chink, and it annoyed him. It wasn't the time for old grudges, though.

'It was a last-minute thing.' Maka glanced around. 'Mind if we use your office to finish our chat?'

Naveed shook his head. 'Of course not. Come on, let's go.'

The trio headed to the office. It was on the second floor next to the VIP section and overlooked the club. It had a comfy looking leather sofa, along with a small dark brown desk and a few spindly chairs. Naveed began smoothing the papers on the desk, apologising profusely as he did so. Finally, he took a seat facing them and invited them to sit. Maka did, but Shorty remained standing.

'Give him that thing,' said Maka. Naveed nodded, unlocking his desk drawer and handing Shorty a thick envelope. Shorty opened it, thumbing through the bands of money inside.

'What's this for?'

'That's your cut.'

'There's about twenty grand here.'

'So?'

'Why is L still paying me?'

'If he wanted your cut to be stopped, he'd have said something. Like I said, his head ain't with it at the moment. He's like the invisible man lately.'

Shorty gave Maka a searching look. 'You think you can bribe me to work?'

'The money is yours. It's your cut. I've told you why the crew needs you, but I've known you a long time. If you don't wanna do it, you won't.'

Shorty wanted to say no again, but Maka had made good points. If he was ever to get a shot at Lennox, he would need the resources of the crew. The money was excellent too, and if he could get the crew clicking again, he would make even more. His kids would get all the money they needed, and Shorty could stay busy. Lamont was the only reason to say no, and if he wasn't around, Shorty wouldn't need to see him.

'Fine. I'll do it.'

Maka grinned, showing all his teeth.

'We're gonna kill this shit, just like we used to.'

Shorty ignored him, glancing at Naveed. He was still watching the pair with a wide smile that Shorty found weird.

'Give us a minute,' he said. 'Need to talk with Maka about some sensitive shit.'

Naveed's smile dimmed.

'This is my office,' he reminded him. Shorty responded with a hard look, and Naveed jumped to his feet.

'I need to go check things are running properly, anyway. Take your time,' he sputtered.

'Bring more drinks on your way back,' said Maka. Shorty had left his untouched drink at their table, but Maka didn't seem to care. 'What's up?'

'K-Bar got a message to me from inside.'

'How? He got a phone in his cell?'

'He got word through his solicitor. About the witness.'

Maka straightened in his seat on the sofa, ready to listen.

'Who is it?'

'Some little party girl called Adele. She was best friends with that Naomi bitch that got dropped. The one Chink was banging.'

'I know which one you mean. Think her surname's *Chapman*. She was joined at the hip with Naomi when she was grinding Reagan. Are we taking her out?'

'I'm not sure,' admitted Shorty. It had been on his mind since the solicitor had contacted him. He wanted K-Bar out of prison, but he wasn't sure killing a potential witness was the right step.

'We drop her, K-Bar's out. Seems pretty simple.' Maka tapped his fingers on Naveed's desk.

'More murders will only make things harder. We need to get Lennox, and that's the only time we need to drop bodies. With the Feds sniffing around Leeds, and all the *OurHood* snitches, we need to play this one differently.'

Maka nodded. This was why he wanted Shorty helping them. He was a hothead, but he was also a street general who was extremely tactical when needed.

'What are you thinking then?'

'If it's the Adele I'm thinking of, I banged her sister years back. *Shanice.* I'm gonna get in contact, see if I can learn anything.'

Maka grinned. 'Okay, fam. We'll meet with Manson and let him know the play with the crew. For now, let's get some more drinks and make a night of it. You down?'

Shorty was. He needed a night to cut loose and forget about the world for a while.

'Yeah, I'm down. Bet we can scare Naveed into giving us some champagne.'

CHAPTER EIGHT

Thursday 30 April 2015

SHANICE CHAPMAN DIDN'T KNOW what to expect. She had been traipsing through social media one evening when she saw a friend request from a blast from the past. Before accepting, she perused Shorty's profile, smiling at several of the photos. When they'd hung out back in the day, Shorty was a player. He was good looking and connected. He'd walk into clubs and buy out the bar, making sure everyone had a good time.

She was under no illusions. She would not fall for a hustler no matter what, and soon they fizzled out. Looking at him now, she was curious. His Facebook wasn't bursting with information about his life, but there was a photo someone had taken of Shorty in a club back in January, with the caption 'fresh out'. Shorty was posing along with K-Bar and Maka. He looked older in the photo than he had when their paths last crossed, but he still had the look, especially in the eyes. It didn't take her long to accept the friend request.

Shorty had immediately turned on the charm, telling Shanice how good she looked. She liked the compliments. Life had grown boring lately. She had two kids, a baby father uninterested in either of them, and a dull office job in town. Despite knowing it couldn't go anywhere, flirting with a thug from the Hood was appealing. She knew Shorty had been through the wars, but she was sucked into the conversation and when Shorty suggested meeting, she was ready.

* * *

Shorty awoke in a good mood. He was taking Shanice to dinner tonight. His day was open, and he planned on using the time to sort out the crew and get things back in line. After some press-ups and sit-ups, he showered, ate breakfast, and left the house after eleven. He had a message from Amy that he hadn't responded to. She didn't know about his plans to help K-Bar, and he wasn't telling her. Whatever was going on with them was separate from this situation.

It had never crossed Shorty's mind that K-Bar would snitch. He wasn't built that way, just like Shorty. When he'd turned himself in, the police tried everything to get him to *cooperate*, but he'd stood tall and when he got out, he had been well compensated. The same would happen with K-Bar, but it made getting things back in line even more of a necessity.

The crew had been going for almost twenty years, and they had amassed a lot of money, but there was a tremendous amount of overhead. There were wages to pay, supply reloads, along with special considerations such as the *hazard pay* for the people behind bars. Their loyalty was bought and paid for, but if those funds stopped, it would make the situation much harder. It was vital the crew continued to profit, and Shorty would ensure it did so.

* * *

Shorty went to see Darren. The young man had come a long way, even in the last few months alone. He was one of Teflon's favourites according to Maka, and one of the last moves Lamont made was to involve Darren in recruitment, recognising the need to replenish the crew and attract the best people. Shorty's only concern was that Darren was a little inexperienced for the role, but he had recently stepped up while Maka was recovering, and was a definite asset for the future.

Darren was holding court outside a house on Markham Avenue with a few of his boys, when Shorty pulled up. Darren nodded when he saw him and said something to his crew, who all dispersed when he climbed from the ride. Shorty approved of the gesture and the young-ster's instincts.

Maybe what everyone said about him was true.

Shorty knew Darren's older brother, Lucas, and he was an atten-tion-seeking idiot who couldn't stay out of prison. It seemed Darren was cut from a different cloth. He touched his fist.

'Everything good?' he asked.

'No surprises so far. Delroy's people are active. They've been driving up and down, looking for any of Lennox's people.'

'How's that working for them?'

Darren shrugged.

'Heard they caught a few people the other night, but no one special. Lennox made a big move getting to Solomon though. No one saw that coming. We thought he had eyes in the back of his head.'

Shorty privately agreed. Solomon deserved his reputation. If he hadn't been so loyal to Delroy, Shorty would have tried bringing him into the fold. They had sparred together a few years ago, and Shorty still remembered being rocked by Solomon's killer left hook. It seemed every day that more of the old guard were dying, and Shorty often wondered if that was a sign he should do something else.

As always, he dismissed the thoughts. He had nothing else. He'd worked his whole life for the reputation he had now, and he saw nothing beyond that. Amy flitted into his mind then, but he forced the thoughts away. He needed to focus.

'Solomon was good. Someone will get Lennox, though. If Del doesn't, we will.'

'What he did to your daughter was fucked,' said Darren. Shorty's stomach lurched. He didn't want to think about that fateful day again.

'He'll get his. Don't worry about that. I need to talk business with you.'

Darren nodded, instantly straightening, his face serious.

'What do you need?'

His attitude impressed Shorty. He'd sent his friends away, knowing

Shorty wouldn't want to speak around them, and he had immediately switched on when Shorty said he wanted to talk. He filed away these facts for future consideration.

'I heard you were looking to bring new people into the crew. I wanted to see who you were considering.'

Darren grinned.

'People are keeping low until the streets cool down. They don't want to be mistaken for one of Delroy's or Lennox's people and end up dead. Maka put me onto some old timers. He's meant to be setting up the meets, so you'll need to talk to him about them.'

'Who've you seen closer to your age?' Shorty asked. They needed young blood in the crew. If they could get more people with Darren's mindset, they would come out of this situation even stronger.

'Roman and Keith. You know them?'

Shorty thought the name *Roman* sounded familiar, but he couldn't place him.

'I think so. Tell me what you know about them.'

'They're independent. They don't rock with any of the big crews, but they've carved out a nice base and clientele. Nothing on our level, but they're making decent money.'

'If they're doing well alone, why would they want to join up with us?'

'I've heard through the grapevine they're having problems with other gangs. I figure we can help one another, and calm the streets at the same time.'

'Do you know the other gangs they're beefing with?'

'I've heard the name *Aaron*, but I know a few. There's one I'm leaning towards, though.'

'I do too,' said Shorty. 'Set up a meeting with Roman and Keith. I'll go with you to check them out.'

'They're squirrelly. They might think it's a trap. I'm thinking we should just roll up on them.'

'Don't you think they might think *that's* a trap?' asked Shorty. In his experience, randomly pulling up on a crew was more threatening than calling to arrange a meeting on neutral ground.

'I think we'll be alright. They're not gonna pull anything with me. I know a few people in their crew.'

'What about me?' asked Shorty, smirking. Darren grinned.

'Everyone knows your rep, fam. Something tells me you'll be safe.'

* * *

They climbed in Shorty's ride. Darren made a call, trying to narrow down a location for Roman and Keith. Shorty tuned out, thinking about his meeting with Shanice and how to play it. He was considering telling her he just wanted sex, but hadn't been able to glean much about her situation when he had spoken to her. He would have to play it by ear.

Darren finished his call and stowed the phone.

'They're local. Someone saw them hanging on Hill Top Mount about an hour ago.'

'Do you have an address?'

Darren told him, and Shorty drove over, knowing the area well. He pulled to a stop outside a red bricked terraced house with a white door. They heard the thumping Drill music as they exited the car. There was a single person in the garden. He was rail-thin and wearing a vest and tracksuit bottoms, smoking a spliff with his eyes on his phone. He looked up as they approached, then straightened.

'Who are you lot?'

'Roman about?' Darren spoke first. Shorty was happy to let him do the talking.

'Who's asking?'

'Tell him Darren's out here.'

The man glanced at Shorty, obviously expecting him to introduce himself. When he didn't, the man shrugged and headed inside, giving one last look over his shoulder.

'Think we're gonna have any trouble with them?' Shorty asked. Darren shook his head.

'They're rowdy, but they know my name. We'll be fine. Worst comes to the worst, the people I left will spray up the spot if we're not back in an hour.'

'A lot can happen in an hour,' said Shorty, but before Darren could reply, the man was back, signalling for them to come in.

The house was stuffy, with a lingering scent of takeaways, cigarettes, and weed smoke. They followed the man through a hallway to the kitchen where four people waited, none of whom Shorty recognised. Two of them — both lanky and hard-eyed — immediately left the room, eyeballing both Shorty and Darren as they did so. Not to be outdone, the pair stared right back.

'Been a while, D. Thought you got too big to be around little guys like us,' one of the seated youths said drily. Shorty guessed this was Roman. He was slender and light skinned, wearing a black jacket and tracksuit bottoms. Something in his eyes reminded Shorty of Darren. There was a confidence that set him apart as the leader of his little crew.

'Never, boss. You lot have done well.'

'Good of you to notice,' said the other youth. He was darker than Roman, with fathomless eyes and closely cropped hair. Broader than the others, he appeared to be the *muscle* of the team, and was eyeing Shorty in particular with dislike.

'You two, go speak to Joey and the others. Make sure everything is humming. We can handle this,' said Roman. The two youths still standing hesitated a moment, then did as ordered.

'You're Shorty,' said Roman when they were alone.

'You're Roman. Your boy there must be Keith,' replied Shorty. Keith's glare only intensified. Shorty wondered if the kid would try him, silently vowing to knock him unconscious if he did. It would take more than a glare and some gym muscles to intimidate him.

'That's right. How come you're here?'

'We wanted to talk business,' Darren interjected himself into the conversation.

'Okay. We're listening.'

'We heard about the trouble you're having with Aaron and his people, and we want to help.'

'What makes you think we need help?' said Keith. Roman barely reacted, rubbing his knuckles, supremely unconcerned.

'If it's the one I'm thinking of, he's banded together with Morby's crew, and Prezzie's. You guys are good, but that's more than you can handle, and you know it.'

'I still don't see how it concerns you,' said Roman.

'We want to present a mutual arrangement. We back you against the other crews, and you become allied with us.'

'Allied with you how? We're our own crew. We do our own thing. There's a reason we didn't go chasing after you lot or one of the other big crews. We handle our own business and stay off the radar. Throwing in with you lot puts us on the stage in a major way, and that brings problems.'

'Brings money too. A lot more money than what you're making now. Money and a responsible organisation that takes itself seriously. You have nothing to lose by signing up with us. Your enemies become our enemies, and we help you get what you want.'

'We don't want to become your lackeys. The only way powerhouses like you lot come looking for little people like us is because you think we're some kids to throw in front of your enemies. That ain't the case and if it's what you want, I'd suggest you speak to Aaron and those lot, and get them to back you.'

Shorty respected the way Roman was responding, but he also liked Darren's negotiating. He'd maintained his composure the whole time, showing little reaction to the things Roman was saying. Keith was alternating his glare between Darren and Shorty, but Darren wasn't fazed. He was focused on his words and on resolving the situation. Shorty also noticed he'd shown some knowledge of Aaron, despite being unsure earlier. He filed it away, not wanting to disrupt the flow.

'I don't know what you know about the crew I roll with, but we don't use people as lackeys or cannon fodder. Like yourselves, we believe in being low key where necessary, and in working with our partners to make sure everyone profits. You've gone further than anyone could have imagined with this team of yours. We're just trying to help you stay around longer. We have the best product. You'll make more money doing less work, and you won't have to take everything on your shoulders.'

Roman shot a look at Keith, who still looked sulky. He shrugged in response to Roman's silent question, and Roman sighed.

'What are you proposing? Who are your enemies?'

'We suspect Aaron and his people recently attacked one of our spots, and jumped one of our runners.'

Roman glanced at Keith again, finally showing annoyance at his partner's lack of effort in involving himself in the conversation.

'We'll work with you, but *we* control the people under us, and we get your supply and backup.'

'In exchange for?'

Roman mulled it over for a moment. 'Thirty percent of our profits.'

'Try sixty. We're bringing the supply, not to mention the protection,' said Darren.

'Fine. Sixty percent *our* way, forty percent yours.'

They negotiated for a few more minutes, with neither man backing down from the other. Finally, they agreed on a fifty-fifty split, which Shorty suspected both had wanted all along. He was impressed with how it had gone. Roman had savvy and street smarts. With him working alongside Darren and backed by the others, it would be the push their crew needed to rise back to their position at the top.

Shorty tuned out of the rest of the discussion, thinking again about his night. Getting K-Bar out of prison would help tremendously in providing both depth and experience to the crew. There was a chance it would all blow up in his face with Shanice, but Shorty would understand more when they were around one another.

'You did well,' he told Darren as they climbed back into the ride.

'He's a tricky one. He's got some serious steel.'

'Reminded me of someone,' said Shorty, as he drove them away. 'When do we get this Aaron kid then?'

'We're gonna give them a few soldiers, and they'll do the heavy work with Aaron and his crew. They'll be on board after that, and we'll get the streets back in line. Should take a day or so to track Aaron.'

Shorty grinned. 'Nicely handled. I thought you'd be louder about it, but you played it subtle. Keith seemed like he had a problem.'

'He's one of those guys that doesn't like anyone but Roman. He's tough though, and he can handle himself. The whole crew can. Probably why they've been left alone.'

'Why would Aaron try it with them then?'

'He's dumb. Doesn't scare easily, thinks that the loudest is the roughest and the toughest. Guess that's how he bullied people into accepting him as a leader. Roman and his guys make money, and Aaron wants a piece. From what I hear, he's part of the reason the streets are so hot.'

'There's a war, D. Lennox and Delroy are trying to kill each other.' Shorty gritted his teeth when he said Lennox's name. Things wouldn't be truly right for him until he had put a bullet or two into the man's head.

'I know that. Everyone does. Aaron isn't quiet, and there's a difference between people knowing not to be on the streets because two gangs are trying to kill each other, and a loose cannon running around those same streets, robbing and beating up everyone in sight.'

Shorty couldn't argue with that. Politics aside, it had been a productive meeting, and was one thing off his mind.

CHAPTER NINE

Thursday 30 April 2015

SHANICE WAS WAITING by the door when Shorty pulled up in the evening. He'd left Darren and chilled for a few more hours before freshening up. Amy had finally got hold of him, and they'd spoken about Grace. Guilt had swirled in his stomach when he hung up. There was nothing between him and Amy, but he'd never stopped caring for her. There was no way he could tell her about what he was doing. While she had accepted his execution of Lutel, he didn't think she would be on board with what might happen to Adele.

'You look good,' said Shorty, when Shanice climbed into the ride. He wasn't exaggerating. She had a cute, round face and a curvaceous figure, having maintained most of the weight she gained after having children. She wore a tight cleavage-displaying blouse and tight grey jeans with a pair of heels.

'You look good too. Even after all these years, you've still got the look.' Her eyes flitted to the Rolex on his wrist. 'Business must be good.'

'I'm gonna get mine regardless,' said Shorty, winking and showing her his cocky side. Although he'd borrowed it from Maka having misplaced his own, Shanice didn't need to know that.

They made small-talk as they drove into the city centre and parked, then walked to the restaurant. It was a fancy Italian spot on Greek Street, with immaculate dark brown floors, white beams, and small, intimate tables with sturdy black chairs. There were plants nearby, dotted with lights. They were shown to their tables and ordered glasses of wine while they waited for the menus.

'This is a nice spot,' admitted Shanice. 'I've never been here before.'

'Same. Came highly recommended, and the food is meant to be amazing.'

'Do you eat much Italian food?'

Shorty shook his head. 'I like my Hood food too much.'

Shanice grinned. 'Same. My kids love Spaghetti Bolognese though.'

'How many kids do you have?'

'Two boys,' said Shanice, watching him closely to see how he would react. Shorty already knew. Her Facebook page was full of photos of them.

'How old?'

'Eight and twelve.'

Shorty didn't ask their names, and she didn't give them. He didn't care, but knew talking about children would make it easier to keep the subject on family.

'How many do you have? I heard you had a girl?'

'One of each. Roughly the same ages as yours.'

Shanice again smiled. 'Must be fate. What have you been doing, anyway?'

Shorty wasn't sure how honest to be with Shanice. He didn't want to lie and have her already know what was going on in the streets.

'I've been keeping things quiet for a while. My daughter had an accident.'

Shanice's eyes softened. 'I heard. I'm sorry. If my kids were hurt like that, it would kill me.'

Shorty bowed his head, the emotions easy to replicate.

'I was right there, and I was powerless to stop it,' he admitted. The images of Grace's prone frame were seared into his brain. He didn't have to search far for them. Shanice put her hand on top of his, gently squeezing. Amy had done something similar recently, but there was none of the warmth he'd felt then now.

'She's lucky to have you.'

Shorty nodded. They were quiet now, waiting for the food to arrive. The small-talk soon started up again, and Shanice spoke about her baby father, and the issues she had with him and his inability to be there for his kids. It made Shorty wonder if Stacey or Amy had ever said similar things about him. Whether they had, he reasoned, he was making up for it now. He and Dionte had spoken numerous times since their meeting, and though the conversations were still a little awkward, it was still progress, and he was thankful for it.

'Why did you really look me up?' Shanice asked a while later. The food was finished, and they were savouring wine and sitting in comfortable silence. Despite himself, Shorty had enjoyed the night. It had been a while since he had been on a date, and even if this was a mission, it was enjoyable. Shanice wasn't as annoying as he remembered, which he guessed was because of her being older and more mature.

Shorty thought about how to answer. He didn't want her getting emotional if he said the wrong thing. Finally, he just went for it.

'Kinda felt like we had unfinished business. I was curious about you,' he said. Shanice blinked, surprised by his words.

'Really?'

'We had fun back in the day and sometimes I remember those days and how free we all were. I had my people around me and the entire world was just *there*, you know?'

Shanice was wide-eyed as she gawped at him and Shorty didn't know why. He'd spoken from the heart. He often thought back on those days and how alive and *whole* everyone was. Their crew controlled the streets, he did what he wanted, and made serious money. Lamont had his back, making sure they mostly stayed out of trouble. He'd been young, carefree and invincible. Now, he was older, guarded, barely surrounded by the remnants of that glorious era.

'I always had a thing for you,' she finally said. 'I know it was never serious, but being around you was something different. You had something about you that drew me in.' She paused. 'You still do.'

Shorty felt a wave of guilt at her words, and this one had nothing to do with Amy. He was deceiving a woman that had potentially never gotten over him. Steeling himself, he remembered why he was doing it. He would not let K-Bar rot behind bars.

'Wanna get out of here?'

* * *

Shorty sat up in the unfamiliar bed, still naked, covered in marks and scratches. Shanice had been an absolute wildcat in bed. Whether it was years of pent-up pining or if it had simply been a while for her, he couldn't say. After leaving the restaurant, the seduction was easy, and the sex had been fun. It struck Shorty how little he had been laid since getting out, and that shocked him. Having sex had once upon a time been the be-all and end-all of his life. Sex and getting money.

Had he changed so much without realising?

Shorty's conversations lately had been tinged with more realism than he was ready for. He'd gotten Amy back on side by being honest with her, and the same thing had worked to a degree with Shanice. He hadn't spoken with her about Adele yet, but he would work it into conversation and take it from there. Scheming in the darkness, he wondered when things would grow easier. He was back in the crew's fold. Grace was steadily improving. He was bringing in serious money, and he had things to live for. It was strange for him to sit and wonder what would come later, and he quickly decided it didn't matter. For now, he would focus on K-Bar.

* * *

'That's him.'

A black Ford 4x4 idled at the end of Hillcrest View in the Hood. The occupants of the ride were watching a group of men hanging outside a house. There were five men passing around a spliff, talking and laughing in loud tones.

'Which one?' said the driver.

'The guy in the grey hoody,' said Roman.

'Okay,' said Manson. 'We go for him. Sharma, make sure they back off.'

'Got it.'

Accelerating sharply, Sharma gunned the ride forward, and they were on top of the group before they reacted. Aaron was the quickest and was already in motion as Manson, Sharma, Roman and Keith jumped from the vehicle. The men froze. Sharma's gun was trained on the group, ready to cut them down if they moved. Aaron barely made it around the corner onto Shepherds Lane, when Roman tackled him to the ground, knocking him into a nearby green electrical box. The pair began tussling, Aaron having the advantage until Keith dragged him off and began kicking him. Roman joined in, his fist repeatedly crashing against Aaron's face.

'Hold out his arm!' shouted Keith. Roman complied and Keith brought all his weight down on the appendage, causing Aaron to scream in pain.

Meanwhile, Aaron's crew were being robbed at gunpoint. They could hear the cries of his beating, but there was nothing they could do. Roman and Keith dragged him back to the group, dumping him on the floor. He clutched his arm, tears of pain in his eyes.

'You lot are fucking dead! Watch when I catch you.'

'This is the end, Aaron. You're out of business.' Manson turned to the crew. 'We'll make a deal with you lot. Work for Roman, or you can try to set yourselves up in another city.'

The four men looked from their beaten, snivelling leader, to the well-organised group that had ambushed them. It was a simple decision to make.

'We're in.'

'Roman and Keith will let you know how this works. Any problems, get them, and they'll handle it. Understand?'

The men nodded. Sharma and Manson zip-tied Aaron's hands behind his back and dumped him in the boot. Without a word, they climbed in and sped away. Roman and Keith turned back to the men, grinning.

'Where were we?'

* * *

Shorty sipped his brandy and coke, looking to Shanice by his side. They were watching a comedy special on *Netflix*, but she was paying more attention than he was.

Shorty had spent every night at Shanice's since their *date*. He'd expected to have to work to wrap her around his finger, but she was wide-open and prime for manipulation.

'How's your family? I haven't seen your brother in years?'

'Trevor doesn't live in Leeds anymore. He got married a few years ago and moved to Wolverhampton. Adele is still around.'

'Yeah, I remember her. Party girl? Liked a drink?'

Shanice kissed her teeth. 'Sounds like her. Don't know if she's still like that anymore.'

'Did she get married too?'

'Nothing like that. I just haven't seen her in a while. She's still in Leeds, but she turned weird. Basically went into hiding and cut everyone out of her life.'

'You don't know where she is?'

Shanice sighed. 'I know. She rang me and told me about three weeks ago. She wouldn't tell me what was going on and we got into an argument. Mum misses her, but Adele won't speak to her.'

'Did you ask her what was going on?' Shorty hoped she said no.

'She wouldn't tell me. Mum is always asking where she is, and it's like she doesn't even care about her nephews.'

Shorty pulled Shanice close and gave her a quick kiss as she relaxed in his arms.

'Take the kids to see her.'

'You think?'

'Don't take family for granted. Cherish them while they're still here. I lost my cousin a few years back, and it sits with me every day. The last time we spoke to each other we argued, and I have to carry that the rest of my days.'

'I'm sorry, Shorty,' she murmured, snuggling closer and kissing his chest. 'You're right. I'll take them to see her at the weekend.'

Shorty hid his smile. He would follow her, learn where Adele was, and how many police officers were guarding her. From there, he would make his move, no matter the obstacles.

CHAPTER TEN

Sunday 3 May 2015

SHORTY WAS PARKED down the street from Adele's place. He had followed Shanice to the spot, watching as she and her two boys were shown inside. Since then, he'd watched the spot for anything out of the ordinary. He had seen Adele leave a few times, returning with shopping bags. Even from a distance he could see the bags under her eyes. Clearly the pressures of being a snitch were getting to her. During his surveillance, he had noticed one thing that had thrown him for a loop.

There was no police presence. Shorty expected them to be well-hidden, but they were non-existent. When Shanice had visited, no one had stopped her, or gone to the premises afterwards. He couldn't get his head around it. Adele was their star witness, but they had left her unattended.

The paranoid part of his brain wondered if it was a ploy to get him out in the open, but that made little sense. Surely it wasn't worth the risk. Jamal had taken an earlier watch, and reported nothing out of the ordinary. This was it. There would be no more waiting. Shorty was going in.

* * *

Adele rarely slept well these days. She lived in fear of the world learning what she had done. Her friend Naomi had been murdered by gangsters a few years ago, and the police tracked Adele down and compelled her to testify. They promised to keep her safe, but it didn't stop her worrying. She had gone against some powerful gangsters and knew K-Bar had been arrested.

Removing herself from her world, she had avoided contact unless absolutely necessary, and had kept to herself. Her sister had visited recently, bringing her nephews along, and it was great catching up with them. It made her feel guilty for neglecting her family, and she'd promised Shanice she would keep in touch more, without going into the detail of why she had remained hidden. Shanice had spoken at length about a new man that had come into her life, though she was coy about giving his name, saying it was early days. Adele was happy for her, but also jealous that her life was so uncomplicated.

When her eyes fluttered open in the middle of the night, it was no big deal. The big deal was the man loomed over her. Before she could scream, his gloved hand covered her mouth.

'Stop fucking moving,' he hissed. 'Keep still and don't make me use this.'

Even in the dark, Adele saw the pistol in his other hand and froze. Her blood ran cold as she realised who the man represented, and why he was there.

'You shouldn't have spoken to the Feds.' He moved his hand from her mouth.

'I di—'

'Don't lie. We know it was you that got K-Bar locked up. Dirty snitch. I should blow your head off right now. Send a message to anyone else thinking of trying it.'

Adele frenziedly shook her head, not daring to speak. There was no doubt in her mind that the man meant it. His voice was full of conviction, and he'd broken into her house with little effort.

'What should I do with you?' he asked. She gasped, tears spilling down her cheeks.

'I'm sorry. They made me do it.'

'Doesn't matter now. We know where you are and how to get you.

More than that, we know where your whole family stays, including that mouthy sister of yours and her two kids. You want their blood on your hands?'

Adele shivered. 'No, please. I'm sorry. Please don't touch my family.'

The man paused, then flicked on her bedside lamp. His face was covered by a mask, and he wore all black. He pressed the gun to her head.

'Tomorrow, you're gonna contact the police and tell them you made up the story. You're gonna refuse to testify and if you do that, you're gonna get ten bags. More than that, you're gonna get to keep your life.'

'Thank you. I'm sorry,' Adele cried, overcome with fear mingled with relief.

'If you don't, I'm gonna kill your mum and dad. Then I'm gonna kill every member of your family that I can find. Even if the police move you, it won't matter. I'll get to all of them, and it'll be your fault. Understand?'

'I'll do it. Please, just don't touch my family.'

'Tomorrow,' the man repeated. 'Ring them first thing in the morning. Don't make me come back. The Feds can't protect you from me and my people.'

With that, he left, leaving Adele sobbing, the terror growing. She couldn't stop shaking. Despite their assurances of protection, the police had left her completely vulnerable, and a man had held a gun to her head while she was in her bed. As her tears grew louder and more frequent, Adele cried for her family, and for her friend Naomi.

* * *

Rigby made his way into work, pumped after three strong coffees. The last few days had been a medley of digging into the gang war and seeing what they could learn. He'd met with Terry, who had clued them in on the situation with Delroy and Lennox. Their other informants were parroting the same story. There had been deaths on both sides, including the murders of Winston and Eddie Williams. A man affiliated with *OurHood*, Malcolm Powell, had also been gunned down, though Rigby didn't understand the connection between an organisation like *OurHood*, and gangsters like the Williams' family.

There was a lot remaining to unpack, and Rigby still didn't understand how any of the above connected to Teflon, but he was determined to find out.

Sitting at his desk after nodding at his colleagues, he'd barely turned on his computer when Piers approached. Piers worked in admin and did a multitude of tasks for Reid and other supervisors. He was in his mid-twenties, with pointed facial features and a grating, nasally voice. Rigby disliked him and knew the feeling was mutual.

'Before you get set up, the boss wants to see you straight away. It's urgent.'

Rigby locked his computer, not even looking at Piers.

'Where is she?'

'In her office. Just knock and go in.'

Rigby clambered to his feet and headed to Reid's office. He began collating all the facts in his head in case she asked for an update on the gang war. He hadn't updated his paperwork yet, but with the facts he knew, it would be enough to get her off his back for a short while. After knocking and walking in, he waited for Reid to notice him. He didn't know how long she'd been in the office, but she looked alert and ready. An empty mug of coffee was on her desk along with a large water bottle, half-full, and a selection of paperwork that the very sight of gave him a headache.

'Good to see you, Rigby. Please have a seat.'

Rigby sat opposite her. She met his eyes with her steely own, but he matched her stare, refusing to let her intimidate him.

'Have you learned anything more about K-Bar?'

'I've focused on the gang war like you asked,' replied Rigby, frowning at her question. She had ordered him to get stuck into the war in Chapeltown. He wondered if there was something he had missed.

Reid nodded, as if he'd confirmed something she already knew.

'The girl recanted her story.'

Rigby's mouth fell open, heart leaping into his chest.

'What?'

'She called in first thing this morning and said she made the whole thing up.'

'No, ma'am. That's utter shite. She's involved. She knew key details about the set up, and the fact her friend Naomi had helped set up Xiyu Manderson, aka *Chink*, back in 2013. Someone got to her. Who has been watching her place?'

'I took the men off her place. We were short-handed on another case, and they were needed.'

'Why the hell would you do that? I told you she was a high-priority witness. She should have been watched twenty-four seven.' Rigby raked a hand through his hair.

'The decision was made based on the fact the case wasn't moving. K-Bar wasn't cooperating, and I and several others believed that the case wasn't strong enough to win at trial.'

'You didn't give me a chance to pressure him. You took me off the case, then sabotaged it by removing Adele Chapman's protection. If you hadn't, we'd have a result.'

'Watch your tone please, Detective Rigby. Remember, you are speaking to a superior officer.'

Rigby was disgusted. Reid's actions had led to the case collapsing, and she didn't even care.

'K-Bar will be released now, you realise that?'

Reid sighed, slowly nodding.

'His solicitor has been on the phone all morning, pushing for the charges to be dismissed. If there is no other evidence linking him to any crimes, we'll have to let him go.'

Rigby couldn't believe it. K-Bar was extremely dangerous. Him being back on the streets wouldn't help anyone, but there was nothing he could do.

'Do you have anything else you would like to add?' Reid asked. Rigby shook his head. There was nothing else they could link K-Bar to. Everything was all hearsay, with no strong evidence. He knew K-Bar was responsible for multiple murders, including Big-Kev's and Chink's, but there was no proof. He couldn't even bring himself to speak.

'I expect a report on the war by the end of the week. I have people breathing down my neck to know where we're at with it. I told them we had our best detective on it. Please don't prove me wrong.'

Rigby ignored the compliment and nodded, climbing to his feet and leaving the office. He wanted nothing more than to go outside and smoke a cigarette, but he wouldn't give Reid any reason to discipline him. Piers was still stood there, watching him with a smug look. Ignoring him, Rigby headed back to his desk, loading his computer. He'd cleared his emails and sorted his schedule for the day when Murphy approached. He had a face like thunder, and Rigby knew why.

'Nothing we can do, James,' he said. Murphy's eyes were blazing, his face almost puce. Rigby hoped he would stay calm and not fly off the handle. The last thing he needed was his partner being reprimanded, even if he agreed with his anger.

'They bloody took them off the house. It's like they wanted the case to get scuppered,' he hissed.

'We'll discuss it later. Her little parrot is watching us. Let's get cracking on this case for now.'

Murphy didn't like it, but he took a deep breath and nodded, taking a seat at his own desk. Satisfied, Piers went back to his own desk, and Rigby began typing up his reports. Now, more than ever, he needed to confirm the link between Teflon and the gang war.

With K-Bar's imminent release, there was a possibility that he would be involved, and that would allow Rigby the opportunity to catch him again. He would get Terry Worthy to keep his ear to the ground for any information regarding K-Bar and his activity.

CHAPTER ELEVEN

Wednesday 6 May 2015

RIGBY WAITED OUTSIDE as K-Bar was processed and released. It hadn't taken long for the motion to take place. Reid and the other bosses weren't bothered about setting a dangerous criminal free, and K-Bar's solicitor was making a lot of noise.

Soon, K-Bar was all smiles as he left the station with his solicitor. His smile only widened when he noticed Rigby. Sending his solicitor on, he stopped in front of the officer.

'I guess you finally realised I was innocent, right Detective Rigby?' he said, his voice oozing smugness. Rigby's fists clenched, but he kept his cool. He would not lose his job scrapping with a criminal like K-Bar.

'We both know what you are, Barrett. I don't care what you think you've escaped from, I'll be here, watching. I caught you once and I can catch you again.'

'If you say so, *boss*. Fact is, I told you I was innocent, and you didn't want to listen. Now, I'm free, so watch away.'

'When you slip up again, I'll be there. I want you to remember that, and I want your boss Teflon to know I am going to bring his entire operation crashing down around him.'

K-Bar nodded, unaffected by the declaration. 'Good luck, mate.

Stay in touch.' With another mocking grin, K-Bar slipped past Rigby and followed his solicitor. Rigby watched them go, growing angrier by the second. His superiors had fucked up on this one, and he felt completely impotent. He'd tried speaking with Adele and convincing her to tell her story. He had all-but promised he would guard her twenty-four seven, but it wasn't enough. Whoever warned Adele had done so thoroughly. There was no getting through to her.

Rigby watched K-Bar drive away, likely going to celebrate his release. He stared at the ground, closing his eyes for a moment. He needed to rise above this. There was still work to do, and if his hunch about this gang war was correct, he would be seeing K-Bar and the others soon enough. Confidence slightly restored, Rigby went back to work.

* * *

Lamont's time as a supplier had been plain sailing so far. Sales in Chapeltown were lower, but this had led to more traffic in other areas, meaning more profit was being made, regardless. He met with few customers, letting Ahmed and Mustafa handle most of it. They had working relationships with many of the customers. Every once in a while, he would go along to a meeting, but it was rare, and he didn't have to talk much. It gave him more time to focus on Lennox and his people. He had a few names of some low-ranked soldiers and workers, but no one major.

It worried Lamont how little the people he got to knew about the organisation. Nikkolo had been worked over by Akeem and others, and hadn't given up any information about Lennox's team. Lamont hoped that with Delroy turning the tide, it would make people open up and reveal more about the workings of the crew. He wondered if it was worth attempting to meet with Ken to learn more about *OurHood*. He was sure the group was key to unearthing Lennox's financial position, but hadn't ruled out the possibility someone could be funding Lennox. All he had at the moment was half-baked theories. He needed more substance.

Lamont was driving from a meeting with his business partner, Martin, when his phone rang. It was Ahmed.

'How are things?' Lamont said by way of greeting. Ahmed hadn't warmed to him anymore since the first meeting, and Lamont had done nothing to bridge the gap, remaining cordial. Mustafa was easier to get along with, meaning Lamont focused more on him.

'Good enough that we will need to put in an order soon.'

'Can we last another forty-eight hours?'

'I believe so. A few people are buying in bulk, especially in Halton Moor and Middleton. There's a lot of traction outside of Leeds as well.'

'I'll make the call tomorrow. You'll have what you need the day after.'

'Thank you.'

There was a brief, uncomfortable silence and Lamont sought to end it.

'Would you like to go to dinner?'

'Excuse me?'

'We're still not seeing eye-to-eye. If we're going to work well together, we need to try to get along.'

Lamont could almost hear Ahmed considering this.

'When?' He replied.

'Tonight.'

'I'm free.'

'Excellent. I'll text you some details. Speak to you later.' Lamont hung up, wondering if it was the right move. It wasn't essential to have Ahmed onside, but it would make things easier in the long run. Lamont was still annoyed at the fact he'd been denied access to the network. He had tried speaking with Mustafa again, but the man had nothing new to say.

Thankfully, Lamont's own attempts to build his personal network were coming along nicely. Several people had come forward, offering to look for information on Lennox and anyone else making waves on the streets. He hadn't heard from Maka or Manson lately, but that wasn't a concern. They had placed an order, and the money was still going to the people he had in place. The pair had impressed him, as had Darren

Lyles. Lamont would arrange for them to get a bonus for their hard work. Maybe giving Ahmed and Mustafa one would get them onside too. It was something else for him to consider.

* * *

That night, Lamont and Ahmed went for a curry in Bradford. Ahmed picked the spot and though Lamont wasn't a fan of curry, he had agreed. The restaurant had spotless white floors, with black tables and white and brown chairs. It was packed, but Ahmed was known and they had procured a nice table near the middle of the restaurant.

The beginning of the meal had been quiet. They ate their food, Lamont sipping his wine while Ahmed had water.

After a while, Lamont spoke.

'How am I doing?'

'Pardon?'

'With the organisation. The new role. You've been part of it far longer than me, so I'm curious to know your thoughts.'

'Why would you care?'

Lamont shrugged, forking a mouthful of food before replying once he'd chewed.

'I've been in the game a long time, and in my experience, things always run smoother when everyone is on the same wavelength.'

Ahmed seemed to accept this, but didn't hurry to respond. Lamont didn't mind. He was using the evening to gain the measure of the man, wanting to see if he could change his initial impression.

'You've done well. You've adapted quickly to the way we do things, and you haven't tried to micro-manage us.'

'Was that a concern of yours?'

Ahmed shrugged now.

'You and Mustafa both began working for the organisation at the same time.'

'Correct.'

'Before this, were you friends?'

'No. We both knew Saj, however. When Akhan was looking for reliable men, we were the first ones Saj brought into the fold.'

'I'm sorry about Saj.'

'Are you?' Ahmed's eyes were ice cold now.

'He was a good man. Unfortunately, he was loyal to someone who didn't have his best interests at heart.'

'That's not for you to say.'

'I think it is for me to say,' replied Lamont, slipping into his element. He had no headaches, aches, and pains or tiredness. Right now, he felt good, and was taking full advantage of this state of mind. 'Akhan and Saj tried to kill me, and they had no reason to do so.'

'You robbed them,' replied Ahmed. Lamont's eyebrow rose.

'Is it really a robbery, if your bosses ask for it to take place?'

Ahmed's eyes widened. He evidently hadn't expected him to say this. Lamont continued.

'Why else would I be here? Why would your bosses want Akhan removed? Do your organisation often promote black men to positions that have always been held by Asian men?'

'What are you trying to say?' Ahmed avoided the questions.

'Akhan brought a level of conflict to the surface that was deemed unacceptable, and that was the end of the road for him. Saj didn't have to go along with that. My question to you is where do you stand in all of this?'

'Trying to kill me too?'

'I'm trying to get to know you, Ahmed. I want us to work together in harmony as we have done so far, but without the tension.'

Ahmed didn't respond, and they finished their food in silence. Both men ordered dessert, and Lamont asked for another glass of wine.

'I think we can work together,' Ahmed finally said. 'You're right about a lot of the things you said. Saj was unflinchingly loyal to Akhan, even when he was wrong. If you are wrong, I will tell you. I won't blindly go along with everything you say, nor will I allow Mustafa to either.'

Lamont nodded. 'I can accept that.'

The conversation became fast-paced, and they spent their time talking about football. Ahmed was a die-hard Manchester United fan and Lamont had supported Leeds United his entire life. The tension slipped away the longer they spoke, and they were soon laughing like old friends. Lamont was under no illusions that everything was fixed, but over time, he would bring Ahmed around to his way of thinking. Mustafa would be pleased that the three of them could meet without friction, and that was enough for now.

'Are you married?' Lamont asked, when they'd grown tired of discussing football.

'I met my wife eight years ago, and we have been married for six years.'

'Kids?'

Ahmed shook his head. 'Soon. You?'

'No marriage. No kids.'

'Why not?'

'I guess I've never seen myself as marriage or parent material.'

Lamont could see Ahmed searching for a response to what he'd said, and grinned.

'I'm guessing you'd pick a boy over a girl?'

Ahmed returned the grin.

'I have seven brothers, so I relate more to boys than girls.'

They spoke for a while longer, drifting back to football and discussing some long term plans for the organisation. Lamont wondered if Ahmed had any access to the information network. He was presuming he did, but he would have to play it carefully if he was going to tap into it. If Jakkar learned of it, the consequences would be devastating.

'Mustafa will be pleased we've had a conversation. Next time, we'll have to invite him too.'

'If you do, be aware you will spend twice as much as you do tonight. He has a tremendous appetite, especially with curry.'

Lamont smirked. 'Maybe we'll expense it back to the company and call it a work dinner.'

Ahmed chuckled, and they finished their dessert. Lamont was tempted to get another glass of wine, but felt two was enough. He instead asked for water, along with the bill. The restaurant had a bar attached to it, and there were various people seated there. Lamont checked them out, noticing a group of attractive women laughing over a story one of them was telling. He instinctively looked around to see if they were attached to any men. He couldn't even explain why he had done it. One of the women turned and met his eyes.

She wore a black dress, with dark brown hair hanging past her shoulders, and she had dark, alluring eyes. They locked eyes for a moment, and she didn't look away. Taking another sip, Lamont returned his attention to Ahmed.

'Who is she?' Ahmed noticed Lamont's wavering attention.

'I don't know. She caught my eye.'

'I'm not surprised. She's stunning, as are her friends. What do you do in these situations?'

Lamont hadn't had to work for a woman's attention in a while, but certain skills never left a person.

'Depends what I want to happen.'

'I think she wants something to happen. Come, let's buy them some drinks and see where it takes us.'

Lamont shrugged. He wasn't eager to go along, but also liked the idea of appeasing Ahmed. They had made some ground in dealing with their issues, but if they were going to be working together for any concentrated length of time, they would need to stay on a positive level.

Maybe women would help them relax.

Lamont let Ahmed make the moves. He went straight for the high priced champagne, with orders to send it to the trio. The brunette was the most attractive of the three; the others both blonde, one taller and leggier than the other, who was curvier. A wave of anxiety shot over Lamont, like he was betraying Jenny's memory by even entertaining this. He took another sip of water, trying to force the thoughts away.

After the women accepted the drinks, Ahmed and Lamont invited them to come and sit at the table. The brunette ended up next to Lamont, giving him an understated smile.

'Thanks for the champagne.'

'Thank my friend there.' He held out his hand. 'Lamont.'

'Anna,' she replied, shaking it. Ahmed was already talking at length with the blondes, leaving Lamont to speak with Anna.

'You all appear extremely dressed up. Where's the night taken you so far?' He asked, getting right to the small-talk.

'It's Sarah's birthday.' Anna pointed to one of the blondes, but he didn't bother checking which. 'We decided we'd go out to celebrate, but the first place we went to was rubbish. What are you and your friend celebrating?'

'We're working together on a project, and we were laying down the groundwork,' said Lamont. Anna looked interested now.

'What sort of project?'

Lamont grinned. 'There are NDA's in place, I'm afraid. I wouldn't want to get sued for revealing the details.'

'That sounds interesting. You've made me curious, which I imagine was your intention,' said Anna. She smiled often, which Lamont found he enjoyed. Reaching out, he placed his hand over hers. It was a move he'd used in the past that he found helped to relax. As Anna leaned in, Lamont's mind skipped to Jenny, a twinge of guilt shocking his system. He pulled his hand away sharply.

'Are you okay?' Anna asked, her forehead creased with concern.

'I'm fine. I just went somewhere for a moment, but I'm back.'

'Are you sure?'

Lamont nodded. He'd slipped into charming mode for a moment, then the guilt had brought him back. There was an opportunity here. A woman he didn't know, who had no expectations of him. This was a chance to get his life back, and to crawl out of the pit of despair that overwhelmed him.

After some more conversation, he went for it.

'Would you like to get out of here?'

Anna gave him a surveying look.

'Are you going to make it worth my while?'

'That's certainly my intention,' Lamont replied, meeting her stare head-on. Smiling, Anna agreed. They hung out a while longer, then said their goodbyes, Lamont shaking hands with Ahmed, who winked at him. He wondered how his married subordinate was going to handle the two blondes, but that was on him. Lamont had done his part and now he was leaving.

* * *

Anna wasn't sure what made her go back to the house of the well-dressed black man she'd known for an hour. It wasn't the sort of thing she normally did, but something had drawn her to him. He was good looking and undoubtedly charming, but there was something behind his eyes that wasn't quite right. She couldn't put her finger on what, but it intrigued her. He was the type of guy she would assume was married, but there was no ring on his finger and the sprawling home he'd brought her back to had no signs of any female element. It was a quandary, to be sure.

The room they were currently in was a medley of dark browns, with Corinthian leather sofas and a luxurious coffee table and bookshelf. There was a drinks cabinet in the corner. Lamont approached it when she'd taken a seat.

'What are you drinking?' he asked.

'I'll have what you're having,' she replied. Lamont fixed them both a gin and tonic. He'd mixed it well, and she enjoyed the taste.

'Are you single?' he asked. Anna nodded.

'Trust me, I wouldn't have come back if I wasn't. Are you?'

There it was again. There was a haunted look for just a second, then it was gone.

'Yes, I am.'

'This is a lovely home,' she said, to avoid the silence that had crept over them. Lamont was like a different man than he'd been in the restaurant. He seemed less sure of himself, more strained. She didn't know what the cause was.

'Thank you. I've lived here for a few months.'

'Where did you live before that?'

'I lived in Adel.'

'Alone?'

'No, I lived with someone.' Lamont's tone was definitely different, and she suspected the *someone* he had lived with was long-gone, and that he wasn't over it.

'Can you tell me anymore about your job?'

'I'm a trader by day.'

'You must do well based on how you're living,' she said.

Lamont thought about that, and it made him wonder. To the

outside world, he had everything a person could want, *so why did he feel so unfulfilled?* He thought about Ken's question at Trinidad's funeral, when he'd asked Lamont if he was happy. *Was it money that defined him, or something else?*

'I guess I do,' he said. 'Tell me more about yourself.'

'Like I said, I work in the city centre. I'm a Data Protection Manager, and I enjoy it.'

'How did you get involved in that?'

'I was a team leader in a contact centre and I wanted a change, so I went for a position when it became available elsewhere. That was six years ago. I've been doing it ever since.'

'Let me ask you something else,' Lamont started. He seemed to have relaxed now from earlier. 'Do you often go home with strange guys you don't know?'

Anna grinned in response. 'I don't, but my friends have been telling me to take more chances.'

Lamont smiled back, but it was strained again. He didn't actually have any friends. He had people that worked with him, and people he associated with like Delroy. Shorty had been his best friend, but they weren't on good terms. He'd lost touch with a lot of the people he'd hung out with in his twenties, and a lot of them were mutual associates of Chink's. After his death, the relationships didn't seem the same.

He wasn't sure how he felt about any of it, but he was sure he should feel *something*, nor did he understand why these thoughts were parading through his mind now. Needing a distraction, he sat next to Anna. She seemed startled by the sudden change in proximity, but didn't back away.

'I'm happy you came back with me,' he said, drawing her in for a kiss. Anna allowed it for a few moments, then gently pulled back, gnawing her lower lip as she watched him. His heart sank at the thought of rejection. A moment dragged by, neither of them speaking. Anna hadn't taken her eyes from him, but after another beat, she returned the kiss, and Lamont deepened it as they snuggled into the sofa.

* * *

K-Bar followed Maka into the house, not knowing what to expect, as loud hip-hop music pumped from the speakers. They were on Francis Street, in a spot K-Bar recognised as a base for parties. When they entered the living room and he heard the cheers before he was doused in champagne, he was elated. The moment was electric, and it was a major sign for K-Bar that he was free. Shorty was there, along with Manson and Darren, among others. Shorty embraced his friend, patting him on the back.

'It's fucking good to see you out, K. For real.'

'It's good to be out, fam. Thanks for sorting that thing for me. I wasn't sure how it was gonna go down for a while, but you handled it.'

'You're my brother. I wasn't gonna leave you in there.'

They hugged again, then K-Bar greeted the others. The celebration continued. Maka called some girls to come over. K-Bar was polite to the ladies, but couldn't move without someone giving him another drink or a spliff to smoke.

Shorty watched his antics with a massive grin on his face. For him, tonight was a major sign things could get back to the way they had been.

He loved the atmosphere and enjoyed seeing people he'd come up with just kicking back and having fun. K-Bar had apparently had a hard time of it when he'd been in charge, but now he was back in his element, and everyone was enjoying the moment. Shorty felt whole with K-Bar watching his back again.

He'd discretely been putting the word out about Lennox, looking for information, but people weren't responding the way he wanted. Lennox's reputation carried more weight than his, and people seemed wary of crossing him. As hard as it was for Shorty to admit, he didn't have the same juice anymore, and that irked him.

Shanice had repeatedly tried contacting him, but he'd finally blocked her number and blocked her on Facebook. He wasn't sure Adele would have told her about the threats, and he didn't care. There was no way she could pin it to him, even if she had recognised his voice. Shanice was nice, but she had outlived her usefulness.

Amy came to his mind then, as he recalled how bad he'd felt for sleeping with Shanice. It wasn't something that had happened to him before, but he wasn't sure where his relationship with Amy was going. When she had coldly told him he wasn't going to see Grace anymore after the shooting, it had felt normal, and he hadn't fought it. After he'd confessed to killing Lutel, her behaviour toward him changed, and he didn't understand why. He was a murderer, and she knew it. *Why would she even want to be near him?*

Getting another drink, Shorty tried to lose himself in the surrounding conversations, not wanting to be overwhelmed by his thoughts.

'What's going on, anyway?' said K-Bar after a while. He'd gone outside to get some fresh air and after gulping down some water, felt better. 'Where's L?'

'I don't think he knows you're out,' said Maka. 'He hasn't really been around lately.'

'How come?'

'Who cares? He's not here, so forget him?' Snapped Shorty, cutting across the conversation. K-Bar cut his eyes to Maka, who appeared unruffled by Shorty's remark. He'd heard things were frosty between the pair, but hadn't known it was so bad.

'What the hell happened with you two?' K-Bar asked Shorty.

'Doesn't matter. We're not cool, and that's that.'

For anyone else, it would have worked. Few people liked being on Shorty's bad side. K-Bar had known him too long to be worried.

'Shorty, just tell me what's going on. There was no point springing me if you're gonna leave me in the dark.'

Shorty shot K-Bar a sour look, but K-Bar glanced back blankly, waiting.

'We had a fight. A proper one. We've argued and come close to fighting before, but this was different. If Akeem hadn't stepped in, one of us would have ended up seriously hurt, maybe even dead. I never thought that would happen.'

'Brother's fight, Shorty. Move on.' Secretly, K-Bar was shocked that the pair had fought. For years, they had a knack for pushing one another's buttons, but it never led to trouble. This was different, and it was worrying.

Shorty kissed his teeth, not replying. Maka saw the mood changing and switched the subject.

'Darren said Roman's doing well. Aaron's people have settled in nicely too and they're not making any trouble.'

'What about Aaron?' replied Shorty. 'Has anyone heard from him.'

'Not since we smacked him around and dumped him in the middle of nowhere. He's dumb, but not dumb enough to come after us by himself.'

'There are plenty of other little knucklehead crews nipping at our heels. This shit with Lennox has made some crews proper brazen. They seem to think they can step up to us now.'

'Let me get out there,' said K-Bar. He wanted to prove to the crew he was still worth something after being on remand. Shorty shook his head.

'Lay low, K. We can handle the street stuff for now. Let the pigs lose your scent, then you can get back out there.'

CHAPTER TWELVE

Thursday 7 May 2015

WHEN LAMONT AWOKE the next day, he winced, his head pounding as he glanced to his side. Anna was awake and looking at him, which he didn't like. Even the fact she was naked didn't sway him. Waking up with headaches was a regular thing nowadays, whether or not he'd been drinking. It made him irritable. Anna was still staring. She didn't look pleased.

'Do you want a coffee?' he muttered, sitting up and rubbing his forehead. Whatever answer he expected, he wasn't prepared for the one he received.

'Who's *Jenny?*'

It was as if someone had poured ice cold water down Lamont's back. He flinched, looking away from her as he climbed out of bed. His eyes flitted around the room, wondering if she'd gone through his things while he was asleep, before remembering he had nothing with Jenny's name on.

'You said her name in your sleep,' said Anna, realising he wouldn't respond. 'Multiple times. I thought you were single?'

'I am.'

'I don't believe you, Lamont, if that's even your name. I don't believe you're a trader, so who knows what else you've lied about. Was it worth lying to try and sleep with me?'

'I don't want to talk about it,' said Lamont, leaving the room. He stormed downstairs and through to the kitchen, splashing his face with cold water from the sink before he put the kettle on.

'What the hell was that, Lamont? Why would you walk out in the middle of a conversation?'

'I didn't want to talk about it. I still don't.'

'You don't think I deserve to know about the woman in your life after you tried sleeping with me last night? Guess that's why you couldn't get it up.'

'What part of *I don't want to talk about it* don't you understand?' snapped Lamont. He didn't want to think about Jenny while he had another woman in his house. Anna's eyes flashed with anger, but he didn't care. He was rattled and couldn't believe he'd said Jenny's name in his sleep. It was twisted on a whole new level.

'You're scum, Lamont. Don't contact me again.'

'Get the fuck out of my house,' said Lamont coldly. Anna stood her ground a moment, then after another look of disgust, flounced from the room and stomped upstairs to get her things. Nausea bubbling in his stomach, Lamont hurried to the downstairs bathroom just in time. He emptied the contents of his stomach into toilet until he was heaving, drawing in deep breaths.

Somewhere in the background, he heard the front door slam, but didn't move. The bodyguards would take care of her. He stayed hunched over the bowl for another few minutes, then shakily climbed to his feet. Forgoing the coffee, he headed upstairs and stood under the shower for as long as he could cope. His head was still banging and he wanted nothing more than to crawl back into bed. He had an afternoon of meetings though, and needed to be sharp. Rubbing his forehead once more, he went to get dressed.

* * *

'You ready?'

K-Bar turned to Shorty as they pulled up outside Marika's. He hadn't told her he was getting out so quickly, and Shorty had taken advantage of that by organising the party the previous night. After they woke up in the morning, Shorty took K-Bar to get his dreads tightened up, then for breakfast. It was Marika's day off from work, so she would be in, but the kids would be at school.

'Course I'm ready. Rika held me down when I was inside. She's a keeper.'

'I'm surprised L left you breathing after you started banging his little sis.'

K-Bar scowled. 'Don't talk about her like that, fam. This is serious.'

'Okay man, calm down. Marika's cool. L's just proper protective over her.'

'He was. They fell out remember? Not sure they ever really made their way back from that.'

Shorty didn't say anything. He couldn't. He and Lamont were basically going through the same thing.

'Come on. Let's get in there,' he finally said. They climbed from the car and K-Bar tried the door, but it was locked. Kissing his teeth, he knocked.

When Marika opened the door and saw K-Bar, her eyes widened and she flung her arms around him. His heart soared. She was as beautiful as ever, and fit nicely against him. They hugged for a few minutes, then started kissing. Shorty cleared his throat when it seemed they had forgotten about him.

'Save all that shit for after I'm gone,' he said.

'Shut up, Shorty.' Marika gave him a hug too. 'I'm guessing you're the reason I didn't see K last night?'

'He needed a night with the boys, and we didn't want to disturb the kids. Is everything good?'

'Everything is perfect now.' Marika gave K-Bar an adoring smile, Shorty pretending to vomit. Soon, they were all sitting in the garden with cups of tea.

'Does L know you're out?'

'Unless my solicitor or someone else told him, I doubt it.'

Marika frowned. 'What's going on?'

'I don't know,' said K-Bar. 'I'm still getting my head around things, but it doesn't appear he's with it at the moment.'

'Of course he isn't. Look at everything he's been through lately.' Marika noticed Shorty looking away with a scowl. 'What aren't you telling me?'

'Shorty and L aren't speaking,' said K-Bar, playing with his cup.

'Why would you fall out now of all times? You need each other. Can't you squash it?'

'It's not that simple, said Shorty, feeling he had repeated those words more in the past week than he had in his life.

'Course it is. He needs you, Shorty. This isn't the time to be falling out.'

'Says you,' replied Shorty. 'How many years did it take for you two to speak after you fell out?'

'That's different. He got shot, Shorty, or did you forget?'

'Look, both of you calm down,' interjected K-Bar, as Shorty opened his mouth to retort. 'We don't need to be fighting amongst ourselves right now. We'll deal with L soon, I promise. I need to meet see him, anyway.'

Marika nodded, satisfied.

'He must be fucked up over what happened to Trinidad too. Lamont looked up to him.'

Shorty lowered his head a moment, remembering his harsh words to Lamont at the gravesite.

'*OurHood* fucked L up. It's like they turned the whole Hood against him,' said K-Bar.

'Someone needs to do something,' replied Marika, hands on hips. 'He's obviously in a bad way. He hasn't even been to see the kids lately.'

Shorty quietly listened to the pair talk, and he liked the way they looked together. Marika had always been a handful, but she seemed different around K-Bar. More composed. For someone who knew her as a bratty teen, it was nice to see her as a grown up. She even dressed differently. More understated, less tight and revealing clothing.

Analysing them as a couple stopped him thinking about Lamont, and the guilt that occasionally slipped through. He slipped his mind to business, and all the work they still had to do in the crew. He didn't have to be cool with Lamont to use his resources.

* * *

Lamont still felt ropey even after he finished getting ready. Anna's departure had messed with his already precarious mindset. Sex was something Lamont always knew he could perform. He had a way with women and he parlayed that into getting what he wanted from them, but if last night showed him anything, he'd lost his mojo, and that made him feel sick. He didn't want to go out and sleep with every woman on the planet, especially with how he was feeling, but at the very least, wanted to know he could.

As he left the house, he tried to put the events into perspective. He'd drunk some wine, but not enough to influence his performance. He trained and worked out, and he was in his thirties. He couldn't think of a single reason behind his *malfunction*, and that irked him.

Lamont's bodyguard's fell in step as they headed for the car. None mentioned Anna, and he didn't ask.

Ahmed and Mustafa were at the warehouse when he arrived. Ahmed gave him a knowing smile, a far cry from the usual scowls he received. Clearly their talk had done him some good.

'How was your night with Anna?' he asked, his eyes glinting. Lamont shrugged.

'I don't remember much of it. Don't think I'll be seeing her again.'

'That's too bad. You two looked good together.'

'How are we looking for today?' Lamont changed the subject. 'The load comes in tomorrow, so I'm assuming we'll be ready?'

Ahmed nodded. 'The people are already in place, and the load will come first thing in the morning. One of Saj's old contacts contacted us today, and he wants five boxes of dark. Also, your representative, Maka, put in an order for eight boxes. Business must be improving.'

'Must be,' agreed Lamont. It was the largest order his crew had put in for a while, and he wondered what the change was. There was the possibility they had moved into some fresh territory, but it didn't matter. It meant more money for him. Maka and co didn't know about the role he'd taken, and he saw no reason to share it with them. As far as they were concerned, the *Asians* were supplying them, and that was still the case.

He spent a while talking business with Ahmed and Mustafa, then went to get some lunch at a nearby sandwich shop. He was finishing up when Marika called.

'Hey sis. What's wrong?'

'Why does something have to be wrong for me to want to speak with my brother?'

Lamont gave her that one. He and Marika were still finding their way back, and he hadn't reached out much lately. They had reconnected at Jenny's funeral, but even that seemed like it was years ago rather than months.

'Sorry, you're right.'

'I wanted to see how you were.'

'I'm fine.'

'K's been asking about you.'

'When did you see him?'

There was an awkward pause.

'K's out. He got out yesterday.'

Lamont was shocked. The last time he'd spoken with his solicitor about K-Bar, they were putting a case together to have his case dismissed due to lack of evidence. Due to the reports of a witness, it was proving more difficult than expected.

What the hell had he overlooked?

'How did that happen?'

'Probably best we don't speak about it on the phone.'

'My phone is encrypted, sis. The CIA couldn't trace this call, never mind anyone else.'

'Still, I'd rather speak with you face to face. Come over later, spend some time with me and the kids. They miss you.'

'I'll come over this evening.' Lamont said goodbye and hung up.

K-Bar was out, and it was clear someone had done some work behind the scenes to facilitate that. He assumed they'd learned who the witness was and taken action, and wasn't sure how he felt about that. K-Bar murdering Naomi had been bad enough, but that was during a hectic time, and no one knew what was happening next. He would need to catch up with him and get the full story.

Anxiety churned within Lamont. The world was moving on

without him, and he felt sick over that. Nothing was going the way he wanted. He had elevated to a new level of power, but that same power had been neutered because of a war that ultimately had little to do with him. If Lennox hadn't gone after Shorty, Lamont would have never become involved in his business. Jenny would also still be alive, but he filed those thoughts away for the evening, where he would have liquor. There was nothing to be done about these things now, so he focused on what he could control. He had another person to see.

* * *

Jukie's was a mainstay in the Hood. There were many gambling spots dotted around, but Jukie's was the most well-known and respected. It was still early, but it would be open. Unless the police had shut him down, Jukie operated twenty-four hours a day and always had something going on.

Lamont headed to his spot and entered, hit immediately by the stench of body odour, hastily masked with cheap air spray. There were a few mainstays in the main room, but all the action was likely in the back rooms.

Jukie was behind the bar, humming along to a song on the radio. He perked up when he saw Lamont, grinning at him. Even knowing that Jukie was neutral in most things that went down in Chapeltown, Lamont felt a surge of relief to see someone in the Hood who didn't immediately vilify him. Heading closer to the bar, Lamont firmly shook his hand.

'Good to see you, L.'

'You too, Juke. Business good?'

'Some people are staying away because of the police, but that can't be helped. Saw you at Trinidad's funeral. I was gonna say hello, but you looked preoccupied.'

Lamont nodded, accepting that. *Preoccupied* was a polite way of putting it. He had publicly argued with Trinidad's family and embarrassed himself.

'It was a tough day.'

'Truly. Trinidad was a great man. What happened to him shouldn't have happened.'

'Agreed.' Lamont bowed his head. Jukie rested his hand on Lamont's shoulder.

'It wasn't your fault, L. You need to understand that.'

'My enemies went after him to get to me. I don't see how that isn't my fault.'

'The only person to blame is the one responsible for the fire, L. You didn't do that. I can see you're not listening though, and I doubt you came here to look at my old face, so how can I help?'

'Lennox Thompson.'

Lamont appreciated Jukie didn't immediately play dumb and pretend not to understand what he was implying.

'Lennox's people don't really stay around the Hood, and they definitely don't come around here. Last one that did got beaten with a stool by Shorty. You need to look outside the Hood if you want to find something.'

'Do you know where I should start?'

Jukie shook his head. 'If I hear anything, I'll pass it on, but people are keeping their heads down. Delroy and Lennox are playing for keeps and no one wants to get caught in the middle of that.'

It was a fair statement and was exactly the sort of thing Lamont would expect from Jukie. He reached into his pocket and laid a stack of notes on the bar.

'You don't need to do that, L. I didn't even give you anything,' Jukie protested.

Lamont shook his head. He respected Jukie, and knew the feeling was mutual. The old man didn't play sides, but he knew and liked Lamont, and they had always looked after one another.

'Keep the money, Juke. Keep me in the loop if you hear anything.'

'I will, L. Thank you.'

CHAPTER THIRTEEN

Saturday 9 May 2015

Bronson zipped down Harehills Avenue, turning onto Spencer Place and nearly running over a kid crossing the road.

'Watch where you're going, you little shit,' he roared over the sounds of the Drill music pumping from his speaker. Taking another turn onto Francis Street, he screeched to a stop and hopped from the car, an imposing square-headed figure in his red designer tracksuit, standing over six feet tall, with a powerful build to match. His baby mother and sometimes girlfriend, Ella, was waiting, and he hoped she had food because he was starving. He was so preoccupied that he didn't see the masked man until it was too late. The blow crunched against his jaw and Bronson hit the ground hard. Dazed, he saw the blur of a weapon, then heard the bang and felt the searing pain as a bullet tore into his left shin.

'Keep your fingers to yourself, or next time you're dead,' warned Shorty. Stepping over the bleeding man, he hurried to his car, which sped away. A few streets away, the car stopped, and Shorty wiped down the pistol, before dumping it down a drain. They drove to Bankside and Shorty's luck was in. There was no one standing outside the spot he was visiting. He took off the mask, stowed another pistol, then approached. He banged on the door.

'Shorty? What are you doing around here?'

'Just came to talk business. Is Dex in?'

The man at the door clearly didn't want to let Shorty in, but he also didn't want to be rude, so he stepped aside and led Shorty into the living room. Two men were there, cracking jokes as they played a game of *Fifa*. One of them, a freckled mixed-race man with reddish brown hair, looked up, paling when he saw Shorty.

'Shorty, what the hell?'

Shorty pulled his gun and smacked the man that had answered the door in the side of the head. He crumpled to the floor and Shorty held the gun on the others.

'I'm here to warn you, Dex. Once and once only; pack it up.'

'What are you talking about? What are we supposed to have done?' The freckled man replied.

'You thought you could badmouth Teflon and get away with it. I'm back now, and old rules apply. You took a few customers, made more money, but now things are back to normal. Buy from our people, or you're out of business. Same deal as that little shit Aaron. What are you saying?' His finger tightened on the trigger. Both men had been around long enough to know Shorty didn't play when he had a gun in his hand.

'We're in. We'll buy from you lot.'

'That's a good choice. Put the word out that I'm back around. I don't care what people think they heard about the crew. We're taking back what's ours. You lot can go back to your game, but you might wanna get some help for your boy there.'

Shorty left, his work done for the day. He had put the fear of God in a few crews to show that no matter what was going on with Delroy and Lennox, these were still his streets, and they were still the best game in town.

Bronson was the most brazen. He'd attempted to muscle in on one of their spots, subtly thinking he could intimidate the workers into working for him. Dex was a small-timer who'd tried increasing his clientele at the expense of their crew.

The gloves were well and truly off, and word would spread throughout the Hood.

* * *

Rigby leant against his car in a parking lot in Seacroft, waiting for Terry Worthy to show. He'd left Murphy behind. He was back at the office, digging into what they had unearthed about the gang war. There were over a dozen murders they had tied to the conflict, including the death of Teflon's girlfriend, and the shooting of Shorty Turner's little girl. If they had attempted to shoot back, Rigby couldn't find the link.

All the attacks were being orchestrated by Lennox and Delroy. Rigby couldn't get a line on either of them, not that it would do any good at this stage. Both men were well-trained in the ways of the street and knew better than to blatantly give orders or hold guns where people could see them. Rigby would have to wade through at least a dozen ranks to get close to Delroy in particular. He hoped Terry was taking his orders seriously.

Terry soon arrived in his Audi. Sliding from the driver's seat, he gave Rigby a cocky smile.

'Nice to see you again, chief.'

'I take it by your smiling face you have some news for me?'

'I'm still working on the gang stuff. People haven't seen Teflon around lately, and they're saying it's because he's going directly after Lenny Thompson.'

'Is that because his girl got knifed?'

'Probably. That and the barber getting roasted. Tef was proper close to Trinidad Tommy. Looked at him like a dad. Used to keep his office there and everything, probably so he could monitor him.'

'We know about the office,' said Rigby. He'd tried getting a warrant to search the place on multiple occasions, but had no probable cause. There were never any incidents on the premises, and Trinidad had been a mainstay in the community. Suddenly, Lamont being outside the barbers on the day of the two deaths didn't seem like such a coincidence. 'What are people saying about Teflon's connection to the death, or to the death of the man who was shot next to him?'

'Nowt, really. Akeem was building a nice rep as a bodyguard.'

'In what sense?'

Terry shrugged. 'He was just capable, know what I mean? That kinda thing always makes people feel safe.'

'We know he was connected to some gangs in London. Any chance any of them are gonna come up here kicking up a fuss?'

'Doubt it. Teflon always had links down there. He has links everywhere.'

Rigby was aware of this, and it was part of the reason Teflon had always worried him. He made money for everyone he dealt with and was practised at staying out of reach. He had tidy relations with a lot of firms, but this seemed to have soured as of late. If Teflon was smart, he would dedicate time to rebuilding these relationships. Another of Rigby's worries was the street conflict overshadowing whatever moves Lamont could be making behind the scenes. He needed to get to the bottom of things as soon as he could.

'What do you have for me then?'

'I know that K-Bar and the lads had a fucking celebration. I wasn't invited, but they invited some lasses around and made a night of it.'

'Why do I care?' said Rigby, running a hand through his hair. Truth was, he did care. It still made him sick that K-Bar had taken advantage of clear disharmony within the police department, and had got himself free of his potential sentence.

'Dunno, figured you locked him up, and that you might care. He doesn't know I'm helping you lot, does he? K-Bar's a fucking psycho when he wants to be. I don't want him coming after me.'

'I'm not Murphy. I don't threaten you with someone killing you. I threaten you with you spending half your life behind bars for the sale of drugs. All jokes aside, Terry; I need more information from you. I want to know who the main killers are on each team, and where to find them.'

'How the bloody hell am I supposed to find out all that?' Terry was aghast. Rigby had no sympathy. He didn't dislike Terry, but he didn't think he was taking the potential threat of prison seriously.

'Work it out. You either help me solve this gang war, or you get us some serious dirt on your crew. I'm talking enough dirt to lock up everyone. The choice is yours.' Rigby didn't even wait for Terry to reply. He climbed back in his car and drove away.

* * *

'Finally, you're here.'

Lamont gave his sister a tight smile and stepped past her into the house. They'd spoken on the phone two days ago, and in that time she hadn't heard from him.

'Sorry. Things came up.'

'It's fine. Better late than never. Go on through, and I'll bring you a hot drink.'

Lamont's niece, Bianca, sat in the middle of the living room, her eyes glued to the television — some goofy show on *Nickelodeon*. She was a smaller version of her mother, but her eyes were darker and her facial features more rounded. When she saw Lamont, she jumped to her feet and ran into his arms.

'Uncle L! You came?'

'Hello, Princess Bianca. How've you been?'

Lamont was made to sit with his niece, and had to pretend to be interested in the show, as Bianca babbled and explained the characters. She curled up next to him, refusing to move even after Marika brought Lamont's drink. Showing great skill, he was able to drink it without spilling any on her.

'I missed you,' she mumbled, after he'd finished and put his cup on the nearby coffee table. Despite everything, this made Lamont smile, and he felt his heart soar. He pulled his niece closer and kissed the top of her head.

'I missed you too. Even when I'm not here, know you're always on my mind, okay?'

Bianca nodded, eyes on her show.

'How come you don't have any kids, Uncle L?' She asked, a few minutes later.

Lamont had figured Bianca to be distracted by her show, and the question stunned him for a moment.

'I don't know, baby. Guess I never figured I would be any good at being a dad.'

'I think you would make a good daddy,' she said, not even turning to look at him. Lamont blinked, feeling oddly emotional after the short conversation. He didn't agree with her. The idea of being responsible for a person he'd created just didn't seem natural to him. With all the issues he had, it wouldn't be fair.

He loved his niece all the more for her attempt to make him feel better, and showed this by clutching her tightly until she giggled and tried to get loose.

Marika watched Lamont and Bianca together, a small smile on her face. This was the reason she'd wanted Lamont to come and see her. She knew Bianca could make him feel better. She had him wrapped around her little finger just like Shorty's daughter Grace did, and he couldn't say no to either of them.

Marika felt guilt for the fallout with Lamont. She had stupidly listened to Marrion and fallen for his manipulations, escalated by their fight after Marcus died. It was mostly behind them now, but they were nowhere near as close as they once were, and seemed to walk on eggshells around each other.

He seemed so different when it was him and Bianca. Unguarded, almost. It was amazing to see, and she didn't want to disturb their time together.

K-Bar and Shorty were out doing something. She didn't know what, and hadn't asked. She'd only told K-Bar to make sure he stayed out of trouble. It would be easier said than done. He was even tempered, but seemed to get caught up in various situations. Shorty and his temper would only escalate that further if it came to it.

K-Bar hadn't spoken with Lamont yet, but they needed to, and soon. Marika wanted things back to normal and hoped K-Bar could bridge the obvious gulf between Shorty and Lamont.

Soon enough, Bianca fell asleep against Lamont, and he carried her upstairs. After waking her so she could go to the toilet, and helping her brush her teeth, he carried the sleepy girl to her bed, and sat with her until she fell asleep. By the time he made it back downstairs, another cup of tea waited for him.

'You timed that well,' he said to Marika.

'It was a lucky guess. I would have microwaved it for you if it went cold.'

'Thank you, anyway.' Lamont sipped the drink and took his seat back on the sofa. Marika had already changed the channel, and was watching the evening news.

'Since when do you watch the news?' he asked, grinning.

'Sometimes it's just good to know what's going on,' Marika replied, lowering the volume and facing her brother. Bianca had revitalised him a little, but he still looked tired. There were visible bags under his eyes, and every so often he would stifle a yawn. Clearly he wasn't getting much sleep.

'I guess so.'

'What's been going on?' she asked.

'Nothing.'

'You look like hell.'

'Thanks. I love you too.'

'I mean it, L. What's going on? Is it Jenny?' she watched Lamont's face blanch at the mention of his former partner.

'I wish that wouldn't happen,' he mumbled.

'What?'

'Anytime someone says her name, I get this jolt, and it's like a fresh reminder she's gone. I just wish I was over it.'

'Why?'

'Why do you think? I'm here and she isn't, and I have it weighing me down along with everything else. If she hadn't met me; if I hadn't pursued her, she would still be alive, and I have to live with that.'

'You weren't responsible for her death, L. No one blames you.'

'*I* blame me, Rika. I should have protected her, and Trinidad. They were innocents in this shit, and I let them die, so that is on me.'

'Jenny wouldn't want you to wallow. Neither of them would.'

'You can't say that.'

'Course I can. I knew them both. Maybe not as well as you did, but still. Jenny loved you, and she knew what you were. Trinidad did too. What happened to them wasn't your fault.'

Lamont didn't want to talk about it. He wanted to push it all away and put it behind him. His encounter with Anna still lingered, leaving a bad taste in his mouth. He should have never invited her back to his house, or attempted to sleep with her. Now, the guilt lingered with the failure of not being able to *perform*. It was a confusing mindset, that was for sure.

'I don't want to argue with you, but you're gonna calm down soon and realise that I'm right. I'm making some food, and you're staying for dinner. K-Bar should be back soon, and he'll want to see you.'

Lamont could have pointed out that K-Bar had been out a few days and hadn't looked him up, but it wasn't important. He hadn't eaten all day and if there was one thing he knew about his little sister, it was the fact that she could truly cook.

By the time K-Bar entered, Lamont had finished his dinner and was on his third cup of tea.

'L, my bro. It's good to see you.' He had a wide smile on his face as they slapped hands. Lamont stood, and they properly greeted one another, hugging like brothers. Marika smiled at the camaraderie between the two most important men in her life.

'You too, K. You look healthy.'

'I kept my head down in there. Wasn't sure how it was gonna go, but I wasn't gonna lose my shit over it.'

Lamont nodded like he had experience dealing with prison. K-Bar took a seat and a few minutes later, Marika put a plate of food in front of him. The three of them stared at the television in silence, waiting for K-Bar to finish. When he did, Marika took his plate despite his protests.

'You two talk. I need to wash up anyway.'

'How have you been?' asked K-Bar after a few moments.

'You're the one that was locked up,' said Lamont.

'Like I said, I kept my head down. I'm sorry about Trinidad and Jen.'

Lamont nodded, swallowing down the lump in his throat. He didn't want to show weakness in front of K-Bar. K-Bar seemed to understand and didn't press the issue. They weren't as close as K-Bar and Shorty, but Lamont had always been able to sit quietly with him, and it was a nice distinction he'd always enjoyed.

'How did you get out?' Lamont asked after a moment.

'Got a message to Shorty through my solicitor. Worked out where the Feds were getting their information from, and I sent Shorty to handle it.'

'Who was the leak?'

'Do you remember Adele? Party girl who was always around town?'

Lamont shook his head.

'You'd know her if you saw her. Anyway, she was the missing link. After the Chink shit and then your shooting, we kinda forgot about her.'

Lamont didn't understand how you could forget about a potential witness, but he'd nearly died during that timeframe. K-Bar had stepped up out of necessity, so Lamont grudgingly accepted it.

'Did Shorty hurt her?'

'Nah. Just words and a bribe. He was on some *007* shit. He used to grind her sister back in the day. Ended up getting in touch with her, sweet-talking her into bed, and then following her to the spot where Adele was staying.'

'If she was a witness, why wasn't she under surveillance?' Lamont was silently impressed with Shorty's actions.

'Who knows? I'm not overthinking it. He got word to her anyway, and she told the police she lied. Next minute I'm out.'

'I'm glad, K. I don't want it to seem like I was neglecting you. Levine was looking into it, and if it came to court, he was confident you wouldn't be convicted. Just be careful.'

'Don't worry, L. I know how to stay low key. You don't need to feel guilty either. These things happen, and it wasn't anything you did that got me caught. I know you would have sprung me like you did Shorty.' K-Bar's expression softened. 'What happened with you two?'

'We both said things and shit got out of control.'

'You'll find your way back to where you were.'

'Do you need anything now that you're out? We have a package for you.'

'Maka already sorted it. Thanks for looking after me.'

'You're part of the team,' said Lamont, realising once again just how out of the loop he was. Thankfully, Maka and the others were all operating at a higher frequency and making up for his lack of attentiveness.

'Still, it's appreciated.'

'Have you spoken to Fiona?'

Some of the light in K-Bar's eyes seemed to dissipate at the mention of his baby mother.

'I tried to see Dwayne yesterday, but she wasn't having any of it. Threatened to call police on me if I didn't leave, so I'm keeping my distance for now.'

'Probably for the best,' Lamont agreed. Fiona was a pleasant woman with a vicious streak, and things had never been plain sailing for her and K-Bar. He could see her using his son against him as a way of keeping him compliant.

'Streets are hot at the moment. Del's making some moves against Lennox. I'm surprised you're not doing the same.'

Lamont didn't see the need in mentioning his current plans to K-Bar.

'Delroy's handling it.'

'I'm surprised Shorty is being calm, after Lennox popped Grace.'

'Shorty's had to do a lot of growing up lately.'

'I just need to get you two back on the same level now. There are some little crews that are talking shit and trying to nibble away at the team. Anyone said anything to you?'

'They can handle things without me,' said Lamont.

'What are you doing in the meantime? I know you. You've always got a plan.'

'I'm playing things quiet at the moment, K. I don't need to remind you to do the same, right?'

'Right.'

K-Bar continued to discuss street politics, but Lamont tuned out. It didn't interest him at the moment. Soon, K-Bar went to sit with Marika when she'd finished washing up. Lamont watched the pair of them cuddling, as he relaxed on the sofa, his eyes growing heavy. He was asleep before he had even realised what had happened.

'Looks like he needed that.'

K-Bar and Marika were watching Lamont sleep, as he softly snored.

'He looks wrecked, Rika. If I didn't know better, I'd think he was on drugs.'

'Not drugs necessarily. Drink maybe. It's been hard for him, like I told you lot the other day. He's clearly not operating at one hundred percent. I think he should speak with someone about his issues.'

'Someone like a therapist?'

Marika nodded.

'L doesn't need to speak to a therapist. He's the strongest guy I know. Give him some time, and I bet you he'll bounce back from all of this shit.' K-Bar hugged Marika against him, planting a kiss on her lips. She returned it, but deep down, she wasn't as convinced as K-Bar. Lamont was in a bad way, and she didn't think it would get better without something drastic happening.

CHAPTER FOURTEEN

Monday 11 May 2015

LAMONT WINCED as he woke up. It was morning, he was curled up on Marika's sofa, and his phone was ringing. Sitting up, he realised she'd put a blanket over him while he was sleeping. He wished she'd woken him up and sent him home, but it was too late to think about that now. Reaching for his phone, he cleared his throat and answered.

'Hello?'

'L, it's Jukie. Did I wake you?'

'No, it's fine. Everything okay?'

'That thing we were discussing the other day. I might have a lead. I heard some people talking about a few of Lennox's guys going in and out of a spot on Jackie Smart Court. Not sure if they're planning a move or if it's a stash spot, but I thought you should know.'

'Thanks a lot, Jukie.' Lamont was on his feet now, aches and fatigue forgotten. 'What's the address? I'll take care of you for this.'

After hanging up, Lamont headed to the kitchen to make a drink and freshen up. This was potentially a tip he had been waiting for. Jukie had previously said that Lennox's people didn't stick around the Hood for fear of detection. If they were changing up their pattern, Lamont could figure it out and use it to track down Lennox.

He was washing up his empty mug when Marika entered the

kitchen. Her hair was still wet from a recent shower, but she was dressed in a shirt and smart trousers.

'Take it you're working today?' he asked. Marika nodded.

'I finish at two. Bianca will be up in a minute so I can get her ready for school. How are you feeling?'

'I'm fine.'

Marika gave him a quizzical look. 'You said you were fine yesterday, but you passed out on my sofa and wouldn't wake up.'

'I was tired, I'm sorry. I'll sleep at my place next time.'

'That's not the point and you know it,' replied Marika, sighing. 'Look, hang around for a bit and I'll make you some breakfast. At least I'll know you've had one good meal today.'

* * *

Shorty was in the kitchen at Amy's. He had come early so they could visit Grace, and was cooking breakfast. Shorty's purging of the streets had been flawless so far. He had pacified Aaron, Bronson and several other crews, and had changed the perception of how the other crews looked at Lamont's organisation.

The money was creeping back up and Shorty had taken advantage, having Grace moved to a private healthcare facility. Lamont's links were wizards when it came to moving money around and making it legit, though Shorty had no idea how they did it. Not willing to forget about Dionte, he sent money to Stacey in Huddersfield. He hoped they were safe, and wondered if it was worth the risk.

'What are you thinking so hard about?' Amy entered the kitchen, stunning in a green t-shirt and black peasant skirt. Shorty checked the eggs he was cooking, and decided to be honest.

'I was thinking about Stace and Dionte. Now that we've sorted Grace. Maybe you should get out of town for a bit, just until things blow over.'

Amy shook her head. 'I want to stay close by in case Grace needs me. Are you really that nervous something will happen?'

'Things are going on out there, Ames. They're not just gonna go away because I'm happy and our daughter is getting better.'

'Make sure you look after us then.' Amy winked, then went to get the plates and cutlery ready for the breakfast.

'Is there an *us* then?' he asked a while later, when they were finishing. The facility had more flexible visiting times, but they wanted to spend as much time with Grace as possible. Amy's face reddened at the implication.

'I think there might be something. I've always cared about you but in the past, it never seemed we were on the same wavelength. Now, we might be.'

'What are we gonna do about it then?' said Shorty, his heart racing. 'I still want you. I've always wanted you.'

'You always wanted sex, Shorty. Don't get it twisted.'

'This is deeper than that.'

Amy looked away. 'It might be. I won't deny that. I don't think we should talk about it yet.'

'Why wait? We're both here now, so let's break it down.'

'Shorty, I just said I don't want to talk about it yet. Please respect that and let's go see our daughter,' said Amy waspishly. Shorty decided he would drop it for now, but would definitely revisit the subject. He still didn't understand what had changed other than Amy knowing the lengths he had gone to in order to avenge what had happened to Grace. It was weird to think that fact alone might have completely changed how she felt about him. He stayed quiet, waiting for her to get ready. She stood in the doorway, smiling at him.

'Are you ready to go?'

'Right behind you, Ames.'

* * *

Lamont was home, thinking about his sister and K-Bar. They looked good together. Far more compatible than any of the men Marika had messed with before. He was still getting used to her changes. The argument they'd had where he'd called her a parasite, had clearly had an effect. He regretted his comments, but was pleased she'd matured.

He'd spent his day pottering around, then had a drink before heading to bed. He switched off the lights and tried to sleep, willing his body to fall asleep at a normal time.

His phone began buzzing, and he fumbled for it, answering without checking the caller.

'Yeah?'

'Hello L.'

'Charlotte?'

He could hear the smile in her voice. Charlotte was the former girlfriend of an old acquaintance, whom he'd spent time with in the recent past. Stupidly, he'd asked her on a date over a month ago, before getting cold feet and avoiding her.

'You sound shocked to hear from me, but I'm the one who has been waiting for you to call.'

'I'm sorry.' Lamont sat up in bed, wincing as he felt his bones creak.

'Are you really? What's going on L.?'

He rubbed his eyes.

'Everything,' he admitted, his head aching. His mouth was dry and he wondered if it was worth going to get some more liquor.

'Talk to me.'

'Look, I'm sorry for getting you caught up in my twisted web, Charlotte, but trust me when I say that you're best off staying away from me.'

Charlotte said nothing for a long moment, and Lamont waited for the click of the call ending.

'This isn't a conversation to be held over the phone. I want to see you and talk to you.'

'Char—'

'You need to speak to someone, L. I can hear it in your voice. I can come to you, or you can come to me. Choice is yours.'

Lamont closed his eyes. Sleep wasn't coming, and it was clear Charlotte wasn't taking no for an answer.

'I'll come to you.'

* * *

Lamont showered and threw on a t-shirt and jeans. After a quick drink, he drove to Charlotte's, two guards following in another vehicle. They would park down the street and shadow him to make sure there were no issues.

Charlotte's Chapel Allerton spot was as well-tended as it had been the last time he visited. She waited by the door, her expression unreadable as she stepped aside and let him in. Charlotte had a regal beauty, similar to Jenny. She had brown hair and eyes that were a startling shade of grey. Lamont tried ignoring this as they walked down the hallway and into the living room. It was wide and airy, with deep red sofa's and throw pillows, a fruity scent punctuated by two candles at the top of a marble mantlepiece. Charlotte signalled for him to sit.

'What are you drinking?'

'Coffee if you've got it. I'd prefer to mainline it into my veins if you have the equipment.'

This got a smile from her. She sashayed to the kitchen and as she walked away, he took note of the pyjama bottoms and sleeveless top she wore, then turned away. Anna had taught him he couldn't rely on that. He'd tried losing himself with her and it had backfired spectacularly. Closing his eyes, he pushed her and their awkward night from his mind.

'You seem the sort who likes bland coffee,' said Charlotte, as she held out a steaming cup. Lamont took it.

'*Bland coffee* is fine.'

'Did I wake you?' Charlotte sat next to him, folding her legs under her. 'You sounded sleepy.'

'I was in bed but I wasn't asleep,' he said.

'What's been happening then?'

'Nothing. Everything is fine.'

'Why didn't you contact me then?'

Lamont shrugged. 'Things got hectic in the streets and I didn't want to get you caught up.'

'Because I'm a defenceless little girl who needs a big powerful man to protect her?'

That irked Lamont.

'Because your ex got gunned down over a street beef, and I didn't think you'd want the reminder,' he snapped.

Charlotte looked down, still clutching her cup. Lamont sipped his coffee to have something to do. He regretted his attitude, but she had asked him to come, despite his attempts to let her down gently.

'I can understand that I guess,' she finally said. 'I suppose what I'm interested in is why you're still doing it?'

'Why would you care about that?'

'Because I'm madly in love with you,' she deadpanned. Despite himself, Lamont chuckled.

'Seriously,' she pressed.

'Because I have to,' said Lamont. 'I lost someone close to me, and I have to make it right.'

'And that means staying around the danger?'

Lamont didn't respond. He didn't need to. Charlotte continued to watch him, and Lamont had the feeling she would survey him all night if needed. He cleared his throat.

'Why am I here, Charlotte?'

'I don't understand why you're trying to cut me out.'

'I already explained why.'

'Tell me what's going on? Whatever you're doing, it's taking a toll, L. When you were at my door, you looked like you were going to keel over.'

'I'm just tired.'

'Tired, but you couldn't sleep . . . how long has that been going on?'

'A while. I haven't exactly been keeping count,' he replied.

Do you think your state of mind might be tied to whatever it is you're doing?'

Lamont shrugged. She was probing and he didn't like it.

Charlotte was shocked at Lamont's appearance. His eyes were bloodshot and it was clear he wasn't in the best way. There was an air of vulnerability about him. The power he normally resonated seemed tapered, diminished somehow.

'L, just talk to me. I won't judge, I promise.'

Lamont took a deep breath, there was no way to avoid the conversation other than to leave, and he was tired of running away. Charlotte was here and wanted to listen. Maybe if he confided in her, she would leave him alone.

'Jenny's death broke me,' he confessed. 'Everyone keeps telling me I shouldn't feel guilty over what happened to her, but I do, and I can't shift it. Every time I think I have, I get deeper into whatever hole I've dug for myself. I lost a business, and more than that, I lost a friend when Trinidad Tommy died. Time after time, he went to bat for me, and now he's gone, and the community rightfully hates me for it. So, I'm here, with no one I can really turn to, and it's no more than I deserve.'

Charlotte didn't respond immediately when Lamont finished. He felt slightly better after letting it out, but the guilt still lived deeply in the pit of his stomach, and the worrying part was that he wasn't sure it would ever diminish. He wasn't sure he would ever be normal again.

'How you're feeling is perfectly normal, L.'

The statement didn't make Lamont feel any better, and he didn't respond. Charlotte shifted closer.

'You're being too hard on yourself.'

'I'm not being hard enough. They're dead, and I'm alive, and it just feels like I've lost something. I hate feeling so fucking helpless, and I don't know how to fix it.'

Lamont's resolve nearly broke, and Charlotte wrapped her arms around him now, hugging him tightly. Lamont initially tried to shift away from her soft touch, but she hung on and he relented, losing himself in her slim curves, and the wildflower scent emanating from her. They sat quietly for a long while, and Lamont slowly felt himself relaxing under her tender touch.

* * *

K-Bar and Marika were laid in bed holding one another, the *Netflix* movie paused in the background. It was shocking for K-Bar how easily things had returned to normal for them. They were out in the open now. Lamont knew about them and seemed to have semi-accepted it, though K-Bar wouldn't be surprised to find a *protective brother talk* in his future. He didn't mind the prospect. K-Bar cared deeply for Marika and her children, and he wanted to commit to her if she would let him. He felt like they were equals, which was a balance he'd never had in any of his previous relationships. Marika had her own baggage to deal with. Her relationship with the Manchester gangster Marrion Bernette had left scars that even years later, she was trying to work past. He admired her inner strength.

'Your bro looks tired lately, don't you think?'

'You want to talk about L now?' Marika giggled, highlighting the fact they were both naked.

'Seriously. I was talking business with him the other day and it was like he wasn't even listening. I dunno what he's got going on, but it's fucking him up.'

'It's Jenny. I told you and Shorty that when we were all here.'

'This is L we're talking about, Rika. We call him *Teflon* for a reason. He's bigger than that, and he's not the sort to let murder affect his business.'

Marika scoffed.

'He loved her. I don't know what that means to you or Shorty or anyone, but this is different. You didn't see Lamont at her funeral. Her death destroyed him. He's not even close to recovering yet.'

'Is it really that deep?'

'Of course it is. Next time you see him, try truly looking at him, and then tell me what you see.'

'Shorty thinks he's shook over Lennox. He thinks that's why he's hiding out from the crew.'

'What do you think?' Marika's tone was crisp and she knew it. Despite knowing K-Bar meant well, she didn't like the implication that her brother was being weak, and she didn't like the fact he was discussing it with Shorty, who he *knew* wasn't even talking to Lamont.

'I don't know. I saw them together and I know L liked her and he was ready to walk away from the game for her, but he didn't. They broke up before she died.'

'I doubt they would have stayed that way. I was friends with her, even when me and L weren't talking, and I think she may have loved him even more than he did her. She stuck by him all the way through his recovery. A woman doesn't do that if there aren't genuine feelings involved.'

'L's rich.'

'So was Jenny. She had her own business and her own money. Plus, her parents are clearly loaded.'

'How do you know that?' K-Bar had never heard Lamont mention Jenny's parents.

'Because I was at the funeral and I met them. They're super rich. Trust me on that. Jenny didn't need Lamont's money and she didn't care about his status. Maybe that's why he recognised it and can't work past it?'

'I think you might be looking too much into it.'

'Maybe I am,' conceded Marika. 'Tell me about the war. What's going on with Lennox?'

'He's something else,' K-Bar admitted. 'I didn't expect him to last so long. No one did. He's basically fighting a war on two fronts. Realistically, he shouldn't have been able to go toe to toe with Delroy, never mind be able to take shots at us like he has.'

'How do you think he did it?'

K-Bar shrugged. 'I'm not sure. Len always had skills. Marcus liked him. So did Shorty back in the day. He was against drugs, but otherwise, he'd have probably been down with the crew.'

Marika mulled that one over. She vaguely remembered Lennox from back in the day. K-Bar was still talking, so she tuned back in.

'We've focused more on rebuilding than going after him directly. Delroy's people are all over him now.'

'Is Delroy in contact with L?'

'I think so. What I've told you is what people told me. I've been trying to get back up to speed with everything going on. This Shorty and L thing is stressing me out too. It's not natural for them to not be talking. Shorty is working with the crew again, and I don't even think L knows.'

'Do you think he would mind?'

'No. L's still the one in charge. If he really wanted Shorty cut off, he'd stop paying him. I just don't think the crew is his number one priority right now, and people are noticing.'

'Can you bring them back together?'

'I think so,' admitted K-Bar. 'The timing just needs to be right.'

* * *

Lamont was sitting around considering his next move. He had men discreetly watching Jackie Smart Court, and they had reported seeing several of Lennox's men there. Lamont had done nothing regarding the spot yet, but he'd had the members of Lennox's team he'd seen there under surveillance. He didn't want to rush any of his moves. Lennox had a knack for countering, and Lamont wanted to make sure that the moves counted.

Jukie clearly liked the money Lamont gave him for the tip, because he'd been in contact again, with another spot, this one a drop-off spot. He didn't know many details, but he had given Lamont a name that more than made up for it.

Sinclair.

No surname, and no real profile, just a young, temperamental kid who'd been bragging about a murder he'd committed. The murder of Akeem. Lamont had flooded the Hood with men looking for him after the shooting, but Sinclair had got away in all the confusion. Now, he was out and about, running his mouth, and Lamont wanted badly to put him in the ground.

For Jukie's trouble, he had given him three thousand pounds, and made sure he put the word out about Teflon's generosity. He admired the fear tactic that Lennox was using to suppress snitches, but cash rewards were always great for testing resolve — one reason Lamont had always paid his people well, lest they get greedy and take someone else's money to work against him.

Lamont had two spots he could move against, but one of them was helping him understand the pieces of Lennox's crew. He'd heard the name *Mark Patrick* rumbling around, but there were few details attached to the name. Lennox was clearly keeping his closest pieces to his chest, having learned after what had happened to Nikkolo. Sharma had been a great help with surveillance and tracking, and Jukie had contacted some freelancers who were always after a payday, meaning

Lamont didn't have to drain the resources of the crew more than he had to.

His talk with Charlotte had been a strange one, and he wasn't sure what to make of it. He hadn't mentioned his failed dalliance with Anna, but admitting how he was feeling about Jenny's murder had felt good. He'd felt clearer and after eventually leaving Charlotte's that night, slept well. The feelings of guilt resurfaced in the morning, reinforcing his belief that he would never feel better. This state of mind was becoming the new normal for him, and that was a terrifying prospect. It made him want to speed up his actions against Lennox. The sooner he got his revenge, the sooner he could focus on making himself strong again.

Where he now stood with Charlotte, Lamont didn't have a clue. He didn't want to rush into anything and his experiences with Anna had shown him that wouldn't work. She didn't seem to expect anything from him other than to be a shoulder to cry on, but that was dangerous. Lamont's life had taught him that people weren't around forever. Whether they were killed, or they fell out, or they simply moved away, you needed to rely on yourself and be strong enough to cope with whatever life threw at you.

Lamont had been that way for a long time. He had been an island; an *army-of-one*, and now he felt like a quivering basket case that needed his hand holding. It made him feel like a weak child, and that simply wasn't good enough.

Forcing his thoughts back to the surveillance situation, he had a decision to make. Leaving the spot on Jackie Smart Court would work for now, but he was considering giving Delroy the tip about the drop-off spot. Delroy had his own men, and was determined to go all out against Lennox's forces. It would be prudent to stay in the shadows, and let him fight off the first waves of Lennox's troops. Whether or not Delroy complied, Lamont would be the one to kill Lennox. Whatever Delroy did after was up to him.

With that in mind, he finished the gin and lemonade he'd been nursing for the past thirty minutes, then called Delroy.

'Good to hear from you, L. How are you?'

'I'm fine. I need to talk to you. It's important.'

'I'm home. Stop by anytime. I'll have a drink ready.'

* * *

True to his word, Delroy had a glass of brandy waiting when Lamont arrived. He wasn't a fan of mixing drinks at the best of times, yet in all the years he had known Delroy, he'd never seen him drinking gin, and there was a chance he didn't stock it. Lamont held out his glass, and Delroy clinked it. They sipped in silence.

'What do you want to speak about?' Delroy asked.

'I have a location for you. It's a drop-off spot Lennox is using. Don't know exactly what for, but I'm guessing weapons or maybe a warehouse for his people.'

'Who'd you get the info off?'

'A trusted source.'

Delroy's eyes bored into Lamont's. He put the glass on the desk in front of him.

'You don't wanna share it?'

'Not yet.'

'Why are you giving it to me?'

'You said yourself last time we spoke face to face. You need this.'

Delroy continued to watch Lamont, clearly trying to understand his angle. Lamont waited him out, in no hurry to rush anything.

'I'll send a team to check it out.'

'Fine. One thing though.'

Delroy grinned. 'Here we go. I knew there was something.'

'Do you know a kid called Sinclair?'

'Heard my people talking about him. He's a little psycho Lennox has running around doing shootings. We haven't caught up to him yet.'

'He's the one who killed Akeem.'

Delroy's eyes softened, understanding immediately.

'If he's there, he's yours. I'll tell my people to capture him alive, but if he won't come quietly, he's dying with the rest.'

Lamont wondered if Delroy had tried interrogating any of the people he'd ambushed, or if they had simply been killed or maimed. In the grand scheme, it didn't really matter.

'How have you been since we last spoke?' Delroy asked.

Lamont savoured his drink. 'Everyone thinks there's something wrong with me.'

'Who do you mean when you say *everyone?*' Delroy settled back in his chair.

'K-Bar, Marika . . . random women on the street,' muttered Lamont. Delroy chuckled.

'Be glad so many people care about you.'

Lamont felt a wave of shame spread through his body. Delroy was right. He doubted Delroy had anyone who cared about him the same way. He'd said his daughter hated him and his wife refused to speak to him. As sad as Lamont's life was at the moment, at least he had people he could speak to.

Delroy could read the look on Lamont's face. He wouldn't let him blame himself for something else he couldn't control.

'Don't feel sorry for me, L. I made some shitty decisions in the past and they're coming back to haunt me. Make sure you make better ones.' Delroy rubbed his head. 'How the hell did you get K-Bar out? I thought he was looking at decades.'

'Shorty handled it. He had a word with a witness and she told the truth about what she knew. They couldn't hold K after that.'

'Shorty sorted it . . .' Delroy rubbed his chin, eyes probing Lamont. 'How do you feel about that?'

'They're friends.'

'That's not an answer.'

Lamont blew out a breath, shaking his head.

'I don't know what you want me to say.'

'Yes you do. Shorty coming back with a bang and helping free his best friend. Do you see that as a threat to your power?'

'No,' replied Lamont, and he honestly didn't. He liked the fact Shorty had done it and until Delroy had mentioned it, he hadn't considered the possibility he would have an ulterior motive.

'This game of ours, it's a show, L. You know that as well as I do. For most people, especially those on the lower levels, the perception is the reality. Shorty is getting involved in your crew politics, but he can't even spare a polite word for you. Does that seem right?'

'I think you're reaching. Shorty and I both crossed the line. Regardless, he helped build that crew.'

'Maybe so, but it's still *your* crew. Without you, he'd have a record longer than my arm. They all would have.'

'You don't know that.'

'You mean, you don't want to admit that. You're in denial because you feel bad over the things that have happened, but you need to pick yourself up and get things back in line, before it's too late. How's the thing with the Asians going?'

'I had a problem, but I resolved it.'

'People not respecting you?'

Lamont chuckled at Delroy's attempts to instigate. 'Respect isn't a problem. The two people under me were proteges of Akhan.'

'Sounds awkward.'

'It was. One of them is fairly laid back, but the other guy was prickly. I took him out for dinner and now we understand each other's position.'

Delroy had an approving look on his face.

'I'm glad it's working out for you. Is it enough?'

'I . . .' Lamont didn't know how to answer. 'I guess it's too early to tell.'

They sat in silence for a while. Lamont expected Delroy to send someone to the drop-off spot immediately, but he was more patient than Lamont had given him credit for.

'Are you hungry?'

'No.'

'When did you last eat?'

'I don't keep count of the hours.'

'You need to keep your strength up. People would probably stop going on about how tired you look if you took proper care of yourself.'

'Everyone said I look tired, not thin,' said Lamont. Delroy wouldn't be dissuaded though.

'It's all connected, and you know it. I'm gonna make us something, and we're gonna hang a little bit. I'll sort this Lennox business later.'

CHAPTER FIFTEEN

Thursday 14 May 2015

DAYS LATER, Lamont was assessing the moves that had been made. Delroy had indeed struck against the spot, sending in a team. There were four shooters there, who were caught completely off guard. Sinclair wasn't among them. Lamont didn't know if he had received pre-warning something might happen, or if he simply wasn't staying there, but regardless, he was in the wind, and this irked Lamont.

Delroy was seeing it as a win. As well as wiping out the team with no casualties of his own, he had seized several weapons along with ten thousand pounds in cash that was hidden upstairs under the bed in the main bedroom. The money was irrelevant, but it was still money Lennox couldn't use against him.

Lamont hoped it would lead to more tips being thrown his way. He had protected Jukie as a source, and even Delroy didn't know about him. He would need to be careful going forward. If Lennox suspected where the information was coming from, he wouldn't hesitate to retaliate against Jukie with extreme prejudice.

It was after midnight, and Lamont was wide awake. He was comfortable, but couldn't sleep, and didn't even want to leave his bed to get another drink.

Charlotte had told him the last time they spoke that he could contact her any time, but he couldn't ring her so late. He didn't even know how to put across how he was feeling and hated the fact he was so conflicted over this situation. He was torn between letting Delroy completely go after Lennox, and doing it himself. Delroy had as much right as he did to pursue Lennox. Two of his children had been murdered by him, and he had outright stated he had nothing else to lose.

So, why did Lamont feel he had an equal right? Why did he feel that he too had nothing else to lose?

He had family that was becoming more distant by the day, and he had associates. There was nothing preventing him from putting his life on the line in the same fashion. There was no Jenny.

Closing his eyes, Lamont searched down deep within himself, wanting to know if there was a way to walk away and leave it up to Delroy. The need for revenge remained all-consuming; he grew angrier the longer he lay there, staring at the ceiling. He felt tears prickling his eyes, wishing he was strong enough to cope with whatever was happening to him. He wished he could be *Teflon* instead of Lamont the weakling.

He thought back to a time he'd done his best to repress.

The time after his parents' had died, and his Aunt had become the primary carer for him and Marika. He remembered hugging Marika as she wouldn't stop crying for their mum. Aunt Carmen had approached with a smile that even as a child he didn't trust and had told him she would look after Marika. When he'd told her he could do it, he had seen her eyes turn cold, and a fear glissaded through his body.

That same night, she beat him with a belt until he cried, for disobeying her. The pain faded, but that feeling of utter helplessness had prevailed, and Lamont felt the same way now. He wanted nothing more than to bury his head and stay hidden, and the feeling frustrated him to his core. There was so much going on that it wasn't a realistic option for him.

Taking a deep breath, he wiped his eyes and tried to relax. He needed to get some rest. Ahmed had set up a meeting with another buyer tomorrow, and he would need to be present for the introduction.

The ringing phone put paid to that idea and he snatched it up without checking the number.

'Yeah?'

'Did I wake you, Teflon?'

Lamont's blood ran cold. He couldn't believe the audacity of the person on the other end.

'You've got some nerve calling me.'

Lennox sounded calm, almost too calm, which Lamont loathed. With everything going on, and the attacks Delroy had made against him, he expected Lennox to sound agitated, but he didn't.

'We need to talk, and I didn't think you would be receptive to a face-to-face meeting.'

'I'd be receptive to it. The chance to tear your head off is appealing.'

'You seem angry. Would you like me to call back in the morning after you've slept?'

'Do you think this is a fucking joke?' snapped Lamont, infuriated by his calm manner.

'Do you want to hear what I have to say?'

'Talk then. Stop wasting my time and tell me what you want.'

'Are you working with Delroy?'

Lamont didn't understand the point of the conversation. *Why would Lennox call him to ask about Delroy?*

'Is that really why you wanted to speak with me?'

'Don't avoid the question. Are you?'

'Delroy doesn't need me to take you down.' Lamont wasn't explicitly mentioning his involvement. If Lennox wasn't watching for him, it would enable him to hit harder later on.

'Do you remember our last meeting?'

'Yes.'

They had met in the city centre after Grace's shooting, and made veiled threats to one another.

'I told you then, Chapeltown was in a funk. Do you think it's any better?'

'You're the one pillaging the streets trying to kill Delroy's men.'

'I can't stop my people from defending themselves. He has a vendetta against me.'

'I'm not re-treading this shit,' said Lamont. His anger hadn't abated in the slightest. 'Tell me what the hell you want.'

'I told you at that meeting that I didn't authorise what happened to Shorty's daughter. In that same vein, my men weren't supposed to kill your girlfriend. Nor were they supposed to kill Trinidad.'

'You expect me to believe that crap? What about Akeem? Wasn't he worthy of avoiding death?'

'Akeem was a soldier. He knew the rules. I instructed my men to kidnap your girl. I needed something to calm you down, to enable you to hear what I was really saying to you that day.'

'How the fuck did she end up dead then?' Lamont knew he needed to calm down, but couldn't. This man was responsible for Jenny's murder, yet he was calmly trying to justify his actions.

'One of my men was overzealous. She was a tiger and fought for her freedom. She grabbed the knife and in the struggle, ended up dead.'

'And now what? You want to apologise?'

'I wanted you to understand that I'm not the monster you think I am, and that our goals are not much different. You care about Chapeltown, and so do I.'

'Trinidad cared about Chapeltown too,' said Lamont through gritted teeth. 'You had him burned alive and for what?'

'He wasn't supposed to be in the building. The barber's was retaliation for what your people did to Nikkolo. I retaliated, but I didn't want Trinidad harmed.'

The entire conversation was surreal, and Lamont couldn't get his head around any of it. There was no reason for Lennox to call and say these things. He couldn't understand his angle, unless it was to keep Lamont from attacking any further. It was short-sighted. Even if he pacified Lamont, there was still Delroy to deal with.

'Do you really expect me to believe anything you say?'

'I expect you to remember my reputation. It was the same reputation that led to you meeting me that day. I have no reason to lie. Whatever is going to happen with us will happen, but it was important you knew the truth.'

Lamont didn't reply. His head was hurting from processing the information he had been given. He wasn't in the right state of mind to deal with this. He felt sluggish, overly tired, and far from his best.

'You can have the one responsible.'

Lamont had zoned out, but those words brought him back.

'What?'

'The man who stabbed her. He should be punished, right? For taking her from you.'

'What's your game here?' Lamont's eyes narrowed.

'Nothing other than what I've already said.'

'I don't trust you or your setups.'

'That's up to you. Regardless, you can have the name and a location, and if you choose not to do anything with that information, that's your choice.'

'What do you want? You never give something for nothing.'

'Like I said, take whatever action you deem necessary. We'll speak again soon, Teflon. Get some rest.'

Lennox hung up. Lamont stared at the phone as if he expected it to make Lennox appear. He didn't even know where to start with the information he'd been given. Lennox hadn't sounded at all rattled by anything that was happening, which was worrying. He couldn't fathom his angle. It took a certain level of balls to call up an enemy and calmly relay information you didn't need to give them. Even after all the hits Lennox had taken, he was still scheming.

Lamont wanted nothing more than to roll over and dismiss his words, but then his phone buzzed, and he had a name: *Ryan Peters*. There was an address too. He recognised it to be in Seacroft. Despite his conflict and the fact he didn't trust Lennox Thompson, there was absolutely no doubt in his mind about his next action.

He couldn't let the chance for revenge go.

CHAPTER SIXTEEN

Thursday 14 May 2015

LAMONT WAS SHOCKED by his change of mood the morning after his conversation with Lennox Thompson. After so little sleep combined with the drama, he'd expected to wake up in a foul, lethargic mood. Yet he hadn't. He'd climbed out of bed at 5am, had a shower, exercised, then had a cup of coffee. He felt sharp and alert in a way he hadn't in a while, and it shocked him.

Lamont was waiting on a phone call back about Ryan Peters. He'd never heard his name before, yet this man had killed Jenny. He'd extinguished the life of someone Lamont loved, and it seemed a little flat that this was him: Some loser hiding out in Seacroft, likely unaware of what was about to befall him.

There was always the possibility he was walking into a trap. He knew Lennox could be trying to set him up, but he'd had his opportunity. Only a few weeks ago, he'd had Lamont at gunpoint, with Sinclair there to pull the trigger. He could have killed him, but killed Akeem instead.

Lennox had got under his skin all over again, and now Lamont was reconsidering what he knew. He had known Lennox a long time ago through Marcus. He was a man of his word, and though he'd hurt people in the past; he wasn't indiscriminate with it. Lennox and

Lamont had met, and he had told him at that stage not to involve himself, but Lamont had anyway. He told him he didn't want Grace harmed, but wanted Shorty dead. It was possible he was even telling the truth about Trinidad.

Adrenaline spiking, Lamont did some more training before his meeting. He would arrange a meeting with Delroy later and get his thoughts.

* * *

Delroy slid a drink across to Lamont. These meetings had become so relaxed that he didn't even ask if he wanted one anymore.

'I didn't expect to hear from you so quickly. You know we didn't find Sinclair at that spot, right?'

'This isn't about that. I received an interesting phone call last night.' Lamont told Delroy what Lennox had said. Delroy listened in silence.

'He's a crafty bastard. He wanted to get in your head, and he's definitely succeeded.'

'Do you think that's all it is?' A day of meetings and work with Ahmed hadn't robbed Lamont of the confusion regarding Lennox's potential motives. He couldn't pinpoint the exact game Lennox was playing, but the man's words had undoubtedly impacted him.

'He could be trying to draw a wedge between us. Turning us against each other is probably the best card he can play right now.'

'He made sense,' Lamont admitted, as hard as that was. He knew Lennox's rep, and *ruthless but fair*, seemed to suit him. Lennox had his own code and had resisted the money being made selling drugs, remaining in his own lane. That took tremendous strength of character.

'Len's not stupid. He wouldn't have lasted as long as he has without that. He must know he's on the ropes now. I'd lay money on that being the reason he contacted you.'

'What do I do then?'

Delroy sipped his drink, then lit a cigarette. Lamont hated the smell, but he could put up with it.

'What do you want to do?'

'I want to find this Ryan Peters guy, and I want to kill him. Right now, my instincts are rusty though. I feel like I've made one wrong move after another this year, and I don't want to make that worse.'

Delroy scoffed, shaking his head.

'You're the smartest person I know, L. Believe me when I say that you were built for the game we play. Never doubt yourself.'

Lamont wasn't sure how Delroy's praise was supposed to make him feel, but *uneasy* described it. The game was tiresome, and lately even the thought of playing it filled him with nothing but dread. He had a long way to go, and eliminating Peters might help in that regard.

'I have to face him. No way around it.'

'Why aren't you using your crew?'

That took Lamont out of his reverie.

'Using them for what?'

'For anything. You have shooters and goons you could send after him. I'm surprised you're not fighting me kicking and screaming to get Lennox.'

'I can't expect them to fight my battles all the time.'

'They work for you. It's *your* crew. Do you think everyone who works with me is happy to be at war? Do you think they like constantly having to watch their backs for danger from Lennox's people? I'm in charge, and they follow me. That's my privilege.'

'I think there's more to it than that with my team. I've had enough people killed.'

'What the hell are you talking about?'

'Chink, Tall-Man, Jenny, Trinidad, Akeem, and those are just the ones I can think of off the top of my head. People around me die, Del.'

Delroy scowled, and the anger made him look ten years younger.

'Maybe I should take back what I said about you being smart. Not one of those deaths is your fault, except for Chink's, and after what he did, he deserved worse.'

Lamont agreed about Chink, but it didn't make the words any easier to accept. As the person at the top, he was responsible for those below him, and he had repeatedly dropped the ball. He didn't want to think about it anymore.

'You've made a dent in his forces. I have a feeling his phone call to me is an attempt to control the situation.'

Delroy topped up his drink. 'I don't know if we're doing enough damage. Lennox has spots everywhere, and his people are extremely loyal to him. It's a war of attrition now, so I guess it comes down to who can last the longest.'

'Would you sue for peace if you had the opportunity?'

Delroy gave Lamont a sad smile. 'Backing down isn't an option. You already know my feelings about the situation. Forget it, anyway. You've made your choice. What's going on with the crew?'

'Shorty is leading by example,' replied Lamont. Word had finally reached him about Shorty's involvement in the crew, and his attempts to retaliate against their usurpers. 'Everyone's supporting him. It's a good fit.'

'How does that make you feel?' Delroy watched him closely.

'I don't have an issue with it. Shorty has always fit in well with the crew, and they can all look out for one another. I expected him to go on a rampage and get killed going after Lennox's forces. He started out that way, but something calmed him. If I was to put money on it, I would say Amy.'

'His baby mother? Didn't think they were together.'

'They're not, but there are feelings there. I could see Grace's accident bringing them closer.'

'Is that why you haven't fought against him being involved?'

'Maybe.' Lamont hadn't considered it. 'Either way, it's best for the crew right now. I can't focus on all areas, and we don't need any more mistakes.'

Delroy continued to study Lamont over the top of his glass and after a few minutes, Lamont grew annoyed.

'Why are you staring at me?'

'I'm worried about you. You don't sound like yourself.'

'How am I supposed to sound?' Lamont's voice rose. Delroy shook his head.

'Get some rest, L. Whatever you do about this Peters' kid, sleep first. Don't rush into anything.'

* * *

Lamont put together a plan for dealing with Peters, having people surveying his spot and reporting to him over a three-day-period.

Jenny's killer lived alone and worked in and around Seacroft, selling mostly weed, but some rock too. Getting him would be easy. The smart thing would be to snatch him from his house, take him to one of their soundproofed locations, and go to work on him, but Lamont wanted to confront him face to face, in his own living space.

That was the plan he was going with. It was just a matter of executing it.

* * *

That night, Charlotte invited Lamont for dinner. She'd prepared a delicious steak, but he picked at it, not having much of an appetite. Peters dominated his thoughts; the need to confront him was hard for Lamont to shake off. Charlotte seemed to be in an odd mood too, and made little conversation, struggling to meet Lamont's eyes.

'Are you okay?' he finally asked her, laying his knife and fork down on the plate. He'd managed around four bites of the steak before giving it up. Looking at Charlotte's plate, she had eaten even less.

'I was thinking about Justin.'

Lamont felt his nostrils flare before he controlled his reactions. Despite his own feelings, and the fact he'd respected Justin, it annoyed him for a moment that he was on Charlotte's mind when she was with him.

'Anything in particular?'

'The book he wrote. The one I told you about, where he mentioned us. I was thinking about the part he wrote about me.'

'Can I see it?' He briefly remembered the conversation they'd had, where she had spoken about Justin's writing, and the book he'd written in prison.

Charlotte nodded after a moment and headed upstairs. She came back down a few minutes later with an expensive looking leather book, which she handed to him.

'I had it bound,' she needlessly explained. 'He gave it to me in paper form, and I didn't want to lose any pages. I still have the original.'

Lamont didn't speak as he read the book. It wasn't particularly long, and was more of a collection of thoughts than a novel, but he was gripped. He felt his stomach flip-flop when he read his name. He'd known Justin respected him, but reading it was different. When he finished, he placed the book on the sofa next to him.

'I saw Justin in a restaurant, a while before he died,' he said. 'We spoke and I offered him a job.'

'Why?' Charlotte asked. She could see from the look on Lamont's face he was right there in the moment.

'He was good. Sounds simple, but people like Justin come around once in a while. He had poise and he made people around him work harder. When you have someone like that you need to cultivate it. He reminded me of myself.'

'How?'

'We both saw things a certain way. We could put our egos aside to work effectively with people, and when I saw him that night, I knew there were issues with King. I even caused some of them.'

'How?'

'I knew the people who were making his business harder. Tunde and Bloon. I used them to make things difficult for him.'

'Why would you do that?'

'King was a virus. He stole his power and flouted a lot of the rules people had in place. We allowed him to do it, but we didn't make things easy. Then, Justin got out, and King calmed down a little and put Justin in charge, but it was clear it wouldn't last long. King had a taste of being the main man, and there was no way he was going to share.'

'Did you tell Justin that?' Charlotte hadn't taken her eyes from him.

Lamont shook his head. 'I made the offer, he rejected me, and I let it go. The fact is, I understand why he had such an effect on you.'

'The night he died . . . he called me. Said I was the motivation behind his words, and that he wrote to avoid going crazy when he was behind bars. He wanted me to know how he felt and the last thing he said to me, was to read those pages and that I would understand.' Charlotte choked back a sob. Lamont slid closer, holding her and letting her cry in peace. She had been dealing with her pain for two years now, and it made him wonder how long it would take for him to be better. He was tired of the grief suffocating him. He just wanted to be better.

'I wish I was okay,' she sniffed. 'I wish I could just move on and leave the memory of him behind, but he's always there, and I'm writing my own words because I think it keeps me connected to him.'

Lamont stroked her back, enjoying the closeness as he had last time. It didn't feel as awkward as his encounter with Anna. Charlotte was broken. He was broken too. When he was around her, he felt more like a protector than a victim. Tilting her head toward him, he felt her breath catch as he stared into her eyes. His lips met hers, and the kiss instantly deepened. He was back in the zone, desire surging through his veins as he pulled her closer against him, devouring her mouth, loving her taste and feel.

Blinking, he pulled away at the same time as Charlotte. Breathing hard, they stared one another down. It went on for a moment that seemed to last forever, and he knew the magnified pain in her eyes was reflected in his own.

He wasn't seeing her. He was seeing Jenny, and he knew Charlotte wasn't seeing him. Like Anna, it couldn't work. He had once again tried to seduce his way out of feeling his pain, and once again, his body had shut him down.

'I'm sorry,' he said, letting her go. Charlotte gave him a soft smile.

'I'm sorry too. It would have been so easy,' she admitted.

Lamont rubbed her hair, smiling despite not feeling particularly cheerful.

'Friends then?'

'Friends,' she repeated.

CHAPTER SEVENTEEN

Monday 18 May 2015

RYAN PETERS HUMMED along to a *Giggs* track, tired from another day of hustling and keeping his head above water. Money had dried up recently and he was having to work longer hours to survive. He had been ostracised from his crew after accidentally killing a woman, and didn't know how to get himself back into the fold. When he wasn't working, he stayed close to home, smoking, playing on the PlayStation, and watching whatever films he had laying around. He had a takeaway resting on the passenger seat, a cheap chicken and chips meal he'd picked up from his regular spot, and had stopped for cigarettes and a few cans from the local shop. There was nothing else for him to do but lose himself to the monotony.

As he turned onto his street, he noticed that a nearby streetlight had been knocked out, cursing the local kids. They were unruly and bored, always causing trouble, knocking over bins and smashing windows; when they weren't smoking weed or robbing houses.

Resolving to smack one or two of them around if he caught them, he grabbed his bags and shuffled his way inside after unlocking his door. Dropping the bags on the coffee table, he switched on the light and jumped back.

'What the fuck?'

A man sat in his favourite armchair, a small grin on his face as he surveyed him. He was well-dressed in a black jumper, trousers and boots. He wore gloves and in his right hand, clutched a gun.

'Hello, Ryan.'

'Who the hell are you?'

'Sit down.' The man motioned to the sofa. Keeping his eyes on him, Peters complied.

'Are you gonna tell me who you are?'

'You don't know?'

Peters frowned. 'I've never seen you before. How would I know?'

'I heard you were sharp, but I'm guessing that was an exaggeration. You don't look very smart.'

'I haven't done anything, mate. If there's a problem, just tell me so I can make it right.' Peters ignored the jibe.

'What if you can't make it right?'

Peters opened his mouth and closed it. He studied the man, racking his brain to see if he knew him from anywhere. He was well-spoken and didn't look like he was from the streets, but he was holding the gun on him with no issues.

'Look, I don't have any money, but you can take the TV and the PlayStation and whatever else you can find, if that will make things right.'

The man shook his head, tutting.

'What makes you think this is a robbery?'

'Why else would you be here?'

'I'm patiently waiting for you to work that out, Ryan. Use your brain — the part you haven't rotted away with drugs, anyway. You're a no-hoper in a shitty little house, with a shitty little existence. Why would I be here? Think to your sins.'

Peters was baffled. The man seemed to have a problem with him but he was far above his level, and didn't fit his usual clientele. He sold drugs to people lower than him, and he didn't sell much. This guy looked like he was a heavyweight. Peters didn't have a patch he was working and he had a feeling that if the man was a drug dealer, they didn't have the same customers.

It took well over a minute before it hit him. Lennox Thompson had essentially cut him loose after the kidnapping went wrong. He paled, nausea swirling, able to taste the bile in his stomach.

'*Teflon*,' he gasped, watching the man's eyes light up.

'I've been waiting a long time to speak with you,' said Lamont, fighting to control himself. He was so angry he wanted to beat him to death with the gun he was holding. His people were surveying the house in case it was an ambush. He wondered if Jenny was watching over him. She hadn't known his hands were stained with blood. He had kept her out of his business with Akhan, not wanting her to get caught up. Now, she wasn't. Thanks to the man currently quailing under the sight of his gun.

Deep down, Lamont knew Jenny wouldn't have accepted him as a murderer, but didn't want to think about that right now.

'I'm sorry. I promise, it wasn't meant to happen. We tried grabbing her, and she fought back, struggling to get free. She grabbed the knife and I tried to calm her down, but she was wriggling around so much that it stabbed her.'

'She was a fighter. She was better than you. Better than me too. She was mine, and you took her from me. I don't care why you were in the house. I only care about what you did, and what you robbed me of. Do you get that?'

'I'm sorry,' Peters tried again.

'Sorry will not cut it here. Do you know my rep?'

He nearly broke his neck nodding.

'Why would you risk it then? Why would you go after my woman? Didn't you think I would do anything?'

'Lennox made me. You have to believe me. Look at me,' gibbered Peters. 'I'd never have done something like that by myself. He just wanted us to hold her. If she hadn't struggled . . .' he couldn't finish.

'How long have you worked for Lennox?'

The sudden subject change caught him by surprise, but he hastened to answer. Teflon hadn't immediately killed him. He wanted information and if Peters could keep himself alive by helping, that's what he was going to do.

'Three years.'

'What sort of work did you do for him? Other than killing women.'

'I . . . I sent messages. Beat people up. Collected money and did robberies.'

Teflon nodded, absorbing the information.

'Tell me everything you know about Lennox and his operations.'

Peters' eyes widened. He wanted to be helpful, but Lennox was equally dangerous, and if he knew he had been telling tales about him, he would hurt him. He was stuck in the middle of a deadly situation and he wasn't sure how he could get out of it. Teflon was his best bet for now. Staying alive was the plan.

'Lennox doesn't keep me close like the others. He was furious after what happened, and I've been on my own ever since. Everyone in the crew abandoned me on his word. I don't know what I can tell you.'

'Tell me what you know. If I like what I hear, I'm more likely to leave without using this.' He waved the pistol for a moment.

Another jolt of fear spread through his body. Teflon was entirely too calm and it was even more unnerving. He didn't know how to deal with this sort of man. Teflon was a mainstay in Chapeltown and was surrounded by deadly killers who would take him out with ease. The only reason he had gone after Jenny was because he had Lennox's backing, and presumed he had a plan for dealing with the man seated before him. Clearly he hadn't.

'I . . . look, I wanna help, but I'm a nobody. I don't see how I can.'

'Do you know why I'm here?' Teflon cut through his babbling.

'Because of what happened. . . what Lennox made me do.'

'No. Well, yes, that's partly true. The main reason is because Lennox called me, and he gave me a *gift*. His words. He told me the address and the name of the man who killed my partner.' Teflon shot him a truly mirthless smirk. 'I'm here because Lennox gave you up, because you mean nothing to him. You were disposable.'

Despite the circumstances, Peters felt a surge of anger cancelling out the fear. Lennox valued loyalty and before the incident, Peters had never put a foot wrong. Lennox was practically in hiding, and there was no reason for him to betray Peters, but he had. This was his chance. Teflon wanted information, and it was his best chance to stay alive. If he could remain helpful, he would live, and then he could leave this life behind and start again somewhere else. He had nothing tying him to Leeds.

'What do you want to know?'

'How does Lennox make money?'

'He does everything. Contract kills. Robberies. Businesses pay him money to look after them. He does security. Anything that makes money.'

'Drugs?'

Peters shook his head. 'He robs them, but doesn't make money from them.'

'How do you know?'

'People talk. Sometimes people want to make money selling drugs on the side, and they try and talk him into getting involved in the drugs game. He has the contacts if he ever needed. Probably make millions if he did.'

'Why doesn't he?'

'No one knows. He doesn't even like people mentioning it.'

'After Nikkolo got murdered, who did Lennox start speaking to?'

'I was out of the fold by then. Lennox wanted nothing to do with me after my fuck up, but I'd say Mark Patrick is the one he would turn to. He did some time in the army and he's good with weapons and shit. Everyone in the crew respects him.'

'Why wouldn't Lennox send him after my partner rather than you? He wouldn't have fucked up.'

Despite his dire predicament, he felt another surge of annoyance at Teflon's attitude. He was used to people outright dismissing him, but it didn't make it any easy to tolerate. It would be over soon. He would give Teflon what he could, then he would flee.

All he needed was Teflon gone from the house.

'Guess he saw the job as beneath him. Mark's a weapons guy. He even knows about explosives and shit, bombs, petrol bombs, whatever is needed.'

'Sounds like the kind of man the army wouldn't want to lose. Why did they?'

'I dunno. All I know is he does well under Lennox, handles all kinds of special jobs. There are a few names that were beneath Nikkolo, but Mark sticks out.'

'I want the other names.'

Peters gave them, tempted to use them to negotiate his freedom. He was determined to show Teflon he was an asset though, and gave the names freely, noting that Teflon made no movement to write any of the names down.

'Going to back to Mark Patrick. You heard what happened to the barber's in Chapeltown?'

Peters shook his head. 'I stay away from the Hood. I've been keeping myself around here, and out of everyone's way.'

'What about *Sinclair?*'

He blew out a breath. 'Sinclair is absolutely nuts. Lennox knew his dad and brother, so he's been around him for years. Schooled him and made him into a killer. He only listens to Lennox.'

'Where can I find him and Mark?'

Peters shrugged. 'I don't know. I promise I don't. Mark will probably be wherever Lennox is, or close by. Sinclair could be anywhere. His family live in Miles Hill, so he might be around there. I'm out of the loop and I didn't spend much time around these lot when I wasn't on the job.'

'Where did you hang out when you weren't working? I want the spots you frequent; the areas Lennox recruits from the most. I want a list of safe houses you could use.'

'The safe houses change all the time, especially with the Delroy shit, but I'll give you what I can. I just want to help,' said Peters, searching Teflon's face for any sign of whether he was to live or die. He was a closed book, his expression inscrutable.

For the next twenty minutes, Peters spilled his guts, searching his brain for every bit of knowledge he could link to Lennox, whether it was a small rumour, or something he directly knew. Still, Teflon wrote nothing down, only prompting him to continue.

'That's it. That's everything I know,' he finally said. Teflon nodded.

'You've been extremely helpful.'

Peters waited, his heart leaping into his throat. He hoped he had done enough to earn a reprieve, but Teflon's expression gave nothing away.

'Stand up.'

Peters did it without thinking.

'Walk outside.'

'Where are we going?'

'Did I say *walk*, or did I say *talk*?'

His mouth snapped shut. Teflon stayed a few paces behind, keeping the gun out of reach. It was pitch black outside without the streetlight. Peters realised Teflon's people had likely done this to lower the chance of any witnesses seeing what was happening. Despite the late hour there were usually people hanging around, talking from their gardens or shouting curses at the little kids wreaking havoc. Now, the street was empty, save for the two large men standing at the bottom of the garden. Grabbing his arms, they none-too-gently dragged him toward a nondescript grey van and shoved him in the back, where another man waited.

'Get on the floor.'

Peters complied immediately, his nose to the floor of the van. It was empty aside from his captor, with nothing he could use to defend himself. Not that he intended to try. The man who had just growled at him was built like Anthony Joshua, and it was clear from his demeanour that he would like nothing more than to tear his head from his shoulders.

The vehicle moved off, and he kept his head down, panic shooting through him. Teflon had given him no sign of what he intended to do after leading him outside. He'd told him everything and hadn't held back. All he wanted was the opportunity to survive so he could flee.

Before long, the vehicle rumbled to a stop. The man guarding Peters signalled for him to stand as the van door opened. Two more men stood there, waiting for him to climb out. His heart slammed against his chest as he descended. They were in a warehouse, the largest he had ever seen. It was filled with machines and a selection of vehicles, mostly random, nondescript cars. In the middle of the room, Teflon stood, still holding the gun.

Peters stomach sank as he glanced left and right. There was no escape. There were half a dozen armed men around the warehouse and Teflon waiting for him, expression still unreadable, ready with a weapon. His chances of escape seemed slim, but he was determined to try. Teflon had kept him alive earlier when he could have killed him. He would need to work harder than ever in his life to convince him and as he drew closer, he gathered his words, searching for something, anything that might work.

'You don't have to do this,' he said, somewhat lamely. Teflon didn't even react. He held up the gun. Peters jerked back trying to run, but two men seized his arms, holding him in place.

'Move, and we'll break your fucking arm,' one of them growled. He immediately froze.

Teflon stepped closer, lightly resting the pistol against his thigh.

'You took the woman I loved from me.'

'Lennox—'

'Is just as responsible as you, and he will get what's coming to him. This is about you thinking you could go after what was mine. You didn't think about the consequences, or what I would do. Instead, you did as you were told, and you got the job done.'

'No, I—'

'Lennox didn't do you any favours. He didn't protect you. He gave you up because you weren't useful anymore. I don't care whether or not you wanted to do it. I don't care if it was an accident and if she grabbed the knife first. She was defending herself,' Teflon's voice rose. 'Defending herself from the men who broke into her house to take her away. I was listening on the phone. I heard her screaming and fighting, trying to get away, as I drove to the house as fast as I could. I had to walk in on her, bloody and dead on the fucking kitchen floor. You stabbed her and you left her there, and you really thought you had a chance at living?'

Peters' mouth was dry. He couldn't even form words. Shaking, his knees knocked together, dizzy with fear. He wasn't seeing the calm man who had interrogated him earlier. He was seeing the deadly criminal who had ruled his own empire for years, who few before Lennox had ever thought of testing. Without warning the bile rose and this time he threw up, emptying his stomach onto the concrete floor beneath him. The guards cursed in annoyance as the vomit splashed against them, but they still didn't let him go.

'I'll make it quick,' said Teflon. 'It's more than you deserve, but there is no reason to prolong this.'

'Teflon, please, I'm begging you, don't do this.' He fell to his knees, the movement forcing the guards to let go. He crawled forward, not caring that he was kneeling in his own vomit. 'I'll go away. You'll never see me again. I'm sorry about your girl! Please don't do this.'

Lamont's face was bloodless with intense rage. His breathing intensified. He couldn't believe Jenny's killer was begging in such a disgusting manner. He felt no sorrow for him. didn't care that he had been duped into doing it by Lennox Thompson. All he felt was the anger he had bottled up from the moment Peters had entered the house earlier in the evening. This weasel, this pathetic excuse of a man had robbed him of Jenny. He raised the gun.

'No!' Peters screamed, foolishly putting his hand out and trying to grab the weapon. Scowling, Lamont's finger tightened on the trigger and there was a loud bang that echoed around the building. The bullet went through Peters outstretched hand, slamming into his chest. It threw him backwards and he crumpled to the ground. Stepping forward, Lamont emptied the rest of the clip into him, still squeezing the trigger long after he'd run out of bullets. He yelled, startling the men present, breathing hard as the smoking gun trembled in his hands. The first bullet would have surely killed him, but the stream that followed had removed all possibility of survival.

For a full two minutes Lamont stared down at his body, then turned to the men present, who were all gawping at him, having never seen such a reaction from their normally stoic boss.

'Take care of this,' he ordered, striding from the spot without another glance at the dead man.

CHAPTER EIGHTEEN

Thursday 21 May 2015

'I HAVEN'T BEEN HERE in a long time.'

Marika had the day off and when Lamont had called around, asking if they could spend some time together, she'd readily agreed. They'd run a few errands, then went for some lunch, and were now at the graves of their parents. She turned to her brother. He was dressed for the warm weather in a crisp t-shirt and khaki chinos.

'When was the last time you came?'

'Two years ago. The day after that dinner party you had. Auntie and I got into an argument and I stormed out and got drunk. The next day, I came out here and spent some time.'

Marika remembered the night. She had announced her relationship with Marrion, hoping to get under Lamont's skin, but the argument with their Aunt had taken all the attention from them.

Looking back, she didn't even know why she invited her. She loved Aunt Carmen and accepted she was hard work, but had long since given up on getting her and Lamont to make peace. Aunt Carmen was the catalyst for their next disagreement. Fuelled by grief over Marcus's death, Marika and Lamont argued, and he had called her a parasite. Other than another argument after an attack at Marika's that she wrongly accused him of orchestrating, they hadn't spoken for almost two years.

Marika learned of his shooting and even through her grief over Marrion, had cried over her big, strong brother, laid up in the hospital and barely alive. She spent time with Jenny, watching over him until he made a recovery, and then she stopped coming.

It wasn't until she was dealing with Aunt Carmen without Lamont around, that she realised just how hateful the woman was. She was bitter about everything and utterly spiteful towards her family. Marika's children loathed her, and many members of the family made excuses to avoid spending time with her. Marika still loved her, but their relationship had definitely changed in the past few years.

She doubted Aunt Carmen had been to the graves since their parents had been buried there. She had certainly never taken them.

'Why did you stay away for so long?' she asked.

'I couldn't face it. Sometimes I would come, and I'd stare at these pieces of stone and speak with them, and then I'd feel guilty, like I knew they wouldn't be pleased with my life choices.'

'I think they would be happy as long as you were,' Marika replied. It seemed like the right thing to say.

'I think I'm happy,' he said. 'I feel better than I have in a while.'

When Lamont said that, Marika glanced at him. He seemed more focused and locked-on than he had recently, more like his old self, and certainly better rested. His eyes were clearer and as he turned to meet her gaze, he had a small smile on his face that seemed to encompass him and make him appear younger. Lamont had never lost his looks. He was a *Jones* like her, and they were a good looking family, but Lamont's sadness had diminished them. Now, he was her brother all over again, and he seemed in that moment to stand taller than ever.

'Have you been sleeping?'

Lamont nodded, his smile widening.

'I've been sleeping well for a few days now.'

'Why?' Marika asked. Turning from the grave, Lamont held out his hand for Marika to take, like when they were kids.

'Good things are happening,' he said, as they walked away. He wouldn't tell Marika about Peters, but since he had killed him, Lamont felt freer, his burden of guilt and despair removed. The bullets he pumped into the killer's body had been cathartic.

The morning after the deed, he'd woken up after a solid eight-hour sleep, and gone for a run. He'd had a stitch and felt exhausted, but it was a pleasing pain, and a sign things were on the up for him.

Lamont hadn't heard from Lennox, but assumed he would know about the death. The Jackie Smart Court address remained under surveillance. He had people in Miles Hill, keeping an eye out for Sinclair and discretely asking questions about the young killer. Lamont reached for his phone, but remembered Marika made him turn it off earlier when it wouldn't stop ringing.

It was all ending. Delroy had Lennox on the ropes, and Lamont had his head back in the game. When his people put the pieces together, they would make a last move against Lennox, root him out of his hiding place, and it would all be complete.

* * *

Lennox was in his safe house, reading over some *OurHood* documents. The organisation hadn't been the same after Malcolm's murder, and didn't seem to have the same pop. Malcolm had been a tremendous waste of potential for Lennox. He was the perfect man to feed Lennox's propaganda about the local dealers, but had fallen apart when he'd sent him after Jenny Campbell. Lennox considered it one of his biggest failures. He'd been warring with Delroy but took advantage of several schemes to ruin Teflon's position, just in case. Breaking up Teflon's relationship was one, but Malcolm had fallen for Jenny and after her murder, confronted Lennox just as he was set upon by Eddie Williams, seeking revenge for the murder of his brother Winston. Malcolm had died in the confusion, and Lennox escaped with his life after murdering Eddie.

With Malcolm being found alongside the son of a major drugs kingpin, it put *OurHood* under an ugly spotlight. A few stalwarts continued to lead the charge, attempting to keep the narrative fixed on police brutality and its effects on the streets of Leeds, but fewer people were getting involved. Even Trinidad's murder had been over-looked and marginalised.

Lennox was leaving the organisation to wither. It served little purpose anymore, and Delroy was moving the goalposts. His people were out in force, all-but suffocating the Hood to draw Lennox out. If it wasn't them, it was Teflon. His people were subtle and just survey-ing, but the pressure was still there. Shorty was still out there, appar-ently leading Teflon's crew, which likely meant rumours of a rift between the pair had been exaggerated.

When Lennox's phone rang, he put the papers to one side before answering.

'Speak.'

'You hear about Ryan?' said Mark Patrick, getting to the point.

'Which Ryan?'

'Our Ryan. Peters. Someone killed him. Probably Delroy's lot, right?'

'Right,' lied Lennox. He'd known about the murder the day after it happened and was surprised it had taken Mark so long to contact him. Peters had messed up, just as Lutel had messed up by shooting Shorty's daughter. The only punishment for such acts was death. Without Shorty around, Lennox was sure he could have negotiated with Teflon down the line, but he'd been forced to escalate the conflict further.

Mark had also messed up when he didn't check if Trinidad was in the building before destroying it. By all rights Lennox could have killed him too, but had held off on that action. Unlike the others, Mark was too useful to be wasted in such a fashion.

Lennox needed him to keep the ranks focused. He'd heard the grumbles about the ongoing war, and the team were chafing under the conditions, constantly having to watch out for ambushes. Lennox spent most of his time reading or thinking, his discipline serving him well. It stopped him making the silly moves others had made.

'Do you want me to investigate? They left him out in the open, so I guess they're sending a message.'

'Don't bother. Keep everyone focused, and stick to the plan. Understand?'

'Understood, boss. I'll keep you posted.'

Hanging up, Lennox went back to his reading.

* * *

After leaving Marika, Lamont called Maka.

'Boss, long time no speak. Tried calling back earlier, but your phone was off. Are you still wanting that meet?'

'Yes. I want Manson, K and Shorty. Darren too, if you think he's needed.'

'You know about Shorty . . . helping out?'

'Of course I do,' replied Lamont. 'I'll leave it to you to organise a time and place.'

'No problem. I can handle that. Are you alright?'

'I'm great.'

Maka paused. 'You sound it. Compared to how you were last time, you sound different. Sharper.'

'I'm feeling it, fam. Set up that meeting and we can talk about it more face to face.'

'Got you.'

Lamont hung up with a smile on his face. The last time he'd felt like this had been the morning after Akhan's death. There had been the sense then that his life was going to change, but this was different. He'd shown Peters true power that night. He had played God with his life and strung him along, making him believe he could live. It had been part of his plan. If he believed he was going to die, there was the chance he would be less willing to give any information on his crew.

Lamont had manipulated him, told him of Lennox's betrayal, and left the slight hope open that he might be allowed to walk away. The death had changed something in him. It had brought his older, more composed self back to the surface, ready to finish what he had started. From there, he would get the crew back in line and everyone would make more money.

With the war over, there would be no reason for Jakkar and Stefanos to keep him out of the loop any longer. The police would move onto new targets. Everything rested on getting Lennox out of the way, and Lamont was making it his number one priority. He share his information with the crew, and they would work together with Delroy's crew to finish the job once and for all.

*　*　*

Shorty was sat by Grace's beside, holding her hand. She had woken a few times over the past week for short periods, but there was still a long way to go before she would recover.

To Shorty's relief, she seemed to thrive under the more personalised care. He couldn't take his eyes from her. Watching her breathing rise and fall was tranquil. If Grace had died, Shorty knew he would have completely lost it. Until he'd gone to see Amy to leave her his money, he had been ready to ride the path to the end, killing any of Lennox's men he saw in front of him.

Amy and the thoughts of being a proper father to Grace had pulled him back from the suicidal edge. He hadn't spoken with Amy in a few days, and had hoped to see her when he visited Grace, but she hadn't come yet. They would normally make the trips to see Grace together, but he had a feeling she was avoiding him. Their conversations had been shorter since he had told her his feelings and let her know he wanted something real between them.

A growing part of him felt she was trying to let him down easily, and it hurt. He recalled the comments she had made a while back about dating other people and believed he had been slow in picking up the signs. It was a bitter pill to swallow. He loved the thought of something real taking place with them, but Shorty was who he was, and she knew that. Whether they were together, he would always be a part of Grace's life, and when it came down to it, that was all that mattered.

Maybe he needed to move on too.

After sitting with Grace for another hour, Shorty placed a gentle kiss on her forehead and left, turning his phone back on when he left the facility. He had numerous messages from Maka and called him back as he walked to his car.

'Yes, Shorty. Everything good? I tried you a few times.'

'I was with Grace, I don't keep the phone on just in case. What's going on?'

'Teflon wants a meeting.'

'Okay. Why are you telling me?'

'He wants you there. Mentioned you by name.'

Shorty frowned. He and Lamont hadn't spoken since their argument at Trinidad's funeral. He couldn't think what he would have to say, and wasn't happy at the idea of being around him.

'I don't need to be there.'

'You're needed, fam. The moves we've made recently are down to you, and that needs to be recognised. You don't need to speak, but at least show up so we know what's what?'

'When are you meeting?'

'Tonight. Haven't arranged the place yet.'

'Can't do tonight. Let me get back to you with a time.'

'Cool. Let me know.'

CHAPTER NINETEEN
Friday 22 May 2015

FOR THE SECOND time in as many meetings, Rigby met Terry Worthy alone. It was barely past nine o'clock in the morning. Murphy was back at the office doing paperwork and covering for Rigby, who had been ordered off any investigations into Teflon and his crew. Despite the spate of shootings and attacks, they couldn't tie them to any of it, and all the intelligence received suggested he and his crew weren't directly involved.

Rigby would have had his usual disdain for meeting with Terry if it wasn't for one key difference: Terry had requested it, and that told Rigby that he had something good to share.

When he arrived, Terry was already waiting, and he was smiling. His posture differed from the last meeting, and Rigby could have sworn he looked like he had just been laid.

'Good to see you, Rig.'

'You too. Why are you so happy?'

'For once, you're gonna be kissing my arse mate, I'm telling you.'

'We'll see. Do you know where I can find Delroy Williams or Lennox Thompson?' Rigby hoped he did. They were sure these were the two gangs responsible for waging war in Chapeltown, but there was no direct proof other than hearsay. They couldn't question them based on circumstantial evidence, and had no witnesses.

That being said, the policy regarding witnesses was currently under review. Rigby had gone over Reid's head and submitted a letter to her boss, showing how the department had messed up pertaining to the misuse of Adele Chapman, and how it would look if the press was to stumble onto this fact. He'd heard nothing back directly, but the station had been awash with talk of DCI Reid being summoned to a meeting. It was a minor victory, but one, nonetheless.

The bodies were still dropping, though. A body had been found a few days ago, one Ryan Peters. He was affiliated with Lennox's crew, but no one was claiming credit for his death. He had been shot multiple times, including once through the hand, suggesting he'd tried to stop the bullet. It was a brutal killing, and the body had been moved, meaning they didn't know where the original location was, making it harder. Thankfully, Rigby and Murphy weren't on that case.

'No, mate. No one does. They're giving their orders and staying out of the way. No one wants to get caught in the middle of that.'

'Why have you called me here then?'

'I don't have anything on Teflon, but he's not really involved in the running anymore. Like I told you last time, Shorty and K-Bar are running the crew.'

'Where is Teflon then?'

'Fuck knows. No one, and I mean no one, is seeing him. He's on the missing list.'

'How is that not causing a panic?'

'K-Bar's back. It's reassuring people. Him and Shorty were always a bloody double act, and now they're running the show.' Terry's tone barely hid his bitterness at the state of affairs. He could tolerate K-Bar, but had never liked Shorty, and knew the feeling was mutual.

Rigby gritted his teeth. The mention of K-Bar made his blood boil. The way he had smiled in his face before his release made Rigby want to knock all his teeth down his throat. He didn't like to make things personal, but getting something on K-Bar would make him infinitely happy, and he had few reasons for such an attitude these days.

'Okay, so you have nothing new then.'

Terry waved his hands and said, 'slow down, mate. I told you I have something you're gonna like. The difference with K-Bar and Shorty is that they're not as squirrelly as my mate Teflon. Much more inclusive, if you know what I mean. They're comfy too; like having their big meetings in the same spot.'

Rigby felt the smile stretching the corners of his mouth. It was impossible to survey places if you couldn't definitively prove the targets were using them to discuss criminal business. Teflon and his contemporaries never had meetings in their houses, or anywhere with any frequency. They had safe houses dotted all over, and homes of mutual acquaintances they could use if they saw fit. If they were getting lazy and using the same spots, it would help with the probable cause.

'Seriously?'

'Serious. Dunno if you know the name *Darren Lyles*, but he's the little bastard in charge of recruitment. Me and him go way back, and I took him for some drinks the other night. We had a chat, and I pumped his ego a bit, told him about how well he was doing. He was telling me about some new faces, bragging really. There's a kid named Roman who they're all in love with. He's got a partner he runs around with . . .'

'*Keith*. I know the pair,' interrupted Rigby. Roman and Keith were smarter and had more common sense than the average little shits. If they were learning under Teflon and his crew, it would only make them more dangerous. 'How did they get those two on board?' He continued.

'According to Darren, they helped them with some problems they were having with local crews. They slapped a few people around and put the word out that Roman and co were under their protection. Now, they're paying a percentage and getting access to Teflon's product. I guarantee Teflon's stuff is the best on the streets. It always sells.'

'You can't tell me anything about where he's getting his supply?' asked Rigby, though he was sure of the answer. At one point it was alleged Teflon was getting his supply directly from Delroy Williams, but those days were long gone. He'd apparently hooked up with some new heavyweights, but all inroads into investigating the chain had led nowhere. It was one of the things he'd planned to pump K-Bar for information on once he had worn him down.

'Okay, so Shorty and K-Bar are switching things up, Teflon is on holiday, and Darren is hiring thugs to keep the crew going into the next century?'

'Pretty much. Things are different now. Teflon kept everything on a need-to-know basis. Shorty and K-Bar are cagey, but nothing like Teflon. They're giving people the chance to prove themselves and get more involved. It means that just by being around certain people, I'm in the know like never before, meaning I have a list of hideouts and locations for numerous people tied to the crew.'

Rigby's smile grew. He gave Terry a lot of crap, but he had come through for them with this information.

'C'mon, let's sit somewhere so you can tell me all about it.'

'I wanna know what I'm gonna get first. I've done you lot a right service here, so it should wipe clean my old record, right?' said Terry.

'That would depend on where the info leads. Is there nothing you can tell me about Teflon, or about the street war?'

'No, boss.'

Rigby nodded. He was satisfied with what he had. He needed to sell his boss on the information, and he wasn't her favourite person after his previous actions. Locking his car, he climbed into Terry's Audi, keeping his head low as he pulled off at speed.

* * *

'Detective Rigby. I understand you have some information for me?'

Reid folded her arms, her eyes boring into Rigby's.

Hours had passed since his conversation with Terry Worthy, and the information was extensive. There were more than a dozen locations, some storage for product and weapons. There was a list of spots that were used for meetings, along with various hideouts for soldiers.

A year ago, he would have already been surveying the properties and getting warrants, but this was a different time It would have been difficult even without him being on Reid's shit list, but now it would be near impossible. It wouldn't stop him from pushing as far as he needed to.

'I met with one of my informants. He contacted me and asked for a meeting, claiming to have vital information.'

'That's great. What did he tell you about the war?'

Rigby paused. 'Everyone knows the players involved, but there is nothing tying Lennox or Delroy to any illegal activity. Both men are well hidden and are giving their orders likely through buffers to avoid any direct links.'

Reid frowned. 'If that is the case, then what is the purpose of this meeting?'

'My informant had information pertaining to Teflon's crew.'

'That would be the crew you were specifically instructed not to investigate?'

'I stuck to that, ma'am. I haven't investigated them, but my informant is part of the crew, and had relevant information. There have been restructures which has led to laxness in certain areas, namely *security*.'

'Get to the point.'

'The point,' continued Rigby, ignoring the rudeness, 'is that I now have a list of locations linked to the crew. I'm talking safe houses, storage spots, places where they hold meetings. This is everything we need.'

'It doesn't involve the main Chapeltown conflict. That is our mandate. To stop that war by any means necessary. It is not our mandate to look into other criminals that have nothing to do with it.'

This wasn't going well. Reid's demeanour was the same, but her words implied she was growing tired of the conversation. He had to push deeper.

'This lead could be the one that nets us the whole thing, ma'am. I still believe Teflon and his crew are involved in the war, and I want to prove it. Shorty's daughter was shot. Teflon's partner was murdered. His business, co-owned with Trinidad Tommy — a man beloved in Chapeltown — was blown up. These incidents connect to the wider issue, and with more pieces behind bars, I will prove that. All I need is a little more time, and warrants and resources for the locations. Give me ninety-six hours and if I have nothing, pull them back. Do this, and we will break the back of the Chapeltown gangs and restore confidence in the area, in our officers.'

Reid didn't reply for several minutes. Rigby didn't turn away, continuing to meet her gaze until finally, she coughed into her fist.

'Ninety-six hours, and not a second more, Detective Rigby. You will have whatever pieces you need but hear this: if this investigation leads nowhere, I promise your career will never be the same afterwards. Do you understand?'

'I do, ma'am. Thank you.'

* * *

Shorty knocked on the door of the address he'd been given, glancing around as he waited for an answer. He hadn't been to Little London in a while, but he'd never liked the area. Unlike Chapeltown, which was full of energy and always bustling, little London felt bleak and sterile by comparison. A few seconds later, the door opened, and a woman smiled at him. Her milk chocolate skin complimented her white blouse, curly black hair tumbling past her shoulders. He'd forgotten how beautiful she was.

'Hey, Shorty.'

'Sienna. How've you been?'

Sienna smiled warmly.

'I heard about your daughter. I'm so sorry, Shorty. I didn't think Lutel would be capable of such a thing.'

'She's alive, and that's all the counts,' said Shorty, remembering Lutel's face before he put a bullet in him. Torturing and killing him had made him feel good, and he only wished he'd had longer to make Lennox's lackey suffer. 'How come you asked me to come see you?'

'Come inside. Can't really speak about these things on the doorstep,' she said. They sat in the living room. It was cosy, though cramped, with bookshelves, two tables, and a selection of trashy magazines, books, and DVD's.

Sienna invited Shorty to sit on the sofa, and she took a seat next to him. Neither spoke for a moment. Shorty was still wondering what her game was. He'd become involved with Sienna a few months ago after meeting her at an *OurHood* meeting. They'd gone out a few times, but she had a jealous ex named Lutel, whom everyone feared. He'd started running his mouth about Shorty taking liberties with his woman, and this culminated in a fight at Jukie's bar, which Shorty easily won, beating the man unconscious with a bar stool.

Undeterred, Lutel fired back, literally, shooting Grace instead of Shorty. Shorty retaliated by killing Lutel and his accomplice, but not before learning of Lennox's direct involvement. With everything that had happened since, he had forgotten all about Sienna, until she had contacted him out of the blue.

'Go on then, what is it?'

'It's about Lennox.'

CHAPTER TWENTY

Friday 22 May 2015

SIENNA HAD SHORTY'S ATTENTION. He leaned forward, brow furrowing as he waited.

'Lennox never spoke much around me, but I knew him through Lutel. I know a girl who used to deal with him.'

'Deal with him how? She was his girlfriend?' Shorty hadn't found a single thread he could pull on surrounding Lennox. He had no family they could get to, and before now, had been linked to no women. This was a massive development.

'Yeah. That's why I contacted you. I want to help.'

'Can you put me in touch with her?'

'I wanted to talk to you first.'

'About what?'

'About us.'

Shorty said nothing. They had barely got off the ground, and he'd forgotten all about her until she contacted. It wasn't worth alienating her, so he needed to be coy.

'Is there an us?' She pressed.

'Honestly, I don't know. I went to a dark place after my girl got shot, and I didn't want to know anyone. I certainly wasn't thinking about the future.'

'What about now?'

'Things are getting better, but there's still work to do. If you wanna talk more after things get sorted, I'm willing to have that conversation.'

Sienna shifted closer to Shorty and when their lips met, he didn't pull away. Instead, he deepened the kiss, his hand entangled in her hair, pulling her ever closer before finally pulling away. Sienna smiled.

'That was some kiss. I'll be in touch,' she said. Shorty nodded. The kiss hadn't made him feel good. Instead, he felt hollow. Amy still hadn't spoken to him and rather than act as a distraction, the kiss only made him more frustrated with the circumstances.

* * *

Lamont's good mood carried on into the next day. He had again slept without issue, and woken up fresh and alert, handling some business with Ahmed, who had become much more receptive to him. They were due to go out for dinner again soon, with plans to invite Mustafa.

There had been no repercussions for killing Peters. His men had been meticulous in dumping the body, and the local news was linking it to the ongoing *Chapeltown War*, suggesting it might spread throughout Leeds.

Ahmed had made some cryptic comments about Jakkar and his displeasure with the lack of resolution in the conflict, but Lamont hadn't responded. When Lennox was taken out, the war would end, and he believed they were close in that regard. He had used the information given by Peters, Jukie, and other sources, along with intel from watching the Jackie Smart Court property, to narrow down where Lennox might be hiding. He didn't think he was in Chapeltown or any of the surrounding areas, but Cross Gates was a possibility as he'd had a base there before. Lennox also had links in Garforth, and Lamont's people were investigating these. No one had found Sinclair yet, but they had found some other little knuckleheads he associated with, and they were being watched.

It was early evening when he made his way to Kate's house. They hadn't spoken since Jenny's funeral, but he had made her a promise at the grave site, and part of it had been fulfilled. She was with Tek, an old friend of Lamont's, when he arrived. Predictably, Tek grinned when he saw Lamont and greeted him with a hug.

'Good to see you, mate. I'm sorry about Jen. I was stuck outta town and couldn't make the funeral.'

'It's fine, bro. I appreciate it regardless.' Lamont noticed Kate behind Tek, giving him a searching look.

'Tek,' she said. 'Can you go to the shop and get me some cigs please?'

'Sure. L, you want anything?'

Lamont shook his head. Patting him on the shoulder, Tek left. Lamont and Kate went to stand in the back garden.

'This isn't a random visit, is it?'

'I wanted to give you an update,' said Lamont.

'How have you been doing with everything? I feel like I lost a part of myself, L. I really do. She was beyond my best friend and not having her hasn't got any easier.' Kate rubbed her arms.

Lamont hung his head. He felt exactly the same way, and that was the hardest part to overcome.

'I know how you feel. Getting used to her not being there hasn't been easy.'

Kate gave him a shy smile.

'It's okay to miss her. You loved her.'

'Ryan.'

'Ryan?' Kate blinked, confused.

'The man who stabbed Jenny. That's his name.' Lamont watched Kate processing this information, her eyes going through a host of different emotions, widening as she realised the significance.

'He's dead?' Her voice croaked.

'Yes.'

Lamont didn't add anymore, and Kate didn't ask him to. She flung her arms around him, and his shoulder was wet with her tears as she sobbed. He tightened his hold on her and for a moment, it felt like Jenny was there with them. They stayed like that even as Tek appeared in the doorway behind them. He locked eyes with Lamont, knowing there was nothing romantic about the moment. With a nod, he went back inside. Tek had known Jenny longer than Lamont, but he knew they cared for her as much as anyone. He wouldn't intrude on whatever was happening between them.

Lamont was in no hurry to let Kate go. This was someone who had been just as affected as him. He remembered how crumpled she had looked at the funeral. He had done this for her as much as himself, and she hadn't judged him for it. Lennox was the last piece. Lamont didn't mention his name. If it reassured Kate to think it was over, he was okay with that.

'What happens now?' Kate mumbled as they finally broke apart. She wiped her eyes.

'I don't know,' he said.

'I know you loved her, L, but you shouldn't hold back. Live your life to the fullest, that's what she would have wanted.'

'I think she would have wanted to still be alive, and the rest is just conjecture,' said Lamont. Kate sounded like the rest of them; hopelessly naïve and trying to predict the actions of a dead person. The fact was, he still had some debt to pay back, and he intended to do so.

'I knew Jenny since we were kids, L. I don't deny what the two of you had and it's so sad it only lasted a short while, but put this behind you and move on. It doesn't hurt her memory, I promise you that.'

Lamont didn't reply. He took his phone from his pocket, noting Maka had tried calling him.

'I need to call someone back,' he said to Kate.

'Stay for dinner. Please. We'll have a few drinks and relax, listen to some music.'

'I think I'll need to jet. I've been waiting on this call,' replied Lamont. Kate nodded and went inside, leaving him in the garden. He called Maka back.

'Are we on?' he said. He'd been waiting days for Maka to get back to him.

'Tomorrow. It took me a second to get everyone together. I'll drop you a message with the location.'

'Catch you then.' Lamont hung up, once again reminding himself that he was almost at the end.

Kate was lighting a cigarette when he entered the room. She looked up and gave him a small smile.

'My plans have changed,' he said. 'If you still wanna chill, I'm down.'

'What do you feel like eating?' she asked, her smile widening.

* * *

K-Bar and Marika were curled up on the sofa, drinking wine and half-watching TV.

'I saw L the other day,' she said, giving up on the boring action movie completely.

'The *invisible man* . . . what's he saying?'

'We went to visit our parents' graves,' replied Marika. 'He looked well. I don't know what changed, but he seemed lighter, like he didn't have the weight of the world on his shoulders for once. When you spoke, did he say anything to you about how he was feeling, or what was going on?'

'You know your bro better than me, Rika. He takes *secretive* to a whole new level. Doesn't talk when he doesn't have to.'

'Something happened, I'm telling you. It's like he got laid or something.'

'Maybe he did. Not exactly difficult for him, is it?'

'His girlfriend died like a month ago. Do you think he could do it?'

'Maybe. Probably. It's hard to tell what's going on with your bro.'

Marika sighed. 'Whatever it is, I'm glad it happened. He looked so much better.'

'I hope that means he's ready to get locked onto the crew, because people are grumbling about him not being around. He's losing face on the streets the longer he avoids dealing with people. They need to see him out and about, leading, or they will lose even more faith.'

Marika pulled away from K-Bar, eyes flashing. 'My brother's mental state is more important than the streets.'

'That may be the case for you, but we came up in those same streets, and me, L, and Shorty, we've been playing that game since we were kids.' K-Bar wasn't backing down from her. 'Fact is, if he doesn't step up in a major way, our way of living could be done.'

'I thought you guys were winning now? You said Shorty was leading.'

'Shorty is like me. He's more of a tactician, but it's easier to smack someone over the head than to be diplomatic. He's doing well now because we're putting ourselves out there on the streets, slapping a few jokers around, but we need the thinkers like L. That's where he shines. He sees three moves ahead, and right now we're only making one. The crew still looks vulnerable and if we don't fix up, people are gonna try us again.'

Before Marika could open her mouth to reply, K-Bar's phone rang. Grumbling, he checked the number. 'It's Shorty. Better take this,' he muttered, before answering, 'what's up?'

'I'm outside. Need to speak to you.'

'Now?' K-Bar was relaxed and hadn't intended on going anywhere. Shorty's response was to hang up. Kissing his teeth, K-Bar clambered to his feet and smoothed out his trousers.

'Gotta go,' he said. 'Don't wait up. Could be a late one if it's business.'

'Okay.'

Giving her a quick kiss, K-Bar grabbed a hooded top and left the house. Shorty's ride was outside, the engine running. He climbed into the passenger seat and slapped hands with Shorty, who immediately drove away, eyes on the road.

'What the hell? You couldn't have come for me in the morning? I was rooted.'

'This couldn't wait, bro. I need to meet someone and I want you to come with me.'

'Who are we meeting?'

'Lennox's ex-girlfriend.'

'What ex?' K-Bar's eyes widened. He couldn't recall Lennox ever being linked to a woman on a serious level.

'Remember Sienna? The one I smacked up Lutel over? She's setting up this meeting with me and the girl.'

'Why?' K-Bar frowned. It didn't sound right.

'Says she felt bad over what happened to Grace.'

'And she's only just contacting you now? Sounds dodgy, fam.'

'Why do you think you're watching my back. Are you strapped?'

'No. I was chilling on the sofa, bro. You didn't even say where we were going.'

'Check under your seat.'

K-Bar pulled out a Glock and checked the weapon. It was lighter than expected, but he could make it work. In their younger days, they had trained with whatever guns they could get their hands on, determined to have the edge in any encounter. It had been years since he had used one, but he would manage.

Neither man spoke the rest of the way. K-Bar recognised the area as Meanwood and hoped there wouldn't be trouble. He had been cool with the older, established gangs in the area, but the newer gangs were as bad as the Chapeltown ones, and they didn't respect anyone.

They parked up outside a pale bricked semi-detached spot. Both men had their guns by their sides in case of an ambush. Shorty knocked on the door and when Sienna answered, he gave her a tight smile.

'Hey, this is my boy, K-Bar. He's watching out for me.'

'Didn't you trust me?' Sienna was almost pouting, but Shorty wasn't in the mood for it.

'We're warring out there. We don't travel light. Is she here?'

Sienna nodded, leaning in for a kiss. Shorty tensed, but returned it. K-Bar gave him a weird look but said nothing.

In the living room, a slim, brown skinned woman was sitting on the sofa, wringing her hands together. She was clearly nervous. Shorty could understand why Lennox would be taken with such a beautiful woman.

'Julia, this is Shorty, the guy I was telling you about.'

Julia's eyes immediately flitted to the guns Shorty and K-Bar were holding.

'I'm not gonna hurt you,' said Shorty, trying to reassure her. 'It's just for protection.'

Julia nodded, but didn't look relieved in the slightest. Sienna made them all cups of coffee and they sat in uncomfortable silence. Shorty was waiting for Julia to start. He exchanged a look with K-Bar, who yawned, probably regretting leaving Marika.

'Jules, these guys are cool. I promise. Tell them what you have to say. Please,' said Sienna.

Julia took a deep breath, resting her hands on her thighs.

'I . . .' she cleared her throat. 'I've known Lennox a long time. We met when I was sixteen. He was twenty, and he swept me off my feet. I . . . he wasn't especially romantic, but he was honest and tough, and said what was on his mind, and I fell for him.'

Shorty was listening, but growing more annoyed by the second. He'd figured Julia would have information, not some bullshit love story. He again glanced at K-Bar who shook his head, silently cautioning Shorty to be patient.

'For a while, we were fine. My mum didn't like me being with an older guy, so he moved me into a flat and he would stop by now and then, but things were different. He was out in the streets building himself up, and he didn't always have time for me.'

Shorty could relate. A lot of his dalliances had fizzled out because he needed to be in the mix, making things happen in the streets.

'I never heard about him disrespecting me with women, but I knew at the same time I *didn't* have him, if that makes sense.

'I was naïve and didn't really understand how deeply he was entrenched in the crime life. Soon, he got locked up, and I was a mess. I didn't know how I would cope, but somehow I kept the flat and kept going. He sent me money, and I dropped out of college and got a job. There were visits, and he looked well, even behind bars. In the visiting room I saw how much people respected him, and it was strange.

'When he got out, he flew me to Egypt and for the entire holiday, he was attentive and loving, and any misgivings I'd had were ironed out. He sucked me back in.'

It was a nice tale, but Shorty was going to go ballistic if there wasn't an endpoint. K-Bar was concentrating, and Sienna looked moved by the tale that she had probably heard before.

'Back in Leeds, he was back out there in the streets, and he seemed harder, more closed-off than before.

'We started arguing, and I guess I thought he would listen to me when I said he was changing, but he just said I could accept him for who he was, or I could leave.' Sienna gathered herself. 'I loved him and couldn't imagine not being with him, so I stayed. He wasn't around anymore, though. He was in and out of town, doing deals. I'd find guns hidden in the flat, along with packages of money, and it all grew too real for me. So, I left.

'I expected him to chase me and beg for me back, but of course, he didn't. I didn't hear from him for a few years and I moved on, but then he sought me out. By this time, I was in another relationship with a guy I liked. Lennox had my heart though, and soon I was cheating on my partner with him.

'Eventually we tried again, but Lennox was way different now. He had gone from strength to strength in the crime game. He wanted me to move in with him. Mentioned marriage and taking care of me, but when I fell pregnant, I saw the other side. He told me I had to get an abortion, and I was terrified. Deep down I knew if I didn't, he would kill me and the baby. I did it, and then I left again. Again, he let me, and again, he went to prison.

'He stayed away for four years now and our paths randomly crossed when I was out with Sienna. She was with Lutel at this point, and when I saw Lennox, all the old feelings came rushing back. I remember him saying I was under his skin,' Sienna's head bowed slightly, but she composed herself. 'We slept together for a while longer, but we drifted apart, and here I am,' she finished.

'What the fuck was the point of that?' said Shorty, unable to hold back. He had listened to her entire pathetic tale of love for no reason.

'Shorty!' hissed Sienna. 'That's my friend you're insulting.'

'Do you lot think I came here to listen to her recount some love story? This is real-life shit.'

'You think I don't know that?' snapped Julia. 'It may not mean much to you, but even my being here is tearing me apart inside. I gave him years of my life, pieces of my soul. I'm here to help.'

'Why did you want to speak to us?' Shorty decided moving past the melodrama was the best bet. He felt K-Bar straighten behind him.

'Lennox will never let me go. I'll never have a life of my own because he's always out there, waiting to prey. Sienna told me about

what he ordered to be done to your daughter. It can't go on. You need
to stop him.'

'We're working on it.'

'I have an address for you. Lennox stays there. He likes it because it
has sentimental value. We lived there on and off for a few years.'

'When was the last time you were there?'

Again, Julia lowered her head. 'Valentine's day.'

Shorty felt a wave of euphoria surge through his veins. That was
only a few months ago. It meant the house was still in circulation, and
Lennox wouldn't know they knew. He shot K-Bar a look, seeing the
same level of understanding etched onto his friend's normally
inscrutable face.

'Do you know who I am?' Shorty asked, wanting Julia to understand
what she was essentially engineering by giving them the address.

'I know you're dangerous, but I also know you love your daughter,
and he should pay for what he caused.'

'Where's the house?'

'Garforth. I'll write down the address for you.'

They didn't stay much longer. Shorty suffered through another hug
and kiss with Sienna, then he and K-Bar drove away.

'What a story,' said K-Bar.

'Fucking nonsense is what it was. Can't believe we're gonna get
Lennox on the back of his ex feeling unfulfilled.'

'Who are we gonna get to scope out the spot?'

'I'll do it myself,' said Shorty instantly.

'I don't think that's a good idea, fam,' said K-Bar. 'When are you
gonna find the time to do that, anyway? We're deep in the streets, and
Roman and that lot need a firm hand. They're not ready yet.'

'You can monitor them. I'm doing this.'

'You don't need to do it by yourself. We can use people for this.
Bring L in on it and come up with a proper plan.'

'We don't need L, and I want to do this myself. Lennox nearly
killed my daughter, and it has to be me that finishes him. Not L, and
not that motherfucker Delroy.' He pulled the car to a stop on a quiet
street and glared at K-Bar. 'I need you to support me. If it was the
other way around, you wouldn't even need to ask, and you know it.'

K-Bar couldn't deny that. As much as he wanted to tell Shorty to use the crew, this was who he was.

'Okay, I'll go along with it, fam.'

* * *

Shorty spent all night watching the address, hoping he would find Lennox Thompson and end him early. He left his surveillance at four in the morning, and no one had shown in that time.

The meeting with Julia had been illuminating. From everything he knew about Lennox, it was strange to imagine him getting caught up with a woman and almost having a child. He wondered how being a parent would have changed Lennox. Ultimately, it was pointless to think about. He needed to get a few hours of sleep to be sharp for the meeting later. Being around Lamont wouldn't be easy, but Shorty would handle it. There were things that needed to be said. Sienna was another matter altogether. She was attractive and seemed interested, but she wasn't Amy, and he couldn't shake that.

Heading to his spot and collapsing on his bed, he quickly drifted off to sleep.

* * *

Naveed arranged a meeting room for the crew in a back room of another club. They arrived separately dressed in *going out* clothes. He had prepared the room accordingly. There was a chocolate brown sofa, along with several smaller love-seat style seats. Bottles of brandy rested on a tray, along with glasses and ice.

'Did you want food?' he asked. Lamont shook his head, and the rest followed suit. Maka and Manson sat on the sofa, making a start on the brandy. Shorty wasn't drinking, and neither was Lamont. He glanced at Shorty, who scowled back. It would not be easy, but he couldn't give up now. Not when he was so close to the end.

'We're all here then, L,' said Maka. 'Are you gonna tell us what this is about?'

Lamont nodded, assessing each man before he started speaking.

'I won't rehash all the things Lennox has done, but he hurt people close to me, and I made it my mission to learn more about him, and the people working for him.' He locked eyes with Shorty again, seeing his old friend wasn't convinced. 'Ryan Peters, the dude that was killed in Seacroft. He did a job for Lennox. It was supposed to a be routine kidnap job, but the woman fought back. She grabbed a knife, he fought with her, and ended up getting stabbed.'

'Jenny,' said Shorty, putting the pieces together. Lamont nodded.

'He's dead now. Before he died, he mentioned the name Mark Patrick. He's the one doing all Lennox's running around. He also mentioned a shooter. *Sinclair*. He gunned down Akeem on Chapeltown Road.'

'Sinclair . . . Never heard of him,' said Manson. Maka looked equally confused.

'Delroy is focusing on shutting down whatever people he can find. I want us to focus on finding this pair. I have men on it, but with our experience, we can do more. K-Bar, you and Shorty are trackers. I want you to go deep underground and smoke them out. Use whatever people and resources you need to do it.' Lamont waited for them to reply. Shorty spoke first, as expected, but his words threw Lamont for a loop.

'Where've you been?'

Lamont blinked, confused by the question.

'What?'

'You've been hiding, doing your own thing, completely ignoring the crew. We've been holding things down, stopping the gangs on the street from pushing us out.'

'I know. I—'

'You come here after all this time, giving us a little speech, trying to get us back in line. It's all about you and your fucking agenda. Typical you, fam. Not caring about anyone or anything but what *you've* got going on. You don't give a shit about the crew.'

'That's not true, Shorty. Lennox is the single biggest threat to this crew.'

'Is he? Or are you?'

'What are you talking about?'

'I'm talking about this! You never letting people in on what's going on. Just expecting them to fall in line.'

Lamont's eyebrows rose. '*Fall in line?* Shorty, taking out Lennox was always the goal.'

'Why haven't you done that then?'

Lamont's mouth fell open. He was familiar with Shorty's temper tantrums, seeing him fly off the handle over the smallest things. This was the other side. The strategic, tactical side of Shorty's personality. It was influencing the room. K-Bar hadn't said a word, but he was nodding along with Shorty now.

'He's in hiding, Shorty. We haven't located him yet.'

'Nothing to do with you being scared of him then?'

'I'm not scared.'

'Explain it then. For once in your life, no sneaky shit. Lay it on the line and tell us why you haven't gone after him.'

'I'm cautious, Shorty. That caution has benefited the crew many times over. When you're at the top, making the decisions, it's different. It's all on you, and you have to pick the right moves.'

'Exactly. That's why I'm here. I've had to decide, because you walked away and left Maka and Manson in the lurch. You left K-Bar to rot, and I had to get him out. Where the fuck were you?'

'I . . .' Lamont didn't have the words for the first time in his life. Shorty shook his head, recognising the indecision.

'Guess that's more *caution* from the boss,' he said. 'You were nowhere. You hid in your house and you didn't care what was going on around you. That isn't leadership. We all put ourselves on the line for the crew and you know what? You don't have the heart anymore. Maybe you never did.'

Lamont looked at each man. Shorty and K-Bar had been alongside him when he started the crew. Maka and Manson had come into the fold later, but this was the first time all pieces had been united so clearly against him. K-Bar was looking at him with something akin to regret. Maka and Manson were staring at him like he was the enemy. He supposed he was now.

Had he been outplayed? Was this Shorty's plan all along?

Ultimately, it was still his crew. He still controlled their supply, but he had wanted them with him on this. He saw them taking down Lennox together and mending old fences.

'Shorty, whatever is going on between us, those are our problems. It doesn't affect crew business.'

'Our problems have grown bigger. You were about one thing: Lennox is a problem, but after he dies, things are gonna change, whether or not you want them to.'

Shorty stood up and left the room. One by one, each man followed, leaving Lamont sitting there, trying to work out what had just happened. He and Shorty had done most of the talking, but the divide was clear, and his crew supporting Shorty spoke volumes.

Lamont poured a drink, a leaden feeling in his stomach as he contemplated the mistakes he had made lately. Instead of gaining centre, he and Shorty were further away than ever.

CHAPTER TWENTY-ONE

Sunday 24 May 2015

THE NEXT MORNING, Lamont was still mulling over the disaster of a meeting. Shorty's words had resonated with him, and he couldn't work out exactly when he took his eye off the ball. He'd known Shorty was helping the crew, but he fully hadn't known to what degree. They were right about his lack of focus. He was determined to kill Lennox, but there was something wrong with him deep down that he couldn't put his finger on.

Lamont was supposed to be more powerful than ever, yet he didn't feel it. He had a loose alliance with the most powerful crime boss in the county. He'd avenged Jenny's murder by killing Peters. Grace was recovering, and he had more money than he could spend. Despite those wins, he felt desolate, and he hated it.

After spending some more time sulking, Lamont went to see Marika again, hoping she would make him feel better. Charlotte would have been useful, but he was giving her space after the way their last encounter had ended. He and Marika were at least on a loving level again, and he was pleased she was back in his life and doing so well. Maybe being around her would influence him.

Lamont knocked on the door, smiling tightly when K-Bar

answered. He wore a vest and tracksuit bottoms, and was holding a protein shaker.

'Easy, L. Everything good? I just finished a workout.'

'I came to see Marika. Is she in?'

K-Bar shook his head. 'She's at work. Come in, anyway. I think we have some things we need to say.'

Lamont could have pointed out that it was his sister's house and that he didn't need to be invited in, but he didn't. He sat on the sofa as K-Bar disappeared from the room, returning with a flannel which he used to clean his face. He remained standing, and the silence stretched on for a minute. It was comfortable despite the circumstances, as it usually was with K-Bar.

'What's going on, L?' K-Bar finally said.

'You'll need to be more specific,' said Lamont.

'That meeting yesterday. You could have said more to Shorty. You basically let him control the crew and I don't for a second think you didn't know he was running it all along.'

'Maybe it's for the best. I didn't say anything because Shorty's making the right decisions. It would be silly to overrule that.'

'You two are best when you're deciding together.'

'I can't see that happening. Shorty can't get over what happened with us. Maybe I can't either.'

'You need to keep talking to him, L. Shorty can be stubborn. You're the same way, and you two need each other.'

'I tried. I apologised and every time I see him, we end up antagonising one another further. He can focus on the crew, and I'll focus on Lennox. Maybe somewhere down the line, we'll meet in the middle.'

K-Bar finished his protein shake, still holding the container and frowning at Lamont.

'You're the mature one. I know it's tough, but you have to keep making the moves until you get through to him. I ain't telling you nothing new here. You know how to get to Shorty.'

'I used to. Me and Shorty haven't been right for a while though, and everything that's happened over the past few years has only made things worse. So, I'll focus on what I need to. I have leads for Lennox's

men, and I'll follow them. That's all I wanted to tell the crew last
night, but you guys supported Shorty instead.'

'Don't look at it like that. You're still our boss and you could have
forced the issue, but you didn't.'

'If I had, what would you have done? Would you have supported
me, or gone with Shorty?'

K-Bar didn't answer, not that Lamont expected him to. The answer
was obvious. Lamont might be the boss, but Shorty had got K-Bar out
of prison, and he had known him longer. Shorty had worked with Maka
and Manson when they were struggling, and used that to push the crew
forward and stop the vultures from swarming. It wasn't an even
situation.

'Do you have a line on Lennox?'

'Not yet,' admitted Lamont. 'Mark Patrick is probably the best bet.
He's the one Lennox is apparently keeping the closest, so he'll know
how to find Lennox. I have a few safe houses that need searching, so
we'll see. Delroy and his people are pushing at the crew, so I need to
touch base with him and see where he's at.'

For a moment, Lamont was sure he saw something in K-Bar's eyes,
almost like a gleam. He blinked, and it was gone.

'I'll watch Shorty for now. You're right about the street stuff.
Meeting got out of hand last night before we could go into it, but the
money is finally on the up. We're reloading soon too, and we're gonna
get twenty.'

'Twenty boxes? Do you have the moves lined up to offload it?'

'We've discussed it,' said K-Bar. 'It's more than we normally move
in a week, but we've got the crews back in line, so we'll knock it out
easily.'

Lamont was uneasy about the increased order. It was likely the
crew had the infrastructure to move it, and it meant he would get paid
twice, as both supplier and boss, but it was a tremendous risk.

'What about the police activity?'

'We'll wholesale it mostly, so it'll be out of our hands. Still gonna be
a lot of profit, and it's worth it. The more money we make, quicker we
get back to where we were, especially with Delroy being distracted
with Lennox.'

Lamont couldn't deny the merits of the plan. The police activity had eased as of late, as it always did with the authorities. All you had to do was wait them out. They had budgets and quotas they needed to justify, and survcillance and long-term investigations were expensive. He had made a career out of out-waiting the police, and it seemed to work for his crew too.

'Just be careful. There's a lot still going on, so eyes in the back of your head. How's it going with my sister?'

'She's a rider, L. Held me down while I was on remand, and we've been close since we got out. Everything is out in the open now, and I've cared about her for a long time.'

'She's changing. In a good way. She seems a lot more focused,' admitted Lamont.

'She's come a long way, L. That fight you lot had made her realise she had to stand on her own two feet. Worked hard on her CV so she could land a job, and then she worked hard in the job to establish herself. She had a rough start. Wasn't used to working, and she had that funky temper. Few times she came back shouting she was gonna quit, but she didn't.'

'A while back, she told me she was studying too, because she wanted to understand money,' said Lamont.

K-Bar beamed, his pride evident. 'She wants to open her own salon. She's been talking about it for a while, and she's working on the qualifications. I'm gonna back her when she's qualified.'

Lamont was smiling now too. Despite his off mood at the start of the day, the thought of his little sister making big moves was something to be pleased about. It had taken her a long time to grow up, but she was making up for it with excellent decision after excellent decision.

'That's amazing. I'm proud of her.'

'That's what she wants. You're always saying we should diversify and invest, so it'll be good for that too. Doing something solid with the money we're making. She really wants you to be proud of her. All the stuff that happened with Marrion and the Manchester boys . . . the guilt has lingered with her. She doesn't talk about it much anymore, but it's obvious.'

Lamont felt a jolt at the reminder of the group that had nearly ended his life. They'd had inside help, Chink pulling their strings in Machiavellian fashion, but they had still almost succeeded, taking advantage of the gaps in the crew to launch their attack.

Two years later, they were all still picking up the pieces.

'I never blamed her for that.' Lamont hated the thought of Marika blaming herself. She'd shown bad judgement, but so had he. He hadn't properly communicated, then he had argued with her when they both needed one another, pushing her further into the hands of the enemy.

'Have you ever actually said that to her?' K-Bar asked.

Lamont didn't reply.

* * *

Despite planning to conduct more surveillance on the spot Julia had given, Shorty hadn't got back to it. He and K-Bar were putting the finishing touches on their order. It had been his idea to order big and spread it around the Hood. He wanted to show all the other crews they were still the biggest, and the profit from moving twenty boxes of food would put them in an entirely different league.

Maka and Manson had said little, but K-Bar agreed with it being a good idea, and had even agreed to be in charge of the delivery.

Since their last meeting, he had spoken with Sienna a few times. She was pushing for something more to happen with them. Shorty couldn't shake Amy though, and if he could work things out and build a future with her, that was what he wanted to do.

Despite this, Sienna was more up front, and Shorty dug that. He didn't have to work hard to understand what was on her mind, and she was more like him. She understood Chapeltown more, having grown up there. Amy was an outsider and had grown up completely differently. Shorty had always looked at her as *better*, but saw Sienna as more on his level. He couldn't work out whether that was good, and that conflict made his head hurt.

Right now, he was getting his weaponry together so he could move on the house tonight. He planned to go in after dark and was carrying both a pistol, and a small knife he'd stashed in his sock. He'd considered going in heavy with a shotgun, but ultimately decided against it. Depending on how many people were there, he could move quicker with a handgun. It was a risk worth taking.

K-Bar called him an hour later.

'Everything in place for the delivery?' Shorty asked.

'The spot is ready. We'll make the calls as soon as it lands. Me and Maka will handle it. Manson and the others will await the calls, and they'll do the drop offs. A few spots are ready for pickups too. They'll sell out quick. Streets are congested, but we have the best goods and people know that.'

'Good shit. We'll move this quick and reload again. After that, we can sit back and focus.'

'How's your thing going?'

'I'm going in tonight,' replied Shorty. K-Bar hesitated.

'I don't like the sound of that, Shorty. Put it off til tomorrow and let me go in with you.'

Shorty was tempted. K-Bar was deadly and with him, the mission would be a piece of cake. He could handle it, however. He didn't need K-Bar. If he could get Lennox tonight and put two bullets in his head, the headlines tomorrow would probably distract from the kilos of drugs flooding the streets. It would work better for them to make the moves all at once.

'I've got it covered, K. Chill.'

'You've been doing your surveillance then? Do you know what to expect?'

'I've done this shit before. Don't worry about it. Focus on what you need to do.'

'Okay, fam. Make sure you ring me if you need me.'

'Count on it.' Shorty hung up, already envisioning what he was going to do with his cut of the money. Most of it would go to Amy for Grace's care, and a significant portion would go to Dionte and Stacey in Huddersfield, but there would be plenty left over. In the old days he'd have spent it on clothes, jewellery and nights out, but he wanted to be more conservative now. If the past few years had taught him anything, it was that it was always important to have money in reserve. If he was arrested again, he wouldn't be able to rely on Lamont to get him a solicitor. He would need to do it himself.

Thinking of Lamont made him recall the meeting. He couldn't put his finger on what was wrong with Lamont, but he'd expected more resistance, and was still surprised Lamont had given in so easily. He hadn't even cared about Shorty essentially stealing the crew from him, which he supposed made sense. Lamont had been trying to run away from the crime game for years, even before Jenny was killed. *What reason did he have to still be doing it now?*

Shorty kissed his teeth, scowling. The last thing he wanted was to think about Lamont. Clambering to his feet from the sofa, he went hunting for his weed and Rizla, wanting to relax and distract himself.

CHAPTER TWENTY-TWO

Sunday 24 May 2015

'W HY DID you allow it to happen?'

Lamont and Delroy were talking on the phone. Needing a second opinion after his conversation with K-Bar, he had called Delroy, filling him in on the meeting and aftermath.

'He needed it more than me.'

'Are you sure?'

'Shorty has done well keeping the crew in line. Fact is, they weren't a priority for me. I just assumed everything was okay, and it was.'

'I've asked you this before, and I'll repeat it now: what do you want? What's the end game for you?'

Lamont considered his reply. The line was encrypted on both ends. It was the only way they felt comfortable speaking to one another over the phone, yet freely admitting his intent to murder someone was ridiculous.

'You know what I want. I want the same thing you do.'

'I think you let Shorty have the crew because you don't actually want to deal with running it anymore.'

'That's not it,' Lamont disagreed. 'I need to get my head in the game. I've been second-guessing myself for the longest. The desire for revenge has gone nowhere, and I figured it would have by now. I guess with Lennox out of the way, that will fix itself.'

'It's not that simple,' Delroy started. Lamont heard him take a deep breath before he continued. 'I would kill to walk away now. Getting up every day, motivating the troops, and trying to keep everyone out of prison is tiresome. I don't have the stamina for it anymore.'

'You should leave it all behind now then. Why wait?'

'I can't.'

Lamont waited for Delroy to add more, but he didn't.

'You want to retire to Grenada, right? So, go.'

Delroy laughed darkly.

'Grenada is a pipe dream, L. All along, I've known deep down I'll never go back. I built land, sent money back home for decades, because that's what I was supposed to do, and because I fucked over many people when I was there. Truth is, I will never leave Leeds.'

'You don't know that.' Lamont didn't like to hear Delroy doubting himself. They had become even closer lately, and he wanted him to achieve his goals.

'L, please hear this if you forget everything else I've told you: Walk away — for real this time. Don't worry about what you *think* you're leaving behind.'

'It's not that simple, and you more than anyone should realise that,' Lamont argued.

'You need to realise it's not as simple as you want it to be. You talk about fixing things and getting back to your old mindset, but that's not you anymore, and your actions lately have proved that. Killing yourself for the streets won't fix that broken part of you.'

Lamont said little more after that, hanging up a short while later with more questions than answers. Delroy was speaking from a different place, but Lamont didn't believe what he said, and wasn't sure Delroy did either. Delroy clearly didn't want him around, and it was likely it was influencing what he wanted from Lamont.

For that reason, Lamont hadn't told Delroy the results of his interrogation of Peters. He didn't know if Delroy knew of Mark Patrick and his role as Lennox's street general, but like the Jackie Smart Court spot, he was keeping it to himself. They both had the same goal, and whoever got to Lennox Thompson first would kill him. It was as simple as that.

* * *

Shorty parked up the road from the spot, checked his weaponry, and headed down the road towards the house in Garforth, hiding behind cars and keeping out of sight. There were no guards when he'd done his brief surveillance, but his caution was justified. There was a man outside the house, smoking a cigarette and looking at his phone. Even if he'd looked up, he wouldn't have seen Shorty, who was well concealed. He would need to get past him to get in the house.

Securing his gun, he crept around to the left side of a car directly outside the house. The man had his back to him and Shorty grabbed him from behind, then turned him, sinking his knee into the man's stomach, hearing the whoosh of air being driven from the man's lungs. He followed it up with a crushing blow to the man's jaw. He was out on his feet.

Shorty dragged him into the garden, dumping the gun he carried, and taking his mobile phone. He was tempted to kill him, but decided against it. He had equipment to break into the house but based on the guard outside, tried the handle instead, grinning when it opened.

Quietly closing it behind him, he took stock of his surroundings. Music was playing upstairs. Someone was in the house and his heart raced, imagining the look on Lennox's face when he walked in on him. He searched the downstairs, gun in hand, ready to shoot anyone he saw. He found no one and silently padded up the stairs. The light was on in one bedroom, so he positioned himself outside the door and wrenched it open, dipping low and charging into the room.

The music was playing from a Bluetooth speaker next to the bed, but the room was empty.

Before Shorty had time to process, he heard a noise from behind and narrowly shifted his weight as someone barrelled into him. He slammed into the wall, the gun spilling from his grasp. Whirling around and to his feet, he glanced at the muscular, smiling man by the door.

'Long time no see, Shorty,' the familiar man said. Shorty tensed.
'Derrigan. Figured you were dead.'

* * *

'What was Teflon saying then?'

K-Bar and Maka were sitting in the back of the van, looking at the product. They'd picked it up from the usual spot and loaded the bricks without issue. The warehouse was a distance away, but Maka had made the trip previously and foresaw no issues.

'How do you know I spoke to him?' K-Bar hated the vans they used for transport. They weren't comfortable and with him being long-limbed, he had no leg room. The van hadn't been properly cleaned out and had clearly been used for another task, meaning there was a lingering odour that grew stronger the longer they were sat there. He and Lamont had talked for a while, with Lamont leaving to attend a meeting. He wasn't sure what to think of the conversation. There hadn't been a real agenda for the meeting, and it had quickly been hijacked by Shorty and Lamont's ongoing vendetta.

'Just a guess. You're the calm one, so it makes sense he would speak to you.'

'He didn't really say much,' K-Bar admitted. 'He's kinda just leaving Shorty to it and letting him do what he's doing.'

Maka wiped his face. 'That meeting was mad. I thought they were gonna get into another scrap. Think they'll ever make up?'

'I dunno. When I got out, I thought I could talk them around, but Shorty will barely discuss L, and L's doing the whole *hanging back and waiting for him to calm down thing.*'

Maka kissed his teeth. 'Never thought they'd fall out. Maybe Tef's way is the best way. You know what Shorty's like he when he's pissed off.'

K-Bar did. Better than anyone. Shorty could be the coolest guy on earth, and then a second later he'd want to fight everyone in the room. He had a hair-trigger temper and for the longest, Lamont had handled him. Somewhere down the line it all fell apart.

'I'll have another go at them. We need the team at full strength.'

'L's not gonna do anything until he's sorted Lennox. Maybe we're best staying out of it for now.'

K-Bar shrugged. Maybe Maka had the right of it.

'D's doing excellent work with those local crews. He's working well with that Roman kid.'

Maka grinned. 'Roman and Keith remind me a little of you and Shorty. Roman keeps Keith calm, and Keith wants to go around splitting everyone's skulls. It cracks me up.'

'We need to do something more with them. Let them have the shine and take the risk. This is a young man's game. We both know that.'

Before Maka could reply, they heard a burst of gunfire, and the van veered out of control. Neither man had a chance to move before they were sent hurtling from their seats, smacking the hard floor of the vehicle. The bricks of product rained down on them. K-Bar struggled underneath a makeshift pile, his head aching. He squinted, just able to make out a car in front of them. The driver was slumped over the seat, bleeding and unmoving.

'Maka,' K-Bar hissed. 'Are you okay?'

'Shit . . . my ribs are fucked,' Maka gasped. 'The fuck happened?'

More gunshots cancelled out Maka's words, smashing through the front window, peppering the back. They ducked back down as several packs of drugs exploded under the bullets, showering them in powder.

'We need to get out of here,' K-Bar shouted.

'Are you mad? We don't even know how many of them are out there!'

'Doesn't matter. I ain't staying here to die,' said K-Bar. He crawled forward and hearing a lull, hoped for the best and opened the van doors. A man stood there, an automatic weapon by his side. He hadn't expected K-Bar to open the van and stupidly gawped. His hesitation cost him his life. K-Bar's bullet smashed through the top of his head, sending him tumbling to the ground. He grabbed his weapon.

'C'mon,' he yelled to Maka. They were on the Ring Road near Moor Allerton. There were woods nearby, and he kept his head low and made for them. Maka was behind him, panting as the gunfire started up again, bullets whining all around them. Gasping, Maka took cover behind a tree.

'You strapped?' K-Bar called. He could just about make his comrade out in the darkness.

'Yeah. Only got a little pistol though.'

'I'll cover you. We need to hold them off and call for backup. We should have had a fucking car trailing us. I didn't even think.'

'Doesn't matter now. Call Shorty.'

'Where the fuck are you going?' A voice yelled. 'Stay and fight, you pussies.'

'Do you recognise him?' K-Bar asked. Maka didn't answer as he tried dialling. He cursed when it went to voicemail. He tried calling twice more and the same thing happened.

'He's not answering.'

'Fuck. Call Sharma and tell him to get some people together.'

'We don't even know where we are.'

'We're near Moor Allerton. We'll hold out here until they come,' said K-Bar, recognising the area. Saying a prayer he would live to see Marika and the kids, he took a better position and lifted the gun.

* * *

Delroy settled into his favourite chair with a glass of brandy. Business was done for the day, and with every passing hour, Delroy was ready for it to end. He realised more and more just how empty his life was, and how little substance he had. He'd tried reaching out to his estranged wife, but she still wouldn't speak to him.

Earlier, he'd visited the graves of his son's, both dead before their time. He'd stared at the headstones with a growing sense of guilt and failure. They'd had no opportunity to be anything but his lieutenants. He didn't hide the life from them and when they showed an interest, he schooled them and taught them the game.

Winston had a wife and kids, but Delroy wasn't allowed to see them anymore, and hadn't since the funeral. Eddie was a hothead with far too much to prove, who was never the same after Winston's murder. He'd made it clear he would track down and end Lennox Thompson's life, but had ended up dead too.

As he contemplated his life, Delroy wondered if keeping Lamont out of the loop was a smart thing. He'd wanted him to get involved earlier in the conflict, but now he was keeping him at arm's length, trying to make sense of the reasons. Lamont was an asset to any organisation. He'd made no secret of his desire to have him on his team, but lately, he'd realised just how damaged Lamont was. He wanted him to be better more than he wanted to utilise him. The deaths of so many close to him had changed him, and he was trying to push ahead, ignoring the surrounding signs to slow down. They'd shared some tough words on the phone, and Delroy hoped he took it to heart. Once Lennox was in the ground, they could both move on.

Staring into the glass at the dark liquid, Delroy's phone rang. He scowled. His men knew not to bother him late at night unless it was life and death. When he checked the number, his heart soared. It was his daughter. Snatching the phone, he hastily answered.

'Alicia?'

It wasn't her.

'I almost feel bad for this call, after hearing that optimism in your tone,' a man said, his tone mocking.

Delroy closed his eyes, his world crashing down around him. This was it. The game was over.

'Lennox.'

'You recognised my voice then? I'm touched. We haven't exactly spoken much in the past.'

'If you touch her—'

'Save it. You're not in control here.' In the background, Delroy heard the muffled sounds of Alicia struggling. His shoulders slumped. 'I want to see you. Now. Don't bring anyone else. If you do, I promise what I do to your beautiful daughter will not be quick.'

'Where am I going?' Delroy growled, fury making his words shake. Lennox had crossed the line going after his daughter. He didn't know how he had tracked her down, but if survived, the gloves would well and truly be off. He would tear apart anyone who even looked like Lennox.

Mocking tone in place, Lennox gave Delroy the address and hung up.

* * *

Aaron was loving this. His team had laid in wait for the van, and taken out the driver. Gary had failed. Aaron had ordered him to secure the back of the van to prevent whoever was in the back from jumping out. Now, he was bleeding out on the floor.

'J-Star,' he said to one man. 'You're coming with me. Grab two more guys and let's go kill these fuckers. There can't be more than three of them. You lot stay here and secure that van for when the backup comes.'

J-Star signalled to two men, and they hurried toward the woods. Aaron grinned, his heart hammering. He had been waiting to get his revenge on Teflon's crew. He had been minding his own business when they'd jumped in the middle of his beef with Roman, beating him down and forcing his crew to abandon him. He'd licked his wounds for a time, letting his injured arm heal, before an opportunity presented itself. Now, he was going to wipe out the whole crew. Following his people, he kept his gun raised, his smile only widening.

* * *

'They're coming after us,' said K-Bar. His heart was racing as he kept the gun raised. Maka had tried calling Manson, Jamal, and Sharma, but he couldn't connect to anyone. K-Bar didn't know how many enemies there were. Other than the gun he'd stolen, he had his pistol. Maka only had the one handgun. They'd had no time to come up with a plan. Despite everything, his adrenaline was skyrocketing. Apart from his assassination of Big-Kev a few months back, he hadn't been in a fight like this for years, and he'd missed it more than he realised. They were outnumbered and outgunned, but it didn't matter. All that mattered was the here and now.

'Get behind me,' he said to Maka. Maka shuffled over just as the gunfire started again, narrowly missing him. K-Bar let go a quick burst with the rifle, moving to another tree nearby, bullets smashing into the surrounding trees. If one caught him, he was done for. He didn't even have a vest on. The team had grown lax, having made the runs so many times without issue. If they survived, he would need to rectify it.

The two teams traded shots. K-Bar needed to be careful not to run out of ammunition. He saw one assailant stupidly step out of cover and put two bullets into his chest. The man dropped and another man foolishly ran toward the fallen man. K-Bar made quick work of him too.

'J-Star,' he heard the voice that had taunted them earlier yell. 'Don't make the same mistake as those idiots. Stay in cover.'

Another voice – *J-Star* – shouted his understanding.

'Maka, start running. I'll cover you,' ordered K-Bar. They couldn't afford to wait around any longer. No backup was coming. There was no way to get to the drugs in the van. He didn't know how they were going to explain it to Lamont or Shorty, but right now, they had to go.

'I'm not leaving you,' said Maka.

'Go. I'm right behind you.'

Maka started running, kicking up mud and twigs in his haste. Bullets followed him, narrowly missing. K-Bar followed the muzzle flash in the dark. He raised his gun, waiting for the opportunity.

* * *

Aaron wasn't smiling anymore. He didn't know exactly who'd been in the van, but it seemed like *Rambo* was tearing them apart. The person was skilled, and he was guessing it was Shorty or K-Bar. They were the most well-known of Teflon's lot, and they were killers. He was regretting not planning the ambush properly. Now, three of his men were dead. He and J-Star had fired guns before, but never to hit anybody. They had fired at cars and windows, but he'd figured it would be easy to use those same skills in a gunfight. Now, he was realising how silly that was.

There was no turning back now, though.

Hearing scuffling sounds from ahead. He began firing wildly, determined to hit the running target. He didn't hear or see the bullets that

hit him, but they caught him in the neck, stomach and shoulder, spinning him around before depositing him on the floor. Aaron's gun fell
from his hand as he gasped for life. There was utterly no chance. He
was aware of J-Star screaming, but it sounded like it was coming from
miles away. Trying to sit up, it was to no avail. His eyes dimmed, and
his life ended on the rough ground.

K-Bar lowered the rifle. He had picked off the man shooting at
Maka, then his comrade right after. The rifle was low on ammo and he
wiped it down and dropped it, gripping his handgun and following
Maka as they crashed through branches and undergrowth. He couldn't
hear anymore gunfire, but it wasn't worth doubling back to the van.
The people in the woods hadn't been the best shooters, but it didn't
mean there weren't more of them waiting. As he followed Maka, a
leaden sensation engulfed his stomach.

Why couldn't they get hold of anyone else?

* * *

Derrigan grinned at Shorty, before he slowly shook his head.

'Not yet, Shorty. I've been waiting for you to come. I know you've
had the address for a while.'

Shorty looked around the room, looking for anything he could use
to get an advantage. He and Nicky Derrigan went way back and had
even once fought after an argument, with Shorty narrowly winning.
That was well over ten years ago though, when he was younger and
more reckless. Derrigan looked solid as he stared Shorty down, a half-
grin on his face. Shorty had been well and truly set up. He didn't know
if they had trailed him, or if Julia and Sienna had sold him out, but he
was leaning toward the latter.

'Where's Lennox? Is he too scared to step to me?'

Derrigan's smile widened. 'Why would he need to do that? You're
not on his level. He has more important business to handle tonight.
You're not the only one getting dropped.'

'He's got you doing his dirty work then, like a little lapdog?'

Derrigan sniggered, unaffected by the insult.

'He's paying me a lot of money for my services.'

'Who set me up?'

'You always had a weakness for pussy. Must be why you ended up saddled with kids. How's your daughter, anyway?' Derrigan's grin was truly sinister now. 'Heard she had an accident.'

Enraged, Shorty charged Derrigan, which was what he'd wanted. He planted his feet, able to absorb Shorty's momentum, then flung him to the ground, kicking him twice while he was down. Shorty forced his way back to his feet as Derrigan took a step back.

'I'm not a kid anymore. You got sloppy, Shorty. There's no way you're winning this.'

Shorty moved forward, faking left and sailing in with a right. Derrigan slipped the hit and drove his elbow into Shorty's back. Shorty cried out in pain but moved quicker than Derrigan expected, kicking him in the stomach. Derrigan doubled over and he caught him with a vicious knee to the face, exploding his nose. He went for a punch, but Derrigan grabbed his hand, driving his free hand into Shorty's stomach, grinning as he felt the air leave Shorty. He hit him twice more, then shoved him onto the bed. Mounting him, he moved Shorty's hands, catching him with two unguarded blows to the face, then dragged him to his feet and threw him into the wall. Unable to get his hands up, Shorty's face impacted against it, blood pouring from his broken nose.

Derrigan was all over him, allowing no time for recovery. He drove a fist into Shorty's kidney, the blow sending him to one knee.

'Lennox played you and your stupid crew,' he taunted. 'You never even saw it coming. I wasn't sure about Lennox when he hired me. Figured he had big dreams but would get dropped, but he saw what everyone else didn't. You and your team are washed up. Delroy's too.'

Shorty struggled to stay upright. He was in tremendous pain, dizzy from the blows to the face and kidneys. He couldn't let Derrigan win, and he again went forward, putting his hands up, ready to box. Derrigan took the bet and threw a sloppy hook. Shorty ducked under it and caught Derrigan with an uppercut that knocked him back. Shorty kept up the pressure, hitting him twice more, but the blows weren't enough to put Derrigan down, who was both bigger and stronger. He grabbed Shorty in a bearhug and Shorty yelled, feeling the air being driven from him, putting pressure on his already injured kidneys and ribs. Drawing his head back, he brought it down on Derrigan's already injured nose, making the man howl in pain. He expected him to back up, but Derrigan instead kicked out, catching Shorty's already injured ribs and sending him to his knees. He followed up with a boot to Shorty's face, sending him crashing to the floor.

'You're done, Shorty.' Derrigan kicked him twice more in the ribs, feeling them shift under his feet. Kicking Shorty onto his back, he looked him in the eye, then brought his boot down on the same injured ribs.

Shorty heard a noise that sounded like a scream. It took him a few seconds to realise it had come from him. He was fading, struggling to stay conscious. It hurt to breathe, and he couldn't focus. He couldn't give up. This was for Grace and Dionte. For Jenny and everyone Lennox had harmed. He couldn't let it end here.

Derrigan looked at the beaten man. He hadn't expected Shorty to present such a challenge. He was older, and hadn't trained as hard over the years as Derrigan had. He was still breathing, and Derrigan had a job to do. Wrapping his hands around Shorty's throat, he squeezed with all his might. Shorty struggled, but Derrigan was too powerful to overcome. He was in so much pain and for a moment, he thought this was it. The intensity grew, but he fought it, unwilling to go down like this.

Still struggling, he jerkily reached for the knife he'd stored in his right sock, and fumbled to get it free. He needed to hurry. A little more pressure and he would be done. His eyes wanted nothing more than to close, but he fought through it, flicking open the knife and jabbing it into Derrigan's thigh.

Derrigan yelled, letting Shorty go. Shorty kicked the man off him, then threw punch after punch at him while he was distracted. He went for the gun he'd dropped earlier, grabbing it just as another man burst into the room with his own raised. Shorty was quicker and put the man down for the count with two shots. Derrigan had already started moving, and by the time the second man hit the floor, he'd limped through the open door.

Wincing in pain, Shorty was about to go after him, when gunfire shattered the windows behind him. He dived back to the floor, his body screaming at him as he crawled along, praying there was no one waiting outside the door for him. He charged into another of the upstairs rooms, which was thankfully empty. There were loud voices and footsteps thundering up the stairs. Shorty didn't know how many were coming, but he couldn't stay and fight his way out. He was barely staying upright as it was. Wildly looking around the room, he saw it was a makeshift bedroom. He could try to barricade the door, but it would take too long and wouldn't last. If Lennox's men didn't get him, the police would. He couldn't risk it. There was only one option available.

As the voices grew closer, he fired a shot at the window in the room, shattering it. Taking a deep breath, he ran to the window as quickly as he could and hurtled through it. He heard shouts, but couldn't stop to think. He slammed down onto a shed roof, his already damaged ribs impacted as he rolled onto a dustbin, then to the floor with a thud. Shorty took a few seconds, his body not wanting to move after everything it had taken, then he shifted to his feet and limped towards a fence leading to the next garden, barely climbing over.

He couldn't wait around. There was no telling what the men would do. He had no choice but to keep moving.

CHAPTER TWENTY-THREE

Monday 25 May 2015

DELROY DROVE himself to the meeting spot. It was a ramshackle house in Bankside, with metal bars on the doors and windows. Two sullen men waited for him. When he climbed from the car, they roughly patted him down, then marched him into the house. It galled Delroy to be treated with such disrespect, but he would take it. Alicia was all that mattered.

Inside, Delroy was led down to the cellar. There were a set of tools propped in a corner. The floor had been wrapped in plastic; the sight making him nauseous. It was a sign he wouldn't be getting out alive. Straightening his shoulders, he stepped into the room. His heart broke when he saw Alicia sat on the floor, gagged, with her legs and arms secured. She looked at him with terrified, tear-stained eyes. She favoured Elaine so much, with her beautiful features, dark eyes and round face.

Lennox was leaning against the wall, a pistol in his hand and a small smile on his face. He was a wiry, hard-faced man, with cold eyes, despite the smile. Delroy couldn't place him. He couldn't recall the last time he'd seen him.

'Delroy. Thanks for coming. Feels weird being face to face after spending the year trying to kill one another.'

'Let Alicia go. You don't need her anymore.' Delroy wanted to charge Lennox and wring his skinny little neck, but there were three men nearby — not counting the two who had led him down here. They were all armed and any attempt at a rescue would lead to him being cut down. He needed to be smart.

'It's touching how much you care,' said Lennox with false sincerity. 'If it wasn't for you, she wouldn't be here. I wouldn't have been forced to murder her brothers. This is all on you, Delroy, and you know it.'

Delroy shot a look at his daughter, seeing the pain in her eyes at the reminder of her brothers. She had blamed him for it, and he doubted what was happening now would make her feel any less angry at him.

'There's no need to drag this out. You got the drop on me. Let her go and do what you will.'

Alicia screamed and shook her head, the sound muffled by the rag in her mouth. Lennox glanced at her, then focused his attention back on Delroy.

'I want you to understand why I'm doing this. Why I win. I'm not led aside by emotional attachments. I go for what I want, and I take it. You're probably wondering how I got you here?'

'I don't care,' snarled Delroy. Lennox was unfazed.

'Yes, you do. You were betrayed. Like so many, you only ever look forward. You were consumed by finding me and never looked to those around you that you marginalised and ordered around. The drug life got you. For decades you polluted Chapeltown, and now I'm going to fix it.'

'You're no better than me,' said Delroy fiercely. 'You might be anti drug, but you're a thug and a butcher.'

'Just like you,' said Lennox. 'You're forgetting, I grew up in Leeds. We grew up on stories of the *Williams' Crew*, and the power you guys had. You killed your way to the top, so let's not pretend you're any better than me.'

'None of this matters. Let her go. You have me.'

'That's not enough. Thanks to my inside man, I know where several of your spots are. My men have already moved in to take the drugs. I want the money too.'

'You're not getting a thing.'

Lennox raised an eyebrow. 'You're not sounding like a loving father right now. Why do you think she's here? You're going to do what I say, or I promise you, I'll cut her to pieces while you watch.'

This was too much for Delroy. With a bellow, he charged, but was easily intercepted by the guards. He tried fighting free, but a sharp blow to the back of his head stunned him, sending him to his knees. Alicia tried to scream and struggle again, but it was to no avail.

'Like I said: you're going to do as I say,' repeated Lennox. 'Make the right decision. Show your daughter you care and give me the information I want. How many spots do you have for collecting money?'

'A dozen,' spat Delroy. The money was collected from these spots and laundered, but they kept the pattern loose in order to fool anyone who might be watching.

'Give me the addresses. No cowboy shit either. I have someone watching your wife, and if I set them loose, you'll wish she was dead.'

Anger flashed in Delroy's eyes, but he again tried calming himself. Getting angry wouldn't help anything, and he didn't want them focusing their attentions on his wife or daughter. Listlessly, he recited the addresses. Committing important information to memory was a must at his level, and he rarely wrote anything down he wouldn't want to be discovered.

Lennox handed the list to one man, who immediately left the cellar. Facing Delroy again, Lennox smiled.

'You did the right thing, Delroy. Take peace in that as you die. Before that happens.' Lennox nodded and one of his men stepped forward, putting the gun to Alicia's head.

'No!' roared Delroy, but his words were lost over the bang. Alicia's head slammed forward as she hit the ground, blood billowing around her. 'You motherfucker!'

'Be thankful I made it quick, Delroy. Your time is over, and mine now begins,' said Lennox coldly. Gun raised, he aimed it at Delroy's chest and fired three times, smiling as the kingpin slumped forward, dead. He took stock of what he had done, and what it would mean.

The war was over. Delroy Williams had lost, and he had won.

* * *

'Is everything in place?'

Rigby ran his hands through his hair as he awaited the response. The best practice was to conduct raids first thing in the morning. Based on the information Terry had provided, the work of the intel team and the surveillance on various locations, it was determined that this was the best time to act.

Rigby had noticed how different Teflon's team seemed. They had increased their reach, new members flourishing in their ranks, but appeared less disciplined. Their surveillance on one location had seen buyers going to the spot directly for pickups, with no attempts at subtlety.

Rigby knew this was the lack of influence Teflon apparently had on the crew at present. He hadn't been able to make any headway into what Teflon's intentions were, but deemed them to be serious if he was essentially abandoning the crew he'd built up.

'Everything is in place over here, chief. Just waiting for you to give the word.'

The operation was a joint one, with several stations involved, and a detachment of armed police. They were hitting half a dozen locations. Four locations housed product and money, and the other two were well-frequented safe houses. Reid had put Rigby in charge of the operation. Her reasoning was two-fold. If it was successful, she would take the credit and if it wasn't, he would be thrown under the bus. She hadn't been joking when she'd said his career was on the line, but Rigby found that didn't bother him. It was worth the risk.

'Hit the spots,' he said firmly.

* * *

Manson, Darren, Roman and Keith were in a safe house on Leopold Street, smoking a spliff and drinking liquor. It hadn't been planned. They had held a quick meeting earlier and ended up staying. K-Bar and Maka were supervising the delivery, and they would be in place to ensure the product got to where it needed to be as quickly as possible.

When the door came off the safe house, they were sluggish in moving as they were overwhelmed by officers. Manson leapt to his feet, ready to fight.

'Manson! Don't,' said Darren. Manson tensed and allowed himself to be forced to the floor. They were secured and read their rights, then hauled away as multiple officers began tearing into the property.

Darren wore a brave face, but on the inside he was panicking. There was no way the police should have known about this spot. There were locations they used to hang out, but this one was off the grid. There were guns on the property, along with drugs and small packets of money. All in all, it didn't present a positive picture.

Sharing a look with his comrades, his stomach lurched as he realised Maka and K-Bar would have no idea what was going on.

* * *

The raids were an undisputed success. They swarmed the locations without interruption, capturing men, product, money, weapons and an assortment of mobile phones and communication devices. It was a better haul than Rigby could have hoped for, and he knew it would damage the organisation likely beyond repair. The downside was the fact he had hoped to grab K-Bar, but he hadn't been at any of the locations.

For a moment, Rigby wondered if he'd had prior knowledge of the raids, but believed if he had, he would have told his people. They had kept the raid quiet for that reason, knowing there were many leaks in the departments. Everything was on a need-to-know basis, and it had worked like a charm.

Back at the station, Rigby grabbed a coffee. There were a host of interviews he would need to conduct. He needed to meet with Reid and debrief her on the operation, and there was paperwork he needed to complete. It was a tremendous amount of work, but this was the best chance Rigby had to finish Teflon's organisation once and for all. The piping hot coffee scalding his lips, he checked his phone for messages.

'Rig.'

Rigby faced Murphy. He hadn't been involved in the raids, with enough people already involved to not warrant his involvement. Instead of wearing an expression of happiness, he appeared stunned. Rigby straightened.

'What's happened?'

Murphy shook his head.

'Chapeltown, mate. Everything has gone nuts.'

* * *

Lamont's head was buzzing with the news being spread. Delroy and his daughter Alicia had been murdered in devastating fashion. It was monumental news. Lamont couldn't fathom it. He had figured Delroy had Lennox on the ropes and never imagined he would retaliate in the way he had. Something wasn't adding up. For Lennox to make such a move suggested a level of backing far beyond what Lamont had worked out he had.

Had he made a mistake somewhere?

All Lamont could do was look at his phone as various people tried to call him. There was no one worth talking to yet. Lennox had made a huge move, and his name was ringing out. Everyone in the know knew who was behind it, and killing Delroy's daughter had been ruthless beyond measure. Lamont knew Alicia Reynolds back in the day. She was a sweet girl who had refused to be involved in the family business. She even used her mother's maiden name, shunning the Williams name completely.

How had she been caught up? How had Lennox found her?

Lamont's immediate thought was that someone had betrayed Delroy. Pouring himself a drink, he turned off his computer and went to sit in the living room. He flicked on the television, but didn't watch it. TV was never the distraction for him it was for others. He was considering reading a book when his phone rang again, and this time, he answered, recognising the number.

He didn't speak, waiting for them to go first.

'Are you really not going to talk?'

'Figured you called for a reason, Lennox. How can I help?'

Lamont could practically feel Lennox's smile on the other end. He stowed his anger. It wasn't the time, and there was nothing he could do without knowing where he was.

'Guessing by now you've heard what happened to Delroy?'

'How did you do it?'

'I'm better than him, Teflon. Better than you too. This proves it. You had your thing with him years back, but you couldn't finish him. I could.'

'You called to gloat then? Seems beneath you.'

'Does it? You don't know me, Teflon. You only *thought* you did. How many warnings do I need to give you before you learn your lesson? Your missus got it. Trinidad got it. Akeem. Still, you keep coming at me — an enemy that you can't figure out. All I wanted was to be left alone.'

'For someone who wants to be left alone, you sure do a lot of damage,' replied Lamont, refusing to be affected by Lennox's mentioning of Trinidad and Jenny. He didn't need those feelings weighing him down again. Not when he was so close to the end. All he needed to do was find and execute Lennox. Delroy had done most of the groundwork, and now he could take over and finish the job for good.

'I was forced to. By you. By old man Delroy. By those pathetic losers who work for you. None of you *are* or *were* good enough, and now, it won't matter. Because this is my time.'

'You can't beat me, Lenny. I am not Delroy Williams. I'm not a tired old man just wanting it to end. You stayed away from me for a reason these past few weeks. Delroy seemed easier, right?'

Whatever response Lamont was expecting, laughter wasn't on the list. It wasn't a snicker either. This was a full on belly laugh that lasted several seconds. His brow furrowed as it hit him for the first time that Lennox still hadn't explained why he had called.

'Delroy was unfinished business. The only reason he lasted this long was because you and your people stuck your noses in. You may not be tired, Teflon, but you are more than broken down. Shuffling around, keeping your head down because the people in Chapeltown don't like you anymore. I could have taken you out when I had your barber popped. Could have had you blasted at the old man's funeral. Like your mentor, you're still here because I have allowed it.'

'What's stopping you then? Let's finish this once and for all,' said Lamont, hoping Lennox took the bait. He was far too calm and controlled, and he didn't like it.

'I don't move when you tell me to. I am as independent as it gets, and everyone will learn that fact. Let's get down to business. I will tear your crew apart. If there's anyone left, anyway. They ran into some problems earlier, so I'm awaiting confirmation.'

'Bullshit,' replied Lamont. 'This act may work with the people dumb enough to follow you, but you're playing in an entirely different league now, Lennox. As I said to you earlier: I am *not* Delroy Williams.'

'No, you're not. I won't refute that. What you are is on borrowed time. You still don't get it, Teflon. It's almost sad really, to be undone by the same mistake twice.'

With those words, Lamont's stomach plummeted, his blood turning cold.

'What have you done?'

'Not me. *You.* You did this. Leaving key pieces unprotected on the board once again.'

'Stop fucking talking in riddles and tell me,' snapped Lamont.

'How many innocents have to suffer before you get the message? Doesn't matter now. When you work it out, just remember; this time, it wasn't an accident. You got her killed.' Lennox hung up.

Lamont stared down at the phone, heart hammering against his chest. He felt like he couldn't breathe, his throat constricting. There was a chance Lennox was just posturing, but he didn't believe it. There was no reason to call Lamont to gloat. He had done something, something that would deeply affect Lamont. Something involving innocents. With a jolt of realisation, it hit him.

Amy.

Hurtling to his feet, Lamont ran from the house, summoning his bodyguards. They zoomed down the drive, driving towards Roundhay as fast as they could. Lamont had his phone to his ear, trying to get hold of everyone. He couldn't reach Amy, Shorty, K-Bar, Maka or Manson, and every time he tried them, the pit of despair in his stomach only grew. There was no way Lennox could reach all of them in a single night. They were well-trained and experienced. They would see Lennox's men coming.

The truth was, Lamont thought, as he hunched forward, willing the driver to go faster, he didn't know his crew anymore. Somewhere down the line, he had lost sight of them. Even when they sided with Shorty after their last meeting, he did nothing to rectify the situation. He had been so blinded by his need to take on Lennox that he'd put them on the back burner. They had proved they could look after themselves. The crew could run without him.

Lamont took a deep breath as the car sharply turned onto Amy's street a short while later. It was quiet and undisturbed, but that meant nothing. Before the car had even screeched to a stop, Lamont was rushing towards her front door, his heart in his throat. He tried the front door, but it was locked, which stunned him. He began banging on the door until he heard Amy's voice.

'I'm coming, calm down!'

Lamont was vibrating on the spot. He needed to make sure she was okay. He had tried Shorty four more times, but each time it rang through to voicemail.

'You're okay?' he gasped when she'd unlocked the door. Amy wore a red dressing gown over pink pyjama's. Her hair was bedraggled and as she stood there glaring, she stifled a yawn.

'I was fast asleep until you started banging on the door like a mad man. What's happened?'

'I thought . . .' Lamont wasn't sure what to say. He was still trying to relax. The scene with Jenny bleeding on her kitchen floor had burned into his mind, and he'd been sure he would arrive to see a similar scene.

'L, what's going on? Tell me?'

'Have you heard from Shorty?'

Amy paled, shaking her head.

'What's happened?'

'Probably nothing. Go back to bed. I'll call you if anything happens.'

'L . . .'

'Seriously. Everything is fine.' Lamont ran a hand through his hair, trying to force a smile onto his face. Eyeing him suspiciously, Amy nodded and closed the door. Lamont hurried down the steps and skidded to a halt, surprised to see Jamal — one of his soldiers — standing by his bodyguards.

'What's going on?' he asked.

'Has anyone been by?'

Jamal shook his head. 'I've been out here all day. Shorty asked me to watch over her. Said he had something to do. What's happened?'

Lamont wasn't listening. Something had jumbled in his mind when he'd seen the enforcer. Lennox's cryptic words had pointed toward Amy, but it wasn't just Amy who fit them. There was another woman, someone closer to Lamont, and like a selfish fool, he had completely overlooked his own family.

'Marika!' he shouted, getting back to the car. 'Drive!' he screamed, giving the driver the address.

* * *

All the way to Marika's, Lamont said a silent prayer. He tried convincing himself that Lennox was sending him on a wild chase all over Leeds for no other reason than to be entertained. Until he pulled onto Marika's street and saw the flashing blue lights. The crime tape. The neighbours watching a particular house.

Marika's house.

'No,' he moaned, nausea bubbling in his stomach. He forced away the sickening feeling and hurried from the car.

'Marika!' he yelled. 'Rika!'

There were several officers stationed around the crime tape. He could see people dressed in white going to and from the house. As he grew closer, he saw the destruction, and it made his heart lurch all over again. This wasn't a knifing. The downstairs and upstairs windows had been completely shot out. Even in the dark, he could see bullet holes littering the brickwork. An officer stepped into his path.

'Sir, you can't come any further. Please step back.'

'My sister is in there. My niece and nephew. I need to get in.'

'Sir, this is a crime scene,' the officer said firmly. 'Please, you cannot come any further.'

'What the fuck happened to my sister? What happened to the kids?' roared Lamont. The officer met his eyes sadly, shaking his head.

'I'm sorry, sir. I can't give you any details. I. . .' he glanced around, pointing at an overweight man talking to two other officers. 'Tanners' is the officer in charge. You can try speaking with him, but I can't promise he'll help.' With an apologetic look, the officer took a step back. Lamont hurried over to Tanners, who had his back to him.

'Are you Tanners?'

Tanners turned to face Lamont. He had a fleshy, jowly face, a pock-marked nose and pale eyes. 'Who's asking?'

'That is my sister's house. No one is telling me what's going on,' explained Lamont, losing his patience all over again.

'What's your name.'

'Lamont Jones. My sister and her two children live here. Are they okay?'

Tanners blew out a breath, but continued to meet Lamont's eyes.

'The kids went with Social Services. It's standard procedure in these situations.'

Lamont closed his eyes, knowing what Tanners was saying, even before he said it.

'Your sister was shot multiple times. I'm sorry to say that she was dead before we got here.'

Lamont fell to his knees, uncaring of who was watching. He couldn't believe it. It had to be a dream. Marika couldn't be dead.

Not his little sister.

'I really am sorry, Mr Jones. Is there anything you can tell us about this situation? Anything at all that will help us catch the people responsible?'

Lamont lurched to his feet, not even trying to stop the tears that were pouring down his face. He turned on his heel and stumbled towards his waiting vehicle, ignoring Tanners calling after him. Marika was dead. His little sister had been gunned down, and it was all his fault.

CHAPTER TWENTY-FOUR

Monday 25 May 2015

HOURS AFTER BEING DRAGGED away from Marika's, Lamont was home, mulling over the utter destruction. The feelings he had over Marcus's, Jenny's, Akeem's and Trinidad's deaths had been magnified. His heart ached. Since her birth, Lamont had looked after Marika, only growing closer to her after their parents' died. He had silently promised them at their funeral that he would keep looking after her.

Now, that promise had been shattered. Marika had been gunned down because once again, Lennox had wanted to get to Lamont. He had reached out and ripped away someone else that Lamont loved, and left her children without a mother.

Earlier, Lamont had spoken to his cousin, Louis, about getting the kids from where they were being held. He didn't know where their father was, but Louis had agreed to pick them up.

Staring at his phone, Lamont felt the tears prickling his eyes and for the first time since he was a child, he sobbed, tired of holding back his emotions. He cried until he was physically spent, then wiped his eyes, overwhelmed by the depths of his grief. This was stark and utter failure, and his family were right to blame him.

Lamont had never truly taken Lennox seriously. He had hated him after he killed Jenny, but he had never truly seen him as a challenge.

His lackadaisical attitude had cost him dearly. Lennox had a game plan from the beginning. He hadn't been intimidated by Lamont's reputation of what he might do in revenge. He had even tried making Lamont compliant by giving up the location of the man responsible for killing Jenny. He had wiped out Delroy Williams, killed his daughter, then eliminated Marika too. Just because he could.

Lamont felt something he hadn't in forever: True and utter doubt. Lennox had been moves ahead of them for months. He had stormed to the top of the crime pile, doing exactly what he'd said he would. Delroy Williams had been an institution for decades, and Lennox had wiped out him and his family. It was ruthless and beyond impressive.

A fresh wave of sorrow hit Lamont. He and Delroy had their differences, but despite everything, Lamont saw him as a friend. They'd grown closer lately, and he had seen Delroy's pain. They were kindred spirits, Delroy an older, broken version of Lamont who had lost his family and had a dream of returning home that he knew would never come to fruition. Like Trinidad, he had put his faith in Lamont. They had seen something in Lamont purely beyond what he saw in himself. They saw a man who could rise above and open doors. It was overwhelming.

Lamont needed an exit plan. Lennox had made it clear he was coming for him now and Lamont would either need to fight back, or escape. He had more than enough money to survive anywhere in the world. Maybe the change of atmosphere would be good for him.

Lennox's levels of clout were off the scale now. Lamont knew how it went. He had gone through the same thing back in the day when he had made big moves. People would fall at his feet to appease him, and what he said and did would set the new standard.

Lamont felt weak. He should have pushed through his issues and been stronger, instead of wallowing in his pain. Now, his niece and nephew had lost their mother over a situation he should have rectified. There was no way around it.

From the moment he had bumped into Nikkolo in the club in January, he had known Lennox was up to something, but he hadn't acted. Deep down, Lennox was just another thug for him to out-think and remove from the equation. When Jenny and Trinidad were killed, he'd had more to pay him back for, but it had never been full-on. Something else always came up. Lennox had taken the hits and the threats, appearing weaker than he was. Like last time, he had countered in spectacular fashion, and changed the entire landscape of the streets.

* * *

Lamont's phone had been ringing on and off all evening, and he couldn't ignore it any longer. He couldn't sit around and wait everything out. Whether he wanted it, the end was approaching. Snatching up the phone, he jammed it to his ear.

'Yeah?'

'L, fucking hell. I've been trying you for ages. Shit's deep, fam. We got rushed doing the pickup. Police rushed bare of our spots. Most of the team got locked up.'

Lamont listened, his stomach lurching as it hit him that K-Bar didn't know about Marika.

'Who are you with?'

'Maka. We're lucky. They were trying to kill us. I tried getting Shorty, but he isn't answering either.'

Lamont rubbed his eyes. Crying had taken it out of him, but he couldn't back away now. K-Bar needed him, and he needed to be the one to tell him what had happened.

'I'm coming to you now. Where are you?'

* * *

Lamont travelled with a team of four bodyguards, another man trailing. He kept looking over his shoulder, expecting to be ambushed. The guards were quiet and diligent, ready to act in case of danger.

K-Bar and Maka had gone to a safe house near Easterly Road. The guards took up positions around the house and Lamont knocked and entered. The pair were in the living room. Both men looked fatigued, but appeared injury free.

'I'm glad you're both okay,' said Lamont. Maka had a bottle of whisky and was pouring it into a glass. In the time Lamont watched, he downed the contents and re-poured. K-Bar yawned, a selection of mobile phones next to him, along with a gun within reach on the weathered coffee table.

'It's mad, L. Everyone is talking about Delroy. Lennox wiped him out. Even took out his daughter. I dunno who came for us. Could be any little drug crew. We dropped a few of them, but we were outgunned. We were lucky to escape.'

'K—'

'We need to regroup, find out who got locked up and who snitched. I'll track the people who robbed us and tear them apart myself. We can't let anyone get away with violating us. They got twenty boxes, and they were waiting on the roads for us.'

'K—'

'Shorty going missing is dodgy too. We had a line on a spot Lennox might have been at. They might have trapped him.'

'K-Bar.'

Finally, K-Bar realised Lamont was trying to speak, and stopped talking.

'Why would Shorty go to a spot of Lennox's alone? Lennox ambushed us last time. We lost Grimer, Rudy, and he got shot.' Lamont motioned to Maka.

K-Bar blew out a breath, not answering immediately.

'He said he could handle it. This is Shorty we're talking about. He's qualified.'

Lamont thought that was beside the point, but there were other things to discuss, and K-Bar would not like the news he gave him.

'Marika is dead.'

Maka's head shot up and he stared at Lamont, incredulous. K-Bar frowned, looking confused.

'What?'

'She . . . Lennox shot up the house. I got there too late, and he . . .' Lamont couldn't finish, his voice breaking.

Maka clambered to his feet and put his hand on Lamont's shoulder.

'I'm sorry, bro.'

Lamont nodded, but kept his eyes on K-Bar. He was looking

blankly ahead, then without a word, he shot to his feet and grabbed his gun, heading for the door. Lamont blocked his path.

'K, calm down.'

'Get out of the way.' The icy chill in K-Bar's voice made the hairs on Lamont's neck stand on end. K-Bar hadn't earned his reputation by accident, and Lamont was aware of this.

'Put the gun down. We need to discuss this.'

'Get out of the way or I will kill you!' K-Bar aimed the gun at Lamont.

'K, what the hell are you doing?' said Maka. He didn't move, and neither did Lamont.

'I'm gonna do what we should have done in the first place and put a fucking bullet in Lennox's head. Move. Now.'

Lamont shook his head, knowing that he was putting himself in immense danger. K-Bar was beyond reason, but he would try. He *had* to try.

'I'm not moving, K. We need a proper plan for Lennox.'

'That was your damn job,' snapped K-Bar. 'You're the smart one. You haven't even fucking checked in lately, so the least you could do was deal with him, instead of hiding like a pussy.' He stepped closer, all-but jamming the pistol against Lamont's face, his finger tightening on the trigger. His words hurt Lamont, but he forced them aside. K-Bar had the right to be hurt, just as Trinidad's family had. He couldn't take that away from him.

'I'm with you, K. He killed my sister, and my girl. Your pain is my pain, fam. We need a plan, and I'm here, ready to work with you.' He paused. 'Believe in Teflon.'

The moment dragged on, Maka's eyes flitting between the pair, the tension spiking. Finally, K-Bar sighed, lowered the gun, and slumped into a seat, tears spilling down his face.

'I loved her,' he mumbled. Lamont too had tears in his eyes, unafraid of showing his emotions. Not now. He placed a hand on K-Bar's shoulder and squeezed. He and his sister had been nowhere near their old level of relationship, but she was the connection to his parents. They had been through so much together, and now she was dead over something she had no involvement in.

K-Bar placed his hand on Lamont's and they stayed like that for some time, united in their grief and giving each other strength, until Maka hesitantly spoke up.

'What's the plan? We're gonna have people out there who aren't gonna know what to do. Add to that we got licked for twenty boxes. I don't even wanna think what that's going to cost us.'

'Don't worry about the cost,' said Lamont, straightening and facing Maka. 'Find out who has and hasn't been locked up. I'll ring my solicitor to get the ball rolling on that end. For now, all dealing is suspended until things are in order.'

'What am I telling people?'

'As little as you can for now. We don't know what Lennox knows, but we know he's coming. There's nothing holding him back.'

'The spots getting hit at the same time . . . gotta be a snitch, right?'

'It's likely,' admitted Lamont. 'They would have to be well-placed to have hit so many areas too. Keep everything to yourself. K, you're with me.'

Finally K-Bar looked up, his posture defeated and his eyes red.

'Where are we going?'

Lamont had his answer ready. He was tired of the facade, and there was one thing he needed more than anything else right now.

'To find Shorty.'

* * *

'I guess that prick Mack wasn't as useless as he looks.'

Lennox had an oily grin on his face. He was with Mark Patrick, sipping champagne in a safe house in Halton Moor as they listened to the reports coming out of Chapeltown. The news about Delroy's death had spread quickly, and everyone knew who was responsible.

Mack had done his part and given them a trove of information about the organisation in exchange for his payoff. Lennox had taken advantage of the petty grudge he had against Teflon's team and had parlayed it into success. His information about Delroy's daughter, Alicia, had been a masterstroke. Lennox hadn't even known he had a daughter and based on the fact she went by a different surname, he imagined that was by design.

'Forget Mack. It's gonna work,' he said to Mark, still grinning. 'This is the breakthrough we've been waiting for. It took longer than I wanted, but Delroy is dead, and his team is ours.'

'Teflon is still out there.'

Lennox waved his hand, spilling liquor on himself in his excitement. 'Teflon is a broken man. We took out his business partner, his girl, and now his sister. Eventually he has to get the message and just back off. If he doesn't, we smack whatever is left of his team and take his shit too. This is what victory looks like, Mark. Savour it, because these levels of win do not come around too often.'

'Are you absolutely sure about Teflon though?'

Lennox's grin faded, his eyes suddenly boring into Mark's. Mark nervously looked away. He hated meeting Lennox's dead eyes for too long. He was combat trained and had been around all types, but Lennox put out a deadly vibe that was like nothing else he'd ever come across.

'I gave him Ryan.'

Mark frowned. 'What the hell does that mean? You sold him out?'

'He sold himself out. I sent him to kidnap Teflon's missus, and he killed her instead. He was dead the second it happened.'

'Weren't you going to kill her anyway?'

Lennox shrugged. 'I wanted her because I knew she would keep Teflon from making a dumb mistake. In the end, I lost Nikkolo because Teflon's people tracked him down. Ryan had to pay for his idiocy.'

'So, you gave him to Teflon?'

'Think of it as a litmus test.' Lennox put his glass on the table in front of him. 'I wanted to see what he would do, and analysed how he did it. Ryan was shot multiple times.'

'So?'

'So, Teflon has enough hitters that know how to do a clean job. One, maybe two taps to the head. Quick and clean. The fact Ryan had multiple bullet wounds, suggests rage.'

'So?' Mark was utterly nonplussed. He wondered if Lennox was losing it.

'*Rage* is an emotion I know how to handle. Shorty was furious after his daughter got popped. He walked into a trap, got a few of his guys killed, and they ended up running off with their tails between their legs. Rage makes you do stupid shit. Speaking of Shorty, has Derrigan checked in yet?'

'No. Maybe Shorty got him,' said Mark. Lennox's eyes narrowed.

'Derrigan was confident he could handle Shorty. If he hasn't, I won't be pleased.'

'Want me to send some people to look for him?'

Lennox picked up his drink again. 'Go for it.'

* * *

When Derrigan was finally led into the room, he was limping, his face bruised. Lennox looked him up and down.

'What happened?'

'He got away.'

'How?' Lennox's expression was one of incredulity.

Derrigan picked up the bottle of champagne and began drinking from it, making a face. Mark glared, but he didn't notice. 'We had a fight. I was winning, then he got the better of me.'

'A fight?' Lennox shook his head. 'I told you to kill him, not have a scrap. What the hell were you thinking?'

Derrigan shot Lennox a sharp look. 'My methods are my own. I wanted to finish Shorty alone. He has a rep. Killing him will be good for future business.'

'You failed. Well done.'

'I'll finish him.'

'You playing *Rambo* has messed up the plan. Your ego cost us the chance to get rid of a deadly enemy.'

'Like when you had your little toy soldier shoot Teflon's bodyguard when you could have finished him?'

Lennox's face paled. Mark's mouth fell open. He had never heard anyone speak to Lennox with such open disrespect. Lennox didn't speak immediately. He locked eyes with Derrigan, neither man backing down. Seconds passed before he spoke.

'Teflon was a broken man after his girlfriend died. The hits ever since have worn him down further. There is a strategy there. We knock all the pieces off the board, then we deal with him. Shorty is a different sort of animal, which is why I wanted him dead. Lutel fucked up, and now you have too.'

'I told you, I will handle it. I don't need to be micromanaged. You sought me out, and you paid me what you did because I'm the best.'

Lennox's eyes hadn't left Derrigan. 'Don't make me regret hiring you.'

'I hope you're not threatening me.' Derrigan's voice was equally cold.

'Call it a reminder of your duties.'

Derrigan finished the bottle, wiping his mouth and dropping it on the table.

'Do you think Teflon got to the top by being weak? Overlooking him is daft.'

'He got to the top because of people like Marcus. I respected Tall-Man and how he played the game, but Teflon has made a life out of getting everyone else to do his dirty work. His team are washed up, and they didn't adapt, which is why we defeated them with simple methods and carved through their organisation. I want you worrying about Shorty. Not Teflon. He will come for you. He's not the sort to let things go.'

'I'll handle him. No mistakes.'

'Good. For now, make sure the troops are accepting of the new regime. Everything goes through us. We'll crush the holdouts who dare to go against that.'

When Derrigan left, Lennox turned to Mark.

'Send her in.'

Mark left the room, returning with a nervous-looking Julia. She stood in front of Lennox, wringing her hands, but meeting his eyes. He gazed at her for a long time before he spoke.

'You did the right thing,' he said softly.

'You didn't give me a choice when you threatened to murder my best friend if I didn't get her to help set up Shorty. Sienna cares about him, you know,' replied Julia.

'The feeling isn't mutual. Shorty doesn't care about her. He never did.' Lennox dismissed her words.

'What do you know about caring for people?' said Julia, her voice growing stronger even under Lennox's intense stare. 'People are just things you force to your will.'

'What use are they otherwise?' Lennox shrugged, acknowledging her words. Emotions and love led to people making mistakes like the ones Teflon, Shorty and Delroy had made. They had allowed emotions and love of other people to lead them, and had been destroyed because of it.

'I pity you.'

Lennox had never seen such a look of disgust on Julia's face. He didn't like it.

'I don't need your pity. You're nothing but a Hood slut,' he spat.

'If that's true, you should be able to let me go.'

Lennox's eyebrows rose before he broke into laughter. 'Do you really think I care about you?'

The look of disgust on Julia's face only deepened. For the longest time, Lennox Thompson had been her world. She had lived for making him happy, but now she saw the real him. There was no humanity left within him. He was simply a dangerous void who cared about nothing and no one. Her heart had truly hardened against him, and she would never view him with love again.

'Can I leave now?'

'You can. Warn Sienna I will kill her slowly if she breathes a word of what happened to anyone, and I promise you that you'll beg for what I do to her before I finish you too.'

CHAPTER TWENTY-FIVE

Monday 25 May 2015

IT WAS WELL after four am by the time K-Bar and Lamont pulled up outside Amy's. For Lamont, it felt like a lifetime since he'd hammered on the doors, thinking Amy was in trouble.

Jamal was waiting at Amy's gate for them. Lamont had left another two men nearby, just in case Lennox tried something. Jamal nodded when he saw Lamont. Despite the late hour, he still looked alert, something Lamont didn't share. He felt like he'd aged ten years in the past few hours and wanted nothing more than to go to sleep. There was still a lot to be taken care of, and so he would persevere.

'How long since he showed up?' Lamont asked the bodyguard.

'About thirty minutes. Didn't say much. Just argued with his missus.'

'Go home and get some rest,' said Lamont. Jamal shook his head.

'I'm good, L. I don't need to be anywhere.'

'You need to sleep. You've been out here for hours, and I have other people watching the spot. I'll get someone to ring you in the afternoon to let you know what's going on. Watch your back. We've taken some hits tonight.'

Jamal patted Lamont on the shoulder, then went to his car and drove away. Lamont glanced at K-Bar. He had spoken little since they left Maka, and Lamont knew what was going through his mind. He prepared himself for the meeting ahead. It would not be easy.

Amy looked pale and drawn when she answered the door to Lamont and K-Bar. She gave both men a hug.

'He's upstairs.'

They traipsed up the stairs after Amy. Shorty was laid up in the spare bedroom, his face heavily bruised, annoyance and pain etched into his face. He glanced from Lamont to K-Bar.

'She made me lay up in bed, even though I'm fine.'

'Please ignore him,' Amy started. 'He has fractured, possibly broken ribs, along with a collection of bruises and injuries that he won't tell me about. Not only that, he refused to let me call an ambulance.'

'I told you I'm fine.'

'Stop saying that!' Amy erupted. 'You're clearly not fine, Shorty. Before you run off and do these things, please remember you have two children you need to stay healthy for. You two can deal with him. I'm going to bed.'

'Shorty, what happened?' K-Bar asked, after Amy had slammed the door behind her.

'I was stupid. Didn't do the homework on that spot, and I got rushed.'

'Where did you get the intel for this spot?' asked Lamont. Shorty glared at him, but answered.

'Lutel's ex. We had a thing a while back, and she reached out. Put me in touch with Lennox's ex, who gave me and K-Bar the info.'

Lamont wanted to point out how stupid it was to rely on their intel, but he didn't. That wasn't why he was there.

'Who rushed you?'

'Derrigan was there.'

'Nicky Derrigan?' Lamont's brow furrowed. 'He doesn't work in Leeds anymore. Hasn't for years.'

'Lennox paid him a lot of money to change his mind. We got into a fight. I got the drop on him, but I had to shoot my way out.'

'You're not the only one,' said K-Bar, recounting the ambush on the drugs van.

'I can't believe all this happened in a single night,' said Shorty, wincing in pain.

'That's not all. Lennox took out Delroy Williams tonight. He killed him, his daughter, and . . . he sent people after Rika, Shorty. She's dead.'

K-Bar's mouth tightened. All the anger on Shorty's face immediately vanished.

'I'm sorry, L. You too, K. I can't believe he went there.' His eyes lingered on Lamont.

'I fucked up,' admitted Lamont. 'I believed Delroy when he said he could finish Lennox.'

'Lennox is a different animal,' said Shorty. 'There's a reason everyone, including Tall-Man and Reagan, respected him. He's ruthless. He's been in and out of prison most of his adult life, but always kept his crew strong.'

'Speaking of crews, ours is fucked. Police raided five or six of our spots. Proper co-ordinated effort. Maka is looking into that, but Manson was definitely arrested.'

'Shit,' cursed Shorty, shaking his head. 'What the hell?'

'We lost twenty boxes. People died, and half the crew are probably behind bars. I can't think of a time things have been worse.'

'I can think of a few times,' said Shorty softly. He and Lamont shared another look, and Lamont knew this was his time.

'I'm sorry, Shorty.'

Shorty's eyes remained hard, but he hadn't completely disregarded Lamont's words, which he took as a good sign.

'I shouldn't have accused you of being responsible for Jenny's death, and I definitely shouldn't have insinuated Grace's shooting was your fault. There's only one person responsible for both. Lennox has infected Leeds. He's gone too far, and we have to stop it.'

'What the fuck do you think we've been trying to do? Me, you, the crew, even Delroy's soldiers. We were all trying to take him out, and he played all of us.'

'We were blinded by revenge, Shorty. I know I was. Len took from me, just like Leader took from me thirteen years ago. Like my Aunt took from me. I thought it would fix me.'

Shorty's face softened slightly. He and Lamont had been friends for nearly thirty years, and he didn't think he had ever heard Lamont talk like this.

'. . . Rochelle broke me a long time ago. She seemed to get me, and I fell for her. The first girl to ever show me any sort of affection. After she crushed me, I was adrift, selling weed with you, wondering what it would take for me to evolve.

'And then we stepped up, and *I* stepped up, and I had something I could get behind. Money would open any doors I wanted, and I would be successful, and I would make myself worth something.

'You know what, though? I was still nothing. I had money and status, but I was still hollow, and all the things and jewellery and champagne, didn't fix me. It was just the best facade we had. I got hurt by a girl once, and I decided it would never happen again. I got women because I didn't care about losing them; they sensed that hole in me, and they tried to fix it, and then they would flee. Jenny was a way out. She was beautiful and had her own brain, and she took no shit from me, and it felt like despite the crime life, I'd found an equal to stand alongside.' The words poured from Lamont. He couldn't even filter them.

'Why didn't you?' Shorty spoke for the first time, his voice low, yet decidedly less hostile than it had been.

'Why didn't I what?'

'Walk away with her. You were gonna, and then I got out of prison, and you were still here. She wanted you to walk away, and that's why you lost her; because you didn't.'

Lamont hung his head. Shorty was correct, but it still hurt to hear. There would always be a pain associated with Jenny, and the possibility of what might have been.

'I couldn't walk away. I was blackmailed and forced to stay in the game.'

'You what?' Shorty's eyes narrowed.

'You remember Akhan the supplier?' Shorty nodded. 'He had something over me, and when I limped into his office after my shooting, I told him I was walking away. Ready to pay whatever cost was necessary, but he played his trump card, and I was trapped.'

'What card? What are you on about?'

'Reagan,' replied Lamont. Shorty looked more confused than ever. He had hated Ricky Reagan when he was alive, and hearing about him when he was dead was even worse.

'What about him?'

'I killed him.'

Shorty's eyes widened. His mouth fell open as he gawped from K-Bar to Lamont, unable to believe what he had just heard.

'You?'

Lamont nodded.

'How? You're not that guy. You kept us around so you didn't have to get your hands dirty.'

'You weren't there.'

'What the hell happened? I thought Tall-Man dropped him?'

Lamont filled Shorty and K-Bar in on the specifics of the night Reagan had ambushed him in the barber's two years ago, and their vicious fight.

'You got the better of Reagan?'

'I was lucky. Marcus cleaned it up, and I figured that was the end. I'd even let myself forget it, until Akhan revealed he knew, and threatened to go to the police.'

'How the hell did he find out?'

'Chink told him.'

'I knew it!' Shorty jerked upwards, then winced as the action put pressure on his injuries. 'I told you all along that he was no good.'

'It doesn't matter now, Shorty. What matters is that I couldn't walk away, and I couldn't tell Jenny that I was a murderer, so I had to deal.'

'Why couldn't you tell her?'

'Would you tell Amy?'

'I *did* tell Amy,' Shorty retorted. 'I thought it would make her hate me, but it didn't. It seemed to help fix things between us.'

Lamont blew out a breath. 'I couldn't take that same chance with Jen. As much as I wanted to, we were on borrowed time after that. Then she died anyway, and I'm still here.'

'Akhan's not around anymore though, is he?'

'I killed him too.' Lamont felt nothing as he told Shorty, save for a slight amusement at the shock etched onto Shorty's face.

'Darren told me about some mission with some Asians, and some robbery. Is that what you're talking about?'

'He tried double-crossing me, and we wiped out his people, and then I finished him.'

'I can't believe it,' Shorty rubbed his face. 'You're telling me you've dropped two bodies?'

Lamont shook his head, remembering Ryan Peters begging at his feet.

'The man who stabbed Jenny. Ryan. I got him too.'

'Who the hell are you?' exploded Shorty. 'You're the guy . . . you talk and negotiate. You don't kill.'

'My back was to the wall, and I reacted. The fact is, I barrelled ahead after Lennox because that's the life we're in, and you have to get revenge, or everyone thinks you're weak. Like you lot told me repeatedly, it's about the message.'

'Yeah, so?'

'Revenge won't fix me, Shorty. It won't heal Grace, or bring Marika, or Jenny or Trinidad, Akeem or Delroy, back to life. I can't hide behind it anymore. I can't hide behind the game, or the rules. Lennox has to go. For the good of everyone.'

There was a long silence after Lamont finished, and both felt as if a weight had been lifted from their shoulders. Lamont had filled in so many blanks for Shorty. He knew why he had remained, and though he would never come to grips with the fact his friend had murdered three men, he understood. He knew why it had been a secret, and he knew why Lamont was hurting in the way he was.

'It wasn't all on you, L. I shouldn't have made out it was. I talked shit about everyone around you dying because I wanted to hurt you. You weren't responsible for any of the deaths.'

'You weren't responsible for Grace's shooting,' said Lamont.

'Course I was. She was with me. If I hadn't smacked around Lutel, she wouldn't have got shot.'

'That makes it Lutel's fault, not yours. You wouldn't have put her in

langer and taken her out if you had known that might happen. Amy
old me you tried to cover her body with yours. How many people
would ever do that?'

'I love her.' Shorty swallowed down the lump in his throat.

'You love both of them,' corrected Lamont. In the background, K-
Bar sniggered, the first noise he'd made during their conversation.
There wasn't much for him to say. He didn't want to ruin the much-
needed talk between two of his closest friends.

'Where the hell did things get so fucked with us? I think I resented
you for years. Thought you looked down on me, and I never knew how
to bridge the growing gap between us. It's probably why I was always
snapping on Chink; you two seemed to get each other, and I was just
lost.'

'We — the three of us in this room — started the crew, and you lot
put me in charge. I thought I was better because I didn't run around
shooting people. Fact of the matter is that it was a collective effort.
When the chips were down, I needed you lot every time, and somewhere down the line, I squandered that.'

'We all needed each other,' said Shorty. 'Tall-Man would kill himself
again if he saw how we fell apart.'

'You're right. We tried making the crime life fit around our lives,
and I should have walked away a long time ago. It wasn't just about
Jenny, or Rochelle or Rika. It was about me.' Lamont took a deep
breath. 'I've felt guilty over what we do, the entire time, telling myself
that by trying to regulate things and by giving the crew *rules*, it made
what I did less deplorable. I didn't need to do it, Shorty. I made
enough money within the first few years to comfortably do something
else, but I didn't. Even beyond that, I tried influencing the decisions
you and others were making, because I thought I was right, and that
you should listen to me above everything else. I made mistakes, and
some of those mistakes led us here.'

'It's not just you. We've all fucked up,' said Shorty. 'Here and now,
you can walk away. Leave the streets to us and get yourself out of the
line of fire. Like you said, you've got the money, and the Feds haven't
tried to arrest you, so they probably can't connect you to any of this.'

Lamont shook his head, not even considering this for a moment.

'Lennox is dangerous, Shorty. We can't leave him unchecked. He doesn't care about Chapeltown. He cares about power, and that will sink the community even further if we do nothing about it.'

'What are we doing next then?' K-Bar finally spoke. 'I still need to put a bullet in Lennox's head.'

'We all have a grudge against Lennox. I have a few theories, so let's talk.'

* * *

Lamont's phone rang again just after nine. He'd left Shorty to get some rest, and they were meeting later to talk with K-Bar and Maka.

'Hello?'

'Lamont, we need to talk. Immediately.'

It was Stefanos. Lamont gripped the phone tighter.

'Where?'

'Come to my home again, please.'

'I'll be there soon.'

* * *

Stefanos waited at the top of his drive as Lamont pulled up. His expression was strained, his face pinched with stress. Lamont imagined he looked the same.

'I heard about your sister. I'm truly sorry about what happened. I know you loved her.'

'Thank you,' said Lamont, not knowing what else to say. It seemed to be enough for Stefanos, who led him to his office. Jakkar waited there, fastidiously dressed in a grey suit. He looked the same as he had the last time Lamont had seen him. His jaw was tight, his eyes boring into Lamont's. Lamont had never seen him look anything less than composed, and it was strange to see.

'Sit down,' he said to Lamont.

'I'd prefer to stand.' Lamont didn't like the hostile environment. He saw the demand to sit as Jakkar trying to dominate the conversation, and he would not allow that to happen. Stefanos slipped into a seat near Jakkar, shooting Lamont a reproachful look that he ignored. Jakkar kept his eyes on Lamont, waiting for him to speak, but he calmly waited him out. Frowning, Jakkar spoke.

'I hope you have some answers regarding what has transpired. Your men were ambushed and robbed of our product. Chapeltown is up in arms over the murder of Delroy Williams, and even now, several smaller crews are vying for power. Lennox Thompson has done massive damage to the stability, and to compound the situation, you've had multiple arrests in your organisation. You messed up, Mr Jones. Not only that, you have failed to live up to your reputation, and I would like some answers.'

'My sister died.'

Jakkar's expression was quizzical. He looked at Stefanos, who remained stone-faced.

'I don't see the relevance.'

'Of course you don't. The relevance is that I've lost more to this life than I can put into words. You want answers? I told the pair of you that Lennox was a problem, and I asked for resources so I could finish him before he could do too much damage. You refused to allow it. You gave me a promotion, but hobbled my resources. My answer is that I'm tired, and that the *reputation* of mine you spoke of, is bullshit.'

'What do you mean?' interjected Stefanos.

'I lost family, friends and lovers to a game I've been reluctantly playing my entire life. I'm done with it. With all of this.'

Now Jakkar spoke, paying no attention to Stefanos.

'I'm not Akhan. I won't blackmail you, but understand that by walking away, your relationship with myself with be severed, as will any link your crew has to our product.'

'Some things are more important. I thank you for the opportunity, regardless.'

'There is still the matter of the drugs that were stolen from you. Half were paid for, meaning there is still a substantial bill outstanding,' said Jakkar. To the surprise of both men, Lamont shrugged.

'Send me the bill, and you'll have the money within twenty-four hours.' He shook Jakkar's and Stefanos's hands, then left. Lamont was

approaching the front door when he heard footsteps following him. He
didn't pause, heading for his ride.

'Lamont.'

He turned to face Stefanos, who remained in the doorway.

'What are you going to do?'

'Clean up the mess.'

Stefanos ran a hand through his hair.

'And after that? What are you going to do without Jakkar's supply?'
He asked.

Rather than answer, Lamont climbed in, and his bodyguard drove
away.

* * *

'All in all a success.'

Reid had an enormous smile on her face, and it was strange for
Rigby to see. Murphy had caught him up on the happenings in Chapeltown, and he had been stunned beyond belief. The actions would have
ramifications in the streets for years to come. It wasn't the time to
ruminate, however. He needed to deal with Reid first.

'We got at least five kilo's, around nine grand in cash, several
mobile phones, and plenty of weapons, along with a few big names
such as Manson and Darren. No one is talking yet, but with these situations, it's usually a free-for-all of who can give people up the
quickest.'

'You did great work, Detective Rigby. You went with your instincts,
and it paid off. I noticed we didn't nab Lamont Jones, Keiron Barrett
or Franklin Turner. Are you confident the people we have in custody
will connect them?'

'I think it's a strong possibility,' replied Rigby, unwilling to guarantee it. This was the best chance they'd had in a long time to connect
the dots, and while he was optimistic, he had been burned going
against Teflon's crew previously.

'Fine. The Williams situation. What do we know?'

'Delroy Williams was murdered, along with his daughter, Alicia
Reynolds. His body was dumped on Chapeltown Road near the Land-

port building. We're canvassing for witnesses, but it's early days at this stage. The next few days will be telling.'

'I'm putting Murphy and Peterson onto that case. You will remain at the station and prepare the evidence for the subsequent interviews of Teflon's people.'

Rigby straightened in his chair, not pleased with this decree.

'Ma'am, with all due respect, me and Murphy could do a better job out there learning the situation. Can Peterson not do the interviews?'

'Detective, you are the one who made it clear how important capturing Teflon was to the betterment of our city. I want you to make sure we get everything and more from the interviews. Murphy can handle the Williams case.'

* * *

Terry was laid up in bed, his arm around the shoulders of a blonde he'd met a few weeks back. He'd been on and off the phone all day, learning more about what had happened to Delroy's crew. For the first time in a long time, Terry was happy with the moves he had made. He had hedged his bets in working with the police and had stayed out of the limelight with the raids, putting him in a fantastic position to move up the ladder. All he needed to do was wait out the storm.

'Are you working today,' the blonde asked. Terry shook his head.

'Got the message to stay off the streets until someone contacted me. The bosses will put their heads together trying to work out how to solve this.'

'The Delroy guy that died . . . he was big time, right?'

'The biggest. There'll be wars now that he's dead. I know at least two teams that are getting guns together, ready to shoot it out for that top spot.'

'Doesn't that worry you?' She asked, snuggling closer to Terry, glad she was connected to such an important man. He'd plied her with champagne and drugs when they met, and had bragged about his connections to big-timers in Chapeltown.

'Course not. Whatever happens, love, I'm fine. I'm connected to everyone, so whoever wins, they'll support me.' Pulling her close, he was ready to return to what they had been doing earlier, when his phone rang. He checked the number, and it was blocked.

'Yeah?'

'It's Murphy. Need to speak to you, right now.'

'Can't it wait? I thought we were done?'

'Meet me at the car park in HareHills. You know the one. You've got twenty minutes, and then I'm coming to your house.' Murphy hung up.

* * *

Seventeen minutes later, Terry pulled up next to Murphy's car in the car park. He was with another man Terry had never seen before. He was tall and bespectacled, with sandy brown hair.

'Who the hell is he? Where's Rig?' Terry jerked his thumb at the newcomer, who gave him a cold look.

'Don't worry about that. Tell me about what's happened lately,' said Murphy.

Terry shrugged. 'Don't you already know? It's been everywhere. Lennox finally got Delroy. Wiped out his daughter too, and now a few of his goons are going around the Hood, forcing away dealers. A few of the little dealers are also gunning for that top spot, so shit's getting bad.'

'I need names. What's your boss saying about it?'

'I haven't spoken to him. Half the crew is locked up, so he'll definitely be in touch, mate. Be patient and let me work.'

Murphy scowled, gripping Terry by the front of his jacket.

'Listen, you little mug. I ain't Rigby. Get out there and find out exactly what is going on. Don't care who you need to speak to, or how you do it. Get me something quickly, or your entire world changes. Don't test me.' Giving Terry a last look of disgust, Murphy and the other man drove away.

Terry spat on the floor, furious. He'd always tried to be respectful, but Murphy had never shown him anything but contempt. He knew Rigby didn't like him, but he was still polite and reasonable in what he asked for. There was nothing he could do. Murphy was vindictive

:nough to make life hard for him if he didn't cooperate, but he swore
his would be the last time.

Climbing into his Audi, he zoomed away, not noticing the car
parked nearby. The driver made a call on his phone.

'Maka, you were right. Terry's the snitch.'

CHAPTER TWENTY-SIX

Tuesday 26 May 2015

'ARE YOU SURE?'

Maka, Lamont, Shorty and K-Bar were in Jukie's backroom. He had been kind enough to let them use it on short notice, and tried to decline the money Lamont gave him, to no avail.

Ever since the raids, they had moved around when needed, not staying in the same spots for too long. They could hear the shouts of a domino game going on next door. The room comprised a table and numerous spindly wooden chairs. On the table rested a bottle of whiskey and four glasses. None of the men had partaken, however. It had been a long few days, and fatigue was clear in all of them. They had rested sparingly, working on putting their plans into action. Lennox's influence was spreading, and it wouldn't be long before they were pushed out completely.

'Positive. I had someone watching him as soon as we had that first meeting. Someone high up had to be the one to give the pigs that info. Worthy was a match. He knew just enough to give up a few spots, but couldn't really implicate any of us directly. My guy saw him meeting with two officers. Didn't recognise them, but one of them was a ginger.'

'*Murphy*,' said Shorty. Lamont recognised the name and description too, knowing the detective to be a partner of Rigby's. Rigby had wanted to lock him up for years. It struck Lamont that Terry might also have an inkling that he was behind the murder of Ricky Reagan. Regardless, he had violated, and would have to be dealt with.

'Do you think Terry knew enough about Delroy's operation to give him up to Lennox?' K-Bar asked.

'Definitely not. Terry is slippery, but not to that level. I spent enough time around Delroy to know he was always surrounded by bodyguards. His mansion was like a fortress, but someone knew enough about him to realise his daughter was the weak link. Alicia didn't even use the family surname. She was well-hidden, but they got to her anyway.'

'What are you thinking happened?' Shorty waited for Lamont's response. He had seen him theorise like this so many times in the past, and his insights were usually accurate.

'My guess is they snatched her to force Delroy to deal, then murdered the pair of them.'

'Who do you think gave them up? Delroy lost a lot of pieces this year. Who was he keeping close?'

Lamont cycled through the active names he knew in Delroy's organisation. Most were solid and dependable, and worshipped the old man. One name stood out.

'Mack.'

An ugly smile appeared on Shorty's face, and even Maka and K-Bar chuckled at the sight of it. Shorty's history with Mack was well-documented. He and Marcus had nearly killed him previously after he'd made threats against Lamont.

'Let's go get him.'

'We need to know where he is first. I'll speak to Jukie and see if he has anything for us. You guys can move onto *Step 2* without me.'

*   *   *

Several days after Marika's death, the family held a gathering. The funeral would take place next week, but it was decided beforehand that the family would celebrate how much she was loved.

To say Lamont didn't want to go was a vast understatement. He didn't get along with much of his family at the best of times and accepted he had unresolved issues where they were concerned. He was determined not to hide away anymore, and this was the first step.

The last few days had been spent locked away with Shorty, Maka and K-Bar, ironing out a plan to go against Lennox. He had asked K-Bar to attend the gathering with him, but K-Bar declined, stating it was a family thing.

Lamont arrived at his cousin Louis's Harrogate home just after seven in the evening. He sat in the car an extra few seconds, staring into space, composing himself for the night ahead.

'Everything okay, sir?' his driver asked.

'I'm fine. Ring me if you need anything.'

Lamont stepped from the car, smoothing imaginary creases in the black shirt he wore. He'd matched it with some black trousers and shoes. His fingers brushed across his old gold watch for reassurance, then he made his way inside after knocking once.

Lamont was the last to arrive, as he'd expected. The family were gathered in Louis's living room, and there was already very little space. There was a picture of Marika that had been placed on a wall, as soft music played in the background. Lamont's eyes narrowed when he saw Aunt Carmen sitting in a chair, surrounded by people, pleased to be the centre of attention. Her eyes flitted to Lamont's, and he held her gaze until she looked away.

After doing the rounds and greeting people, Lamont made a beeline for his niece and nephew. Bianca clung to him and he held her tightly. She was still coming to terms with what had transpired. She and Keyshawn had been in bed when the shooting started. Keyshawn had run to her room and dragged her to the floor. They heard gunfire, screams, and then silence. It had been Keyshawn who had discovered his mother's dead body. She had been shot three times in the back, and once in the back of the head. He kept Bianca from seeing it, then called the police.

Lamont had seen them as soon as Louis secured temporary custody, and had told Keyshawn how proud he was of him. He still felt that pride even now, as he squeezed his nephew's shoulder. Keyshawn's face was an emotionless mask, and it was disconcerting for Lamont to see. He would help him push through if it was the last thing he did. Maybe speaking to a professional would help.

'Princess Bianca,' he said, lifting her so she could wrap her arms around him in a tight hug.

'I want to stay with you, Uncle L,' she whispered.

'That's fine. You can stay with me while I'm talking to the grownups.'

Bianca shook her head. 'No, Uncle L. I want to stay with you. Forever.'

Lamont's heart wrenched in his chest. No child should have to go through something of this magnitude. The sadness in his heart for his dead sister mingled with the joy of his niece wanting to stay with him. He hadn't considered where the kids would stay. Louis was happy to have them, but he was married and already had two children of his own. The more Lamont considered it, the more he wanted it to happen.

'I told you I wouldn't leave again,' he murmured. Bianca clutched him tighter. Keyshawn gave him a look, showing he'd overheard.

'Let's go outside,' he said to his nephew. 'Bianca, go play with your cousins for a few minutes.'

Bianca didn't like it, but did as she was told.

Lamont and Keyshawn made their way to the front garden. Keyshawn stared at the floor, kicking at the ground with his shoes. Lamont watched him for a moment, still shocked at the similarities between them. Keyshawn reminded him so much of himself that it was uncanny.

'How are you doing with things?' he started, somewhat lamely.

Keyshawn shrugged. It was the level of answer Lamont had expected, yet he persisted.

'Is Louis looking after you?'

'Yeah.' Keyshawn finally found his voice, but added nothing else. Lamont continued to watch him. He was toeing a line between not wanting to make his nephew uncomfortable, but also wanting to avoid what had transpired during his own upbringing. Lamont vividly remembered being ignored by his Aunt in the aftermath of his parents' death. There was no opportunity to properly grieve or show his emotions. He'd needed to be strong for Marika, and it was clear early on that Aunt Carmen didn't want to hear him complaining. He wouldn't allow that to happen to Keyshawn.

'I wanted to tell you once again how proud I am of you. The way you've looked after your sis during all of this is fantastic, and I hope you realise that.'

Keyshawn nodded, and silence descended on them again.

'Why did she die?'

The question threw Lamont for six, and he was unsure how to answer. Despite his maturity, Keyshawn was still a child, and he couldn't tell him what had transpired.

'A bad man went after her,' he finally said.

'Because of you?'

'Because he wanted to hurt your mum,' said Lamont delicately, before adding, 'he wanted to hurt me too.'

Again, Keyshawn nodded.

'Your sis said she wants to live with me.' Lamont paused to see if Keyshawn would react. Other than glancing Lamont's way, he didn't. 'What do you think about that?'

'I . . . don't want bad people shooting at us anymore.'

Lamont hung his head, his heart breaking all over again. Straightening, he pulled his nephew in for a hug.

'I promise you, that won't happen, K.'

Keyshawn stiffened at the beginning of the hug, but slowly relaxed into it. After a few minutes, they composed themselves and headed back inside.

Lamont kept his distance from Aunt Carmen, but felt her eyes on him several times over the course of the evening. Drinks were made available, and she consumed her fair share.

It was almost ten in the evening when the conversation took a sudden turn. Bianca had already gone to bed, but Keyshawn was still up, playing on his mobile phone in the corner. Lamont was nearby, listening to Louis talk about his job. Aunt Carmen and Aunt Pat were holding a loud conversation that Lamont did his best to tune out until he heard words that chilled his blood.

'I'll take them. I raised Rika, and I raised her right. I'll do the same with her kids.'

'That's not going to happen,' said Lamont. His voice carried around the room, ending all conversations. Keyshawn glanced up at him, but Lamont kept his eyes on Aunt Carmen. The sight of her drove him to rage as it always had. He'd told her the last time they spoke, that he would never see her again, but he'd been forced to break the vow. Her eyes were bleary as she glared at him.

'Excuse me?'

'Keyshawn and Bianca will never live with you. They're going to live with me.'

A low murmur broke out around the room after Lamont's declaration.

'You must be crazy, Lamont. Why on earth would the kids live with you? It's your fault their mother is dead, dragging her into your crazy mess.'

Louis opened his mouth to defend Lamont, but froze when he saw the expression on Lamont's face. The family all knew what Lamont did. They knew his background, but few had ever seen him like this. The cold fury in his eyes as he stared down his Aunt was chilling, sending shivers down their spines.

'Keyshawn,' Lamont started, his voice level despite his rage. 'Go upstairs, please. Take your cousins too.'

Keyshawn didn't argue. He took the hands of his younger cousins and led them from the room.

'You vile excuse for a woman,' he said to Aunt Carmen, still speaking in the same level tone. 'You didn't even have the common decency to speak softly around Keyshawn? Do you really think I would ever expose my niece and nephew to your awful parenting?'

'You're ungrateful. You always were. I went without so that you and your sister would have everything you needed, and never received any thanks for it. I refuse to be judged by a disgusting criminal.'

'I'd rather be a criminal than be the things we all know you are,' he retorted, taking great pleasure at seeing her face pale. 'Whatever I am, I would never mistreat or abuse those children, and I doubt that is something you could say with any honesty.'

'L . . . maybe we should—' Aunt Pat spoke up, but Lamont silenced her with a vicious look.

'No. You all let this woman do what she wanted. You let her take me and my sister without considering what would be best for us. That's bad enough, but you went one step further and practically ignored us. You kept your heads buried in the sand because as far as you were concerned, it wasn't your problem. Do not interfere any further.'

Aunt Pat's mouth opened and closed. She looked at her husband for his reaction, but he was equally stunned. None of them knew how to deal with this side of Lamont. Aunt Carmen's chins quivered as she shot her nephew a look of loathing. It didn't matter. He'd said his piece, and no one in the room would stop him from getting what he wanted. Without another word, he went outside again to get some fresh air, needing to be away from his family. He took several deep breaths, trying to calm himself.

The comments about being responsible for Marika's death still stung, but he was working past it. He wasn't to blame. Lennox Thompson had decided to leave Marika's kids without a mother. Lamont didn't know where her baby father was, but he would track him down in due course, and ensure there were no roadblocks in him being named the carer for his niece and nephew.

'You really got some stuff off your chest in there, didn't you?' Louis headed out and stood next to his cousin. They had similar features, but Louis was shorter and thicker around the middle. His hair was also thinner on top, but he had the piercing eyes and facial features many of the Jones' shared.

'Sorry for bringing all the drama to your house,' said Lamont, running a hand through his hair.

'Don't worry about it. Wouldn't be a family gathering without an argument.'

They both chuckled, comfortable in the silence.

'You're right, you know,' Louis said, moments later. 'You're the best one to look after them. I think you need Bianca and Keyshawn as much as they need you.'

Lamont didn't respond, but he agreed, and it was nice to know Louis was on his side.

'I just need to survive,' he said.

'Is it that bad?' Louis knew little bits of what Lamont was involved in, and the deaths that surrounded him this year, but not much of any substance.

'I'll handle it. Watch the kids for now, especially Keyshawn. I don't want him internalising his pain.'

'Leave it to me, cuz. Nothing will happen to them.'

CHAPTER TWENTY-SEVEN

Monday 1 June 2015

THE DAYS FOLLOWING the execution of Delroy went well for Lennox. Led by Nicky Derrigan, his forces were pushing out numerous drug dealers with little resistance. The ruthless way he had dealt with the Williams' crew had left a fissure on the streets of Chapeltown, and no one wanted to get in his way.

Despite the successes, he had heard no response from Teflon or any of the other larger crews. Teflon had completely pulled his people back, and there were no signs of them selling any drugs, which was surprising. He brushed it off, however. He had shown Teflon time and time again that he was superior, and would destroy him and his team if they stepped up. Teflon was soft at heart, and every time he had gone against Lennox, he had lost someone close to him. He would be silly to risk that again.

Lennox was firmly looking to the future. Soon, Chapeltown would be united under his control. To restock the war fund, he had raided Delroy's drug spots, planning to sell the product, along with what he had stolen from Lamont's team. It went against his credo, but he consoled himself with the fact he wasn't selling the drugs in Chapeltown.

Through Mark Patrick, he had arranged sales with several out-of-town buyers that would flood their own areas with the high-quality product. Sitting comfy in his safe house, he poured himself a drink with a smug smile on his face.

* * *

Mack sat in his front room, glaring at a western on the TV and chain smoking. It was late evening. He had tried calling Lennox numerous times, but hadn't received a response, and it was making him antsy. Mack had resented Delroy and his treatment of him over the years, culminating in him sharing information about Delroy's family, namely his daughter Alicia. He had expected Lennox to use her to lure out Delroy, but had been sickened when he murdered her. There was nothing to be done about it now. He had to think about his own future, and that meant getting the rest of the fortune Lennox had promised him for his involvement.

Once he got the funds, he was done with England. His family had land in St Kitts, and he would live like a king with the money he earned. Mack was so lost in his musings that when his door was kicked open, he didn't immediately react. By the time he'd made it to his feet, Shorty and K-Bar were in the room, dressed in all-black and armed with pistols, both trained on his head. He raised his hands, shivering with fear in the middle of his living room.

'Where's Lennox?' asked Shorty.

'I don't know!'

Shorty shook his head. K-Bar — usually the calm one — stepped forward, cracking him around the head with his gun. Mack crumpled to the floor as K-Bar stood over him, a murderous look in his eyes.

'You better talk, Mack. We know you set up Delroy. If you don't start talking, the beating is gonna be worse than the last one I gave you, and that's before we get into some special shit.'

Mack shifted back, terrified by Shorty's words.

'H-He threatened m-me. Said if I didn't go along with it, he would kill me,' he tried.

'He threatened all of us too,' replied Shorty. 'He took out people close to all of us, but we'd never back down from him. You sold out a man that fed you for decades. If you hadn't been so shit with your money, you'd be retired now. Who did you deal with in Lennox's crew? There's no way he'd deal with a prick like you directly.'

'. . . Sinclair. This young crazy kid who works for Lennox. He made the offer and gave me a direct line to his boss.'

'Bet he's not taking your calls anymore now that you're useless, is he?' said K-Bar dryly. Mack pretended not to hear.

'I want all the information you have on the crew. Don't piss around either,' Shorty demanded. Mack didn't hesitate. He spilled information about potential hangouts, and descriptions of the people Sinclair was with. He even gave a description of the car he'd driven. K-Bar stored all the information in his phone.

'Guess we got what we came for,' he said to Shorty, who nodded.

'What happens to me now?' stammered Mack. His eyes widened when Shorty's finger tightened on the gun.

'This is for Del and Alicia.' He fired twice, bullets exploding into Mack's neck and cheek. Standing over Mack's prone frame, he fired twice more. They quickly left the house, jumping straight into the waiting car, which drove away at speed.

* * *

Terry waited in his Audi. Maka had contacted him in a panic, saying he needed help after all the problems with the crew. Terry had arranged to meet with him, an oily smile on his face, as he plotted how he was going to profit from the situation.

Maka told him Lennox had made his moves against the crew, robbing them of product, and murdering Teflon's sister, along with Delroy and his daughter. Terry had gleefully passed all the information onto Murphy, hoping it would keep him off his back.

Maka arrived a short while later. He looked harried, shiftily looking in all directions. Hastily greeting Terry, he got to the point.

'We're fucked. Supplier's cut us off after all the shit that's happened. Teflon's fucked off and left us in the lurch, and half the team is locked up. I need you to step up if you can handle it.'

'Course I can handle it, mate,' replied Terry, trying to keep his voice level. 'Where's Shorty and K-Bar?'

'Shorty's injured. One of Lennox's guys beat him badly. K-Bar's all depressed because Rika Jones got blasted, and he was loved up,' said Maka, his tone full of scorn. It surprised Terry. Maka was normally calm, but all the stress had seemingly got to him.

'Shit . . . you shoulda called me earlier, pal. I could have helped.'

'I know. It's been bad though. Taken a while to get things relatively back in line. That's what I need you for.'

'Go on.'

'I've had to scrape a deal with some Slovenians. They've got links all over, but they've been struggling to crack into the Hood.'

Terry nodded. 'I've heard of a few of those Russian lot trying to make moves. Do you want me to meet them?'

'Yes. We're likely to get ripped off, but see what you can do. I know you've wanted more responsibility for a while. This is your chance to be a player again, and show what you're made of.'

Terry grinned. 'I won't let you down, Maka. When's the meet?'

Maka handed Terry a piece of paper with the details.

'Everything is on there. Make sure you burn that paper too. Ring me after you're done, and we'll discuss next steps. Cool?'

'Leave it to me, mate.'

Terry watched Maka drive away, his grin widening. This was what he had been waiting for. He had Maka dependent on him, and had more titbits he could feed the police. Climbing into his ride, he motored away, already calling Murphy. Hopefully this would keep him off his back.

CHAPTER TWENTY-EIGHT

Tuesday 2 June 2015

TERRY ARRIVED at the spot where he was meeting the Slovenians just after ten in the evening. It was a house on Brownhill Crescent in Hare-hills. He hadn't told the police about the meeting. He wanted to use Maka a while longer before he gave him up. The information regarding Lennox and Teflon had been passed onto Murphy. It matched up with a lot of the talk going around the Hood regarding Lennox and his crusade against dealers. Terry was hoping the police arrested them quickly, leaving the path free for him to keep climbing the ladder.

As he climbed from his car, he thought back to his initial arrest. He'd been caught red-handed doing a deal, and he'd thought his life was over. Now, through cunning and solid moves, he had made it work.

Knocking on the door, he planted a smile on his face when a woman answered. She wasn't the nicest, with slightly crossed eyes and crooked teeth. The body was ridiculous, however, and she wore a plunging top showcasing her tremendous cleavage. He forced his eyes back to hers.

'Hi love, I'm here to meet *Ivan*,' he said. She nodded and let him in, pointing to the room ahead. Terry entered with a stroll, turning up his nose at the sight of the living room. There were dirty plates on the flimsy coffee table, a small LCD television on a spindly stand in the middle of the room, and creaking floorboards that sank under the weight of Terry's feet. He glanced back at the woman, who was pointing to the next room. Hoping for her sake she wasn't wasting his time, Terry wrenched open the door and entered the kitchen, where he froze.

'Good to see you, Terry,' said K-Bar, his gun raised and pointed at Terry's chest.

'K, what's going on? What's all this?'

'Guess you could say we're tidying up,' replied K-Bar.

'I don't get you,' said Terry, feeling a bead of sweat at the top of his head. He needed to pick his words carefully here. As nice as K-Bar could be, he was deadly. Slowly, he raised his hands, trying to show K-Bar he wasn't a threat.

'Yeah, you do. *Informer.*'

Terry's blood ran cold as he realised instantly that the game was up. If they knew he was a police informant, there was utterly no way out.

'Listen,' he started, thinking on the spot, 'the Feds followed me here. You kill me, they're coming straight for you.'

K-Bar's smile both terrified and confused him.

'Wouldn't be the first time you've sent them after me, right? Was it you who told them about some of my other moves?'

Terry shook his head jerkily, nausea bubbling in his stomach.

'Please . . .' he started, only to be cut down by a single bullet to the forehead. Not even giving him a second glance, K-Bar left the house. The woman who had set Terry up was long gone, and there was nothing connecting her to the house.

Shorty waited for him in a car down the street.

'All done?' he asked. K-Bar nodded.

'Pity we can't take his car too. Fucking snitch.'

'It's done. I'll call Maka and let him know.'

* * *

Sinclair was next on the list. They tracked the car he was using to a spot in the heart of Miles Hill. Shorty had two men with him, named Kareem and Majid. Both men were strongly built and could handle themselves. They all wore masks to cover their faces and prevent detection. The driver kept the car running and the three men hurried to the house. There was no time to worry about unlocking the door. Kareem kicked it in with ease and charged into the living room, gun raised.

Shorty and Majid hurried upstairs. Shorty took one room, Majid another. Bursting into the bedroom, Shorty found Sinclair shrugging off the woman he was with, trying to go for a butterfly knife that rested on the bedside table.

'Don't do it to yourself,' Shorty warned, ready to shoot if he moved. Sinclair looked like he was still thinking of going for it, but stopped moving. The woman he was with screamed as Majid entered the room, followed seconds later by Kareem.

'Oi, shut it, before I shut you up,' snapped Shorty. Trembling, she complied.

'What the fuck do you want?' Said Sinclair. If he was scared, he wasn't showing it. Lamont had mentioned the young assassin who had killed Akeem, but he had thought he was exaggerating. Sinclair looked around fourteen years old. He had no facial hair, a tapered fade, and a bony chest and skinny frame. It was hard to imagine him being able to lift a gun, let alone shoot it.

'Darling. I suggest you wait downstairs. Don't leave before I've spoken to you. My people are waiting outside,' Shorty told the woman. Unconcerned about her nakedness, she hurried from the room as quickly as she could.

'Get on with it then!' Sinclair was still showing no fear. Shorty was impressed.

'You have to answer for what you did to Akeem.'

'Who the hell is Akeem?'

The men beside Shorty tensed, but Shorty ignored them for now.

'The man you shot on Chapeltown Road.'

'What about him?'

'This guy here,' Shorty motioned to Kareem. 'He's his brother.'

Sinclair shifted slightly in the bed. Other than his bottom lip quivering, he showed no reaction.

'This guy,' he motioned next to Majid, 'is a good friend. I'm gonna eave them to deal with you, while I go speak to your pretty little girlfriend.'

The men advanced on Sinclair. As Shorty headed downstairs, he heard the first scream. The naked woman had done as ordered, and was sitting on the cherry red sofa, using a small throw-pillow to cover her nakedness.

'Is this your house?' Shorty asked.

She shook her head.

'Get some clothes and go home. If I hear you've said a word about what happened here, I'm gonna come and find you. Write your name and address.'

After a few minutes, he called Kareem and Majid off. Both men looked like they wanted to do more damage, but they were on a tight schedule. Sinclair was left face-down on the bed, after being half-strangled, with wounds to his genitals, arms, and legs, and a large in the hole back of the head. It was a grisly revenge for Akeem's murder.

'I hope this makes things right,' said Shorty, after they had cleaned up and changed their clothes at a safe house in Scott Hall.

'It does,' replied Kareem. 'My brother was a soldier and knew the rules, but I'm glad we made it right.'

'Give Vincent my regards when you go back home,' said Shorty. 'Teflon's too.'

'We will. You need any more help up here?'

Shorty shook his head. 'We're nearly done, fam. Thanks for the offer.'

After slapping hands with both men, Shorty left to link with K-Bar and Lamont.

* * *

The executions of Mack, Terry Worthy, and Sinclair, was a co-ordinated effort that took place within a 24-hour period. Rather than resting on their laurels, the crew was committed to finishing Lennox. Teflon had put up twenty thousand pounds in reward money, wanting all addresses linked to Lennox and his men. His surveillance of the Jackie Smart Court property had paid dividends when his men saw

Mark Patrick show up to give orders to the men staying there. After a quick phone call, they had tailed him discretely to a spot in Archery Road.

Ten men were ready to rush the spot. They had no confirmation Lennox was there, but it was deemed to be worth the risk.

Lamont, K-Bar and Shorty were all present, armed and focused.

'He doesn't even have people watching the spot,' K-Bar remarked.

'He could have people watching from any of these houses. We go in quick and heavy, and we don't leave anyone alive,' said Lamont. K-Bar and Shorty both shared a look, grinning at Lamont. They trusted his combat instincts much more now that they knew he had some kills under his belt.

'Quick and heavy is fine. Let's make it happen and finish this swiftly.'

* * *

'What the hell are you trying to tell me?' Lennox snapped. He was with Derrigan and Mark Patrick, and neither had good things to say. Lennox had been at the house for the past few days, wanting to remain close to the action in the Hood. During that time, he'd added little touches to the spot, adding an X-Box, a widescreen television and games and DVD's to stave his boredom.

As they spoke, Derrigan kept glancing over at the console, clearly bored with the conversation. He had his feet up on the coffee table, hoping the others would stop talking soon.

'Teflon and his team are coming back on us,' said Mark. 'They've attacked a few spots, and they got Sinclair. Tortured him pretty badly before they killed him too.'

'I don't care about Sinclair,' said Lennox. 'He was a tool, and he outlived his usefulness. Mack is dead too, so I'm guessing they found out about him giving up Delroy.'

'What are we doing now then?' Derrigan asked. Before Lennox could reply, gunfire ensued. Mark knocked over the coffee table, using it for quick cover as a group of men swarmed into the room. Mark saw K-Bar lining up a shot on Lennox, and let go a burst of shots. They all

pped into K-Bar, who did a stutter-step like movement before falling
ackwards. Enraged, Shorty blasted Mark before he could move, four
bullets putting him down for the count. Lennox was scrambling away,
with Derrigan watching his back. Lamont fired a shot at him, but it
missed. He and Shorty exchanged a look and ran after Lennox, chasing
him into the next room. Two goons waited for them. Shorty cut them
down, but the distraction gave Lennox time to slip out of the door.

'Go!' Shorty shouted. 'I'll handle Derrigan.'

Nodding, Lamont ran after Lennox. Derrigan eyed Shorty, then
smiled. Both men aimed their weapons at one another.

'Round 2 then?' he said. 'We never got to finish our fight.' He
lowered his gun slightly, which was a fatal mistake. Shorty pumped the
rest of his clip into him, sending him crashing into the wall.

'I don't have time for that shit,' he said to Derrigan's prone frame.
He turned to one of the men who had followed him. 'Finish this piece
of shit off.'

Running back through to the main room, Shorty hurried toward K-
Bar, who was unmoving on the ground. Two of their goons were
standing over him.

'K . . .' Shorty whispered, knowing it was too late. His long-time
friend and comrade was dead. Mark had clinically put him down. The
bullets to the chest had finished him. Blinking away tears, Shorty took
K-Bar's gloved hand in his own. 'I'm sorry, fam. You deserved better
than this.'

After squeezing K-Bar's hand one last time, Shorty hurried after
Lamont.

* * *

Lennox hurtled from the house during the confusion. There had
always been a chance of getting caught, but he had never actually
expected it to happen. Somehow, Teflon had tracked him down and
from the sounds of things, had wiped out his two remaining pillars in
Derrigan and Mark Patrick. He was absolutely furious at the turn-
around. This was his time. He'd murdered Delroy and his entire family
to earn this, and yet Teflon had surprised him once again.

As he rounded the corner onto Blackman Lane, he heard footstep
following, slowly growing closer.

'Stop, Lennox.'

Lennox heard the click of a gun and complied, turning slowly to
face Teflon. They stood in the middle of the quiet streets staring one
another down. It was the first time they had been face to face since
their brief meeting in March. For a man he'd believed was steps away
from a breakdown after his sister's death, Teflon looked remarkably
composed. He stepped closer to Lennox, gun aimed at his chest.
Lennox noticed his hands weren't shaking.

'Have you killed before?' he asked.

'Does it matter at this stage?' Teflon replied. 'You're finished.'

'You think?'

'The police are hitting several of your known spots. They want you
for various murders, and we've taken out your main team. This has
been a long time coming.'

Lennox found his anger growing in the face of Teflon's calm
demeanour.

'You're nothing without your people, Teflon. Your bitch screamed
for you before she died. Your sis and that old barber probably did the
same, if they even got the chance. All deaths I orchestrated, because
you weren't strong enough to stop me.'

Teflon nodded, seemingly in agreement, which was a shock.
Lennox didn't like this side. They'd spoken on the phone when he'd
given him Ryan Peters' location, and he'd sounded frustrated.

'The deaths hurt me. For too long, I forced myself into thinking
having those feelings was a weakness. I envied you at one point,
because you have no feelings, and you're truly ruthless. Now, I pity
you. People don't weaken me. They strengthen me. My connections to
people have kept me going, even when I thought it was money, or the
power I had at my fingertips. In the end, power nor money stopped
those close to me from losing their lives.'

Lennox shook his head, not wanting to listen to Teflon's redemp-
tion bullshit.

'You're not strong enough to be at the top. You don't have the
stomach to do the things needed to lead.'

'I agree. It's a *strength* I don't want. I've been on borrowed time for too long.' His finger tightened on the gun.

Fear welled within Lennox, but was instantly quashed. He refused to be afraid of Teflon.

'No matter what happens here, you don't win. You can't walk off into the sunset with your bitch. I took her. I took your sister.'

'I'll never truly be over their losses, but I know I'll be okay,' Teflon's response again took him by surprise. 'Jenny loved me. She saw something in me, and we were happy for a time. I want to experience that same happiness again.'

Despite himself, Lennox snorted. Teflon smirked.

'I don't expect you to understand. Like I said, I pity you. You couldn't hold onto your woman without threatening her. I'm guessing your mum scarred you.'

Lennox was still. Then he roared and stepped toward Teflon, before coming to his senses and remembering the man was armed. He snarled, wanting to tear him apart.

'You—'

'She was a prostitute. You couldn't take that she cared about getting high more than she cared about you. You never had a role model, and it made you into some cold, unfeeling husk. Your plans failed. You can't have Chapeltown, because you're even worse for the community than I am. You don't care about anything but yourself.' He paused. 'I care more about them than I do myself. Never thought I would say that.'

'Fuck you,' Lennox spat. 'If you pull that trigger, you're truly no better than me, no matter what you say, or how you try to justify it.'

Teflon shook his head.

'I can honestly say I'm doing this not for revenge, but because it's the right thing for everyone else.'

The gun fired once, the bullet slamming into Lennox's stomach and sending him careening into a nearby wall. Aware they were out in the open, Teflon stood over him. Lennox coughed, blood dribbling from his mouth, his eyes dimming.

· · ·

Lamont wasn't leaving it to chance. The final bullet smashed into Lennox's forehead.

He glanced down at the fallen criminal, the ramifications of what he had done washing over him for a second. He turned and saw Shorty nearby, gun by his side. The two friends shared a nod, acknowledging what had transpired.

'C'mon,' said Shorty. 'Let's get out of here. Someone will have called the Feds.'

Looking at Lennox's body one last time, Lamont followed Shorty away from the scene.

EPILOGUE

Wednesday September 9 2015

'You need to cheer up, mate.'

Rigby let Murphy's words drift over him as always. They were on their way to a crime scene, and the March weather was particularly cold. Wind whipped through the open window on the passenger side door. Murphy embraced it, closing his eyes and breathing it in deeply. Rigby zipped his jacket up as far as it would go, shaking his head and muttering as he navigated a left turn.

'Seriously, it's been months,' Murphy continued, knowing Rigby wouldn't reply. 'You can't dwell on things forever. I mean, we did bloody outstanding work. We smashed a few crime rings and locked up dozens of people. That's a win.'

'Teflon and Shorty got away. Worthy ended up dead, meaning they probably learned he was the grass.'

'Worthy was never the sharpest knife in the drawer, was he?' Murphy scoffed.

Rigby finally glared at his partner. 'That's a callous attitude to have. Even for a hard bastard like you.'

'I'm not wrong though, am I? He was a screwup all of his life, and look where it got him. At least he tried to leave us a parting gift.'

'Even with his help, we failed. Teflon and Shorty got clear away.'

'Their crew is finished. Delroy's crew is finished. That's the two biggest crews right there. That's a win, so you need to shake the misery and move on.'

Rigby didn't reply. He wasn't sure he could do that. To him, it seemed like yesterday they had found the bodies of Lennox Thompson and several of his men. Rigby never had the chance to fully go after him for the murders he *knew* he had ordered, but the brass were happy. They had closed multiple murder cases, causing a significant dent in street traffic in and around Chapeltown.

Relations between the community and the police were thawing, but there was still work to be done. He wondered if Teflon was done for good, or if he would try to take advantage of the power vacuum the way other crews were attempting to, and become stronger than ever.

They were approaching the crime scene though, and as Rigby brought the car to a halt, his mind shifted from Teflon as always. It was a new day, a new crime, and it demanded his full attention.

COSTA DE ORO, URUGUAY

'Gracey, let your dad hold the phone. You're shaking it!'

The smile on Lamont's face couldn't get any wider. He was on a beach on the other side of the world, talking to people he loved via FaceTime. Grace Turner's face took up most of the phone screen, but Lamont knew Amy and Shorty were with her. She had recovered well enough to go home, but was still taking a truckload of medication, and had weekly hospital trips for check-ups. Shorty and Amy were trying again and though it was early days, from what Lamont could see, they were doing well. They seemed more open with one another, which was good to see.

Shorty had followed Lamont's example, stepping away from the life of crime. He had saved his money over the past year, and wanted to set up his own business, but he wasn't sure what he wanted to do. For now, he was content staying with Grace and catching up on the time he'd missed. There had been a few trips to Huddersfield, and a few

wkward meetings between half-siblings, but it was all progress, and it
ll made Lamont smile every time he heard more about it.

The pair were still finding their way back to the level of brother-
ood they once had, but they were taking steps to repair their relation-
hip, one day at a time.

'Gracey, go get a drink with your mum, let me talk to Uncle L in
peace.'

'Okay, daddy. Bye, Uncle L.'

'Talk to you soon, Gracey.'

Shorty took the phone and went to sit outside in Amy's back
garden. There was a moment of silence between them, neither forcing
any conversation.

'You look good, L,' Shorty finally said. 'Down there agrees with
you, man. You look healthy.'

'I feel it,' Lamont admitted.

'Being away has done you the world of good.'

Lamont wiped his eye with his free hand. 'I still have a lot of work
to do. It's hard sometimes, dealing with everything that's happened.
Gets overwhelming. What I'm learning is that I need to accept the
fact I'm not superman, and that it's okay to be down.'

Shorty didn't fully grasp what Lamont was saying. He still had
issues communicating with Amy, resisting the urge to storm out when
they argued, but like Lamont, he was learning to live with it. All that
mattered to him was that Lamont finally looked like he was healing.

'I don't really get it, fam, but I'm glad that *you* get it.'

That was enough for Lamont. He wouldn't have been able to be so
open with Shorty in the past. They were the best of friends, but hid
parts of themselves from each other, allowing resentment to fester
until frustrations overflowed. Now, their friendship had evolved. It
wasn't as deep as it had been, but it was realer, and it was still
developing.

'What's going on with Bianca and Keyshawn then?'

Lamont's stomach plummeted when Shorty mentioned Marika's
kids. Thinking about Marika was hard, and it had taken some time for
him to truly come to terms with the fact his little sister was gone. He

pointed the blame at Lennox, but deep down, he still had some issue to work through with his guilt.

'When I'm back in the city, they will come with me. Bianca i happy. Hard to tell with Keyshawn.'

Lamont didn't have to say more. Shorty knew Keyshawn was like Lamont in temperament. They both internalised their pain, and Keyshawn was clearly feeling the pain of his mother's murder. He had lashed out at Lamont a few times, blaming him for what happened, but he always apologised. It would take time, but Lamont would help him through it.

They would help each other through it.

'They're gonna be fine, L. You're gonna do good by them; give them what you never had.'

Lamont lowered his head for a moment, overcome by emotion. He and Shorty had never really spoken about his upbringing, and the influence his Aunt had on him after his parents died, but he was right. Lamont was new to parenting, but vowed to be there for both of them, and to raise them right.

'Thanks, Shorty.'

'Anytime, fam. I'm gonna see what those two are up to. I'll speak to you soon, though. If you don't come back to Leeds, we're coming down there to find you.'

Lamont chuckled. 'I'll hold you to that.'

The connection was cut, and Lamont put the phone down. Stretching, he stood up and looked over the balcony of his hotel. He had a gorgeous view of the pale sands, and the seas that were almost turquoise. At night, it was a place of wonder, with the music and dancing, and the carefree attitude of the locals. It made Lamont feel tranquil and without his responsibilities back home, he would give serious thought to living here. As he stood there in his light blue vest and khaki board shorts, Lamont remembered a few years back, sitting in Jenny's back garden, speaking of a want to travel, having already purchased tickets to Uruguay.

Tickets that were never used.

For a fleeting moment, he wondered how things would have changed if they had made the trip, but he closed his eyes and took a deep breath. The pain would always be there. In spite of that, he would be okay.

Staring out at the lapping waves, Lamont felt a wave of content he never thought he deserved to feel, then looked up at the sky, closing his eyes with a small smile on his face.

DID YOU ENJOY THE READ?

You can make a huge difference

Reviews are immensely powerful when it comes to getting attention for my books.

Honest reviews help bring them to the attention of other readers.

If you've enjoyed this I would be very grateful if you could spend just five minutes leaving a review (it can be as short as you like) on the book's Amazon page.

Thank you so much

ALSO BY RICKY BLACK

ABOUT RICKY BLACK

Ricky Black was born and raised in Chapeltown, Leeds. He began writing seriously in 2004, working on mainly crime pieces.

In 2016, he published the first of his crime series, Target, and has published three more books since.

Visit https://rickyblackbooks.com for information regarding new releases and special offers and promotions.

To everyone who believed in me, and helped me bring this series to fruition.